"A uniquely inventive novel. . . . How splendidly the author has balanced art with environmental obligation. . . . It is exciting in literary circles when a first-time novelist does as well as Brandeis does with *The Book of Dead Birds*."

—*Rocky Mountain News*

"What a shimmering and accomplished first novel! The landscapes of Korea and southern California, and the territories of a mother's fierce dreams and her daughter's tentative flights, are all rendered with graceful language and stark, affecting honesty."

—Susan Straight, author of *Highwire Moon*

"The vivid tale of a woman learning to save and cherish life."

—*San Francisco Chronicle*

"A moving and perceptive first novel."   —*O, the Oprah Magazine*

"*The Book of Dead Birds* is a story of healing—a skillful, textured weaving of dark and light."

—Donna M. Gershten, author of *Kissing the Virgin's Mouth*

"An emotional story forged in crystalline prose. . . . Brandeis channels Ava with the precision of a poet, creating an elegant tale . . . in which beauty is rendered from brutal sources."

—*Bust* magazine

"A sad, funny debut. . . . The plight of the mother and daughter is heartbreaking. . . . A wrenching tale."   —*Kirkus Reviews*

"Brandeis has a poet's ear for the music of language . . . [her] characters and their fledgling flights of the heart stay with readers long after the book is closed and set aside."

—*January* magazine

About the Author

GAYLE BRANDEIS is the author of *Fruitflesh: Seeds of Inspiration for Women Who Write*. Her work has appeared in *Salon* and *HipMama*, among other publications. She lives in Riverside, California, with her husband and two children. *The Book of Dead Birds* is her first novel.

The Book of
Dead Birds

[A NOVEL]

Gayle Brandeis

Perennial
An Imprint of HarperCollins*Publishers*

First Perennial edition published 2004.

Designed by Nancy Singer Olaguera

The Library of Congress has catalogued the hardcover edition as follows:

Brandeis, Gayle.
    The book of dead birds : a novel / Gayle Brandeis.—1st ed.
        p. cm.
    ISBN 0-06-052803-6
        1. Women conservationists—Fiction. 2. Birds—Effect of water pollution on—Fiction. 3. Korean American women—Fiction. 4. Mothers and daughters—Fiction. 5. Racially mixed people—Fiction. 6. Salton Sea (Calif.)—Fiction. 7. San Diego (Calif.)—Fiction. I. Title.

PS3602.R345 B66 2003
813'.6—dc21

2002032894

ISBN 0-06-052804-4 (pbk.)

04 05 06 07 08 ❖/RRD 10 9 8 7 6 5 4 3 2 1

for Matt

I had a dove and the sweet dove died;
   And I have thought it died of grieving.
O, what could it grieve for? Its feet were tied,
   With a silken thread of my own hand's weaving.
                              —JOHN KEATS

If you go back far enough in my family tree there are birds.
                              —SUSAN MITCHELL

The Book of Dead Birds

I remember the first time I flew.

I was four years old. My mother decided to take me to Balboa Park for the afternoon. I watched the back of her short-sleeved blouse as we crossed the parking lot to the playground; the sky-blue fabric tightened, then loosened, tightened, then loosened, across her shoulder blades, pointy as chicken wings. I tried to catch up, but my mother was too fast. Even then, I knew she didn't like to be seen with me in public. I knew it was because of my skin—so much darker than my mother's, dark like the treats she made out of dates that morning, the ones that stuck between my teeth, filling my mouth with a prickly sweetness.

We didn't go to the park very often, but this day was special— New Year's Eve, 1975. Not December 31, when midnight bullets flew through our San Diego neighborhood and we crouched together in the closet; this was a few weeks later—the lunar New Year, the Korean New Year, the day when girls stand up on seesaws and swings.

At four, I was already as tall as my mother's ribs. I broke into a run and tugged at my mother's shirt, pulling it out of the elastic waistband of her lime-green pants. She shook herself loose and kept walking. I could see the scar on her lower back as her shirt flapped up—a crescent moon, beaded with pale tooth marks. I reached to swipe a finger over it, but she walked even faster.

She let me catch up to her when we reached the grass. Without looking at me, she looped two fingers around my wrist and guided me over to the swings. She lifted me by the armpits with a grunt and deposited me, standing, on a swing strap. I clutched the chain while she moved the swing lightly back and forth, but I couldn't keep my balance. I wobbled, then tumbled into her arms.

She glanced around to make sure no one was watching, then shifted me onto her hip and lurched over to the seesaw. With her foot, she tilted one end of the peeling yellow plank to the ground; I grabbed on to her sleeves.

"No, Omma!" I yelled, as she set me, standing, on the edge.

"You stay here." She twisted herself away from my grip.

"Omma!" I jumped off the seesaw. The plank rose into the air. She pushed it down again and set me back on.

"You stay now." Her voice was firm.

I couldn't breathe as I watched my mother walk to the other side of the playground. I wanted to step off the seesaw but my feet felt bolted to the plank. When she finally stopped and turned around, my throat filled with air.

"Omma!" I spread out my arms. She began to run toward me.

I had never seen my mother run before. She was fast. I watched her cheeks jiggle and her mouth sway loose and her small breasts swing around as she came closer. Then she jumped. She jumped as if there were a trampoline in the grass. She shot up so high, I worried she might get tangled in the jacaranda branches above. There was a determination in her eyes that scared me. It scared her, too. I could see her hesitate as she began to fall. She pedaled her feet backward like a cartoon character who realized he had just walked off a cliff, but she landed on the seesaw anyway, a crumpling blur of limbs.

That's when I flew.

I flew straight over my mother's head, flew like a bullet across the playground. I felt as if I wouldn't ever stop, as if I would keep on flying, past the park, past the zoo and the stores and the ocean. I felt as if I would be a flying girl forever. Then a eucalyptus tree zoomed toward my face. My mother tackled me to the ground just as I was about to hit the molting trunk.

Neither of us spoke on the car ride home. We barely even breathed—it felt as if one loud exhale would make some invisible seesaw between us lose its precarious balance. As soon as we got into the apartment, I stumbled off to bed. I felt my end of the ghost board clatter to the ground, felt my mother float untethered behind me as I drifted into a deep, dark nap.

When I woke, my whole head throbbed. My forehead had banged into the dirt pretty hard when we fell. In the gray light of dusk, I could see my mother sitting by the window, rocking a bit, as if she had to go to the bathroom.

"Omma." My voice was a puff of air.

My mother turned toward me, then crept up to the bed. Something about her looked different, scary. Her eyebrows, I realized, were completely white. She had put some kind of powder on them; flecks of it dusted her eyelashes, her cheeks, her collar. After I walked to the bathroom, I was startled to find my own eyebrows white, as well. They looked strange on my much darker face, like a powdered sugar decoration, frosting on a gingerbread cookie. A scrape ran across my forehead, an oblong abrasion, speckled pink and red. I touched a finger to it; pain shot behind my eyes. I began to feel dizzy. My mother grabbed me by the arms and led me back to bed.

"If you take nap at New Year," she told me as she tucked me under the covers, "the story says your eyebrow turn white. Is joking to put on flour if you fall asleep."

My mother didn't look happy to me, not like someone telling a joke. "Did you fall asleep, Omma?" I asked.

She shook her head. A tear carved a streak through the light dusting of flour on her face.

I pressed a finger against the damp trail, then stuck my finger in my mouth. It tasted like paste, like salt.

She was silent for a moment before she whispered, "I want to show you."

"Show me what?"

"I want you can see . . ."

Specks of flour drifted past my eyelashes. My mother smoothed the pilly bedspread over my thighs.

"Long time ago," she said, "girls and women live in walls."

"We live in walls." I rubbed at my eyes. "If we didn't live in walls, we'd live in the sky."

"Stone walls," she said. "A big fence, all around the yard. Girls, women, not able to go to the world."

"That's silly." I wanted to go back to sleep. My whole skull throbbed.

"New Year's different."

"They could go outside?" I could still see my mother running toward me as if in slow motion, her whole body rippling like gelatin. I could still see my mother jump. My stomach pitched with the sudden rush of flight.

"They had the *noldwigi*. Long wood on a bag of rice straw. A seesaw."

"So?"

"So they see."

"Omma." I winced. My forehead felt like it would crack open if I tried to think too hard.

"The girls, they jump on the *noldwigi*, they jump the other one up, let her see over the wall. Just a little look. Once a year, over the stone. They show each other."

She sank to her knees.

I turned my pounding head to the window. A pigeon landed on the ledge outside. Its throat shimmered with the sunset.

My name is Ava Sing Lo.

I am a bird killer. The killer of my mother's birds. An accidental killer, but a killer nonetheless.

Someday I'll probably end up like Prometheus, chained to a rock, birds pecking away at my liver. Appropriate karma. Birds should peck at all my vital organs. I should be tarred with bird droppings and copiously feathered. I should be forced to swallow a whole sack of birdseed dry.

My mother named me Ava because she liked how the English letters looked—the big A a beak pointed upward, the v a sharp slash of wings, the small a round and flat as a parrot's eye. She chose the name even before she knew it had anything to do with birds—the letters spoke to her with their own hollow bones. Her family name was Song, but she chose Sing for us because—and this may be more my interpretation than hers—it sounded more active, like something that is happening, something alive in the throat, not something that has already been written down, sung a million times. I'm afraid I haven't lived up to that part of my name yet.

The "Lo," which I know I've lived up to (or, I should say, lived *down* to) comes from my mother's mishearing of the song "Swing Low, Sweet Chariot." She had seen an American movie where a man in prison sang that song, and she thought he was saying "*sing* low," his voice was so low, so gravelly and dark. That's how she felt twenty-five years ago, she's told me—low and gravelly and dark right after I was born. That's how I still make her feel, it seems, again and again and again, awkward as the "l" sound in her mouth.

* * *

Kane is my most recent victim. Psiticin Kane, who I named after I discovered the scientific name for parrots. Kane of the red tail feathers. Kane of the stunning bilingual vocabulary. Kane of the lemon pulp eyes. Kane, the African gray my mother thought would be her companion the rest of her life.

My intentions, as usual, were good. My mother was on a Las Vegas bus tour, and I arranged to have the carpet cleaned. She grew up on smooth stone floors and the seed-studded carpet grated on her nerves; I thought she would be thrilled when she came home and found soft clean shag beneath her feet. How was I to know parrots are so sensitive to cleaning products? I thought I had taken precautions—I had covered Kane's cage with a towel before the carpet cleaners came. He was nervous around new people and skittish about strange sounds. I always covered his cage before I pulled out my *chang'go*. I thought I had done enough.

When I got back home and took off my shoes to walk across the slightly damp carpet, I could tell something was wrong. Kane's normal greeting of *"Annyong hashimnikka?"—"Are you at peace?"*— was conspicuously absent.

"Animal crackers in my soup," I sang off-key. Unlike my mother, I am not much of a singer.

I had bought a package of animal crackers for Kane, his favorite treat. He liked to walk around the cage with the string of the circus-train box dangling from his beak, like a handbag.

"Monkeys and rabbits loop de loop," I continued.

Usually at this point, Kane joined in with "Gosh oh gee but I have fun . . . ," but there was no Shirley Temple response from under the terry cloth. I hoped it was because he wasn't used to singing with me—my mother was the one who usually shared this duet—but I had a sinking suspicion this wasn't the case.

I softly added the next part, despite Kane's silence: "Swallowing animals one by one."

I took a deep breath, then pulled the towel from the cage. Kane lay on the spattered newspaper. His pale yellow eyes were glazed. He trembled as if he had just taken a dip in freezing water.

The box of animal crackers fell out of my hand and burst open on the ground. I opened the cage, pulled Kane out, wrapped him in the towel, and ran downstairs without putting my shoes back on.

"Has your bird recently been exposed to any chemical or caustic fumes?" Dr. Miller asked me as he listened to Kane's chest.

"I just had the carpet cleaned." I watched his freckled hands.

"Bird's lungs are very sensitive." The vet moved his stethoscope. A strand of his curly orange hair fell on Kane's belly. I brushed it away. "You should never expose them to industrial cleaning products."

I should have known Kane had weak lungs. He had come down with psittacosis a couple of years before. My mother came down with it, too, and I had to take a week off from San Diego State, walking between sick mother and sick bird, administering droppersful of antibiotics and ginseng and seaweed soup.

"We're going to have to do an aspiration," Dr. Miller told me. "It would be best if you wait outside."

I bounced my heels up and down as I sat in the small waiting room. A pug drooled on my shins, but I couldn't find the energy to shoo him away. Dr. Miller walked through the swinging doors, and a small surge of hope rose inside my chest.

"I'm afraid we weren't able to save your bird," he said. "We did everything we possibly could. The damage was just too extensive."

All I could do was nod. My heart clattered against the bottom of my rib cage like a fallen plate.

"There was a last word." The vet's voice brightened a bit. "I don't know if it was a word—it was actually more of a sound. Something like hee hee hammy something . . ."

My whole body suddenly turned cold. "I don't understand."

"I'm afraid I don't either," he said. "I thought it might be gibberish, but . . ."

"*Ihae mot hamnida* is probably what he said. It means 'I don't understand' in Korean." My voice cracked like it does when I sing.

Dr. Miller looked at me strangely—trying, I'm sure, to figure out why a dark-skinned, barefoot woman like myself would know Korean.

"Kane used to say it a lot." A tear slid into my mouth. "It was like his little joke."

Do I have it on tape? I wondered. I sometimes recorded my mother's birds' voices to use as MIDI samples. I hoped I had something left of Kane for my mother to press to her ear.

The vet cleared his throat.

"I'm sorry for your loss." He briefly touched my shoulder. "I'll have the receptionist bring the body out shortly."

I watched him walk back into the clinic with a flap of white coattails, flounce of orange hair. I thought of the strand of his hair that fell on Kane's belly, brassy against the pale gray, as shocking a contrast as Kane's red tail feathers had been. My mother loved those feathers. She had saved the brown baby ones in a Ziploc bag and was so excited when the red ones came in, even though she usually associates red with the Korean Book of Death and never wears it herself or writes with a red pen.

The receptionist brought Kane out in a white paper bag, my name scrawled across it in thick black marker. One red feather poked past the crinkly paper lip. The immensity of what I had done suddenly bowled me over.

Oh, Omma. I closed my eyes. *Oh, Omma, I am so, so sorry.*

When I got home, my mother was picking pieces of animal cracker off the floor.

"The carpet wet," she said.

"I had it cleaned." I held Kane's bag behind my back.

"Smells." My mother pinched her nose, fanned her other hand in front of her.

We stood together in silence. The empty cage in the middle of the room spoke louder than either one of us could. My mother cocked an eyebrow up at me and I handed her the bag. She looked inside, nodded, and walked to her room.

"Omma." I stood at the door, but my mother didn't answer.

I knew what my mother would do. She would add Kane to her Book of Dead Birds. She would tape a feather onto a yellowed scrapbook page, write her reminiscences, paste in a photograph. She would press the cracked maroon leather cover to her chest and wail. She would yell that I was as bad as the army, storming in, killing every living thing in sight.

I knew what I would do, too. I would listen outside my mother's door. I would feel wave upon guilty wave of nausea. I would apologize until my jaws ached. I would search through my MIDI files for the bird's voice. I would—despite my most diligent efforts—most likely kill again.

Omma, I don't know if you'll ever read this, my own under-the-bed book. (Funny, isn't it? Should I paste in a bit of your hair? A nail clipping?) Everything you sing, I remember, I write down—

frantic notes and scribbles I hope I can flesh out on these pages, even if it scorches my own flesh in the process, even if the words have to claw their way out. I don't know if I'm getting it right—I know you think I don't get anything right—but this is what I've gleaned so far. Omma, if I can't save your birds, maybe I can save a little bit of your story.

Hye-yang wasn't sure she could hold her breath much longer. She watched her mother and grandmother swim five feet deeper underwater, scooping sea urchins off craggy volcanic rock. Their hair streamed around their faces as they turned to place the creatures into rope baskets strapped to their backs. Hye-yang swam toward them, bubbles escaping from her mouth. Just as she reached for an abalone shell, a sharp pain shot through her ribs. She pushed herself toward the surface, leaving her mother and grandmother behind.

Hye-yang broke through the skin of the water, gasping. Three white pelicans flew past her, eyeing her basket. As they swooped down a few feet away, Hye-yang noticed a man sitting on a rock on the shore, silhouetted against the gray sky.

Uneasy, Hye-yang swam toward him.

"You are not allowed here," she said to the man as she walked out of the water. It was unlawful for men to watch the women divers on Cheju-do. Hye-yang, at eighteen, had just started to dive.

"I heard you singing, before, before you went underwater." The man stood up on the rock. He wore a dark, shiny blue suit and tie, not the traditional clothes worn on Cheju-do. His hair was slicked back. A cigarette dangled from one hand. "You have a beautiful voice."

Hye-yang crossed her arms over her chest. She knew the loose white diving garment turned see-through when wet. She hadn't been singing; she had been letting the air out of her lungs, sending out an *eieieieieieie* that filled the whole cove before she dove underwater.

"I would like to offer you a job," he said. "Singing. At a nightclub, on the mainland. Our girls do very well."

"I am a diver, not a singer." Hye-yang set her rope basket onto the rocky ground.

"You could be very famous." The man threw down his cigarette and jumped off the rock. He walked up to her and pulled a pink card from his inner jacket pocket.

Hye-yang did not reach for it.

The man stepped even closer. He slid the card beneath Hye-yang's wet collar, then reached his hand deeper. Hye-yang froze as his fingers grazed her nipple.

"You will call me." He smiled as he drew his hand back out of her clothes, but his eyes were cold.

Hye-yang felt the card, plastered to her skin, start to slide down her left breast. She began to shiver uncontrollably, but she couldn't move. She watched the man light another cigarette and walk away.

Hye-yang's mother and grandmother soon came up behind her. She could hear the water drip off their bodies, a light patter against the ground.

"Hye-yang," her mother said sharply as she dropped her heavy bag. "Was a man talking to you?"

"I told him he wasn't supposed to be here," Hye-yang said.

Hye-yang's grandmother gestured to the card glowing through Hye-yang's clothes. She reached in and pulled it out.

"What is this?"

"He told me I could be a singer."

"Well, you're not much of a diver." Hye-yang's mother laughed gruffly. She picked up Hye-yang's rope bag and shook the small number of abalone shells out onto the rough dark sand.

Hye-yang's grandmother threw the card back at her. She and Hye-yang's mother walked away, dragging their rope bags full of hard and spiny animals. Hye-yang could hear them saying something about more and more shame.

Hye-yang crumpled to the ground, tears spilling down her face. She had brought shame to her family's house even before she was born. In utero, she was promised as a bride to a neighbor's two-month-old son, but a week and a half before she was born, the boy succumbed to crib death. Hye-yang came into the world a widow, a fallen woman. No man would ever want to marry her, her mother was always quick to mention.

Hye-yang scooped the abalone shells back into the bag. Still shivering, she made her way back home, past the barley fields and acres of yellow rapeseed flowers, the pink card curled soggy in her hand.

A spray of gulls flew overhead, crying into the wind. Hye-yang walked faster. Tall *harubang,* grandfathers carved from volcanic rock, lined the dirt path. Despite their goofy faces, the stones looked menacing to Hye-yang, dark and foreboding against the gathering storm. The abalone shells clacked together in her rope basket in time with her steps.

Hye-yang looked at the pink business card. It was written in English, except for one Korean phrase that meant "we hire entertainment ladies." Her face smarted when she remembered the man's hand in her clothes. No man had ever touched her skin before, not even her hands. Her father may have held her, but he died when Hye-yang was three, and she couldn't remember anything about him.

Hye-yang turned the bend and her family's small stone house came into view, its thatched roof battened down with ropes and rocks. One pole was gone from the gate, a sign that her mother and grandmother were out, but not far. Hye-yang took down the other two poles and went inside. She peeled off her wet diving clothes and stood shivering before the kitchen fire as she looked at the business card again. If only the man had not touched her, Hye-yang would call. Maybe she should call anyway, she thought, eyeing the strange English letters. Hye-yang knew she was not helping her family as a diver. She was nothing but an embarrassment. If she went to the mainland and got a job, she could send money home, more than she could ever earn with her small catch of abalone. Plus, she loved to sing. When Hye-yang sang at the Snow Blossom Festival a few months before, her first time in front of an audience, she felt like her heart would soar right out of her skin.

Hye-yang put on some dry clothes. She brushed out her salty hair and thought about the phone at the farmer's coop kiosk, the closest one to her family's house. Hye-yang pulled on her jacket and grabbed a pouch of coins. Then she noticed an envelope on the floor, addressed to her, already opened, its contents jutting out.

Hye-yang recognized the handwriting immediately. The letter was from Hye-yang's friend Sun, who left Cheju-do four months before to work at the Korean Folk Village in Suwon. Hye-yang wanted to go with her, but her mother refused, saying she needed to stay and learn to dive.

There is still lots of work available here, Sun wrote, on paper thin as onion skin. Sun played a bride each weekend in a traditional wedding ceremony put on for tourists. During the week, she demonstrated women's seesaw. *Come visit me,* she pleaded. *I need a friend from the island. My best friend.*

Hye-yang missed Sun terribly. She missed their cave, the dark craggy cave they found together behind a waterfall, the one that led to strange tunnels and cold little pockets of space. They often took candles and red bean buns and explored the passages, bumping into each other in the dark, giggling with the fear and thrill of it. After Sun left, Hye-yang passed the mouth of the cave almost every day, but she couldn't bring herself to go inside of it alone.

If she were to leave the island, it would make sense to go to her friend, not to some nightclub in Kunsan where she didn't know anyone but a man with a shiny suit and rough hands. Hye-yang tossed the business card into the fire beneath the pot of rice. The soggy paper sputtered for a while, sizzling and twitching, before it collapsed into flames, sending black tongues of smoke up the sides of the pot.

Hye-yang's mother came through the door, waving her hand at the smoke that began to fill the room.

"You want to go?" she asked Hye-yang sharply, gesturing to the letter unfolded on Hye-yang's lap.

Hye-yang nodded her head. Across the room, her mother slowly disappeared into the swirling gray smoke.

"You go, then." Her mother's voice cut through the haze. "But don't you come flying back here. Don't even think you can come flying on back."

Red Lored Amazon (Name: Pippy)

Ava, daughter, 11. Kill bird with candy.
He sit on shoulder when she do homework,
give him MM out her hand. Every day
she give him some. One day he fall
back off shoulder, hard stone to the floor.
I don't know candy poison for bird.
Ava, she know?

[yellow-shelled chocolate crushed under tape]

[small red feather]

10/16/82
Helen Sing Lo's Book of Dead Birds

M y mother works in bent silhouette, framed by the bright window across the room.

I rustle the newspaper, yesterday's, to try to get her attention. "Omma," I ask her, "where's Estonia?"

"Estonia Hotel downtown," she says, her voice muffled by her surgical mask. Between this and the sudden whir of the dentist's drill, I can barely hear her.

"The *country*, Omma." I flinch at the reminder of her knowledge of downtown hotels and glance again at the blurb in the *San Diego Union Tribune*, the one I've been saving for her. "Do you know where the country Estonia is? The article says it's Baltic, but I'm not really sure what that means. I think it's near Russia."

My mother grunts and presses a magnifying glass against her goggles. She stares intently at the scrollwork she's just drilled into an empty ostrich eggshell, the one she's turning into a music box. Her eggshell change purses, night lights, ships in bottles, picture frames sell at a small circuit of local craft fairs and gift shops.

"I have something for your book," I tell her. My mother's back slowly unhunches itself.

"Listen to this." I lift the paper. "'Thousands of swans are in danger of dying along the Baltic coast in Estonia as one of the harshest winters in years has frozen the shallow waters where they feed. Hundreds of swans have already starved to death. The remaining 5,000 are in danger of dying if, as forecast, the waters stay locked in ice for many weeks to come.'"

It sounds like my mother is saying something, but when I look up, her mask is still, collapsed against her lips. A wispy glow emanates from her backlit head, through the slim gaps in her teased-up hair. I am momentarily stunned by its corona. My own hair, cropped close to my skull, feels like a sudden, dense weight. No light could ever pass through it.

"They're trying to help, Omma. Here." I clear my throat and start to read again. "'In an effort to save the swans, rescue teams have smashed holes through some sections of the ice, frozen nearly two feet thick along the coast. A public appeal has also been made for people to feed bits of bread and potatoes to hungry swans languishing near the shore.'"

"Do you think swans would like *Oh-Jing-Uh Bok-Um?*" I try to joke a bit. "Birds eat squid, don't they? It's too bad we don't live closer by. Maybe we could ship it there."

My mother looks out the window. Her shoulders start to rise to her ears.

"The pepper paste might be a bit much for them . . ." I bite my lip and walk toward my mother, but she quickly flips her goggles back down, turns the drill back on, and starts to carve again.

I wave my hand in front of my face to keep the eggshell dust out of my nose and mouth, then trudge off to my room. The room I moved back into after I finished my masters in communications at San Diego State and couldn't get enough steady work as a sound engineer to pay my own rent. The room I'm not sure I'll ever quite escape from.

The fact that I have a degree—two degrees—in communications is a bit of a joke. I spent most of my time at school behind a soundboard with headphones clamped over my ears. I didn't have to communicate much with anyone. I'm just grateful for my drum. Without it, I don't think I could communicate with my mother at all.

The article about the Estonia swans will end up in my mother's scrapbook by the end of the day, I'm sure of it. I flop down on my bed and grab a lump of candied ginger from the bag on the nightstand. My mouth fills with its bright, soapy flavor. I can imagine flying off to Estonia, wherever it is, with bushels of bread and potatoes and covered dishes of spicy squid. I can imagine standing at the frozen shoreline, tossing food everywhere, crumbs disappearing like light down one cygnet throat after another. I can imagine hefting swans under each arm, carrying them back to my tiny hotel room that smells of borscht and wet wool.

I can almost feel the birds' solid weight strain against my biceps as I work a fibrous strand of ginger between my teeth. I can see myself folding the swans into dog carriers for the long flight back to San Diego. I can see myself filling my mother's bathtub with the birds, the living, unharmed birds, their long necks swooping against the shower curtain, their beaks cool and smooth as plastic against my palm.

I swallow the broken threads of ginger and listen to my mother's drill buzz like a mosquito in the next room. Kane's recorded voice occasionally rises above the hum—*I don't understand. I don't understand. Are you at peace?*

Ava, daughter, age 6.
Go to park together.
No seesaw,
pond full of birds.
Bring bread from home
to feed in pieces.
Ava walk up to goose—
soft brown body,
black head, black neck,
stripe of white under chin.
She gives bread.
Too big piece, maybe?
Ava lift up hands,
bird fall down,
stick pink tongue
from black beak.
Look like person tongue,
so pink. Didn't know bird
could have pink tongue.

—5/23/73

Against my better judgment, I buy my mother a zebra finch, scrabbling madly inside a Chinese take-out container, from a man on a blanket outside the Tae Kwon Do studio. My mother names him Yukam, "Regret." She keeps him in a cage by her bed and bars me from her room.

I wake up around 3:00 A.M. to the sound of my mother's singing. It is the *pansori,* of course. I grab my *chang'go* and sleepily carry it out into the dark living room. My mother is sitting there on the floor, Yukam settled squarely on top of her head.

My mother once told me that *pansori* singers train by standing underneath a waterfall and singing until their voices cut through the rush of water. They practice until they spit up enough blood from their throats to fill three large jugs. Listening to her voice, it's easy to believe this.

I sit cross-legged and begin to thrum at the hourglass-shaped drum in response to my mother's song. *Pansori* songs can go on for hours; my mother always weaves her own words in with the traditional lyrics. Often, she forgoes the traditional lyrics entirely. Bits of her life stream out of her, in English, in Korean, of which I unfortunately have very limited knowledge. She periodically stands up, whips her folded fan around, lifts her arms in sweeping gestures, then she sits back down, her voice a touch quieter, her face still blazing with her story. I talk with my mother through the drum—soft, sympathetic, thrums at times, angry thumps at others. The song doesn't stop until the room is tinged with the first wash of morning light. I go back to my room and write down as much as I can remember.

Hye-yang told her mother and grandmother it was her bleeding time, so she would be excused from diving for the day. She imagined the women were reaching for sea urchins as she stuffed her clothes into a bag, looped her archery bow over her shoulder, and walked through the open gate without replacing the three wooden poles behind her.

As she hiked along a rocky ridge above the ocean, Hye-yang thought she could see figures in white garments traveling parallel to her under the water. She wondered if her mother and grandmother were following her, echoing her steps with their ghostly glide. Hye-yang sped up her pace, hoping to lose them, when a gull dove through what she had thought was her mother's head. Hye-yang's feet froze beneath her until the bird came back up, a fish thrashing in its beak. The billowy image in the water shuddered, then righted itself again, and she realized it was only the reflection of some clouds.

When she got to the ferry docks, Hye-yang half expected to find her mother and grandmother, dripping and angry, waiting for her, but aside from the ticket taker and some uniformed workers, only a few honeymoon couples milled around by the boat. Hye-yang paid her fare, then climbed aboard the ferry.

She rested her bow against a bench and leaned her stomach against the railing at the front of the boat. The water stretched out forever in front of her, vast and blue and brilliant. A surge of excitement, laced with fear, rushed through her body as the boat lurched, then began to pull away from the dock. Hye-yang had never left the island's orbit before. She waved at some pelicans as they flew by, their wings fully open, white feathers glinting in the sun.

The ferry arrived in Pusan eight hours later, at dusk. Hye-yang was stunned by the sight of the large city, already lit up for night. As she walked down the ramp off the boat, Hye-yang's sea legs buckled beneath her; she had to brace herself with the tip of her bow as she walked toward the terminal.

Inside, Hye-yang bought a bowl of buckwheat noodles in sweet radish sauce, and a cup of walnut tea. Hungry as she was, she found it hard to eat, overwhelmed by the number of people around her, all moving so fast. Human voices filled the space like bird chatter. The air smelled strongly of smoke and armpits and fish. Every time someone walked by, it stirred up a new layer of scent. Hye-yang hugged her bow to her body to keep it from getting smashed.

She slurped up a few noodles, then pushed her way through the crowd until she found the bus with a SUWON placard hanging above it. She squeezed herself, her bag, and her bow on board and fell into the last available seat.

The bus smelled like the terminal, but even more intense. Hye-yang tried to get comfortable in her narrow seat, her bow tipped against her chest and shoulder, but she wasn't quite successful. An elderly woman sat next to her, sound asleep. The scent of squid drifted from her open mouth.

Hye-yang gaped out the window at the tall buildings as the bus pulled away from the station and made its way slowly through a maze of streets, sound and smoke pouring through the scattered open windows.

Just a few minutes into the ride, the bus got snagged in a traffic jam. Hye-yang noticed a crowd of men milling on the street outside, standing in front of windows, going in and out of buildings; men in Western business suits, mostly, but a few wearing old-fashioned *chogori*. The street was lined with storefronts featuring huge window-panes, all of them glowing inside with a harsh pink light. In every window sat at least one woman wearing an elaborate *hanbok* and makeup, posed in a little traditional tableau.

The old woman next to Hye-yang stirred.

"Ahhh, Wanwol-dong," she sleepily muttered to Hye-yang.

"Excuse me?" Hye-yang asked.

"This area—its name is Wanwol-dong," the woman yawned.

"What are the women doing in those windows?" Hye-yang asked.

"You don't know?" The woman looked at Hye-yang, surprised.

"Is it some sort of cultural display?" Hye-yang asked, thinking the street might be some urbanized version of the Folk Village she was traveling to in Suwon.

The woman snorted.

"Are they selling those *hanbok*s?" Hye-yang looked at the colorful costumes, the large sleeves trailing to the ground.

"They're selling what's in those *hanbok*s, daughter," the woman said matter-of-factly before she closed her eyes again.

Hye-yang stared for a second at the white whiskers sprouting on the woman's upper lip before she looked back out the window, shocked.

Traffic began to move again. Hye-yang tried to see the faces of the women as the bus drove down the street, but their features smeared together in the pink glare of the endless storefronts.

Hye-yang's lids still pulsed with colored light when she closed her eyes. The business card the man had given her at the beach flashed into her mind. It had left a pink stain on her breast, like a bright little window to her heart. She wasn't able to wash it off for days. Hye-yang opened her eyes again and grimaced as her seat-mate made a few more wet smacking sounds. As the bus picked up speed, she turned her head and watched the pink haze recede into the background, garish as the sunset.

When I wake up a few hours later, my hand is still a bit numb. I flex and blow on my fingers to limber them up before I get out of bed and join my mother in the kitchen.

She is standing over a pot of *Hae-jang-guk,* "morning-after" soup. Her eyes are red and puffy. I figure it's from lack of sleep until I realize she is crying.

"Omma, are you okay?" I lightly touch her shoulder. "Did something happen to Yukam?" I feel overwhelmingly guilty, even though I know I've done nothing wrong.

My mother shakes her head. She spoons out a bowl of soup for herself and walks across the kitchen with it steaming in her hands.

"Omma?" I follow after her, but she goes into her room and closes the door.

I stand in front of the door for a moment before I return to the kitchen. I ladle up my own bowl of soup and bring it to the low coffee table in the dining area. The *Union-Tribune* is folded on my mother's cushion; I pick it up and shake it open. Two holes are cut out of the front section—one a small square, the other a long rectangle with a thin arm jutting out on top.

No longer hungry, I dump my bowl of soup into the sink. Three robins' eggs sit on a dishcloth by the basin, ready to have their insides blown out. I carefully move them, then the soup pot, into the refrigerator so that they won't spoil.

In the evening, my mother finally comes out. Her eyes are practically swollen shut, her skin blotchy.

"Omma, what can I do?" I ask from the kitchen. My head feels fuzzy, my hands sore. All day, I've been trying not to listen to the sobs coming from my mother's room. All day, I've been keeping myself busy, napping, practicing my tae kwon do *hyung*s, drumming a bit to keep my hand from cramping up. I set the pot of soup back on the stove to reheat it.

"No soup." Her voice is raspy. She grabs her purse and keys and heads for the door.

"Where are you going?"

"To drive."

"Do you want me to come with you? It's getting dark."

My mother shakes her head. She slips on a nylon windbreaker even though the air is still warm.

"Are you sure?"

She nods, not looking at me.

"Chosim haseyo," I tell her. "Be careful." Kane used to say it whenever he saw her leave the apartment.

She pauses for a moment.

"Don't go near Yukam," she warns before she closes the door behind her.

I stir the soup, but I'm no longer hungry. I put the foil back over the pot and turn off the burner.

If I want to see the new entries in her scrapbook, I'm going to have to be quick about it. Who knows how long she'll be gone?

The brassy doorknob to her room looks like it will give me an electric shock, but it feels cool against my hand, flimsy, almost too easy to turn. I open the door a crack. The bedroom is dark and smells of seaweed. I push the door a bit further and stick my head inside. Yukam's wing brushes my cheek as he flies out.

"No, Yukam!" I yell. "No no no! Come back!"

The bird flies in circles around the apartment, lighting briefly upon the curtains, the coffee table, the back of the sofa. He flies into the kitchen and bombs droppings onto the foil that covers the soup pot. I chase after him, looking up, arms outstretched. I trip over the cushions on the floor, hit my shins on the coffee table, bang my ribs into the kitchen counter. Yukam lands on a windowsill.

"No!" I yell when I see the window is open. I dive toward him.

Just as the bird is about to escape, I clap both hands over his small body. When I lift him to my chest, it feels like I'm holding my own wildly fluttering heart.

The sound of footsteps approaches the front door, then the jangle of keys. I race to my mother's room, throw Yukam inside, and shut the door. When my mother enters the apartment, I lean against the wall, attempting to look casual. I'm panting like crazy.

"I forget something." My mother looks at me suspiciously.

I nod, trying to catch my breath.

"What you have going on?" she asks.

"Nothing, Omma," I tell her. "I just thought I'd get some exercise. I was jogging in place . . ." I pantomime running.

She squints at me, then walks to the kitchen. I sag back against the wall, hoping she won't notice the droppings on the soup pot.

"You have my eggs?" Her voice rises.

"The robins' eggs?" I walk over to her. "I put them in the fridge to keep them fresh."

She lunges for the refrigerator. She pulls out the dish towel that cradles the three tiny blue eggs. Carefully, she puts each one on her tongue and closes her mouth.

"Omma, what are you doing?"

She glares at me, her mouth full.

"The air is so warm," I tell her. "I thought you'd want me to keep them fresh for you. I know you don't like blowing rotten eggs."

My mother opens her mouth. The three blue shells wobble precariously inside. She lifts them from her tongue and puts them into another dish towel, then tucks the small bundle under her shirt.

"I find the eggs on the ground," she says. "The nest fall down. I try to hatch, but you freeze to death!"

"Oh, Omma." My knees buckle. I sit down on the floor. "I thought you wanted to turn them into a necklace or something."

"I want to turn them into birds!" she yells.

I put my face in my hands.

The door slams behind my mother as she leaves the apartment again.

I sit on the floor a few minutes, my palms mashed against my eye sockets, a bright blizzard sparking behind my lids. When I open my eyes and stand up, the fierce speckles are still there, swarming the whole kitchen, dissolving everything for a moment into atoms, or dust. I wad up the soiled tinfoil from the soup pot, throw it away, and dump the rest of the soup down the sink. The broth scent wafts from the drain like bad breath.

I walk back to my mother's room, open the door without hesitation, and slip into the darkness, closing it behind me before Yukam can fly out.

The bird swoops past, stirring up the scent from my mother's half-eaten bowl of soup as I click on the light. I kneel down and pull the *Book of Dead Birds* out from under the bare mattress. I flip through the thick pages, turning my head so that I won't have to read about my murderous past. When my finger finds a page still a bit squishy with glue, I let myself look. Two articles, their shapes corresponding to the holes in the morning paper, cover the yellowed paper. The glue shines dully through the newsprint.

The first headline blares, "GI Not Charged in Death of Korean Prostitute." A woman was killed in the U.S. camptown of Osan, it says. A soda bottle had been jammed so far up her vagina, it perforated her uterus. The handle of an umbrella had torn open her rectum. Her neck had been broken, her face badly bruised. The U.S. Army chose to not press any charges against the GI responsible for the crime. Even though the people of Osan vehemently protested the inaction, the article suggests nothing further will be done.

No wonder my mother was so upset.

I set the book on the bed and stretch my arms out, shake them to shake the story out of my limbs. One of my hands flops against my mother's soup bowl. It wobbles precariously on the dresser, sends a fat wave of broth over the edge. I steady the bowl, then quickly grab some of my mother's crumpled tissues to mop up the spill. They wither and dissolve in the cold salty puddle. I use the edge of my shirt to clean up the rest, then pick up the bowl to wipe underneath it. A black-and-white photograph sits there, the edges and bottom lightly stained with soup. I carefully lift the picture and set it on the leg of my pants. The paper is a bit soggy, but the image itself is clear.

Two women stare up from my thigh. Their arms are looped around each other's waists, their smiles broad. An egret stands on one foot behind them, off to the left. Another bird's wing blurs over their heads. One woman, who I don't recognize, wears a traditional Korean wedding ensemble. The other is dressed in an old-fashioned-looking *hanbok,* a large archery bow tilted against her hip. I recognize the bow, but I barely recognize my mother. I've never seen a photograph of her smiling before. I've never seen her smile before, period—not like this. Usually she keeps her lips closed, straight, her upper lip puffed out a bit, as if stuffed with dental cotton. The smile in this picture is large and unguarded. It takes my breath away. I run a finger lightly over my mother's sodden face before I move the photo to the back of the scrapbook. Hopefully it will press dry.

A greenish square remains on my pants where the photo sat, matching the stain that spreads across the bottom of my shirt. I pull the seaweed-flecked cloth away from my body and begin to close the scrapbook, eager to change into some dry clothes, but then I remember I haven't read the other article yet. I twist the bottom of my shirt into a knot and spread the book back open.

"Poison Link Suspected in Bird Deaths," reads the next headline. The dateline is the Salton Sea, an inland lake eighty miles north of San Diego, in the middle of the desert. Over three thousand birds have died there in the last two weeks, 597 of them endangered California brown pelicans. I glance at the small map at the bottom of the article. The body of water is shaped like a lopsided *chang'go*.

The birds have been dying of botulism, the article reports. Officials believe the outbreak may stem from fish killed by pesticide misuse, since endosulfan had been illegally sprayed on private agricultural land south of the sea and had recently leached into the wildlife refuge. Thousands of fish showed up dead in the runoff ditches that drain into the sea; many sank to the bottom but were churned up by a fast, fierce thunderstorm, then cooked rancid in the returning desert sun. Contaminated maggots washed out from the rotting fish and were gobbled by pelicans, who started to show signs of sickness shortly after the storm. The surviving birds, the article states, are now being treated by volunteers.

Yukam lands on my lap. I close my hands around him and carry him to his cage.

"No more flying the coop for you, buster." I click the wire door shut.

"The surviving birds are now being treated by volunteers," I read again. I close the scrapbook, lift up a corner of my mother's mattress, and slide it back underneath.

Ava, daughter, give me book for birthday,
BIRDS OF AMERICA by John James Audubon.
Little flags stick out of book. "These are birds
that died," she tell me, "birds that are extinct
any more. Please note I do not kill any of them."
She run out of room, eat no cake.

I open book to flag at ivory-billed woodpecker:

When wounded and brought to the ground, the Ivory-bill immediately makes for the nearest tree, and ascends it with great rapidity and perseverance, until it reaches the top branches, when it squats and hides, generally with great effect. Whilst ascending, it moves spirally round the tree, utters its loud pait, pait, pait, at almost every hop, but becomes silent the moment it reaches a place where it conceives itself secure. They sometimes cling to the bark with their claws so firmly, as to remain cramped to the spot for several hours after death. When taken by the hand, which is rather a hazardous undertaking, they strike with great violence, and inflict very severe wounds with their bill as well as claws, which are extremely sharp and strong. On such occasions, this bird utters a mournful and very piteous cry.

3/13/86

The sound of the drill wakes me in the middle of the night. All I can see when I walk into the living room are my mother's hands, carving in the dim pool of her gooseneck lamp. When I see a robin's egg under the drill, my heart drops. I flick on the ceiling light. My mother flinches.

Without looking up from her work, she points her arm back toward the kitchen counter. A shoebox sits there, a desk lamp bent over it. I walk closer and peer inside. Nestled in a mishmash of cotton balls and scarves lies another robin's egg.

"It's still alive?" I reach a finger hesitantly toward the tiny speckled shell.

My mother turns off the drill and pulls the top of her surgical mask down to her chin.

"Don't touch," she says sharply. "Two die already."

She lets the mask snap back up. The drill whines back to life.

I can't contain a smile. A living egg!

"Omma?" I walk over to her. "Omma? I want to talk to you about something."

She continues to work as if she can't hear me.

"I think I'm going to go to the Salton Sea," I tell her. "I want to help those pelicans, Omma, the ones that are sick. I think I can help them."

My mother's drill jerks to the side. The blue eggshell shatters. A few yolky fragments spray my soup-stained shirt.

"See what you made me to do," she scolds, but when she looks up at me, her eyes are filled with something other than anger.

I have this dream quite often. A large egg sits in the middle of the living room, shining like water. It shudders, then hops, then fills with a wild tapping, like the roll of a snare drum. A sharp elbow, a familiar-looking elbow, pierces the shell from the inside. It is so slick with blood and yolk, I can't tell whether it is my mother's or my own. It flaps around, then stills. I wonder if it will find the strength to break all the way through.

The morning sun is surprisingly hot; the air conditioner in my Sonata staves off only some of it as I run errands, picking up things I'll need for the trip—toothpaste, deodorant, tampons, blank tapes, adapter cable, a fresh bag of candied ginger. Sweat drizzles down the back of my neck. I know the desert heat will be even more intense; I feel parched at the thought of it, my mouth dry as the sheets of seaweed my mother keeps on top of the refrigerator. I park in front of Luk's Market so I can get something to drink before I head home.

The window on the door of the market is broken, covered by a black garbage bag and duct tape, but an OPEN sign is looped over the doorknob. I push the door lightly.

"Hello?" I step into the dim store. No one answers. The only sound comes from the coolers humming in the back. I work my way toward them. A blast of cold air hits my skin as I slide a glass door open. I close my eyes to feel it better and reach in blindly for the bottle of raspberry sparkling water I know is right in front of my face.

"What you doing here?"

I am startled by Mr. Luk's voice. The bottle slips out of my hand and shatters against the floor. Cool water bubbles up between the straps of my sandals.

"I'm sorry, Mr. Luk." I bend over to pick up the pieces. I've been to this market dozens of times, but he is never happy to see me.

"You break, you buy," he says.

A small woman I haven't seen before comes running through a door near the coolers. One of her eyebrows is missing, replaced by a long puckered scar. She stands behind her husband and stares at me like she thinks she knows who I am.

"That girl Korean," I hear her tell him.

"What?" Mr. Luk barks back at her. "Are you a crazy woman? She no Korean girl."

"She is from Helen!" the woman says. She looks straight at me. "You are from Helen?"

"Yes!" I tell her. "Helen—that's my mother—Helen Sing Lo . . ."

The woman whispers frantically to her husband.

"This store is closed!" he says sharply.

"There's an open sign on the door. I was thirsty . . ."

"You pay for the drink!"

"Of course." I rummage through my wallet. I pull out a five-dollar bill, thrust it at him, and walk out of the store.

The woman comes running after me with change.

"Keep it." I open the car door.

"Your mother Helen old friend of mine." The woman pushes the bills and coins into my palm. "I sorry for my husband. Bad things happen here sometime. He just scared; just scared man."

I slide into the car, lean my head back. "I'm sorry . . ." I close the door.

The woman taps on the window. I roll it down.

"Have you eaten rice yet?" the woman asks.

I shake my head.

"I work with your mother when you was little girl," the woman says in a low voice, and digs into her deep apron pocket.

"Is there any problem?" The husband's voice is wound tight as he steps through the door of the market.

"No, no problem here!" the woman calls out. Her eyebrow scar twitches a bit.

"Tell your mother to see me," she whispers. She throws a handful of miniature Crunch bars onto my lap before she runs back to the market. Her husband ushers her brusquely back inside and rips the open sign from the door before he slams it shut.

I unwrap a Crunch bar, let my teeth pass through the deep brown chocolate, the pale crisped rice inside. Such an easy balance between these two flavors; such an uneasy balance in my own life—chocolate and rice battling it out, creating something different, something neither flavor can really claim. When I'm around other Korean people, even my mother—maybe especially my mother—I feel so black. When I'm around other black people, I feel so Korean. When I'm around anyone else, I just feel Other. The only time I really feel at home in my skin is when I'm slamming against the skin of my drum, but even then I know I'm doing it all wrong.

My sophomore year of college, a man, Dr. Park, came to my ethnomusicology class to give a talk on Korean music. When he got to the section on *pansori,* I made the mistake of telling the class I play the *pansori* with my mother. I usually never spoke up in class—the words just popped out of me. My professor was stunned; Dr. Park was even more stunned when I mentioned I use the *chang'go*.

"The *chang'go* isn't for *pansori*." He shook his head at me from across the lecture hall. "You know that, right? The *puk* is the traditional *pansori* drum."

"I don't have a *puk*," I stammered. I had no idea that I had been using the wrong drum. "My mother taught me on the *chang'go*." I didn't mention she had stolen the *chang'go* from the massage parlor where she worked at the time. It had been used as an end table there, the deerskin cluttered with plastic bottles of oil.

"Come up here." His voice was somewhere between a cajole and a bark.

I walked to the front of the room, my face burning.

He pushed a shiny red *chang'go* against my stomach, a stick into my right hand. "Show me," he said.

I looped the strap of the drum over my shoulder and began to tap out a few rhythms. I usually drum in response to my mother's song; my hands felt awkward, stiff in the quiet classroom.

"No, no, no." He watched me closely. "You are supposed to inhale when you strike the *kungp'yon,* exhale when you strike the *yolp'yon.*"

My breath caught in my chest. "This is how my mother taught me," I told him.

"Your mother taught you wrong." He took the *chang'go* back.

I shift and the small Crunch bars fall onto the floor of my car. The candy in my mouth suddenly feels cloying, like sweet mucus. It catches in my throat as I try to swallow it down.

At home, after about five glasses of water, I tell my mother I met a woman she used to work with. She looks suddenly suspended, like she is balanced on a thin wire.

"What woman?"

"Her married name is probably Luk. She works at Luk's Market, near Washington. Short woman, only one eyebrow . . ."

My mother wrinkles her face for a moment before her eyes light up. "Anchee?"

"She didn't say."

She grabs her keys and purse and races out of the apartment.

When I go into my room, I catch a glimpse of myself in the mirror over my dresser. My mother's sad eyes—the same shape, just with more of a lid—stare back at me. Her high, broad cheekbones rise under my skin. Three gulls flap past the window behind me. Their doubles skim across the mirror.

I bow shakily to myself and assume the *Choom Be,* the tae kwon do ready stance. I look at my reflection, fists waist high, held tight next to my body, shoulders square, legs wide, feet planted on the carpet. I wonder what in the world I could possibly be ready for.

A chicken darted in front of Hye-yang's feet as she passed through the stone walls that bordered the Folk Village. She stumbled to avoid the bird and pitched forward. The tip of her bow clunked against the ground like a cane; her bag of clothes threatened to come undone, the strap biting deep into her shoulder. The chicken fluffed itself and scurried away.

Hye-yang remained bent over a moment to catch her breath, amazed by how easily a small bird could knock her over. She readjusted her belongings and headed toward a row of craftspeople who were practicing their arts in front of small farmer's huts.

While tourists watched, women spun silk from cocoons roiling in an iron pot; a man swirled his calligraphy brush over a scroll; blacksmiths bent over their anvils; grandmothers tied expert knots, teenagers pounded rice into flour. How strange, thought Hye-yang, that people pay to watch other people work. People pretending they weren't being watched. Hye-yang felt dizzy—so much movement, so much concentrated staring, all around her.

She felt even more disoriented when she noticed a small stone house up ahead, built to resemble a home from Cheju-do. It looked just like her family's house—the same thatched roof held down with ropes and stones, the same volcanic rock fence. It was as if the house had been ferried over from the island with her and dropped onto the village grounds. Hye-yang stood before it, heart knocking wildly; a woman stepped outside the house, wearing a white diver's outfit. Hye-yang almost expected to see her mother's face, but the woman was young, around her own age. Hye-yang closed her eyes and took a deep breath. The air smelled like honeycomb and dry grass, not seaweed and wet rocks. She finally realized how far she was from home. She wasn't sure whether the lightness that filled her head was freedom or fear.

A sudden burst of gong and drumbeat fractured the air. The steady stream of visitors turned and headed toward the music. Hye-yang let herself get carried along. As the crowd parted to let the musicians through, she noticed they were part of a wedding procession. A priest walked behind the *chang'go* player, holding a wooden goose on a small tray, two ribbons tied around its neck. The groom walked solemnly behind him. Hye-yang's heart lifted when she realized that her friend Sun, the weekend "bride," was probably inside the elaborately carved wooden box carried on the shoulders of four men who followed the groom.

The men set the box—a wooden bird perched on each corner—onto the ground. Two women attendants in pink *hanbok*s helped the bride out. Even though her head was bent traditionally down, her face hidden behind her sleeves as the attendants led her to the proper place, Sun's forehead, the back of her neck were unmistakable. Hye-yang would know them anywhere. She pushed through the crowd to the front as the two women lowered Sun to her knees. The priest placed the wooden goose by her feet, then bent to the north and bowed twice.

Sun's face was covered for most of the ceremony, even during the several times the ceremonial cup was brought to her lips. When she finally raised her face above her sleeves, Hye-yang could see small pink circles painted on her cheeks. Without realizing what she was doing, Hye-yang began to wave frantically. Sun, who had looked so radiantly solemn, glanced over.

"Hye-yang!" she cried, a smile bursting across her face. Hye-yang waved harder.

The priest bent down and whispered fiercely to Sun. She nodded and the ceremony resumed, but Hye-yang could see Sun's shoulders quaking with laughter under her *hanbok.*

Hye-yang waited for Sun by the empty platform after the wedding was over. Sun came out soon in a plainer *hanbok,* the bright circles rubbed off her cheeks, her hair loose.

"I can't believe you're here!" Sun cried. "Are you staying? I can get you a job!"

"That's why I came," said Hye-yang.

"Come on." Sun grabbed Hye-yang's hand.

Before the day was out, Hye-yang was an employee of the Folk Village, slated to sell cuttlefish at a stand the following morning, slated to room with Sun in the village dormitory that night.

The two of them stayed up late, catching up on island life, village life, sharing smuggled bottles of OB beer. Around five in the morning, unable to sleep, Sun pulled Hye-yang outside. They hopped a couple of low stone fences and ended up in the area where Sun performed seesaw demonstrations. The moon, full as a grapefruit, bathed the field in a pale, pulpy light.

"How high can you go?" asked Hye-yang.

"I'll show you." Sun led her to the wooden plank. Hye-yang stepped onto the end of it.

Hye-yang watched, a bit nervous, Sun walk pretty far away before she turned, ran toward the seesaw, and jumped onto the other end.

A giddy, weightless feeling opened in Hye-yang's chest. She tilted her head back, spread her arms out wide, and let the night embrace her whole body as she rose into the air. If she opened her mouth, she thought, the moon would slide right in.

"What can you see?" Sun called up to her.

"I think I can see the whole world!" yelled Hye-yang, before she hit the ground and toppled over on her side.

Sun ran over to her. "Are you okay?"

Hye-yang nodded her head and started to laugh. She yanked Sun's leg until she crashed down next to her.

"Let's do it again." Hye-yang grabbed Sun's face.

They ran back to the seesaw.

"What can you see?" they yelled, as they flung each other into the air as high as they could.

"I can see the governor's palace!"

"I can see Hollywood, California!"

"I can see Cheju-do like a pebble in the ocean!"

"I can see the stars spell out my name!"

Dawn began to leak over the horizon. Hye-yang rose and rose with the spreading light.

The inside of the windshield is hot as an electric blanket against my palm. It's easily over a hundred degrees outside the car. I click the air conditioner up a notch and begin to navigate another 168-mile loop around the Salton Sea, my third continuous circle in the past six hours: Highway 86 until it curves into the 195 near Oasis, until it curves into the 111 near Mecca, until it curves, at Brawley, back into the 86 again.

The sea glints beyond scrubby, cracked acres of desert. I see it out of the corner of my eye, but I can't quite convince myself to drive any closer. As long as I keep circling, I haven't committed to anything—my car is just following the pull of gravity, a small planet orbiting a wet oblong star.

Splintered telephone poles line the road, forked open by lightning or wind. Dust devils spiral lazily over empty fields. Farmland turns into trailer park turns into citrus grove turns into date farm turns into vast expanse of sand and grit and nothing, the whole valley ringed with dark mountain ranges, looming brown parentheses of earth. I had thought this was a resort town, but there is not a golf course or fancy spa anywhere in sight. Maybe they're hiding somewhere between the highway and the water. Maybe they've evaporated in the desert heat.

I find myself anticipating certain landmarks I've already passed twice—the ancient liquor shop near Bombay Beach, the rusted-out motorboat in a field by Salton City, the soldier rows of date trees near 100 Palms. I begin to predict the name of the next passage of sand and gravel that will course beneath the road—*Alki Wash, Bee Wash, Cedar, Frink, Butter Wash, Wister, Sand, Signal Wash, Polo, Skee, Salt Wash, Gravel, Bug, Cattail Wash.* Near the horizon, the road wavers—

the asphalt, the land around it smearing into oily waves of vapor. I feel slightly dizzy, like my own edges are blurring out into the desert air, coagulating into dark distant hills.

I didn't say good-bye to my mother before I left. I didn't have a chance—she wasn't home when I woke up. I waited around longer than I planned to, but she never came back. I was worried I wouldn't go at all if I didn't go soon, so I wrote a quick note and left it on the counter by the robin's egg shoebox. As I loaded my *chang'go* into the car, a small slip of paper tumbled out from beneath the strings. Four lines of poetry were written there, in my mother's hand:

> *That fall the wild geese flew so far south*
> *they took the sky with them.*
>
> *Stay just as far away as you can;*
> *time will keep or lead you back.*

I recognized the lines from a library book I had once checked out, a collection of Korean courtesan poems from the Chosun dynasty. She must've looked at the book, must have copied some of the poems down, without me knowing. The thought of her reading those poems, poems written by *kisaeng,* women who had been used and ostracized by society six, seven centuries ago, was almost too much to handle. I put the poem in my pocket, loaded up the car, and pointed it, eyes brimming, toward the Salton Sea.

I have no idea how long I'll be gone—one week? A month? Long enough to try to set things right—whatever that means—if only I can bring myself close enough to the birds in the first place. The sea sparkles in my peripheral vision like a mirage. I know I can't keep circling like this, but for now it's all I can do.

Parakeet, Blue (Name: Lee Lee)

Ava, daughter, 13. Kill bird.
Forget to close cage after clean.
Lee Lee fly out window, into sky. Good bird,
like to eat seed in my mouth.
Songs in morning. No words.
Find him on patio, smack himself
dead on glass to get back in.

[birdseed captured under cellophane tape]

[pale blue feathers]

[bit of soiled Korean language newspaper]

2/11/84

Highway 111, as I come to know it, seems appropriately numbered—a row of three thin digits, each one almost invisible, spare and pale as the landscape it cuts through. Scattered patches of white—salt, I guess—gleam dully from the dirt like snow. Even the sky seems white, as if the blue had been taken by geese flying south, or, more likely, burned blank by the relentless sun.

I feel incredibly conspicuous in my shiny green car. The only other color along this stretch of the road comes from the occasional string of boxcars stopped on the Southern Pacific railway. The trains are pretty muted, too—dusty wine, dirty mustard, black sandstormed down to gray. The few cars I pass are equally eroded—pickup trucks painted with primer, twenty-year-old weather-faded sedans, eyes trained on me from inside, loaded with curiosity and threat. If I don't make some sort of decision soon, I worry that my own car, my own face might get sanded down to dust.

I crank the steering wheel and veer off the highway onto Desert Beach Drive.

The water spreads out before me, miles of flat shimmer. It looks refreshing, but as soon as I get out of the car, the heat and stench almost knock me over. An overpowering smell of bird and fish decay mixes in the air with something equally rank and environmental. I grab a piece of ginger to try to mask the scent, but the odor molecules still find a way to seep inside.

What planet have I landed on? I stomp a sleeping foot against the pavement, slap some life into my face, look around to make sure no cars have pulled into the lot behind me. The area is completely deserted. An empty fifties-style motel sits on the other end

of the parking lot, all of its doors open, the rooms bare. The building is so utterly abandoned, no one has even bothered to vandalize
it. Dusty tufts of overgrown bougainvillea seem incongruous
against the walls, random bursts of fuchsia life.

A marina up ahead, partly underwater and long deserted, touts
sandwiches and live bait from its sun-bleached awning. An old
yacht club, shaped like a ship with broken porthole windows and
faded nautical flags painted around the border, silently faces the
water. It looks like no one has dined or danced there in decades.
What happened here? *What happened?*

Holding my breath, I walk toward the sweeping span of water.
As I get closer, the sea begins to looks less sparkly—it is the color
of tea, the color of mud. The beach is not a sandy one, either, as it
had seemed from the parking lot. The ground is completely
heaped with barnacles, small white tubes that crunch beneath my
sandals, making me shiver even in the intense heat. I remember
reading somewhere that barnacles had been introduced to the area
by WWII aircraft that used the sea for dive bomb practice. I feel
like I'm walking across a bone yard.

Every few steps, I come across dead fish in various stages of
decomposition—some still silver and wet with missing eyes, some
dry and brown like the cuttlefish my mother buys in Koreatown,
some dissolved down to bone, bleached white as the barnacles
beneath them. Pale-green bird droppings offer the only other color
on the ground. I walk up to an old swing set and steady myself
against one of its hot metal legs. The end of a small slide disappears into a mass of barnacles nearby.

What am I doing here? I wonder, queasy from the rotten air.
Then I see the jetty up ahead, covered with dead and dying pelicans.

The birds, dozens of them, are heaped against each other, a
seething clump of beige and brown, long beaks jutting out like cac-

tus spines. Some pelicans convulse violently, others have already started to decompose, their speckled breasts caved, split open. My eyes feel seared. Bile rises in my throat. I don't know what I expected—some ballet of languid wings, something remotely beautiful. Anything but this.

One bird lets out a horrible screech. Its head lifts briefly off the ground, then collapses, its beak wide open. I bend over and retch a small splash of orange onto the barnacles and fish bones, my contribution of color to the landscape.

I stumble back to the Sonata and blast the cold scent of Freon into my nose. My throat, my eyes are raw. I pop another sugary clump of ginger into my mouth, lean my head against the steering wheel, and take some deep breaths. It would be so easy to go home, so easy to hit the road and never look back. It would be so easy, but when I pull back onto the 111, I can't seem to drive toward San Diego. I find myself pulling off the highway again onto a street not far down the road, one I've passed three times already, a driveway with a sign that reads VISITOR'S CENTER.

I avoid the stuffed-animal displays inside the deeply air-conditioned building—my stomach feels wrung out like a rag; the glassy eye of a barn owl could easily twist me dry. A short, stocky woman behind the information counter, her face deeply creased by years of sun, looks up as she straightens a display of maps that look like they were printed at least three decades before.

"Can I help you?" Her voice is gravelly, cigarette-thick. She stares at me suspiciously.

"I'm here to help the birds?" I swallow the sweet acid that wants to rise up my throat again.

"You with Fish and Game?" the woman asks.

I shake my head.

"Fish and Wildlife?"

I shake my head again.

"Bureau of Land Management?"

"No . . ."

"The prison?"

"No!" I shake my head more emphatically.

"We're getting people from all over." The woman spreads her thick arms out to encompass them all. "Where'd you say you were from?"

"San Diego." I cough out the words.

"Oh, so you're from Sea World, then!" The woman's wrinkled face brightens. "I heard they were coming down to get some of the pelicans. I just love Sea World . . . took my friend's grandkids there not a month ago. Shamu had some kind of infection. Kids were mighty disappointed—show was canceled. How's he doing now?"

"I don't know . . ."

"Oh, of course not—you work with birds, not whales. Those flamingos you got are something else, aren't they?"

"Actually . . ."

"Can you imagine sleeping on one foot like that? I don't know how they keep their balance."

I shrug. I feel off balance on two feet.

"My friend's granddaughter wants to dye her hair like a flamingo . . . you think they dye those birds? Some looked pinker than others."

"Maybe . . ."

"And those penguins—aren't they darling? Like little Charlie Chaplins . . ." The woman starts to waddle around in imitation behind her desk.

"I'm not from Sea World," I finally blurt out.

The woman stops her penguin walk. She looks crestfallen, as if I had deliberately misled her. Her gaze turns suspicious again.

"I'm here on my own," I tell her. "I figured they'd need more volunteers . . ."

The woman takes a moment to compose herself. "You want to speak to Darryl Sternberg over at the hospital." Her voice is suddenly businesslike, her face flushed.

"And where would that be?" I ask.

"Just beyond the dock we got out back, and up the beach a ways." She busies herself again with her map straightening.

"Thank you." I dig into my pocket, hand a dollar to the woman, then take a map from the front of the display. The woman nods curtly before the whole display stand tumbles over again. I start to help her pick up the maps.

"You better go see Darryl before it gets too hot," she says. "It got up to one-twenty yesterday. He's gonna be cranky."

"Thank you," I tell her. "I'm sorry about this . . ."

The woman nods and slaps the maps together as I take a sip

from a water fountain to soothe my aching throat before I walk back out into the blast of heat outside.

A temporary structure is set up a few hundred yards ahead on the barnacled shore—chain-link walls covered with UV-protectant fabric. The air gets heavier, thick with the scent of something gone wrong, as I get closer. My stomach twists tighter.

Through the opening between two of the chain-link panels, I can see at least fifty people inside. Some tend pelicans in a child's wading pool, others unload trash bags full of dead birds. Some weigh the birds, catalog them, slit their bellies open, put hearts and livers into clear sandwich bags. In a small red tin structure adjacent to the enclosure, two men throw bodies into an incinerator that sends more heat into the sweltering air. A pile of dead birds taller than me stands in the corner. The stench is unbearable. I fan myself with the folded map.

"Can I help you?" A harried-looking man comes up to me.

"I'm looking for the hospital."

"You found it," he replies, then races off to the plastic pool full of birds, syringes of some kind spilling out of his vest pockets.

"This is the hospital?" I ask another man who is hefting a dead pelican onto a scale.

"You were expecting private beds?" he asks as he records the weight, then throws the bird in a pile.

"Running water, maybe." I look around. No sink, no fans. Dirt floor. Flies everywhere.

The man laughs and points to a long hose that snakes across the ground.

"Could you please tell me where I could find Darryl?"

"He's over there." He points to the man by the wading pool, the man I had first talked to.

"Thank you." I try not to breathe. My voice sounds the way I've heard people speak after they've inhaled pot, all tight in the throat.

I walk over to the pool. A woman holds a pelican's floppy neck while Darryl squirts something from one of the syringes through a tube into its beak.

"Excuse me." I tentatively tap his shoulder.

He snaps his head around. Part of the liquid from the syringe squirts out, splashes against my jeans.

"Dammit!" he shouts.

"I'm sorry . . ."

"That syringe was measured out perfectly," he says. "This bird only got about sixty milliliters of electrolytes, thanks to you. Those forty milliliters on your calf aren't going to do you any good, are they?"

"I didn't mean—"

"Who *are* you?"

"My name is Ava. Ava Sing Lo. I'm here to help the birds."

"Well, then." He hands me a wet cloth. It is blessedly cool in my palm. He gestures to a pelican sitting at the edge of the pool, its neck draped languidly over the edge. "Wipe out this bird's eyes. I need to get more solution." He storms off.

I tuck my map into my pocket. "What do I do?" I ask the woman, stroking a pelican's head. The woman's light-brown hair is starting to come out of its hasty ponytail. Sweat streams down her forehead, trickles behind her glasses, down her freckled nose, over her chapped lips.

"Just wipe its eyes with the cloth," she says. "They fall down and can't hold up their heads, poor things. Their eyes get all full of mud and salt and crap before we can get to them . . ."

I swallow and walk to the other side of the blue plastic pool, which I now realize has circus animals printed all over it, almost mockingly festive. I kneel down beside the bird. Its eyes are so caked, I'm sure it can't see a thing. I tentatively raise the cloth to the pelican's head. I can feel the bird startle a bit, but it is too weak to do much. I gently touch the cloth against its covered eye. The bird flinches, shudders. A wing brushes lightly against my arm, sends a shiver down my spine. I wipe at the hardened crud, then run some water from the hose over the cloth so that I can loosen it some more. Eventually the dirt smears off. The pelican's eye looks right into mine. My heart starts to pound.

"It's okay," I tell the bird, then move over to the other side. The bird relaxes a bit as I wipe at the other eye. Once that one emerges from the layers of mud and salt, though, it is glassy, vacant. It takes me a moment to realize the pelican is dead.

"Oh, no," I whisper.

"We lose a lot of them," the woman says, raising her arm as if to signal someone.

"I have sort of a history of killing birds," I tell her.

The woman doesn't say anything, but I can feel her recoil.

A man in an olive-drab jumpsuit comes up to the pool and whisks the bird away without a word.

"How can you stand this?" I ask the woman.

"It doesn't get any easier," the woman admits. "Believe me."

"Are you a volunteer?"

"No, I'm with a wildlife refuge in Colorado. They shipped a few of us out here to help with the effort. I'm supposed to be here another two weeks, but frankly, I'm not sure I can hang on that long."

I wonder how long I can stand it myself. It would be so easy to just walk away. I know I can't, though, not yet.

"How many birds have been affected so far?"

"Over three thousand already—a few hundred brown pelicans among them. They're endangered, you know. It's kind of ironic, really—earlier this year, the browns were getting close to getting off the list, but now with this outbreak, it's possible we'll have to add the western whites to the list now, too."

I look around. The pile of dead birds is almost too awful to comprehend, big enough to fill the pages of several scrapbooks.

"I'm Abby, by the way," the woman extends her hand. "Abby Westin."

"Ava Sing Lo."

Abby's fingers are waterlogged and wrinkled against the back of my hand.

"Where are you staying?" Abby asks.

"I'm not sure. This whole thing was sort of a split-second decision. I figured I would find something once I got here."

"There aren't any hotels nearby," Abby says. "Not anymore, at least."

"I saw the one off Desert Beach Drive. It's like a ghost town over there."

"It's like a ghost town everywhere," says Abby. "If you want, you can bunk with me. They've set up big army tents for all the people who've traveled here to help."

"I'm just a volunteer."

"I'm sure you could stay with me," says Abby. "There's an empty cot. The gal who was sharing the place couldn't deal with all this. I was this close to leaving with her."

"No time for chitchat, girls." Darryl reappears. "We have to tube these birds. The van from the Pacific Wildlife Center is going to be here any moment to bring them to Laguna Niguel."

"What do they do with them there?" I ask.

"Rehabilitate them some more," he says, as he sticks a tube into a pelican's beak. The pelican is weak, but it has enough gumption to give him a bit of a struggle. "More electrolytes, then a multi milk solution—half milk, half water—eventually fish. When they're strong enough, up and preening, they get released." He hands Abby a tubed syringe. I watch her feed it to a pelican easily, like she has done it hundreds of times. She probably has.

"Darryl," asks Abby. "Would it be possible for Ava to bunk with me? She's not with the refuge—she's here as a volunteer—but she needs a place to stay."

"Don't see why not." Darryl tubes another bird. "We appreciate your help—it's the least we could do in return—not that the accommodations are all that spectacular."

"That's fine," I tell him. "Thank you."

"Welcome aboard." Darryl tosses me a syringe.

An hour later, after I struggle, and fail, to tube several birds, Abby tells me about a weekly boat tour for new volunteers and refuge workers. If I hurry, she says, I can make it. I have a feeling she just wants to get rid of me, but Darryl says it's a good opportunity to get a sense of the sea's expanse, its history, its flora and fauna. I stumble to the dock, where I am shuttled onto a boat with about ten other shell-shocked people. They sit like zombies, silently facing each other on the two benches that stretch the length of the boat. My arms feel raked by resistant pelican beaks; my biceps sting, but I can't find any scratches when I examine my skin.

A perky woman in a tan uniform hops on board and starts up the motor. As the pontoon pulls out onto the sea, she launches into her regular tour spiel like she has a boat full of eager vacationers, not a group of death-stunned workers.

"The Salton Sea," she says grandly, "was created by mistake! In 1905, water diversion dikes along the Colorado River collapsed, and water flooded into the ancient Salton Basin for almost two years, leaving behind the largest inland lake in California! Today the lake is about thirty-five miles long and fifteen miles wide and straddles two counties! It boasts one of the best fisheries you could ever find!"

She rattles off the varieties of fish in the sea as if they're all swimming happily in the depths, ready to be snared by some lucky wrangler's hook. As if they're not bloated and wasted by botulism, clotting the surface of the water.

When she mentions that the tilapia originally came from Africa, the whole crowd in the boat mutely swivels around to face me, as if I'm responsible for the slew of fish myself. I look down, my face hot. Brownish water seeps up through some little grommeted holes on the floor of the boat and slides over to my feet. I tense my toes inside my shoes. When the woman says that tilapia are mouth brooders, that their babies swim into their parents' mouths for protection, I can feel everyone stare at my lips.

I don't hear much else until the woman mentions gulf croakers. The fish actually croak when they die, the woman says, as the pontoon journeys toward the center of the sea; they make a froglike croaking sound. When they're alive, they make a sound like a drum. It's because of their modified air bladders. The woman sounds a bit embarrassed by this last word.

I try to listen for the fish drum, fish croak, but all I can hear is the motor of the boat. I never knew fish could make sounds. I'll try to record some later for my MIDI, maybe mix them with Kane's voice. With all the dead fish floating around, I'll probably have a better chance hearing them croak than I will hearing them drum, although I would much prefer something percussive. My hands feel restless for the skin of my *chang'go.* I thrum my fingers against the edge of the boat until someone shoots me a dirty look.

I started drumming on my first birthday. I can't remember the actual event, but I remember my mother's telling of it.

In Korea it's traditional to have a huge first birthday feast, during which objects are set before the child—coins, a calligraphy brush, a dancer's fan. The first object the child reaches for supposedly determines his or her life's path.

That day, so the story goes, my mother brought me to McDonald's. She set a few things on the table—some pennies, a shell, a small doll, a comb—but I reached for the chopsticks my mother had brought from home. She had been using them to eat her french fries, dangling each strip of potato in front of her mouth like a worm before she bit it away from the pinch of wood. I grabbed the sticks right out of her hand and banged and banged them against the yellow Formica.

Table drum, floor drum, chair drum, bed drum, knee drum, eardrum, heart drum, *ba dum, ba dum,* the whole world became a drum for me that day. When I was three, I got my first real drum— a feathered tom-tom my mother bought at a dime store. When I was six, she found a used set of bongos at a garage sale. Then, when I turned eleven, my mother gave me the *chang'go,* the drum that quickly became my home, my heart. That night was the first night she sang the *pansori* to me, the first night she began to let her story spill. Sometimes I think my whole life has been a silence punctuated by drum beats and MIDI samples and tae kwon do grunts. In between, I feel blank as the desert sky. Only sound can pull me into sharp relief.

A loud motor, like wire brushes on cymbals, whirs into earshot. I look up as an airboat speeds by, its floor heaped with pelicans, a man in an orange jumpsuit standing above them. The sight of the birds is sickening, but the huge caged fan mounted on the back of the boat sends a welcome blast of slightly cooler air across my face as it passes. Out in the water, the air is not quite so stifling, the stink not quite so lethal, but it is still hotter and smellier than anything I'll ever be used to. I'm grateful to at least have some space around my head, some open sky, after being walled in at the bird hospital for the last hour. The mountains that ring the sea are too far away to feel like walls.

The woman points out the line that cuts across the hills like a belt. A waterline, she says, from an ancient sea. This basin has been filled many times, with both salt- and freshwater. Freshwater snail shells can still be found up there.

The pontoon passes the top of a telephone pole that juts out of the water like a thick finger. The water level, the woman explains, keeps rising because of agricultural runoff from nearby farms. The sea won't reach those watermarks up in the hills anytime soon, but it does sometimes rise enough to cause problems. Several resort areas were inundated in the seventies. Whole buildings are now underwater.

"The Salton Sea has no outlet!" she explains to her catatonic audience.

The phrase sounds incredibly foreboding, even though I know the sea could be just the outlet I've been looking for. The boat passes some dead treetops pushing up through the wet surface. The branches are covered with birds. Living birds. Common cormorants, says the woman.

These birds are diving birds, she says, great fishers, but they're clumsy on the ground. They jump off trees to fly so that they won't have to run. See their legs, way back on their bodies, like they're coming out of their rumps? They'd tip over if they tried to run. In the Orient, the woman continues, people keep these birds as pets.

I expect everyone to turn and look at me again, but no one does. I am amazed they can't see my mother shining through my skin. My whole body feels like a watermark, a dark salty line left behind by the unknown soldier who fathered me. Only my eyes, my cheekbones, carry traces of my mother, like snail shells left behind, fragile memories of freshwater.

That night, I leave the heat of the canvas tent I share with Abby in search of a phone. I follow a narrow trail, cut through some pungent-smelling brush, silvery in the beam of my flashlight. The trail ends at a wall of dirt, chest-high. When I walk up to it, I am startled to find water on the other side, mushrooming dark over the lip of earth. If the dirt barrier were to crumble, the sea would come pouring out, knocking me over. I turn and run back down the path, branches scratching at my clothes.

As I pass back through the encampment, I catch sight of the ranger station and find my way to the pay phone. From here, the sea looks flat, nonthreatening. I watch the water shimmer in the moonlight and let my breath return to normal as the answering machine clicks on in San Diego. My own generic "please leave a message" recording is gone, replaced by a squawk, then Kane's voice crowing, "*Yoboseyo?*"

I can't remember Kane ever saying the special phone hello before; I certainly can't remember recording it. Either my mother impersonated his voice on the tape or she bought another parrot. Both possibilities make me feel strange. So does the fact that my mother changed the message so quickly after I left.

"Omma?" I ask after the beep. "Are you home?" I picture my voice trailing out into the living room. "Hello? Are you there?"

No one picks up.

A train rattles in the distance.

"I'm at the Salton Sea, Omma." I try to raise my voice above the train's whistle. Hopefully my message will be audible. "I just wanted to let you know I got here okay. I helped out in the bird hospital for a while. Tomorrow they want me to walk around the beaches to find more birds. Hopefully I'll find some that can be saved. I don't know how—"

The answering machine beeps and cuts me off. I consider calling back, but I'm not sure what else I would say. The trains keep coming.

The tent is like a sauna when I enter it, shining my flashlight ahead of me. Abby, asleep in her clothes, frowns and flips over when the light hits her face. I flick it off and find my way to my cot in the dark. I strip down to my underwear, fold the hot top blanket down to the bottom of the cot and scoot under the scratchy sheet beneath. It takes me a long time to fall asleep. Right after I finally drift off, around 2:00 A.M., Abby cries out in her sleep. I wake up, heart pounding.

"Omma?" I ask, ready to grab my drum. Then the heat hits me, the smell, and I remember where I am. I wait for my heart to calm down, wait for it to feel steady as the trains that seem to run all night, a rhythm of steel against track that echoes across the hills. I slide back into sleep, clack clack, clack clack. Every couple of hours, Abby cries out again.

Dried squid dangled around Hye-yang's head like stiff mittens from clothesline strings. The flat brown bodies brushed against the tips of her ears, her forehead, her hair, as she navigated her way around the stand. She enjoyed selling the cuttlefish to hungry Folk Village visitors, but after a few weeks, she began to feel restless in her little booth, tired of the fish reek that began to waft from her skin. During a lull, she wandered over to the archery area, picked up a bow, and shot an arrow straight into the heart of the rice straw target. A manager saw; one of his archers was going to marry a GI and leave the village, he said. Would she be willing to perform demonstrations? Hye-yang was quick to accept the offer. She saw the squid lift off her skin by the dozens, a whoosh of leathery wings in flight.

She soon spent long, satisfying hours pulling her right arm back, squinting her eyes into fierce focus. All the shame she had caused her family on the island distilled into one thin, sharp point after another, then flew straight out of her arms.

At Sun's urging, Hye-yang also began to sing a few times a week. She sang most often for the traditional farmer's dance troupe, but her true moment of glory came when she was allowed to sing the *pansori,* accompanied by a single drum. Her voice wasn't ripped raw like a trained *pansori* singer's, but she could feel lament and longing thick in her throat. She knew the crowd could feel it, too—she often saw men and women cry when she sang. Their tears fed her, filled her heart near to bursting with wet diamond drops. Her whole body sometimes felt ready to explode into song, shimmering like a handful of glitter in the air.

Every night, she and Sun pushed their sleeping mats together; their hair, their hands tangled like dreams as they slept. Every day, Hye-yang woke up eager to go to work. She never felt so happy, so deeply at home in her life.

A year after Hye-yang arrived at the Folk Village, Sun planned a trip back to Cheju-do for her grandmother's sixtieth birthday celebration. Hye-yang felt torn. She missed the island, missed the jagged cliffs, the salt air, the fields of yellow rapeseed flowers, but she hadn't heard from her mother and grandmother since she left. The only time she let herself remember their faces was when she wrote their names across the envelope she sent home each month with a portion of her earnings. The women often appeared in her dreams, though, swimming deep underwater, grabbing at strange sea creatures. When she tried to reach for them, they dissipated like clouds.

A storm brewed while Hye-yang watched her friend pack for the weekend. Rain began to explode against the ground as soon as Sun kissed Hye-yang good-bye and left the dormitory. Through the window, Hye-yang watched Sun bend against the wind while she made her way toward the bus station. With weather like this, Hye-yang knew she wouldn't be able to perform outdoors at the Folk Village for days, with either her bow or her voice. She would have to spend the weekend shivering in the cuttlefish stand, water dripping through the straw roof, turning the strands of squid slick and even more pungent. Hye-yang suddenly realized how empty the Folk Village would feel without Sun around. She grabbed some clothes, threw them into a small bag, and ran through the storm to catch up with her friend.

Peach face lovebirds (2) (Names: Lulu, Soo)
Ava, daughter, 21. Kill birds with pan.
She buy me pan at flea market for scrambled egg.
When she cook it, birds fall down. Gas comes from pan
(called Teflon). Smells like nothing to person,
make birds into nothing.

[small feathers, lime green and peach]

[foil wrapper from stick of butter]

[receipt from flea market]

7/18/93

I walk along the beaches, my hands stuffed into hot gloves, garbage bags sweating against my legs. A week on the job, I have yet to find a living bird among the barnacles, but there is no shortage of dead ones. Every couple of hours, another one of my bags is full, bulging with feathers and bones. Beaks strain against the plastic; some poke all the way through. I leave the bags on the beach so someone from the hospital can pick them up later in a golf cart. The heat and stench that permeate each hour of my day slowly become familiar, but never less disturbing.

After dinner, Darryl suggests we all have a scent party to get the death smell out of our noses. Everyone rushes off to their tents and comes back with various bottles and cans and candles and baggies to put on the picnic table. We all circle it, leaning over to sniff the various objects, walking slowly, hesitantly, like we're playing musical chairs.

I deeply inhale Old Spice deodorant, a stick-on air freshener disk, a bayberry scented candle, a handful of eucalyptus seeds, citronella insect repellent. I can feel Darryl's eyes linger on me as I bend over an unlit incense cone, a plastic jug of baby wipes, a tube of coconut suntan oil. The way he looks at me has changed since I've been here—his eyes turn soft in my direction. My shoulders tense, and I feel him turn away, but our heads knock into each other as we both lean toward a lavender-scented sachet. I jump back, bumping Abby's face into a jar of instant coffee. When Abby lifts her head, her nose is coated in brown powder.

"Sorry," Darryl and I both say at the same time. I don't look at him, but I can feel him hesitate for a moment, then move further ahead, toward some cedar chips, anise-flavored toothpaste, rose-petal potpourri.

"No problem," laughs Abby, brushing herself off. "I love the smell of coffee."

She plunges a finger into a pot of Vicks VapoRub and smears it under my nose.

The menthol fills my skull, cools my face, burns the touch of Darryl's eyes off my skin. I can barely smell the packet of Kool-Aid, ripped open, or the paper wrapper that once held salt taffy that comes next. I rub some of the slick goo off my upper lip. When I look up again, Darryl is gone.

I stumble, scent-drunk, back to the tent and pull the small box of candied ginger from my purse. I almost brought the box to the scent party but in the end decided not to. The ginger is for me alone. I didn't want it to get touched, changed, by so many other smells. I crush a bit between my fingers and breathe in the sharp scent of it, like smelling salts, to clear my swooning, aroma-swimming head.

"I think Darryl likes you," Abby says as she comes into the tent, a few dark grains still on her nose.

"I don't want to be liked right now." I pop a piece of ginger into my mouth, then close my eyes, heart pounding.

"Do you have a boyfriend at home?" asks Abby.

I shake my head.

"A girlfriend?"

"No." I open my eyes again.

"Darryl's a nice guy." Abby takes off her shirt and rubs her face with it.

"I know. I just don't want to get involved with anyone right now." I don't tell Abby that I've never really been involved with anyone before—just a few ridiculous dates in college. I don't tell her that I'm scared my mother will rise up like a ghost between me and anyone I try to touch, that she'll get between me and any pleasure I may hope to feel. I don't tell her my nipples are inverted, the tips sucked back into my chest like a turtle pulling its head back into its shell, like something shying away from the light. I don't tell her that whenever I touch myself, whenever I try to bring myself to that place of shiver and sigh I've heard so much about, my mother's voice shrieks inside my head and my body shuts down. I don't tell her my mother's story is so heavy in my bones that I can't even begin to think about writing a new story for myself.

"Good night, Ava." Abby slips into her cot.

"Sweet dreams," I tell her, although I'm sure they'll be anything but. I try not to think about Darryl trying to sleep, maybe thinking of me, just a few yards away.

I can see my mother's heart. It glows inside her chest in the dark, a hummingbird feeder filled with bright-red liquid. Two tubes swoop out from the bottom; the rubber tips poke through the droop of her breasts. I bend and wrap my lips around one. The hollow pellet is hard, like a bead on a cheap necklace. I press it between my palate and tongue and begin to suck. A thin, sweet liquid pours into my mouth. Hungry, I pull harder with my tongue, but only a feeble stream flows out. My mother's rib cage contracts—painfully, it appears—with each vacuum pull of my mouth. The hummingbird feeder rattles inside. I can tell if I suck too hard, the glass will shatter. I relax my lips and pull away. My mother spins around and walks back into the night.

I wake up starving, a film of sweetness on my tongue. I don't feel hungry, exactly—more hollowed out, like some of the birds I find, ones that have been gutted by wild dogs or the steady jaw of decomposition. My appetite has been gone for days, so I am glad to feel some semblance of hunger, but at breakfast I can barely swallow down a bite or two from a tin of military-issue corned beef hash. I don't think I can stomach eating near the hospital anymore. I can't stomach eating with people who handle dead birds, can't stomach these Meals Ready to Eat, the containers sealed like small coffins. Maybe if I could find a real meal, one made with actual fresh ingredients, I'd be able to force something down.

By lunchtime, the heat is so unbearable, it almost takes away my appetite, but I ask for some suggestions anyway.

"There's a place out by Bombay Beach, just south of here," Darryl says. "I've heard it's pretty good."

"Maybe I'll give it a try." I look at my feet.

"Would you like some company?" he asks.

I feel myself blush.

"No, thanks," I tell him. "I just need to get away by myself for a little bit."

"I know the feeling," he says. "But I probably need to stay here, anyway—I am Mr. Supervisor Man, after all." He affects a superhero pose—legs out wide, hands on hips, chest puffed out.

I pretend not to notice his stance. "I'll tell you all about it."

Darryl's chest deflates, his arms drop.

Bon appetit!" he calls out as I walk to my car.

* * *

In the rearview mirror, I watch Darryl watch me drive away. I shift my thoughts to the road ahead, the familiar blankness of the 111, the heat that the air conditioner can't quite seem to dispel. I wonder if Bombay Beach is an East Indian colony, although I can't imagine people in saris at the Salton Sea, eating samosas and chewing on cardamom seeds. After all, Mecca Beach certainly isn't an Islamic spiritual destination. Still, I find myself excited by the prospect of some real food. Even more excited by the prospect of getting away from the birds, the bird people, Darryl's slow warm gaze.

The Aloha Room sits in the middle of a salt-encrusted parking lot near the water. Inside, the air is blessedly cool and smells blessedly clean—no trace of bird. Hawaii memorabilia straight out of the fifties is tacked to bamboo-lined walls, interspersed with photos of John Wayne and other Hollywood cowboys. Neon beer signs sputter their light into the dim room, along with the paper Japanese lanterns in orange and green and pink that hang from the ceiling. A counter spans one wall by the kitchen, shaded by an awning made of straw. Red and black vinyl booths line the other walls. A revolving pie rack gleams near the cash register, peaks of meringue rising inside like clouds. I feel my mouth begin to water for the first time in days.

In one booth, a woman, the only customer in the restaurant, sits hunched over a cigarette. I glance at her offhandedly, then do a double take. She appears to be wearing a tiara and a huge plush tomato costume. I wonder if I'm hallucinating from lack of sleep, but even after I rub my eyes, the woman is still in the strange outfit, along with black fishnet stockings and bright-red pumps.

"Hey, Miss Tomato!" a heavyset woman with salmon-colored hair calls out from the kitchen window that opens out to the counter. "Show some vegetable spirit, why don't you?"

"A tomato is a *fruit*," Miss Tomato answers sullenly, her voice raspy, as far from a tomato voice as I could have imagined. "You should know that, Frieda, you work in the food service industry."

The woman steps out from behind the counter and walks over to where I'm standing by the front door, unsure whether or not to seat myself or wait for some sort of permission.

"She won the Miss Tomato Pageant at the Tomato Festival over in Niland today, and is she celebrating?" She gestures to the woman in the booth. "Is she whipping herself into one big salsa party? No, Miss Tomato Emily Lawrence is moping around the Aloha Room like a great big rotten vegetable."

"Fruit, Frieda!" Miss Tomato repeats before she takes another big drag on her cigarette. "I wouldn't be no stinking vegetable."

"Are you from the health board?" Frieda asks. I shake my head.

"You should put out that ciggy anyway, Emily," says Frieda. "I don't want to get busted. You're not supposed to be smoking in here."

Emily gives her the finger and takes another drag.

"Have a seat," says Frieda.

I walk over to a duct-taped counter stool. The woman presents a coffee-and-grease-stained menu with a flourish.

"Specials today are patty melt with chips, breaded veal cutlet, and Cobb salad, except with no ham, but I could do double turkey."

"Veal is cruel, Frieda." Emily gets up from her booth and squeezes herself into a stool two away from me. Some of the soft tomato costume smooshes over, presses into my elbow. I'm seized with the urge to wrap my arms around it like a big stuffed animal and fall asleep. "You know what they do to make veal? They lock poor little baby cows up in cages and don't even let them walk around or nothing."

"Well, I don't do *that.*" Frieda shakes her head knowingly at me. "We buy them frozen from the Price Club."

The tomato woman snorts and takes another puff. "Give me a Bud," she says. "Lite."

"I always did like pickled tomatoes." Frieda winks before she shooshes the beer from the tap into a large plastic glass and hands it to Emily.

"You would think he would at least show up for the pageant." The tomato woman turns to me, her tiara slightly askew on her bleach-blonde hair. Dark roots sprout from her jagged part. "You would think that if he cared about me one friggin' iota, he would be there to see me at least do my tap dance number."

"Her boyfriend didn't show," Frieda says in a stage whisper.

"He's a Tomato Adjuster, for god's sake," Emily says. "All the tomato people got the day off."

"I'm sure he had a good excuse," I pipe up, suddenly aware I haven't said a word since I walked in.

"Oh, so you know where he went?" Emily scrunches her eyebrows at me. "You tell me, where the fuck was he?" She slams her cup against the counter. Beer sloshes out onto her costume, darkens and mats it in a series of blotches.

"I'm sorry . . ."

"Don't you pick on this poor girl," Frieda scolds Emily, then turns to me. "She's just pissed off, sweetheart. Don't you listen to her."

"He's probably off porking some other little tomato, the slime bucket." Emily guzzles the rest of her beer. "I owe you, Frieda," she says, then hefts herself off the stool and strides toward the door, red plush bobbing around her. It takes Emily a few tries to get out—the sides of the costume won't fit through the jamb. She has to turn sideways and scrunch the tomato with both of her hands before she can leave.

"What'll it be, honey?" Frieda asks.

I quickly scan the menu, my brain a bit addled from the tomato woman.

"The Cobb salad sounds fine." I point to the hand-printed specials paper-clipped to the menu.

"Good choice," the woman says, "even without the ham."

"Is she gone?" A man's voice booms out of the kitchen.

"It's safe, you can come out now," Frieda chimes back.

"Thank god." He pokes his head in the window.

"Oh, she's not that bad, Ray, come on." Frieda leans over rows of glasses to kiss him.

"She's a man-eater." Ray ducks out of the kitchen, rubbing his short salt-and-pepper beard with one hand, holding the large plastic salad bowl with the other. He wears the same kind of Hawaiian shirt that Frieda does. They are about the same size, too, in girth, the buttons straining against their bellies. "And I don't mean that in any pleasurable way." He sets the salad on the counter in front of me.

"I should hope not," Frieda laughs. "This is my husband, Ray," she tells me. "Ray, this is . . . I didn't ever get your name, did I?"

"Ava. Ava Sing Lo."

"Well, isn't that a pretty name, now?" Frieda says. "Sounds Oriental."

"Hmmm." I spear a cherry tomato.

"So, what brings you into these parts, Miss Ava Sing Lo?" asks Ray.

"The birds. I'm helping out at the hospital."

"Oh, isn't it a shame?" Frieda's face washes over with sadness. "It just about breaks my heart. Not so good for business, either. Just this morning, in fact, we carried about eight or so dead pelicans, and one tern, to the dumpster. They were just lying there on the parking lot by the beach."

"You should call the hospital about them," I tell her. "We're doing statistics, and we have an incinerator."

"Oh, I wouldn't want to get in the way of you doing your job, honey," says Frieda, "but we were about to open for breakfast and we sure didn't want to turn the stomachs of our customers. It's hard enough getting people to come here as it is, off the beaten track and all."

I force down the lettuce and strips of processed cheese I held in my mouth. These people had been carrying dead birds a few hours ago; who knew how well they washed their hands? My appetite quickly withers.

"And the smell—that's enough to turn them away," adds Ray.

I push my salad bowl toward a glass sugar container.

"It's worse even than the algae tides, and those can stink up the place like you don't want to know," says Frieda. "Which do you think is worse, Ray? The green tides or the red?"

"Nothing stinks like these birds." He pinches his nose. "But you get used to it, you know, just like you can get used to pretty much anything." He leans his elbow on the counter; an anchor is tattooed on the inside of his forearm. POPEYE, I think, even though Ray's arms are not nearly as big as the cartoon character's, and both his eyes seem serviceable.

"I think the green tides are worse than the red." Frieda scrunches up her face. "The green are algae, the red are little dinosaur germs."

"Dinoflagellates," Ray corrects.

"They turn the whole sea red, or green, depending on the tide. Sometimes it gets so bad, all the oxygen gets sucked out of the water. People come and load all the fish on big trucks so they won't suffocate."

"Where do they bring them?" I ask.

"Don't rightly know—some big pond somewhere? They bring them back when the tide dies down. There's always plenty of fish here."

"Looks like there might not be too many after this die-off," I say. "There's more dead fish than birds, I think."

"Is that so? That's a shame, truly. I guess I've heard that if the water keeps getting saltier, the fish might not survive too much longer anyway."

"This is some kind of place." Ray tugs at his beard. "It's amazing anything can survive out here at all."

"But we do, babe, don't we?" Frieda pinches his stomach.

"That we do." He smiles at her. "Barely," he adds, looking at me. I suddenly feel guilty and dig into my pocket for enough money to cover the tab.

"So where do you hail from, sweetheart?" Frieda asks as Ray wanders back to the kitchen. "I'll bet it's someplace exotic—you look a little like some of the girls we have on the wall here. Are you from Hawaii?"

"San Diego, actually." I put some crumpled bills on the counter.

"Where you staying?" Frieda ignores the money. I feel self-conscious about it and lay my palm over the dollars, so just small edges poke out, like my hand is on a bed of lettuce.

"I'm sharing a tent with one of the rescue workers," I tell her. "I haven't been sleeping much, though. My roommate has bad dreams. Screaming dreams."

"That's no surprise," says Frieda. "It's a real nightmare out there."

"I hope I'll be able to stay awake." I try to stifle a yawn.

"Honey," Frieda says. "If you need a place to stay, we got a trailer you could use."

I cock an eyebrow.

"I have an old double-wide here in Bombay that's just sitting there empty. I haven't lived there in years, myself. My sister stayed in it for a while, but she moved to Arizona a couple of months ago. You'll like the place—it has a view and everything. Just needs a little airing out."

I bite my lip, which tastes disturbingly of turkey juice, and take another sip of water. "I don't know . . ."

"It's paid for already, so it's not like we really need a rental income or anything," says Frieda, "so long as you eat here every so often and don't trash the place. Utilities are up to you, too, of course."

"Of course." I nod, mulling it over. "It's very generous of you to offer—I suppose I could at least take a look at it."

"It's nothing." Frieda winks as she slides the bills out from under my hand. "You done with that rabbit food?"

I nod again.

"Well, then. Let's skedaddle!" Frieda hits the counter with her palm. "Ray, I'm taking Miss Ava Sing Lo here out to see the double-wide!" she calls as she ducks under the counter door.

"Hurry back, sweet cakes," Ray says with a deadpan voice, as Frieda grabs me excitedly by the elbow and leads me to the door.

"I'd already forgotten how hot it is out here." I squint as we blast out into the sunlight. In the heat, I feel like Miss Tomato myself, encased in a huge, sweaty orb of fake fur. "You have a good air conditioner in there."

"*Refrigerated air,*" nods Frieda. "We make sure to put that on all of our signs." She leads me to her car, a white Nova, at least twenty years old.

"I haven't really been around Bombay Beach yet," I tell her as she pulls her seat belt across her lap. "All I've seen so far is your restaurant."

"There isn't a whole lot to it." The car chugs through the salty lot.

I adjust the vent on the dash, but all it does is pour out hot air.

"It takes a while for the AC to kick in," says Frieda.

Sweat trickles down my face as I look out the window. A few people are, unimaginably, fishing at a small inlet. As the car turns the corner, I see huge piles of dirt, at least ten feet tall, heaped up along the length of the shore. KEEP OFF SIDES OF DIKE USE STEPS say signs every few feet. Obviously people haven't been paying much attention. The dikes are crumbling in places, loose dirt scattered everywhere.

"Why are these here?"

"The water just keeps rising," Frieda says. "This town is actually below the water level right now—if you look on the other side of that dike, the water would be up to your navel, at least. It's all the runoff from the farms and everything—it keeps making the sea grow taller."

"Are people worried the town is going to get flooded?"

"Well, the dike's been holding up pretty good," says Frieda, "but lots do get washed out sometimes. If you look around later, you'll see there's a whole trailer park half underwater, all rusted out on the other side of the dike—kind of creepy. A hardware store's underwater, too, and a bait shop. Pigeons live there now. Did you know we have pigeons around here—just like a real city!"

I haven't seen any pigeons come into the hospital so far; I wonder if they've been affected at all by the die-off.

"See how all these trailers have platforms built on top of them?" Frieda asks.

Some trailers do indeed have small porches hoisted up over the roofs, some covered with Astroturf and plastic lawn furniture.

"Those places used to be primo property—you used to be able to see the water right out your window—but after the water went up and they put up the dikes, all you can see anymore is a load of dirt unless you put up a platform."

"You said your place has a view. How'd you manage that?"

Frieda just grins.

We drive a few more blocks, past empty lots covered with abandoned salt-encrusted boats and trailers. There are a few small cinder block houses, but most of the homes are trailers, most of them pretty rusty, their gravel yards full of dune buggies and shabby golf carts and old car parts. There are few lawns, fewer flowers, although there

is quite a bit of cactus, and many chain-link fences have an assortment of flat, sandy-looking stones propped up against them. We
drive by a hot-pink trailer with white iron scrollwork and a green
gravel lot full of lawn ornaments, which I instinctively know is
Emily's. Sure enough, Miss Tomato, out of her costume, although still
in fishnets and red high heels beneath her white shorts and striped
tube top, comes out onto the front steps and waves her cigarette at
us. Frieda honks and waves back. Emily does a little tap dance, wiggles her hips, sticks out her tongue, and disappears back inside her
house. Frieda laughs and shakes her head.

Could I actually live here? I wonder this even more as Frieda
turns another corner and eases the car into a driveway. I crane my
head to see out the windshield. Frieda's double-wide doesn't have
a platform erected over it. The whole trailer itself has been somehow hoisted up onto a platform, eight feet or so up in the air.

"Pretty nifty, huh?" Frieda says as we get out of the car.

"How did you do that?" I tilt my head back to take it all in.

"Boat hoist," Frieda says. "A friend of ours works at the marina.
Another friend works at the railroad—he got us the tracks for the
substructure, here . . ."

The frame of the platform does indeed appear to be built of
railroad tracks.

"And the railroad ties for the planking."

"These boards?" I look up at the slightly greasy-looking wood.

"They're the best," Frieda says. "They're soaked in pitch, so
they're weatherproof. Won't rot or nothing, ever. Some black stuff
oozes out of them sometimes, so just wear shoes when you go outside."

"Wow." I walk around under the platform, around the cast-iron
sewer pipe and copper water pipes and gray electrical conduit that
reach from the platform into the ground. "Are you sure this place
is safe?"

"The safest," Frieda says. "We went through that big quake a few years ago in there. Could barely feel it sway."

I walk back out from under it and look up. "What's that?" I point to a large metal tray that hangs off the edge of the platform.

Frieda unlocks a small metal box attached to one of the railroad tracks and pushes a button inside. The tray lowers down on pulleys until it is knee level in front of me.

"It's for groceries, luggage, what have you," says Frieda. "It could probably even lift you up there, but don't overdo it—I'm not sure how sound the motor is right now. The ladder is probably the best bet for you, yourself, but feel free to use the lift for your stuff. I'll give you the key."

"Can I take a look inside?" I can't tell if I'm fascinated or scared by the place. I can't quite imagine living inside of it.

"Of course." Frieda starts up the ladder. I follow her. A drop of sweat peels down Frieda's back, drops out the tail of her Hawaiian shirt, and hits me squarely on the nose. I want to wipe it off but feel too unsteady on the ladder to take my hand away. I turn my head and rub my face, as best I can, on my shoulder.

"It does need some airing out, like I said," Frieda says as she climbs up onto the platform and fumbles with the keys. I pull myself up behind Frieda. There isn't much room on the platform— about two feet sticking out from the trailer on all sides—and no railing. I feel a wave of vertigo. I move beside Frieda and steady myself against a window.

Frieda opens the door. "Phew," she says. "It smells like an old thermos in here."

It does smell a bit like old milk in the trailer, mixed with dirty socks and rusted, liquefying, lettuce. Not as bad as dead bird, but close. I hold my breath. It is hot inside, too, stiflingly so. Frieda sets to opening up windows and turning on fans.

"All the utilities should still be on," she says.

I go to the small kitchen sink and lift up the faucet lever. Water spurts a bit, hot, but soon it starts to flow and cool off. I run my wrists under the stream, wipe them across my forehead. The kitchen has dark wood cabinets, a microwave that was probably among the first on the market, and green, orange, and tan flowered wallpaper. I walk around the rest of the texturized shag carpet in the trailer. There's not too much furniture. A small breakfast nook right outside of the kitchen, an olive-green couch in the living room, a couple of end tables next to it, one boasting a faceted amber glass lamp with a nubby beige shade.

It wouldn't be so bad to live here; it would be nice to get away from Abby's shouts, away from Darryl tossing and turning in the next tent. I peer into the bedroom. An afghan stretches over a bare full-size mattress; the bed stand next to it holds a clock radio and a lamp like the one in the living room. A low dresser sits across the room. And, lo and behold, an air conditioner is mounted in the window. I run over and turn the knob. Cold air blasts against my face.

"I'll take it!" I yell to Frieda, who is in the bathroom. The toilet flushes, water runs, and Frieda walks into the room, smiling.

"Well, then. Welcome home, sweetheart!" She grabs my hands in her wet ones.

The ferry ride to Cheju-do was choppy, the clouds overhead threatening to burst open. Sun snored against Hye-yang's arm, but Hye-yang barely slept through the night crossing. As the first morning light crept into the sky, Hye-yang watched the island grow bigger and bigger on the horizon, rocky and dark, until it threatened to engulf the whole ocean. She shivered as the air filled with a light gray mist.

Sun's family came to greet her at the dock. They swallowed her up like some great organism, a human amoeba. Sun's head poked up over the crowd as she was being swept away.

"Are you coming with us?" she yelled to Hye-yang.

Hye-yang shook her head and waved her friend on. At the bus station, she had wired her family to tell them she was coming home for a visit. Even though her mother had told her to never come back, Hye-yang didn't believe she meant it—especially since she was contributing money to the family; more than she ever could have made as a diver.

After she stood in the drizzle for two hours, a dock worker just ending his shift offered to give her a ride. Drenched and grateful, Hye-yang climbed into his car. They drove in silence for the first few minutes. Then, on a precarious road that overlooked the ocean, the man suddenly stopped the car with a jerk and unzipped his pants. He pushed Hye-yang's head toward his lap, but she screamed and tried to get out of the car. He clamped her mouth with one hand and grabbed her left hand with the other. Crushing her knuckles, the man forced her to move her hand up and down over his semierect penis until he spurted all over the dashboard. With his pants wide open, he started the car again, one of his hands still tight over Hye-yang's mouth. She looked out the window as a gull swooped toward the water, then disappeared under its dark husk.

The scent of the man's semen hung in the car like a sour rain. Hye-yang thought she might throw up. She tried to bite his hand, but she couldn't move her mouth freely enough. When they were half a mile from her family home, the man leaned over Hye-yang, popped open the door, and shoved her out. She tumbled on the ground a few times before she landed on her side. The car showered her with dirt and pebbles as it peeled away.

Hye-yang sat, stunned. Her right leg and hip were badly scraped from the fall. In a daze, she brushed herself off, wiping her left hand repeatedly against her coarse skirt. She spit onto the ground several times before she stood up, but couldn't get the acrid taste of the man's hand off her lips.

Hye-yang limped down the dusty road. She ran her hand along the rough edge of the long, low volcanic rock wall until the skin started to scrape off her palm, but she couldn't get the memory of the man's body off her palm.

In the distance, she could see a cluster of new houses, their corrugated tin roofs glinting through the light rain like an optical illusion. The houses were painted candy colors—tangerine orange, sea blue—so bright, they hurt her teeth. She was surprised by how glad she was to finally see the muted stone and straw of her family's house.

All three poles were up at the front gate, one crossed over the other two. No one was home. Hye-yang squeezed awkwardly between two of the poles. Her hip and hand throbbed. The front door was locked, which surprised her—there had never been a lock on the door before. With a great deal of discomfort, she pulled herself through an open window and collapsed onto the stone floor.

The house looked much the same as it did when she left, except for a small transistor radio on a windowsill and a black rotary telephone that rested on the ground beside her. Hye-yang picked up the receiver and let it hum into her ear. She could barely remember her mother's voice. Her mother and grandmother must have bought these small concessions to technology with the money she sent home. She set the phone back on its cradle and curled her body around it.

Several hours later, Hye-yang woke up sore and hungry. It was dark, but her mother and grandmother were still not back. She washed her hands several times in a bucket of water and lit a fire, then tore into a bowl of rice that was crusting by the stove. When she found no other food in the house, Hye-yang remembered the jar of kimchi that her mother always kept buried by the back door. She dug the crock up in the dark, her hands aching, dirt working deep into her scrapes. The vinegary cabbage was still crunchy, so Hye-yang knew it hadn't been fermenting long. It tasted good— spicy and familiar—even though it burned her raw hand. For the next two days, it was all she had to eat.

Hye-yang limped down to the beach a couple of times each day to search the choppy water for a glimpse of her mother's bobbing head, her grandmother's white diving clothes. Nothing moved but the waves and the occasional swooping bird. Walking back home, Hye-yang once caught a glimpse of what looked like a familiar face in one of the new tangerine-colored houses. As soon as she walked closer, the face disappeared. When she knocked on the door, no one answered.

Hye-yang wrote down the number on her mother's phone before she met Sun at the ferry docks. Sun looked well fed, happy.

She offered Hye-yang a handful of warm chestnuts. Hye-yang held out her torn palm.

"What happened?" asked Sun, concerned, as Hye-yang devoured the nuts like a starved animal.

Hye-yang told Sun about her family's absence. When Sun asked about Hye-yang's limp, Hye-yang told her she hurt her hip sliding down a hill. She didn't mention the ride with the dock worker, but he loomed large in Hye-yang's mind, dirty in her hand. She looked nervously around the area, but couldn't identify him among the uniformed men by the ferry.

"You should have come to my house," said Sun.

"I didn't want to disturb your grandmother's celebration," Hye-yang told her. "It was time for your family to be together."

"You *are* family." Sun put her arm around Hye-yang. "You are always welcome at my home—you should have known that. I wish you had come. If I had only known, I would have pulled you with me by the hair."

They stood together in silence for a moment.

"This will cheer you up." Sun suddenly smiled. "I met a man yesterday. A man from Kunsan."

Sun showed Hye-yang a tattered, familiar-looking pink business card. Hye-yang's breath caught in her throat.

"'Wild Ting Nightclub Establishment,'" Sun read slowly. They had both picked up some English in Suwon. The village managers wanted U.S. Air Force business and offered cursory English lessons to all employees. Hye-yang squinted at the words. English did not come as readily to her as it did to Sun. The looped letters made her dizzy. The skin on her chest began to burn.

"He told me I could be a famous dancer," said Sun. "He said many entertainment scouts from Hollywood, California, come to these clubs. The pay is good, too—more than three times what we make in Suwon."

"No." Hye-yang shook her head emphatically as they boarded the ferry. She thought of the man, his slick mustache, his tobacco breath, the way he slid the pink card into her clothes, her small bag of abalone crashing to the ground. "No, the Folk Village is a good place to work. The best place."

"They have shiny costumes there, and colored lights . . ." Sun pushed her way through the crowd to get them a seat at the front of the boat.

"I'm staying in Suwon," Hye-yang said. "You should, too. Everything we need is there."

"Suit yourself." Sun's hair fluttered back in the breeze as the boat began to move. "But I'm going. We live in the past in Suwon, Hye-yang. I want a future for myself. Think about it. Record players! Fancy makeup! Hair spray! Maybe even a paper star on our door! Some rich American movie man may fall in love with me, take me to Hollywood, California, yes?"

Hye-yang closed her eyes. The salt air entered her pores, sour as the scent of the man's semen. She felt herself swim in a million directions inside, like a sea full of fish.

John James Audubon: The Passenger Pigeon (extinct now)

Everything proved to me that the number of birds resorting to this part of the forest must be immense beyond conception. As the period of their arrival approached, their foes anxiously prepared to receive them. Some were furnished with iron-pots containing sulphur, other with torches of pine-knots, many with poles, and the rest with guns. The sun was lost to our view, yet not a Pigeon had arrived. Every thing was ready, and all eyes were gazing on the clear sky, which appeared in glimpses amidst the tall trees. Suddenly there burst forth a general cry of "Here they come!" The noise which they made, though yet distant, reminded me of a hard gale at sea, passing through the rigging of a close-reefed vessel. As the birds arrived and passed over me, I felt a current of air that surprised me. Thousands were soon knocked down by the pole-men. The birds continued to pour in. The fires were lighted, and a magnificent, as well as wonderful and almost terrifying sight presented itself. The Pigeons, arriving by thousands, alighted everywhere, one above another, until solid masses were formed on the branches all round. Here and there the perches gave way under the weight with a crash, and, falling to the ground, destroyed hundreds of the birds beneath, forcing down the dense groups with which every stick was loaded. It was a scene of uproar and confusion. I found it quite useless to speak, or even to shout to those persons who were nearest to me. Even the reports of the guns were seldom heard, and I was made aware of the firing only by seeing the shooters reloading.

No one dared venture within the line of devastation. The hogs had been penned up in due time, the picking up of the dead and wounded being left for the next morning's employment. The Pigeons were constantly coming, and it was past midnight before I perceived a decrease in the number of those that arrived. The uproar continued the whole night; and as I was anxious to know to what distance the sound reached, I sent off a man, accustomed to perambulate the forest, who, returning, two hours afterwards, informed me he had heard it distinctly, when three miles distant from the spot. Towards the approach of day, the noise in some measure subsided: long before objects were distinguishable, the Pigeons began to move off in a direction quite different from that in which they had arrived the evening before, and at sunrise all that were able to fly had disappeared. The howlings of the wolves now reached our ears, and the foxes, lynxes, cougars, bears, raccoons, opossums and pole-cats were seen sneaking off, whilst eagles and hawks of different species, accompanied by a crowd of vultures, came to supplant them, and enjoy their share of the spoil.

* * *

It was then that the authors of this devastation began their entry amongst the dead, the dying, and the mangled. The Pigeons were picked up and piled in heaps, until each had as many as he could possibly dispose of, when the hogs were let loose to feed on the remainder.

From the couch, I watch the wind whip across the water. It's already eleven. I must have dozed off again. I've had a headache off and on for a couple of days; Darryl told me to take a day or two off to relax. I admit—it feels nice not to have a bag full of birds in my hand, nice to have such free, empty palms, such light biceps. My headache has already dwindled considerably. A day off is probably just what I needed.

On my way to the Aloha Room for some breakfast, I see a girl—seven, maybe eight years old—building a sand castle on the barnacle-strewn shore. Thick, straight bangs shadow her Coke-bottle glasses, her tea-colored face. She wears a brightly colored, ill-fitting bathing suit with a ridiculous little flounce of skirt in the back. Her legs splay out at strange angles, the skin withered looking, unused. A couple of battered metal canes with arm braces lie on the ground beside her, one on top of the other, like an X.

I realize I haven't seen any children since I arrived at the Salton Sea. It seems strange—wrong, somehow—to see a child here, in this desolate landscape.

The girl continues to pat the mound in front of her. As I get closer, I see it is spiraled with little bits of different plants—drooping marigold, a strip of dyeweed, some ghost flower petals, desert velvet. Her brow is wrinkled in concentration. A putty-colored hearing aid sits in her ear.

The girl looks up, startled. Her glasses make her eyes look extra big, slightly lopsided themselves, the frames askew on her small nose.

"Sorry to bother you," I tell her. "That's quite a castle."

"It's a burial mound," she says, her voice high in her soft palate.

I look more closely at the heap of sand and barnacles and shreds of plant. Something sharp pokes out—the end of a beak. On the other side, the corner of a wing juts through, the feathers dusted with sand. A few other feathers push to the surface around the pile.

"I think maybe this is how the Cahuilla buried people, but maybe I made it up," says the girl.

"You shouldn't be touching these birds." A shiver runs through me. "They have all sorts of awful germs."

"I know." The girl rolls her eyes. "I'll wash my hands as soon as I'm done."

"Is your mother around?" Who would leave their child alone with dead birds? In a bathing suit when the water is contaminated?

"She's in the Aloha," she says. "She said she'd come get me in a little bit."

I suddenly remember being left alone on the beach when I was a girl, a bag of lobsters squirming around by my feet, the claws nudging my skin.

"Are you going to be all right?" I ask her.

"I'm fine." She pats down another plant.

"Don't touch any more birds, please." My headache comes back, a strong pinch between my eyebrows.

She crosses her heart with one slightly shaky finger and goes back to her work.

After I walk into the dark restaurant, I go straight to the bathroom and wash my hands for a long time. I splash some water on my face before I go to the counter.

"There's a little girl playing outside with a dead bird," I tell

Frieda. I can see her through the window, putting something on top of the mound.

"Oh, that's Jeniece," Frieda says. "I've been keeping an eye on her through the glass as best I can. I didn't notice she had a dead bird, though. Damn."

"You know her?"

"Of course I know her, you goofball." She hits me on top of the head with a laminated menu. "She's my daughter!"

"Oh." I fiddle with the napkin dispenser, trying not to flush. "I didn't know you had kids, Frieda."

"Just the one," she says. "My mom usually watches her when I'm at work, but she had a doctor's appointment today. I didn't want her bringing Jeniece to the clinic—Jeniece spends enough time there as it is, and there's all those germs . . ." She looks out the window at her daughter playing with a botulism-infected pelican.

"I better go." She wipes her hands on the apron and rushes outside.

I watch her run to Jeniece. I watch her put her hands on her hips and yell. I watch her turn and walk back to the restaurant. I watch Jeniece stand up and follow after her mother, her metal canes clunking against the barnacles, kicking up dust, her legs dragging behind her as she struggles to catch up.

As soon as they get inside, Frieda points to the bathroom and the girl shuffles off to wash her hands.

"Hi, Ray," Jeniece mumbles as she passes the counter.

"Hey, darlin'." Ray lifts a spatula like a peace sign.

"She was playing with a dead bird!" says Frieda, exasperated.

"She's just a kid, Frieda." Ray goes back to his frying.

Frieda sighs and sits down in the booth across from me. "Ray's so patient," she says. "We got together when Jeniece was three, and from the start, it was like she was his kid more than mine. I mean, of course she's my daughter, of course I love her and everything, but she was just so sick when she was a baby, I didn't want . . ."

"Babe." Ray gestures to Jeniece, who is coming out of the bathroom.

"Hey, kiddo." Frieda raises her voice a notch so that Jeniece can hear her. "Did you wash your hands long enough? The whole ABC song?"

Jeniece shuffles over to a stool at the counter. "'Next time won't you sing with me.'" She rolls her eyes.

On my way home, I stop in front of Jeniece's burial mound. I know I should dig the bird out, bring it back to the hospital, but I can't bear the thought of destroying the girl's intricate decorative work. It almost reminds me of one of my mother's carved eggs, so painstakingly rendered. I replace a bit of desert velvet that has fallen out of place and start to walk back to the trailer.

Wind sweeps across the sea as I walk down Bombay Beach. Dead fish shuttle to the shore by the bucketful. I hold my breath and remember how, when I was around Jeniece's age, my mother and I often went to Casa Cove so that she could skin-dive for lobster.

My mother wore an Esther Williams–style suit, cut low on the hip, bandeau-halter-style on top. I thought she looked like a movie goddess as she came out of the sea, her hair dripping wet over her face, a laundry bag of lobsters hanging by her side. I would hand her a towel; she briskly rubbed it over herself before the lobsters could claw their way out of the bag. She held the towel out, and I draped it back over my shoulder. She walked to the car; I trailed wordlessly behind.

One day, an old surfer—grizzled beard, big tan belly—came up to us as we climbed the sandy slope to the parking lot.

"You skin-dive?" he asked my mother offhandedly, gesturing to the lobster bag at her thighs.

"Forty dollar," she said, her voice suddenly hard, businesslike. The man looked at her quizzically.

"You make a date later, one hundred dollar," she told him.

"Whoa, lady, I'm not asking you for a date," he said, "I just saw you diving without a tank, and—"

"You dive my skin, one hundred dollar," she repeated.

The man shook his head and walked toward the water. My mother didn't talk at all the whole way home. I leaned my head against the window and drummed on the loose door of the glove cabinet, my thumps punctuated by castanet clicks from the lobster bag.

The next time we went to the beach, we ran into the same guy. He said something to my mother about reconsidering her offer. After she caught her lobsters and a tangle of deep-green kelp, she told me to keep playing. She had somewhere to go.

I watched her climb up the hill in her wet swimsuit flecked with sand. I watched her flick a stray piece of seaweed from her shoulder and yank the suit higher up her hip before she disappeared into a Winnebago parked by a date palm. I saw the man's hairy face flash briefly in the doorway before the door clicked shut. The top of his RV was covered with seagulls.

When my mother came back, she was wearing a blue terry cloth robe I had never seen before. Her swimsuit dangled limp from her wrist, like a purse. Her breath had a weird fruity smell, and she wavered a little bit when she walked. When we drove home, the robe slipped aside and one of her breasts drooped out. Her nipple was the same color as my knee. It was the first time I saw myself reflected in her body.

* * *

That night, I try to call my mother again.

On the answering machine this time, the parrot voice says *"Chal chinaesumnida."* "I am fine."

"I'm glad to hear it, Omma," I say into the phone, "but are you there? Hello? Are you ever going to pick up when I call?"

I wait, but no one answers. I hang up the phone and flop onto the nubby couch. Maybe my mother doesn't want to talk to me until I've saved at least one bird. Maybe she doesn't know what to say. Maybe she just wants to keep the house silent. Maybe she's too depressed to talk to anyone.

Jeniece flashes into my mind but I will her back out. I grab my *chang'go* and slap out a few rhythms. My pulse surges thick in my ears, my headache thick in my brow; I set the drum back down and close my eyes. *No thought, no thought, no thought, no thought.* I follow the slowing beat of my heart, the rise and fall of my own breath, until the waves finally swell and drag me under.

The flowered suitcase in Sun's hand repeatedly banged into Hye-yang's knee as they walked together to the bus station. Hye-yang struggled to keep up with her friend, who walked with quick, eager steps. Sun had just given her notice at the Folk Village. She couldn't stop talking about the outfits she knew would be waiting for her in Kunsan, dresses full of spangles and sequins designed to catch the light. Clothes that sparkle like stars. Clothes that turn girls into stars.

Hye-yang's skull felt stuffed with dirty rags. She couldn't pull together enough clear, clean words to answer her friend. She couldn't move out of the way to avoid the drumbeat smack of the suitcase.

Sun spun around and gave Hye-yang a quick kiss on the lips.

"You're sure you won't come with me?" she asked. She wore sunglasses, a scarf poofed over her hair. Hye-yang turned so that Sun wouldn't see the tears that stung her eyes. When she looked back, Sun had already boarded the bus. She blew a big, stagy kiss from the closing door as the driver pulled away from the curb. Hye-yang watched Sun make her way toward the seats in back, watched her flutter a garish pink handkerchief through an open window until the bus disappeared from view.

Without Sun around, Hye-yang fell into a depression. Her hip hadn't healed completely, and she wasn't able to assume the correct archery stance. She could still feel the dock man's body, its squishy heft, in her hand. Her palm felt dirty—she clenched and opened her fist over and over, but she couldn't shake the man off. Her arrows missed the rice straw target, one wayward fling after another.

During the farmer's dance troupe performances, Hye-yang sang so quietly, no one could hear her voice over the drums. In the middle of the *pansori*, she burst into such violent tears that she couldn't continue the song. When she wasn't working, she wouldn't leave her room. Within a month, she was asked to leave the Folk Village.

Hye-yang packed and vacated the room she used to share with Sun, rolling up the sleeping mat that still held some of their twisted-together hair. She walked across the village for the last time and set down her bow and bag of clothes by a pay phone near the cuttlefish stand where she used to work. Trembling, she dialed the number she had copied down at her family's house. Her mother answered after one ring.

"Omma?" Hye-yang asked, her hands, her voice shaking.

"Who is this?" The voice was sharp, clipped.

"It's Hye-yang, Omma. I'm calling you from Suwon."

Hye-yang could hear her mother hold her breath.

"It's your daughter, Omma. It's me, your daughter, Hye-yang." Hye-yang bit her lip.

"My daughter drowned in a diving accident," Hye-yang's mother said before she hung up the phone.

Hye-yang slid to the dirt, cradling the receiver until it pulled from her grasp like an arrow from her bow. The phone swung against a pole, then shot back precariously close to her head. It swayed around for a while before it dangled limp, squawking in Hye-yang's ear.

The dead, fishy scent from the stand overwhelmed Hye-yang.

She wondered if maybe she really had drowned in the ocean, if her body was undulating somewhere underwater, tangled in kelp, gulls swooping down to scoop chunks of her skin into their beaks. Maybe she was a ghost; maybe she had been one even before she left Cheju-do the first time. Maybe the man on the beach with the shiny suit had only wanted to show her the way to the afterlife, show her where she needed to go.

Fighting nausea, Hye-yang stood slowly and hung up the phone. She hesitated for a moment before she pulled a pink business card, the one Sun had given her, out of the folds of her jacket. Her fingers felt cold, waterlogged, heavy with the dock man's flesh, as she lifted the receiver again.

I wake before the sun rises. My headache seems better, just the faint ghost of a throb. I turn on the air conditioner, bow to the cool rush of air, and begin to practice some of my *hyung*s before it gets too hot. The trailer is too small for all my favorite kicks, all my thrusts of arm and heel, but there is enough space for a small repertoire. The first couple of times I practiced tae kwon do in the trailer, I worried I might rock it right off its platform, but now I feel slightly more steady, slightly more rooted this high in the air.

I bow once again to the AC, then sit on the bed and listen to my heart pound. I tell myself it's because of my vigorous blocking moves and not the fact that I'm going to see Darryl soon. I'm surprised by how excited I am to get back to work, dismal as the work itself may be.

I decide to walk to the bird hospital. It's not too hot this early in the day, and I can always get a ride later if I don't want to walk home. I grab some extra bags and rubber gloves before I leave, in case I find a bird or two along the way.

A diffuse light teases the sky as I climb down the ladder. The pigeons are already awake in the rusted-out, half-drowned trailers on the other side of the berm. They fly in and out of the windows with rushing gurgles of throat, sharp ruffles of wing. I wish them well as I step down to the rung where they disappear from view.

My feet register the place where the asphalt turns to barnacle. The Aloha and its parking lot stand silhouetted, still dark in the distance, as I crunch across the beach. More pale light leaks into the air. I see Jeniece's burial mound a couple of yards away. It has been destroyed. The pelican has been dragged away by wild dogs, maybe a coyote. A few bones are scattered about—curve of skull, tip of wing, bits of skin and feather clinging to strewn white shards. The desert plants Jeniece had so carefully arranged are flung all over the barnacles. The site looks like the aftermath of a wild party, or an amateur paleontology dig.

I nudge a bird rib with my shoe. When I was ten, I wanted to be a paleontologist. I thought my future was in dirt, in bones. My class had just finished a unit on dinosaurs, and I was filled with awe. As I had my after-school snack, I told my mother there had been two classes of dinosaurs in the world—bird-hipped dinosaurs and lizard-hipped ones. I told her that birds probably came from the bird-hipped dinosaurs long after they died away.

She grabbed my arms. "What will come after all the birds die?" she asked, her eyes fierce. "You tell me. What will come then?"

A piece of my little walnut-shaped cake caught in my throat.

"Omma," I coughed. I pulled myself away from her grasp, stumbled to the sink, and tilted my head under the faucet. As I looked up at the water, I imagined that's what birds would turn into next—a clear ribbony rush, stippled with light. If something as big as a dinosaur could turn into something as small as a bird, wouldn't that be the next logical step—from scale to feather to pure liquid shimmer? I turned to try to explain this to my mother, but she had already left the room.

I rest my toe in part of the pelican's hip bone. I put my hands on my own hips, feel their contours, the ridges of bone that swell beneath my khaki pants. I have lizard hips, dinosaur hips—so much broader, more earthbound, than my mother's slight bird-hipped frame. I squat down, slip on my rubber gloves, and begin to scoop the bones into a plastic bag. Better for Jeniece to see things flattened down to normal than find her work in such grisly disarray. I smooth out the sand and barnacles with my covered palms.

A small hunk of bird flesh and feathers tumbles away toward the shore; I follow it. The garbage bag feels so light—it's amazing how little the bones weigh. A whole dead pelican in these same bags feels like a stone.

I pick up the piece of bird as the sun lifts over the hills. The air instantly feels about twenty degrees hotter. The sea begins to sparkle like root beer. I wipe away the sweat that pops onto my forehead and notice a shell on the ground up ahead. I haven't seen any like it here before—a pale pink disk among the barnacles. I put the bird remains in the bag and reach for it. It squishes between my gloved fingers, resists when I try to pick it up. I jump back. Some of the surrounding barnacles fall away. The shell is attached to skin. The shell itself *is* skin—a nipple, I realize with a bolt of nausea. A breast. I stumble backward over the bumpy ground, kicking loose more barnacles. A collarbone. A bruised throat. An open mouth, filled with small white shells.

I drop the garbage bag and run to the Aloha Room. I bang on the door, but Frieda and Ray aren't in. I race to the bird hospital. Inside the chain-link enclosure, the temperature rises. Everything seems to spin.

"Ava, hi!"

I can hear Abby, but I can't see her.

"Are you ready to be back yet? It looks like you still have a headache . . ."

I bend over. "A woman." I gasp for air.

"I'm sorry?" Abby asks.

"I thought she was a shell . . ."

"Do you have a fever?" Abby touches my forehead with her gloved hand. "I think she's delirious," I hear her say to someone else.

"Ava, are you okay?" It's Darryl, his voice full of concern.

"I saw a woman." My breath begins to steady. My eyes begin to focus again. Darryl's generous lips, Abby's freckles zoom into sharp relief. "A dead woman on the beach."

"What?" Abby asks, alarmed.

"She was in the barnacles. I thought she was a shell."

"Oh my god," says Darryl. "Ava, are you okay?"

I nod my head, sit down on the dirt floor.

"I'm calling the police," says Abby. "Which beach was it—Bombay?"

I nod again.

"Let me get you some water." Darryl lightly touches my hair.

I dip my head between my knees. My pulse pounds loud in my ears. I flash again on the woman on the beach, the woman with no pulse, no breath. I think of the woman's open mouth; my own tongue fills with chalky barnacle grit.

"Here you go." Darryl holds a water bottle out to me. I sit up and take a long, grateful swallow.

"The police are on their way," Abby says. "Did it look like heat stroke or something?"

I shake my head. "She was naked. Someone tried to bury her . . ." The room begins to spin again.

"Annyong hasnimnikka?" is on the tape when I call home a few hours later—Kane's voice, from the recording I had given my mother after he died.

"No, Omma, no, I'm not exactly at peace," I say into the yeasty-smelling receiver. "I found a body today. A dead woman. Murdered." I close my eyes. I'm sure I can feel every corpuscle that scuttles through my veins. "I don't know what I'm doing, Omma. I don't know what I'm doing here anymore. Maybe I should come home . . ." The machine cuts me off.

A while later, I try again.

"Tell them you know the language of birds," my mother's

voice, her real voice, crackles on the answering machine tape—a command, not a suggestion. My heart flip-flops at the sound of it. I wait for more, but there is just the sizzle of static, then the beep.

"Omma," I say into the phone. "If I knew the language of birds, I probably wouldn't be here in the first place. Are you there? Why won't you talk with me? Omma? Hello?"

The machine beeps, cutting me off again. I press redial and listen to my mother's voice one more time, but I can't think of anything else to say.

It is only later, as I'm trying to sleep, that I remember the folktale my mother used to tell me, the one about the two brothers who knew the language of birds.

One day these brothers were walking down the street when a crow let out a plaintive caw. From this, they knew a man was being stabbed a couple of blocks away. They ran to the scene of the crime to see if they could help and found the man splayed in a pool of blood. One brother put his head to the man's chest to try to detect a heartbeat; the other put his hand over the man's nose and mouth to see if he could feel any breath. The police arrived, and seeing the brothers kneeling over the body, their hands covered with blood, they immediately charged them with murder.

At their trial, the brothers tried to explain what had happened. They told the judge about the crow, his message; they told about their attempt to help. "So you know the language of birds," the judge sneered. "Tell me, then, what the crane perched in the persimmon tree outside is carrying on about!"

The brothers looked at the bird through the window and listened intently. They turned to face each other, unsure of how to proceed. One brother flushed and cleared his throat.

"Your Honor," he stammered, "the bird says, 'Please return my eggs to me, the ones you have hidden inside your sleeve.'"

The brothers grasped each other's hands. They knew they could be sent to their deaths, saying such a thing to a judge. The guards rushed toward them, but the judge held up his palm. He rolled back the long sleeve of his *chogori;* three eggs balanced there inside the crook of his elbow. The crane beat its wings wildly. A shower of persimmons fell from the tree. The judge let the brothers go.

My mother must think I will be accused of this murder. The police did question me a long time, much longer than necessary, it seemed, but they let me go with nothing more ominous than a snide thank-you, a slightly leering "we'll be in *touch.*" They had asked all sorts of personal questions—questions about my sexual preference, my sexual history (when I said "none to speak of," they just laughed in my face). They asked if I was a U.S. citizen, they asked if I was born in this country; they asked my reasons for being in the area; they wanted to know everything I've done here, everyone I've talked to. They asked me why I had touched the victim—specifically why I had touched her nipple, why I had gloves on my hands. They asked if I had touched her genitals. They asked if I had touched her neck, if I had kissed her. They asked if I liked it rough. They asked questions until I was shaking so hard, I thought my skull would vibrate right through my scalp. I doubt it would have helped much had I told them I know the language of birds.

Hye-yang looked through the window as the bus to Kunsan cut through acre upon acre of rice paddies. Rows of slender green plants spread out in all directions, as far as she could see. The shoots, hip-high, were tinged a brassy blonde, almost pinkish, in the sunset; the bus exhaust parted some of them, revealing their dark-green roots, the damp scalp of earth underneath. Hye-yang watched white ducks walk between the rows, dipping their beaks into narrow furrows of water, tilting their heads back to swallow.

A few olive military vehicles passed the bus. Hye-yang leaned off her seat and watched the fortified camp town come into view through the windshield. The bus pulled up to the gate and stopped. Hye-yang made her way to the front, hesitated near the driver for a moment, then stepped out into the dusty air. The stone wall that surrounded the town cast a broad shadow across her face.

She started to walk through the gates, when a U.S. Air Force guard put his hand flat on her breastbone to stop her.

"Excuse me, Miss? Your registration card?"

Hye-yang stared at him.

"You can't come in without your card." He left his hand there.

Hye-yang looked back at the bus. She had the urge to jump back on, to go back to Suwon, but it began to pull away, spewing a cloud of exhaust in her direction.

"All the girls need their cards," the guard said, slowly this time.

"Card?" Hye-yang pulled the pink card out from her jacket and showed it to him. "I come sing here," she said.

"Oh, a new girl." He looked her up and down with a sly smile that reminded her of the dock man, then let his hand trail down the front of her shirt before he pointed her through the gates.

Hye-yang felt disoriented as she entered the camp town. The dusty road, lined with shops and clubs, was busy, but not in the same way the Folk Village had been. Even the weekend crowds there had felt polite, friendly. This was a frantic busy. A dark, noisy, careless busy. American men, some in uniform, some not, barreled up to her, one after another, speaking too fast for her to understand, putting their hands on her body as she rushed by. Small children, some strangely pale, others strangely dark, played unsupervised, barely clothed, in the street. Neon lights began to sputter on over the clubs, spelling out words she could barely understand—SHANGRI-LALA, SEXXY GIRL, PASTIES PLACE. She finally spotted the hissing sign that carried the name she recognized from the business card—WILD TING. Under the yellow letters, an orange neon woman jerkily shook her hips from side to side, a pink tail sprouting from her bikini bottoms. The light that formed her face was burnt out, the tubes dark, dirty looking.

Hye-yang pushed her way inside the dim, smoky club. The air was filled with the sweet stench of rotten fruit. A woman's shrill, false laughter rang out over the flat din of voices, the tinny jukebox music. Glancing over the heads of dark-skinned military men and the women who leaned toward them, Hye-yang caught a glimpse of Sun, standing on top of the bar. As she pushed through the crowd toward her friend, she felt a rush of relief, of happiness, wash over her.

"Sun!" she yelled. "Sun!" She remembered seeing Sun at the Folk Village for the first time, Sun the bride, with pink cheeks and flowers in her hair. She remembered the way Sun's face broke into joy when she saw Hye-yang in the crowd. Hye-yang edged her way closer to the bar. She called Sun's name again, but her friend didn't look her way. She looked like she couldn't see anything, like she was looking at something far beyond the walls of the club. Her hair was frizzed out, a big puffball around her head.

"Sun!" she yelled, frantically this time. She began to wonder if she was indeed a ghost, if her edges had already started to disappear.

As Hye-yang pushed her way through to the bar stools, she realized with a shock that Sun was wearing nothing but a T-shirt, not even panties. She watched, stunned, as Sun squatted down and lifted a coin from the sticky wood veneer of the bar with her vagina. Sun wiggled around, then dropped the coin into the waiting mouth of a GI who stared at her from a red bar stool, running a hand up her bare leg. Hye-yang turned her head. She had never seen Sun's naked body before, had never seen any woman's naked body before, not even her own, not between the legs. When she and Sun shared a room at the Folk Village, they always changed behind screens, never showing each other anything. Hye-yang wondered if her own body looked so purplish down there, so wrinkled and tired.

"Sun," Hye-yang said again. The name sounded like a sob.

Sun looked down.

"Hye-yang," she said dreamily. She bent down so her crotch was right in Hye-yang's face. A strong smell wafted out, like cuttle-fish. Hye-yang suppressed a gag. Sun reached out and touched Hye-yang's face. The man who had taken the coin in his mouth put his hand on Hye-yang's hip.

Hye-yang pulled away and pushed back through the crowded bar, back out into the dusty air. She collapsed against the side of the building and tried to take a deep breath.

"Are you okay?" A man with dark skin crouched down beside her.

She looked up. "My friend," she started, not sure what to say in English.

"You work with your friend?" He licked his upper lip and smiled.

"At Folk Village," she said, glad to have someone to talk to, someone with kind eyes.

He nodded.

"In Suwon," she said.

"Your friend's named Sue?"

"Sun. In Suwon."

"Soon, hell yeah—in Sue, on Sue, anytime sounds good to me. How much?"

"I know her since little girl."

"Just like sisters. Damn! What's the damage?"

Sun sidled up next to Hye-yang. "Fifty, for both," she said, then put her arms around Hye-yang and kissed her. Hye-yang felt Sun's thick tongue in her mouth and jumped back. She was glad to see Sun had put on a skirt, even though it barely covered her hips.

"That sounds more than reasonable. Fuck Village. Damn!" He tapped the wallet in the back of his pants, then put one arm around Hye-yang, one around Sun. Hye-yang resisted as he tried to pull her away from the wall.

"Come on, baby," he said, his lips against her ear.

"Come on, Hye-yang," Sun said, then glanced back nervously at the front door of the bar. "I be with you."

Hye-yang didn't budge.

A familiar-looking man with a thin mustache and a shiny suit burst out of Wild Ting.

"Sun! Where are you going?" he yelled.

"My friend is here," she said. "My friend come to visit me!"

"You are still on my clock." He glared at her. "You make sure you bring me my cut."

Sun flipped her middle finger at him, then tugged at Hye-yang. Hye-yang couldn't move. She wanted to tell Sun about the man at the dock, but it was like the man's hand was still clamped over her mouth, shoving her voice somewhere deep inside, somewhere she couldn't access. She wanted to tell Sun about her phone call with her mother; she almost wanted to believe her mother's story.

I am floating in the ocean, she thought as the man stormed toward them. *I had a diving accident and now I'm a ghost. I'm covered with kelp. Birds are tearing me apart. He's here to show me where to go.*

Albino Cockatiel, Name: Man Jang.

Ava, daughter, age 14,
see bird look at self in window.
She find Sun's old face make up
under my bed, put in birdcage,
circle open like a shell.
He love mirror inside,
bob head up and down,
watch white feathers
flick and spread on top.
Next day he tip over, pink dust
all over cheek. Maybe he try
to eat powder and choke.
Maybe sun hit mirror
and burn him with too much light.

5/17/85

I don't know where I should be right now. Part of me wants to go back to San Diego. Being here is ridiculous—so much death. The woman, the birds. The birds I haven't helped yet. And how can I go back to San Diego if I haven't helped the birds? And how can I stay here, walking around by myself on the beach, knowing some murderer is out there? Darryl probably has people teaming up now. He probably won't let anyone go out on their own. Maybe he'd volunteer to come with me on my rounds . . .

I want to see what's going on at the hospital, but I can't seem to get out of bed. I can't seem to answer the phone, even though it rings several times, even though I know it may finally be my mother, finally calling me back. Frieda eventually comes over to check on me.

"It's a shame, what happened to that girl." She puts a Tupperware batch of chicken and rice soup in the fridge for me to microwave later. Her hands still smell of broth when she comes over to the bed.

"And, Ava." Frieda's breath smells of broth, too; it wafts over me like a chicken-scented humidifier. "It's a shame you had to find her, but life goes on, honey . . ."

I bury my head beneath the pillow. Frieda pulls it off.

"We're all scared, Ava, all of us. There's still a killer out there somewhere. Emily's gone near out of her mind with fear, and what's that gonna do for us? Nothing. Nothing! Lying around feeling sorry for yourself isn't gonna help that girl you found none. She's gone. We here gotta keep on living, even with some maniac running around. So stop feeling sorry for yourself and get out of that bed!" Frieda slaps a hand against my blanketed thigh.

I keep my eyes closed as my body gently rocks on the bed from the reverberation of Frieda's slap. I don't think it's myself I'm feeling sorry for. I think of my mother, the blank look on her face when she read about the prostitute killed in Korea. I remember the way she closed her bedroom door behind her.

"Ava, open your eyes." Frieda shakes me by the arms, but I can barely feel it. "Snap out of it! We need your help."

I let my eyelids slide open; they feel like they are about a mile long the way they drag over my irises.

"What kind of help could I possibly give you?" I ask Frieda before I flip onto my stomach. So far I've only helped the statistics people, the cleanup people. I exhale loudly into the musty sheets.

"You know that kung fu stuff, right?" Frieda asks. I roll back over and sit up. Frieda cocks a knowing, penciled-on eyebrow.

Now, every Tuesday and Thursday morning in the Aloha Room after the regular breakfast crowd leaves, I find myself teaching tae kwon do lessons for women. At around ten, Frieda shoos Ray out of the restaurant and puts a cardboard sign on the door that says CLOSED FOR SELF-DEFENSE PURPOSES, under which Emily has scrawled "Yea, we girls are gonna kick your butt!" Someone else has crossed out "girls" and written "WOMEN!" over it with a green pen.

The regular group, besides Frieda and Emily, consists of four women in their sixties—Betty, Pat, Myrna, and Sue, who normally play bridge those mornings but decided to try something new; Lonnie, a gravelly-voiced park ranger; and Rayanne, who owns the Pretty Poodle grooming shop in Salton City and looks a bit like a poodle herself.

I have never taught a self-defense class before. I have never *taken* a strictly self-defense class before, just the straight martial art. I hope the women in her class can't sense how lost I feel.

I start each session with a formal bow, just as all of my tae kwon do classes have begun. The bowing atmosphere in the Aloha Room is vastly different from that at the *dojang*. I remember how solemn the bows had felt there, how quiet, and almost sacred. Here, the bowing is accompanied by a bunch of groans and "Oh, my back!'s," plus pseudo-Asian voices saying "Ah so," and variations on "Confucius say bend over." I consider scrapping the whole bowing thing but can't bring myself to do it. I bow even when I practice by myself.

The bridge ladies, in their soft pastel jogging suits, are surprisingly intense once it comes time to do the *hyung*s, the forms. I would not want to be cornered by them in a dark alley. Frieda, still wearing her Hawaiian shirt, is amazingly focused, too, although her blocks and punches lack a lot of oomph; she looks more like she is dancing than learning how to protect herself. Emily spends much of the time with her hands on her hips, exasperated, which is strange, since she is a tap dancer and must be at least somewhat coordinated. Short, stocky, windburned, Lonnie is almost frightening in her ferocity; she lets out harsh yells with every kick and punch, like someone from a Godzilla movie, if not the monster itself. Rayanne looks near tears half the time and approaches each new form with timid hands and feet, a poodle trying to avoid a puddle.

"So when are we gonna start the *fighting?*" Frieda asks one Thursday morning, after an hour of *hyung*s. "We've just been kicking the air . . ."

"Yeah, we could beat up a light breeze just fine, is about it," adds Emily, who hasn't even been beating up the air very much.

"I wanna feel some *booty* under my foot!" Frieda slaps Emily's hand.

"Sparring is kind of tricky," I hesitate. "You have to be really careful not to hurt the other person. It takes a while to learn the kind of control you need—you have to use full power, but deflect it, not use it on the other person, pull away before you hit."

"Kind of like Rick," says Emily. "He needs to work on that—he always says he's gonna pull out in time, but sometimes he just can't control himself, you know how he is. It's a good thing I can clench myself up tight in there, so those sperms of his don't get through."

"Clenching isn't gonna stop any babies from starting, sweetie pie," Frieda says. "You need to get that boy some condoms."

"Do you mind?" Rayanne blanches, puts a thin hand over her pursed mouth.

"Well, this *is* a *protection* class, is it not?" Frieda demands. "We gals gotta look out for each other."

"Besides." I clear my throat, try to veer the conversation back into its original direction. "We need some mats. This floor is too hard for sparring."

"I know a gym teacher down at the high school in Indio," says Lonnie. "I'm sure we could drag some mats over here, no problem."

"You look into that," I tell her, "but we still need to work on our forms some more before we start getting at it."

There is a collective groan.

"This is important. We don't want to hurt each other, right?"

"Couldn't we get one of those guys that dress up in big foam suits with a big foam head and everything and you can just pummel away at 'em and they don't feel a thing?" Frieda asks. "I saw one on a rerun. *Roseanne,* I think."

"Yeah," a few other voices murmur. The bridge ladies nod in assent.

"I don't know where we'd find a costume like that," I say.

"Well, I volunteer Rick, costume or no," says Emily.

Frieda slaps Emily's hand again, then looks at her watch.

"Okay, girls," she says, "time to clear out. I gotta start the lunch stuff."

The crowd of women suddenly disperse, like a drop of dye spattered onto water.

"Hey," I call out, "we haven't done our closing bow!" But no one hears me. The bridge ladies are already out the door, and Lonnie and Rayanne are struggling with their shoes. Frieda and Emily have disappeared into the kitchen. As the grill hisses on, sending the hot smell of grease into the air, I bow to the plastic hula woman who swivels from the ceiling, slightly deflated, her left foot almost flat as she bows subtly back.

A couple of nights later, Emily and Frieda invite me to join them for cards at Emily's place. I'm not much of a card person—my mother often played the flower card game, just never with me—but I say yes, if only to avoid another nervous evening alone in the trailer. I'm surprised by how nice it is to spend time with other people, surprised by how sad I was when I found out that Abby went back to Colorado shortly after the body was found. I've never been much of a people person before. Maybe the birds are shoving me into human company.

At the faux-wood laminated table, Emily is holding an open package of ramen. She crunches a corner of stiff, pale noodles off the folded block, still in their cellophane wrapper. The foil flavor packet peeks precariously out of the corner. Either it will fall or Emily will bite into it by accident and get a mouth full of monosodium glutamate.

"I didn't know you could eat ramen raw," I tell her.

"It's not *raw,* exactly." Emily's teeth pass through the noodles with a sound I wish I could sample. It could be used for part of an iceberg breaking off, or someone walking on leaves. I have to remember to carry my little recorder with me at all times. "It's already fried and everything. It's just faster this way."

"Ramen only takes three minutes to cook, Emily." Frieda shakes her head as she shuffles the deck of cards.

"I just like it, okay?" Emily crumbles off a chunk of noodle, holds out her hand to offer it to anyone. Frieda and I decline. "Plus they're cheap—eleven cents a pop, cheaper than those chow mein noodles, and it's pretty much the same thing. So deal already."

"I don't know if I can," says Frieda.

"You don't know if you can what?" Emily washes the dry noodles down with a swig from her bottle of peach wine cooler.

"Deal with your ramen-eating shenanigans." Frieda sounds mournful.

"Deal the *cards*, you idiot!" Emily sits down. A spray of hard white crumbs land on the table in front of her as she rubs her hands together. "I wanna take you girls for all I can get."

I wonder how many packets of ramen noodles I have consumed in my lifetime. They were a staple in my house growing up—sometimes my mother and I had them for dinner every night of the week, sometimes with a bit of Buddig's paper-thin lunch-meat turkey, the cheapest meat we could find, sliced in. This was usually after there had been a sting at the massage parlor where my mother worked, when she went for weeks without pay before the business opened up again in another location. When I was ten, she stayed in jail for two days after one of those stings. I pooled all of my change together and bought eight packs of ramen at Lucky's so that I would have something to eat until she came home. I avoid ramen whenever possible now.

Frieda dusts some of the crumbles off the scratched-up table and dives into the card game with a fierceness I have not seen in her before, certainly not in self-defense class. I have trouble focusing on the cards—the smell of the noodles between Emily's teeth is too distracting—and I'm quickly out, owing three dollars.

I drift away from the table, leaving Emily and Frieda to battle to the death themselves. I look at the knickknacks in the china cabinet—Precious Times figurines, little blonde angel babies—the dusty silk flowers, the Miss Tomato ribbon, a Kmart portrait of Emily with her boyfriend, his hand up her shirt.

I step outside. The sky is clear, the smog swept away by a warm breeze that makes the palm trees sway gently. They look like women dancing while they do the dishes—humming a little tune, not performing, not even aware they are moving, just following the music in their heads, their hands full of suds. A few orangey dates, too small to eat, are strewn about on the ground. I roll one around with the toe of my sandal. Somewhere a bird calls out, a sweet, healthy cry, and I try to telepathically tell it to fly away, get out of here; this place won't support your song.

"It's *hot* out here." Emily steps outside. She lifts her arms over her head, as if to take the heat in, and I catch a whiff of her deodorant and the sweat it isn't entirely preventing. Emily wiggles around a bit, like the palm trees, but I can tell Emily is conscious of her own little dance. Emily is used to being watched, and she moves accordingly, sashaying her hips from side to side as she climbs a few stairs when a man is behind her, throwing her head back to laugh when some guy tells a joke, bending her leg up onto the chair, so whoever it is can get a peek of her panties. She holds a wine cooler out to me, and I take it hesitantly, twist off the top. It is sickeningly sweet, but it is cold.

"Where's Frieda?" I pick at the label on the bottle.

"She's cleaning up."

"You let Frieda clean up your house?"

Emily takes a swig. "I sure as hell don't like to do it."

We sit down on the small concrete platform by the front door.

"The stars are amazing tonight." I look at my bottle. The wine looks like it is glowing inside, radioactive, the way Emily's porch lantern shines through it. The bubbles stream up like shooting stars.

"That's Cassiopeia up there," Emily points out. "And Cygnus, the swan."

I look up and lift my bottle to the sky, sending a toast to all the swans in Estonia. I wonder how they are doing—the news never followed up on the story, and the Estonian consulate never answered my letter. I hope they are faring better than my poor pelicans.

"Plus the dippers are out, Ursa Major and Minor." Emily's hot pink fingernail skitters around more. "And Draco's right there, too."

"How do you know so much about stars?" I ask.

"Well, actually . . ." Emily arches her back to see the sky better, and probably to stick up her breasts, although if it is for my benefit, it isn't working. All it does is show me the line of sweat beneath them on Emily's neon-green tank top. "I don't know if I told you how I lived in San Bernardino for a while?"

I shake my head.

"I was living with this guy who owned a billiards and bar stools store, Kenny. I worked there part time for a while. My main thing was to wear these little skirts and bend over the pool tables. I sold a lot of pool tables." Emily demonstrates, sticking the back of her white shorts into my face.

"I'll bet." I turn away, swallow down some more of the sweet wine while Emily sits back down.

"Kenny was very into me making something of myself, you know? So I took some classes at the junior college. I signed up for world history or something or other and film appreciation—like you have to go to college to learn how to watch a movie! I flunked out, though. The classes were at the same time as my soaps."

"Hmm." I can feel the alcohol kicking in; I don't drink very often. My shoulder blades tingle.

"Kenny was furious. He said how am I going to be an educated woman if I don't go to class? So I signed up for this class—I thought it was cosmetology, you know, makeup and all that? So I signed up, but when I went to the first class it wasn't about lipstick or hair care or anything!"

"What was it?"

"It was *cosmology*." Emily shakes her head and laughs. "Stars. The universe and shit."

"And you took the class?"

"The teacher was cute. We did it in the planetarium this one time. He put on the stars and everything. It was cool."

"And you learned a lot?"

"I got a B, but that's only because I didn't do the homework. He told me if I was as good a student as I was a lay, he would have given me an A-plus-plus!" Emily lights up a cigarette, obviously pleased with herself.

"What about Kenny?"

"That asshole? I found him doing it on a pool table with this floozy from accounting. She didn't even look good in a short skirt!"

"Well . . ." I don't know what to say.

"So I moved back here. I figured that's all the bettering of myself I needed to do."

"I see . . ."

"So anyway, that's the Corona Borealis." Emily points back up at the stars with her cigarette. The lit end of it whizzes like a comet in front of my face. I wonder if I should ask her about the two constellations that supposedly come together once every summer, the ones from the Korean folktale about the star-crossed lovers who can only see each other when birds form a bridge across the Milky Way.

The screen door suddenly opens against our backs. Emily and I scoot out of the way to let Frieda through.

"Jeez, it's hot out here," she says. "Why don't you girls come back inside?"

"Just what I was thinking." Emily throws her wine-cooler bottle out into the yard. It crashes against something, but Emily doesn't seem to care. She just stubs out her cigarette, and with a swivel of hips she is back inside.

"I think I'm going to head back home." I stand up. "Tell Emily I said thanks for the hospitality."

"Will do, hon." Frieda gives me a little hug. "You be careful now. Keep your keys out in front of you."

"Sure thing. See you tomorrow."

Frieda goes back inside. The screen door clinks behind her.

I look for Emily's bottle so that I can bring it home and put it in my recycling bin along with the bottle I have almost finished myself, but it had shattered in pieces on Emily's green gravel yard. The force of it had taken part of the ear off one of Emily's little gnome statues. I suddenly flash on Jeniece, her hearing aid. She must be with Ray tonight. I wonder what they do together—watch TV, play cards, build burial mounds?

I look up again at the sky, my hands full of glass. I try, and fail, to find the swan again before I get into the car.

The ride home is a bit squirrelly; I try to focus on the road, but I feel like the tires are sliding over ice. By the time I make it back to the trailer, my mouth is completely dry. I pound down a glass of ginger lemonade, then a glass of water, but it doesn't help. My thirst doesn't feel connected to my tongue, the back of my throat; it's a tipsy thirst that shoots through my bones.

I pick up my *chang'go,* and with each thrum of my fingers, each slap from the heel of my palm, I feel drenched in sound, my heart bursting open into a million drops of water. I feel my mind sharpen back into focus.

The phone rings. I tuck the receiver between my shoulder and my ear so that I can continue to play.

"Hello?" I drum softly so that I can hear who called. No one responds.

"Hello?" I drop the drumming down another notch. Still no answer. I am about to hang up when someone clears their throat.

"Hello?" I ask again. "Is someone there?"

Then the person starts to sing.

"Omma?" I whisper.

My mother's voice swirls out of the holes of the receiver, a mournful sound. I close my eyes and begin to play the drum with stronger hands.

Hye-yang quickly learned the way of the *kijich'on*:

- ∿ No throwing up inside the club. No throwing up outside the club. No throwing up where the GIs might see you.
- ∿ Stay in the DMZ. The Dark Man Zone is where you work. You are a Dark Man girl. Black GIs only. Don't even stick your head in a white man club.
- ∿ Bring your money directly back to the bar. You owe the bar for your room and board, your clothes, your television, your radio, all of your cosmetics. You will be paying the bar back for a long time. Don't even think about keeping the money for yourself. Don't even think about trying to escape before you have paid back your debt. They have a peephole into your bedroom. They'll know if you're planning any funny business. They'll always track you down.
- ∿ Sell drinks to the GIs. As many drinks as you can. Water them down before you bring them to the table. Get the GIs to buy you drinks. Water those drinks down even more.
- ∿ You will choose an American name, one the GIs can say and remember.
- ∿ You will keep your ID on you at all times, with the name of this bar on the front, your menstrual calendar on the back. You will go to the VD clinic every week to make sure you

are clean. If you are infected, you will be sent to the Monkey House; this is not something you will enjoy.

~ You will bleed the first time, maybe the first several times. You will hurt for a long time between your legs. Your jaw will ache. You will think you are going to die. You will think that you want to die. Don't worry. Before too long it won't hurt anymore. Before too long, you won't feel anything at all.

~ Your friend will take pills. Lots of little orange pills. It will look like someone has pulled your friend's heart right out of her body. She will float around you like a ghost. She will grab on to you and cry; other times she will pluck at your hair and laugh like a machine gun. She will talk about being a star. She still believes one day she will be a star. She will take little orange pills and drink tall glasses of watered-down vodka. She will tell you stories you won't even want to begin to believe.

Does that girl have a silver face?" Frieda gapes at the teenager walking into the Aloha Room—a surprising sight in itself, silver face or no.

"Either that or I'm hallucinating right along with you, babe." Ray squeezes Frieda's shoulders.

"Maybe there's something in the water today." Emily lifts her eyebrows and holds out her glass for more.

I imagine Emily in her Miss Tomato costume. I imagine a bunch of pelicans hoisting themselves up onto the bar stools. Anything's possible inside these walls.

The girl stops at the hostess stand. She looks like a cartoon, a smiley face smeared with metallic paint, her blonde braids streaked with green. A stretch of skin sparkles between her tank top and flannel rocket-ship pajama bottoms. Just behind her, another girl comes in, sporting tufts of bright-pink hair, a purple sports bra, army pants with a baby-doll face sewn on to each knee. Both girls have about two dozen candy necklaces bunched around their throats. They are smiling, smiling, almost demonically smiling, their teeth a dazzle of orange and blue from the neon by the door.

After being around dead birds all day, I almost can't look at these girls—they seem too full of color, too full of life.

"It's too early for Halloween, isn't it?" Frieda asks.

Ray sings the theme from *The Twilight Zone*—"do do do do"—under his breath.

"What a funky place!" The girl with pink hair looks around the room in awe.

"Yeah," says the girl with the silver face. "It's got that retro tiki thing going." They pounce on each other, rub each other's hair.

"Retro means washed up, right?" Frieda asks, eyes fretful.

"Retro's cool, Frieda," Emily whispers back. "Like old T-Birds and stuff."

"I ain't no old T-Bird, yet," Frieda says. She puts her hands on her hips and glares at the girls.

Silver Face pulls a menu from the stand. "I knew it!" she says. "Check out the 'Diet Plate'!"

Pink Hair reads out loud, "'Ground beef hamburger steak, cottage cheese, peach half, dinner roll.' No way!" The girls laugh so hard, they have to hold each other up.

Frieda sidles out from behind the counter. "Can I help you?" she asks. She looks stung; I know she eats that Diet Plate just about every night.

"Yeah—do you have any vegan chow?" Silver Face asks.

Frieda crosses her arms below her breasts. "Is that like Puppy Chow?" She arches an eyebrow. I've never heard her voice like this before—snide, almost mean. Somehow I get the feeling Jeniece has heard it plenty of times.

The girls laugh even harder. "We don't eat animal products," says Pink Hair.

"We have fried fish," says Frieda, and they fall on the floor laughing, their platform sneakers churning the air. Frieda throws up her hands in exasperation and storms back to the counter.

Silver Face links eyes with me. She stops laughing.

"Oh my gosh," she says. "You are soooo beautiful." She makes a beeline for my stool. My breath catches. She wraps her arms around my shoulders. Her makeup presses damp against my cheek. I can feel the heat of her body pass through my clothes. Pink Hair giggles from the ground. The baby doll's eyes open and close on her knees. I can't move.

"Get off her already," Ray barks after what feels like a year.

Silver Face glides away as if on roller skates.

"Are you okay, Ava?" he asks.

I nod, my nostrils full of her greasepaint-bubble-gum scent, my skin suddenly cool.

Silver Face beams at me. "No one can see how beautiful she is, but I can!"

"Me too," says Pink Hair from the floor. Baby eyes blink, blink in my direction. She blows me a kiss.

Why can't I move?

"Okay," Frieda shouts. "That's enough! You both get out of here right now!"

"But we're hungry," says Pink Hair.

"Eat your goddamn necklaces," says Frieda. "Shoo!"

Silver Face looks straight at me again. "You're beeeeautiful!" she trills. She grabs Pink Hair's hand. A square piece of paper flies out of her back pocket as they fly out the door.

"They're on X," says Emily.

"They're on something, that's for sure," Frieda scoffs.

"Ecstasy, definitely." Emily nods her head. "I did it once. It makes you all huggy and lovey and everything. It makes you want to grab everyone in sight."

"You must have X running through your veins, then, woman." Frieda starts to wipe off the counter.

Emily picks up the piece of paper and snaps it in the air like a flag. "I knew it—they're going to a rave!"

"Around here?" asks Ray.

"On the Indian reservation." Emily scans the flyer. "'Desert Dogma Smash.' We should go!"

"No way," says Frieda. "I'm not hanging around a bunch of whacked-out, technicolor teenagers."

"Oh, come on. It'll be fun. Raves are like outside discos!"

"Have you ever been to one?" Frieda asks.

"No, but . . ."

"We told Jeniece we'd rent a movie tonight," says Ray.

"Frieda, you can blow it off, right?" Emily begs.

"Sorry, hon," says Frieda. "I'm too *retro* for such things."

"Well, I'm going!"

"You can't go by yourself," Frieda warns. "They still haven't found that guy . . ."

"Ava will come with me, won't you, Ava?" Emily winks at me.

"Well . . ." I still feel frozen.

I'm beautiful?

"You have silver on your cheek—you'll fit right in!"

"I don't know . . ." I touch my hand to my face. The smear of makeup feels warm and sticky, like blood.

"There will be tons of drums and stuff, right? You're a drummer, right?"

"It would be nice to hear some music, I guess . . ."

"Cool!" Emily jumps up. "I'm going to go change!"

I hang around while Frieda and Ray close the Aloha down.

"I think I'll go pick up that video before it gets too late," Ray says to Frieda. "Be careful on your way home, all right?"

"I'll see you in a bit." Frieda gives him a smooch and locks the door behind him.

"I don't know why I said I'd go to this thing." I slide the flyer around on the counter.

"It should be fun." Frieda collapses into the stool next to mine. "Just don't let Emily get in too much trouble."

"I'll try not to."

"'The Torres-Martinez Reservation,'" she reads from the flyer as she unscrews a salt shaker cap. "Jeniece's dad was from there."

"Really?" I hand her the carton of salt. "Are you still in touch with him?"

"He's long gone, honey." Frieda pours in the crystals, twists the lid shut.

"Did Jeniece ever know him?"

"He took off right after she was born." She opens another lid. "Couldn't handle the fact that she had so many problems. I haven't heard from him since. We were never that tight anyway. Not like me and Ray."

"Does Jeniece ask about him?"

"She thinks her daddy was a migrant worker," says Frieda. "I told her we had a fling when he was here picking spinach in the valley. I told her I didn't even know I was pregnant until he had already moved on."

"And you feel okay about that?" My heart starts to pound. I know I have no right to pry, but I can't help myself.

"About what?"

"Lying to your daughter." My heart thrums even harder.

"Honey." Frieda keeps pouring the salt as she looks at me, keeps pouring it long after it spills over the lip of the shaker. "She's much better off not knowing what a no-good shit-head that dad of hers was."

"Don't you think she'd want to know where she really comes from?" I remember the burial mound Jeniece built. Maybe she has some inkling already, knowledge prickling up in her muscles, her bones . . .

"She's from the Salton Sea, and she's like the Salton Sea. That's all she needs to know." The salt keeps pouring. It forms a pile on the counter.

"In what way?"

"She was made by mistake," Frieda says.

I feel a twinge in my belly.

"I mean, it was a good mistake. Think of all the birds that come here on their way to Mexico. They wouldn't have a place to rest if it wasn't for that mistake."

"It's more of a final resting place right now, Frieda." The pile of salt is almost as high as the shaker.

Frieda follows my gaze to the counter. "Would you look at that?!" She stops pouring. "Why didn't you say anything, Ava?"

"I'm sorry . . ."

Emily bangs on the door. Frieda shakes her head as she goes to unlock it. I sweep the pile of salt into my hand and dump it in a dustbin, then brush the rest off on my pants. Emily sashays in, wearing a black mesh tank top with a lime-green bra underneath, a short patterned skirt in blues and yellows and high-heeled gold sandals. Her makeup is cranked up to a new pitch, her hair piled high on her head.

"Are you ready to get down?" She shakes her hips.

In my car, Emily jabbers away about who knows what, but all I can think about is Frieda and Jeniece. Jeniece, who thinks her father bent over rows of spinach, pulling green leaf upon green leaf out of the earth. Jeniece, whose father himself is rooted to the same patch of soil.

My mind reels. I knew mothers could be silent, I knew mothers could keep things tamped down inside themselves, but I didn't know mothers could tell such big lies. Did my mother make up the stories she sang to me, the ones I've been writing down, the ones that have been tearing me up? We never talk about those stories outside our *pansori* sessions. We act as if they don't exist, aside from in the song, in the drum, in my pen, but I can always feel them, rattling under our skins, ready to spill. What if her story, my story, has a completely different rhythm than what I had been led to believe? What if my father is not a total mystery, but someone with a name, an address, someone I could easily track down?

"Turn here," says Emily, and I crank the wheel so hard, I almost run us off the road.

The hills glow in the distance, a strange pink sheen, as I follow the tire ruts down a stretch of sandy dirt. A few cars pass us, showering my windows with pebbles. Kids whoop inside, heads rocking, arms pumping the air. They look scary to me, vaguely sinister.

"Emily, I don't know if this is such a good idea." I check the rearview mirror to see if it's safe to turn around.

"No, you're right, it's not a good idea." She sighs and reaches one leg over the hump between our seats. "It's a fucking fantastic idea!" She presses her gold heel onto the accelerator. The tires spin madly; the car lurches forward.

"Emily!" I press the brakes, sending us fishtailing over the dirt.

"Just kidding, sheesh!" She pulls her foot back, turns on the radio, and starts bopping to the ranchero music that blares out. Another rhythm—a driving techno beat—seeps into the car from the outside. I can feel it more than hear it, the rhythm pounding erratic as my heartbeat as I manage to gain control of the steering wheel again.

The dirt road curves; the pink glow intensifies. We reach a makeshift parking lot. Tents are scattered among the cars. A few kids sit on beach chairs; others lie on the ground looking at constellations. When we get out of the Sonata, the music hits me full force, electronica buzzing my breastbone. Emily grabs my elbow and pulls me toward the sound.

The wind is insane. Emily's carefully blow-dried hair flies all over the place. I can feel my own hair grow heavy with sand. A bunch of people, I notice, are wearing surgical masks. I think of my mother in her mask, protecting her lungs from eggshell dust. I clamp my lips shut tight, shield my face with one of my hands. The music is incredibly loud, and fast—at least 120 beats per minute. My heart rate speeds up in response as we walk toward it.

Even in this wind, people are dancing like crazy, jumping up and down, swinging limbs at wild angles. It seems like almost everyone is wearing huge pants—the legs so wide, they look like ball gown skirts. Lots of people are glowing, bright tubes looped around their heads, necks, wrists, neon paint all over their skin. Some people on dunes and rock formations swing glow sticks from the ends of ropes, tracing arcs, circles, blazing figure eights in the air. Several people have silver faces. Several have pink hair.

On the stage, alien cowgirls do a spastic square dance. Lights swivel from the scaffolding, sending shafts of color across the desert. Emily starts to circle her hips, slowly, not at all in time with the music—more like she's listening to some burlesque number inside her head. A few people come up to her to compliment her "totally eighties" clothes. She looks confused but flashes them a smile anyway. Everyone is smiling here—you can see it even with their surgical masks on, even with the way they squint against the wind. It hurts my face to see so much smiling. It makes me feel even worse. All I want is to go back to my trailer and go to bed.

"I'll be right back!" Emily yells over the music.

"What?" I stare at her. "You're not going anywhere! How will we find each other again? There must be a thousand people here."

"Just go over by that tarp thing." She points to the DJ booth. "I'll come right back, I promise."

"But . . ."

She waves and slips into the crowd. I head over to the tarp. The DJ has pretty impressive equipment—two DAT machines, a mixer, two turntables, two CD players. I envy the headphones clamped over his ears. He's off in some world of his own, head bobbing like one of those figures on a dashboard. He has no idea I'm standing here, wishing I could get my hands on his DATs. I finger the small tape recorder inside my purse.

Everywhere I look, people are hugging each other. I don't think I want anyone to hug me, but an all too familiar feeling of invisibility kicks me in the stomach. I don't know what I want anymore. I stick my head outside the tarp; my face is blasted with sand.

"Ava!" Emily comes running. "See? I told you I'd be right back!"

I am surprised by how glad I am to see her. Maybe we can head back home now.

"I got some X!" Emily is breathless. I can tell she's already taken the stuff—her eyes are extra wide and I can see more of her teeth than usual. She hands me a water bottle. There is so much grit in my mouth, I am happy to have a nice long drink.

"Have you ever tried Ecstasy?" she asks.

"No, and I have no intention to ever do so, thank you very much."

Emily bursts into giggles. "Too late!" She slaps her hands on her thighs.

My stomach dips.

"I just dosed you!" She can't stop laughing.

"What?!"

"I put it in the water bottle!"

"Emily!" I spit out what's left in my mouth. "What should I do? Is there an antidote or something?"

"Just enjoy it, Ava," Emily says. "You need to loosen up!" She lifts up her arms and starts jumping up and down to the DJ tracks. A group of teenage boys gather around her.

"Emily!"

She is too busy showing off for the boys to answer.

I don't know what to do. I race over to the closest tent. A bunch of kids are lounging around inside, sucking on pacifiers. I can't bring myself to ask them anything. I run over to three relatively normal-looking guys sitting on beach chairs.

"Excuse me?" I ask, panting. "Can you help me? I just took some Ecstasy!"

A hefty guy with a goatee and a kind face stands up and slips a surgical mask over my nose and mouth. The inside is slick with Vicks VapoRub. It smears on my skin, makes the inside of my nose burn. I flash on the night of the smell party, Abby's fingers, Darryl's eyes. I take a deep breath and start to cough.

"Does this counteract it?" I ask, my voice muffled.

"No, man," the guy smiles, "it *enhances* it!"

I rip the mask off my face.

"What?!"

"It makes you feel it better. I thought that's what you wanted." He adjusts his ski cap.

I run off, furiously rubbing the slick stuff from my face. I don't know where to go. The music is so loud, I can feel my diaphragm vibrate inside my ribs.

I push myself through the crowd and into some open space. The air is wild, a mad rush of prickly seeds and candy-wrapper scraps. My body begins to feel funny, like my bones are melting, like the wind can pass right through me. Only my feet feel solid, slogging through the sand. I climb up a dune. A small crowd gathers by a bonfire at the bottom on the other side, nestled in a grove of cottonwood trees. The leaves shimmer in the firelight, flashing silver like some sort of code. I can hear a single voice singing, the shake of a rattle. The techno music recedes into the background. I stumble-slide down the dune, my body streaming in all directions.

My mother balances on a star at the far edge of the Milky Way. The swirling swath shimmers between us, a river of glitter in the dark. From where I stand on my own small star her body blinks in and out of focus, but the nightingale that hovers over her head shines in sharp relief.

"I can teach you a song," I hear the bird tell her, and my mother's voice floats out into the empty space.

A crane touches down next to me and whispers, "I can teach you a dance." It lifts its strange ankles, and my hands involuntarily slap against my drum.

Crows and magpies swarm the milky span and spread their wings. Their bodies drown out all the glimmer. "Use us as a bridge," they say, then clip their beaks to each other's tails and wings, weaving together a huge hammock of bird. I place a blind foot on a crow's back. The bird bobs down, then rises back up, like a buoy. I move my other foot onto a magpie's wing. The ridges of its feathers are jagged; my foot slips, knocks against another bird's skull. I'm scared I might fall; there is nothing to hold on to but my drum as I slowly step from one bird to another. A few bright specks seep up between their wings, but it is too dark to see anything else. I can't tell whether my mother is navigating this bridge, too, trying to reach me halfway.

I wake up to a strange, buttery light—much softer than the light in the trailer, where even the sun seems harsh and fluorescent. Outside the window, a hummingbird hovers over a bird of paradise plant, then darts away, an emerald flash. Beyond it I can see hills, cactus. I'm on a futon, covered by a down comforter. The room smells of cedar and coffee. I have no idea where I am. My head pounds. My mouth is completely dry.

"Good morning." Darryl kisses my cheek. "It's so amazing to see you here."

I sit up fast. The cover slides down to my waist. I'm relieved to see that I'm still wearing my clothes.

"Are you okay?" He hands me a cup of coffee. "You were really out of it last night."

I struggle to remember what happened. Then it all comes back to me in a rush: a bunch of rave kids sitting in a scraggly semicircle on the ground, the cuffs of their enormous pants pooling together in the sand. In front of them, by the fire, a woman, around sixty years old, sang in a language I'd never heard before. She danced in small steps, half bent over, her arms and hands shaping the song. A younger woman, maybe in her twenties or thirties, obviously related to the singer, sat on the ground, shaking a large gourd rattle. She watched the singer intently as she accompanied her. My heart pounded. I fished around in my purse for my small tape recorder and pressed the red record button. I wondered if the singer was telling the truth; I wondered if the other woman hung on every word, if they rang inside her long after the song ended. I felt myself melt into the music, into the sand.

"Ava?"

I looked up. The warmth of the bonfire flooded my body.

"Darryl!" I grabbed his hand and pulled him down to the ground next to me. "I didn't expect to see you here!" My cheeks hurt, all of a sudden I was smiling so much.

"I heard there were going to be bird songs tonight." His voice was quiet so that he wouldn't disturb the singer. He looked down at our hands, linked together, and cleared his throat. His hand felt so good. I lifted it up and kissed it. *Did I really do that?*

"This is a bird song?" I whispered. I was melting, melting.

"Traditional Cahuilla," he said. "Only a handful of people still know the language . . ."

"I don't know the language of birds," I told him. "My mother told me to say I know the language of birds, but I don't!" I started to laugh.

A bunch of rave kids turned to me and said, "Shhhh!"

"Are you okay, Ava?"

"I'm fiiiine." I flopped my head against his shoulder. His shirt smelled wonderful, like soap and fire smoke. *Oh my gosh . . .*

I felt his arm stiffen. "Did you take something?"

I nodded. "Emily tricked me." I laughed even harder.

The singer spread her arms like wings. I wrapped my arms around his waist.

"Ava, this is weird," Darryl said. "You're not yourself. Maybe I should take you home."

"But I want to hear the music . . ." I pressed my ear against his chest. *Did I actually do that?*

"Ava . . ." Darryl's eyes were confused. He'd been wanting me to touch him, he's been wanting to touch me, for weeks, but now he pulled away.

I brushed the back of my hand against his hair. I wanted to say something, but I couldn't. My jaw clamped shut tight; my teeth ground together, my mouth suddenly turned dry, salty as soup mix. Only a growl could pass through. *This really happened. How could this have really happened?*

"Are you okay?" Darryl looked panicked. I shook my head. Something between a laugh and a cry bubbled up inside my chest.

"Don't sweat it." The guy sitting next to me squeezed my jaw at the hinge and opened my mouth. He slid in a pacifier, slick and wet, tasting faintly of candy. I wanted to spit it out, but it felt nice to have some space between my molars, some saliva beginning to flow.

"First time on X?" he asked me. I nodded.

"Wait till you have sex." He looked at me, then Darryl. "You'll flip out."

Even in the dark, I could see Darryl flush.

"Let's go," I whispered, the pacifier still in my mouth. Then I stood up too fast, and the world disappeared.

I pull the covers up over my chest. I'm too embarrassed to even acknowledge the night before. I have no memory of anything after the bonfire.

"I thought you lived in a tent," I say, feeling like a complete idiot.

"I'm just staying down there during the rescue effort," he says. "I want to be close by in case anyone needs me. This is my regular house. I come up here to unwind."

"It's nice," I say, and it really is, full of space and light. Through the open bedroom door I can see the main part of the house, the high open beam ceiling, the simple furniture.

"I picked it up for a song." He sits down on the bed next to me. The mattress tilts; my hips slide toward him; I try to hold them back. "It's all solar. There's so much sun out here—it makes sense to take advantage of it."

I take a sip of coffee. Is it possible he put ginger in it? It tastes amazing.

"My hat goes off to anyone who can live here," I say, but this house, this view, away from the stink of the shore, seem surprisingly, wonderfully livable.

"I really thought I wouldn't be able to hang—I'm a northern California boy, so this is a pretty intense climate for me—but they need me here. The birds. And the place has grown on me, actually. It's where I'm supposed to be right now."

I wonder what it's like to feel such certainty. My body has a hint of it—my skin feels warm, almost like it's glowing from the inside out; I wonder if the Ecstasy is still circling through my blood, or if it's just the coffee, or maybe it's from being in Darryl's bed, from Darryl being so close. It's scary, how good it feels. I'm not sure I can handle it.

"You know, there's a bird song about the first people who came to this area," Darryl tells me. "Maybe the woman sang it last night—I don't know Cahuilla, so I wouldn't have recognized it. I've just read that this song is supposed to be about the first people who came here, the first people on earth, supposedly. They could fly, so the mythology goes. They circled this place three times before they decided to touch down, to try to make a human world."

"I did that." I take another sip. "I mean, I didn't fly, but I drove around the sea three times before I decided to stay."

"I'm glad you decided to stay, Ava." Darryl leans toward me. He closes his eyes; his lips reach for mine.

I jump up, spilling the coffee all over the bed.

"I should probably go." My heart is hummingbird-fast.

"Ava . . ."

"I'm sorry about the spill—I hope it doesn't stain."

"I'm not worried about the spill," Darryl starts.

"I'll pay for it, I promise." I race toward the door.

When I get outside, I realize I have no idea where I am. My car is nowhere in sight. There is no discernible road, even, just ruts on the hill where Darryl's Jeep has gone in and out.

"Let me give you a lift." Darryl comes outside, holding my purse. He is still wearing pajamas. "I can take you home, or I can take you to your car. Just let me know what you want."

"I don't know . . ." I want to sit down on the dirt and cry.

"You don't need to go," he says. He stands a step closer. I can feel heat move between us like a hand. I close my eyes.

"Oh my gosh!" I step back. "Emily! I gave Emily a ride to the thing last night! She had no way to get home!"

"If I know Emily, she found a way," Darryl chuckles.

"You know Emily?"

"Who doesn't know Emily around here?"

"Could you take me to my car, please?" I was supposed to be keeping her out of trouble, not falling into trouble myself. "I want to make sure she's okay."

"Sure thing." He hands me my purse. "Hop in."

At the site of the rave, only a few stragglers, a few tents and cars remain. At first I can't find my car; then I see it has been turned into some sort of art piece. The top is covered with glitter. A few beer bottles and candles sit altarlike on the hood, along with a couple of condom wrappers. The top of the trunk is littered with flowers and surgical masks. The car is so spattered with dirt from the unpaved road, I can barely tell it's green. In the dust on a window, someone has written the word "beautiful." I stand, frozen, before it.

"I'll work on cleaning this up," says Darryl. "Why don't you look around for Emily."

"Are you sure you don't mind?" I ask. "I've given you a lot to clean up already."

"It's my pleasure." He smiles. "And it's true." He points to the dusty word.

It is eerily quiet here, eerily still, after the wind and noise of last night. My sternum has some sort of Pavlovian response—I can feel it buzz as if the music is still thumping through the air. I can't find Emily among the small clusters of kids sitting on the sand or in beach chairs, toasting marshmallows for breakfast and drinking sodas and beer. I peer inside the few tents that are open. Many kids sleep with pacifiers in their mouths, huddled together like puppies. In one tent, a girl with pink hair—the girl from the Aloha,

I'm pretty sure—is asleep, naked. Her pants are on the ground out-side, baby-doll eyes wide open on the knees. I try not to look at her nipples, but I can't seem to help myself—she must have dyed them; they are almost as pink as her hair. Her eyes fly open; I race away, wondering where Silver Face is, wondering if I still have sil-ver smeared on my cheek.

Darryl is lifting a condom wrapper off the hood when I get back.

"She doesn't seem to be here," I tell him, blushing. "Maybe we could check the Aloha."

"That's the restaurant you always go to, right?" he says. "I still haven't checked that place out."

"The food's not the best, but it's homey," I tell him.

"Are you sure you don't just want to go home?"

"I want to see if Frieda knows where she is," I say.

"Okay," he says. "I could use some breakfast, anyway. I'll fol-low you there."

I've never been so aware of the back of my head before, the backs of my arms. I can feel Darryl driving behind me, his car bouncing on the same potholes as mine, changing lanes when I do to stay right behind me. I'm glad I'm surrounded by so much metal. My body feels way too soft and fluid and warm to hold itself together.

The Aloha is surprisingly busy—at least half a dozen tables are filled, the most I've seen at one time. Emily is sitting at the counter. Relief floods through me at the sight of her. She looks at me, then quickly glances away.

Darryl touches my elbow. It feels funny to be here with him;

it's always been the place I've gone when I've wanted to avoid catching his eye. One wall crumbles down after another . . .

Frieda runs up to me and gives me a hug. Her hair smells like bacon. "Ava!" she cries. "We were so worried about you!"

"I think I passed out, but I'm okay." I glance over, but Emily won't look at me.

"*I* didn't pass out." Emily fiddles with her fork. "You only had a little bit—I barely put anything in the water."

"Did you give her something?" Frieda spins toward Emily.

"I just wanted her to relax," she says, her face pale. "Looks like it worked." She gestures to Darryl's pajamas with her head.

"Emily! How could you do something so stupid? That's totally illegal!"

"Don't lecture me, Frieda, okay?" Emily storms off to the bathroom.

"I didn't know she did that," says Frieda. "That's bad. That's really bad. That's not even what I was worried about, though—not before now, at least. We heard another body was found, not too far from that rave."

"Oh, no" tumbles out of my mouth, Darryl's mouth, together.

"When Emily said she couldn't find you last night, I got scared . . ."

"I had no idea," I tell her. "I'm glad Emily got home okay."

"Yeah, well," Frieda says, distracted. "Oh, we got some other news from the cops, too—that first body, the one you found, Ava? Turns out she was a hooker."

My heart falls to my knees.

"I didn't even know we had prostitutes in these parts." Frieda hands Darryl a laminated menu. She knows I don't need to look at the menus anymore.

"World's oldest profession," Ray says from the grill. "They're everywhere you go."

"I'm not even going to ask you how you know that, babe," Frieda says.

Heat rises up my neck and into my cheeks. The words "my mother was a prostitute" tap the inside of my teeth like Braille, then slide back down my throat. I've never said them out loud before. If I say them out loud, I think I might spontaneously combust. I can write the words, but if I say them, it would make them real. If I say them, I would have to deal with them. On the page, even in my mother's song, they are in a safe little box. In the air, from my own lips, my own breath, they would rip my heart out.

"Have they identified the second body yet?" Darryl asks.

Frieda shakes her head. "It's a woman, that's all I know."

"I figure I'm gonna ask Rick to start paying." Emily walks back to the counter. "He calls me a slut so much, I might as well make a few bucks out of it."

"You're kidding, I hope," says Frieda. She gives a customer some change. He glares at all of us before he leaves.

Emily laughs unconvincingly. I wonder how she got home last night.

"You shouldn't put up with that crap," Frieda says to Emily. "Rick is no good. You could do so much better than that little asshole."

"I have." Emily grins slyly at Darryl. He looks down. My stomach bunches up.

"Excuse me," I say, then race toward the bathroom. Frieda meets me in the hallway by the cigarette machines.

"Emily's clean," Frieda says. "I make sure she goes in for a test at least every six months. You have nothing to worry about in that regard."

Emily shows up in the hallway. "She's got plenty to worry about," she says.

My knees weaken.

"With the bodies and the birds and everything." Emily rustles in her pocket for some change. "We all got something to worry about around here."

"You know, I'm not really hungry," I tell Darryl when I come back from the bathroom. I hope my eyes aren't too red. I can barely look at him. "I think I'll go on home."

He stands up. "Ava," he says. "I'm really glad we found each other last night."

"Thanks for looking out for me," I tell him.

"Can I see you again?" He steps closer.

I tilt back. "I'll be at the hospital tomorrow."

He opens his mouth but no words come out.

I run for the door.

I can barely see the road, I'm crying so hard. I don't know why Emily's news upset me so much. Everyone has their dating history. I didn't expect Darryl would be a virgin, too. The back of my head feels cold, naked. The unsaid words in my mouth are heavy, invisible stones. When I look in my rearview mirror, all I see is empty space.

Someone has left a package on my elevator lift—a large one, it looks like, as I drive toward the trailer. Maybe it's a boulder. Maybe it's a bag full of birds. I pull into my parking spot. Closer up, it looks like a large pile of clothes. A shuddering pile of clothes. I sit inside the car, heart pounding, ready to drive away again. I'm not ready to find another body, dead or almost dead. I'm not ready to find the person who killed those people, either. I shift into reverse.

A head pops up from the bundle, and a scream involuntarily tears through my throat. I press the gas. The tires spin fruitlessly in the dirt. The person sits up; the metal pan of the lift tips back and forth. The person grabs on to the chains.

"Come on, come on," I tell the car. "Go, go, go, go!" Then I catch a glimpse of the person's face, the shape of the person's shoulders. I suddenly feel like I've been drenched in cold water. I throw the car back into park.

"Omma?" I whisper.

My mother shakily lowers herself to the ground. The tray of the lift swings. Jumbled clothes, shoes, a birdcage covered with a towel remain on it, along with a few pillowcases filled with hard-looking things.

"Your hammock work wrong."

"It's not a hammock, Omma." I walk toward her, my limbs fizzing with adrenaline. "It's like an elevator. To bring stuff up to the trailer."

"Hard on the back." She rubs her spine. She seems to be wearing several layers of clothes.

"Omma, aren't you hot?" As usual, it's at least a hundred degrees today.

"It's more easy to carry this way."

"Don't you have any bags?"

She just shrugs. I turn the key and push the button to send her scraggly pile up to the trailer. I want to ask her what she's doing here, but my tongue has retreated into silence; the effects of the Ecstasy have evaporated completely, it seems.

"Watch for Yukam!" she yells. The birdcage wobbles a bit but stays upright.

"How did you get here?" I ask. Her car is nowhere in sight.

"Anchee drive me," she says.

"Is she here, too?" It looks like someone could be hidden under the stuff on the slowly rising lift.

"She drive back home. Why you give me so many questions?"

"I'm sorry, Omma. I just wasn't expecting to see you today. You caught me off guard." *This is my mother. My mother was a prostitute. This is her. This is real.*

She reaches inside two layers of pants, pulls a tattered article out of the pocket closest to her skin, and hands it to me. My name is there, in smudged newsprint: "The body was discovered by San Diego native Ava Sing Lo, 25." I'm surprised my mother hasn't put this inside her Book of Dead Birds yet. I'm even more surprised to see myself listed as a San Diego native. I've lived there all my life, but I've somehow never considered myself native to the city, never thought anyplace could ever claim me as its own. I've always felt alien there. I've always felt alien no matter where I go.

"They think you kill her," she says.

"No, Omma, they don't," I tell her. "No one thinks I've killed anyone."

"You watch out," she says. "They think you kill her."

I scan the article quickly to make sure there aren't any accusations that I'm not aware of, but the paper gives no indication of this.

"Omma, why would anyone think I killed that woman?"

The lift shudders as it reaches the top of the chain. A stuffed pillowcase wobbles at the lip; the contents begin to spill from it like vomit. A few stray feathers take to the air. A large dark square zooms down toward me. I jump back; it lands with a thunk at my feet. Some papers fly out, some seeds and scraps of paper. It's my mother's scrapbook. I bend down and try to pick up all the loose things that have fallen out. My mother stares at me as if I've just killed another bird.

"I'll fix it, Omma, don't worry," I tell her. She looks at the feathers from Kane and Lee Lee, along with a sunflower seed hull and part of a candy wrapper, in my hand. She runs for the ladder.

"Omma, there's not much of a ledge up there," I tell her. "Let me unlock the trailer before you go up."

She creeps up to one of the highest rungs anyway and puts a protective hand over the top of Yukam's cage. She could easily fall. My heart feels like it's full of bees. I think about Darryl's house, the easy, buttery light, and wonder why I was so fast to run away.

Ava, daugher, 12,
come home from school,
give me this on yellow paper:

A siege of herons or bitterns
A wisp of snipe
A desert of lapwings
A sord of mallards
A skein of geese (flying)
A muster of peacocks
A murder of crows

[Part of yellow page torn off, taped in,
"A murder of crows" written
across it in loopy script]

11/2/83

I am not able to get much sleep with my mother in the trailer. I finally drift off in the wee hours of the morning, but am awakened shortly afterward by the smell of morning-after soup, made with sheets of seaweed and various kitchen implements my mother brought in a pillowcase. The smell makes me want to cry; I have to hide my face in my hands after I take the first taste.

"I'm teaching a self-defense class this morning, Omma." I set down my spoon. "You can stay here or you can come with me. It's like tae kwon do, for women. For women to protect themselves."

She gives me one of her sidelong glances, then snorts. "*You* teach this class?"

We haven't talked about tae kwon do since I was sixteen. I had stopped going to class after my teacher's son grabbed my breasts once after practice. I didn't tell my mother about this; she never knew why I refused to go back. After two weeks, she tricked me—she said we were going to go clothes shopping, a rare event—and drove me to the *dojang*. I refused to get out of the car. She tried to pull me out, but I was already six inches taller than my mother's five-foot frame, and thirty pounds heavier than her hundred. I didn't budge, even though I knew the teacher and his son were watching from the door of the storefront. My mother screamed at me, but I crossed my arms in front of my chest and wouldn't move.

My mother eventually exhausted herself and sat down on the sidewalk. My teacher came outside and helped her into the back of the car. She lay down across the seat and fell asleep, or pretended to, immediately. Embarrassed, I nodded my thanks, then slid over to the driver's side of the car and strapped on the seat belt. I was so eager to leave, I didn't scoot the seat back. By the time we got home, my legs were cramped from trying to fit into my mother's position. I had to shake them out and slap them to bring them back to life.

My mother brewed a pot of peacock tongue tea after we got home. We sipped from our cups together on the couch, but neither of us said a word.

I didn't practice tae kwon do again until graduate school, when I noticed classes were offered at SDSU. I was amazed by how glad I was to be doing crescent kicks and down blocks and the crane stance. My body remembered everything. I didn't tell my mother I had taken it up again. I practiced in secret in my room.

My mother slurps up the last of her soup. "I go with you," she says, a glitter of challenge in her eyes.

The self-defense group has dwindled the last couple of weeks. The bridge ladies decided, in their words, that they can now sufficiently "kick ass" and have gone back to their cards, and Rayanne never returned after Emily's comments about her boyfriend. Most weeks it's been just me, Frieda, and Emily, with Lonnie showing up every now and again.

The Aloha smells of sausage and syrup when we walk in. The breakfast crowd, if you can call three men a crowd, is still there, huddled together over their last cup of coffee. Jeniece is there, too, sitting by herself in a booth. She looks away before I can wave hello.

"Frieda, Ray, Jeniece, I'd like you to meet my mother." My mother stands behind me. They probably can't even see her.

"Howdy!" Ray lifts a spatula in greeting.

"Ava! I didn't know your mother was coming out!" Frieda wipes her palms on her apron and steps around me. "So nice to meet you," she says. My mother stands stiffly, shakes hands with Frieda like a robot.

Emily comes through the front door wearing a grayish sports bra and faded paisley bicycle shorts, holding a frayed hand towel. I almost can't look at her. Darryl put his lips on her lips. Darryl touched her skin. I feel nauseous just thinking about it.

"Emily, look! This is Ava's mom!" Frieda calls out.

"I didn't know your mom was Japanese." Emily drops her towel and stares at my mom like she's part of a sideshow. "Ava, I didn't know you were part Japanese!"

"Korea," my mother says. "I from Korea. No Japan."

"She speakee English!" Emily squeals.

"Emily!" Frieda glares.

My mother looks almost frantic. "Where you put your eggshells?"

"*My* eggshells?" Emily points to herself. "I don't have any eggshells!"

My mother turns to Frieda. "What you do with them?"

"We toss them out, I guess," she says as she gives the men their change.

"Why you not blow them?"

"You blow eggs?" Emily laughs. "Ooh, your mom's dirty, Ava!"

The three men drool at Emily before they get up to leave. She pretends to ignore them but tilts her hips in their direction. Is that what Darryl likes?

"My mom makes art out of eggshells," I say quickly. "She puts a pinprick on each side and blows the stuff out. She makes amazing stuff."

"We did that once," Jeniece pipes up. "Me and Ray. Remember, Ray? That Easter? We blew the stuff out of the eggs."

Ray winks at her.

"The house smelled like vinegar for days," says Frieda.

"Can't raw eggs make you sick or something?" Emily asks. Half

her attention is on the men walking out the door. She runs her fingers through her hair to maximum effect. Is that what drew him
in? "They give you botulism or something?"

"That's what the birds have," I tell her. I'm sure there's more
vinegar in my voice than necessary.

"Well, the birds have eggs!"

"I think it's salmonella . . ."

"Oh! Knock knock," says Ray.

"Who's there?" Jeniece asks.

"Sam and Ella. I mean, Sam and Janet."

"Sam and Janet who?"

"Sam and Janet Evening," he sings.

"I don't get it," says Emily.

"Some enchanted evening," he sings again. "Sam and Janet
Evening. Sam and Ella Eeeeevening . . ."

"You work here?" my mother asks. Ray scrapes the grill to the
tune of the song.

"I eat here," I tell her.

"Where the tae kwon do?"

"Oh, the self-defense class—that's here, yes."

"You know, Ava," Frieda says. "I don't think we can do the class
today. I have to take Jeniece to the doctor and we're going to have
to lock everything up. I'm sorry—I should have called you."

"Damn, Frieda!" Emily picks up her towel and dabs her forehead. "I was gonna kick your butt today, too!" Did he touch her
butt? Did she touch his butt? Where did they touch each other? His
house? Her trailer? The fish bone–studded shore?

"Sorry, kiddos," Frieda says. "This was the only time we could
get her in. We better get ready to skedaddle."

"What do you make with your eggs?" Jeniece asks my mother.
My mother walks over to the booth.

"Purse, box, ship in bottle, many kinds things." She sits down across from Jeniece.

"I can't picture it," Jeniece says.

"I show you sometime," she says. "You a sick girl?"

Frieda rushes over to the booth. "Jeniece isn't sick," she says. "She just has some problems."

"I'm defective," Jeniece says.

"A birth defect doesn't mean you're *defective*," Frieda says.

"Mom, look at the word, okay? It's the exact same thing."

"I use *all* the eggshells," my mother says. "Defect one, broken one. I make things with all the one."

"Mosaics," I say, remembering the picture frames she spangles with tiny bits of shell, intricately pieced together.

"See? You're not defective," says Frieda. "You're a mosaic."

Jeniece rolls her eyes behind her thick glasses.

"I show you sometime," my mother says.

"We better go," Frieda says. "It was so nice to meet you." She shakes my mother's hand again. "Come on, Jeniece."

Jeniece tussles with her canes and pulls herself out of the booth. "See you later," she says to my mother. My mother nods and smiles. I can't remember when I last saw her smile.

"Well, Omma," I say. Her face drops when she looks at me. "Do you want to see the bird hospital?"

"If you want," she says.

"I want to do whatever you want."

She shrugs, watching Jeniece stomp-drag her way to the door. Emily watches my mother.

"So, what brings you to the beautiful Salton Sea, anyway?" she asks. Did Darryl call her beautiful, too? Did he spike her coffee with ginger? Did he look at her the way he's looked at me?

"They think Ava kill her."

"Who thinks you killed who?" Emily crinkles her eyebrows at me. Frieda stops at the door to listen.

"They think Ava kill that girl."

"Ava, have you been killing people?" Emily says with mock horror. "I thought you were just breaking hearts!" Me? *I'm* the heartbreaker?

Ray turns off the light in the kitchen.

"They put Ava in jail," my mother says.

"What?" Emily asks.

"No one's putting me in jail, Omma." I touch her elbow. It feels hard and dry, even through her windbreaker. "Let's go, okay?"

My mother lets me lead her to the door. I can feel all eyes on us as we walk back out into the light.

"It always so hot here?" She fans herself with her purse.

"Maybe we're closer to the sun than most places." Emily shields her face with her hand as she comes outside. Her nipples jut through her pilly sports bra. I feel a rush of shame about my inverted nipples. Who would ever want to touch such weird and backward things?

"We're farther, actually," I say, hating the snotty tone of my voice. "We're lower than the ocean here. We're about as low as we can go in this country."

"Oh, no." Emily sashays past us with a wink. "Believe me. We could go much, much, lower."

I forget to warn my mother about the stench at the bird hospi-tal. I forget to warn her about what she's about to see. When we walk into the enclosure, she freezes. Then she starts to swoon. She sags against me, dead weight. I lower her onto a folding chair.

"Ava?" Darryl rushes up to us.

"This is my mother," I say, grateful to have her as a shield between us.

"Is she okay?"

"Omma, are you okay?"

She looks dazed.

"I guess passing out is a family tradition." Darryl tries to laugh, but I see the concern in his eyes. I try not to look at his hands.

"I not pass out," my mother says. Her voice seems to come from a tiny place deep inside her chest, a voice echoing from a well.

"I think she's just overwhelmed," I say. "She's never seen so many dead birds before." The pile by the incinerator is especially tall today.

"Let me get you some water," Darryl tells her. He walks off. I'm tempted to follow him, but I don't.

"Omma." I touch her shoulder. "I'm sorry. I should have prepared you better for this."

"You prepare me for this." She glares at me. "Your whole life you prepare me for this."

"Omma, you know I never meant . . ."

Darryl comes back with a water bottle, a bendy straw poking out the top. "Here." He bends down and offers it to my mother. "Have a sip."

She lowers her head and wraps her lips around the straw. I have to look away, it seems so intimate—the bottle resting on his knee, her practiced mouth. What did Emily do to Darryl with her lips?

"Omma, why don't I take you back to the trailer," I say. "I think you need to take it easy."

"Will you come back later?" Darryl asks me.

"I should probably stay with my mother," I tell him.

"Ava, about Emily . . ."

"We should go." I help my mother to her feet.

"You don't have to keep rushing off . . ."

"I'll see you later." We start to walk away.

"I just want—"

"We need to go," I tell him. "Thanks for the water."

"Nice to meet you," he calls to my mother as we hobble off to the car. I'm not sure which one of us is holding the other up.

There was no red ribbon around Sun's doorknob, so Helen walked into the room. Sun was curled up on her bed. A bruise peeked through the rouge on her cheek. She didn't acknowledge Helen's presence. Helen climbed onto the bed and wrapped her arms around her.

"I wish we were back in our cave," she said into Sun's shoulder. It hurt to talk, her jaw was aching so much.

Sun didn't say anything.

"Don't you wish it, too?" Helen closed her eyes so that she wouldn't see the blink of the neon sign outside; the light bled through her eyelids anyway. "Don't you wish we were back in our cave on Cheju-do?"

Sun pulled herself off the bed. Helen toppled over.

"Don't you know what happened in that cave?" Sun lit a cigarette.

"Our life happened in that cave." Helen sat up. "All our dreams, everything we told each other . . ."

"You're still so naive, sometimes, Hye-yang." Sun took a deep drag.

"What are you talking about?"

"Haven't you ever heard of April third?"

"Of course I've heard of April third."

"The April third massacre, the one on Cheju-do?"

Helen stared at Sun, confused.

"Thirty thousand people were killed, and you haven't heard about it?!"

"That isn't true," said Helen. Surely she would have heard something if that were true.

"People never talk about it!" yelled Sun. "Why can't people ever talk about anything?!"

"You're making this up." Helen rubbed her aching jaw.

"It was 1948. Rebels were hiding in our cave, Hye-yang! Whole families were hiding in our cave! But the army found them! The army found them and killed them, Hye-yang, right there, right there in our cave!" She took a swig of vodka from a canteen one of the GIs had left behind. "You know those bones we found? People!"

"Why are you saying this?" Helen asked.

"It's true! It's all true! Women were raped! Babies were killed! People were tortured, Hye-yang—buried alive, whipped like dogs!"

Helen covered her face with her hands but the neon still seeped through.

"My grandmother pretended to be retarded so they wouldn't rape her, but they did anyway! Two policemen put a plank on my mother's stomach like a seesaw and sat on either end, Hye-yang. She thought they were going to crush her to death. She was bleeding for days. She thought she'd never be able to have children. I was her miracle, she said, even though my real father was one of the rapists! The man I call Father was in Japan for a year before I was born, so how could it have been him?!"

"If this is true, why didn't you tell me before?" Helen cried.

"They told me not to tell! They told me not to talk about it! I didn't think I'd ever be able to say anything, but here I am! It's just words! It's easy!"

"My mother never said anything about this," said Helen.

"But she was there, Hye-yang! She was there! For all you know, your father was one of the rapists, too!"

"Sun," Helen started.

"Don't you see?!" Sun grabbed Helen's hands. "We're not supposed to say anything! What if we started talking about what they do to us here?! What if we started asking for better treatment?! They'd kill us! We can't talk anywhere!"

"Sun, you're scaring me," said Helen.

"Good! You should be scared!" screamed Sun. She jumped up and started to pull shirts out of her dresser drawer, fling them around the room. "This is scary! This is scary!"

Someone banged on the door. "Shut up in there!" he yelled.

"See? You see what I mean?" Sun said, her voice steely now, mascara running down her face.

Helen rubbed her jaw again. If words were inside her mouth right then, she couldn't feel them at all.

Another Audubon bird, gone.

The Parrot does not satisfy himself with cockle-burs, but eats or destroys almost every kind of fruit indiscriminately, and on this account is always an unwelcome visitor to the planter, the farmer, or the gardener. The stacks of grain put up in the fields are resorted to by the flocks of these birds, which frequently cover them so entirely, that they present to the eye the same effect as if a brilliantly coloured carpet had been thrown over them. They cling around the whole stack, pull out the straws, and destroy twice as much of the grain as would suffice to satisfy their hunger. They assail the pear and apple-trees, when the fruit is yet very small and far from being ripe, and this merely for the sake of the seeds. As on the stalks of corn, they alight on the apple-trees of our orchards, or the pear-trees in the gardens, in great numbers; and, as if through mere mischief, pluck off the fruits, open them up to the core, and disappointed at the sight of the seeds, which are yet soft and of a milky consistence, drop the apple or pear, and pluck another, passing from branch to branch, until the trees which were before so promising, are left completely stripped, like the ship water-logged and abandoned by its crew, floating on the yet agitated waves, after the tempest has ceased. They visit the mulberries, pecan-nuts, grapes, and even the seeds of the *dog-wood, before they are ripe, and on all commit similar depredations. The maize alone never attracts their notice.*

Do not imagine, reader, that all these outrages are borne without severe retaliation on the part of the planters. So far from this, the Parakeets are destroyed in great numbers, from whilst busily engaged in plucking off the fruits or tearing the grain from the stacks, the husbandman approaches them with perfect ease, and commits great slaughter among them. All the survivors rise, shriek, fly round about for a few minutes, and again alight on the very place of most imminent danger. The gun is kept at work; eight or ten, or ever twenty, are killed at every discharge. The living birds, as if conscious of the death of their companions, sweep over their bodies, screaming as loud as ever, but still return to the stack to be shot at, until so few remain alive, that the farmer does not consider it worth his while to spend more of his ammunition. I have seen several hundreds destroyed in this manner in the course of a few hours, and have procured a basketful of these birds at a few shots, in order to make choice of good specimens for drawing the figures by which this species is represented in the plate now under your consideration.

My mother starts to come with me on my route. Every time we find a bird, she looks at me balefully, as if I have killed it myself. I have to keep reminding her that I'm not responsible, that I'm trying to help, but she just shakes her head and sighs. On the first day, I catch her trying to pluck some feathers from a pelican, and then a grebe—to put in her scrapbook, I'm sure—but I convince her that even the feathers need to be burned. I can see her scanning the ground for some evidence she can bring home and paste onto a page. I'd hate to see what she would write above it.

"Omma, have you heard any stories about pelicans?"

She strokes the top of a brown pelican's head with her gloved hands before I scoop it into the bag. "The girl-who-kills-the-pelicans story? That one I know."

"Omma." I stop for a moment. "I mean the myth about mother pelicans. People used to think that mother pelicans broke their own chests open with their beaks and served their babies pieces of their heart."

"You think I don't do this?" She smacks her palm against her chest. I remember my dream, the hummingbird feeder, the taste of diluted sugar . . .

In graduate school, some of my colleagues had babies. They were so hyperaware of how every little thing they did affected their children—they were worried about each second they spent away from their babies, each second they spent *with* their babies. They were certain they were setting their kids up for either a life of therapy and crime or a life of superstar genius fame and glory. I can't imagine my mother worried like that when I was an infant. She certainly didn't seem to when I was a child.

I wonder what my mother's heart really looks like. I imagine a wrinkled leather pouch, something mummified and dry; she could tear it into strips and serve it as jerky—chewy, saturated with salt. My mouth feels parched by the thought of it. I look at her, picking her way along the prickly shoreline, and wonder what my own heart must look like in her eyes. Sometimes I don't think I can feel it in my chest at all. Maybe that's why I keep turning to the drum, trying to find something, anything, that has a real pulse.

"I'm glad your mother is going with you, Ava," says Darryl when we return with our lumpy bag. "I've been worried about you going out there all by yourself."

"I don't go anymore," my mother says flatly.

"Why not, Omma?" I ask. I wonder if she's ready to get away from me, go back home.

"I go with not-dead birds now." She points to the kiddie pool full of sick pelicans.

"Well, we could definitely use more help here," says Darryl. "We'd be happy to have you. I'd love for Ava to come back and work in the hospital, too, get out of the sun a bit. Not that it's any less hot in here, but . . ."

"I like my route," I say quickly. I realize how stupid it sounds, saying I like my daily death march. I still have trouble looking at Darryl. Emily rises between us like some sort of lurid neon-tinted phantom.

"You know what's best for you, Ava." His voice is tired. I feel a blip of panic. I don't want him to give up on me, but I can't reach out. Not with my mother here. I don't want her to see me wanting anyone. Maybe that's ridiculous. I keep thinking about how Emily asked me if I had ever tried Ecstasy before. *No,* I told her, *and I don't have plans to ever do so, either.* I was so certain about it, so closed off to the possibility. What is it with me? Why can't I give myself the chance to have a little ecstasy—real ecstasy, not the drug—just because my mother has never been given the opportunity?

Darryl's name pops out of my mouth, barely louder than an exhale, but he's already on the other side of the hospital. My mother gives me a suspicious look, then turns to stare at a woman trying to wrestle a pillowcase over a pelican. Many of the Salton Sea residents have donated pillowcases to the hospital to use as pelican restraints—there is only one pillowcase in the trailer because Frieda has given so many away. I think I recognize the faded pattern of flowers, the rusts and yellows and greens.

The pelican puts up a good fight, but the woman finally manages to get the pillowcase over its head; in one swift pull, the pelican's head emerges from the hole cut into the top seam. The pelican tries to open its wings, but it is foiled by the funny little dress, the drab muumuu, it suddenly finds itself in. The bird snaps at the woman, knocks the syringe of electrolytes out of her hand. It's wonderful to see such a feisty bird, a bird with so much spunk. The woman grabs its beak and forces the tube down its throat. When I look over at my mother, she has tears in her eyes.

The two of us soon fall into a rhythm. I take her to the hospital in the morning, then leave for my route. My mother hasn't saved a bird yet; the pelicans keep dying in her hands. She seems to think I've jinxed her somehow, but it's a relief to know I'm not the only one without a magic touch. Every day, we go home for lunch together, then back to our respective bird trenches, then back home for dinner. I am grateful to eat her meals, her kimchi, again—she brought out jars and jars of it, along with her other favorite ingredients, wrapped in pants and jackets. I am grateful, too, to be able to avoid the Aloha. I don't want to see Emily, not yet. I cancel my classes for the time being, even though the killer is still at large. Frieda has left several messages on my machine, but I haven't had the energy to answer them. I keep expecting her to show up at the trailer, but so far she's giving me space.

I've been feeling very quiet. My mother and I don't talk much. I don't talk to anyone much anymore. I keep waiting for my mother to burst into song, to start a *pansori* session in the middle of the night, but so far it hasn't happened. I drum in the evenings, hoping to spark something in her, but she usually turns on her drill and does some carving, or takes Yukam's cage into the bathroom and lets him fly around for a while with the door closed. I want to know more of her story, even though I have enough notes to keep writing for a long time. Not that I've written a whole lot since she's been here.

It had become a ritual for me to write almost every day, even just a little bit, before I went to bed, or right when I woke up, but now I feel so self-conscious. I can hear my mother breathing, and it reminds me that I am writing about a real live person, that I am most likely taking all sorts of liberties with her past. Her true past is breathing right along with her; I will never fully know it, no matter how hard I try, no matter how closely I bend in to listen, how wet her exhale against my cheek.

I have all these scattered notes, these scattered words, these scattered feelings. They're like the tapes I've been making—snippets of bird squawk, snippets of engine hum, snippets of throat clearing and fork dropping and wind blowing through saltbushes. Who knows if they'll ever come together into something that means anything.

Before my mother showed up here, I used to be able to shut off my mind when I wrote about her. The words just poured through me. I almost couldn't control them. I never thought of myself as a "writer." I was more a historian, a scribe; it was almost like I was channeling.

Now the words have slowed themselves down. They come out one at a time, solid, separate; there is no longer any doubt they are coming out of me. It's a very different feeling. They catch in my throat and I feel like I'm going to choke. They catch in my hands and I have to play the drum harder to try to get them out, because the pen is not enough on its own. Still, as awkward as it feels, I have to keep writing. I have to chase these stories out of me, exorcise them from my body. From our bodies.

I find myself wanting to inject myself into the story sometimes, to scream out "Omma, don't go there" or "Omma, why can't you say anything?" as I write. I find myself wanting to scream the same things to myself. It's getting harder and harder to talk; at the same time, it's getting harder and harder to keep silent.

Even my dreams have changed since my mother has come here. She never enters my sleep anymore. Her presence in my trailer, on these pages, seems to be enough. I still can't seem to talk to Darryl, but he sometimes floats through my sleeping landscapes; when I wake up, he dissipates like mist—all I can hold on to is a color, sometimes a smell, a light pressure against my lips.

The bird dreams, I remember.

Last night, I dreamed I was standing in the water, naked. A pelican touched down on a wave in front of me. It poked the tip of its beak into the center of one of my breasts and gently drew out my nipple, like it would a worm from the soil; it did the same with the other one before it flew away. I woke up in the dark, my nipples tingling but inverted still, pointed inward toward my ribs, my lungs, my heart. I reached inside my T-shirt and pinched at my areolas until my nipples slipped out of their caves; I rolled them between my fingers until they were hard as pebbles, until I thought they might begin to glow. I started to feel a warmth travel through my body, slide between my legs, but when I reached down there, my mother made a sound, the couch creaked, and I pulled my hands away.

"Omma," I call to her. She's in the bathroom with Yukam.

She opens the door. The finch flies out. I do a quick scan of the windows to make sure they're closed. Yukam settles on the faucet of the kitchen sink.

"Whatever happened to that egg? That blue egg?" I ask her.

"Anchee have it."

"She's the one from the market, right?"

"I work with her when you was little girl."

"So the egg is okay?"

"I no want to bring in the car. Too much move it around," she says.

"It didn't break or anything?"

"Not everything break, Ava," she tells me.

"Did it hatch yet?" I ask her.

"Anchee have it," she says again. I decide not to press the issue. She scoops up Yukam and puts him back in his cage.

"Your omma is not here to help you!"

Helen woke up, disoriented, in her clothes, on Sun's bed. She could hear Sun yelling, in Korean, in the street. She looked out the window and saw Sun standing outside, wearing jeans, a GI's shirt, no shoes; she held a sign high up in the air. One word, in English, was written across it in large marker: UNFAR.

"Women, your omma is not here! We have to help each other! Women, women, we have to help each other!"

"Shut up!" a man's voice yelled from a room nearby.

"I will not to shut up!" Sun yelled in English before she switched back to Korean again. "We have to help each other! Do you think the clubs are going to help us? Do you think the U.S. Army, the Korean government, are going to help us? They check us for diseases, but do they care about us? Of course not! They just care about their precious soldiers—they just don't want their dicks to fall off! That's the only reason they want to keep us clean!"

A woman called out in response.

"Shut the fuck up!" a male voice yelled.

A few women ran outside to join Sun. Helen watched through the window, too scared to move, her heart bursting with fear and pride. Sun must not have taken any pills this morning, must not have lifted the flask. Her voice was crisp and fierce and awake.

Helen wished she could yell out to Sun, support her, but her own voice was hidden somewhere, salted away deep inside. She hadn't been able to sing for weeks. It was an effort to even talk; it was as if the words had to climb out of a dark, slippery well just to get to her tongue.

"What happens if someone beats us up?" Sun shouted. "Nothing! They get off scot-free!"

Women yelled and nodded in response.

"These men can hit us, punch us, rape us, kill us, and do they get in trouble?"

"No!" the women called out.

"We have to say this! We have to talk about this! If we stick together we can talk about this!"

Can we? wondered Helen. *Can I?*

"We have to show them that we're not just some little hole for their garbage!" Sun yelled. "We deserve to be treated like people! We are stars! We are superstars!"

Men shouted insults from the windows; the women in the street shouted back. The air was soon so thick with voices, it sounded to Helen like a million drums pounding. Then a gunshot rang out and the group of women scattered.

Sun came back to her room, breathless, followed by a few women from the crowd outside.

"Helen!" she beamed. "I mean *Hye-yang*! I won't call you by your American name, not anymore, ever! I promise! Did you hear me out there?"

Helen nodded, embarrassed that she hadn't come outside.

"We can do this!" Sun said to the women. Her eyes glittered. "If we work together, we can change things!"

The women began to speak about better cuts in pay, less barroom debt, accountability for the GIs who are their customers. Helen wanted to join in, but she couldn't even catch her breath. She looked outside at the jeeps patrolling the area. She didn't want to be in Sun's room when they came looking for her. As Sun scribbled furiously on a piece of paper, the other women looking over her shoulder, Helen slipped past her out the door.

The sky was a rich, clear blue, the air not too warm. All the voices earlier had obscured Helen's view out the window; she hadn't known what a lovely morning it was. She tried not to notice the jeeps honking at her as they passed, tried not to notice the men with their rifles, tried not to notice the way the dust from the ground jumped onto her ankles, leaving a thick rime, tried not to think about Sun in her room, starting something that Helen knew could never really work. She told herself to just soak in the sunshine for once, just enjoy the soft touch of it on her skin. She closed her eyes and lifted her face to the sky.

A blow to the hip jarred her out of her reverie before it really even began. A group of children ran past, chasing a small dark-skinned girl down the dirt road.

"*Ggum-doongi!*" they chanted. "*Ggum-doongi!*"

The girl ducked, teary, into the empty Shangri-La-La bar. The other children stood in the doorway, taunting her. "Yeah, run off to your Dark Man omma," one said. "She's nothing but a *ggum-doongi* fucker, just like you're gonna be!" yelled another. They picked up handfuls of dirt and tossed them into the dim room.

"Stop that!" Helen yelled at them.

The children turned toward her. "Are you a *ggum-doongi* fucker, too?" the tallest one sneered, his eyes a disconcerting shade of blue. "Do you have little Dark Man babies running around, stinking up the place?"

Helen spit on the ground right in front of his feet.

"Filthy whore!" The boy threw a handful of dirt in her face before he raced out of the DMZ, his arms raised in victory, the other children trailing close behind him. Helen blinked some of the dirt out of her eyes, spit some out of her mouth.

The girl stuck her head through the bar doorway.

"Are you okay?" Helen asked.

The girl just stared into space, her lips chapped, her hair a wild, frizzy tangle. A cold weight dropped down to the floor of Helen's stomach. Of course she wasn't okay. How was anyone going to be okay here?

Helen wondered if she should go back to Sun's room, see what they could do to make things better, but the more she thought about it, the more her feet refused to move in that direction. It's better to not even get our hopes up, she decided.

The girl slunk out of the doorway, her long Coca-Cola T-shirt badly stained, her legs and feet scabby and bare. She picked her way down the street, arms across her body as if she had a stomachache. Helen wondered if any of the GIs had gotten to her yet. She swallowed down the nausea that swept through her whole body like a wave. She wiped some more dirt from her face, brushed off the front of her short orange dress and headed over to Wild Ting to see if any GIs had stopped in yet for the morning.

Ava, daughter, 19.
Come into house with poem
book. She stand and read
in front of me. Her voice
big, not regular squeak voice.
Loud. Her hands flap around.
After she finish,
she put down book
and run out the house,
pages still spread open
on table. The book
heavy in my hands
when I pick it up.
These words covered
with pink pen:

**And I had done a hellish thing,
And it would work 'em woe:
For all averred, I had killed the bird
That made the breeze to blow.
Ah wretch! said they, the bird to slay,
That made the breeze to blow!**

Another bird? Another?

10/17/90

I am about to add another pelican, a brown, to my quickly bulging bag when the bird twitches. At first I think it's my own hand twitching, a sudden surge of pulse beneath my glove, but a tremor shakes through the bird and it falls from my grasp.

I drop the bag. Some of the beaks clack as they knock into each other, the ground. I kneel over the bird that had moved in my hands. It is nearly still on the ground, but I can see a slight rhythm thrum in the pelican's throat. I take off my glove and touch two fingers to the pulse. It is weak but steady. I spit on my hand and wipe at the pelican's encrusted eyes. A pale gray eye looks back at me warily.

Please, please, be okay, I try to tell the bird telepathically as I scoop it up. I leave the bag of dead birds on the shore, even though I know I'm going against standard protocol. I can come back for them later—they aren't going anywhere.

I run with the bird up the slight sandy embankment to my car. I put it on the floor mat in front of the passenger seat. I know I should bring the bird to the hospital, have Darryl take a look at it, but I feel compelled to go home instead.

"Hang in there," I tell the bird the whole way home. "Just hang in there, baby, please, hold on . . ."

Fortunately, the drive isn't too far from Mecca to Bombay. I lift the pelican out of the Sonata and carry it up the ladder into the trailer. It seems to get heavier and heavier with each step. I plunk it down in a heap on the floor of the shower. Still breathing, a good sign, but it can't seem to lift its head. I wet a washcloth in the small sink and wipe the pelican's eyes more thoroughly. The bird starts to shake.

"It's okay, now, just hold on. You're safe here," I turn on the shower and watch layers of silt and salt swirl off the feathers and spiral into the drain. I rub the feathers smooth beneath the water, cup my hand beneath the pendulous beak. *This bird is alive,* I think in amazement as the pelican starts to calm down, to shake less. *This bird will live.*

I turn off the water and slide the rippled vinyl doors shut.

"Don't go anywhere," I tell the pelican. "I'll be right back."

I drive back to Mecca Beach to get the bag of dead birds before I go to the hospital.

"Just a few on Mecca," I tell Darryl, as I drag the bag to the weighing area. "Seems to be slowing down."

"Glad to hear it." Darryl gives me a sad, lingering glance before he races off somewhere.

I feel like a criminal as I make my way over to the supply area and slide several tubed syringes full of electrolyte solution into my purse, along with some eye lubricant so the bird's eyes won't dry out before its eyelids can move again. I hurry away before anyone will notice the supplies are gone. They are going through them so fast, I'm sure a few won't be missed. My mother eyes me from the wading pool.

"Omma," I start.

She lifts her hand. A man comes over and carries away the now dead pelican she had been tending.

"Come home with me," I whisper. "I want to show you something."

"Is Yukam okay?" she asks.

"Yukam's fine, Omma. This is a good thing, a surprise."

She stands reluctantly and follows me out of the hospital. Darryl watches us leave.

"I'll bring her back later," I say, then grab her elbow and pull her to the car.

"Don't be dead, don't be dead, don't be dead," I chant inside my skull. I pull a clump of candied ginger from my purse and let the sharp flavor crystallize my thoughts as I zoom down the highway.

The bird isn't dead, although it is shivering in a skim of now cold water, oily droppings floating all around it. I move the bird so that the water will drain and run a warm shower to send the poop down the pipes and take the chill away. My mother stands in the doorway of the bathroom, not saying anything.

"You doing okay?" I crouch down beside the pelican. The warm water mists all over my already sweaty face. "I got something for you." I pull a syringe from my purse. "I am not an expert at this yet, so bear with me." I lean toward the pelican and fall onto the floor, drenching the side of my shirt.

"It's alive!" I say to my mom. She bites her lower lip.

"Okay, now, we got your favorite sports drink here." I'm sopping wet by now, the shower beating down upon me. "It'll give you that get-up-and-go—you'll be playing soccer in no time flat."

The pelican, to my amazement, opens up a wing. It unfolds over my head and bangs into the opposite edge of the shower stall, although it is not nearly open all the way. I feel like I'm beneath the bar awning at the Aloha Room. I scoot out from beneath the feathers.

"Come on, now," I coax. I get the tube into the bird's beak and squirt the 100 ml of electrolyte down its throat. "There you go. Much better."

"I'm just going to get some dry clothes on, okay?" I tell the bird. "You hold tight now. Make yourself at home . . ." *Oh my god, what am I doing?*

"Omma, can you keep an eye on him while I change?" I ask. She nods as I race to the bedroom. My heart is pounding so hard, I can barely use my fingers. I have to rebutton my dry shirt three

times before I get the holes in the right order; I almost fall over
trying to put on my pants. When I glance in the mirror, I hardly
recognize myself—a shimmer seems to come off my skin, like part
of me is moving so fast, so frantically, it creates a halo effect.

"It want to get out," my mother says when I get back into the
bathroom. The pelican, still on its side, is flopping its one wing
around. It looks much healthier than it did even a few minutes ago.

"Are you ready for some more?" I pull out another syringe. I
can't remember what the timing is supposed to be with the electrolytes. It couldn't hurt to rehydrate the bird, could it?

I try to get closer to the bird, but it is beating its wing too hard.
The wing seems so separate from its listless body, like a flag whipping around on top of a mountain.

I finally get underneath the wing and ease the tube down the
bird's throat. It looks at me with great distrust; its wing slows down
and eventually folds back into its side. For a moment I worry the
bird has died, but I can see its breath rise and fall. My breath rises
and falls right along with it.

The next few days are a blur of rehydration and eye lubrica-
tion, a blur of wet feathers and cautious hope. I feign illness so
that I can stay home with the pelican; my mother pockets more
supplies as needed during her shift at the hospital. The bird gets a
little stronger every day. It can start to move its eyelids; then it
can start to move its neck; then it can stand on its hocks; then it
can stand on its feet. Then it begins to get feisty.

"Omma, could you get the pillowcase off the pillow on the
sofa?" I ask her. "I think we're going to need it."

She nods and races out. She comes back with a pillowcase
from home, the one that was filled with pots and pans when she
first got here, covered with bleached-out geometrical patterns.

"We're going to need to cut a hole in it—do you mind?"

She shakes her head, then puts the pillowcase to her mouth and tries to pull the seam out with her teeth.

"Maybe we should get some scissors," I say, but she shakes her head again and yanks harder. I hear a ripping sound. She holds up the pillow. Blue threads dangle from her lips. The pillowcase gapes open—a perfectly sized hole.

"What we do now?" she asks.

"We put it over the bird's head," I tell her.

"After that. What we do with the bird?"

"I don't know, Omma," I tell her. "We'll figure something out."

"I do the bird, you do the pillow." She leans into the shower, drenching herself, sending water spraying out of the stall. The bird hits her in the face with its beak. She pulls her head back out; a bit of blood trickles next to her eye.

"Are you okay, Omma?" I ask.

"I fine." She leans in again. I lean above her and turn off the shower. I try to put the pillowcase over the bird's head, but it is moving around too much. A wing smacks my mother in the mouth, cutting her lip.

"This bird very not-dead," my mother says.

"Yeah—hopefully we can manage to stay not-dead in the process ourselves," I tell her. I get the pillowcase partially on the bird, but I can't get it all the way over. An eye peers out of the head hole like a child dressing up like a ghost for Halloween. I rustle with the cloth until the gap slides over his wet skull; the pillowcase bunches up like a collar around his neck, his wings still free beneath it.

"Omma, can you fold in his wings?"

"How I do that?"

"I don't know—just try!"

We struggle with the bird until finally my mother squeezes the two wings in like someone playing a concertina and I yank the cloth the rest of the way down. The pillowcase doesn't look like a dress on this bird, it looks like a sausage casing. The poor bird struggles to keep its balance, its wings tightly pinned.

"I'll try to give it some more stuff." I hold out the tubed syringe. The bird snaps and snaps, but I manage to slip the tube into its beak and press the plunger down. I'm soaking wet; my mother is sopping and bloody. We collapse back against the sink.

"I think it's ready for fish," I tell my mother.

"I think I ready for bed," she tells me.

I wet a washcloth and gently rub her temple. I smear some of the same antibiotic ointment we've been putting on the bird's "bedsores" on the cut. She closes her eyes. I don't think I've ever touched her like this before, so tenderly. I don't know if anyone ever has. I dab some more with the washcloth, wanting to keep the connection, wanting to keep touching her like this. I dab and daub until she begins to squirm.

"That enough," she says, and leaves the bathroom.

"What do you think of that?" I ask the pelican. It struggles inside its pillowcase. I ease the material back over its head and let it spread its wings.

A couple of days later, the pelican is hopping all over the bathroom, preening, roosting on the edge of the sink, knocking our toothbrushes all over the place. It is swallowing fish without spitting them back up. Its hocks are free of sores. Its eyes are clear. It is time to set it free.

My mother and I begin to make plans. We decide to drive down to Casa Cove, her old skin-diving haunt, and release it there.

"We bring the mosaic girl," my mother says.

"The mosaic girl?"

"The girl with the sticks," she says. "The girl at the tae kwon do place."

"Jeniece?"

"I think that the one."

"Why do you want to bring Jeniece?"

"She want to see my eggs."

I've barely spoken to Jeniece, other than our encounter at the burial ground. My mother hasn't seen her since her first morning at the sea. I don't know whether Frieda would want us to take her so far away, especially when we haven't spoken for a while ourselves. Still, I remember the way my mother smiled at Jeniece, the way Jeniece seemed so easy with her. "I'll talk to Frieda about it," I tell her.

"You do it soon." She points to the pelican, flapping madly on top of the toilet.

"Will you be okay alone here for a few minutes?" I ask her.

"I not alone. Go!" She shoos me off with her hands.

It feels weird to pull into the parking lot of the Aloha. It's like it's been lifetimes since I've been there, even though it's been less than two weeks. The light seems starker on the salty pavement; the bamboo sign looks shabbier than I remember. Now that Darryl has been here, I feel his not-being-here acutely. It takes me a while to touch the handle of the door, pull it open.

"Ava!" Frieda rushes up to me after I finally come in. "How are you? How's your mom?"

"We're doing okay." I want to sink into her hug, but I shrink away from it instead.

"We've been worried about you." Frieda pulls back and searches my face.

"I'm fine," I say. "I've just had some stuff to sort out." I look around the room. Much to my relief, Emily isn't there.

"I'm so sorry Emily did what she did," Frieda said. "I want you to know I've given her a good talking to."

"It's okay . . ."

"No, it's not! Giving someone drugs without telling them—there's no excuse for that! I almost called the police on her!"

I've been so focused on Emily and Darryl together that I had almost forgotten about Emily dosing me. I remembered my refusal when she first asked me about whether I'd ever tried Ecstasy more than my panic after I realized what she had done. I've tried not to let myself remember how good it felt after things kicked in . . .

"Listen, Frieda, how's Jeniece doing?"

"Jeniece? She's fine . . ." She looks at me quizzically; we haven't really talked about Jeniece before.

"Is her health okay?"

"Her eyesight is deteriorating a little, the doctor says, but for the most part, she's doing pretty good."

"Great." I'm not sure how to broach the subject. Frieda absently runs her hands over the laminated menus in their wooden pocket, fanning them out; they make a *fwap fwap* sound when they fall back in place. I almost want to ask her to do it again so that I can record it.

"Anyway," I start. "My mom and I are going to San Diego tomorrow morning—just for the day—and we were wondering if we could take Jeniece with us."

"San Diego?" Now Frieda looks even more confused.

"Just for the day. My mom wants to show her her egg carvings. Jeniece sounded pretty interested, and . . ." I can't bring myself to mention the pelican.

"I'm not sure," says Frieda. "I'd need to talk to Ray about it. And Jeniece, of course, to see if she'd even want to go."

"Sure," I say. "I know this is kind of weird, Frieda. We'd take good care of her, I promise."

"I don't doubt that, Ava. It's just that she's never been that far away from home. Other than a couple of hospitals, but one of us was always with her."

"She's never been to San Diego?"

"It's not like she hasn't ever been away from the Salton Sea or anything," she says quickly. "We've taken her to the Date Festival in Indio and stuff like that. It's just kind of hard to get out . . ."

"My mom never took me out much, either . . ."

"Anyway, I'll talk to them and let you know. I'm not promising anything but I'm not saying no."

"Thanks, Frieda. I better go . . ." I start to back away.

"Aren't you going to stay for breakfast?"

"I can't today," I tell her. "My mom is already cooking something. I'll be back soon, though, I promise. I know it's part of our deal, me eating here."

"Don't worry about that, Ava. I just like to see you around."

I feel myself start to tear up. "Well, we want to get a pretty early start tomorrow." I try to wipe my eyes discreetly. "If you could call me before it gets too late tonight, I'd appreciate it."

"I'll do that," she says. "You take care of yourself, Ava."

I nod and rush outside before I start bawling.

We plan our departure. My mother packs her things in case she decides to stay in San Diego. We hydrate the pelican. We get Yukam's cage ready. We stay up fairly late, but Frieda never calls. I can't tell whether I am sad or relieved.

In the morning, just as I start to load up the car, Frieda pulls up and rolls down the window.

"She wants to go," she says. Jeniece cowers in the backseat.

"I never said I *wanted* to go." She crosses her hands over her chest.

"Come on. It will be good for you," Frieda tells her. "A change of scenery and everything."

Jeniece scowls as she undoes her seat belt. "You just want to go to the movies with Ray or something."

"Well, we don't have a lot of time just the two of us . . ."

"So you're just going to pawn me off?"

"Jeniece, this is a great opportunity for you. You'll get to see more of the world!"

Jeniece rolls her eyes and sighs. I think I've seen her eyes rolling more often than I've seen them any other way.

"We'll have a great time!" I say, my voice a little too bright-sounding. "You'll get to see the ocean . . ."

"We have the sea right here." She opens her car door, sticks the canes out first.

"And my mom wants to show you her eggs."

Above us, my mother opens the door of the trailer. I can see the pelican scuffling around behind her. I make a motion for her to close the door. Frieda looks up after the door is shut.

Jeniece sighs again as she heaves herself out of the car, the cuffs of the canes around her forearms.

"We'll have an adventure!" I imagine this sounds like something a person should say to a child, but I don't really know. I've never really spent time with kids before. Even when I was a girl, I rarely spent time with other kids aside from school and tae kwon do class, and even then I pretty much kept to myself.

"I didn't ask to go, you know," she says.

"This wasn't an easy decision for me, either, honey," Frieda tells her. "But Ava here was so generous, and—"

"Forget it," says Jeniece. "It's fine. I'm glad I don't have to look at you today, anyway."

Frieda turns to me. "Is this a way a daughter talks to her mother?"

I'm not the right person to ask, that's for sure.

"It's fine, Mom." Jeniece's voice softens a bit. "I'll be fine."

"If she gives you a hard time, you give one right back to her," Frieda tells me.

"We'll be great," I say, even though I have no idea what I'm getting myself into.

"I love you, sweetie." Frieda kisses the top of Jeniece's head. "You be good now."

She opens her car door. "Thanks again, Ava," she yells out the window before she pulls away, spraying salt and gravel in her wake.

"She couldn't wait to get rid of me," says Jeniece.

"I'm sure that's not true," I say, but what do I know?

The door to the trailer opens. "I come out now?" my mother asks.

"I'll be right up," I tell her.

Jeniece waves at my mother; she smiles and waves back. Then the pelican tries to get outside and my mother quickly closes the door.

"What *was* that?" Jeniece asks.

"It's a pelican," I say.

"I thought so!" she says. "Why do you have a pelican in your house?"

"We've been taking care of it. It was pretty sick, but now we're going to release it."

"Today?"

"That's the plan."

"With me?"

"I didn't tell your mom because what we're doing is kind of illegal."

"Cool!"

"So why don't you wait in the shade under the trailer?" I say. "I'll go get the pelican and we'll hit the road."

"Awesome!" She shuffles off beneath the landing.

The pelican is in a pillowcase, but it's still hard to get it out the door. It will be too much of a handful to try to carry down the ladder, so I put it on the metal lift. It maniacally scrabbles around the metal square.

"It scared!" my mother yells. She steps onto the lift, sits down, and tries to hold it in her arms. The pelican gets more frantic. The lift sways dramatically. I push the button, and the metal pan falls, way too fast, to the ground. It lands with a crash just inches away from Jeniece.

"Cool!" Jeniece yells again.

"Are you okay?" I call down to my mother.

"I fine!" She grabs hold of the sack of bird before it runs away.

We wrestle the bird into the backseat floor well of the car. My mother wants to sit back there with it, but Jeniece says she can't sit in the front seat if there's an air bag. Before we even make it to the highway, the pelican starts attacking Jeniece's canes with its beak, making a great clanking sound that I surreptitiously record before Jeniece completely freaks out. I pull over to the side of the road; we move the bird to the floor of the passenger seat in front, and my mother moves to the backseat. The bird thrashes its head around occasionally, nicking my legs with the tip of its beak, getting in the way of the stick shift every now and then, but the drive is otherwise fairly uneventful. My mother and Jeniece talk intently in the backseat, their heads bent toward each other; I try to hear what they're saying, but I only catch little snippets—"egg," "mother," "bird." A song rises up in me like hysteria. I can't help but sing it out loud:

"Sing Lo, sweet chariot, comin' for to carry *you* home." I point to the pelican. Before I know it, my mother and Jeniece are joining in, singing to the bird, filling the car with music. The pelican looks confused—it slams its head against the door a couple of times, but then it settles in. I almost think I can hear it hum along.

It feels funny to pull into the Casa Cove parking lot as a driver; I've only been a passenger here before. A passenger leaving with a squirming bag full of lobsters, not a driver arriving with a squirming bag of pelican.

"Omma, do you still come here to skin-dive?" I ask her.

"I go sometime," she says. "Not so easy anymore. Not so easy hold my breath under water."

"Do you like to swim?" I ask Jeniece.

"I don't know how," she says. She looks at the ocean, awestruck. I had forgotten that she's never seen it before. I open the door and the ocean air floods the car. It smells amazing—the scent is big, open somehow, not claustrophobic like the smell at the sea, with its death stench and algae tides.

"Will you be okay going down the hill?" I ask. I had forgotten that the parking lot overlooked the beach, that there is quite a big trek both ways.

"I think so . . ."

My mother gets out and opens the door for the pelican. I open the door for Jeniece. The pelican starts to bound down the sandy hill, but with its wings straitjacketed, it keeps losing its balance and tumbling for yards at a time. My mother runs after it. I keep an eye on them as I help Jeniece sidestep down the hill, her canes slipping every once in a while, unable to find purchase. Eventually we all make it down to the bottom. I'm grateful the beach isn't too crowded—I'm sure the four of us make quite a sight. People begin to gather round.

"Why you got that pelican all trussed up?" a teenage boy asks. "Are you gonna cook it or something?"

"You should set the poor creature free!" a woman says, distraught.

"We are," I try to assure her. "We're from the Salton Sea. We just rehabilitated this pelican and now we're going to release it." I know we don't look very official, but that seems to appease her.

My mother bends down by the pelican. She gets the pillowcase partway up its body, but it thrashes around and shakes the cloth back down. I give it a try, but the pelican won't even let me get close. Finally, Jeniece lowers herself to the ground and lays her canes a few feet away. The pelican is distracted by them; my mother eases the pillowcase over its head as it tries to eat one of the metal cuffs. The pelican stretches its neck, spreads its wings. We all scooch back. It opens the feathers at the end of each wing tip like fingers. My heart starts to pound in my ears. I look over at my mother; her hand is at her throat.

The pelican starts to run. The small crowd cheers it on. The pelican runs and runs, wings open, until it gets to the water. Then it stops. It waits a little bit, then takes a tentative hop into the waves. It stays there, bobbing like a buoy near the shore, for the longest time. I want to urge it to keep going, to fly away, but it doesn't seem to know what to do. The teenage boy runs out into the water and chases it further out into the surf. It keeps bobbing there, bobbing, bobbing, bobbing. We sit on the sand and watch it for a good portion of the afternoon. I almost want to swim out there and bring it back with us, take it back to the Salton Sea, but I know how crazy that would be. We finally shout our good-byes. Only as we're making our way back up the hill, Jeniece panting with the exertion of it, does the pelican lift off and head for the setting sun.

* * *

The car is incredibly quiet as we drive back to the apartment. It's as if a great weight has been lifted; I thought I would feel relieved, and I do, but I'm surprised by how empty I feel, too. I'm sure my mother feels the same way. The exhilaration has yawned open into something else, something big and wordless and more than a little sad. Jeniece fidgets around uncomfortably in the backseat. I'm sure she's eager to see my mother's eggs, to get our attention focused back into something small, something with definite edges.

As we pull up to the complex, I can see the door to the apartment is wide open. My heart drops.

"Omma, did you give someone the key?"

She shakes her head.

"Did you lock the door when you left?"

"Of course I lock it!"

"Uh-oh." Jeniece's face in the rearview mirror is filled with fascination and dread.

"You don't think you left it open by accident?" I know it's ridiculous to say this—she's been gone for three weeks; even if she had left it open, a neighbor surely would have closed it by now.

"Ava! You think I not know what I do?"

"You two stay in the car." I open my door. "I'll go check it out."

Jeniece lifts up her hands in surrender. "You're the black belt," she says.

"Black brown belt," my mother corrects her. "She not make it all the way." Already it's as if the whole stirring drama with the pelican never existed.

It feels weird to go up the pebbly steps again, to see the dingy stucco walls, as if I'm stepping back into a skin I thought I had shed. I can feel my body gearing up for the possibility of a fight, my muscles gathering potential energy. I've never had to use my

tae kwon do in a real-life situation before. I'm not sure I'll be able
to go through with it.

"Hello?" I say as I near the open door. No response.

"Hello?" I say again. The scent of my mother's seaweed soup
pours out of the apartment like an exhale, even though she hasn't
been there for weeks. I peer inside, my heart perched in my throat
like an Adam's apple.

The floor cushions by the coffee table are slashed and—my
heart sinks at the sight of this—eggshells are everywhere, but otherwise the living room looks okay. I step through the doorway.
Everything seems to be in its place. Nothing is missing, as far as I
can tell. My mother's room is stripped bare, but I'm pretty sure it's
because she brought everything with her when she came to see me.
In my room, my mixing boards are still under my bed; my MIDI
keyboard is silent on its stand. I'll have to remember to bring them
back to the trailer with me. If I go back to stay any longer, that is.
I'm not sure where I belong now. Probably not here. My room feels
weird, fake, like the set of a TV show I once watched but am now
embarrassed by. I don't feel any trace of real life inside these walls;
I don't think it's only because I've been gone for so long.

I go back into the living room. Who would tear up some cushions and break some eggshells and leave? Was it kids? Cats? My
mind starts to spin—maybe it's the Salton Sea killer, maybe he
found out my mother was a prostitute . . .

A strange sound shakes the apartment, a weird metallic
thumping.

"Hello?" I ask. No answer. I stand behind the door—which I
stupidly left open—and assume the ready stance. The thumping
gets louder, closer. My muscles feel ready to spring. So ready to
spring, in fact, that when the sound gets even closer, like someone
is clomping across the balcony with coffee-can stilts, I jump out
from behind the door and let out a "Hi-*ya!*" kind of sound.

Jeniece and I scream at the same time; she scoots back and almost topples over the railing. My mother grabs her by the elbow and helps her steady herself.

"I thought you were going to stay in the car!" I can barely breathe.

"She need to pee," my mother says.

"Too late," Jeniece says. A wet patch spreads along the inseam of her pants.

"Oh, Jeniece." I usher her into the apartment.

Jeniece nods; she's trying not to cry. My mother pushes past us; when she sees the eggshells all over her room, she drops to her knees. She scoops up fragments and lets them fall again to the floor, somber confetti.

"Who do this?" she whispers.

"It wasn't me, Omma . . ."

"I know it not you! You think I think you come up here and break my eggs?!"

"I wouldn't be surprised . . ."

"I wouldn't be surprise, too, but you not do this."

"The eggs were pretty, I can tell," Jeniece's voice trembles. She bends down and picks up a piece, tendriled with carvings. The sharp scent of pee wafts up; the stain on her white pants is orange, from vitamins, maybe, or dehydration. I'll try to remember to offer her some water later.

"They pretty—they beautiful!" My mother runs her hands across the carpet; little pieces of eggshell jump up like popcorn. "They take hour and hour of work—hour and hour! All gone!"

"But you can still use them, right?" Jeniece says. "You can still use the broken ones, you said."

"This too many broken." My mother crunches some in her fist. Jeniece's face drops.

I go to look for some clothes for Jeniece to change into. Most everything would be way too big. I finally find an SDSU T-shirt that's just about the right size for her to wear as a dress.

"I hope this will be okay." I hold it out for her to peruse. "I'm afraid I don't have any underwear that would fit you, but this should go down past your knees, so I don't think you have to worry."

"Thanks." She takes it from my hands.

"Do you want to take a bath or a shower?"

"I take baths."

"Well, the bathroom is down the hall," I tell her. "Feel free . . ."

She looks hesitantly down the hallway.

"I'll get you a towel." I hope there is a clean one somewhere in the apartment.

"I don't know . . . ," she starts. "I mean, sometimes I have a hard time . . . I mean, could you maybe set up the bath for me?"

"Not a problem." Her face just about breaks my heart. "I'm happy to do it."

"I don't do this all the time, you know," she says. "I mean, we were in the car for a long time . . ."

From the floor, my mother says mournfully, "It okay. When I laugh, I wet my pants, too."

She must not wet her pants very often.

"It's certainly nothing to be ashamed of," I say. "We all do it every once in a while. I don't think we have time to run a load of laundry, but we can rinse out your pants and bring them home in a plastic bag . . ."

She nods, a little teary. I go to prepare her bath.

The bathtub is filthy, coated with dirty soap scum and hair. I find some scouring powder and the desiccated remains of a sponge under the sink and set to work. The ghosts of Estonian swans float above my scrubbing hands. I never imagined this tub would hold a girl from the Salton Sea, never imagined my Salton Sea shower would hold a pelican, never imagined I'd go to the Salton Sea in the first place.

As I fill up the tub, I can hear my mother's voice over the rush of the water. Her *pansori* voice, not her regular voice. I race out into the living room. Jeniece looks terrified. My mother's voice can get pretty scary-sounding, low and guttural and torn.

"Your bath is ready," I tell her.

"Is your mom okay?"

"This is just something she does sometimes," I tell her. "It's a Korean way of singing. She used to be a performer, a long time ago."

"Can you call my mom?" Jeniece starts to cry.

"Why don't you go take your bath and we'll call her after you get out," I say, trying to listen to my mother's words at the same time. "There's a towel hanging on the rack."

Jeniece nods tearily and sets off for the bathroom.

My hands itch for my drum. I lower myself onto a torn cushion and smack the coffee table twice.

"They kill her!" my mother wails, her voice rising and falling in wild swoops. "They kill her!"

I catch my breath and pound the coffee table again. I wonder if she's talking about the woman at the Salton Sea. I kind of doubt it.

"They break her like eggshell," she sings. "They break her. She try to help us. She make a union, and they break her!"

Pound pound slap.

"She call union Silky Domestic Fowl. Korea protect this bird, make this bird a treasure, but who gonna protect us? Who gonna make us a treasure?"

Slap pound slap.

"I don't help her. I get too scared. I don't help her. I don't help her!"

Tap tap tap tap tap tap tap.

"They say she get killed 'cause she go out with white man. She don't go out with white man! She try to get us more better life!"

Slap slap slap.

Her voice drops to a whisper. "I don't help her."

Tap.

"Sun . . ." She starts to cry.

My palms throb, but they can't respond. My mother grabs eggshells in both hands and rubs them over her face, her mouth trembling, her breath jagged. I inch over and put my arms around her. She tenses, then collapses against me, sobbing.

"Omma," I whisper into her hair. "I'm so sorry. I'm so sorry . . ."

"I so sorry," she says, but I don't think she's talking to me.

My mother decides to stay in the apartment to clean up the eggs. I unpack her stuff from the trunk and bring it upstairs before we take off for the sea. The mats in the car are completely plastered with pelican poop.

"Thanks for coming with us today," I tell her.

"It was fun," she says unconvincingly. Her hair is still wet. I can't tell if the streams running down her face are tears or bathwater.

"Are you hungry?" I ask her.

She nods her head.

We get some drive-through on the way to the highway. She's asleep before she eats even half of her burger.

It feels funny to drive back to the sea in the dark. It's almost as if I know where I'm going.

Frieda is outside, waiting for us, when we pull up to the Aloha.

"Thank god you're okay," Frieda says when I roll down the

window. "I was worried sick." She looks frantic. I don't know why—we told her what time we were going to leave San Diego, and we made good time. Jeniece wakes up at the sound of her mother's voice.

"Frieda, are *you* okay?" I ask.

"I need to talk to you."

"What's up?"

"Not in front of Jeniece."

"Mom . . ."

"It's grown-up stuff."

I get out of the car. Jeniece does, too, her movements slow, groggy.

"What's that you're wearing?" Frieda asks her.

"It's Ava's shirt."

"Everything's fine." I hand her the plastic bag with Jeniece's rinsed-out clothes. "Jeniece had a little accident, but everything worked out okay."

"Jeniece?! What's gotten into you?! Are you two years old or something?"

"I'm not a baby!" Jeniece screams, instantly more awake. "It was an accident! Why do you always want to pick on me?!"

"Go to your room, young lady!" Frieda yells at her.

Jeniece opens her mouth in protest.

"Now!"

Jeniece groans and clomps off.

"I was looking forward to seeing her, too," sighs Frieda.

"She's a great kid," I say. "She didn't give us any problems at all."

"I guess she just saves it for me." Frieda rolls her eyes.

I want to defend Jeniece, but I don't know what to say. "You had something you wanted to tell me? Grown-up stuff?"

Frieda's face drops. "It's Emily."

I feel queasy. She and Darryl must have run off together. Maybe they got married. Maybe she's having his baby . . .

"She's in ICU. It's pretty bad."

Despite myself, I feel flooded with relief. "What happened?"

"Someone tried to kill her. The police think it was the same guy who killed those two girls. She had the same marks on her neck."

"Oh my gosh."

"They have her boyfriend in custody, but I don't think he did it. I mean, he roughed her up a couple of times, but he's too much of a chickenshit to try and kill someone . . ."

"Why is he in custody, then?"

"He has a record. When he beat her up, I called the police on him. No way was I gonna let him get away with that. Plus, his fingerprints were all over her, and some of his semen was in her and on her lips and everything . . ."

I feel another wave of nausea.

"Are there any other suspects?"

"Not that I know of. I think the guy's out there still, I really do. I think he's close by. Maybe you should stay with us tonight, Ava."

"No, thanks," I tell her. I'm looking forward to having some time in the trailer alone. "Thanks for letting me borrow Jeniece for the day. She really is a great kid, you know."

"I know," Frieda says softly.

"I don't think she knows you know." I bite my lip.

Frieda clears her throat. "Well, anyway, thanks for taking her."

"Good night, Frieda."

"You be careful now, all by your lonesome."

"I'll be fine, Frieda. Don't worry about me. I'm a self-defense teacher, remember?"

"I don't think the class helped Emily none," Frieda says. "No offense . . ."

"None taken. Good night, Frieda," I say again, then go to the car.

When I get to the trailer, the hairs on my arms stand up. Everything looks okay—the door is closed, the lift is empty—but I feel nervous. The stress of the whole day must be getting to me. I take a deep breath and get out of the car. A rustling comes from under the trailer, where all the pipes are. I tell myself it's only a cat, only a dog, only a bird, but a person—a large person, a man—steps out of the shadows. My limbs turn fizzy with adrenaline; I shakily assume the ready stance. I wish I could see better—without the headlights, it's hard to distinguish anything, but I can tell he's coming closer, with an intensity that almost takes my breath away. When he gets within a yard of me, I jump into the air and kick him in the throat. He falls to the ground with a huge thud. I race up the ladder of the trailer to call the police and hide behind the door. A police car and an ambulance pull up. I wait until I hear a knock before I stand up. When I open the door, I recognize one of the policemen who questioned me at the station.

"So you find the bodies *and* the guy who killed them, huh?"

"I just found one . . ."

"What kind of racket do you have going on here?"

"There's no racket." I have no idea what he's talking about. He fingers his handcuff.

"You two working in cahoots? He takes the tumble for you? What's the deal?"

"I'm sorry—I don't understand . . ."

"Sure you don't," he nods slyly. "The guy down there says he knows you."

"He what?" I run to the window.

"He says he works with you."

In the squad car's headlights, I can see the man sitting up now, the back of his wavy hair . . .

"Oh, no."

"Are you two like Bonnie and Clyde or something? Or like those two in that movie with the bartender from *Cheers*? The dumb one? That movie where the couple goes around killing people?"

"Officer." Words start to tumble from my mouth. "There's been a mistake. That's my friend out there. I didn't recognize him in the dark . . ."

"Slow down," he says. I try to take a deep breath.

"That's a friend of mine," I say. "He didn't do anything. I just got scared and kicked him. I thought it was the killer, but it was just my friend . . ."

"Why don't we come down and have a little chat, then, all of us?"

I nod.

We step out onto the narrow landing together.

"Strange place you have here," he says. He goes down before me—probably to keep me from bolting.

"Darryl," I call out. "Darryl, I'm so sorry!" This seems to be my catch phrase these days—maybe it always has been: *I'm sorry.*

Darryl looks up at me and tries to smile. He is obviously in a lot of pain.

"Ava," he croaks out.

I jump off the ladder and run to him.

"I'm so sorry, I thought you were the guy . . ." I crouch down before him. He reaches out a hand. I grab it. I feel a jolt go all the way up my arm.

"I know," he says, his voice whisper-soft, strained. "I should have let you know it was me." He stops to cough; my hand falls when he lifts his to cover his mouth.

"Do you want to press any charges?" the cop asks Darryl.

He shakes his head. "It was an honest mistake."

"Is there anything I can do?" I ask him.

"Let me take you to dinner tomorrow," he wheezes, like the air coming out of a bellows. He coughs again. Some blood flies out.

"Oh my gosh, Darryl, I really hurt you."

He puts his hand to his chest and winces out a smile.

"We need to take you in," one of the paramedics says. They wheel a gurney toward him.

"And we need to ask you some more questions," the officer tells me.

"But—"

"No buts about it," he says.

"But I know the language of birds," I say. He stares at me like I'm crazy. I feel a crazy laugh bubble in my chest, but I don't let it out.

As he leads me to the squad car, I turn to Darryl, who is being strapped in to the gurney. "I should take *you* out to dinner, not the other way around . . . ," I start.

He smiles—a real one breaking through the wince—then coughs up more blood.

I drive to the hospital after the police are done questioning me, but Darryl has already been released. I want to check up on him, but I don't know his number and I don't know how to get to his house. There is a message on my machine when I get back home. "I'll be there at seven tomorrow," he says, his voice strained but amused. "In full body armor, of course." His laugh turns into a coughing fit, and then the tape is quiet. I think the message is over, but after a couple of beats he says, "I'm really looking forward to this, Ava." I can hear him breathe for a while before the tape clicks off.

I take another step on the bridge of birds. White pelicans, gray mourning doves, are scattered among the crows and magpies. I can see a few feet in front of me thanks to their light feathers, but my mother is still out of my range of vision. I hear the nightingale over her head tell her to sing; all that comes out of her mouth is breath. I wobble toward her exhale, my fingers thrumming soft.

The bridge sways under my feet. The nightingale's eyes flash in the dark. "Chosim haseyo," it tells me from a distance.

The birds who make up the bridge open their beaks and fly away. The Milky Way sparkles back into view, a flurry of flashbulbs. I have to close my eyes against the sudden dazzle. My mother's silhouette burns inside my eyelids. I can't figure out what's under my feet, now that the bridge is gone. I can't figure out why I haven't started to fall.

The next day goes by like a blur. I spend an embarrassing amount of it in front of the mirror. My hair has grown a lot since I've been out here. I've always kept it cut close to my skull, barely there; even when I was a little girl, my mother cut it that short. She didn't know how to deal with my hair. Mothers of black kids would shake their heads in dismay at my almost bald head. Now my hair is poufing up like a mushroom. I tie a scarf around it to hold it down a little. After changing a zillion times, I finally decided on simple—white shirt, tan pants, which I hang in the shower to steam the wrinkles out. I am trying to decide whether or not to put on earrings when I hear the car pull up. I keep my earlobes bare, take a deep breath, and go outside.

"Should I be scared?" Darryl calls up to me as I climb down the ladder.

"I'm so sorry," I tell him again.

"Hey—I was impressed." He grins. "I didn't know you pack such a punch—er, I mean, kick!"

"How's your throat?"

He holds my door open for me, then runs around to his side of the car.

"It still hurts a little when I swallow, but I'll be fine, Ava. It looked a lot worse than it was. I bit my tongue—that's why there was so much blood."

"Maybe you should just go home and rest tonight," I tell him. "We could do this some other time."

"Are you kidding?" Darryl says as we pull out of the parking spot, sending scraps of salt and dirt flying. "Not on your life. I've been waiting a long time for this opportunity. A little esophageal discomfort isn't going to keep me from showing you the town."

"I think I've seen pretty much all there is to see around here . . ."

"You'd be surprised," Darryl says.

We drive in silence for a while.

"Ava," he starts to say. "I know you're upset about Emily . . ."

"It's okay," I tell him. I'm not sure I want to hear about the gory details.

"I just want you to know it was a long time ago," he presses on. "Five years maybe. It wasn't long after I first came out here."

I stare at the Chocolate Mountains, trying to quell the queasy feeling.

"I was going through a rough time. My wife had died about a year before that."

My stomach lurches again. "I didn't know you were married."

"For three years," he says. "Everything happened pretty fast after she was diagnosed with ovarian cancer."

"I'm so sorry . . ." My mantra. It feels different this time, though.

"I was completely lost. I didn't know what to do with my life. When the position down here opened up, I jumped at it. I wanted to get away from all the memories up north, you know, but when I got here, it wasn't any better. This place looked as desolate as I felt."

I nod, my voice stuck in my throat.

"I was drinking when I met Emily—drinking way too much those days. It was just so nice to have someone smile at me, you know? So nice to have someone want to touch me again."

I shudder involuntarily.

"It lasted less than a week, Ava. It just didn't feel right. We had nothing to talk about. I felt emptier than ever."

I open my eyes wide to keep from crying.

"To tell you the honest truth, I was worried I'd never be able to love anyone again . . ." He looks over at me. I meet his eyes for a second, then turn my head to look out the window again, dizzy. We drive in silence until Darryl pulls the Jeep into the driveway of Shield's Date Garden.

"I thought we'd stop for a little movie before dinner," he says. "Make it a real date."

I look at the rows upon rows of date palms. "When you say date, you really mean it." My voice feels scratchy, like I haven't used it in ages.

"I always say what I mean." His eyes find mine again. I worry I won't remember how to breathe. He gets out and opens my car door.

"They have a great film here," Darryl says as I hop down to the dirt. "It's the only movie theater for miles, you know. No popcorn, but it's nice and cool inside. Don't get put off by the title—I don't mean anything by it, Ava, honestly. It's just fun, you know—a bit of local lore."

I can't imagine what he could be talking about until I notice the sign advertising the film *Romance and Sex Life of the Date.* I can feel sweat begin to form on my upper lip. I wonder if I should turn around, feign a stomachache, a heart attack. The sign, however, also touts the air conditioning and the 108 COMFORTABLE THEATER SEATS. It would be good to get out of the heat.

In the empty theater, I find myself strangely stirred by the erotic life of the date. I don't like the fact that the palms are divided into "harems," an acre of forty-eight female plants with one male "presiding"—it sounds too much like my mother's life as a bar girl—but the actual date reproductive process makes my body respond in ways I wouldn't have expected.

When the film's narrator speaks of how each female blossom must be pollinated by hand, I become acutely aware of Darryl's fingers, folded neatly on his lap. I am tempted to touch his sleeve, his arm, his wrist, but I hold myself back. *I've never tried Ecstasy before and I have no intention of ever doing so.* I have a feeling those words will haunt me the rest of my life.

After the movie, we wander over to the gift shop and taste samples of Medjool, Zahidi, Khadrawy, Halawy, and Deglet Noor dates, along with dates rolled in coconut and little date pellets dusted with oat flour. Darryl points out a package of dates stuffed with walnut pieces. The way the fruit is spread open, with the little nubbin of nut in the center, makes it look like a tray of plastic-wrapped vulvas. My pulse drops down between my legs.

"So, you mentioned dinner . . ." My voice is wavery.

"Well, I just thought we could eat dates all night."

I look at the package again and involuntarily gasp.

"Just kidding!" he grins. "I should ask, though—are you vegetarian?"

I shake my head. I've barely eaten meat—certainly not bird meat—since I've been out here, but I couldn't live without my mother's *bulgogi*.

"I mostly am, myself," he says. "But I suspend all dietary considerations for this place. Everything's dripping with lard."

"What place is it?"

"It's a little tacqueria in Mecca," he says. "My own personal Mecca de Manteca."

"Sounds good," I tell him, even though I'm hesitant to replace the taste of the dates with something else. The prickly sweetness reminds me of the Korean New Year, seeing over walls.

"Oh, it's more than good." He grins broadly. "It's ecstasy."

The tacqueria is a tiny place—a kitchen with an outdoor ordering counter and four picnic tables, all filled, on a little patio glutted with plaster statues and tubs of cactus. Christmas lights twinkle from the wrought-iron fence. The air is rich with the smell of meat and grease and onions, tempered by the powdery scent of fresh tortillas. Music, heavy on the accordion and horns, crackles out from a small speaker mounted by the roof.

"They have amazing *jamaica* here." Darryl points to a huge glass jar on the counter filled with garnet-colored liquid and ice cubes. Dark reddish things that look like tongues and sea anemones float around inside. The handle of a ladle hangs over the top of the jar.

"What in the world is that?" I ask.

"It's like a punch," he says. "It's made out of hibiscus flowers."

"Those things look more animal than vegetable," I say.

"I'll get us some," he says. "Is there something you really want to try, or do you trust me to order for you? I know what's really good here."

The menu, handwritten on a dry erase board, is all in Spanish. I recognize "taco" and "burrito," but beyond that, I'm lost. "I trust you."

"Good," he grins. "I'm glad to hear it."

"I'll go save that table," I tell him, as a couple of men get up—day laborers, probably, bandanas loose around their necks. When my route took me to Mecca, I would often see groups of men lined up along the side of the road, waiting for people to drive up and offer them work—in the fields, on a construction site, wherever under-the-table work was needed. One of them tips his cowboy hat at me as he leaves.

Darryl comes to the table with two Styrofoam cups of *jamaica*. The drink is musky and sweet, like perfume that has been on someone's body.

"That hits the spot," he says after a long gulp. "*Muy bueno.*"

A woman comes to the table with a tray of food.

"*Gracias,*" Darryl says.

"*De nada,*" she tells him. She looks at me curiously. I look away until she leaves again.

The table is covered with plates, food swimming with blobs of orange oil, sour cream everywhere. Pickled carrots and jalapeños are scattered along the edges of the entrées. I can't make sense of most of it. I pick up what appears to be a taco and take a bite. The meat, wrapped in a greasy corn tortilla, is the most tender I have ever tasted. It seems kind of like beef, but kind of not, satiny and mellow.

"What is this?" I ask.

"*Lengua,*" he says. "It's amazing, isn't it?"

"It's delicious." I take another bite. "I've never heard of it before."

"It's tongue."

I spit my mouthful of it into a napkin. "Tongue?!"

"They have tripe and sweetbreads and brains here, too, but I didn't order them."

I feel light-headed.

"Tongue is the best thing on the menu, Ava, honest. You said you trusted me, right?"

"I just wasn't expecting . . ." But I was hoping, wasn't I? Haven't I imagined his tongue—the texture, the taste of it in my mouth? *His* tongue, not a cow tongue. I feel dizzy, but I can't tell if it's from disgust or desire.

"I'm sorry, Ava," he says. "Try this—there's no meat at all, other than the lard in the beans . . ." He points to what appears to be a large shoe made out of cornmeal, filled with beans and a crumbly white cheese, sprinkled with lettuce and tomato and onions.

I take a bite from the plastic fork he holds out and close my eyes. The cornmeal is chewy and satisfying, the beans are like velvet, the cheese adds the right salty bite.

"It's a *sope*," he says. "It was my wife's favorite. There was this place in the Mission we used to go . . ." He trails off, misty.

"I'm so sorry, Darryl . . ." Those words again—they keep rising into my mouth like heartburn.

"So." He wipes his eyes. "I've told you my saddest story. You tell me yours."

I take a sip of my *jamaica* and practically choke on the piece of hibiscus that comes through the straw.

"Are you okay?"

I nod, my eyes tearing. I chew the flower bit, rubbery and sweet between my teeth.

"So, tell me. Who's broken your heart?"

I don't know where to begin. "I've broken my own heart, I guess."

"How's that?"

"I've never had a real relationship before," I tell him.

He puts his hand to his heart. "You don't strike me as someone who just fools around."

"I've never really fooled around, either . . ." The choking tears slip into real tears. I hope he won't notice the difference.

"Ava, are you okay?" He touches my hand.

I nod. The tears are streaming now.

"What is it?" he asks.

I can't answer.

"Did someone do something to you?"

He must think someone molested me when I was young. I shake my head. "My mother . . ." I start crying so hard that I almost throw up—I can feel a petal climbing up my throat.

Darryl comes around the table and puts an arm around me. I collapse into him, sobbing. We sit like this for a long time.

"Hey, do you remember that old commercial?" He fingers a pink packet in a chipped bowl on the table as I start to calm down. "'Wherever you go, Sweet 'N Low'?"

"I think so," I say, my voice trembling.

"It's like that for me, you know," he says. "Wherever I go, Ava Sing Lo."

I don't know what to say.

"I can't stop thinking about you, Ava," he whispers into my hair.

"You don't know anything about me." I start to cry again.

"But I want to," he says. "I want to know *everything* about you. I want to know your favorite color, I want to know what you looked like when you were a little girl, I want to know what kind of toothpaste you use and why you always smell like ginger and how you got that scar on your kneecap, and—"

"My mother was a prostitute," I blurt out before I realize I am going to say it.

I feel like I'm going to die, or at least explode into a million pieces, but nothing happens. I've said the words and the world didn't end. I feel exhilarated, like a ton of new oxygen has been pumped into my blood. I feel like now that I've said this, I can say anything. But I don't. Darryl wraps me in his arms and I let my lips speak to his without any words at all.

Helen stumbled down a dirt alley, holding her stomach. Bile rose fierce in her throat; she had to keep it burning there, she had to keep moving, at least another block. The night air skimmed her face like angry sweat as she rushed past a row of small tin-roofed houses, her shirt slipping off one of her shoulders.

"Are you okay?" A man's voice startled her. She stopped in her path. Before she could answer, Helen threw up—a white, clotty arc that hit his polished shoes.

"Come on," he said. "You need to lie down."

Men often said that to her, but not with the same tone of voice, not with such soft concern. Usually it was a terse command. *Lie down*. Or *Kneel, Bend over, Stand against the wall.* Like something someone would say to a dog or a naughty child. Just an hour before, Helen had been asked to squat under a table at Wild Ting and suck off five GIs, one by one, rotating between them like a windup toy beneath the cheap gum-studded particle board.

Helen threw up again, this time all over the man's pant leg. She hadn't been able to hold anything down lately. Helen figured she was pregnant; she recognized the symptoms she had seen in other pregnant bar girls—the queasiness, the deep fatigue, the darkness across the bridge of the nose—plus, her period, normally so regular, was already almost two weeks late. She had started throwing up the day Sun was killed.

"It's okay, it's okay," she could hear the man say, as he grabbed her elbow. He was pale, almost colorless, she saw as she turned her head, his hair a pelt of beige stubble, his eyes slate gray. His face was as smooth as it was white, his hands were, too. Helen cringed as he guided her through the dark walkways to a clinic, his large warm palm wrapped just beneath her bicep. She hoped no one would see her, a DMZ *kijich'on* with this ghost of a man.

The clinic was one she had never been to before, far different from the clinic where she checked in each week to be tested for an assortment of venereal diseases. A nurse put a check mark on the back of her identification card there, beneath the chart of her menstrual schedule, to show she was clean. She brought the card back to the club and put it in a cardboard box beneath the bar, where Knute kept the IDs handy. The last club owner, after the shiny suit man, was Madame Karen Carpenter Cher, an ex–bar girl from Pusan who never let her girls work when they had their period. The new owner, though—Knute, a squat American expatriate and ex-GI—just put the "bleeders" on extra blow job duty. "Their mouth ain't bleeding," he would joke to the GIs as he sent them off with their chosen orifice. When Cher was the boss, sometimes Helen stained the back of her dress with ketchup or chili sauce after her period was over, just so she could get a couple of extra days of rest, but with Knute there was no such reprieve.

The clinic the man brought Helen to was so white inside, it dazzled her eyes, made the middle of her forehead burn. She threw up again, on the man's lap this time, as he sat next to her. He stroked her hair, and she let herself be lulled beneath his long fingers. As she drifted in and out of consciousness, she could hear the man argue with the Korean women at the desk about whether or not they could treat Helen. It was a GI clinic, not some hootchy-kootchy joint you bring a date to, they said. Helen threw up another time. The man made a passionate plea, and a woman at the desk sighed and finally ushered them into the back part of the office.

Helen sat down on an examining table covered with crinkly paper, a cushy table, not like the hard wood one at the VD clinic. The man put a hand on her shoulder and lowered her down.

Another white man, dressed in mint green, came and spoke with the man, who referred to Helen as his fiancée. Helen felt a needle enter her upper arm where her princess sleeve ended; the fluid inside made her whole muscle sting. She bit her lip hard, grabbed the man's hand. He squeezed back, and she could see tears spring to his eyes. A second needle went in at her hip, where the doctor had yanked down the elastic waistband of her lilac polyester pants, her rosebud underwear. Demerol and Compazine, the doctor said to the man—one will calm her down, the other will stop the vomiting, but she'll be sleepy, so you better take her on home to rest.

The man thanked the doctor profusely, took Helen by the arm again, led her outside. She leaned against him, barely able to stand, the drugs circling woozy through her blood.

"You'll be okay now, you'll be fine," he whispered into her hair. He led her to what she supposed was his apartment and laid her down on a sofa. Before she could say a word of thanks, she fell into a dead sleep.

It was still dark when Helen woke up. She touched the blanket the man had draped over her. It was soft, like a stuffed animal splayed open. She rubbed her left hand up and down the fleecy material and tried to go back to sleep, but something felt wrong. She couldn't move her right arm. At first Helen thought it had fallen asleep, like it often did when some GI slept in her room, the weight of his head pressed against her bicep, but she didn't feel any tingles or pinpricks under her skin. Her whole arm seemed to contract itself into the spot the needle had gone in; her shoulder was drawn tense up to her ear. She cried out a little bit, a mewl of fear, but her voice felt strange. It was as if her tongue had grown while she slept, had filled up her mouth. When she called out, tentatively, "Help me, please, sir," her words sounded like Regina's, the deaf bar girl who worked at Wild Ting with her. Helen's jaw pulled itself over to one side and wouldn't go back. She screamed another garbled cry for help.

The man, soft with sleep, stumbled out to the couch. He flicked on a light and looked at Helen with alarm.

"I can't talk," she said, although the words came out without any clarity. She knew the man hadn't heard her voice before, and she was worried he would think that was how she always spoke. She gestured to her mouth and shook her head violently. Without another word, the man scooped her up and ran her back to the clinic, in his pajamas.

"Something's wrong," he said, panicky, as soon as they got through the door. "She's having some kind of seizure, her mouth is all twisted . . ."

"Does she have a history of this kind of episode, sir?" the woman at the desk, a different one, asked coolly, as she ruffled through some files.

"I don't know."

Helen shook her head.

"No," he said. "She doesn't. She was in here before, they gave her a shot, two shots. She was puking . . ."

"Is she pregnant?" the woman asked.

"No, of course not," said the man, and Helen didn't correct him.

"I'll get the doctor, sir," she said. It was a good five minutes before she came back, and during that time Helen felt like her jaw was going to crack open, to shatter apart. It felt unhinged, worse than after giving five blow jobs in a row; it felt like her lower jaw was planning on leaving the rest of her in the dust, like it was trying to break through her skin and fly away. Helen understood; she wanted to fly out of her skin herself. The first shot made her feel like she was floating for a while, but she fell asleep before she could travel very far, her friend Sun's voice warbling in the distance.

A doctor came out a couple of minutes later, right after Helen's jaw spasmed and she bit into her tongue. Blood filled her mouth, dripped over her lip. She had tasted her own blood slightly less than a year before when a GI punched her after she sneezed with him in her mouth, and her teeth clamped into his penis. A thin scar lay jagged on her top lip where her tooth had passed through. Madame Karen Carpenter Cher was in charge then and had let Helen rest until her mouth healed up, in her own room. If anything happened to a girl that couldn't be covered up with makeup under Knute's command, she was sent to the squalid Monkey House in the mountains, where they sent all the bad VD cases, until she was presentable again.

"She's having a stroke?" the woman at the desk asked the doctor.

"I'm not stroke on him!" Helen wanted to defend herself, but she couldn't get the words out. How could that woman think she would stroke the doctor at a time like this, although his zipper was within reach, and she could have if he asked.

"She's having a dystonic reaction to the medicine Dr. Salinas gave her earlier today," the doctor said to the woman, to the man who brought Helen in, to everyone but Helen. "I'm going to give her some Benadryl intravenously. We'll keep an eye on her for a while. She'll be fine."

"She's my fiancée," the man piped up. "Can I stay with her?"

"If you want." The doctor strode off to get the IV equipment. "Good luck," he said under his breath.

The nurse guided the IV needle into the back of Helen's hand; she felt herself fly out of her body with the shock of it. The Benadryl burned in, worse than the injection earlier, stinging its way down her vein, and she was sucked back into her skin. She willed herself to fall asleep as the man held her other hand, stroked the path of each vein, one by one, up to her wrist.

* * *

Later, back in the man's apartment, Helen dozed on and off on the couch. The man—James, he finally told her—was never far from her side, bringing her juice and tea whenever her eyes opened.

"Will you marry me?" he asked Helen as she forced some tea down her raw throat. She had not spoken one word to him yet other than her garbled cries for help.

"What you know from me?" Helen asked. "Why you want to marry this?"

"I knew the moment I saw you," said James, "when you threw up, it was just so white. The puke of an angel. I saw that, and I knew, yes-siree, that's the woman for me. Everything inside of her is pure as the driven snow. Don't find that too often round here, you know."

"You not know me." Helen shook her head. She considered asking him if he wanted a good time, giving him the price rundown, but she resisted.

"I'm flying to the air force base in Miramar, near San Diego, in less than a month—that's in California, you know—and I'd like you to come with me," James persisted, his gray eyes earnest, near tears.

You crazy boy, was all Helen could think, but then she remembered Sun's desire to go to California. *Hollywood, California,* she heard Sun's voice—Sun's Folk Village voice, not her Wild Ting voice—ring out, full of hope. Maybe Miramar was near Hollywood, California. Helen would find it for Sun, she decided. She would get out of this place alive.

Helen soon found herself attending classes at the USO Bride School, where she learned about such things as the military lifestyle, the U.S. health care system, and how to prepare American-style breakfasts and instant pudding desserts. She found herself trying not to lock eyes with the other bar girls in the class, the ones who stirred up scrambled eggs with extra care, trying not to look coarse, trying not to arouse suspicion. She found herself throwing away her *kijich'on* ID. She found herself saying "I do" in the chapel. She found herself leaving all her clothes and makeup behind at Wild Ting, never to look at Knute's ham face again. She found herself on an airplane, bound for the United States of America.

Helen couldn't believe how her heart fluttered, like wings in her chest, when she was up in the air, flying over the ocean. All around them, newlywed couples kissed and pawed at each other. Some GIs had blankets over their laps, their wives' heads moving underneath. James tentatively put his hand on Helen's knee, touched her hand as if he didn't believe she was real. She wasn't, in a way, wasn't there in the cramped seat next to him. She was out in the thin blue air, out in the pale wisps of cloud, where she always knew she would feel at home.

Darryl and I have been spending a lot of time together, but we are taking it slow—my choice, I'm afraid, not his. I love being near him, I love kissing him—the warm wet rush of it—but whenever he puts his hand on the front of my shirt, or high on my thigh, I clench like a fist. My whole body clamps down. I can't bring myself to put my own hands anywhere but his back, his face, his hair. I tell him I'm sorry again and again—I can't seem to stop myself from saying it. He's patient, but I can tell he's frustrated.

Emily is doing much better now. She came out of her coma after a couple of days. The doctors were worried about brain damage, but as soon as she woke up, she made a huge stink, demanding that someone bring one of her negligees from home; no way was she going to be caught dead in a hospital gown. After Emily started her physical therapy, Frieda showed up with the Miss Tomato tiara and sash and makeup kit; she glammed Emily up and pushed her around the hallways of the hospital; Emily waved from the chair as if she were queen of the parade. She's the same old Emily, pretty much. Her speech is a tiny bit slurred, and she seems to drag her left foot a little, but overall she's doing much better than anyone expected. I told her I've forgiven her; it seemed like the right thing to do, although part of me feels like I should have thanked her—Darryl never would have known how I really felt, *I* never would have known how I really felt, without that little chemical nudge. She says she doesn't remember why I would need to forgive her, says she doesn't remember the rave at all, and *drugs? Whatever would she be doing with drugs?* Her memory seems fine otherwise, for the most part, although she says she doesn't remember the attack. She insists she was hit by a car, but I don't know how even she could convince herself that a car would leave finger marks on her throat.

The birds are doing much better, too; the botulism seems to have run its course. We find very few dead birds now, and the pelicans that survived have all been rehabilitated and released. The out-of-state workers have gone back to their home posts. The bird hospital is eerily empty, the incinerator silent and cold. Bird organs have been shipped off to research facilities. The statistics people are firming up their calculations. The death smell is slowly fading away.

Now that I don't have to do my route as often, I find myself with more time to work on my mother's story, to fiddle around with the tapes I've been compiling. I bring my sound equipment to Darryl's house and play with it with my headphones on while he does his paperwork. It feels so easy being there with him, working side by side. It feels so easy until he reaches for me. I look at his bed, his fingers, and my mind flares, but my body can't seem to catch up.

"Ava, it's okay to feel good," he tells me, as I pull away from his hand yet again. I bite my lip to keep from crying. No one's ever said this to me before. I certainly haven't been able to say it to myself.

"You feeling good isn't going to hurt your mother."

Adrenaline shoots down my legs, a cold river.

"Think about it," he says. "She had such a rough time. You don't have to. She probably wants you to feel good, don't you think? Wouldn't she want that for you? I know I do . . ." His fingers trace the inseam of my jeans.

"I'm sorry, Darryl . . ." I can still taste his mouth—rich and dusky as cedar—inside mine. I can still taste my mother's sorrow, my own contribution to her pain. I want to chase her out of my head, but it's like she's rooted there.

"If you don't want to be here, just tell me, Ava. You don't have to humor me along."

"It's not that," I tell him. "I want to be here. You know I do. Just give me some more time, okay?"

He kisses the top of my head and walks off to the bathroom, a little hunched over. I know he is going to try to will his arousal away, maybe touch himself to relieve the pressure, and I feel so guilty, but I just can't go there with him, not yet.

I keep missing my mother's calls. She calls to tell me she saw some of the pelicans being released at Casa Cove, dozens of them being ushered out of dog carriers, unfolding their wings, taking to the sky. She calls to tell me I have been offered a job—a temporary one, a well-paying one—as a Foley person for an animation studio project in Los Angeles. She leaves the number on the answering machine. I haven't called them back yet. It makes sense to take the job—my savings are not deep enough to support me much longer— but, much to my surprise, I'm not sure I'm ready to leave here.

I finally call my mother to give her Darryl's number in case she needs to reach me in an emergency. "I'm not sleeping there or anything," I tell her. "I'm just spending more time there now."

I am prepared for her to give me a lecture, to say "*Chosim haseyo*"—"Be careful," like Kane always used to squawk at me—but she just says "He a nice man" before she hangs up. Her time with him in the bird hospital must have impressed her. I don't think I've ever heard her use the terms "nice" and "man" together before in my life. When I exhale, I feel like it's a breath I've been holding a long, long time.

James had lost his virginity to Helen their wedding night. Helen pretended to, too—she cried out like she had a hymen to break. She had a hard time acting inexperienced; she was tempted to pull out her bag of tricks, ask him if he wanted anything kinky, offer herself like clay or mud, not porcelain.

It almost annoyed Helen how grateful James was for her. When he stroked her inner arm or her neck like it was a marvel of nature, she wanted to swat his hand away. Helen was grateful for the fact that he never lasted very long—five minutes at the very most. Less than a minute the first time.

James was adamant about having a baby, so when Helen pretended like her period was late a couple of weeks after they were married, he was ecstatic. She was glad she wasn't that far along when they met—she wouldn't have too much to explain when she started showing earlier than she should have. James was more involved with the pregnancy than Helen was. If Helen had laid an egg, which she would have much rather done, James would have been the one to keep it warm.

Helen *ate* eggs, though, one after another—hard-boiled, fried, scrambled. Her husband was thrilled—a good source of protein, good Western food for the growing baby. She never told him she had heard her mother advise a pregnant neighbor to not eat eggs—they slip the spine right out of the baby's body, her mother had said, so the baby is born floppy, no backbone to support it; the baby will not live long. If the baby were born strange, maybe James wouldn't notice the color of its skin. Although she normally didn't eat bird flesh, Helen asked her husband for the money to buy duck meat—her mother had said it would fuse the baby's extremities. He was tickled by her gourmet wishes but told her it was too costly. "I'll bring you chicken," he said. "Everything tastes like chicken anyway. And it's cheap."

He came home the next day with a bag full of chicken thighs and a scrapbook, so that Helen could keep track of how many calories she ate each day, how many vitamins, and, later, so she'd have a place to paste in baby pictures and note first smile, first words. Her first impulse was to rip out the pages, but she swallowed that down and pushed the book under the bed. She felt the blank paper wait underneath her, silently taunting her when she tried to sleep, when James crawled on top of her large belly. She felt the pages daring her to write. She felt herself fill with words, new jagged English words, words she could never say to James. One day, when James was on duty, she spread the pages open like wings across her lap. She found a new place to hide the book, under the ironing board, where she knew he would never look. She let the words spill . . .

Bird fall out of nest. Baby.
Find on sidewalk, on way to commissary (milk).
No feathers, eyes purple with skin cover.
Pink yellow body to see inside. Heart stopping.
Big head, neck bent bad, little wing open.
No want to touch it. Leave there. Walk home
other way.

Sun, friend Sun, neck bent bad same way,
purple all around. Sun, where they take you?
You fly away? You go over wall?

White husband drive silver plane, make me
drink milk milk milk.
Dark baby flutter inside.

Helen knew the baby's father was black, although she wasn't sure which black man in particular. She hoped that the baby would favor her skin color, that it wouldn't be too dark. Some of the men she serviced had lighter skin than she did, freckled yellow, honey brown. One man had even been an albino, his skin chalky, his afro a frizzled, jaundiced-looking white. Maybe it was his baby. Comments from James had made it clear that he did not like black people—niggers, he called them, darkies, spades, even *ggum-doongi*. When James prayed for the baby to be healthy, Helen prayed for it to not be black.

While she was pushing the baby out, Helen went crazy. The baby got stuck, and she had to push for over an hour. Things flew out of her mouth she couldn't control. "I suck you, ten dollar," she yelled. "You put it in my asshole?" "What you want? You want good time?" She couldn't stop. A nurse tried to reassure James that women said the strangest things during labor, it wasn't her talking, it was the pain, but he sat, blanched even whiter, on a chair next to the bed, dumbfounded, his hands in his lap. He had held her hand the whole labor until she had screamed out, "I suck that big black cock? You put that big black cock in me?" and he dropped her hand like it was a pile of dog shit.

Then the baby was born black, and Helen watched James's lips press themselves into a thin blue line. She watched his hands clench and unclench. She watched the warmth of his gray eyes melt down into steel. He didn't say another word, got up, left for three days without calling. When he came back after the hospital called him to come get his wife and baby, he showed up stubble-faced, beer on his breath, his clothes rumpled. Helen held the baby wrapped so thoroughly in blankets, her face was engulfed in deep layers of cotton. Helen hoped the white cloth would reflect off the dark face, lighten the baby, but if anything, it accentuated the contrast.

James pushed the wheelchair down the hallway with such force, Helen thought her episiotomy stitches would split open, thought the baby would fly out of her arms.

"Sir, it's regulation that hospital personnel push the wheel-chair," said a young black nurse.

"Fuck off," James grunted, and ran the rest of the way. Helen closed her eyes and pulled the shrieking baby close to her chest, just starting to prickle with milk, as they hurtled their way toward the bright automatic doors.

I stop by the trailer to grab some more tapes when an unfamiliar car—a gold Mercury Zephyr, early eighties, probably, spotted with Bondo, pulls up. My mother gets out, along with another woman—Anchee, the woman from Luk's Market. She has a bruise around her left eye. Both of them look at me slightly perturbed.

"We look all over for you!" says my mother. "We drive around, look at bird hospital, look at restaurant, look at here, you not anywhere!"

"Three time we come round here!" Anchee says. I can't help but smile, thinking of the Cahuilla myth.

"I'm sorry—I was at Darryl's house."

"We not know where that is!" Anchee says. Her hand flutters up to her bruise.

I look in the car. It is stuffed to the gills with clothes and pots and pans and houseplants and two birdcages—Yukam's, and one with what looks like a small robin inside.

"Don't you touch those birds!" my mother says.

"No you touch the birds," Anchee echoes. "Your mother tell me what you do. Shame in you!"

Shame in me, yes, I think to myself. So much shame. Too much shame. So much I can't even bear to think about it.

"Omma, it looks like you're moving in."

She and Anchee nod. "Good for work on egg," says my mother. "Palm Springs nearby, many craft fair, many people want to buy fancy egg."

I open the car door and start to unload some of her stuff, stunned.

"What about the apartment in San Diego?"

"I move out," she says. "I don't wanna stay in broken egg place."

"What did you do with all the furniture?"

"I call someone, they take it away," she shrugs. "They give me a few dollar for it."

"What about your car?" I ask my mother.

"I sell it," she says.

"For how much?"

"Your mother get seven hundred dollar," Anchee says proudly.

"Omma," I groan. "You could have gotten three times that much!"

My mother shrugs.

"Don't you think you should have warned me about all this first? What if there wasn't any space in the trailer?"

"You say you at Darryl house . . ." She has a hard time with the syllables of his name—it sounds like a gurgle in her mouth.

"I'm not sleeping there . . ." I don't know what else to say. I turn to Anchee. "It was nice of you to drive her out."

"Anchee stay, too," my mother says.

"Here?"

"Me and you sleep in bed," she says. "Anchee sleep in couch. Or me and Anchee sleep in bed, you sleep in couch. Or just me sleep in bed, Anchee sleep in couch, you sleep in Darryl house."

"Omma!" I'm shocked she would even suggest this. Every time she's noticed me even look at a man before, she's jumped down my throat.

"He don't care if you a black girl." I can't tell if this is a statement or a question.

"No, of course not," I tell her, although I've wondered if that's what initially attracted him to me—a whole different kind of skin to touch. I'd like to think it was more than that, that some mysterious force brought us together, but I don't really know.

"People always surprise you come out of me. When you little girl, sometimes I pretend I a baby-sitter for you so people don't say nasty thing."

"Omma, I'm sure people didn't care as much as you thought they did. I don't know if people ever really noticed us at all."

She looks at me like I have no idea what I'm talking about, then starts to pile the contents of the car on the trailer lift.

Over the next week or so, I sleep on the couch and let my mother and Anchee take the bed. They moved all of my clothes into kitchen cabinets so that I won't have any reason to go near the birdcages in the bedroom. I go over to Darryl's house to get away, but I feel a different kind of pressure there.

"Maybe you should take Ecstasy again," he says, only half kidding, as we sit on the edge of his bed, rumpled and breathing hard after another marathon kiss. "Maybe it would help you get over this hump."

"No pun intended, right?" I lean into him. He laughs and kisses my forehead.

"I can give you a better kind of ecstasy myself, Ava. I like to think I can, at least."

I bite my lip.

"My version is a lot less dangerous than X, too," he says. "It's all natural, no side effects. There is, however, a chance that you'll find it addictive. A good chance, I hope."

I'm sure he knows this feels way more dangerous to me than any pill ever could. My mother's whole history, my whole history, weigh on me like a bag of dead birds. She's essentially given me her blessing to be here, but it's a heavy blessing, almost a burden. I don't know how I'll be able to shake it all off. I want to, more and more all the time. I want to be able to shake it all off.

Darryl scooches off the bed and kneels in front of me. I hold my breath.

"I want to help you feel good, Ava. It's driving me crazy."

"I know . . ." *Go away, Omma. I don't need you here.*

He touches the top button of my shirt. "Is this okay? Please tell me this is okay."

My mother's outline hovers inside my head. *This isn't going to hurt you,* I tell her. *I don't have to hurt like you.* Her molecules shimmer like dust. When I breathe out, some of the particles scatter. *This is a good thing, Omma. Please go away.* Her outline begins to fade. I start to feel guilty for chasing her off, but before she can gather herself together, reassert herself again in my mind, I turn to the warm real bulk of Darryl's body.

"I should warn you," I tell him, my heart at a furious boil. "I have weird nipples."

He looks amused. "Do they shoot root beer? Do they talk?"

"They're inverted. They point in." I flush. I've never told anyone about my nipples before. The only conversation I've ever had about them was when I was about eleven and my mother came into the bathroom when I was in the tub. She looked at my chest and told me no man would ever want a strange girl like me. She seemed happy about this, relieved, like I had found a way to save myself.

"They're yours," he smiles, and slips the button through its hole.

My breath catches. "I'm really scared, Darryl."

"And you think I'm not? Look at this . . ." His fingers tremble as he undoes another button.

"Just the shirt, okay?" I lie back on the bed, more stiffly than I would have liked. I think of the woman I found on the beach, her nipple lifeless between my fingers, her body rigid. I think of my mother in Kunsan, the first time she was with a man. Her body must have been stiff then, too, contracted against his foreign body, wooden with fear. I've never let myself visualize that exact moment; I skimmed over it when I wrote that part of her story. She's never given me any specific details about that night; I don't know if I could handle them.

I shouldn't be thinking about this right now. Omma, please forgive me if I'm not going to think about this right now.

Darryl kisses my lips, then parts the fabric at my breastbone and kisses there, too. My muscles loosen, turn warm and fluid as the night at the rave. I begin to feel far from dead, far, far from my mother. Wherever Darryl's mouth touches, my skin unfurls like wings.

My mother has filled up all the pages of her Book of Dead Birds. She keeps the book prominently displayed on the coffee table so that I'll see it as soon as I wake up on the couch each morning. She doesn't want me to forget all the evidence stacked against me.

I buy her a new scrapbook, one with a bright-green cover. I tell her she can use it for bird-watching, for recording all the birds, the live birds, she notices around the sea. I pick up some binoculars, a guidebook, for her at the visitor's center. People travel from all over the world to watch birds here when there's no die-off in effect; if she decides to do this, she should have no problems filling up the pages.

Anchee has been busy with her own books, keeping records of her snack sales. She stole boxes and boxes of candy from her husband's store before she left. She convinced Frieda to let her set up a little candy display by the cash register. She is at the Aloha now, arguing over Frieda's percentage.

I don't know yet what I'll do with my notebook about my mother's life, don't know if I'll ever show it to her. I still have so many questions.

My mother finishes blowing an egg. A final teardrop of albumen hangs from the shell; she sweeps it off with a rag.

"Omma," I say. "You've never told me what happened next."

"What happen next when?" She wipes her lips with the back of her hand, sets the eggshell down.

"What happened after I was born. After you left the hospital."

"Oh, that." She turns away, picks the eggshell back up, looks at it as if it is the most interesting object on earth.

"Omma, you don't have to tell me. I mean, of course I want to know, but if you don't want to . . ."

"It okay." She puts the eggshell back down.

I reach for the drum, but she doesn't start to sing. She starts to talk. She has never told me her story in her regular speaking voice before—it has always been the *pansori,* the drum, the wild fluctuations of the song. Now her voice is level, calm. I fold my hands in my lap to keep them quiet.

"He beat me up," she says. "After the hospital, he beat me up. I still bleeding from you being born and he stick his thing in me. He bite me, he hit me. He do all kinds mean thing to me."

"Oh, Omma," I say. "What did you do?"

"I run away," she tells me. "I take you and I run away. The army place so big. I not know where to go. He try and look for me. I see him run around, look for me. I run into plane."

"You crashed into a plane?" I'm confused.

"I go inside. A plane open. I go inside. He run past it, not see us there."

"What happened then?" How could I have not known about this?

"The plane go up in the air."

"With us in it?"

She nods.

"Didn't they know we were in there?"

"We in the bottom. In like a little bubble. The place where they shoot guns out."

So *that* was the first time I flew. I guess my maiden launch wasn't from a seesaw after all. "How long were we in the air?" I ask.

"Not long, but it go up and down a few time," she tells me. "It take off, go around over water, come back, come down. I think we gonna get out and then it go up in the air again. It go up and down, three time, maybe four. Up and down, up and down. I not know what gonna happen."

"Were you scared?"

"I scare they gonna find us. You scream like crazy. I think your ear hurt. My ear pop and pop. I thought they try and scare us, go up and down like that, try and make us sick."

"Maybe it was a test for a new pilot, or something."

"Who know? But I see San Diego from air. I see all kinds thing from air. Is good to see so many thing, open your mind. I see some sign, know there is place we can go."

"Did he ever find you after that?"

She shakes her head. "I one time see him, when you was 'bout five year old. I see him walk down street with yellow-hair woman and yellow-hair baby, but I not say anything."

"Omma." I touch one of her hands. Her skin is so dry. "I wish your life had been easier. I'm so sorry you've had such a hard time. I'm sorry if I've made it harder for you . . ."

She stands up, brushes herself off, and goes to get her drill. Through the open bedroom door, I can see Yukam and the baby robin stir as she walks by.

Anchee comes through the door. The way she and my mother look at each other makes me catch my breath. I wonder if they are lovers, if they are helping each other find their own pleasure, the way Darryl has been helping me. I kind of hope so, although I doubt it. I have a feeling my mother wouldn't care if no one ever touched her again. She and Anchee are probably just glad to have found a home together, to have escaped. Either way, this trailer doesn't feel like mine anymore.

* * *

Before I give myself a chance to chicken out, I call the Foley people to find out if the job is still available. The one they originally called me for has been filled, but my timing is good—another temporary position just opened up. I tell them I'll take it. It's just for a few months, and I can definitely use the money. I'm sure my mother will appreciate it, too—it will be a while before she has enough eggs to hit the craft fair circuit again, and Anchee's candy money, while helpful, is not going to amount to a whole lot. Plus, I enjoy Foley work—crushing potato chip bags into a microphone to simulate feet walking across gravel, waving my hand around in a bucket of water in time with the character's movements in the tub, coming up with new ways to create everyday sounds.

Darryl promises he'll come visit me in L.A., and I'll try to spend some weekends back here if I don't have too much work. Where I'll stay when I visit, where I'll stay when the job's over, I'm not sure. We'll see how it goes. The job should be done just as the Date Festival opens in Indio. Darryl and I have plans to meet there. I can already feel us going over the top of the Ferris wheel, our feet dangling in thin air, the bench lightly swaying back and forth, dizzy as the rush of flight. I think about the walnut-stuffed dates that will be waiting for us when we reach the ground, and I feel even dizzier.

As I pull my clothes from the kitchen cabinets, a small piece of paper flutters out from between some socks. It's the poem, the *kisaeng* poem my mother tucked into my drum before I left San Diego. The last two lines haunt me:

Stay just as far away as you can;
time will keep or lead you back.

I never thought there would be anything to keep me here, never thought it would be so hard to leave this place. I feel like I need to do something, something special, to mark my time here, to bring some sort of closure to the rescue effort.

When I was at SDSU, a portion of the AIDS quilt came to campus. People signed up to read names of AIDS victims over a microphone that projected out onto the quad. Each person read for five minutes. I sat in the grass, too shy to get up and read. I let the names wash over me like ghosts, felt waves of sadness at each syllable, each name that meant more than itself, that encompassed a whole person, a whole history, a past of favorite foods, deepest fears, a past of music and pain and love, each name meaning so much more than the words suggested. There were so many names, and I tried to honor each one I heard, let it travel through me, leave its mark.

It all suddenly makes sense. For the first time in a long time, maybe the first time ever, everything finally seems to make sense. I start working on my tapes in earnest.

The Aloha is dim; the only light comes from the inflatable hula girl, a soft glow in her belly. The self-defense class is assembled; everyone is here—Emily and Frieda, the bridge ladies, Lonnie, Rayanne with her pink poodle hair piled high. Everyone is wearing a traditional white Do-Bok. We stand in a circle, ready.

The door opens. A man walks in, wearing a self-defense suit, padding everywhere, a huge puffy helmet. We charge at him. He tosses Emily across the room, throws the bridge ladies over the counter all in one swoop. Rayanne pummels him with her dainty fists. He picks her up and hurls her through the window. Lonnie kicks him with the side of her stocky leg; he grabs her calf and pile-drives her headfirst into the floor. Frieda and I stand together, ready. He reaches for us. I know the world is about to go black, but the door opens again and the room is flooded with light. My mother stands in the doorway, holding her bow and arrow. She lets an arrow fly. Frieda and I jump back. The arrow pierces the chest of the man's self-defense suit. Blood gushes from it like a geyser. She must've hit him in the heart. He crashes to the ground.

When we're sure it's safe, we remove the man's helmet. It's not a man at all, it turns out, but a bird, a huge bird. An albatross, its head turned to the side, its beak open. "It not bother you anymore," my mother says. A chain falls from my neck. I float up to the ceiling, suddenly weightless. Free.

I stand at the end of the pier at North Beach, where I first saw all the dying pelicans. Darryl and Frieda and Ray and Jeniece and Emily and Anchee and my mother all cluster around me. We each hold a sheet of paper, different lines highlighted on each one. My drum is strapped around my neck. My hands are ready. I give my mother the signal and she turns on the tape player. The tape I have put together, the one full of birdsong and bird silence, whirs into the air.

I hold the piece of paper out in front of me, the list of bird die-off victims Fish and Wildlife has compiled. I begin to read, out loud, with all my voice, with all the feeling I can muster. "Snowy egret, two hundred seventy-one, cattle egret, fifty-five, unidentified egrets, two hundred eighty-seven, green heron, five, black-crowned night heron, one hundred sixty-nine." I punctuate each bird name, all the bird names to come, with a drumbeat.

Darryl's voice buckles around the names, "White-faced ibis, seven, fulvous whistling duck, one, brant, one, green-winged teal, fifty-three, mallard, five."

I fiddle around on the drum until Frieda begins: "Northern pintail, twenty-seven, gadwall, seven, canvasback, two, redhead duck, twelve, lesser scaup, five."

Ray takes over: "Common merganser, two, red-breasted merganser, five, ruddy duck, twenty-seven, unidentified ducks, thirty-seven, osprey, two."

Jeniece is next: "Sora rail, one, American coot, one hundred and four, black-bellied plover, four, semipalmated plover—did I say that right?—eight, killdeer, one."

Emily clears her throat, tosses her hair, and says in her best Miss Tomato voice, "Black-necked stilt, one hundred twenty-five,

American avocet, one hundred and seven, greater yellowlegs, one, lesser yellowlegs, six, willet, thirty-one."

"Why'd you give me yellowlegs, Ava?" she asks. "Are you saying something about my legs? Are you saying something about my gimpy leg?"

"No one's saying anything about your legs, Emily," Frieda says.

"No offense or anything, Jeniece," Emily says.

Jeniece rolls her eyes.

I turn to my mother. "Go ahead, Omma."

She stumbles over the words but stays remarkably calm: "Spotted sandpiper, one, whimbrel, ten, long-billed curlew, six, marbled godwit, eleven, ruddy turnstone, one."

When it's Anchee's turn, she shakes her head. "You do it," she tells me. "I not know how to say these name."

I let the words rise from the page: "Western sandpiper, one hundred ninety, dowitcher, seventy-three, sanderling, four, Wilson's phalarope, two, unidentified phalarope, nine."

Darryl touches my elbow, then reads, "Unidentified shorebird, sixty, Bonaparte's gull, twenty-three, ring-billed gull, six hundred fourteen, California gull, twenty-five, yellow-footed gull, three."

"Herring gull, eighty-six," Frieda continues, "unidentified gull, twenty-seven, gull-billed tern, one, Caspian tern, thirty-two, Forster's tern, eight."

Ray takes over. "Unidentified tern, eighteen, black skimmer, eighteen, American crow, one, belted kingfisher, one."

I tap a faster rhythm onto my drum.

We all read together: "Brown pelicans, eleven hundred twenty-nine, white pelicans, eight thousand five hundred thirty-eight."

I lift my hands off the drum, let the resulting silence fill the air. The tape is still whirring, offering a smattering of coos, the whoosh of the airboat. We take a collective breath, then send the names of the two women who were murdered echoing over the hills.

* * *

I am glad I can picture most of the birds we named. A few months ago, all I could identify was a crow, a sparrow, humming-bird, blue jay—common birds any child can name. Now I feel the dignity of all 14,131 lost birds, the dignity of the two lost women, pass through me like the breeze behind a hawk's tail feathers. I feel my own heartbeat trail after them.

I take a long look at the water, the water that stretches out before us, blue for once, not affected by any algae tides. I suddenly love each wrinkle, each shimmer of it. I love the mountains that rise up on each side, the Chocolate, the Santa Rosa, the Orocopia, the Superstition Hills. I love the pale-green birdshit that plasters the barnacles by my feet, the birds that circle overhead, out of danger for now. I love the people who surround me, these broken, beautiful people . . .

"You should have seen this place in its heyday," says Frieda. "All the movie stars came here—Frank Sinatra, Doris Day, all the biggies. The water was so full of people, you could barely move sometimes. There were always parties on the beach, water-skiing competitions, boat races, fishing derbies, you name it. It was spec-tacular. We thought it would last forever."

"We're going to try to save it," Darryl tells her. "It may come back."

"It would be a miracle," says Ray.

"That would be so cool if the stars came here again," says Emily. "Can't you see it, Frieda? Tom Cruise walking into the Aloha?" She tosses her hair as if he's going to show up any moment.

Darryl squeezes my hand.

"Maybe I skin-dive here," my mother says.

"Gross!" yells Emily.

"If the water get cleaner," my mother tells her. "No more fish floating around."

"Good luck," Ray says under his breath.

"You skin-dive?" Frieda asks.

My mother nods. "Women in my family dive. That what they do."

Frieda turns to me. "Do you skin-dive, Ava?"

I shake my head, surprised by the pang I feel.

I'm not the only one to end the tradition. I've read that women divers are becoming a dying breed on Cheju-do, that fish farms are setting up shop, sending their wastewater into the diving areas. The water is becoming so polluted there that the rocks change color. Now the normally abundant sea urchins yield less than a teaspoon of bright-orange meat each. Abalone are getting harder and harder to find. People are concerned about it, I've read. Maybe things will change if enough voices are raised.

"Did you hear?" Frieda pulls me aside. "They have some guy in custody. I'm supposed to take Emily in to ID him. She says she doesn't remember anything, but maybe if she sees him . . ."

I look over at Emily rolling around some barnacles with the toe of her sandal. She looks a lot shorter, more vulnerable, almost childlike, without high heels on.

"You'll have to keep me posted."

Frieda gives me a hug. "We're gonna miss you, Miss Ava Sing Lo."

I breathe in the scent of bacon from her hair. My mother is watching us, watching Frieda crush me to her body in a way she herself has never done. She blinks a few times before she turns her head; Jeniece is there, ready to catch her attention. I hear her ask my mother if she'd teach her how to swim.

When I emerge from Frieda's embrace, Darryl is waiting.

"This was perfect," he says.

I reach for his hand. The warmth of his skin travels all the way up my arm.

"It was the right thing to do," I tell him, and it was. The exact right thing. I lean my forehead into Darryl's and close my eyes. The desire to create this memorial, this new sensation of desire, a sensation I'm just learning to heed, was sharp as my palm against my drum. Insistent as the drum of my heart. Keen as the pull that first brought me to this parking lot, reeling me in like gravity, telling me that after all my circling, it's time to create my own human world.

Acknowledgments

I could fill a whole book of live birds with my gratitude.

Thanks to the Money for Women/Barbara Deming Memorial Fund for supporting me and the novel in its very early stages.

Thanks to my mentors and workshop leaders at Antioch who challenged and encouraged me as this novel was finding its form—Karen Bender, Leonard Chang, Jill Ciment, Tara Ison, Jim Krusoe, Darrell Spencer, and the magical Alma Luz Villanueva, with worshipful bowing to Diane Lefer who guided me through a radical revisioning of the book. All of my friends at Antioch were equally important to the process—thanks to each and every one of you, with special gratitude to Laraine Herring, Peggy Hong, and Sefi Ransome-Kuti; your collective talent and support amaze and sustain me. Eloise Klein Healy was such sublime mother hen for the program; I was so fortunate to have been under her wing.

Thanks to the family I was lucky enough to be born into—my parents, Arlene and Buzz Brandeis, for being my steadfast champions, my sister Elizabeth Brandeis for being my partner in crime, plus Jon and Magdalene Brandeis, Sue Ball, Craig Morrison, Mollie Morrison-Brandeis, Mimi Perretz, the Perretz-Gonzales', and all the rest of the famn damily for rooting me to this earth. Thanks to the family I was lucky enough to marry into—Patricia O'Donnell, Dick McGunigle, Sharon McGunigle, Heather McGunigle, Maggie McGunigle, Tim Ormsby, Eula Palmer, Jack Cotter, Diane and Paul

Reardon, and all the rest of my *Makheteyneste*. I'm so blessed to be part of your clan.

I can't thank my husband, Matt McGunigle, enough. This book would not exist without his belief in me. Thanks, too, to my kids, Arin and Hannah, for being the loudest members of my cheering section. I love you all so much.

Thanks to all my friends, on and off line, for your support, with special hugs to Kate Anger, Denise and Dave Brown, Jennifer Calkins, Lucia Dick, Chris Fullerton, Christian Harder, Jianda Johnson, Vicki Kelley, Donna Kennedy (Miss Salton Sea, herself!), Catherine Kineavy, Judy Kronenfeld, Kristin Kucia-Stauder, Caroline Leavitt, Kris Lovekin, Kathryn Morton, Bernadette Murphy, Cati Porter, Sakada, Sue William Silverman, Jacque Smillie, Rob Stauder, Susan Straight, Katherine Thomerson, Greg Walloch, Valerie Carlene, Susan Ito, Keta Hodgson, Linda Rigel, Lakin Khan, Greg Hyduke, Mary Sharratt, Alex Lang, Liz Newman, all my friends and beloved professors from the Johnston Center at the University of Redlands, the folks at Readerville, all writer-mamas and everyone at MYWG.

Thanks to Sonja Johnson for participating in my first dead bird ritual when we were in first grade. Thanks to the strep germs that gave me fever dreams that changed the course of the novel. Thanks to the dead crow that appeared on my patio just when I was ready to throw the story away.

Thanks to folks who gave me the lowdown about the Salton Sea situation—Norm Niver of the Salton Sea Citizens Advisory Panel, Jake Vasquez of the Salton Sea National Wildlife Refuge, and Linda York of the Coachella Valley Wild Bird Center. Your first-hand perspective was invaluable. Thanks to the documentary *The Women Outside* by J.T. Takagi and Hye Jung Park for first alerting me to the plight of women on U.S. military bases in Korea; thanks to Katharine Moon's book *Sex Among Allies* for deepening my understanding.

Thanks to the great people at James Levine Communications, especially my agent, Arielle Eckstut, for being such a marvelous force of nature (as well as a supreme mensch!). Thanks to Terry Karten and Andrew Proctor at HarperCollins for all of your wisdom and guidance and enthusiasm; I can't believe my good fortune in getting to work with you. Thanks to my posse at Harper-SanFrancisco and their continuing beneficence—Renee Sedliar and Calla Devlin, you are goddesses.

I am deeply, deeply, grateful to everyone associated with the Bellwether Prize. Barbara Kingsolver, Toni Morrison, and Maxine Hong Kingston have all been longtime idols for me, models for how to serve as a writer in the real world, how to balance art and social responsibility. To be able to acknowledge them here makes me weak in the knees. Thanks to all of you for your generosity in your work and in your life. I am humbled to have been given this incredible honor.

Kamsahamnida.

CHILDREN OF PARADISE

ALSO BY FRED D'AGUIAR

FICTION

The Longest Memory

Dear Future

Feeding the Ghosts

Bloodlines

Bethany Bettany

POETRY

Mama Dot

Airy Hall

British Subjects

Bill of Rights

An English Sampler: New and Selected Poems

Continental Shelf

The Rose of Toulouse

PLAYS

High Life

A Jamaican Airman Foresees His Death

Days and Nights in Bedlam

CHILDREN
OF PARADISE

A NOVEL

Fred D'Aguiar

GRANTA

Granta Publications, 12 Addison Avenue, London W11 4QR

Published in Great Britain by Granta Books, 2014
First published in the USA by HarperCollins Publishers, New York

A portion of this book has appeared, in a slightly different form, in *Caribbean Ghost Stories*,
by Martin Munro, ed.

A CIP catalogue record for this book is available from the British Library.

1 3 5 7 9 10 8 6 4 2

ISBN 978 1 84708 861 1
eISBN 978 1 84708 863 5

Offset by Avon DataSet Ltd, Bidford on Avon, Warwickshire
Printed and bound by CPI Group (UK) Ltd, Croydon, CR0 4YY

www.grantabooks.com

TO THOSE WHO LOST THEIR LIVES AT JONESTOWN

And now these three remain: faith, hope and love. But the greatest of these is love.

—I CORINTHIANS 13:13

CHILDREN OF PARADISE

ONE

Adam leans against the bars of his cage and watches the settlers. It's his favorite pastime. He sees everything from the vantage point of his living quarters, stationed in the central clearing of the commune. The children gather a little distance from his cage for their late-afternoon play. They spring about and gesticulate and talk over one another and seem to shriek and shout for no other reason than they have tongues in their heads. The light loses its muscular glare and drops in at a soft slant that's more tolerable to his eyes. Adam peers without creasing his face.

He listens to a small group boasting about which one among them fetches water the best. Ryan, the biggest child, thinks he has the natural advantage. He says that because of the way he carries the bucket, clean without a spill, he should get a medal from the president. Rose, a sprig of a girl with missing milk teeth, counters that if fetching water from a well with two buckets were an Olympic event, she would win gold. Trina, who is bigger than Rose but not by much, points out that the constant heaving of full buckets makes their arms longer than the commune gorilla's. They glance over at Adam. Trina breaks into a combined foxtrot and canter to mimic a loping, armpit-scratching, and chest-thumping gorilla. The others join her with teeth-baring grunts, leaps, and scratches of torsos and thumps of chests.

They look around for someone in authority—a prefect or a disapproving adult—who might reprimand them for being boisterous, and see no one, so they continue with an improvised song that they sing under their breathes, for fear of detection. Trina leads with the first line:

—Hear no evil.

The rest of her group adds the well-rehearsed response:

—Ears of the prefects behind you.

The chant goes back and forth between Trina and the group.

—See no evil.

—Eyes of the forest above you.

—Speak no evil.

—Or the commune gorilla will get you.

They glance over at Adam in his cage, watching them. Without missing a beat, Trina adds another of her lines and continues the group song.

—For this jungle far from the U.S.

—Sees all for Father.

—And this jungle that's a test.

—Hears all for Father.

—And this jungle paradise.

—Knows all like Father.

They check Adam's cage again and search for an older child nearby to start organizing their game. Other groups in the clearing argue among themselves about which one did not work hard enough and who was careless or a slacker. Their urgent whispers sound like feet kicking through leaves. They uncross their fingers and whisper thankful prayers and affix grateful smiles that they are not the ones sent away from the clearing by the prefects to redo chores. Two prefects from among the older children pick the teams for the game. Rose and Trina and most of the younger children edge to the front of the gathering to get chosen for the first team.

According to the rules, the first team must keep running, no standing still and no hiding, until the second team catches all of the first team. When the last person gets caught, the game ends.

The members of the first team shriek as they sprint in every direction to put as much distance between themselves and the second group. Running in pairs, they head for more remote parts of the compound, away from the rows of dormitories and the preacher's white house surrounding the square, and so farthest from the group designated to chase them. The chasers count, poised like runners at a start line. The smaller children try hard to keep up with the bigger children. Adam watches the game as the younger children stretch their legs and pump their arms and drink deep of the rarefied green air, damp and steaming.

The energy in the sprung bodies of the children seems to come from the thick vegetation, energy that bears no relation to their bodies. It looks to be energy reserved expressly for play, a newfound lease on life, that defies the many hours spent at the laundry house near the dormitories, where those on laundry rotation wash and fetch clothes to and from the network of clotheslines strung from pillar to post; or sweeping and mopping the plain wood floors of a dozen dormitories, the schoolhouse, dining hall, and assembly hall; or polishing the varnished wood floors of the main house where the preacher lives; or tidying the compound by patrolling its many pathways and central open area with the large gorilla cage, each child armed with a bag for litter and a can for any sharp objects, such as nails, broken glass, and wood splinters; or working in clusters around giant basins as they peel hundred-pound bags of potatoes and drop them in for a sound of tin muffled by shallow water; or slicing heaps of onions with faces streaming, and if they are lucky to be unobserved, whisper jibes to pick each other up from the misery of that onion burn, jibes about whose eyes suffer most and how the driest face among them makes that person the champion peeler; or scraping carrots to a clean orange shine, hands stained orange; or shelling peas until their hands are so green, they seem grafted from the vines and leaves, properties not of children but of creatures formed by the jungle—all this industry to fill pots to feed almost one thousand mouths.

The children play. The preacher frowns. Pat, Nora, and Dee, his three personal assistants, copy his look of disapproval. They frown as they stare out of a living room window of the preacher's house. Dormitories to the left and right frame their view and flush before them the gorilla cage and the large clearing populated with the fiery atoms of children. Each assistant tries to outdo the other based on some private calculation about what the preacher wants to hear. The only thing logical about their approach is that Pat, who has been with the reverend the longest of the three, always precedes Nora, who always precedes Dee, the most recent of the reverend's triumvirate of most trusted converts.

—You see how joyfully they run.

—Yes, Reverend.

—Yet they complain of always being hungry, and they drag their feet at their chores.

—Yes, Reverend. Maybe we need more discipline.

—Hungry or not, they're flying because they're doing something they really want to do.

—Yes, Father. Maybe they need to hear more lessons from you.

—If I preach any longer, I won't get any sleep.

—Yes, Reverend. I mean they need to hear your wisdom more often.

—The success of this mission cannot solely depend on me. I need help.

—Yes, Reverend. We must all teach the children.

—Look how happy Adam is to see them play.

—Yes, Father. A dumb animal is easy to please.

—Adam is smarter than you think.

—Yes, Reverend. I mean he reacts to things more easily.

—Not just react, my child. The gorilla is infected by the children's joy.

—Yes, Reverend, positively possessed.

—That's the kind of enthusiasm I want to see in all things that we do at this mission.

—We have no better guidance than yours, Father.

An older child in the chasing group latches on to Trina and closes in on her. Trina has a wide-eyed look, as if she cannot believe she is about to get caught so soon and left standing on the spot to stew in her failure, while the other children in her group run far and wide and take a long time to enjoy the feel of the ground at their feet and the air in their faces and no one to tell them not to do this simple thing of running when everything that they do, night and day, is subject to regulation. Trina narrows her eyes as if resolving on the spot that she cannot and will not get caught so soon, that she will do whatever she needs to do to avoid the older girl on her heels. She heads straight for Adam's cage. Trina must calculate that the older girl will give up the chase, because there is not a single child or adult, except the preacher, who is not afraid to get close to Adam. The children usually hurry past the cage at a safe distance and pause only to pick up something loose to pelt at Adam before running away. The thought of running close to the cage, of disobeying every adult warning, makes the little girl tremble, must make it hard for her to breathe, but Trina behaves as if the dangerous approach is her sole option. Just this once, she says aloud to herself, or I sit out the rest of the game.

The older girl lunges at Trina, stretches out her arm for the child in order to bring an end to the chase. Trina twists her body away from the older girl's outstretched hand and jumps toward the cage. The older girl, her first capture almost within reach, abandons her pursuit and veers toward another target at a safer distance from the gorilla. The older girl shouts:

—I'll tell a prefect you're too close to the cage.

—There's no rule against it.

As she replies to the older girl, Trina appears pleased about the success of her gamble; there's a half-smile starting little fires around the corners of her mouth and eyes, and the tension of her body's spring-loaded joints loosens, and just at that moment she stumbles in a stop-and-start move that turns out to be too gymnastic even for her lithe, spidery frame. Adam watches her body as it collides with the cage at the gorilla's favorite spot where he presses against the bars and watches the children and perhaps sees himself out there with them, running, jumping, and dodging.

The second Trina crashes into the cage, she realizes her mistake. She does not bother to look for the gorilla. No time. She pools all her energy into making one leap away from the cage, back into the thick of the game, renewing the chase, no one about to shout at her to stop her wildness.

But Trina needs eyes in the back of her head to see Adam. She cannot hear him, either, not above the din of the children chasing one another, the children chased by their sounds, their shouts and laughter powering their chase. But surely she smells gorilla: a strong, distinct nose-sting of a smell that she finds impossible to ignore, less an outright stink and more a case of some secretion that sits on the skin too long, so long that it becomes a layer of its own, a suit of armor that commands a wide aromatic field. Adam's smell turns the child's mind to the tomato vine that stains her hands with summer, vines that fail over and over to bear fruit, despite the soil's legendary fecundity. She has to rub paraffin on her hands to take away that smell of a lost season in the abandoned country of her birth. Paraffin followed by copious amounts of soap and water, which soon give way to sun, steam from the trees, grass caresses, red earth, sweat, and the rare luck of her mother's rosewater smell transferred by an embrace.

Adam leans there at that very collision point. He follows the flicks back and forth of the children. His eyes dart from one to another as each body with its signature sound flies this way and that across the open and vies for his fleeting attention. In that split second Adam, accustomed to seeing a child draw near and then dart away, marvels at the audacity of this particular child, closer than usual and now so near that only the bars of his cage separate their bodies. Adam simply opens his tree-trunk arms and clasps them around the child. She screams and right away begins to wriggle, twisting and elbowing to free herself. Adam tightens his arms a little to keep her from slipping away. His face creases as he narrows his eyes against her ear-piercing screams, no longer a child's shriek of excitement that informs play but something harmful. The children in both groups freeze and stop and stare at the cage. They add their voices to Trina's screams. And from one child's fear, and her small voice that announces it, comes a collection of children's voices raised in terror. Some call their mothers. They grab each other, and some of them shout:

—Miss Joyce! Miss Joyce!

Ryan and Rose run to help their friend, who threw them one-liners for their response not long ago. They join in the call for Trina's mother:

—Miss Joyce! Miss Joyce!

Until this moment anyone seeing the proliferation of children, all in the open, might mistake the place for a colony without any grown-ups. Not one of them can be seen, busy as they are doing all the things the children cannot manage on their own. Cooks at fires balance the flavor of giant pots. Nurses attend to the sick in the infirmary. Carpenters operate the sawmill or climb ladders to perilous rooftops or feed garbage into the single-minded incinerator. Guards patrol the vast boundary of the compound and check fences and secure gates with rifles slung over shoulders to free their hands for a hammer and nails, or large sticks that they set alongside them as they repair a fence post or tighten barbed wire around the commune perimeter, or they simply stroll and scan everywhere and everyone within range, their arms draped over the ends of sticks balanced behind their necks. The men and women and some older children on farm duty stop their swilling and cleaning of the outlying pig and cow pens. All abandon their duties and run toward the screams. The preacher's advisers stop their paperwork and radio communications with the faraway capital and make their way to the exit of the main house at the front of the square, unsure what the reason can be for this commotion among the children. Even the commune leader who looked out the window moments earlier at a scene of enviable joy, even he registers something different and decides on the basis of what he hears that his intervention is merited and heads directly for the front door.

—Miss Joyce! Miss Joyce!

Joyce never heard her name called this way, more like a summons, a repeating alarm. She knows right away that her daughter is in trouble. She jumps up from her ledger of supplies for the commune and covers her mouth to trap a scream. Her chair falls to the floor, and receipts scatter from her makeshift desk. She scrambles to the exit of the main house. She prays quickly and quietly for Trina's safety, more a thought than an utterance, since her lips move but there is no sound.

God, please. Keep my child safe.

This is how Adam earns his second beating. He holds on to Trina and refuses to release his grip. The perimeter guards are the first to approach the cage. They push the circle of children out of the way. They carry long sticks and rifles. They shout at Adam and lash his arms, careful to avoid hitting the child. They swing their sticks and jut the butts of their rifles. A carpenter among the guards swings a hammer. Joyce runs up to the cage and screams at the guards to stop. She fears a badly aimed blow as much as the predicament of her child in the grip of a gorilla. The guards slow a little but do not stop. Adam switches arms around Trina, from his right arm to his left to avoid the pain brought by the men. Trina spots her mother.

—Mom, help me.

Trina stops looking at the men gathered to rescue her. The sight of her mother close and yet far helps to calm her a fraction. She hears children crying, picks out her two close friends, Ryan and Rose, calling her, but they sound farther away than their bodies look. The bodies and voices of the crowd near the cage begin to blur into one mass of sound and movement as Adam tightens his arms around Trina. She cannot keep her mother in focus. She struggles to breathe. Adam's grip moderates Trina's screams. She becomes quieter. Her screams shorten to less frequent bursts of air from her constricted frame. Trina's eyes drift down to the large hairy arms alternating around her body. Adam's arms feel heavy on her chest and stomach. Under pressure, Trina's mind switches from the reality of her predicament with Adam to the weightlessness of a dream built from memories of trunks of fallen trees. The kind of tree trunk so big across that she cannot jump over it cleanly but must step up onto its bulk before she leaps down the other side. Mass she views as truly immovable because the large span of one such fallen tree remained for ages lying across a path, and chain saws had to cut it into pieces to clear that path, and several men together could not pick up one such trunk. She feels trapped under a fallen tree. The trunk presses on her chest. She waits for the hands of adults to free her, but they appear to need more time than she can spare.

Trina twists her head to her extreme left to catch a glimpse of Adam's face, perhaps to put an expression to the strong arms or with her own look of a desperate plea to convince the mind behind the face to free her. The men continue to strike Adam's arm, and he switches Trina from his left arm to his right. His grip tightens around Trina's torso more as a natural reflex to the blows than out of any intention to harm the child. Her cries stop. She slumps in Adam's embrace. The guards lessen then and cease swinging their sticks. Joyce begs someone to free her child. The preacher in charge of all things at the commune pushes his way to the front of the crowd, which parts for him, and in a soothing voice, he offers Adam one very ripe plantain, the yellow skin streaked with black. Adam grabs the fruit with his left hand. The preacher offers a second fruit, and Adam grabs that one as well. He holds Trina in one arm and two plantains in the other hand, both arms stick out between the bars of his cage.

The cage door opens, and Adam sees a tempting variety of treats, bananas, oranges, breadfruit, a head of lettuce, and mangoes, just beyond his reach. Adam tries to work the child's slumped body along the bars while maintaining his grip on her so that he can reach the fruit basket. But he loses patience with the trickiness of moving Trina along while supporting her slack body and feeding his arms in and out of the bars as he progresses nearer and nearer the hoard of treats. In his haste to move closer to the basket and keep hold of the child in one arm and the two plantains in his other hand, he tightens his grip and squashes the fruits. Adam keeps his eyes on the preacher, who beckons him to come nearer and nearer. Adam, Adam, Adam, the preacher says in a soothing voice. Adam hardly notices his arms slacken around the silent child. He drops her without looking at how her body falls in a heap, one leg under her, the other stuck out to the side and twisted the wrong way, malleable as wire or clay.

The preacher orders the guards and his assistants to take Trina to the infirmary and wait for his orders. The men and women, Joyce first among them, rush to retrieve Trina. Two of the guards drop their sticks, push Joyce to one side, and scoop Trina off the ground somewhat clumsily because they are partly attentive to her and partly mindful of Adam's exact location in relation to them. They lower Trina to the ground a safe distance from the cage. Joyce drops to her knees and pulls Trina to her chest and sobs. A nurse and the commune doctor separate Joyce from Trina and begin to examine the girl for a breath and a pulse. Two women restrain Joyce and urge her to let the nurse and doctor help. No one is allowed to approach the circle of nurses, the doctor, the personal assistants to the preacher, and the guards surrounding Trina. A heated discussion ensues in hushed tones.

Adam leaps on the treats and scoffs them. The preacher stands less than three feet away. Adam turns once or twice from the food and growls at his benefactor to stay away. The preacher seems not to care about the gorilla's threats. Adam gathers his treats and moves sideways to the back of his cage, away from his brazen master, then crouches beside the collection of treats and does not notice the preacher exit the cage. Adam looks at the cage door just as the commune leader loops a chain around the door and the bars of the cage and threads the catch of a padlock through holes in the last two links of the chain. It hardly crosses Adam's mind that he should ignore the treats, charge at the exit, and escape from the cage. Instead he thinks it wise to watch the children more closely the next time they play in case another child approaches his cage. He plans to grip that child as well and take the beating that comes with it just to earn himself more treats.

The preacher orders his guards to clear the area and his men to brandish sticks and lash at the legs of the children who fail to move away quickly enough. Next he orders that Trina be taken to the infirmary, and he allots two other guards to escort Joyce to the main house. Joyce acquiesces quietly. She knows better than to protest against an order from the commune's leader, even if it means being separated from her injured daughter. The preacher holds up his arms, and the array of guards in the middle of clearing the compound, as well as the many children and adult onlookers backing away, come to a standstill and hush.

—The child is no longer with us. Get back to your work of serving God.

He turns and marches to the infirmary, his walk an odd mix of soldier and sailor, of rigidity and inebriated spasticity. Joyce screams, No. The men and women around her grab her as she lunges toward her daughter. They lift and drag Joyce away from the clearing and steer her to the main house. One of the women, a personal assistant to the preacher, thrusts her face close to Joyce's and speaks in a rapid volley that is almost a whisper. Joyce nods as she keeps her eyes locked to the woman's stern gaze. Whatever Joyce hears from the preacher's assistant, whatever the nature of the threat or inducement, it is enough to make Joyce assume a cooperative demeanor. She nods. She stops her struggle. Her shoulders drop. She takes the arm of the nearest person to her and barely lifts her legs as she is led back to the house. Her lips move and issue a small sound. It would take someone standing very close to her, as close as it takes to stare into a pocket mirror, to hear Joyce's lips forming her daughter's name. Trina, said over and again, Trina.

—Guards! Guards!

A prefect shouts for help to come right away and deal with his rebellious mother. Two guards approach the teenager and his mother. She tries to tell her son to be quiet, that she meant nothing by what she said to him. But the prefect, in keeping with his training to listen and report anything suspicious that he hears, no matter the source, tells the guards that his mother said the child could not possibly be dead, that she had to be in a faint or a state of shock. The guards congratulate the prefect on his loyalty to Father and the commune, over and above any loyalty to blood, and second only in loyalty to the Most High. They grab the woman and march her away. The teenager looks satisfied but not completely so. He looks around for someone else, anyone else, nearby to tell him he did the right thing in reporting his mother to the guards. He did as he was trained to do, as all the children are trained to do: Report anyone who expresses any opinion that goes against the teachings and orders of their leader. Another prefect comes over to the teenager and pats him on the back. The teenager watches his mother for a moment as the guards march her to the infirmary, where the commune leader and his inner circle of advisers and assistants have Trina. The other prefect hits the teenager gently on the arm, gently but with sufficient purpose to jolt him back to the business at hand, and the two plunge themselves into the fray of clearing the compound of idling children.

Guards raise their sticks and swing them at children and shout at others to move away from the area. Ryan and Rose and the other children who share a dormitory with Trina begin to cry aloud and ignore the sticks. Poorly aimed blows, meant for the legs, connect with backs and arms. Rose ducks too low in an effort to dodge a blow, and the bamboo stick hits her on her head and splits the thin flesh. The quick flow of blood heightens her screams and attracts more lashes to quiet her. Ryan rushes forward and grabs Rose, steering her away from the square, and both draw a few more lashes from the guards, who continue in their quest to carry out the preacher's orders. Parents do their best to pull their distraught children away from the raised sticks. The adults around Joyce wipe their eyes and avoid her empty stare. They fight an impulse to stand and look in the direction of the infirmary. The whole thing has happened so fast that many of the children appear puzzled, and some of them repeatedly ask the older children nearby and the adults they can trust if it can really be so that the girl, Trina, just died in the arms of the gorilla. The same reply emerges from each responsible older child and adult as if learned by rote: If Father says the child is dead, then it has to be so.

And from being a clearing in the jungle where moments ago children ran in wild abandon, the compound converts into an empty mausoleum, no children in the open. Whimpers emanate from the oblong dormitories where the children dived for cover. An older girl soothes Rose while Ryan dabs the cut on her head. Several boys and girls covered in welts from the sticks sit with friends who comfort them and urge them at the same time to be quiet as they struggle to recover their composure. Their cries are discernible only by standing directly outside the dormitory's log building and listening for signs of distress. Guards practice this act of listening and leaning with an ear against a door only to bang against the door for absolute silence. The guards repeat the trick at other dormitories, and that proves sufficient, for soon the settlement returns to calm and industry, an air overlaid by the metronomic thrum of the power generator and an occasional splash of parrots mapping their flight paths with screeches or the ferocious tapping of woodpeckers pausing to squawk with delight at their progress drilling holes in the trunks of trees.

Adam peers through his bars around the empty compound and up at the sky, where the bales of cloud have all too soon begun to whittle away and become translucent and invisible in the dropping furnace of the sun. Branches on the zinc roof of Adam's cage deflect the heat and create an illusion of a natural habitat; tarpaulin curtains guard two sides of the cage against the sun's flame. A pile of bedding furnishes one area, mostly straw, small branches, old clothes, and, for entertainment, a large tree limb on the floor and an old tire suspended from a rope at the center of the cage. Adam avoids the trough of pig swill but tolerates his water bowl. On occasion he enjoys treats of fruit and confectionary.

It was not always like this. At one time the cage was never locked, and he could roam around the compound getting into mischief. Monkey business, the preacher called it. He wrestled with the commune guards, who seemed content to roll around with him on the floor until he clobbered them unintentionally, intending to fend off a blow or beat someone to the punch. This resulted in fewer romps on the floor of huts or in the grass, though there was always someone willing to challenge him and risk getting knocked around. Denied a watermelon, the gorilla became angry and took it anyway, cuffing the commune guard who stood between him and his food. The dismissive wave of his hand translated in human terms into a perfect sucker punch. A couple more guards approached, and he fought them off with a few well-aimed sweeps of his arms. Others arrived to chase him out of the storeroom when he was grabbing at one treat after another, some of which he ate in just one bite. He attracted more guards, and their numbers turned into a crowd. The cheers and smiles turned to jeers and curses.

Adam simply stopped reacting and bent his head and kept his eyes glued to the floor, forgetting half a mango and part of a watermelon, loaves of bread with just one chunk missing, bags of flour, rice, and sugar ripped open and sampled, vegetables scattered about. The guards prodded him with their sticks, and he moved from the storeroom, as directed, toward his cage. They shouted at him to keep moving and move faster. They herded him into his cage and added a chain and padlock, and that was the last day he tasted freedom.

On occasion, he gets scratched by the preacher on his preferred spot between his shoulder blades, just as his mother had scratched him before his capture. Every time he thinks about her he stares at the jungle as if she might walk out into the clearing to end her long search for him.

The preacher scratches him with a hand that feels a bit like hers but through the bars of a cage, and Adam has to offer his back as a sign that he welcomes a scratch and therefore it is a safe undertaking. He held a child in his arms, and that earned him his second beating. The child's mother screamed at him. He wishes he had his mother. She would scream at somebody to unlock her son's cage, and she would scratch his back with more affection and accuracy than the preacher.

TWO

The unpainted wooden structures nearest the preacher's house contain multiple families who are associated with the preacher in some personal capacity or have high standing in the commune. The doctor and nurses and the preacher's personal assistants and top bodyguards all live with their families in shared houses set apart from the other commune members, whose children sleep together in dormitories. Other buildings serve as the laundry, carpentry, foundry, sawmill, schoolroom, and numerous dormitories, all joined by walkways. Close to dusk, with the low sun filtered by the forest, four guards march to Adam's cage carrying long poles and a large piece of tarpaulin balanced between them. They spread the tarpaulin on the floor, thread the poles through two ends of the fabric, and hold up the sheet in front of Adam's cage to block his view of the compound and main house and infirmary. Adam hears a lot of activity coming from behind the screen. He sees, around the sides of the tarpaulin, a number of people approach his cage from all parts of the commune. The activity behind the tarpaulin stops, and the four guards collapse it, pull out the two poles from the ends, and fold the sheet by having two guards walk with their ends to the other two guards. Adam recoils from the scene that greets him. He stops seeing the guards in front of his cage as they untie the ends of the tarpaulin until the sheet shrinks to the size of a suitcase. All four guards drag the folded tarpaulin to one side and come back to the front of the cage, waving again their sticks and rifles, and order the people assembled to take a few steps back. Few people need any further motivation. They comply quickly. They know it is never a good idea to stand too close to an armed guard. Still, the assembly swells, bringing the work of the commune to a standstill. Expressions of astonishment and loud gasps fly around the gathering as new arrivals catch sight of the scene in front of the cage.

An open coffin sits there on a plinth. Two armed guards stand attention beside Trina's lifeless body. A third person, a nurse, fans flies from the child's face, powdered into a mask. Trina is adorned in an ornately laced full-length white cotton dress. Her mother pushes past the perimeter of guards in front of the cage and throws her body against the bars and bawls and implores Adam to take her life as he took her daughter's. Some women in the crowd start crying, too. Ryan and Rose lean on each other in disbelief. Joyce cries and pounds her fists on Adam's cage. She looks over at the community leader's house and only incidentally at Adam, and she hardly glances at her decorated child in the oblong box. Adam retreats to the back of his cage, suspicious of her performance. He worries that his proximity to her might get him into some sort of trouble. Perhaps a third beating. A group of the preacher's personal assistants and guards half-heartedly approaches Joyce, and she surrenders readily to their touch as they coax her away from the cage and the exhibit of her daughter.

Adam stares at Trina. He cannot be sure of his senses. She lies perfectly still. Her face is bone-white. Her lips have darkened with the lids of her eyes. Her hands clasped across her chest: white as well. And yet he expects her to leap onto her feet at any moment and resume her game of running from another child trying to catch her. Adam remembers how his mother grew just as still and how she failed to move no matter how much he implored her to attend to his cries. He thinks the girl might be in the same condition of helplessness. Could his grip have made her still the way his mother was long ago? He held her. Yes. She became still in his arms. Yes. Now she lies in a coffin in front of his cage. He turns away from the coffin and pictures a banana grove and a waterfall and his mother by his side. But his mind comes back to the child in the coffin. He sees himself in that box with his body reduced to the size of a child's and his mother not there to scream for him. He sees his mother as that child. And he howls and rattles the bars of his cage.

Everyone in the commune wipes away tears of approval at their distant cousin's display of remorse; sad as they are, they display gladness to see that Adam understands the meaning of his actions. The commune's spiritual leader stares into the cage through the bars. Adam entertains an impulse to grab the man and keep hold of him just as he grabbed the child and earned a pile of treats. But he shakes the thought from his head and avoids the preacher's dark, unblinking eyes. He knows this is the only man in the commune who does not fear him. He understands this lack of fear to mean that their fortunes are intertwined. If Adam knows one thing from his beating after he grabbed the girl, it is that his well-being depends on the preacher's: As long as the preacher leads this community, Adam will prosper with him; just as only the preacher's word can halt Adam's beatings, only the preacher's actions can alter Adam's fate.

The preacher walks to the coffin and waves his arms over the face of the girl. Two more guards approach, taking turns pushing forward a woman in their custody. She stands beside the coffin, and the preacher announces to everyone that a good prefect, the very son of this woman standing before him, exposed her for expressing doubts about the tragedy that has befallen Trina and her mother, Joyce. He gestures to the prefect, who takes a step forward and bows his head, and the people applaud. The preacher turns to the woman and asks if, in her layperson's opinion, she thinks the child is not really dead. He wants to know from her lips, because the report from her son, a trustworthy prefect, says that she thinks the child is pretending to be dead. The woman shakes her head. The preacher wants her to check for herself and tell the people gathered around them what she thinks she sees. The woman says she is not a doctor, and if the doctor pronounced the child dead, then it must be so, the child must be dead and gone, since the doctor is the expert. She apologizes for expressing any doubt and explains that her doubts were not said in disbelief but in a refusal to accept the loss of one so young.

The preacher invites various people in the crowd to come forward and see for themselves whether the child is pretending to be dead. He picks out individuals at random. Two guards are among the chosen. Each files forward and looks closely at Trina lying still as a log in her cot-sized coffin. Some start to cry, while others shake their heads in despair and make the sign of the cross, and one woman takes the preacher's hand and kisses it. The woman who kisses the ring of the preacher lunges for the woman branded as a disbeliever, but the guards block her path and gently restrain her and steer her back into the crowd. The doubting woman cowers. Except for the two guards pulled from the crowd, who take up positions near the preacher, all the other witnesses are sent back to their places. They look at the woman as if she is the devil incarnate. The preacher raises his thick eyebrows and stares at the woman. His act of looking at her lasts no longer than a second. She falls to her knees and begs the preacher's forgiveness. She tells the assembled crowd that the child is dead indeed. She says through her loud crying that it is a tragedy, but Trina is most definitely in the arms of the Almighty. The preacher nods in approval. He reminds her to keep her faith at the very moment when the devil of doubt and disbelief rears his ugly head. She says repeatedly:

—Thank you, Father. Thank you, Father.

The guards usher the woman back into the crowd. The people standing nearby edge away as if to avoid some form of contaminate. Her son, newly promoted from a prefect to a guard for demonstrating his loyalty to the preacher over loyalty to family, puts his arm around her. She stands there with her son's arm around her but keeps her arms by her sides and cries. The commune leader returns his attention to Trina in the coffin. Again he waves his hand over her head.

—God's child, listen. I speak to you as God's messenger.

He looks at Adam and nods, and Adam returns the nod. For a third time the preacher waves his arms over Trina and places his palms on her face and issues his order to her at the top of his voice:

—Arise, my child. God, rise up this child, release the pangs of death, because it is not possible for one of your children to be held by it.

The crowd leans forward, eyes darting from the preacher to the coffin and back. Adam mimics the movement. Joyce stands at the front of the crowd and stares at her daughter lying in the coffin. Two women flank Joyce and keep their hands on her as if to check any sudden movement.

The preacher stretches his hand toward Trina and pushes with his spread fingers at her head, roughly, the way a hand might make contact with someone who has slept through an alarm and the calling of a name.

—Arise, my child!

Joyce tightens her lips and narrows her eyes. She takes care to lower her head and hide her disapproval of the way the commune leader is handling her daughter. Only the preacher looks away from the coffin. He searches the faces of the crowd for any trace of defiance, and finding his scrutiny met with cowed compliance, from averted eyes to heads lowered into shoulders, he returns his attention to the coffin fitted with Trina.

—Get up out of the coffin, child!

What happens next takes a couple of seconds to begin, seconds that appear to slow down and stall just long enough for the crowd to come to terms with the possibility of an impossible occurrence. Eyes search the sky just in case some external force might actually come into play. The people glance at one another and back to the coffin and preacher. Adam's eyes chase the people's stares from the heavens to one another and then the coffin. Joyce keeps her eyes on her daughter. The preacher repeats his action, pushing his fingers against Trina's forehead as he speaks.

—Arise, my child, and take your rightful place among the living!

A gasp escapes the crowd as Trina jerks awake. She rises staggeringly to her feet. People faint. Small children scream and hide behind their parents. Ryan and Rose cling to each other. Rose buries her face in Ryan's shirt. The prefect, who betrayed his mother for expressing doubts about Trina's condition, falls to his knees, and his mother hesitates for just a moment before she drops to her knees beside him. Adam grabs the bars of his cage and thuds his head against them, eyes wide. His nostrils flare as he sniffs the space between Trina and him. The preacher offers an arm and Trina takes it, steadies herself, and steps out of the coffin as gingerly as one might step out of a bath. She curtsies and smiles to ecstatic applause. She leans against the coffin and shades her eyes, looking into the crowd for her mother. Joyce runs to her with open arms and scoops her off her feet and squeezes her nearly as hard as Adam. Mother and daughter sob. Ryan and Rose walk up to Trina and Joyce. Trina sees them and smiles. They stretch out their hands slowly and touch Trina lightly and quickly retract their arms. Joyce pulls them close to her and all four embrace. Rose feels Joyce's arm around her shoulders and imagines it is her banished mother, not Trina's, who hugs her. The people keep up their cheering and applause and bow their heads repeatedly in the direction of their leader. Some of the women fall to their knees and forcibly drag their children down with them. Others follow suit, their arms busy making the sign of the cross. Whispers of praise the Lord and Father begin and spread throughout the crowd, and a chant builds and rises to a crescendo of: Hallelujah. Praise Father. Bless Father. The preacher nods at them and looks proudly at Adam and bares his Tic-Tac teeth.

—You are all witnesses of how God works His miracles through me?

—Yes, Father.

—I am flesh and blood like you, but my faith in God is strong, and God feels it and works His miracles through me.

The crowd says over and over, Praise the Lord.

—Repeat after me, my children. We will die . . .

—We will die.

—... But we will rise again.

—But we will rise again.

—Repeat. We are destined to die ...

—We are destined to die.

—... And surely we will rise again.

—And surely we will rise again.

—For the kingdom of heaven is ours. Repeat!

—For the kingdom of heaven is ours.

Spontaneous applause and more shouts of hallelujah ripple through the crowd. Several hundred adults hug one another, and the children take the cue and clasp hands and jump up and down. The preacher steps up to the bars of the cage. Adam suppresses an impulse to leap at the bars and grab his master, not to capture him but to feel if he is the same as the girl and the guards, the same soft flesh and pliable bones. Adam notices that the man's left arm is behind his back. Adam focuses on that arm, interested in whatever surprise might be stored there. The preacher nods again, and Adam copies the nod and cracks his face with a smile. Next, the commune leader produces a banana and pushes his arm through the bars. Adam does not hesitate. He grabs the banana, taking care to touch part of the man's hand. He finds that the hand is softer than he expects, almost as soft as the proffered fruit. Adam thinks, Father, just like everyone in the commune.

Joyce leads her daughter from the cage through a forest of arms tapping them on the head and shoulders and through a sea of smiles and wet faces. Joyce lifts her dress and wipes Trina's face with the hem.

—Let's clean you up and get you out of these clothes.

—Can I keep the dress for a special occasion?

For an answer, Joyce looks at one of the assistants, who nods her approval and tells Trina to go to the house and pick up a brand-new flute. They march inside, and Trina admires the walls hung with masks and carvings of oddly shaped figures and paintings of campfire scenes and spies; propped in one corner is a large glass case that resembles a fish tank, divided into four compartments housing two tarantulas and two scorpions. Trina walks her fingers and thumb along the glass, over one of the labels, *Guyana Pinktoe*, written in neat cursive, and a tarantula creeps toward her hand before she hurriedly withdraws. She taps on the glass of the Gormar scorpion, and it scuttles to meet her hand, and she withdraws again. She hesitates and reminds herself that even scorpions cannot sting through glass, then reaches forward and presses against the place where the scorpion rests. The guard warns her not to tap or touch if she wants to remain in the reverend's good books. An assistant appears and hands Trina a wooden flute. Joyce nudges her.

—What do you say?

—Thank you very much.

Trina turns the flute over in her hands and hugs it. She wants to try out a few notes, but she thinks better of it because her lips are covered in dark lipstick. Her mother leads her out of the house and Trina hangs on to the flute with one hand and her mother's hand with the other. They head from the main house to the infirmary with the nurse and the doctor, who says he wants to make sure the child is all right.

Very few people remain in the wide clearing between the preacher's house and Adam's cage. Most have dissolved into the surrounding buildings, back to the kitchen and food hall, the bakery, the schoolhouse, the laundry building, the separate dormitories for adults and children, and the mill with its adjoining incinerator and chimney stack, or else farther out to the fields and outlying pig farm. The preacher retreats from the cage, dips his hands into a basket, and returns to the side of the cage with his hands full of fruit and bread. An assistant carries a bucket of water. Father unlocks the cage. Adam thinks fleetingly that he should dash for the exit and keep running until he is far from this place of sticks and whip and back with his mother among the trees, vines, and chatter of birds, in her embrace before she was knocked to the ground by a nail hole he tested with his finger hoping to wake her moments before a net pinned him down and he was dragged away from her. But his Father cares for him in a way that makes him want to stay in his cage and hope for more gifts of fruit and back scratches, maybe even for his master to return the life robbed from his mother's body. As his master steps into the cage, Adam holds out his hands and lowers his head to make it clear that all he wants are the treats and nothing else. Nothing bad will happen, no grabbing, no sudden movement, not even a growl. And it works. The preacher hands treats to Adam and pours a bucket into his drinking bowl, and all seems to return to the harmony of before, except Adam remains confined to his cage. No mother for him but Father. Many people visit his cage, and he turns his back, and a friendly hand that is not his master's scratches him.

The children exercise the utmost care in the vicinity of Adam's cage. They still stone him if an adult is not nearby to catch them. Not Trina. She walks close by if her mother is not looking, almost within an arm's length. She asks Ryan and Rose not to pelt Adam. Ryan wants to know why her change of heart. Trina says being locked in a cage is bad enough for the beast. When she looks at Adam, she says she feels lucky to be alive. Adam could have crushed her after she fainted in his arms and the men continued to lash him. But he did not.

—He killed you.

—No, Rose. All Adam did was squeeze me a bit too hard.

—Ryan wants to know if Father really did that to you, Trina.

—Yes. We must never speak about it. I am a ghost.

Trina holds up her arms and shakes her hands:

—Boo!

Ryan and Rose recoil from her and laugh, hands over mouths to stifle the sound, eyes roving left and right for any prefect or adult sure to object to such levity.

Adam likes to watch the children at work or running and screaming with delight. Their missiles puzzle him. He never meant to hurt the girl. He feels sorry that he grabbed her and held her too tight and she ended up in a box on display in front of his cage, lying as still as his mother when she fell with a finger-sized hole in her head.

THREE

The preacher hands Joyce an envelope containing a list of names of government officials with sums beside their names.

—Go to the capital and disperse these funds for me.

—Yes, Father.

—Come straight back. I need Trina and you here.

—Of course, Father.

Joyce and Trina almost break into a run to get to the landing pier, restrained only by the presence of the two guards assigned to accompany them. They see the captain again for the first time in weeks. He is glad, though he, too, keeps his enthusiasm from erupting in front of the guards. Nevertheless, they hug quickly. Each has to wrench away arms that do not wish to let go. Each pulls back from resting a head on a familiar shoulder for too long. The first mate joins in as well. The captain and the first mate shake hands with the guards, Eric and Kevin, who take turns announcing to Joyce within earshot of Captain and First Mate that relations should be seen as more formal between the commune and outsiders, no matter how friendly the outsiders. Joyce apologizes.

The first mate unmoors the boat and throws the two rope anchors on board and hops back from the wharf onto the *Coffee*. The captain sweeps the vessel around and the river pulls at the craft and the engine goes up an octave as they embark. Parts of the river's surface capture the faint blue that pushes through thin cloud cover. Parakeets swoop their rainbow banners left and right, moving fast in orchestration and with what might be construed as raucous group laughter.

The captain and Joyce separately ponder the idea of more formality between them. Trina takes out her sketchpad and pencils and sits, looking all around at the shifting scene of the riverbank, the tumble of the water and the slide of sky, two skies to be accurate, and this starts her pencil scribbling, one sky above and another reflected on the river's glass.

Kevin and Eric look at their charges every now and again but mostly they chat with each other as they play cards for secret stashes of commune-proscribed loot. They confine their exclamations to outward apparel in lieu of mild cursing since none is allowed by the community.

—Jacket!

—Oh, skirt.

First Mate Anthony demonstrates the latest disco moves to a bunch of eager young passengers, moves that he claims rule the clubs in L.A. and New York. He gets the passengers to begin a slow clap while he gyrates and thrusts out his arms and spins on the spot, and without knowing what unfolds there, a viewer might mistake the first mate for an epileptic in the throes of a seizure, being egged on by a set of cruel witnesses.

Joyce launches into an attempt to convince Kevin and Eric of a cool impartiality toward the captain. She winks at the captain before she draws him into a typical debate between a commune devotee and an outside skeptic.

—But Captain Aubrey, all this sensory stuff to do with the boat ride is an illusion.

—What you call an illusion, all this, is all there is, Miss Joyce.

—Paradise is all this and more, everlasting life, but you settle for material well-being, which is transitory, and sacrifice spiritual wealth.

—Food, clothing, and shelter come before pursuit of an afterlife.

—The only true calling is a study of the ways and means to get closer to God.

—I run my boat and mind my own business and live my good life as best as I can.

—Your so-called good life is nothing without a belief in paradise, why settle for less?

—This life is rich and more than enough for me.

—The reverend teaches us that the material pursuit is such a powerful illusion that those who believe in it cannot see beyond what is in front of their eyes.

—I have my charts and a compass, and I know where I am going.

—But you don't have love in your life, you don't have God, and you think that the life you see all around you is all the life that there is, and you are wrong.

—No more wrong than those who believe in what they cannot see as the only thing to aim for in the blind belief that they will wake up and find it waiting for them. Meanwhile, they neglect the precious world around them or treat their flesh with disdain.

—What's flesh when compared with the spirit? Nothing. Spirit is everything.

Both Eric and Kevin cast satisfied glances at Joyce and give the captain a triumphant stare that tells him he has met his intellectual match. They are pleased to have Joyce on their side.

—The captain's on the ropes, nah, the canvas, and he doesn't have the grace to surrender.

—Joyce's our smartest emissary.

—After the reverend.

—Goes without saying.

The *Coffee* cuts a path through the river, and the wake fans out behind the boat and holds out the promise of permanence, but only for a while, only as long as it takes the current to obliterate that wake and restore the river's mirror as if the boat never cut through there.

Two guards meet Joyce's party at the city port. One acts as a driver, the other bears a rifle for their protection. They pack into a seven-seat jeep. The streets of the capital—lit somewhat selectively, since the national grid functions at an historical low—present a tableau of shadows interspersed with islands of luminosity. Most of the big houses operate generators, and the engines make parts of the city sound like an all-night Formula 1 race. The reality is different, few cars and even fewer people on foot. Army jeeps patrol with searchlights that they direct down dark alleys and at pedestrians who shield their faces and answer questions about their destinations and sometimes are searched at gunpoint and relieved of a sizable portion of any currency found on them, which the locals refer to as being taxed, since there is an official dimension to this heist, as distinct from being choked and robbed or mugged by a gang or kidnapped for ransom.

Fights break out between territorial dogs, thin mangy strays as fierce as bulls. The barks and yelps, though sporadic, are as distinct as gunfire in a shoot-out. On a couple of occasions an army jeep challenges the commune jeep before quickly waving them on their way, sometimes even with an apology. The unwritten practice is never to impose an impromptu tax on commune people, because they operate a system of bribes as efficient as any corporate payroll.

The headlights pick up men walking in the dark. The men wear their shirts rolled up to expose their midriffs. They shield their eyes from the glare and wave at the jeep for it to stop and give them a ride. The jeep passes garishly dressed women brushed fleetingly by the foraging headlamps and erased by the pursuing dark. Parts of the women's bodies appear for a moment to be plucked from anonymity by the sweep of the headlights and thrown back into it, as the headlights move on: a bare thigh or near-exposed breast, a red-lipped smile, a wink. They are watched over by men's shadows lingering near cars with open doors and loud music.

The jeep pulls up in front of a large building with a wooden sign stating that it is the headquarters of the People's Commune. Trina sleeps, exhausted. Joyce carries her while Kevin and Eric diligently open and close various doors for Joyce's smooth conveyance from jeep and street to front door to parlor, into corridor, and upstairs to a guest bedroom. Joyce deposits Trina in bed with a kiss, freshens up with a quick shower and change of clothes, and heads back downstairs for the business of the commune with the names on her list, business that lasts late into the night.

She looks over the bookkeeping for the commune office building with the secretary stationed there and says she cannot ratify the accounts due to several irregularities. She runs her finger on a countertop and shakes off the dust and looks at the secretary for an explanation.

—We had to fire the cleaner. She stole from us.

—Well, hire someone else. This place represents us. First impressions are lasting ones.

—Yes, Miss Joyce.

Cars with ministerial or other official government plates, some with army and police escorts, including the interior minister's, pull up outside the headquarters in a steady stream. Joyce greets the officials while surrounded by Kevin, Eric, and other commune guards and leads them to a back room where envelopes swap hands and instructions pass from mouth to ears and understandings are understood and little pleasantries lead to warm partings and more greetings for more of the same and the same old same old.

On the early drive back to the port, they meet an unusual traffic jam. A cart has broken down in the road, and it seems the driver might be waiting for volunteers to amass in sufficient numbers to help him drag the cart and horse to one side. But when the jeep pulls almost to the front of the queue of vehicles inching around the accident, it becomes clear that the long cart laden with huge logs looks fine, with all four of its wheels upright on the two axles, but the horse that is supposed to pull the cargo slumps on all fours even as the owner repeatedly lashes the unresponsive beast with a long and very thick stick.

The noise of the beating makes Trina cover her ears. Joyce holds on to Trina to gain comfort as much as to offer it. The stick sounds like it should snap in two or the horse's flesh tear free or its bones shatter. Each lash seems to reverberate in the jeep. Joyce slams her fist on the front of her seat and orders the driver to unlock the doors. The driver says he knows things out there must look bad, but the commune cannot get involved with the daily life of the city. Joyce tells the driver that unless he unlocks the door immediately, she will break the glass and climb out the jeep's window. Trina stops cringing, distracted by Joyce's protest. The driver looks at the other armed guard in the front seat, who avoids his eyes, and so he sends his visual appeal to Kevin and Eric, who shrug. He presses the button and unlocks the doors. Joyce storms out of the jeep. The driver implores her to ignore the melee, which he says is going on right now on every street, and would she want them to solve all of them? Joyce pushes her way to the front of the onlookers and shouts at the man:

—Can't you see the beast is spent?

—Spent? This beast owes me.

The man is indignant. He turns and again swings his stick at the horse. Joyce hurries back to the jeep and asks Eric for his rifle. The guard looks at her with enough incredulity to stop a charging elephant in its tracks. But Joyce pulls the rifle away from his grasp, through the open window. It is the same incredulity in the co-driver that keeps him from resisting her. Joyce marches back through the crowd parting for her, and she approaches the cart. The horse now lies on its side, and the cart man looms over it with his long stick and swings away. He might be beating dust out of a carpet or driving a large stave into the ground. He grunts with the effort of his lashes. This time Eric and Kevin brandish their rifles and follow Joyce. The crowd ducks out of her way. She aims shakily and fires. People nearest to her dive and run. The man swinging the stick stops and turns to face Joyce. She lowers the rifle and thanks him for his undivided attention and says the next bullet will not be into the air.

—Drop the stick.

Joyce supports the rifle with palms that move about the barrel as if trying to recognize by touch exactly what it is that those hands bear. She aims it straight at the driver of the cart. The man curses and drops the stick.

—Thank you.

The cart owner shrugs. Murmurs sweep around the growing group of bystanders. He glances at them but cannot make out if the whispers condone or condemn Joyce's actions or his. Joyce hands her rifle to Kevin, who now has two of them to handle.

Joyce snatches the whip from the cart owner. She lifts the stick and brings it down hard on the legs of the cart driver, who skips and moves toward her as if to retaliate but thinks better of it as he sees the guards aiming rifles at him. Joyce hits the man two more times, each blow harder than the one before. She is crying, and the cart driver capitulates and says he is sorry for being rude and promises to take better care of his horse.

—The blasted animal is letting me down. I got deliveries to make; many mouths to feed.

—You're destroying your livelihood in a cruel fashion.

Joyce hands his stick to him and dries her eyes on her dress and asks the cart driver how much it would cost him to rest the horse for a couple of days and hire another beast of burden to finish his day's work. The cart driver rubs his bruised leg and names a price. Joyce suggests a lower price. The cart driver throws out a third figure a little above Joyce's. They agree. Joyce asks Kevin and Eric to hand over the notes, and the crowd applauds and Joyce finds extra notes for all of them, and the cheers follow them as they drive away.

FRED D'AGUIAR

On their way to the port, they joke about the look on the cart man's
face. The guards tell Joyce that she is a true representative of the People's
Commune, and brave. They pass vendors with ripe fruit hanging on string
from rickety stalls, a gauntlet of honey and flower smells and loud inducements to stop and taste and buy a little something with wide gestures and
smiling, inviting faces. They pass schoolchildren in pressed uniforms with
satchels, filing along the roadside with combed hair and neat plaits and
oiled faces, elbows, and knees. And sheep and goats meandering into the
lane of traffic, some dragging a rope they must have chewed through or
pulled free from some pen. Chickens peck at minuscule grub in the roadside pebbles. Dogs trot from shade to shade and eye each other cautiously,
more so than the deadlier vehicles passing inches from them. Joyce hugs
Trina, and Trina keeps hold of her mother all the way to the port.

The captain and first mate look glad to meet them again, and the
return journey includes much respectful trust shown by Kevin and Eric to
Joyce. They tell the story of the cart man and his horse, and the captain
and first mate nod and look at Joyce with new eyes.

The first mate jumps into the conversation:

—Captain, tell Trina one of your Anansi stories.

—Cousin, you want me to bore the child to tears.

—What's Anansi?

—You mean who, Trina. He's a spider character, and he likes to play
tricks on everyone.

—Did you make him up?

—No. He comes all the way from Africa.

—Trina, you're making your mother look bad. Don't you remember
those Brer Rabbit stories?

—I know, Mom. But I want to hear an Anansi story from Mr. Captain. Please.

—The captain's busy, Trina. We're almost at the commune.

—I'm never too busy to tell Anansi stories. We could start one and
finish it next time.

—Yes, Mr. Aubrey Captain, tell me one.

—Just Captain will do, Trina. So you want to hear about Anansi?

—Yes, Captain.

Trina sits next to the captain as he commands the *Coffee*, and she listens to one of his Anansi stories, something about the spider having to share a hand of bananas with his wife and four children and he gives one banana to each of them and he has none left for himself and so he hangs his head and waits and his family feels sorry for him and each child and his wife break off a quarter of their banana and give it to him and he ends up with the most banana. The captain ends by saying:

—What a clever scamp!

Trina agrees. The captain hands the wheel to his first mate and strolls over to talk with Joyce. Later they dock to eat and stretch their legs, and the captain makes sure he finds Joyce and Trina for company. The first mate sits with Trina to look at her sketches, and this gives the captain time with Joyce. Kevin and Eric no longer look warily at outsiders, at least not their present company; instead, they seem engrossed in conversation with each other.

As the *Coffee* sidles up to the commune's dock, the captain swears it is the fastest voyage he has ever made. They shake hands. All agree with some regret in their voices that this particular journey has come to an end until the captain says in jest:

—As must all our journeys in this sweet life, my friends.

Joyce, Eric, Kevin, and Trina stop and look at the captain for a moment, and they leave with a darkened demeanor, a gloom that the captain and his first mate puzzle over after their friends have left.

—The feeling that comes over you when someone walks over your grave?

—Like they saw a ghost.

—You mean us?

—No, themselves.

FOUR

The settlers battle the wild every day. Light crawls up the trunks of trees all around the settlement. Red flames lick the branches and leaves as the sun buries itself in the horizon. A flock of parakeets spreads a bright palette across the stretched canvas of sky. Their notes are sharp and wild, like an orchestra warming up. Trina cranes her neck for the swirl and picture of them. The flock disappears into the trees, and the forest echoes with the cutting sound of birds playing hide-and-seek. She waits for clouds to sweep by with sketches of a city. Each group of buildings that shifts in and out of view in that cloud drift resembles the city she left long ago. Sometimes she sees hills, faces, and animals. But never the millions of trees that surround her. A forest has no reflection. And it reflects nothing. It only absorbs.

The preacher emerges from his house; the two bodyguards stationed at the front door jump to attention, and the children freeze in the middle of their trash collecting. He looks around and calls for Trina. She steps forward and quickly wipes her face and hands on her dress and tries to smooth it in an effort to look presentable as she approaches him. He waves at the other children to carry on. The children spring back into action. Ryan and Rose resume their work after positioning themselves so they can look at Trina and the preacher. He hands Trina his handkerchief. She seems reluctant to take it, and he nods and pushes it at her a second time, and she takes it and wipes sweat from her face, neck, arms, and hands. She tries to hand the handkerchief back but he tells her to keep it. He leads her toward the cage, but she pulls against him. He releases his grip on her arm and walks up to the cage and swivels his back against it. Adam charges toward the bars, where the man presses his back. Trina covers her eyes and peeps through her fingers. Adam reaches the bars and spins around and fits his much broader back to the preacher's. Adam turns his head to the side and glances over his right shoulder to catch a glimpse of his master and of Trina, to see what they will do next and what will be required of him. The commune leader gestures to Trina. She takes small, slow steps toward the cage and freezes as Joyce screams:

—Trina! Come to your mother right now.

The two bodyguards at the house take a couple of steps toward Trina's mother with the butts of their rifles ready to stop her. The preacher raises his arm and they stop in their tracks. They look at him to see what he wants them to do about Joyce's public display of parental insubordination. Father beckons again to Trina to come to him, and this time he trains his eyes on Trina's mother. His stare works its ministry on her. His way of looking without blinking and with his black eyes apparently devoid of emotion prefigures instances of huge upheaval in the commune, long scenes of public humiliation for a follower gone astray and in need of correction, hours of sermonizing from the evening into early morning. He stares at something hidden in Trina's mother, something deposited by him in her skull for safekeeping, and now he wants to see that hidden thing again to make sure not only that it is still there, just where he left it, but that the secret property remains in the same mint condition in which he deposited it. She gave him her love and this love was not hers to take back, just as she trusted his teachings and that trust would be taken to the grave. Trina's mother abandons her summons of her daughter. Her lips stop working. All the strength in her body drains from her and takes her legs from under her. She flops to the ground right there in the dirt.

Trina reacts by quickening her pace toward the preacher. He holds out his arms and she offers her outstretched hands to him. He grasps her hands, pulls her next to him, and turns around to face the cage. He pushes her arms into the cage and places her hands directly on the back of the gorilla. Rose wants to rush to Trina's aid, but Ryan holds on to her. Joyce waves at them. The two walk over quickly to Joyce's side, and she holds on to them as they help her to her feet. Trina feels giddy. But the man's arms are warm, and the gorilla's back warmer and hard, and the hairs on it bristly like something she should pull away from. But she stays very still and tries to keep breathing, inhaling more deeply with each breath. Adam's broad back lifts and falls. Trina feels the man's hands on hers. Her hands under his direction can touch anything, even fire, and remain unscathed. He is Father to all. He plucked each and every one of them from their mad and aimless ways and brought them to the wilderness and placed them one step closer to paradise. The man moves her hands around on the gorilla's back and releases his grip on her hands and begins to scratch the gorilla's back, and Trina scratches as well, the same action of sinking her fingers into the tough hair and muscle. The gorilla slumps to the floor of his cage, and the man and Trina stoop and keep up their scratching. The man gives Trina a mango; her empty belly growls and her mouth waters, but she knows what she has to do without any instruction. She pushes the mango. He takes the fruit between his pouted lips before steadying it with his hands.

—You are practicing with your new flute?

—Yes, Father.

—You should practice right here by the cage. Adam likes music and he likes you.

—Yes, Father.

The preacher stands. He is dirty. He helps Trina up and they walk to her mother. Ryan and Rose take a few steps back from Joyce. The preacher offers his hand to Trina's mother, and she takes it in her dusty condition with her face wet and her nose running. He takes his handkerchief from Trina and offers it to Joyce. She shakes her head. He keeps his hand extended toward her. His eyes soften. He smiles. She smiles back. She takes the dirty handkerchief and wipes her eyes and nose. The preacher places Trina's hand in her mother's hand, and before he turns from them, he asks that they make sure they sit in the front row at his evening sermon. He disappears with his assistants and two bodyguards close behind him before Trina's mother can return his soiled handkerchief. He walks in long urgent strides as if late for another appointment but heads straight back to his private quarters, the only building in the compound painted white and standing apart from all the others.

Trina and Joyce remain on the spot until the preacher enters his house with his three assistants. The two bodyguards close the front door and station themselves on either side of it. Joyce looks at Trina's face and plants a kiss on each cheek. She shakes her head and gazes up at the sky and back at the white house with the guards, where the preacher who brought them over the ocean to their retreat in the middle of the jungle dreams up his plots for their lives. His eyes and his words led them all to this remote location. He promised them it would be temporary. Not him so much as his eyes and his words. No one she knows can resist the two. And everyone around here, including Joyce, hopes his words and his certainty will bring them salvation right here on earth.

Until her arrival in this country, Joyce cannot remember meeting another man to compare with the preacher. Her view of him as someone who stood at the apex of a pyramid with everyone else stacked on a broad plain below remained intact up to the day she met the captain onboard the *Coffee* with his young first mate for that first journey upriver from the capital to the commune. Her nonstop talk about the preacher and his vision for their community hid the fact that in her head, the captain grew to share that privileged position on the highest plinth. Every detail she and Trina clamped eyes on in their first trip upriver, from the city to the commune, confirmed the miracle of the place. They wanted to know everything about everything they saw, heard, felt, smelled, and tasted. At the time, the captain appeared glad to indulge them, even if mother and child were indistinguishable in their unbridled enthusiasm for the interior of the country.

The preacher emerges again from his house earlier that evening and visits Adam, who nods and smiles along with the man's nods and smiles. Father lingers and Adam offers his back. The preacher scratches it. Adam's eyes relax. After the preacher scratches Adam's back, he turns and offers his back to Adam. Surprised, Adam takes a step away from the bars of the cage. His eyes shift in rapid thought. But the preacher waits, and Adam steps close to the bars and scratches the man's back the same way the man scratches Adam's, with both hands at the same time. Adam tears Father's white shirt, and red spots blossom on the preacher's back, and he moves away quickly. The commune leader steps out of reach of Adam's arms, smiling. Adam returns a mirror image of that smile as if his face looked exactly like Father's face. The preacher yawns and stretches and heads back to his house. Adam yawns loudly, stretches, and lumbers to the bed at the back of his cage.

The preacher and all the people, children included, move and make noises that Adam feels mimic his movements and sounds. He thinks his body splinters into a thousand pieces to occupy a large clearing in the forest. He watches the entire commune's comings and goings and feels parts of him leave the confines of his cage and roam the compound at will. Looking at the people going about their business leaves him feeling he is all of them rolled into one. This feeling, that his body mirrors a thousand fragments made of people, intensifies when he peers at the sky and follows the splayed wings of solo birds, or latches on to a flock, as the whole assembly swirls in the breeze. Adam believes his body belongs to their bodies. They are all the parts of him.

FIVE

Adam's bones ache. His skin tingles with a small current rising to the surface. Storm clouds gather and block the sun. Darkness drops without a parachute. A crack of lightning and drumroll of thunder stop the adults at their chores and the children in the middle of school. Commune members working in the open, trimming bushes, uprooting weeds, tending to farm animals, securing barbed wire fences, all dart for shelter. A few large drops bang on the tin roofs. Fat drops, wide apart and able to kick up dust and slap it down again. The drops stitch together and wall up space. They multiply and become a barrage of stones on the galvanized zinc. The pigs squeal and the dogs bark. Adam hoots and stands back from the front of his cage. The guards shout to the heavens to be quiet before they wake Father, but more lightning flashes and a tree tumbles to the forest floor. The thunder persists, rolling across the compound in a stampede on the ground and in the air, above the heads of the guards. Some guards grab their rifles, aim at the sky, and make firing noises with their mouths. Children scream with each rip of thunder. A guard accidentally pulls the trigger on his rifle, and it barely registers above the storm. Adam jumps into the air and shrieks and curls up in a tight bundle with his arms around his head to hide his face and cover his ears. The sound of the rain lashing at vegetation and earth reminds him of his back getting beaten by sticks and the butts of rifles.

Though the thunder rolls away into the distance, still the dark clouds deluge the compound. Usually, Adam likes to stick his hand through his bars and collect the ropes of rain as they lash his arm. But the lightning and thunder have made him shiver. Rain beats on everything. Adam listens to the drums, and finally begins to relax and unfold. Soon he dozes. People expect the preacher's door to open at any moment and for him to add his bellow of disapproval to the general upheaval. But his door remains closed. His personal nurse and assistant, Pat, tiptoes into the living room and finds him fast asleep, curled on his side with his hand over his ear. She picks up the cover he kicked off and drapes it over him, and he does not even stir. She leans in to make sure he is breathing, and she smiles. She opens the front door with less care this time and reports to the guards in a normal speaking voice that the preacher is fine and asleep, and in his present condition he can sleep through an air raid. She sits with them on the front porch and watches the rain lash the life out of things and choke gutters and pour down walls and well up in drains and spread outward and create instant rivulets that snake in every direction. As the thunder echoes in the distance and the rain continues to spread sheet after sheet, the children run out into the open and turn their heads to the sky and spread their arms and drink the rain, bolting left and right to catch as much as possible. The guards hold up their arms in protest, but the children prove too many for the guards to corral. A few of the children obey and turn for indoors but just as soon run back outside again and sprint from the guards and rejoin the large group dashing around and screeching. The downpour washes the children, the leaves, grass, and vines. All appear sprightly, polished, and renewed.

—Mom, can I go out?

—No, Trina.

The air smells fresh and lighter to breathe. The rain switches off, and the children move from running in the rain to playing in the instant mud pools. They run through the wet and mud and stop looking for a prefect, guard, or adult to shout at them. They dive into the freshly filled pond. Trina stares, wide-eyed, from a window as Ryan and Rose and many more of the children gather in the pond. Trina makes a move for the door but sees her mother shaking her head disapprovingly.

—Mom, can I go out? Please.

—No, Trina.

—But all the other children are out there having fun.

—Use your head, child.

Her mother taps her skull as she speaks:

—That kind of fun will only bring them trouble.

—I never get to have any fun. I'm the only one left out of everything.

—Trina, that's nonsense, and you know it.

—But it's true. Why can't I go out and play with the other children?

—You know why? You know how things can take a bad turn in this place.

—Just this once, Mom, please.

Trina runs to her mother and hugs her. Joyce keeps her arms by her sides.

—Please, Mom.

Trina stares into her mother's face. Joyce keeps shaking her head.

—Please, Mom. Please.

—I said no. Practice your flute.

Trina's big black eyes fill with water, and rather than loosen her embrace, the child holds on even tighter. Joyce feels her conviction dissolve.

—Please, Mom. I can practice later.

Trina tightens her hug even more. Joyce finds her arms leaving her sides, seemingly powered by their own need to return Trina's affection. All the sensible arguments for keeping Trina safe under her watchful eyes turn to powder and dissolve as she embraces her daughter.

—Okay. But I thought you were hungry.

—I am hungry, and I want to play. I'll practice my flute later.

Trina kisses Joyce, who smiles and kisses her back.

—Promise.

—I promise.

—And remember, not a word to anyone about Father's business.

—I won't. Thanks, Mom.

Trina dashes from her mother's arms. She sprints into the muddy fray. Joyce walks over to the window. She tries to keep track of Trina, but her child quickly disappears into the thick of other children all covered in mud and not distinguishable by name or face except in varying degrees of height and whether the mud-slicked creature wears a dress or a pair of shorts.

Adam opens his eyes and shuffles up to the bars of his cage and presses his body against it for the best view of the children. Maybe another child will trip into his cage. The children splash in the mud and pelt each other with clumps. Ryan and Rose greet Trina. They hug briefly and hop on the spot, beside themselves at the prospect of all this fun.

—What kept you? Ryan knows but asks Trina anyway.

—You know my mother. Everything's too dangerous until it isn't.

Her answer makes Rose and Ryan laugh. A few others gather around. Trina, since her resurrection, is the most popular child at the compound. The children spontaneously grab her. They lift her off the ground. They swing her and count one, two, three, and fling her into the water. Her limbs fly as she splashes down untidily. She springs to her feet with a broad smile and triumphant waves of her arms, which produce raucous laughter all around. Adam somersaults in appreciation and rattles his bars and leaps about as if he, too, frolics amid the throng and has several hands swinging him into the pond. Trina stands up and falls back into the pond.

She stands in the muddy water and looks at Adam, who somersaults and claps. She keeps her arms by her sides and her back and legs straight as she falls backward, shouting:

—Timber!

Again, Adam somersaults, claps, and hoots. A third time and a fourth, and each time the same appreciative gymnastics and applause and gutturals from Adam. More children join Trina in the pond. Ryan organizes the children in lines and gets them to count to three, and a forest of young trees fall into the water and Adam somersaults, claps, and guffaws.

But prefects must be perfect, and guards designated to guard something or other feel compelled to do their duty. Each watches the next and waits for one of them to do something, to take it upon himself to file a report with the preacher, who is nowhere in sight, and become the one who benefits, perhaps with a promotion from speaking up, while the rest would face questions and criticisms for allowing such a demonstration to take place. The young man recently promoted from a prefect to a guard, who enjoys punishing the children at every opportunity, says he has a job to do and he will do it rather than try to second-guess their leader or anyone else. He grabs his stick and runs to meet the children. The other guards, adults, and prefects follow him and pour out of doorways and from under awnings with their sticks raised. The prefects and guards lash the children on their arms and legs and make them hop and skip and cry and beg.

A child screams with joy and a child screams in pain, and the difference is in the timbre of that scream. Decibels of joy strike the inner ear differently from those of pain. The children's cries wake the preacher from a deep sleep. Tuned to the distress calls of children, he wakes with a start, not as a man in charge of multitudes in a commune of his own making but as a child in the Midwest, left in a tornado shelter while his father retrieves something from the house, and covering his ears and crying for his father as the ground over his head thunders. The preacher wakes and shakes off the image and staggers to the front door, his limbs not quite his. He fumbles for the handle and throws the door open. The newly washed sun blinds him with its tentacles burning through remnants of cloud, turning the puddles to mirrors aimed at the preacher's face. He barely makes out the figures of children flailing their arms and hopping to avoid the lashes of adults and older peers, but the cries sail unimpeded into his ears, and to stop it all, he bellows at them:

—Cease and desist!

He shocks the guards and prefects to a standstill. Pat, his nurse, jumps to attention. He repeats the three words over and over. Everyone freezes, and some of the prefects drop their sticks. The children dive into the buildings to hide from the preacher's voice. Many cover their ears.

—Cease and desist!

He keeps shouting. Anyone in the commune not able to see the preacher must hear him. All of those able to see him standing in the doorway of his house must wonder what they should do next to show him they have heard and obeyed. They have ceased and desisted. A few voices say:

—Yes, Father.

This spreads among them and a chorus grows:

—Yes, Father.

He covers his face with his hands and appears to cough repeatedly into them. His entire body shakes but he does not make a sound. He stamps his right foot then his left then his right then his left, not quite marching on the spot more like trying to drive some stubborn thing into the ground. Every adult in the place chants.

—Yes, Father.

Many cry openly. Others fall to their knees and sob and keep repeating:

—Yes, Father.

Every adult in the place chants it, and many cry openly for the upset they have caused in their Savior. The doctor and nurse and several assistants run to him. Pat grabs one of the preacher's elbows, the doctor the other, and they steer the preacher back into the front door. The doctor places a firm hand in the small of the preacher's back, and Pat calms him in her most soothing voice:

—Yes, they will do as you say, Father, they will do exactly as you ask, you can relax now, let me make you a nice cool drink. You sit and put your feet up and relax, they will do as you say, you do not need to worry about them.

Her words and her touch combined with the doctor's prove sufficient to fade from the preacher's mind that image of the child all alone in an underground shelter and the roar of a twister overhead from which his father never returns.

—Tell them they must not beat all the children at the same time. Tell them the children sound like a tornado when all of them cry together. They must not beat all of the children like that. They'll destroy this place. This place is too small, too fragile, to contain so many children screaming at once. Tell them.

He pushes away Pat and the doctor.

—All right, we will, Reverend.

Pat nods emphatically and backs away from him along with the doctor. They leave him sitting with his head in his arms. The nurse mixes him a cocktail of sweet iced tea with a few drops added of what the doctor calls a picker-upper. The doctor tells her to make sure the preacher drinks all of it right away, and she must see to it that no one bothers him. The other assistants and guards agree.

They leave the nurse in the house, promising to return soon, and scatter to the four corners of the compound with the message from the preacher that the children must never again be punished as a group, that the life of the commune depends upon it, meaning the sanity of the man and therefore their sanity, their lives. Some adults look disapprovingly at the children and blame them for this new surge of ill will in the commune. Others think the children are a blessing to the place, and as the future of the place, they are worthy of better treatment. Since it is the word of Father, it must be obeyed if they are to thrive as a community. They must love the children but not spoil them; punish them justly but not in a blanket fashion; see to it that the children do not cry as one body, since their collective distress holds a peculiar sway over Father.

Trina and her dormitory companions talk in hushed tones. The young guard apologizes for having to lash at them but says it is better that he lashes them and they find out this important thing than no lash and no new crucial information about Father. He says he used as little force as possible. That an adult guard could deliver a bad lash to any one of them. The children nod and wonder if the young guard could aim for their legs next time rather than their arms and heads. He promises that he will. He leaves, and they make rude signs in the air behind his back. Trina wants to know if Ryan is the only one to get hit repeatedly by the guard who loves to wield the stick. The young guard calls the stick his rod of correction. The children avoid him as best as they can, since he finds the slightest opportunity to correct with lashes from his rod any behavior that he judges to be deviant. They return to examining and comparing the welts on each other's arms and legs and bodies. Ryan wins first prize for the biggest welts, all down his left side. They question him about the focus on his left side. He says he tried to squeeze through a gap in the fence and half of him, his right side, made it through the gap before the rest of him got stuck. He says the guards came along at random and hit him a few times and wandered off as others queued to take a few swipes at him and marvel at the easy target he made of himself by choosing to be still rather than the usual squirming, dodging, jumping. The children agree.

Trina worries about their leader. He cried because they cried. He appeared to be one of them. But he is their father. What would become of them if he stopped being their father? The children fret about this and about how they will be treated by the guards and teachers and other prefects from now on. Ryan says that the evening sermon should answer all their questions. Trina urges them to be on their best behavior at the meal and to complete all their chores quickly and with as little talk as possible and certainly free of any horsing around. All agree. Rose says today's rain is the best she has seen since her arrival six months earlier. The children nod. Rose imagines that she sees her absent mother's face in the bark of a tree and blinks and looks again and again until the image fades from that tree though it remains burned on her retina. She becomes glum. Trina asks her what is wrong.

—I miss my mother. I wonder if it's raining in the capital. She likes the rain. Will I ever see her again?

Both Ryan and Trina jump to offer Rose an answer. Trina wins out by being louder with her more strident tone.

—The capital isn't far. I'm sure she's thinking about you right now in this rain.

Rose likes the idea that the same rain soaks her mother in the capital. The many other children whose parents are not living with them in the commune say that this is true for them as well. Their parents left the commune or were thrown out of it. Like Rose, they were all told they belonged to the commune and Father was their sole parent. The children bring the talk back to how good it feels to run out into the wall of rain and feel it lash the arms, legs, body, and face. And rainwater swallowed directly from the sky tastes just like fresh coconut milk. They rub their hungry bellies and lick their lips.

—Yummy.

Trina follows with another assertion:

—It's worth a beating, isn't it?

A few of them hesitate to agree, but most think she is right, there is nothing like running out into this kind of rain and nothing sweeter to drink than sky water.

—Like bread just out of the oven, Ryan says. And they agree:

—Yes, just like fresh bread.

Trina wonders how the rain might be improved to make it even tastier. Rose says it would be great if, on the way down, the rain could hit bees and strip them of their honey, then the rain would arrive in their mouths honey-sweet. This gets everyone wild with speculation.

—What if the clouds were cotton candy and the rain flavored strawberry?

—Or any other flavor we could wish for?

—How about chocolate?

—Chocolate?

—Yes, chocolate.

—And strawberry.

—And vanilla.

—Vanilla?

—Yes, vanilla.

Trina thinks that, for there to be vanilla, there would have to be vanilla being transported somewhere by some flying creature that the rainwater could come into contact with on its looping, swaying descent toward their upturned faces and into their open mouths.

The children leave for their chores and try to maintain the hush made by the preacher's outburst. So many feet shuffle over wooden walkways and wood floors with so little noise. So many hands handle cutlery, plates, and cups with hardly a clatter and whisper, yet keep the sum of those hands, feet, and eating utensils no louder than a heavy breath, collecting trays of dirty dishes and running them under water with just a sound of a splash, and exit or enter rooms with a similar demeanor of, say, the wind taking the opportunity to explore an open space, or an inquisitive dragonfly or hummingbird. Those sounds. The noise of a child amounts to as much as that wind or that insect and no more; not one foot drags, not one collision of shoulders, not one foot finds that one loose floorboard in a parade of feet on the floor, not one body trips, nothing drops to the floor, not even a knife or fork or spoon. All of the commune's utensils are collected one at a time from a tray of such things without the usual clash and scrape of metal. All this deliberate cultivation of quiet sums up the lesson to the children of their collective beating and the preacher's outburst.

The children chew with their lips sealed. They pick up each spoonful or forkful of food with such deliberation that they seem to be in the middle of using the fork or spoon of food to thread some kind of needle. They drink and do not slurp. They replace their cups on the tabletops with a deliberateness that slows time and kills sound. They burp and silence it by keeping their mouths shut, and only briefly do their puffed cheeks give way to that occurrence. Their joints crack and click involuntarily and make them a new breed of living thing, utterly quiet in all actions except for this noise in their joints. Bellies grumble with digestive juices, but even this is muffled and sounds like a building settling on its foundations or the air making some adjustment in temperature or pressure, if such a thing can be heard as much as it can be felt. Adults look at the children and nod their approval. A few of the parents think it might be high impudence on the part of their children to obey and in such an ostentatious manner. But most agree that this is a new set of children.

The adults approve and return in their various work groups to their various allocated chores: to feeding the pigs on the farm, to cutting up trees at the sawmill to sell as timber for construction, to collecting eggs from the chicken coops, to milking in the cow sheds, to washing clothes in the laundry room, to mending and sewing in the tailor shop with its bolts of cloth on giant rollers, to the infirmary with its sick and mostly elderly patients, to the mechanic and carpentry shops, the bakery, the large kitchen with its vats for pots and battalions of potato peelers and legions of sobbing onion slicers, and washers of dishes clattering pots and pans in a carnival of stacking and soaping and rinsing, and somewhere a lone voice launches a couplet and gathers a chorus of voices all lifted in praise of the Lord as routine continues to be pressed on a daily basis into the service of the commune's heraldic purpose.

Supply trucks arrive leaving deep mud tracks, their big wheels caked in mud and the whole vehicle sprayed with it. Men unload bags of rice, sacks of flour, sugar, salt, barrels of cooking oil, vinegar, bottles of wine and spirits (kept out of sight and shuffled away directly to the preacher's whitewashed house) and medical supplies in white plastic bags and sealed containers, from syringes to mobile coolers with ampoules of penicillin, analgesics, narcotics, and all of it walked directly to the pharmacy situated beside the infirmary and all of it kept under lock and key and properly refrigerated with an emergency generator ready to chug into action should the main compound generator choke to a standstill.

The children chant in the schoolrooms, divided by screens easily wheeled around to accommodate additions or subtractions of children, and the chants vary from multiplication tables to Bible psalms to swearing allegiance to Father and the church of eternal brotherhood, sisterhood, parenthood, to singing hymns with verses interspersed by one-liners shouted by a teacher or rotated between the children so that the songs last for hours of head-spinning enchantment. A class moves outside and sits under a tree. Adam hears these alphabets and numerals, and he absorbs the stories of sinners redeemed and the lost found by the Holy Scripture, and he somersaults and claps his hands as the children clap theirs to a hymn. As they recite a psalm, so Adam listens with parted lips. This is the glory of heaven made on earth, of watching the day begin with putting back into place the trees and the birds hurled from limbs into flight and the animals erased by the dark, now redrawn with morning light and released from the traps of sleep: set free to buck, scamper, and roam.

Daylight brings peddlers to the compound in defiance of the hand-painted signs warning that Trespassers May Be Shot and listing pork knockers and speculators and encyclopedia sellers as examples of subjects who qualify for target practice and listing indigenous tribes such as the Akawaio, Mawakwa, Warrau, and the Wapishana as the only exceptions because of their wood carvings that decorate the private dwelling of the preacher, and their medicines kept in leather pouches and gourds carved from calabash, and refrigerated in the commune pharmacy for emergencies in case supplies of the Western remedies run out. The indigenous natural therapies bear neat labels handwritten in ink bled from berries, and the remedies—some of which smell as if taken from fish guts or pig feces, others like peppermint or rosewater—stave off fevers, cure snakebites, spider bites, water ague, sun poisoning, berry and mushroom poisoning, foot and stomach worms, crotch-eating mites, and nightmares. The preacher breaks his own rules and, from time to time, entertains jewelers from the capital whose handmade bangles are famous as far away as Australia and whose amulets are worn by babies from Berbice to Bangladesh to protect against night raids by witches out to rob babies of their spirits. The preacher believes in the enduring value of gold and diamonds, but he instructs his guards to aim their rifles at the speculators because they offer the world nothing but bad ideas and appear at the gates of the compound only to contaminate this great community devoted to redeeming a lost humanity.

The preacher allows encyclopedias into the grounds to update the school library or to add to his small collection, but only those hand-picked by him. Books on the history of capitalism and communism and the making of the industrial revolution and the rise, rise, rise of Cuba and the demise of kings and queens and stories about the elevation of the downtrodden status throughout history of the poor and powerless and the heroes who fight for them from John the Baptist to Robin Hood to Che Guevara. Many of these books arrive in multiple volumes, hardbound with gold leaf painted into the covers. The commune library remains as well stocked as the food storeroom, for without feeding the mind and spirit, the preacher reminds them at nightly sermons, without exercising the mind with a strident and stringent vocabulary and facts about history and a Euclidean numeracy, the body can never feel satisfied, no matter how lavish the dining tables or how heaped the enamel plates. For the cup that runneth over is not physical but spiritual.

The long loud blast of the horn of the captain's boat with its weekly delivery climbs up from the river, floats over the trees to the commune, and lands in the ears of Trina and Joyce. Trina lowers her flute from her parted lips and looks in the direction of the preacher's house, where her mother helps to keep the commune's accounts straight, not quite the commune's bookkeeper but one of the people the preacher credits with keeping his books in order. Trina thinks of the boat with her mother, their first time, before Eric and Kevin accompanied them and the captain introduced her

to his tall tales about the trickster spider. Trina refits her lips to the flute
and repositions her fingers and breathes, dreaming of Anansi.

Joyce stops her work and raises her pencil to her lips and stares into
the distance, and a tune springs to mind: Captain, Captain, put me ashore.
Her captain did just that. Put her ashore. Left her there and continued
on his merry way. Left her with what? An appreciation of life on the water
and the days measured by tides; sighting swaths of land from the river, a
view of the land that will make it never the same once she sets foot on the
muddy banks again.

—Why did you call this boat *Coffee*? Why not *Tea* or *Hot Chocolate*?

—Coffee was an eighteenth-century enslaved African who ran away
from his plantation and led a slave rebellion. He lived in the interior and
evaded capture.

—Sounds like my kind of guy. I mean I like his trailblazing spirit.

—I get you.

Joyce asks him about his family and he says he has no one and she
refuses, point-blank, to believe him. This annoys him, albeit teasingly.

—You calling me a liar?

—Yes. A man of your, how shall I put it, obvious qualities must have
someone to love and who loves in return.

His anger dissipates. He is a liar to her because he is someone whom
somebody cannot help loving. He says he likes the way she insults him, and
can she elaborate a little?

—Well, you have a sound trade, and you have all of your teeth and
your fingers and, I bet, even your toes.

He laughs and coughs and gives the wheel to his first mate so that he
can find a drink to stop himself from choking.

—All my teeth! You will be entering me for a steeplechase next.

She says that is not what she means. Other women might use the word
"handsome" or "good-looking," but that would give him the wrong idea

about her estimation of his attributes. Trina looks up from her sketchbook at this juncture in the conversation. She has not heard her mother talk like this to a man. Joyce sounds playful, with a higher-pitched, lighter voice, none of the usual grave warnings or thinking geared to praising the preacher and his mission. The captain says there is someone but that things have cooled between the two of them. Joyce says she does not mean to pry, but by "cool," does he mean over or simply in cold storage and liable to be brought into the light and rejuvenated at any moment? The captain says cool as in stone-cold dead, cordial but not intimate, no longer romantic, in fact, a frosty cordiality and therefore no light and no such sustenance at all. Joyce says a lot must have been asked of him for the whole thing to be shut away and starved of light. Trina looks puzzled by all the photosynthesis talk and returns her attention to her sketchbook. The captain says that this person wanted him to settle down with her in the city and give up his boat. She wanted him to make more money than a river captain.

—How could I give up all of this?

He spreads his arms at the river and the surrounding country and the light bathing them all.

—Do you ever regret it?

She hates herself for saying this the moment it jumps out of her mouth. She looks at her feet, rubs her hands down the front of her dress as if to smooth out the pleats, and shakes her head. She wonders how her talk about God and the commune and her leader has turned to this intimate conversation with a man whom she's known only a day.

—Never. Not for one moment. Especially at times like this, with someone new and surprising on my boat.

She stands next to him as he steers. Trina sits nearby and draws two adult stick figures standing on either side of a child and holding the twigs of that child's arms.

—You're not like a white woman, you behave different.

She makes a surprised O of her mouth and covers her widened eyes with her hands.

—I really want to know what a white woman is supposed to be like and just how many of them you've met to help you form this expert opinion about me.

He confesses that he met few of them on his boat but encountered some in the city, and they were all bossy know-it-alls and seemed cross-eyed when they talked to him, as if looking down their noses at something unsightly hanging from the end of their vision.

—What makes you think I'm white?

—Your skin is a dead giveaway, though your jet-black hair is something of a puzzle. Do you have something mixed with your European blood?

She says she has yet to meet someone who is not tainted with some mixture or other. Her father came from Spain to Florida on business and met her mother, a Miccosukee, in an illegal casino at West Palm Beach. Her mother thought he was an awful gambler, but he stayed at her table just to be dealt cards from her hand with her smile.

—He lost a lot of money that night, but she slipped him her phone number by dealing seven cards to him in a sequence that she said was an awful-looking hand but a number of some import to him if he cared to remember it. And the rest was history, as they say.

The captain smiles at this beautiful answer.

—That explains your hair and your ways.

—And what exactly do you mean by that, Captain?

—Well, you seem more open to me as a human being. You don't see me as black first and human second.

He wonders if she feels an affinity to nature. He says everyone knows that the tribes in this forest have lived here for thousands of years without interfering with the place, while the Europeans with their enslaved Africans and indentured Indians from South Asia ruined the place in just four hundred years. Right on cue, a barge floats by with a red flag warning them that logs would follow, and they pull to the side as a half mile of felled trees floats past them with hired indigenous tribesmen running acrobatically across the logs to keep them together and hopping back into small motorboats that zip up and down alongside the flotilla of felled trees.

The captain says he has one more thing to ask her, and ordinarily he would wait a little longer, but the dock for the commune is coming up around the next bend in the river.

—Trina's father?

This makes Joyce laugh. She calls Trina and asks if she would kindly tell the captain about her father. Trina set down her sketchpad.

—Oh, show me that.

Trina holds up the double page for the captain, who sees an S for their river filled with logs. Instead of trees, lines of bulldozers are parked along the river's banks, and instead of flocks in the air, just airplanes.

—You have a gift, Trina.

Trina says her mother met her father at college.

—He was a football star, and he abandoned us for a life of women and drink.

—Trina!

—But Mom, that's what you say about him.

—I know, but you're not allowed to repeat it.

They are smiling, and the captain takes off his hat and raises his eyebrows at the first mate who seems equally amused and mildly shocked. Trina sees none of this and blithely carries on.

—He looked like you, but you seem a lot nicer.

This surprises the captain.

—Like me?

—Yes, Captain.

Joyce adds that Trina's father always maintained that his ancestors were never enslaved.

—They arrived in Florida as free people from Haiti. He played for a few years and a knee injury ended his career and he got locked up for tax evasion and that was that. He's back there somewhere, wheeling and dealing and, mercifully, out of our lives.

—Any regrets?

—Not a one.

Joyce hugs Trina. A natural lull follows with some searching out of objects in the river. A log floats like an alligator, just submerged in the water. The current billows and mimics shape-shifting cloud. They pass herons nesting in the mangroves, pure white splotches against bright green and the green rising out of the mineral-stained water.

A watch repairman who sells clocks and watches and peddles his wares in a cart ignores the No Trespassing sign and tries to sneak around the commune gates. The guards fire at his cart, alarmed by the noise coming from it. He opens the cart to show them that it is full of harmless clocks and watches. He tells the guards that by shooting at his cart, they try to kill time but succeed only in ruining his merchandise. The commune leader purchases a kitchen clock and a schoolroom clock from the watch repair specialist to compensate him for the damage and for the fright of being fired upon. The seller of timepieces trudges from the compound, dissatisfied. He grumbles.

—Time wasted on you people.

The man feels he knows time from the inside out.

—Nobody can beat time. No matter how grand he think he is.

On his way out of the compound, the time seller waves at Adam.

—I feel sorry for you, forced to live here and watch them day and night.

The time seller's sweeping gesture takes in the rain forest, whose clock is the rain made in the trees and the mist grazing and a sun crawling in a blue sea fished by birds and sailed by cloud.

Adam looks around at the industry of the commune that surrounds him. The people's unceasing labor is a testament of their higher calling, and by their treatment of him, keeping him close to them and giving him a central place in their lives, he feels elevated from his humble position of a dumb beast to honorary citizen of the commune. The people want him here so that he can witness their toiling. All he has to do is look up at the giant monocot trees that fringe the compound to see how much labor it takes to clear this place and erect buildings and weed and pluck the wild greenery every day to keep it from encroaching and swallowing the compound. He, too, could pluck, chop, and carry if they would let him. He cannot see himself sitting around in a clearing or propped against a tree picking fleas from some other gorilla's fur as another hand combs his fur for ticks to nibble. He knows nothing of that life. He was captured too young. Saved from his preordained station in the order of things, his fate tied to that of the compound and its inhabitants. His place in the world is narrated in the creation stories read aloud by the children seated in a semicircle in front of a teacher and sheltered from the flames of the sun under the inclusive canopy of a tree. But he will prove destiny wrong.

SIX

The entire community of more than one thousand souls is required to attend nightly sermons unless someone is bedridden in the infirmary. Everyone aims to finish chores early to find a chair. Latecomers end up seated on the floor. The singing of hymns begins right away and continues as the place fills up, and soon those who have missed finding a chair simply squat on the ground beside a row of seats and shelter under the tarpaulin from the cool night breeze, the mosquitoes, and the general feel of discomfort of sitting too close to the thick jungle dark. Citronella coils burn. Bulbs strung around the tented structure attract kamikaze moths. Guards stand around the edges of the congregation to keep children in their place and wave off with big sticks and much gesticulating of arms and whistling and curses any curious night life that will arrive, mostly in the form of snakes, wild boar, and the occasional hungry panther. The preacher remains in his house waiting for the right time to join the congregation and deliver his sermon. He paces the corridor behind his front door and warms up for the service. He clasps his leather-bound Bible to his right breast and utters verses aloud, gesturing wildly. He hears the singing and clapping and waits until he is satisfied that the congregation has reached an optimal volume. And if joy in a clearing means anything in the pitch black of the jungle, it surely amounts to the preacher's flock of devoted followers in full swing, vocals at a maximum, hands red from vigorous clapping, feet hot from stamping on the ground, and wide smiles on sweating faces invigorated by chanting and movement and pooled enthusiasm.

His appearance results in shouts and whistles and prolonged applause. He holds up his arms and calls for calm and thanks his congregation for its unbridled welcome. But he takes a full five minutes of saying thank you, and please, and okay, and praise the Lord, before his followers settle and wait for him. They erupt once more the moment he lifts his arms and praises the Lord, which is always a signal for the congregation to repeat his words in unison and throw their arms collectively into the air and start the applause all over again. The preacher cannot begin his train of thought until ten minutes after his arrival. He spends the time standing there and watching and smiling. Gradually, his people settle and become still for him and concentrate on him to the exclusion of everything else, from the whirring fans and jungle shrieks and coughing from those who turned up sick, to the discomfort of the metal folding chairs with no elbow room between one person and the next.

—How far we have come, my children.

—Praise the Lord.

—Look around you. Look at the strength of our numbers.

This results in many heads turning from side to side and lots of peering up and down rows of seats. A fresh wave of applauding, whistling, and shouted praise the Lords erupts. Chairs shift, shoulders bump, bodies press together to fit everyone under the big tent. The preacher tells his followers that they cannot be governed by earthly time. Unlike the rest of ordinary humanity, busy putting to no good use its time on earth, the commune must bide theirs until such time as the calling from on high comes for their salvation to eternity, to a place of timelessness and an existence free of want and pain.

—Repeat after me. We are destined for a place of timelessness.

The congregation repeats as instructed but in disarray, parts of the response starting too late and other parts finishing too early to create the effect of a loud jumble. The preacher ignores the confusion and carries on.

—Repeat after me. Eternal life free of want and pain.

This time the congregation works in concert. Those who are late starting the repetition simply skip a word or two and join in with the majority. The effect sounds much smoother, and the preacher nods approvingly and smiles at Trina and her mother seated in the front row. He gazes at them and they bow their heads, Trina's mother more deeply. Trina's eyes remain wide. She sits forward in her seat. She stays so still, she looks frozen to the edge of the metal chair. Blinking or slouching in her chair might rob her of some crucial detail. Trina expects something to happen, since her mother supervised her as she washed and made her wear a clean, ironed dress and one of the preacher's assistants walked them from the dormitory to the tented meetinghouse and seated them in places vacated by two other assistants who said they were keeping the seats warm for Trina and her mother.

—My children, another day is over in a calendar of days dedicated to the glory of God.

—Praise the Lord.

He says they are disciples of the Savior. Their devotion to Him is surely proved by their challenging location in the jungle and by the daily hard work.

—All of you demonstrate your dedication to the Lord by your hard labor every day.

—Praise the Lord.

—All of you demonstrate your spirituality by your daily study of the Scripture.

—Praise the Lord.

—All of you are ripe and ready for paradise.

Applause and cheers in waves, dying down and rising up to spill from the tent and ricochet off the walled dark that joins the trunks of trees. The preacher asks if, in such an environment, doubters might still be found, skeptics might abound, and cynics thrive. The congregation shouts a variety of expressions of disbelief. No. No way. Never. Impossible. They look around, knitted brows meeting wide-eyed amazement.

—If a man asked you to place your head in the mouth of a lion, would you do it?

The congregation is slow to respond. His assistants say no, loud and clear, and the rest take the cue and add their voices to the mix.

—No. Of course you wouldn't. Not if asked by any man. And why would a man ask such a thing of you? Such a man might mean to do you harm, and to follow his instruction would be foolish to the nth degree, right?

—Right!

—But what if the request came from your Savior? What if the voice that asks you to perform such a feat comes from within? Not from flesh and blood standing in front of you but from a guiding spirit inside you? What would you do then? Would you place your head in a lion's mouth?

—Yes. Yes. Yes.

—God's work is a miracle, and we see it in a myriad of ways, and God is everywhere in all the beauty of the things we see around us and in ourselves. But God cannot do everything for us. Right?

—Right!

—We have to help ourselves to prove we are worthy of His salvation. We have to work for His light to shine in us and through our example of discipline and dedication to the strictures of the Scripture. Right?

—Right!

—Repeat after me. Strictures of the Scripture.

—Strictures of the Scripture.

—Remember that phrase and find a tune for it to recharge you in your daily work. Are you with me?

—Yes.

—Do I make myself clear?

—Yes.

—So how can there be a doubter in our midst, a skeptic, who does not see these obvious truths, a cynic who thinks these precepts are mere tricks of the mind and not facts of life. What do we live by and what must we die by? Repeat after me. Strictures of the Scripture.

—Strictures of the Scripture.

—These are not man-made rules like the signs around the compound devised for your physical safety. The strictures of the Scripture are for your spiritual security. What are they for?

—Spiritual security.

—And the spiritual dictates the physical. No matter how challenging the physical may appear to be. So ask yourselves this question every day in your hard work, what is the most challenging plane of existence? And answer unequivocally. The spiritual, not the physical. Repeat.

—The spiritual, not the physical.

He hoists up his trousers with both hands, pulls a pressed handkerchief from his back pocket, and mops his brow. Keeping a firm grip on the handkerchief, he sets his thumbed black Bible on the dais next to the high chair and picks up the microphone and resumes.

—We delude ourselves when we pursue comfort and believe our bodies rule our lives. We neglect the more important spiritual plane when we get caught up in gathering around us the comforts and luxuries of physical life. But we are not trained to believe in the spiritual plane of existence. And we are not trained to think that a spiritual assertion is profitable or more important than the physical. We think if we are hungry, that is the most important thing, and we start to dream about banquets, don't we? We picture tables of food and goblets of wine. But if, instead of the belly, we pictured the mind and then the spirit, we would not be hungry. If, after a large meal, there is still something missing in us, we know that thing must be some quality that no number of banquets can satisfy. Are you with me?

—Yes.

—I think our banquet is God's Holy Scripture. We are put here to feed on His guidance, and our reward is everlasting life. What is our reward?

—Everlasting life.

—Now, here is a practical lesson tonight for all to see what I mean by food of the spirit over and above food of the body. Who am I to you? Am I not a messenger of God?

—Yes, Father.

—Am I not among you to bring to you the message of God?

—Yes, Father.

—I come to you with God's word, unadulterated and unexpurgated, two big words, but they mean unedited and not tampered with by inferior human hubris, another big word, meaning human presumption. Will you accept God's words, big or small, given to me from God directly?

—Yes, Father.

—Tonight's practical lesson is about trust. I come to you as God's messenger, and throughout history, God has sent many messengers, and we know what an unready and ignorant humanity did to those messengers, right?

—Right, Father.

—They killed the messengers but not the message. Repeat.

—They killed the messengers but not the message.

—Tonight's practical lesson is about trust. You trust me.

—Yes, Father.

—You believe in me?

—Yes, Father.

—But still I say to you that there are doubters, skeptics, and cynics among you, even after I delivered you from hell on earth to a paradise on earth that is a shadow of the real one waiting for us all. Even after all this, there remain doubters and skeptics and cynics among you.

—No, no, no.

—Yes, even after I plucked you from degradation and transported you across the sea to a place that is an Eden on earth but only a morsel of the feast that awaits you in heaven. Even after all that, you doubt me.

—No, no, no.

—Yes. Among you. Sitting right beside you. You know deep in your hearts about that doubt. I do not have to point you out in the crowd. You know who you are, and God knows who you are, and if God knows and I am His messenger, then I know who you are. But do not be afraid. Our God is a loving God. Tonight's lesson is about what?

—Trust, Father.

—Yes. If you trust in me, I will make you what?

—Fishers of men.

—And what will be your reward?

—Everlasting life.

—Yes, everlasting life. And that is a long time, isn't it.

—Yes, Father.

—Try to imagine eternity. You cannot. Not in your limited body. How can you? You live on a physical plane, and eternity is about the spirit and about time without end. Do not blame yourself that you doubt, but blame yourself if you do not trust me, after all I have done for you and shown you to be the evidence of God's work. Right?

—Right.

—What an evening, my brethren. What heat.

The preacher beckons to an assistant and exchanges his soaked hand-kerchief for a hand towel.

—What heat and what promise. The Lord's work may be difficult, but it is never in vain.

He gestures to Trina and Joyce to approach him. They move quickly from the front row up onto the stage. He motions for them to come closer and stand next to him.

—I don't bite. Ladies and gentlemen, tell them to come closer.

The audience shouts at Joyce and Trina to move closer to the preacher. The shouts are half playful and half in anger. He asks Joyce and Trina to say their names into the microphone, even though everyone knows them. He pushes the microphone close to their lips.

—Trina, Father.

—Trina. Indeed. Who does not know Trina! Our miracle child.

He nods at Joyce to speak into the microphone.

—Joyce, Father.

He says there is no greater trust than between a mother and her daughter, since the mother brought the daughter into the world and serves as her mentor and spiritual guide until the daughter can fend for herself in a harsh world. The congregation murmurs its assent, and all gaze at Trina and her mother in anticipation of their central role in some lesson based on trust.

The way the congregation concentrates on mother and daughter, looking at the two with a variety of open mouths, raised eyebrows, and widened eyes, makes it clear that people believe Joyce and Trina are the two doubters-skeptics-cynics. Joyce looks bewildered. She is about to be tested, and she trembles, not for herself but because Trina is a part of the experiment. Joyce glances around and keeps her arm on Trina's shoulders. Trina leans against Joyce and fights a strong impulse to burst into tears. She cannot think what she might have done wrong. She played her part as instructed and rehearsed. She breathed nothing of it to anyone, as promised. She waited like an obedient corpse for the right touch and the key words from Father before she opened her eyes, even though she was thirsty and tired from holding the one posture of stillness and barely inhaled and exhaled to hide the fact of her life.

Trina remembers her resurrection by the preacher in front of Adam's cage. Immediately after Adam drops her to the ground, Trina experiences a metamorphosis in the hands of the commune's leadership. First, the guards scoop her off the damp earth, and Trina regains consciousness as they carry her to the infirmary. Second, the nurses and guards form a screen around her. She begs for her mother. And third, one of the nurses fires an order at Trina:

—Be quiet. Go back to sleep.

Trina flops in the guard's arms. She wants to see her mother but knows it is foolish to disobey a direct order from a nurse or guard or prefect. In a room in the infirmary, a nurse takes Trina's pulse and listens to her heart and asks her to breathe in deep and hold it. The nurse taps Trina's back and chest and left and right sides.

—And exhale.

The nurse asks if any of it hurts. Trina says she is a little sore in places. The doctor walks in, and the nurse reports to him that Trina is as good as new. But he goes ahead and shines a small torch into Trina's eyes and makes her open her mouth wide and say ah. As he pokes at the back of her tongue with a small flat stick, he asks Trina her age. She gags.

—Ten, Doctor.

—Good.

The doctor asks the nurse to come with him to help with the patients, and both leave the room. Trina remains sitting on a small table with two guards and two of the preacher's personal assistants, Dee and Pat, around her. The preacher walks in with a retinue of helpers and everyone comes to attention, not like soldiers do, but from slouching and looking relaxed one moment, they switch to a springiness coupled with the jitters. The preacher walks up to Trina and ruffles her hair and says he needs her to do something very important for him and for everyone at the mission. He assures her she will be fine. She should not worry about anything. Her mother is fine, too, and will be along soon.

—Will you help to do God's work, Trina?

—Yes, Father. Anything, Father.

He explains to her about what will happen next to convert her into a beautiful corpse, and all she has to do is play along, but she must never speak to anyone about it. For her obedience and cooperation, she and her mother will gain many enviable privileges.

—Will you be my little disciple?

—Yes, Father. Yes.

—Good girl. Nurse Dee tells me you play the flute.

—Yes, Father.

—Do what I say and you will get a new flute.

—Thank you, Father.

—Very good. Now lie down and be as still as you can.

The preacher signals for the doctor and Dee to draw nearer to him and Trina. The preacher strokes Trina's hair and she opens her eyes and sits up, bewildered. She looks at the adults around her and buries her face in her hands.

—Please can I see my mother now, Father?

—Of course, my child. Don't cry. You're in good hands.

—Thank you, Father.

He ruffles Trina's hair, thumbs tears from below her eyes, and kisses her on the top of her head. He turns to one of the guards and says:

—Go and fetch Joyce.

To his many eager assistants, he says:

—Fetch the seamstress, the undertaker, the carpenter, and what's her name? The old lady who does excellent makeup. Come on people, chop-chop. We have a show to put on.

His people rush to carry out his orders. The seamstress pulls a tape around Trina's waist and up and down her arms, body, and legs. The carpenter takes one look at Trina and says he has just the right box for her. She is not much bigger than a doll, he says. Just a few pieces of wood for this one. The old lady responsible for making up the faces of the deceased wonders how she will make such a sprightly face look dead.

—Death never looks convincing on a young face.

The old lady decides she will apply plenty of white powder, as if summoning the ghost of the child from the depths to the surface.

—Usually, I make the dead look as if they live. With this one, I have to make her look dead.

The preacher and his assistants begin rehearsals with Trina. One of the assistants lies on a table and pretends to be Trina so that the child can see exactly what she needs to do and at what time. The preacher talks, and the woman acting as Trina reacts at the appropriate time. When Trina takes a turn, the preacher issues his order and she moves too soon. The preacher curses under his breath, spins away from Trina, and pulls a handkerchief from his pocket and swipes his face. Dee steps in. She encourages Trina to listen carefully to Father, to concentrate and wait for the third command before she moves a muscle. Trina nods and lies back, and again the preacher faces her and speaks. She twitches, and he curses aloud and asks her if she is a mental incompetent. Trina begins to cry. Dee calms Trina with a hug. Pat steps in and suggests that perhaps the preacher should touch Trina. That his words may be too powerful for the child to do anything but listen, enthralled by his voice. The preacher smiles. He likes this line of reasoning. Pat adds that if he makes contact with Trina, actually lays a hand on her, it might provide the extra clue for the child to obey his command. They rehearse this suggestion. He speaks. Trina ignores him. She counts each time he touches her. On the count of three, she sits up and they congratulate her but remind her to wipe the smile off her face. They run through it again. Trina is perfect. Everyone smiles. The preacher tells Trina to remember to blink many times in the light and shade her eyes. Remember to breathe deep. Breathe as if she has just come up for air from a long dive.

The carpenter arrives with an oblong box and rests it next to Trina, who climbs into her coffin. She lies on her back and wriggles to a settled position, and the assistants arrange her hands by her sides, and straighten the pleats of her dress, and the makeup woman dabs Trina's face one last time.

—Keep your lips sealed and your eyes closed. Picture your eternal spirit looking down at your empty shell of a body. Make Father proud of you.

The carpenter lowers the lid on the coffin with a wink and a promise to Trina that it will be lifted in no time and she will be reborn as a star among her peers.

The fans whirr and clank and shake, but the night air merely stirs the heat generated by the congregation. An elderly woman faints and the guards bar her husband from leaving his seat to tend to her. The guards ferry the old lady out of the tent and a nurse fans and mops the elderly woman's brow and offers her a sip of cold water. No one is allowed to leave the tent except for an emergency or in obedience to a direct order from the preacher or one of his assistants. The guards aim their sticks at anyone who shifts too much in a seat or looks around at the exits instead of toward the front of the tent, at the preacher. The mosquito coils dotted around the tent burn down to cinders, and the jungle settles with just the preacher's voice over the loudspeaker coupled with the response of the congregation. The quiet outside the tent creates the impression that all life secreted in the jungle might be listening to the sermon. A hand held in front of the face in such a thick and absorbing dark would be severed from the body. Trees lean in closer to catch whatever emanates from the tent. Wild animals in that dark move around, if they move at all, with ears inclined toward the commune. The dark listens. The night adds to the audience for a preacher who measures the success of his conviction against the degree of loyalty demonstrated by his followers. To the preacher, the surrounding jungle is merely indifferent. The jungle fights against being cleared according to his settlement plans, though the success of the settlement makes the jungle an ideal location and adversary. The natural camouflage is an ally. The opposition to human habitation presents the right opposing force to the communal effort. If things go wrong, the people simply need to work harder to secure their environment. If his teachings do not make sense, it is because the people focus too much on the details of what he says at the expense of his meaning.

He is their spiritual guide. He instructs them in the deep and varied meanings of his inspired teachings. Any time spent questioning his motives amounts to time subtracted from work on behalf of the commune. To question him is an act of disobedience. How can anyone find the time to doubt him? A person who expends the right amount of effort to hold back the jungle from reclaiming the compound has no time to cultivate doubt. He reminds them of their hostile and isolated jungle location and of the even more hostile forces ranged against them beyond the jungle.

—Many people in high places, people who think they are high and mighty but who do not know about the Almighty, these deluded people want to bring down our commune and see it fail and break up our holy alliance.

His people must have absolute trust and absolute faith in him. The preacher nods at Trina and Joyce. They give him a half-smile and wide-eyed look. He turns toward the exit left of the makeshift stage that is no more than a few wooden plinths covered with a thin green carpet. He lifts his right arm and shows a thumbs-up to two guards stationed at that exit, and they disappear into the textured dark. Joyce hugs Trina. Trina looks up at her, questioning. Joyce seems just as puzzled by what they could have done that would be construed as mistrust, especially after Trina's recent resurrection and induction into the inner circle of those who appear to have won the faith of the preacher. Trina starts to recite the Lord's Prayer, not out loud to attract more attention, but to herself with barely a move of her lips. She prays in the hope that whatever lies in store for her and her mother is at worst a public dressing-down, some humiliation from the preacher's tongue, even a public beating by one of the guards. But not time at the bottom of the old well full of spiders. Not sentenced to run the length of the dissenter's passage, as it is called, made up of two long lines formed by guards and prefects who kick and punch at the head and body. At least a public beating ends fast. Trina knows from the many reports of other children that the key is to be quite still. Trying to dodge or fend off the blows with lifted arms only prolongs the beating. The guards, armed with long sticks, seek a worthy target area and take longer to score a satis-factory hit on a chosen site.

Trina and Joyce stare at the entrance to the tent. The preacher drinks from a tall flask and dries his face and neck with his towel. People stand and stretch, and a few of them ignore the guards and dash out of the tent for a bathroom break while others whisper about what might happen next. The wait makes Trina giddy. Add to it the puzzle over their part in the lesson, and it proves too much for Trina. She begins to shake from head to toe, and her mother holds her tight and tells her to think of the two of them together at the happiest time in their lives, to just picture that time and place. Trina thinks of California, a clump of trees in a back garden. A hummingbird feeder hangs by the back door. She reclines in a hammock beside her mother. They swing gently and watch the hummingbirds zip to the feeder, balance in the air with wings that beat fast as propellers, and make a small engine noise as the birds direct their long needles of beaks into the syrup before they dart away. Trina trembles less and breathes better.

Trina and Joyce hug each other, and the people at the front of the room scream and scramble from seats and topple chairs and trip over each other. Guards rush forward and use their sticks to nudge and prod people back to their places. The large black figure of Adam lumbers into the tent on the end of a rope held by three guards. Adam appears sleepy and swipes at the rope, which the men keep at arm's length. They pull him toward the stage. The preacher nods and smiles at Trina and her mother. He steps close to Adam and presses one hand to the gorilla's back and offers a banana with the other hand. Adam grabs the banana somewhat clumsily and allows the man to scratch his back as he peels and eats the fruit in one mouthful and hurls the peel at the three men holding his lead. The guards, armed with sticks and stationed at the exits, poke at anyone who does not return to a chair or take a seat on the floor and keep still. The preacher waits for the congregation to settle, and then he gestures to Trina and Joyce to approach him and Adam. Joyce steps forward ahead of Trina. The preacher urges them to step closer. He waits as they edge forward, holding on to each other. He hands mother and child one banana each and indicates that Trina should offer her banana to Adam. Trina holds the banana by the tip and stretches her hand toward Adam. The gorilla swipes the banana. He peels and scarfs it. Again he pelts the guards with the peel. The preacher points and says:

—Now you, Joyce, offer your banana to this magnificent creature made by the Creator.

Joyce closes her eyes and holds her banana up toward Adam, and he grabs at it, but his grasp is oddly timed and he overreaches and seizes Joyce's left hand instead of the banana. Joyce screams and tries to pull away. Adam wants the banana. He simply tightens his grip on her hand for her to surrender the fruit. Joyce screams as Adam crushes her hand. The preacher steps away from the gorilla and gestures to his assistants to bring more fruit for Adam, but Adam appears to want just the fruit that Joyce offered him and none other. He releases her left hand and grabs at her other arm and looks around the stage to see what has become of the fruit. Not seeing it, he thinks Joyce has concealed it somewhere on her body. He proceeds to tear at her clothing. Trina screams along with her mother, and several of the women who stand near the front of the room add their cries to a chorus of panic. The guards beat people with their sticks to restore order in the room. The preacher signals the guards to drag Adam from the tent. When Adam slaps at them, he seems to be slow in his movements, awake but not fully alert.

The preacher points at Trina and Joyce and says that one of them trusts him and the other does not, and he asks the congregation if they can guess which one is which.

—Who trusts me? And who does not? Mother or child?

Everyone points at Joyce, shouting that only the child, Trina, is full of trust. Trina hugs Joyce, who struggles not to whimper and shiver. Joyce's torn dress reveals several scratches on her arms and body from Adam's nails. The preacher asks two of his assistants to take Joyce to the infirmary, but he tells Trina, who tries to follow her mother, that she should remain by his side. He kisses Trina on top of her head and tells her that she is much too close to her mother. He places his index finger over his lips, which silences Trina and the congregation. He asks everyone to give Trina a round of applause for her bravery. She did not know what would be asked of her, he points out, but she withstood the test of her trust of him over her fear of what was asked of her. Again the congregation applauds.

—Trust is so basic an instinct that even a gorilla can detect it. Imagine what God knows about our inner thoughts and feelings if a gorilla, a dumb beast, can detect if we trust him or not, or fear him more than we could ever trust him. Work on bolstering your trust, people.

—Yes, Father.

The preacher dismisses the congregation with a wave of his hand. He tells Trina that Joyce will be fine but that she must remain calm and remember everything they talked about earlier. He promptly leaves the tent with four guards and three assistants. The congregation sits for a moment, unsure about the abrupt end to the evening; they begin to move only when the guards point toward the exits with their long sticks. They walk slowly, drained by the harrowing sermon. They ignore the prod of the sticks and barely hear the guards' orders to move faster and hurry to their beds. They trudge through the dark in a somnambulant state, dreamless because incapable of another nervous impulse, emptied into mere echoes of themselves.

SEVEN

Ryan and Rose try to console Trina in the dormitory. They say her mother's wounds are just scratches and will be cared for at the infirmary. Trina shakes her head and cannot stop her tears. Ryan hugs her and asks if she wants him to get her and the others some bread. His bold offer makes Trina smile. Rose says he should bring two loaves and jam to go with them. A third child says the treat would go down nicely with a cup of tea if he could manage that as well. Trina chuckles along with the others. A quick rap on the door banishes all the children's smiles. They adopt a variety of miserable expressions, from hangdog looks to sour faces to blank impassive stares, just in time to see an assistant to the preacher stride into the dormitory with a paper bag that she hands to Trina. She tells Trina that the preacher himself wants Trina to know he is proud of her conduct at the sermon and that she is a fine example of trust.

—Is my mother all right?

—She'll be fine, only a few scratches and a slightly sprained wrist.

—Can I see her?

—It's very late now. In the morning.

Trina thanks her and waits for her to leave the dormitory, then opens the twisted top of the brown paper bag. Inside she finds a chocolate bar, a pack of sweet wafers sandwiched with cream, a packet of salted peanuts, chewing gum (which the children are never allowed to have without special permission), and a bag of salted potato chips. Trina offers the treats to the entire dormitory of sixteen. Some of the children accept. Rose says that she cannot, that Trina should enjoy her hard-earned treat. Ryan insists that Trina should enjoy her treats by herself, since she paid a high price for them with her mother in the infirmary and her life almost lost for real. But Trina says she will be happy only if she can share her unexpected bounty. She says she did what any one of them would do if ordered to do so by the preacher, and any other course of action would have been insane and accompanied by one of three outcomes: the well, the gauntlet, or a group beating. She divides the chocolate and hands out a few peanuts and offers the potato chips to eager hands. Ryan and Rose see her logic and think her brave and very generous, and with that they help themselves to a part of the chocolate bar, a stick or two of gum, and a wafer. They nibble their treats to make them last. They talk in between chewing for longer than they should as they try to stretch the time the snacks last. They say how they could not breathe and could hardly look and almost passed out in shock as Trina offered the gorilla a banana. How did she do it? How did she manage not to pee herself? Ryan says he was with her all the way, beside her in every move she made. Rose agrees and adds that she was like Trina's shadow if Trina had a shadow in that tent. Trina smiles and then stops in the middle of the smile and starts to cry. She says she hopes Adam dies in his sleep and ants crawl over him and eat his gorilla body. She says she wishes she were big and could wield a large stick so she could beat the snot out of those guards and make them cry for their mothers. She drops her treats as she says this and pulls at her hair. The others stop nibbling and look alarmed. She begins to say something about the preacher, and Ryan drops his snack and rushes to her and covers her mouth with his hand. He pulls her to him and cuddles her. She shakes in distress.

—I will get you a real treat, Trina. Promise me you won't say bad things and get yourself into more trouble, and I will get you some fresh bread hot out of the oven. Promise.

Ryan looks into Trina's face, and she stops shuddering and nods, and he smiles at her and she smiles back.

—You'll get me bread? I don't want you to run that risk for me.

—You have no say in it, Trina. The choice is mine, and I'm going to do it right now.

—I don't want you to steal bread for me.

—It's not stealing if you're hungry.

—What if you get caught?

—I'm hungry. We're all hungry, right?

The children in the dormitory nod at Ryan and ignore Trina. All except Rose.

—But the guards will hurt you.

—Only if I get caught, Rose, which I won't. We all want some bread, right?

Ryan extracts a promise from each of them that they won't ever tell anyone. All agree. Trina says she felt strong back in the tent because of them; otherwise she would have wet herself without a doubt. She says her mother told her that as long as they think of one another and behave as if they are together and help one another, they are bound to make it through the nights and days in this jungle.

Adam submits to the tug of the rope around his neck. Three men grip it. He allows them to drag him back to his cage. He is glad to be left in peace. He feels drowsy and cannot keep his eyelids from drooping. His arms belong to some other creature with poor aim. How else was he unable to grasp a banana held up in front of him? His mind did not belong to him. It still feels that way. He tried to do what the preacher wanted of him and failed. Take a treat offered by a child and a woman. Follow the lead he was strapped to for the safety of everyone. Watch the preacher and do what was asked of him. But in his drowsy state, he could not think. His body is numb and heavy. A weight presses against his muscles and makes movement slow and his aim poor. He wants to be left alone. He needs to sleep. In the morning everything will feel better. A good sleep will recharge his body, sunlight invigorate him. The children at play with their speed and happy noises will surely lift his spirits. Adam surrenders to sleep that stakes its claim on him. He allows sleep to take him wherever it wants. His last thought of the night is of Joyce, Trina, and the preacher, three people he feels he has to obey from this night on no matter what they ask of him. And with that, Adam finds himself bounding through the trees with his legs and arms, able to run along a lane cut through the air, a headlong straight line forged through the jungle. He moves in this effortless way at high speed without colliding with a single object. He overtakes flocks of parrots. Crows swerve from his path. He runs in the air high in the trees and drops to just above the height of the man without slowing. The jungle blurs as he runs, and he does not feel tired or breathless in this sprint without end. At the precipice of a waterfall, all he has to do is run in the direction of the headlong plunge of the water, since its downward trajectory continues this lane for his rocket arms and legs. He wishes never to wake from this sleep, where his cage is no more and nothing and no one impedes his path, his will. Coming up in front of him, only a speck to begin with, he can just about make out a figure, another gorilla, waiting for him as he gallops near. The head and body look familiar, and before he can put a name to the form, he finds himself tumbling through the air into the arms of his mother.

Trina, Ryan, Rose, and the rest of the children in the dormitory sit up in their beds in the dark and talk about hunger. About the small last meal of the day, said to be shredded beef and rice but in actuality masses of rice and ladles of gravy with nothing in it but colored water. A paltry meal digested hours ago. What they wish for ranges from entire roasted pigs to chocolates with three layers to the box. The smell of the bakery begins to drift into the dormitory. Ryan shifts the talk to cutting a fresh loaf and spreading it with creamy butter. What would it be like to watch that butter run off a slice and catch the runoff in a wide mouth and bite into the not too hot but more than just warm baked dough. Ryan moves to the door. Trina volunteers to go with him. Rose says they should draw straws to be fair to everyone, since all of them stand to benefit.

At this point the talk swings to what will happen to the bread scout if he or she gets caught. Pictures of the bread evaporate from heads at the mention of discovery. The children know what that means. Rose says how terrible it would be if one of them got caught and all of them were punished. To be lowered one at a time into the well, moist and dark with a spiders' enclave of webs in sufficient quantity to wrap a child in its shroud. Or be made to run the community gauntlet of fists and slaps and kicks. Or face a public beating by the guards. This makes everyone swear to protect the rest of the dormitory by saying he or she acted alone. All agree that whoever gets caught must take the punishment on behalf of everyone, no matter how terrible. They interlace fingers and cross hearts and hope to die. Trina adds that whosoever succeeds in bringing back bread gets the biggest slice first and the rest will be shared among the other children. Ryan thinks of another thing. He says that if anyone betrays the group, the punishment will be an endless dousing in a well, a perpetual running of a gauntlet formed by the group, and a beating with sticks from the group at every opportunity rather than one measly sentence at the bottom of the well, or one short sprint along the line formed by the commune, or one instance of a beating by a few men armed with sticks.

Ryan pulls straw from a mattress and breaks it into pieces of varying length and puts the pieces in a hat and holds out the hat for everyone to pick a piece. The children each draw a straw from the hat. Trina and Rose examine theirs. Everyone knows how hard it is to make it along the gangway all the way to the bakery and back without bumping into one of the guards patrolling the walkways and standing in lookout towers with bin-oculars and rifles, towers dotted around the perimeter of the compound. The bravery required might be too much for a child's body to contain. But what a loaf to win if that journey in the blackness could be made and the cooling loaf slipped from its tray and returned to the dormitory, hot enough that the booty has to be shifted from arm to arm to stave off the burn. Trina announces that Ryan picked the shortest straw. He does not hesitate. He hugs Trina and Rose. They wish him luck and urge him to be extra careful. Others say much the same thing and pat him on the back. He tiptoes to the door, opens it a few inches with the greatest care, and slips sideways into the dark.

Trina stands by the door and listens for footsteps. Rose and the rest of the children fall silent, almost listless in concentration. Each walks with Ryan in the darkness. Each squashes the belief that evil jungle spirits roam on such a night on the hunt for young hearts to tear from chests, and the most venomous snakes crawl up to the dormitories under the camouflage of darkness to catch the foot of a sleepwalking child and drag that child off into the jungle, and worst of all the dark scrambles the head of a child who becomes disoriented and walks toward the trees whose thick trunks and massive canopies and tangled undergrowth grab legs and wrap vines around the neck and pull a child's body up into the trees, never to be seen again. Trina imagines she accompanies Ryan in that dark. She holds his hand, and they tiptoe in matching steps and press into the dark, which, despite its thickness, parts for them in the face of such conviction.

As Ryan draws close to the bakery, his eyes grow accustomed to the night. He sees a post that resembles a sentry. The night air is like a veil draped over a shy face. The shy face retreats as Ryan approaches it, and the bakery smell thickens and he has to swallow the saliva that pools around his tongue. He feels brave, thinking of Trina and Rose and the others salivating and swallowing, just thinking of him getting nearer and nearer the hot loaves. The baking crew plucks the loaves from the giant oven with long paddles shoved under the baking trays, which they turn over with a swift tilt of the hands. The loaves are lined up in neat rows on shelves to cool beside open windows. Ryan reaches an open window and ducks under it. He hears adults talking inside the bakery not five yards from him. A dog barks a little distance away. A guard smokes, contrary to commune rules, at the same distance as that dog. A red light shines like a bright night insect and dulls and shines and dulls. Ryan reaches up and grabs the first hot solid thing he feels and does not bother to look at it in the dark. He wants to grab another but can barely breathe and control a gross tremor from head to toe. He tries to reach up again but cannot. His arms refuse to obey him. He tries to turn away, but his legs feel pegged to the ground.

He conjures Trina and Rose waiting for him. He sees the bottom of the well with him in it and the cluster of sticks descending on his head. The fear proves sufficient to unlock his muscles. He crouches and tiptoes away. The barking gets closer. Ryan cannot look back. He speeds up his escape. The loaf burns his side where he clutches it. He hears more dogs barking and the clicking of crickets and a hoot he credits to an owl and a chattering of some sort that could be any wild animal. A strand touches his face. He swipes at it and thinks of a web and hopes it is the web of an absent spider. Heat from the hugged hot bread travels from his side up to his forehead and down to his toes. The air grows hot. The soil and the wood walkway burn his bare feet. He feels as if he is walking inside a giant oven heated by a close darkness. He cannot look back. He can barely see his hand in front of him. He counts, almost by touch, the rows of buildings full of sleeping children separated from their parents. The solid wood buildings, though spaced several feet apart, appear to be bridged by the dark. Ryan feels the dark gliding with him, its density creating the sensation that he was moving with the night rather than through it. At last he stops at his dormitory door. He turns the handle and slips inside and starts to breathe heavily. Everyone inside almost cheers at the sight of him with a loaf under his arm. He holds the block of gold high into the air.

They surround him and clap him on the back. Trina and Rose hug him. Everyone looks at the loaf, not sure how to begin to address its baked perfection. The hot smell spins their heads. The tanned rectangle shines like a gold bar, a work of art with a heavenly scent. They look on and cannot believe what they must do next, and quite fast if they are not to arouse suspicion. Ryan reads their minds and breaks off a chunk of bread and offers it to Trina. She passes it to Rose.

—Youngest first.

Rose looks around and decides to keep the gift. She holds the portion up to her face and takes a long deep breath and holds it in and waits as if inhaling is the point and actually eating her share an afterthought. Ryan works his way along the group, going by age. He breaks the bread and hands a piece to each child in turn. At last he takes the remaining chunk for himself, and on Trina's count to three, they begin to nibble and chew long and slow, turning the bread to liquid in their mouths before swallowing it and keeping this silent chewing circle of smiles and nods and amazement in their eyes. How can bread taste so sweet? It's only yeast, flour, water, and a pinch of salt. Bread must be the number one food in heaven. They mop up crumbs and lick wet fingers. They speculate about the vital importance of bread. That's why Catholics offer a wafer for the body of Christ. That's why each morning it is bread that breaks the night's fast. Bread should be a world currency like gold. The Bread Standard! To bread or not to breathe! They sniff the bread smell, still in the air. Bread for air. Air bread. Trina calls Ryan the bread liberator. Rose says he is her hero. And mine, another child adds. Mine, too, says a fourth and fifth. Trina teases Ryan, and he teases her back.

—The Bread Liberator!

—The Resurrected One!

—Will you put the bread into verse?

—Yes, something about myrrh and frankincense.

The whispers die down and the children settle in their bunk beds with smiles. Trina asks Ryan in a whisper how he felt out there alone in the night. Ryan tells her and Rose about it.

—The night's so thick, you can chop it like it's a tree. You can climb up into it as if you're dreaming, like the dark is a ladder. You lie down in it and it feels heavy on you, like you're at the bottom of a lake. You hold up your hand and you rest it against the giant body of the night and you can't tell your hand from the dark flesh. It gets to you so much that if you move in the night, you begin to see you're not the one moving but the night's carrying you forward and you leave no trace behind and there's no path in front for you to take, there's just the night moving forward and pulling you with it.

They pause and listen for the next person to say something. They slow and quiet. Trina interrupts the silence by wondering in a low whisper if the community, even the gorilla in its cage placed at the center of the compound for all to see, belongs here in the middle of nowhere, isolated like this. They can easily disappear without a sound, absorbed by the trees, with little or no trace. Trina tells them that her mother says everything at the commune is a test. Ryan waits for a moment in case Rose might wish to speak, but hearing nothing from her, he says that Father preaches much the same thing, that everything about their lives in this place is a preparation for life in the next. They say nothing for several seconds. Trina asks if they are still awake. Rose and Ryan whisper back that they are but only barely.

Trina whispers that Ryan's magic trick with the bread matches the kind of thing Anansi would do. Several voices chime in, not knowing what Trina means.

—Anan-who?

—Anansi!

She explains that, in one of the captain's many spider stories that he told her on his boat to pass the time, clever Anansi goes out and defies all the odds and defeats many foes and returns with plenty of food for his hungry children. Just like Ryan. Everyone agrees.

Trina thinks about her mother but says nothing. She remembers

Joyce telling her about being tested and about the next place waiting for them.

—That place is paradise, free of worldly cares. Focus on passing the test rather than on the reasons for having to take it; understanding will come with time.

Trina can barely keep her eyes open as her thoughts about her mother's advice blur and fade: Work with a smile on your face no matter what's on your mind and no matter how bad you feel.

The alarm sounds at the bakery. Searchlights comb the compound. Guards begin their search of each dormitory. Before anything can be done, the door bursts open and torchlights illuminate faces. The guards sniff. The smell of fresh bread lingers in the air. The children rub their eyes and feign a slow posture of interrupted dreams. The guards check inside a few mouths. Nothing, not a shred of evidence, not even a crumb to be seen anywhere. Just the persistent smell. More guards arrive and sniff the air. They see Trina. They ask if she knows anything about this. Trina shakes her head. The guards tell the children that the whole dormitory is in big trouble. That it is obvious from the evidence in the air that stolen bread was in here not so long ago. That they will all be punished and shamed. That not even the twice-born Little Miss Trina can save them from this one. The children squirm and twist in their beds and look around at the ceiling or directly down in front of them. The guards continue to lambaste them: They should think about the shame they will bring down on the heads of their parents in front of the whole community. Such shame never goes away. If anything, it grows with each passing day. Trina inhales and seems about to speak up. Ryan sees her and jumps up on his bed and says he took the bread and he just finished it, just that second, and all the others were sound asleep. He opens his mouth wide. The guards surround him, shine a torch in his mouth, and sniff. They are convinced by the smell but cannot see any actual pieces of bread. Nothing in the teeth or the crevices of his mouth. No stray crumbs. This puzzles them. Bread crumbles in children's hands. The guards confer. With Trina in the room, she cannot be involved in this transgression. They agree Ryan is the sole greedy culprit. They grab him and, ordering everyone to stay in bed, march him out of the dormitory.

EIGHT

Morning arrives in patches of red light trembling on the trunks of trees. The night rolls back its giant black linoleum to reveal buildings, fences, meandering night watchmen, and the prone quest of wild boar, the odd jaguar, pigs in their pens, cows, sheep, chickens, and goats. Light sidles between leaves to end in broken-glass formations on the forest floor. Doors open and people stagger into the open, looking more asleep than awake. The tintinnabulation of aluminum buckets and iron pots and pans. Stoves cough up flames and coax pots to the boil. The children wash, big boys supervise the washing and dressing of younger boys, older girls instruct younger girls.

They head to the breakfast hall, long tables and aluminum plates and cups and steel spoons and the orchestra of children handling these implements without a conductor, warming up and then launching into their meager breakfast score, some tea and a piece of bread (sometimes buttered) for the children, occasionally a shallow bowl of cereal with watered-down milk. Before morning school there are chores like washing up, making beds, picking up rubbish, emptying bins and emergency night pots, sweeping floors, big girls combing the hair of younger girls, women and men overseeing the whole enterprise with a harsh word or two for any child who moves too slowly or with too much talk or too sloppily, or whose knees and elbows need to be oiled or whose face should be washed again to remove the sleep crusted in the corners of the eyes or whose mouth is white with toothpaste not washed away properly, and hurry, hurry for school, for canteen, for time is not to be wasted among the godly, since time is precious and in this blessed life there is never enough of it to waste even one second, so move.

Joyce tries to hang wet clothes on the clothesline with her sore left hand in a bandage. She keeps several clothespins in her mouth and throws an item of clothing over the line. She arranges the item with a few adjustments and pins it in place. Trina runs up to her and hugs her. Joyce pushes her daughter away and looks around in a panic. Seeing no one, she pulls her daughter back to her embrace and apologizes several times.

—The guards took Ryan last night.

—I heard. I'm sorry. They'll use him as an example to test us. You must be strong.

They look at each other for a moment and nod. They tell each other they are fine and that they love each other. Trina offers to help hang the wet clothes. Joyce asks Trina to hold up her hands and decides at a glance that she needs to wash before she handles clean clothes. Joyce asks her to fetch more clothespins; she is about to run out, and then where will she be? Trina heads to the laundry room, where a group of women and girls attend to a dozen or more washing machines while others hand-wash certain items that cannot be machine-washed. More clotheslines are strung about the yard behind the laundry room with the clothing at various stages of being sunned. A breeze passes through, and the clothes flap like flags, and as the breeze picks up strength, the sound of the clotheslines mimics clapping or people slapping their thighs.

The clotheslines fall into four distinct groups: women, men, girls, and boys. No one owns anything, so the aim is to find something that fits.

The different dormitories and houses apportion clothes in the sizes of the children and adults living in them. This simplifies finding a clean item only a little, since the enormous task remains for a child or adult to wear something that is not too tight or too baggy.

The commune's rules against vanity discourage complimentary remarks about a person's appearance. The preacher maintains that the beauty that matters most happens to be within and not in any outward appearance. The exterior look should attend to good hygiene, and that is the end of it. For cleanliness, says Father, is next to . . . He trails off and waits for the collective answer. Trina's mother makes sure her daughter understands what size dress she needs to find and to pay particular attention to her choice of underwear—it should be clean and free of holes before she steps into it—and never to wear clothes that stand out and invite covetous eyes. The mending crew operates in a room packed with sewing machines. They make new things and repair old ones, cut large items down, and patch elbows and knees with pieces cut from items too damaged to restore to decency. Ironing is kept to a minimum, for the commune leader and his cadre of assistants only, and for the others to welcome an important visitor, perhaps a politician or other government delegation, to the compound. Clean clothes can be found in a series of storehouses with large shelves built in to walls, some fitted with drawers. Each section has a label according to age group and a one-word description. For Trina, the area to hunt for clothing is the girls' section and the six-to-ten age group; she has to hunt for underwear or dress or skirt or blouse (never the immodesty of trousers for the girls) in the drawers with those labels. A folding crew is responsible for keeping everything tidy, down to ensuring that fresh adhesive or tape holds those all-important labels in place.

Trina and her mother end up on laundry duty together. Trina washes her hands at a bucket beside a water barrel not far away. She shakes the excess water from her hands in the warm morning air and finds a bucket full of clothespins, just inside the door of the laundry room, and grabs it. But the bucket is so heavy, she has to walk back to her mother by gripping the handle with two hands and carrying it between her legs. This keeps her legs wide apart. As she steps, she rocks her body from one side to the other with the bucket kept very still between her legs. Trina's mother looks around and sees her daughter swaying toward her, laden down with pins in a bucket, and she has to hold her sore ribs and cover her mouth to stifle her laughter, since levity is not encouraged outside of sermons. Trina reaches her mother, who looks around to be sure they are not observed before she hugs and kisses her daughter several times in quick succession and tells her that she loves her in a rapid volley and, with the same lightning speed, resumes her task of hanging wet clothes.

—Mom, can you help Ryan?

—I don't know if I dare say anything, much less do something.

—We can't just abandon him.

The postman's van enters the compound. The approaching engine grabs everyone's attention. The postman drives into the main clearing that separates Adam's cage from the preacher's house. He stops his van at the front steps of the preacher's house, and people doing chores in the vicinity of the main clearing glance surreptitiously at the vehicle. The two guards stationed at the preacher's front door help the postman with his many sacks of mail for the commune. Trina's mother looks without looking, as she calls it. She knows it is considered slovenly and wayward to stop work and watch anything that does not relate directly to the task in front of her.

—Maybe you can help him.

—Me?

—Yes, Trina. You.

—But how?

Joyce whispers to Trina to keep her eyes on her work while she steals a glance or two in the direction of the mail van. The fact that so much mail arrives and none of it for anyone other than the preacher, including more than two hundred checks signed over to him by pensioners, makes everyone think of their homes and relatives who must be curious about them. Seeing the mail van induces a longing in Trina for another place more than for a father. She never knew her father, but she remembers another country. She misses the fact of never knowing her father less than she misses the country that she left to come to the jungle. A faraway land fathered her. Her mother never talks about him except to say he was a drinker and gambler and ungodly and unworthy of her love and loved no one but himself. If Trina asks where he came from or what he looked like, Joyce says he told her he came from all over and he looked like any man with selfish intentions. And that now the preacher is Trina's father and no man on earth would do for them what he has done for them and for everyone at the commune.

Trina's longing remains undiminished despite what her mother says. She sees the mailman and thinks what she feels must be multiplied in the bodies of everyone on the compound. Combine all that longing and hope and they should fill those huge mailbags, each longing in the shape of an envelope, each hope a sheet of paper filled with writing and sealed inside. Trina glances about and sees how everyone nearby, from the kitchen to the laundry to the cleaners and yard workers, lingers and tries to look at the mailman without making it obvious, how slow they become with half of their attention on the job and the more important half on the mailman. The van turns in three points and accelerates away and raises a little dust that disperses while it raises those seeds of longing and hope.

Trina and Joyce exchange looks of resignation and a smile. Trina decides to cheer up her mother and herself. She switches from slow to fast. She looks around, and seeing no prefect or guard's eyes on them, she slaps her mother on the behind and says that the clothes hanging like this in row upon row of lines resemble a theater full of headless people. Her mother looks about, and seeing that the coast is clear, she asks Trina if it could be that ghosts occupy the clothes. Trina replies that must be it exactly, an open-air theater of ghosts, an audience of ghosts looking at the two of them onstage, putting on a show. Joyce likes this. And what kind of a show are we in? her mother wonders. Trina says it is a show about a mother and her daughter lost in a forest and waiting for rescuers destined to come someday. Joyce asks if she can try harder to be happy as she waits to be rescued. Trina promises that she will be happy and will make a bigger effort to be happy if she can be sure of rescue someday and if it will please Joyce.

—Yes, it will please me to think that my daughter is happy with me no matter where we happen to be.

Trina passes pins to her mother, a couple at a time, and wet clothes, one at a time. They edge sideways as they fill the line. Trina asks her mother how the play they are in will end.

—Happily, therefore be happy. But the exact details of the happy ending aren't known. Not even by the actors.

—The ghosts know, don't they?

—Nope. They are in the audience because they don't know the ending, either.

This makes Trina laugh and squash the laugh with her hand to her mouth. Joyce drags the basin of wet clothes along with them while Trina pulls her bucket of clothespins, a two-handed pull with her legs far apart, and the bucket of pins grows imperceptibly easier to drag as the line fills and dips with the weight of the clothes, and some drip and pockmark the dirt.

Trina hears her name from more than one source. Joyce looks alarmed and tries to hide her concern with a smile at her daughter, whose entire frame stiffens at the sound of her name. A prefect runs up to Trina and says she must come right away, at Father's request. Seeing the concern on their faces, the prefect tells them not to worry, that this time it is a good thing. The prefect leads Trina to the dormitory, where she collects her flute. He leads her from the dormitory to Adam's cage; the preacher waits there for them. He wears a starched and well-ironed white shirt and white pants with a prominent leg seam. He is about to give Adam his breakfast. The preacher greets Trina with a smile and says he hopes she will be his helper. Two guards, rifles slung over shoulders, stand a few paces from the preacher and Trina. One of the guards carries a bucket full of vegetable and fruit peels, some limp salad leaves, and lettuce and ripe bananas. The other holds a bucket of water.

—You play the flute while I feed him.

—Yes, Father.

At the sight of breakfast, Adam scrambles from his bed to the gate of his cage. The man points to the back of the cage, and Adam retreats there. The preacher takes the basket of food from the guard, fishes a bunch of keys out of his trouser pocket, flicks through them with a jangly sound, and stops at a large silver key. He inserts that into the fat lock and turns his wrist, and the lock flicks open. He sinks the bunch of keys in his pocket and stifles their song. Next he pulls the chain from the coupling and places lock and chain on the ground next to the cage door. A guard leaps forward and opens the door for the preacher, who steps inside with the basket of gorilla goodies. The guards become edgy. Trina plays and looks at the sandals on the preacher's feet, crisscrossed black leather polished to a shine and held in place by a spotless silver buckle. His toenails are cut in a straight line and longer than she thinks they should be, with sharp edges on account of the straight cut, nails that could burst a balloon if one landed on his foot, or cut someone if he kicked them.

The preacher pours the contents of the basket into a trough and comes back out for the bucket of water, which he carries into the cage and pours into a large bowl. He stands inside and looks at Trina as she plays. Trina lowers the flute. He nods to Trina to resume playing and beckons her to join him in the cage. Adam eats, but his eyes follow Trina as she comes. He pauses with a mouthful of lettuce and remembers that he should view the two of them right there in the cage with him as his most important allies in the community. This man and child bring him food and music. The preacher watches Adam eat while Trina plays her flute. People around the compound stall in their chores and steal glances their way. Joyce stoops to pick up wet clothes and pretends to sort through the laundry as she fights to breathe and keep her head clear and see what her daughter is doing with the preacher. Adam reminds himself that all he has to do is obey the preacher, carry out orders from him to the letter. Adam pretends to eat as he looks askance at the preacher and at Trina playing her flute.

—A friend of yours did something wrong to me, to himself, to everyone at this commune, and to God.

The preacher's words pound Trina's body. She feels her energy drain from her. Her arms weaken, and she lowers the flute and stares with wide unblinking eyes at the preacher.

—You know his actions cannot go unpunished, don't you, Trina?

—But Father. He won't ever steal again.

—That's not the point, Trina. Listen to me.

—But he's good, Father. He made one mistake.

—If you say "but" to me again, I will lock you in this cage with Adam. Do you understand?

—Yes, Father. Sorry, Father.

—If I don't make an example of him, others will take it as a sign of weakness, and anarchy will spread like wildfire through this community.

—Yes, Father.

—I need your help to restore order. You're this boy's friend, so you're the best person for the job.

—What job, Father?

—Play some more.

He tells the guards to stand a little farther away. Trina makes up a tune that comes from listening to the wind in the trees and then the rain made by trees and the arrival of sunshine through that rain. Adam again stops chewing and listens. The preacher nods in time to the tune or some thought that roughly matches Trina's playing. He touches Trina's shoulder for her to follow him, and he walks backward out of the cage, so Trina steps backward as well. She glances behind her to see where to place the ball of her foot while avoiding the preacher's razor toenails. After they're out of the cage, the preacher replaces the heavy chain and big lock and keys it shut. The preacher walks away, leaving Trina standing next to the cage with the guards holding a bucket and a basket between them. The guards pass the basket and bucket to the nearest passerby and follow the preacher at a safe distance. The preacher pulls a notebook and pen from his pocket and, every few steps, notes something that is wrong, an eyesore in need of someone's attention. He frowns throughout. A smile and a nod break out on his mask of distemper the moment Trina scoots beside him and curtseys. He takes her hand in his, and she wants to look at his hand to check why it feels soft and warm, but she just returns his grip and stifles an instinct to break into a skipping step. She knows her mother sees all this, so Trina tries to act as she imagines her mother would instruct her to act, with engagement but not unseemly enthusiasm. Therefore no skipping. Therefore she swallows the nursery rhyme brimming in her throat.

—Your flute playing's coming along.

—Thank you, Father.

He places his pen in his shirt pocket and ruffles her hair and points in the direction of the school building for Trina to head there, and she runs toward it and looks over her shoulder at him and he waves at her and she waves back. She glances at the clothesline. Though Joyce stoops over a basin of clothes as if sorting through for the right item to fit on the last space left on the line, Trina knows her mother crouches at that particular angle to take a good look at how her daughter is conducting herself with the preacher and the beast.

Trina waves at her mother by pretending to wave away a fly. Trina even says, Shoo, fly. And she speaks quite loud. Every muscle in Joyce's body wants to wave back at Trina, but she knows better than to attract the attention of a prefect or guard. Like every parent at the commune, she has to downplay public displays of affection toward her child. Trina belongs less to her and more to everyone in the community. Every adult is a parent to her child, and therefore Trina belongs to everyone as much as she belongs to her mother. And everyone in the community belongs to God, whose prophet is Father to all of them. Joyce allows herself a brief smile that she smothers by burying her face in a small wet shirt. She sniffs at the shirt as if she detects a sweat stain on it and, certain she has wiped that smile from her face, holds the shirt up to the light in an ostentatious act of inspection. A breeze whips through the rows of clotheslines, and the garments flap in a burst of applause. Joyce marvels at Trina seeing the ghosts in the clothes hanging on lines, and takes a bow to her audience. What a child. She has worked out already at her delicate age that everything they do at the commune, each chore or demonstration of loyalty, has to carry with it like a shadow a performance for some other thing that can never be shown. The chore can never be that Joyce simply hangs wet clothes on the line; Joyce tries to perform the chore as if she were Trina. What would Trina do on a stage in front of an audience of ghosts? Joyce thinks for a moment. She pauses and listens to the clothes. How to find the rationale for bowing in the open to no one in particular? She thinks like the mirror image of her daughter. It comes to her in a flash. She drops her clothespins, reaches down to retrieve them with a slight bend in her knees, and straightens again before the clothes. Her disguised genuflection is as good as taking a bow. The wind picks up. The clothes flap. Joyce sings to herself, barely a song, more a hum:

—Captain, Captain, put me ashore . . .

She sees her daughter with her on a boat with a man in a sweat-stained captain's hat standing at the helm. The picture of the captain makes Joyce's temperature rise. She replaces the captain and his boat with an image of Trina playing her flute.

NINE

In the schoolhouse, the head teacher asks the assembly of children who walks them from calamity to safety. Father, the children reply. With so many voices saying the word, it booms from the building and resembles many other words: fatter, farther, fadder. The youngest children sit in the front rows and the older children at the back. Teachers brandish four-foot-long flexible canes and stand around the sides with a few older prefects drawn from the most obedient of the children to help keep the others seated, looking straight ahead, and still, no fidgeting, no whispering, or else a quick flick of a cane on the arms or legs. The prefects decide one child is guilty of a gross infraction when he continues to whisper after a warning hit and fidgets unduly despite a tap of a cane on his legs. They pull the child out of the assembly and make him hold out a hand, and the cane tastes his flesh six times, three licks on each outstretched palm.

Trina sits at the front and waits for the preacher, as instructed. She spots Rose a few rows back; no sight of Ryan. Trina looks without looking at a mirror image of her mother. Trina has perfected the act of staring straight ahead with her eyes thrown to the corners to catch glimpses of things to her extreme left and right. She times her survey of the room to coincide with any disturbance that might occur. The moment another child is reprimanded, in the middle of the lash or extraction from the row of seats, usually through pulling that child by an ear, Trina looks behind and away from the focal point of the room to see what else is happening and who is doing what to whom. She finds it much more interesting to consider the events that will happen next rather than the events that are almost done and over with.

Where is Ryan? She maps the position of each teacher and prefect. The farther away from her the prefect or teacher, the more she can scope out her environment undetected. All she wants to do is scratch if she feels like it or cross and uncross her legs without someone shouting at her or lashing her arms and legs. Trina spots Rose, who looks particularly unhappy, barely able to stop herself from crying. Trina knows if Rose bursts into tears, she risks a beating. It happens all the time. The prefects beat a child who they think is crying for nothing. They say by beating the child, they are giving him or her a real reason to cry. Trina tries to catch Rose's attention and smile and cheer her to save her from punishment.

First, she thinks, distract the prefects. Trina bumps the child to her right with her shoulder. That child bumps the child to her right, and the bumping runs along the row of seats until a prefect shouts at the children to stop their nonsense and two more prefects leave their stations and come over to investigate. Second, Trina turns to face Rose and beams to her the biggest smile she can fit on her face. Trina also crosses her eyes and sticks out her tongue and curls it up toward her nose. Rose smiles, and so do many other children who witness Trina's antics. The prefects shout and tap at more children.

Trina scans the faces around her to take her attention away from the front of the room. She hates how an adult asks a question in order to occupy the thoughts of a child minute by minute. It seems every adult in the commune is bent on emulating the ways of the preacher. Trina sees it as rude, because she has enough things to think about already. She cannot bear setting aside all her thoughts for a relay of questions everyone knows the answers to. As the assembly shouts a reply to a question, Trina moves her lips soundlessly. She creates the impression of her engagement and full participation in the proceedings. If the teachers and prefects are far from her, she does not bother to move her lips. She uses the time to examine how the other children look, and she weighs on scales in her mind just how much happiness there is among the children as opposed to misery. This morning is ruled by misery. Ryan is missing. To get through her day, she decides to smile at as many children as possible.

—Who puts food on your table?

The head teacher paces across the front of the room and makes an arc of her cane in front of her chest and lashes the sides of her legs as if to spur herself on with her interrogative formulations. The children reply:

—Father.

Trina moves her lips, since she is seated three seats from the end of the row and easily observed by a prefect who stands nearby and stares at every child in the vicinity for seconds at a time, as if looking for some sign on the child's body that will indicate imminent rebellion.

—Who protects us from our wicked ways?

—Father.

Trina lip-synchs some more.

—Who will guide us through the gates of paradise?

—Fadder, farther, farter.

Trina moves her lips and keeps a smile away from her mouth and confines her glee to her narrowed eyes. The children bow their heads, and the head teacher asks the Lord to forgive them their evil ways, for they know not what they do in their actions that serve the devil and their thoughts that invite evil into their minds and hearts, and only the preacher can save them from themselves, amen. Amen, the children reply. The prefects and teachers order the children to clear the central space of the assembly room. Beginning with the front row, each child takes a chair to a corner of the hall and adds it to a stack. Older children help the young ones, who cannot lift their chairs onto the stack. The children stand to the side. It takes five minutes of scraping and bumping to clear the hall and gather all the children around the sides of the room. The head teacher calls Trina to the middle of the room. Trina stands and looks around to see if she can spot Rose and whether this concerns Ryan. The head teacher extends her cane to Trina, who hesitates. The teacher says Trina had better take the cane or taste some licks from it right there in front of everyone. Trina considers the ultimatum. The head teacher leans in close to Trina's ear and whispers that this order comes from the preacher, and not to obey it would mean terrible things for a lot of people, not just Trina. The teacher urges Trina to think of her mother. Trina takes the cane and holds it beside her. The cane is as tall as Trina.

The head teacher calls on the assembled children to pay special attention to this exercise. Prefects step forward and form two lines, one on either side of Trina. Each prefect wields a similar cane. She says that a child among them went against the communal ideal by committing a crime of theft. Two guards march into the hall and join the front of the two lines. One of the guards is the young man recently promoted from a prefect as a reward for snitching on his mother and who likes to beat children. The head teacher says that the only appropriate lesson for a thief is a public beating. The young guard lifts a whistle to his mouth and waits for the head teacher to finish her speech. The whistle hangs on a plain piece of string around his neck. The head teacher says that by special decree of the preacher, Trina is to head the group who will carry out the punishment. The head teacher nods at the young guard, who looks at the door and blows his whistle. A shrill beaded sound reverberates in the hall. Trina's ears ring. The whistle seals her ears tight. All eyes train on the entrance to the hall. Trina feels her body become limp, her blood drain, her air vacuum, her legs lose their polarity of bones. She looks for Rose in the crowd. She thinks of her mother. If only Joyce could walk in and put a stop to things.

Four guards march in with Ryan in the middle. The hall full of children harvests whispers, gasps, shuffling feet. The youngest of the children begin to whimper, Rose among them. Trina finds Rose, squeezes her eyes almost closed, and barely nods. Rose stems her tears. For Trina. Rose inhales deeply to calm herself. For Ryan. He looks around the room. His eyes are red. His clothes dirty. He stares blankly at Trina without showing the slightest sign of recognition. The guards position Ryan at the end of the two lines. He faces Trina, who stands at the other end. The young guard tells Ryan to walk to Trina and turn around and walk all the way back. He must stay in the middle of the lines. He must not bump into any of the prefects or guards. He must not run, he must not fall to the ground, or the whole thing will happen again from the beginning. He wants to know if Ryan understands. Ryan nods. Ryan looks at Rose and nods. This must happen. Ryan nods at Trina again. And the best way for it to happen, the smoothest way, is for everyone to play his part to the best of his ability. Trina nods back. The prefects and guards raise their canes and sticks, and Trina follows their gesture. She lifts the leaden weights of her arms with the cane in her hands. The young guard's whistle slices the air to ribbons, and Ryan's punishment begins.

Ryan walks like an automaton, slow, joints stiff, his arms by his sides. He winces and blinks from shadows of sticks, from the involuntary register of a heavy object brought down fast and hard on his body. His eyes fill with tears, against his will to keep them clear and empty of his surroundings. Each strike approximates to a hard punch or kick. His body jolts with the blows. He hears his name attached to curses. He meets Trina with her arms raised over her head and a stick in her hands. He sees her through eyes full of water so that she looks blurred in parts and bulbous and wavy, almost boneless. More sticks rain down on Ryan, and Trina's image runs down Ryan's face. He sees darkness with no sound and feels numbness all over his body.

Outside the school building, Adam shakes the bars of his cage and howls. Joyce and Ryan's parents edge close to the school to pick up what they can of the events going on inside. A guard stationed outside the building orders them to move away. He walks with them and repeats his order, and they move slowly ahead, just out of reach of his stick.

A convoy of four army jeeps pulls up in front of the preacher's white house, and several uniformed men hop out. One of the soldiers carries a light but big briefcase, light from the way he swings it around with ease as he moves. Four pairs of soldiers each grab four large cases and head for the front door of the preacher's house. They huff and puff with the cases and call directions to each other about which one should start up the steps and which one should follow. Another soldier pins under his left arm what looks like a foot-long sandwich in a brown paper bag. The guards at the front door push the door wide and hold it open for the soldiers to enter. The group files into the house and leaves the driver of the first vehicle to keep watch. The guards close the front door and admire the vehicles from afar. The soldier steps from behind the wheel and stretches. There is a pause during which the driver unbuttons the left breast pocket on his pressed uniform and fishes out a cigarette pack decorated with a camel. The two guards' attention wanders from the four jeeps to the soldier. He peels off the clear plastic seal, shakes the pack until one cigarette frees itself, takes it between two fingers and taps it on the packet, pulls a lighter from the same pocket, shields it with a cupped hand, and lowers his head to the flame. The guards step down from the porch to join the driver, who offers them each a cigarette. They look around and decline. One guard says somewhat perfunctorily that the commune considers cigarettes to be devil sticks. The soldier shrugs and draws deeply and looks away from the guards in the direction of Adam's cage. The guards watch as smoke from the cigarette climbs out of the nostrils of the soldier and scatters to enviable invisibility. They quiz the soldier about the capital. He says things are tough in the city. People cannot find work. Basic supplies like flour, sugar, milk, and rice are hard to come by. The driver marvels at the compound around him. He says the guards are lucky to have food, clothing, and shelter guaranteed. Even in the army, a soldier has to buy his uniform. The only free things are ammunition and a gun. The guards say that the most difficult food to find is food for the spirit. The army driver agrees and blows a smoke ring whose halo drifts above his head and evaporates. Is army life good to him? It takes the driver two puffs, the first short and the second long, to consider the question. He says he has a regular wage and a roof over his head, but the things that he has to do to make ends meet, to supplement his wage, none of it is to be found in any army training manual and yet all of it has to be practiced. Such as what, the guard wants to know. Well, here he is in this compound in the middle of the jungle, and why is that. The guards shrug. The driver asks them to think about it. He puffs twice and squints through the smoke as he looks at the guards. He lights up another by gently meeting the fresh cigarette with the ruby stub, then drops and mashes the stub into the soil. He offers the packet absently, and the guards liberate two cigarettes each and conceal the little devils under their cloth hats.

He says that the guards must answer why here and now for themselves, and he continues to speak as he exhales smoke. How is it that a group of almost one thousand foreign nationals could end up with permission to clear three thousand acres of prime jungle and build on it and do whatever they want? He leans on his jeep and waits for the guards to say something, but they shift their weight and glance away or stare at the ground and examine the toes of their boots. He keeps puffing and speaking through the fumes. He says they must know more about it all than a mere driver and army private. How can all this happen—he waves his cigarette to take in the compound—and not have anyone in government or the police bother them from one end of the month to the other except for this little house call. The guards nod. The private keeps his cigarette between his lips as he pulls and puffs and talks. Wisps snake up to his eyes and make him squint. The guards add nothing. They know it is better to remain silent. They nod and twitch.

Talk switches to the dangers presented by the compound's juxtaposition with boa constrictors, vipers, caiman, wild boar, jaguars, red ants, and killer bees. Is there an antidote to be found anywhere on the compound for each of these mortal threats, the driver wants to know. The guards pat their rifles.

—You need a lot of bullets to get rid of killer bees.

—No, just shoot the queen and you kill the colony.

—You fellas must be marksmen.

They chuckle. The front door opens and the guards run up the steps of the porch to meet the departing retinue. One soldier carries the same large briefcase he arrived with, but it appears much heavier, since he lets it hang by his side. Another soldier follows, minus the sandwich in the brown paper bag. Others emerge, and each soldier carries in a rather casual way one of the three metal suitcases they struggled with earlier in pairs. The preacher emerges last of all in his brown slacks, white jacket, and open-toed slippers. He shakes hands with the soldiers, and they salute, hop down the steps, and leap into the jeeps, seemingly sprightlier than when they arrived. They drive off and wave to the guards and the preacher. They pass Adam's cage and stare as they fix sunglasses in place. Adam stares right back at them. They do not wave, so neither does he. The preacher turns back to the front door the moment the jeeps disappear along the road that leads to the entrance of the commune. A guard crouches and retrieves a flattened cigarette stub from the soil, brushes it off, and tucks it under his cap.

Two guards at a barrier that is no more than a tree trunk on two upright forks lift it to one side for the four jeeps to drive through with a casual exchange of salutes. One of the guards says into his two-way radio that the rooster has flown. Kevin and Eric, the guards at the improvised gate, take up their cards from under cloth caps and place them on the table next to a small hut and resume their game of gin rummy. There is no need to keep a constant lookout. They can hear an engine's approach a mile away. The straight road cleared of trees and bushes makes it possible to see someone coming from half a mile. They spend more time looking at the compound for someone who might be trying to leave.

Playing cards is illegal. If someone sees and reports them, the card-players will be beaten. The number of lashes depends on the preacher's mood and how many people need to be punished and whether there are any witnesses to the deed. The careful calibration of crime and punish-ment depends on reasoning exclusive to the preacher. At the gates to the commune, on the fringes where its rules begin, seems just sufficiently far away to make it a lesser crime, not as much a broken rule as a way of pass-ing the time. Every guard at the gate is sworn to secrecy, and each shift stores the pack of cards under a loose floorboard in the guards' hut. Kevin and Eric play for matches and cigarettes. Smoking is a sin. So the guards take turns lighting one cigarette while the other guard keeps a close eye on the road. Swearing is a sin. The guards obey this rule because speech, especially words generated by excitement, is such a spontaneous thing that they worry they will say something bad within earshot of someone who has the power to get them into trouble. This makes the talk around their game of cards a somewhat restricted linguistic enterprise, no expletives, just the names of animals and people's apparel substituted for the usual proscribed words. Women's apparel for curses to do with women's bodies and men's apparel for men's private body parts and rats for what adults do in private. Kevin slams a bad card on the table.

—Oh, panties.

Eric responds with a trump card, which he delivers as if threading a needle.

—Rats to you, my fine-feathered friend.

Eric casts a baleful eye toward the road leading from the compound and slaps a mosquito on his neck and collects the cigarette and three matches that accrued as the stakes grew and grew. They play again and the fortunes reverse; Kevin wins back his coveted cigarette and two of three matches from Eric.

In the school building, the older students position screens to carve out classrooms; they wheel in chalkboards and distribute exercise books. At every turn, some teacher or prefect congratulates Trina on her display of loyalty to the commune over personal friendship. Trina smiles and feels numb and cold. She cannot speak. A teacher asks if she is all right, and she nods and smiles. The teacher tells her she is a brave girl and will go far. That her courage means she is destined to climb the ranks of the commune and command new heights next to the preacher. Trina wants to swing her flute at the teacher's face. She smiles and nods. The younger children repeat instructions and information; the older children write answers to quizzes and copy dictation into their books. The children in the school band—Trina included, with her flute—walk out of the building and shelter under a tree and practice their scales. To the jaguar or panther prowling in the forest, they sound like every species of bird gathered in one area, all singing at the same time. The children's instruments empty the trees of parrots, woodpeckers, and crows. Even the sloth inches farther away from the compound. The music teacher calls out the hymn for the class to begin, and the instruments chime in synchrony. The entire forest of wildlife draws nearer and grows quite still. Some of the birds join in with their own musical improvisations. Trina takes the lead with a flute solo. Images of Ryan fill Trina's head. Her arm raises a stick and brings it down on his talk, his walk, his smile, and his arms holding her. Her eyes water as she plays. The teacher assumes she is moved by the music. Joyce hears the flute and knows as long as her daughter plays, she will not feel alone without her mother. Adam pulls on the bars of his cage, raises himself to his full height, stretches his neck, aims at the sky, and howls.

TEN

The preacher in his painted house puts up his feet and accepts two clinks of ice into his glass of fifteen-year-old red rum. He knows what the evening sermon will be about. Temptation, the vagaries of it, the certain ruin that it brings to the unwary spirit, the need to police temptation with priestly rigor. Who among them is not tempted? he thinks as he sips on the rum and tastes the cane in it, the molasses and the syrup that slow the flow of the over-proof spirit. He rolls it on his tongue and swills fire and ice into every nook and cranny of his mouth to produce a gentle burn that saliva eases and repeated sips reduce, and he swallows for the same pleasant burn down his throat and for the feel of a gentle furnace in the pit of his gut. He holds his glass over his head, and his three assistants and two bodyguards set aside their two pistols and a rifle and toast to his health and touch glasses and throw their heads back. He says the country they are in surely must be a wicked place, with rum of this high a caliber. What he could do with a big country like this if he held the reins. The vast forest overflowing with minerals, precious metals, diamonds, and timber. He says that, were he El Presidente, he would build a road through the jungle to connect every country on the continent, from the top to the bottom of the continent and from east to west, linking all the nations and uniting them under one flag, the flag of worship of the Most High, for a heaven on earth, for the equal rights of all regardless of sex or standing in life. He would minister to every tribe in the rain forest, every conquistador, every missionary, every gold digger, diamond prospector, and gaucho, until the whole lot united under him as one family and paid homage to God and to His number one agent under the sun, yours truly. His followers applaud. He nods for a refill and complains how shallow these rum bottles are and what robbery to put something so good in a receptacle so parsimonious.

He asks his assistants, Dee, Pat, and Nora, if they are happy. They reply in unison:

—Yes, Reverend.

He asks them if he did the right thing to drag them across the sea and deep into the jungle, just for a little respite from the devils out to get him. Yes, they say, again in unison. They take turns cementing their assent. Dee first, followed by Pat and then Nora:

—No doubt about it.

—The best thing we can do with our lives.

—Prior to meeting you, Father, we lived life without meaning.

He drinks to that.

—Amen.

They toast to that. He asks for two more pieces of ice and holds his glass with both hands next to his right ear for the music of the cubes dropped one at a time from silver tongs. A queue forms at his front door as the various scouts from every corner of the compound appear with some important news.

—What's the fuss?

—Ryan's gone, Father.

—The bread stealer?

—Yes, Father.

—How dare he run away from me!

The preacher jumps out of his chair and knocks it over and flings his glass at the fireplace. He curses the child in a long string of obscenities akin to a spell, the worst words imaginable from the mouth of a preacher. An assistant touches his arm and leads him back to his chair, set upright by another assistant. A fresh glass finds his open hand.

—Should we send some guards to find him?

—No. Forget it. He won't get far. Where will he find food and water? He can barely button his pants, much less survive in this jungle.

He takes out his handkerchief and mops his face and neck, both corded with veins. He shakes his head and takes a long drink from the glass and exhales loudly with the rum burn that reddens his neck as if staining it.

—Should we notify the army in case they come across him?

—No, absolutely not. Not a soul outside this compound must know about him. He'll come back with his tail between his legs. And upon his return, whatever his condition, he must be taught a lesson for running away.

—His mother and father are at the infirmary. Should we notify them?

—No. They have lost their privileges. I'm his father. I'm his mother, too, come to think of it, and I say we do nothing.

—Sorry, Father.

—No one is to do a thing, you hear me? The gauntlet was apparently too easy for him. Not sure a spell in the well would have any effect on a child of his temperament. My sermons had no effect. A visit with Adam should straighten him out.

—Yes, Father.

—Let me know the second he crawls back here.

—Yes, Reverend.

He dismisses the others with their daily reports of commune behavior. They file out of the house. A minute later he asks his assistant to call them back. The communications manager heads the line; he looks directly into the dark eyes of the preacher and says the local tribes keep calling to tell the commune to stop polluting the river. The preacher interrupts the report. He waves at an unseen irritant in front of his face and says he does not wish to hear another syllable about the local tribes and that he did not come all the way out into the wilderness of the Amazon to be dictated to by primitives, and will the communications manager please stop taking calls from the tribes, and will he please do his job and just hang the hell up on them.

The infirmary nurse is second in the queue. She waits for a minute as the preacher's assistants clear away broken glass and return rum bottles to the drinks cabinet. The nurse launches into her report to the preacher, but the glint from pieces of glass on the wood floor catches her gaze, which wanders from the preacher's face and scrambles across the floor. He stops the nurse's report and asks what she finds so interesting about his house to make her take her eyes off him and pry into things that are of no concern to her. Before she can say anything, he raises his voice. Did she wish to live in his house and do his work and take on his worry while he lives in her lodgings, free of the pressure of steering one thousand souls to salvation? Of course not, he answers before she can say anything. He waves his hands in her face.

—Keep those beady eyes of yours on me.

The nurse apologizes profusely. Tears spring to her eyes.

—Don't! Don't you dare cry!

She blinks rapidly and inhales deeply and picks a spot to look at on the man's forehead, just above his eyes, since she finds that his dark stare undresses her. She says last night's emergency patient, the woman injured by Adam, had only superficial scratches and a couple of metacarpal fractures, nothing a painkiller and bandage could not rectify. He interrupts the nurse to let her know that "rectify" is a good word to use to a rector in his rectory. He laughs. Everyone in the room laughs as well. The nurse laughs longest of all. She continues, telling him that one child has colic and a second diarrhea, after eating two sticks of green corn.

—Serves him right.

—Not him, Father. Her.

—Serves her right. Greedy guts.

He laughs and everyone follows suit. The nurse resumes. Yet another child needed a tetanus injection for a rusty nail she stepped on that pierced her shoe and went into her foot. Miss Taylor, the old lady responsible for putting makeup on the dead, is sick. She says she has no feeling in her left leg and left arm. The doctor thinks she may have had a stroke in her sleep without even realizing it. She complains of stomach cramps and asks to see you, Father. She says she wants to see you before she faces her Maker. The preacher asks the nurse if he really needs to see the old lady; if today for certain will be her last day of taxing the miserable air with her miserable litany of complaints. The nurse says no, the old lady is sure to live another forty-eight to seventy-two hours but might not be compos mentis, since confusion is a symptom of a stroke. Okay, he agrees to see the old lady soon. He looks at the nurse and chews his cud and furrows his brow.

—There might be a birth soon, but it might end up as a cesarean.

—Ha, an impending death and an imminent birth; the Lord giveth and the Lord taketh away. What about our two dissidents?

Here the nurse seems to choose her words very carefully. She says they are still heavily sedated and catheterized and quite helpless, that they come around but do not know where they are and still go on about crossing the sea and getting back to the surf and beaches and home to burgers and fries and the people who are their blood. The two remain so far from their immediate surroundings that neither one has mentioned Ryan once. The preacher instructs her to keep them under the fog for a few more days, after which the drugs should be reduced and the reeducation program started in earnest.

—We are their family now, and I am their father, and that is all they need to know.

He pounds the arm of his chair. He takes a deep breath and straightens and presses his back into the chair, whose padding squeaks under the pressure. His agitation gives way to a broad smile, and he rubs his hands together and turns to the pharmacist.

—Right, how are the supplies doing?

—We have lots of cyanide and a shortage of penicillin.

—There are a lot of rats around, and the language of rats, the only language rats understand, is poison. This commune has a jewelry license, you know. Cyanide works wonders on gold and silver.

He reminds the pharmacist that too many drugs cause more damage than good and that the tetanus and other important vaccines may be ordered in sufficient quantities. Any disease in the camp would send the wrong signal to the mercenaries out there. He gestures at the window framed by the forest. Mercenaries, ready and eager to destroy our little experiment in paradise.

He instructs the pharmacist to stock up on cyanide before the prices increase and a shortage ensues and to keep it all under lock and key.

—Thank you, my trusted pharmacist. Keep up the fine work. Who else? Bring me some good news, someone.

He talks aloud to no one specifically and pounds the arm of his chair with a friendly fist. The prefect for the women in the kitchen says supplies remain good, and the various cooks and washers and cleaners jibe and fuss at one another, but none of them has any grumbles about him or about the place. He says that is good news.

—Something's working in this community.

She wonders if there can be more meat for the evening meals. He knits his brows and makes a big effort to maintain an air of cordial impartiality. He says that while many among them may believe that he can turn bread and salted fish into loaves and shoals, he cannot produce mutton from mud and steak from sticks. He urges her to remind them that the animals on the compound are commercial undertakings, that meat is bad for the soul, and that the meals assigned to them are well balanced and exceed the recommendations of the World Health Organization.

—Ask them if they see any rickets in this camp or malnutrition, and then ask them why not? The more people have, the more people want. Why oh why can't people be satisfied with what they have, compared with the poverty I plucked them from, the meaningless squandering of their days back in that land run by infidels.

He asks the prefect to tell all the other prefects to talk up the original reasons for coming here, remind the people where they came from compared to what they enjoy now. He says he feels worn out by just listening. He is tired. He dismisses the young guard recently promoted and assigned to listen in on the talk of the guards and report to the preacher personally. He tells the farmer he will hear from him another day but he should keep up his work of eavesdropping on other farmworkers. He shakes the hand of the carpenter, whose ears are as primed as the pumps on the well whose wood he repairs. He pats the head of the child prefect trained to ingratiate her way into every conversation to check that none of the talk denigrates the preacher. He waves them all away with a promise to hear from them another day. And to each of the commune reporters, his assistant gives a reward of a paper bag full of treats. He needs to sleep.

—Everyone out! Get out!

The house empties fast. He asks his personal assistant and nurse to give him something to help him get a little rest, for he is weary of his burden and his head will explode with it and his mind turn to porridge because of it, and he needs just a little respite. His assistant and nurse turns his left arm, palm up, teases a vein into prominence with a few flicks of her middle finger, and injects him. He looks at her and says she is beautiful and good to him and the only one he can trust. She says that is what he says to all the girls. Yes, he says, but he really means it when he says it to her. She is beautiful and good to him. She runs her fingers through his hair until he slumps into his armchair. She shakes out a folded blanket and drapes it over him and shuts the blinds to his living room and tiptoes away, signaling to the guards stationed at the front door with her index finger over her lips that the preacher sleeps. The guards nod and tiptoe off the front porch and set up a perimeter of silence. They shoo Rose away from the house without listening to her reason for being there, and as a tractor approaches, they make the driver describe a wide arc away from the house.

They turn the volume of their radios to the lowest setting. They signal to everyone who walks nearby that they must be extra quiet, for the preacher who never sleeps is actually asleep and his rest is as precious as diamonds and gold. Rose fails to heed the warning fast enough, so they remove their belts and chase her and threaten to beat her, and when she cries out at their threats, they threaten to beat her for making that noise. They command her to be quiet and suffer her punishment in silence, for Father demands tranquillity. Quiet for the preacher who parted the sea and guaranteed them safe passage and brought them to an unspoiled promised land and delivered them from evil, just as he will guide them unscathed to the king-dom of heaven. But for now he needs and must catch forty winks.

In the rush to clear the space in front of the house, the guards chase Rose around the corner to the back and leave their rifles on the ground by the front porch. They catch Rose and stop the chase and beat her, even though she is too far from the white house for the drugged preacher to heed her noise. They grow tired of the sport of Rose's dancing feet trying to avoid their belts and race back to the house, holding up their trousers and threading the belts back around their waists. They search for their rifles and cannot find them. They scratch their heads and look around but cannot see anyone in the vicinity. They swear to each other to say nothing about the loss to anyone. The punishment for losing a rifle would result in a demotion, at minimum. They grab two sticks, usually the preserve of prefects, and wait at the front door for the end of their shift.

—If anyone asks about our weapons, say we left them inside the armory.

The reinforced basement room in the preacher's house holds many weapons and ammunition, and since the preacher sleeps and no one except God Himself should disturb him before he is good and ready to wake, those guns can wait to be retrieved.

—Sleep and the preacher are strangers who need to get acquainted.

The guards shake on it. Not a word. Demotion minimum and likely some hurt, some public humiliation. They keep looking around in disbelief that two rifles can grow legs and walk off. They whisper that someone in the community must be up to something. Is the child whom they chased and whipped involved in some way? No. The rifles must turn up. They cannot disappear into thin air. Other guards must be playing a practical joke on them. That must be it. The change of shift should solve everything. Their replacements will turn up and admit they hid the rifles to see the guards' reaction. The guards wonder, if they do not say anything and it really is a practical joke, whether they might look bad or devious. No. If their rifles do not turn up, something big and bad happens for sure, because a rifle thief lives among them.

ELEVEN

If the commune located beyond the reach of history sought to give history the slip and start from scratch, there could be no better setting than a realm where myth rules the order of night and day. In a place where trees big and plentiful create their own rain cloud and downpour and it is possible to walk in a stride through a wall of rain into a bright room of sunlight. Where mists hang with nothing to hold them up. And those mists graze in fields and nuzzle and scratch an itch against the trunks of trees. Cloud percolates between a handful of trees and disperses an aroma of humidity that makes it difficult to swing an ax without feeling breathless in an instant and persuades the native tribes in the forest—the Macushi, Waiwai, Arawak, Patamona, and Waurá—to drop their tools and hunting weapons and retreat to their huts and hammocks and carve out new faces buried in the fallen trunks of trees, new faces for their gods or old gods with new faces, and wait out the weather, surely a god for cleansing, for enveloping, for conjuring life, and wait out the trees inhaling until their lungs fill and exhaling to quench the thirst of their roots buried in the soil, shake out cloud from the green and flower-threaded plaits of canopies and placate the gods of the soil and air for granting space to tribes, haul up the rivers and streams with ropes invisible to the human eye until the water reveals itself in mountain ranges, in clouds too heavy for their moorings in air and so sent back down to earth by gusts, drumrolls, rods, and staves of flint-made light and other inducements.

A delegation picked from eight of the local indigenous tribes and loaded into two jeeps approaches the entrance of the compound. On guard duty, Kevin and Eric hide their cards, aim their rifles, and ask the occupants of the two jeeps to step out and keep their hands in clear sight. The indigenous people, dressed in a mixture of traditional and Western-style clothes, comply. None bears any arms but all wear some form of decoration, from earrings to nose rings to paint and elaborate facial tattoos. All smile at the guards. The guards open a channel on their radio for the preacher to hear what business the delegation wants with the commune. The speaker for the delegation says he has farming matters to discuss, and these matters are of the utmost importance to the health of the community and everyone who lives around it. The preacher's assistant asks how many make up this delegation and says the preacher will grant them one hour of his time. They are to wait at the gate for fifteen minutes before proceeding to the white house at the middle of the community.

These are not the usual indigenous traders who bring along medicines and artwork for the preacher to preview and purchase. The preacher calls his various heads—of security, farming, education, community relations, and Joyce in accounting, among others—to gather at his house right away to meet the delegation. His assistants put out a call over the radio for all the guards to look sharp around the place and for everyone else to look purposeful. The assistant calls for eight schoolgirls to dress in their Sunday best right away and come to the preacher's house. The assistant summons Trina and reminds her to bring her flute.

At the main entrance, the delegation stands around their jeeps and chat. Kevin and Eric watch them. One of the Indians detaches himself and walks over to the guard's hut where Kevin and Eric planted themselves and asks if the mosquitoes still treat them like they are newcomers with sweet blood or if the pests ignore them. The guards laugh and say they still burn mosquito coils and rub mentholated spirits on their hands and necks and even their clothes and boots and put up with the stink just to keep away the mosquitoes, whose proboscises are as long as knitting needles.

—What's a knitting needle?

Just as Kevin and Eric are about to explain by holding hands a foot apart, the Indian says he is joking.

—My wife has lots of them, and at night I sit with her and we knit together.

He winks heavily. The guards warm to him right away. The Indian says pee is just as effective against mosquitoes as mentholated spirits, and cheaper. And it stinks just as much, the guards add. They introduce themselves and shake hands. Sid, the Indian, recommends that Kevin and Eric try a local weed and points to some in among the grass only a few feet from the guard hut. Sid strolls over, plucks a handful, spits into his hands, and squashes and rubs and works up a bright green paste. After some reassurance and coaxing, he applies the concoction to the hands of Kevin and Eric. Both say if this voodoo really works, it will be a miracle. Sid says it's medicine, not magic. Kevin and Eric cannot believe they sat day in and day out at their post with the plant growing wild right under their noses all this time and suffered without knowing anything about it while the high-pitched whine and itchy bites tormented them night and day. Sid offers Kevin and Eric cigarettes, and they thank him and take the offering and say to Sid that he did not see them accept those cigarettes. What cigarettes, says Sid. They all laugh and light up and puff for a minute and examine the sky for rain, which one of the visitors says is far off, and Kevin asks exactly how far off, and Sid is about to take a guess when Kevin says he is only joking and again they laugh. The laughing dies down and Sid says two hours. And they laugh again. The delegation points out the direction of the location of each of the eight tribes. You got us surrounded, Eric says. The delegation trades words for "welcome" and "goodbye" with

Kevin and Eric and climb into the two jeeps and drive through the lifted barrier and into the heart of the compound.

At the white house, eight girls dressed in matching white frocks give a jar of honey and a single rose to each of the eight visitors, curtsy, and accept carved wood statues, masks, and dyed clothing from each member of the delegation. The assistants collect the gifts from the girls, who retreat. The preacher emerges from the white house and speaks:

—Honey from hives right here at the commune. Welcome, gentlemen.

He stretches out a hand to greet each of the delegates. The girls in white return to dormitories to change back into their everyday clothes and run back into their classes, careful to keep out of sight of the visitors. Sid points to the cage with Adam in it and Trina beside it, playing her flute. The preacher leads the delegation to the cage. He tells Trina to keep playing and explains to the visitors that Adam is the commune's little attempt at a zoo. Sid spreads his arms and indicates that the whole rain forest is a zoo and all of the people, the commune included, are in it. The preacher nods and says true, true. Sid asks Trina if the tune is Bach's B-minor sonata. Trina nods and keeps playing. Sid tells her she has a good feel for the instrument. He leans in close to Trina and lifts the middle finger of her left hand and instructs her to drop it a little more quickly behind the leading index finger. Trina pauses and regroups and tries the trill as advised, and Sid nods, and Trina stops and thanks him for the helpful tip. He promises her a Macusi flute the next time he sees her, a flute so fine it almost plays itself.

The delegation follows the preacher to the house. He asks Sid if he plays.

—I dabble. That little girl plays.

The assistants offer carbonated drinks or something a little stronger, and with everyone holding a glass and settled on mats on the floor in a big room at the back of the house, the commune leader asks them to state the exact nature of their business concern. The chief spokesman thanks the preacher for his gift and hospitality and says that the ways of the preacher match ancient Indian practices of civility and one of the preacher's ancestors may have originated from one of the indigenous tribes of the Americas. The preacher thinks this is not true for him but is the lineage of one of his group. He points to Joyce and says she has roots in the Miccosukee tribe of central Florida. The Amerindians look at Joyce and smile and bow. The preacher says he must be channeling his good vibrations through Joyce. Everyone smiles. The chief says the river feeds all life near it and wonders how much the commune relies upon it. The preacher says a boat arrives once a week with supplies from the capital, and the commune draws water from the river for irrigation. The children swim there sometimes, but he is not supposed to know about that. This raises much laughter. The things I don't know about my people, the chief says, are usually not worth knowing or are things best left to the people. The preacher nods at this wisdom. The chief asks about the pig farming. He wants to know the size of it, how many holdings, and the method of cleaning the sties and disposing of the waste.

—The blood and guts are fine, the piranhas and caimans take care of that, but the chemicals and the shit are another matter.

The preacher calls on his farming manager to answer on his behalf. The farming manager says water is pumped from the river by a generator and the waste sent down drains to the river. The chief shakes his head, though he keeps his pleasant smile. He says this is not acceptable, that he lives downstream and the water is contaminated, smells awful, and makes his people sick. He wonders if pits can be dug and the waste placed there, along the same principle as a community latrine or a rubbish dump. As the chief speaks, he does not seem to notice the response of his host. The smile disappears from the preacher's face, and his face and neck redden. The chief says he notices the commune owns a bulldozer and a tractor, so the solution of digging pits for the waste is easy for the commune. He adds that the government inspectors will visit the area soon and do not approve of this practice of dumping pig waste into the river. This is all very direct and good, the preacher says, but every activity on the three thousand acres of the commune, every commercial and civil practice, is approved by the government and exceeds governmental standards. The preacher says he will consult with his manager and others about the feasibility of the chief's suggestion and inform the delegation of his decision in a few days. He thanks the chief for his candor and asks if there is anything else of concern to the delegation. The chief says there is not, and before he can add any word, the preacher stands and abruptly leaves the room. The delegation instantly loses its relaxed posture. They straighten and raise their eyebrows. Some drain their glasses. Others push their glasses away. The chief stands, and the rest of the coterie follows. They march out of the building.

Sid says to the chief:

—That went well.

The chief ignores Sid and says to the commune representatives:

—Thank the preacher for me. We did not mean to offend him. We look forward to hearing his answer in a few days.

The delegation members climb into the jeeps and speed away. At the entrance to the compound, only Sid waves to Kevin and Eric. They wave back, aiming their parting gesture at Sid only.

—I should have filled those jars with pig shit.

The preacher hurls the masks across the room and stamps on the clothing and tears some into shreds and spits on the pieces and tosses a few more until he runs out of breath and is covered in sweat. He inhales deeply at the urging of one assistant while another massages his shoulders. He takes off his sweat-soaked shirt and holds out his arms as an assistant hangs a clean one on his body. He waves off the assistants and radios the capital, and an official puts him through to the president's office. The preacher demands to know who sent a delegation of the local tribes to his compound to stir trouble. The first secretary to the president says he has no knowledge of any such delegation. The man wants to know if foreign nationals put the Indians up to this mischief. The first secretary says the president is overseas currently, but he will pass the matter to the minister of the interior and that the preacher is not to worry another minute about it. The preacher says he needs to speak with the interior minister right away because he hears from the Indian delegation that a government inspector is scheduled to visit the area. The preacher stays on the radio as the first secretary connects him to the Ministry of the Interior, who in turn connects him to the interior minister's secretary, who says that the minister is in a meeting and will have to call back.

—Not so.

The preacher shouts into the two-way radio that he is a personal friend and this is an urgent matter and if the secretary values his job, he will interrupt that meeting and get the minister on the line right away. There is an elongated pause of static as the preacher waits and his breathing comes back to normal. He complains aloud that he pays these people good money made by the honest sweat that drips from the brow of the commune, and this is how he is treated. At last the interior minister materializes on the line and apologizes immediately and asks the preacher what the nature of his emergency might be. The preacher explains about the delegation, the rumor of a looming inspector visit, and the commune's pig-farming practices. The interior minister says the preacher should forget about the inspector.

—Poof, he's gone.

He promises that there will be no inspection of anything pertaining to the commune. The indigenous delegation, though, will require a little appeasement, since the treaty about the treatment of natural resources directly affects tribes in the area, and that treaty is ratified by the United Nations. The preacher says he does not give a rat's ass who ratified what. He just wants to know that no one will interfere in the business of the commune. The minister repeats the need for some gesture of appeasement from the commune to the indigenous delegation working on behalf of the local tribes.

—How much?

—Let us not talk about such matters on the air. I will meet with someone at your office here in the capital, and we can come to an amicable arrangement. Satisfied?

—Okay.

And that is the end of the matter as far as the preacher is concerned. He slams the radio receiver onto the table.

—These people think I can pull a golden calf out of my ass.

He paces back and forth and rails against the forces he perceives as direct threats to his dream on earth, his rainbow coalition of the poor and the powerless ennobled and lifted nearer to God by his communal enterprise. His assistants keep out of his way and move valuable or dangerous objects out of his reach. He says if he bulldozed the forest, there would be no delegation. If he gouged deep holes in the landscape to extract minerals, there would be no delegation (though one would be justified). But the second he deposits a little innocent pig shit in the river, whose currents sweep the shit away anyway, all hell breaks loose, delegations from eight tribes put aside their usual squabbles, he says, and they have the gumption to petition him and threaten him with government scrutiny. He will fix their indigenous backsides, he shouts at the furniture. He says they have owned all this land for centuries and done nothing with it. He flings his dark glasses across the room, pounds the table, and looks around for something else that is loose and within reach that he can throw, and seeing nothing, he knocks over a chair and kicks it and curses and limps in a circle and stoops to examine his throbbing big toe.

And he wails for his assistants.

—Nora, Dee, Pat, anybody.

TWELVE

Everyone gathers early for the evening sermon in part to find a chair but more out of helpless anticipation based on the day's events with the children. Adults and children move in such an economical and orderly fashion that they force the guards to keep their sticks by their sides and languish next to entrances. Even the sick in the infirmary ask for help to get to the meeting. Miss Taylor, the commune's makeup artist and seamstress, says she wants to be there if they can wheel her in her bed. The doctor says that is out of the question. The recent rain-softened ground would prove unsuitable for any such attempt. She accepts the doctor's explanation and tells the nurse to make sure an assistant powders the preacher's forehead, which has a tendency to shine in the congregation tent's fluorescent lights. And he should wear something bright for the occasion.

A few sick people enter the tent and a number of people jump up to offer their seats. These instant displays of sacrifice result in many offerings of blessings from the sick, God bless you, brother, sister, child. The air becomes more akin to a carnival atmosphere than the usual tense wait for the unpredictable twists and turns of the preacher's sermons. People know not to show any levity that is unrelated to a specific instance of spirituality, but they cannot hide or disguise a collective sense of movement with a common purpose. The cooperation is instinctive, the consideration for the children, the elderly, the infirm, exemplary. No one has to ask for anything. They anticipate one another's every need: a proffered chair, a gentle hand steering an old elbow, a need for someone to scoot over and make a bit more room, all met instantaneously and accepted with abiding grace.

Waiting for the preacher to appear is no less a gracious affair. The talk remains hushed, and the moment the band and choir strike up, every pair of lungs in the tent pitches in. The hymn promises that someday the singers will meet Jesus in heaven. The singers declare this repeatedly. The tambourines, drums, and various flutes make it clear that such a place includes these very instruments; they, too, will be brought up to meet Him. Trina is among the church band, but an assistant pulls her from the group and seats her beside her mother, who sits in a chair at the end of the second row. Trina tucks her flute in the space between chairs, and the two clap along with the congregation and sing. The joy and happiness that the congregation swears is theirs, along with peace, really seems possible at that moment. But not for Trina and Rose, who worry about Ryan, and not for Joyce, who wonders what may be in store tonight for her and her daughter.

More than joy and happiness and peace thrive in the room. The air seems positively ecstatic. Each voice, each instrument, lifts the other up to a place that makes everyone's spirit soar. Trina looks along her row and encourages Rose with a smile.

The preacher hears the glorification, all in his name, as he prepares for his sermon. He thinks how early it is for the congregation to reach such a crescendo. He calls for Dee, his most trusted assistant. She looks with raised eyebrows at Nora and Pat and lifts her shoulders in acknowledgment of their complicity. They know her name is on the preacher's lips tonight, but tomorrow it may be either of their names. The man is in the shower. He asks her to soap his back. She knows what that means. She removes her apron and nurse's hat and rolls up her sleeves. He draws the shower curtain and leaves the water running and causes it to sprinkle the stone floor. He gestures for her to come over to him, but she says she does not want to get her uniform wet.

—Well, what are you waiting for?

—But there isn't time, Father.

—I make the time around here, come on in.

And with that, she kicks off her shoes.

—Slow, slow, imagine you're wading into the sea on the Pacific coast.

She moves like a sloth as she steps out of her dress and unhooks her bra and peels off her stockings and, last, her underwear, which she wriggles out of from side to side as the scant fabric moves along her hips and thighs and over her knees to her ankles. Naked, she curtsies. He holds out his hand, and she grasps it daintily as she steps into the shower. He pulls her to him. She flicks the curtain shut to keep the floor from getting soaked.

Adam sits in his cage in the semi-dark. A little light dribbles his way from the tent and a few of the buildings strewn about the compound. He claps, clucks, and sways along with the worshippers in the tent. Though he dearly wants to be in the tent, enjoying the band and the people straining at the top of their lungs, he hopes the preacher will leave him out of the evening's proceedings. He does not appreciate the way he is put to use. He can do more for the preacher. The last time they roped him and injected him and bribed him with fruit and hauled him to the tent. He hates needles and the indignity of ropes and handlers who clearly fear and despise him. If they turn up again, he will not let them near him. Adam grabs the bars of his cage and shakes them. He leaps up and imagines landing on the heads of the guards who tug him to and fro at the end of a rope. His only friends are the preacher with his treats and his backscratching and the girl with her flute. All the rest are his wishes splintered into a thousand pieces and sent hurtling around the compound. Now they sing the night into being. Their voices pull this dark veil over the trees, vines, flowers, shrubs and stitch everything into one seamless fabric that joins him to them and unites everything so that distance means nothing and nothing can come between them, least of all the bars of his cage.

The preacher, pelt freshened by his shower, tells Dee that he wants his Elvis look: slicked-back hair, dark glasses, a white sequined shirt, and tight white trousers made to measure by the commune's tailor, with pointy-toed cowboy boots stitched by the commune's shoemaker. He sneers at the mirror one last time and heads for the front door, Bible in one hand and pistol in the other. Pat, Nora, and Dee and two bodyguards follow him.

—To the infirmary! I need to say goodbye to my makeup lady.

The boards that pave the walkway rattle as they march along. He bursts into the infirmary, and the doctor and nurses bolt to attention and swarm around him. He touches the bed of each patient as he passes and makes the sign of the cross. They thank him and cry with joy. He looks at the parents of Ryan, labeled as dissidents and locked in a chemical prison of sedatives. Both are hooked to drips with bags feeding liquid into their taped arms. The preacher moves on and stops at the bed of the old woman. Who will put on her makeup? he wonders. He cannot see himself getting so old. She opens her eyes and says, Praise the Lord. The preacher leans over and kisses her.

—I miss my makeup lady.

He sets aside his Bible and pistol and hugs her for a long time. She sobs with great heaves of her chest and gasps.

—Do not cry. You're going to make me cry. You are heading for paradise, and I cannot wait to meet you there. You will wait for me, won't you?

—Yes, Father.

—You have nothing to fear. You know that, don't you?

—Yes, Father.

—Thank you for your service to this community; you kept us looking good and feeling good to the end. Don't think I have not noticed it, and if

I have noticed it, the Lord has surely taken note of it and awaits your services. We will meet again in the kingdom of the Most High.

—Yes, Father, thank you, Father.

—Do not thank me. I thank you.

The reverend falls to one knee and keeps his grip on the old lady's hand. Everyone's eyes close. Miss Taylor grabs her compact with powder and sponge and dabs the forehead, cheeks, and nose of the preacher. He rises and thanks her. The old seamstress and makeup artist smiles through her tears, and there really is not a dry eye in the infirmary. He leans over, kisses her again, and turns and marches out of the infirmary with his Bible and pistol.

Just before he enters the tent, he hands his Bible and gun to his assistants, who duck into the tent's entrance ahead of him. They make sure everything is in place: his jug of ice water, his towel. They place his Bible next to the jug on a small table beside a large high-backed chair. The music and singing stop. Everyone looks at the exit left of the stage where his assistants entered. The congregation fully expects the man to follow at any moment. The preacher walks with a bodyguard around the outside of the tent to the exit. He takes care to avoid the sticks that he orders his guards to pile at each exit. He straightens, takes a deep breath, pushes his dark glasses up the bridge of his nose, rolls his shoulders, flicks both arms out in front of him, and steps into the hall's fluorescence.

The people seated near the entrance turn their heads and cry out, and everyone, even the guards at the front of the room, jumps and grabs their weapons. The man touches people's heads and grasps their outstretched hands as he walks to the front of the congregation, careful to step over the legs of children scrambling to their feet along the aisle.

—Bless you, bless you.

He tries to catch the eyes of each person and maintain his leisurely, impeded walk to the stage. Those seated too far from the aisle to benefit from direct contact stand up and applaud, and the entire room jumps to its feet and surges forward, clapping and hollering:

—Praise the Lord.

He repeats each phase as he marches forward. About halfway up the aisle, with the preacher's touch and blessing part and parcel of his forward trajectory, the band strikes up "When the Saints," and the congregation begins to clap in unison and sing. The guards put aside their sticks and rifles and clap and sing, too.

The preacher hops up onto the stage and claps his hands and waves and points at individuals in the congregation. He grabs the microphone and sings "I want to be in that number," more as a sound test than anything. He signals to the music teacher doubled as band leader, and she waves her arms for the band to come to a close with a long flourish intended to settle the congregation into their seats. Everyone finds a chair or a spot on the floor, and the guards lean on their sticks and rifles.

—Thank you, thank you, and may God continue to bless your lungs, good people.

Laughter and applause.

—We had plenty of rain these last few days, didn't we?

—Yes, Father.

—Another thirtysomething days of that deluge, and we would have been boarding the ark.

More laughter and applause.

—But it was good, wasn't it? It was bountiful. It was proof of the glory of the Lord. Yes?

—Yes!

—Finish my thoughts for me, good people. I know you all know what I am about to say. So speak for me as I speak for you. Our children are our own and not our own. I know and you know that they can try us sometimes, and heaven knows we have to work hard to keep them from turning into sour apples, fruit picked too early and ripened too fast for their own good, forced-ripe fruit. But the good Lord says, suffer the little children . . .

And here he cups an ear in his hand and inclines his head toward the congregation, who complete his sentence:

—To come unto me.

—That's right. And though they may test us and we need to keep them on the straight path. We must not spare the rod and . . .

He cups his ear at the congregation again, and they shout:

—Spoil the child.

—We must see them in their innocence as already admitted into the kingdom of heaven. Tonight I want us to think about temptation, in all of its many disguises. It is a snake.

—Yes, Father.

—It is the flesh.

—Yes, Father.

—It is the promise of riches on earth.

—Yes, Father.

—But do not worry yourselves about riches. You know what the Good Book says about the rich man. It is easier for a camel to stream through the eye of a needle than—finish my thoughts for me, brothers and sisters— than . . .

—For a rich man to enter the kingdom of heaven.

—Very good. A camel is easy to see, right? But the effort required from a rich man to be able to enter the gates of paradise is close to a miracle, isn't it? Picture the huge camel to my left, and in my right hand see the little needle, and not just the needle, but the eye of the needle. Can you see it, madam? You, yes, you in the front row.

—No, Father.

—No, you cannot. If you had said yes, I would have asked you to go and see the doctor, for you would be seeing things, madam. Wouldn't you?

—Yes, Father.

—You might be able to see the needle, but the eye of the needle is so small and the camel so big that it would take a miracle to feed that camel through that needle. Look, even I have to close one eye and lick the thread several times to get a thin piece of cotton through a needle.

Here the man mimics licking a piece of thread and aiming at a needle, and he closes one eye and tries a few times to perform the task. The congregation laughs and claps.

—You see how hard it is to put what should be put through a needle's eye?

—Yes, Father.

—Well, where is that camel? Okay, now picture the enormity of that task, a camel through the eye of a needle, and that is what riches collected in this short life on earth put between you and your rightful place in heaven, eternal life, free of any want, free of all aches and pains, free of all worries. So do not wish for riches that will make it impossible for you to gain your place in heaven which is like nothing seen on this earth, not just a palace but all palaces, not just a vault of wealth but all the mountains of the world piled with wealth. That is the kingdom that awaits each and every one of us in this room. But temptation has an invisible side, a face that we cannot see and a force that is as strong as the wind and present everywhere.

He stops smiling at the end of his sentences. He takes off his dark glasses and points at the congregation.

—All of you were tempted. And all of you gave in to temptation.

The audience hushes. Their faces cloud.

—Your children, our future, ran into the rain, and what did you do? You did not watch them to make sure a coral snake did not crawl among them and bite them. You did not keep a lookout for a jaguar, panther, or viper, with your rifles ready to protect the children. You did not ask them to play but play safe. You intervened in their play in the rain by beating them. That was temptation, people. That was giving in to cruelty. That was spite. Let me tell you something. I am the first to beat one or any number of our children who misbehave, if they break the rules, if they are wicked and evil in the myriad of ways available to us all. We must not spare the rod. But that does not mean we beat the children for playing in mud. That signals surrender to temptation. That is the wrong thing to do at the wrong time. Now, I asked the guards to bring along a pile of sticks, which you all saw and must have taken for firewood or something. Well, this is what I want the children to do. I want each child to take a stick, all three hundred of you or however many of you are here tonight. Go on. Take a stick.

He waits for the guards to pass sticks to the children, who hold them as if they are strange unrecognizable objects.

—I want you children to stand next to an adult. Include the guards in this little exercise. They are adults, too. Leave the sick and infirm out of this lesson. I want each child with a stick to hit each adult, on the arms and legs only, not on the head or breast.

The adults in the room open their eyes very wide, and some of them gasp.

—Make it a good hit, or we will be here all night.

Several parents look at the child standing over them with a stick and wide eyes and flared nostrils and lean away from the child as if confronted by a jungle predator. The preacher orders the guards and the parents to stand closer to the children brandishing sticks. He makes the adults in the band and choir put down instruments and lyric sheets and take up places next to children with sticks. Several children surround the young guard and lift their sticks high above their heads.

—Children, on my count of three, I want you to go ahead and hit an adult with your stick. One. Two. Three!

The children tremble so much at the prospect that they can barely operate their arms. They raise their sticks above their heads, as ordered. Their gazes follow the sticks up into the air to avoid the faces of the adults. The children bring their sticks down on the astonished bodies of the adults, and then the children drop the sticks. They drop the sticks so quickly that the action seems to bear no relation to their previous grip of those sticks and their wielding of them over their parents and guardians, a rapid act of disassociation that some of the children follow up with a small kick to push the sticks farther away. Trina touches her mother with her stick and drops it right away and rubs her hands on her dress in an exact repeat of her actions at Ryan's beating. She blinks rapidly to keep her eyes from filling. Joyce gives Trina that soft, resigned look of understanding, an apparently unfocused stare with the hint of a smile around compressed lips to let Trina know that an order is an order and not to obey Father would result in something even more frightful.

The guards collect the sticks, and the children slink off to their places on the ground next to the seated adults. Many parents wipe their eyes, squeeze them shut, shield their faces with two hands, pull clothes up to bury their faces, but nothing stops the flow. Children cry with them. Only a few adults fume and shake their heads and hug themselves and rock in their seats as if at sea or trying to right a capsized vessel. The children cry with a trace of panic in their vocal cords. The guards and many assistants look quizzically at the preacher. They wait for his next move to make explicit the usefulness of this latest manifestation of his wisdom. He nods and lifts his hands to settle the congregation. Even in their shock and distress, their obedience of him does not falter. The man places his dark glasses on the table and picks up the Bible. He directs his gaze at the adults in the room.

—I was a child like these children. You were all children like them. Have we forgotten? Someone had to see to our needs. Each of us was helpless and needed guidance once. How could we forget? I have not forgotten. When I was a boy living in the middle of the country, a tornado warning stopped my play. My father had this serious look on his face, and I knew something was not right. All he said was tornado, and he collected me, and together we went down into the shelter dug in the backyard and lowered the trapdoor. I asked my father where our dog might be. My father took one look at my face, and I do not know what he saw, but he knew he had to find our dog for me. He said he would be right back and I should stay put no matter what I heard, and he climbed out of the safety of the shelter and closed the trapdoor. Well, you know where this is going. The tornado arrived. A dozen freight trains, a herd of stampeding elephants, that tornado took what seemed like forever to pass by. All the time I cried for my father. I forgot about my dog. I waited and could not wait anymore, and I pushed the trapdoor up and climbed out, and the house was gone, I mean torn from its foundations, and my daddy and the dog were gone. There was wreckage as far as I could see.

The preacher pauses to wipe his eyes with the towel. Some of the adults in the congregation cry with him.

—I was alone in the world, and my daddy and the dog were together somewhere waiting for me. I had to believe that, because I blamed myself for my daddy's death. I blamed that look that I had on my face that made him leave the safety of the shelter to find my dog. That look, ladies and gentlemen, is the look of the innocent. That look is the expression that all of our children have, and we, all of us adults in this room, do not need a mirror to know that we carry the same expression when we think about our Lord God and Savior.

The reverend swallows some water and dries his face and neck with the towel. He looks at the wet faces in the room. Many of the adults reach for the children seated beside them to touch them softly, caress their arms and pat their heads.

—You see what I mean. Suffer the little children . . .

—To come unto me.

—You see that a blow from a child with a stick is nothing compared to the look on a child's face, all of our faces, as we search for salvation from our Father in heaven, our Maker. That look is the rich man, ladies and gentlemen; that expression wants to enter the kingdom of heaven, but we may as well be a camel and try to stream through the eye of a needle. We must suffer the children because we are the children.

The preacher slumps into his chair and dries his eyes. His assistants surround him. The music teacher waves at the band, and they strike up a racy arrangement of the hymn "In the Sweet By-and-By." Adults lead the old and the sickly out of the tent, followed by very young children and their parents and the older children up to the eldest. As they disperse, they clap and sing and sway. Children apologize to their parents, and many of the adults say it is the right thing to do and there is no need to be sorry, all the children need to do is listen to what adults tell them and conduct themselves like children of God. Remember what Father said about temptation being invisible and all around. Some of the adults laugh at having been hit with a stick wielded by a child. Others say it is a miracle that the preacher survived losing his father the way he did, and look how mysteriously God works. Trina walks beside Joyce.

—If you ever lift your hand to me again, it will be the last thing you do, child.

Trina freezes and darts an alarmed look at her mother, who, seeing the damaged reaction in her daughter, immediately switches from serious to happy and nudges and hugs Trina, who wants to know, as she returns her mother's nudge:

—I did not hit you hard, right?

—Ooh, it still stings. I might need to visit the infirmary.

Joyce hugs Trina to make sure she knows it's a joke. Trina gives her mother a playful elbow. They step in the dark and hold on to each other as they walk on the elevated log footpath. The logs rumble with all the marching feet. Trina's mother holds up her bandaged hand and says they should count their blessings because the gorilla played no part in the evening.

—Imagine a lash from that beast!

Trina assents but does not confess that she prefers to face Adam any day rather than lift a stick and hit her mother. She imagines she feels Adam's eyes on her, his gaze licking her back.

The preacher asks his assistants and guards: How was it?

The head teacher responds:

—Well, you had me worried for a while.

—Parents think it is their right to hit their children, but I've never seen a child exercise the right to hit a parent. That's bold and original.

The reverend nods. He laughs aloud and runs his hand through his thick black hair.

—You have to surprise them, and keep surprising them, or else they lose interest in you and you lose them.

Everyone nods at his impermeable logic. He says he needs a drink, and as his assistant reaches for the ice water, he says:

—No, woman, I mean a real drink.

They head back to his house where a meal, and an array of real drinks in ample volume await him and his party. On the way, he stops at Adam's cage.

—Come here, Adam, it's me.

The gorilla scampers to the front of the cage and half turns away from the man, who pushes his hand through the bars and scratches Adam's back. He fishes a stick of chewing gum out of his trouser pocket and hands it to Adam, who removes the paper with pursed lips before pulling the gum into his mouth and chewing gleefully. The reverend pats the gorilla on the head, says good night, and heads to his house. Inside, a record player perks up with Elvis followed by Little Richard, volume set low. And more than a dozen glasses with ice and half full of rum scatter from trays into the hands of the doctor, pharmacist, head nurse, chief accountant, chief electrician, project manager, head of security, head teacher, and various assistants and guards. All toast to the man's health and the longevity of the community. They carve chunks from the roasted carcass of a lamb and open cans of Coke.

He asks the pharmacist about the quantities of cyanide in stock, and the pharmacist replies that there is enough for farm use. The preacher's next question, how much is enough, leaves the pharmacist flummoxed, and instead of saying he does not have an accurate measurement for the poison but he can come back with an answer, he feels compelled to provide an answer that instant, and so he says off the top of his head that there is enough to kill about half of the community.

—Only half? Double our supplies.

—Yes, Reverend.

This remark causes the room to hush and pay attention but with each person assuming a demeanor of disinterest. The preacher wants to know, just out of curiosity, how lethal cyanide works: the dose, the taste, the speed. And here, the pharmacist, as the lone expert about the more lethal aspects of the periodic table, needs to speak as the sole protector of the commune responsible for ordering adequate supplies of medicines and industrial chemicals and not as the next candidate for most-favored-person status in the eyes of the community's spiritual guide. But the pharmacist, also acting as the commune's sole licensed jeweler, replies as the person who could prove most useful. And on the basis of the pharmacist's advice, the preacher makes certain decisions about the chemical holdings in the commune based on the secret workings of his mind.

In a switch of topic and mood, the preacher takes a gulp from his glass, smacks his lips, grimaces, and utters, Praise the Lord, and slaps his chest as the rum shocks its way from his palate to his stomach, and asks no one in particular if this is not as good a place as any to be free from prying eyes and interfering hands.

—With our beliefs.

The preacher waves his glass as he speaks.

—No human and no government or state is qualified enough to dictate to us. No army on this earth is mightier than the heavenly gospel. Am I wrong?

—No, Father.

Murmurs of assent flick from mouth after mouth, full of meat and drink. The preacher belches and farts very loudly and calls his assistants' names admonishingly.

—Nora, Dee, Pat!

The three giggle and cover their mouths and look their coyest.

—Oh, Father.

—Praise the Lord.

From outside the house, it is possible to hear faint traces of music and laughter. Figures move in front of the windows as if dancing and hanging on to each other for support. The rest of the compound wishes each other good night, and most of the generators switch off to save fuel and to increase the peace and tranquillity of the jungle setting, spoiled only by the loudspeakers that the preacher operates in the day at a whim and at night to broadcast his sermons. Night watchmen working in pairs take up positions around the perimeter of the compound armed with a flask of something hot, rifles, a radio, a flashlight, and proscribed playing cards. Some oil lamps flicker weakly, their flames like insects in the giant pitch black. Besides the preacher's white-painted house, only the bakery and infirmary burn electricity. Inside the bakery, tables are taken over by bodies of dough, fists cuff the mixture and flip it over and break off pieces and roll them into loaves, and oil and flour pans for the oven, and feed the hungry flames of the giant oven with shovels of coal until the oven crackles and blazes with low gutturals. The guards glance at the man's house with envy at their exclusion from the festivities.

—Blouse.

—Trousers.

—Skirt.

—Panties.

—Socks.

—Garters.

—Garters?

—You don't want to know.

—I think I do.

The envy fades fast, eased by the knowledge that it will be their turn on another evening to join in the revelry, and someone else will be in their shoes on overnight guard duty.

Adam listens as he sticks to the back of his cage and waits for the guards to find comfortable positions of studied diligence and doze. The commune soon settles to sleep for the remainder of the night. Adam pokes his fingernails into the soil and digs, and the earth feels soft. He scoops handfuls of soil. He looks around, and the guards in the distance stop their chatter. Adam stands still and listens for any other sounds from the commune. Hearing none, he retreats to his bed area and pulls back the straw, leaves, branches, and tarpaulin to resume his widening of a large hole in the ground.

THIRTEEN

Trina faces the wall on the bottom bunk of her bed and cannot stem the flow from her eyes. She thinks of Ryan. Her stomach hurts. She wishes she could spend the night with her mother. Trina thinks of Joyce going to sleep in the adult sleeping quarters, and she sees herself lying in a narrow bed with her mother, or not even on the same bed, perhaps on bedding on the floor. No words, just listening to her mother's breathing and trying to match what she takes for an outward breath with her own exhalation. At some point she imagines she drifts off with her mother on a boat with the captain, who takes the three of them to a place where no one watches them and they can be together as mother and daughter from one end-of-the-day to the next.

—Trina.

She comes back to her name and reoccupies her place in the room and registers her stomachache. The breathing from the other children makes her think of the pipes of a church organ, but unlike an organ, each child operates independently from the others. She listens and hears her name again.

—Trina.

She recognizes Rose's voice. Rose wants to know if Trina is still awake. Trina keeps very still and adds an audible pipe of her sleep to the organ of pipes. She wants Rose to do the same: not think about Ryan and grab what little time remains for sleep before the early-morning call on the community intercom. Trina tells herself that she is not the only one. She repeats the community mantra that all the children sleep away from parents and every adult is a parent to every child. And the preacher is Father to them all.

Child without parents. Parents with no memory and no mind left for a challenge. Parents up from a fog of sedation swear they have no son and the priest is the father of them all. No one speaks about Ryan in the company of his parents. They walk around dazed. Numb. Dumb. They pray that soon their work on this earth will be done.

Jungle for clothes on tree-stump legs, uprooted and gangly. Perambulation of vines and shrubbery. Child no more. Beast of sorts. Tongue forked for dicing air of smells, threats. Head full of matted weeds. Ryan shakes his head to scare off the devil of the dark, the devil of animal grunts and howls and roars, the devil of cold, the devil of thirst, the devil of an empty belly, the devil of trembling with every thought. He eats termites. Drinks from clear springs. Crouches and adds to the forest manure. Wipes himself with broad leaves. Runs on all fours to look worse than wild. Growls to deny sense sounds from his mouth. Jumps from a high rock into waterfall white roar and tumbles downstream with current. Climbs back to earth. Wanders far among trees without end. Green light. Blue cut above shine in forest floor pools. No words for this. Speech to shadow. Over. Shadow, come in. Over. Nothing but echoes.

In the commune's infirmary, a nurse and two patients sit around the bed of the old makeup lady. They hold her hands and read from the Bible and fan her face. She breathes, irregular and very shallow. Once or twice she takes such a long time between breaths that those around her bed lean in close to see if she has left them, sneaked off under their noses or tiptoed off the world. But she draws heavily on the store of medicated oxygen in the room and puts them at ease. They whisper to each other about the evening's sermon; they wonder what next? The patients talk about their aches and pains and the nurse about the work rotation ahead of her. It is at this moment of distraction, as they grow comfortable with the old woman's brinkmanship, her way of reaching a precipice and balancing there, half on, half off, and in need of the merest flutter of breeze to tip her over the edge of the world, right then when all of their eyes avert from her face and they touch her hands absently because she recedes a little from the front of their minds, at that moment the old woman in the infirmary, a faint smile at the corners of her mouth and eyes, gasps her last and the man's image fades in her head with the susurration of his name on her lips, Father.

Which will find Ryan first? Anaconda, panther, jaguar, wild boar? Or madness? The trees take him into their enclave. He is green from his days in their midst. Days he eats nothing but the bark of trees. Days a termite grows into a nutritious possibility. He chews leaves for brine, licks them for salt. Uses vine to hold up his pants and bind his feet. Vine for a lasso. Nights he sleeps a little and only lightly on a bed of leaves. Panther or jaguar on his trail. Some way off. They take the measure of him by the strength of his scent. He swings a stick to clear a path. He makes enough noise for three of his kind, his age. Panther or jaguar hesitate and circle Ryan as if he is not alone. Ryan smells good in the wild and a good deal worse than most: funk soil, vine sap, leaf smear bag of bones, veins cord his face, neck, and arms, tendons string the out-of-tune instrument of his body. Still the panther or jaguar persists in tracking him by keeping a respectful and safe distance from Ryan and his powerful scent.

Trina wakes with a stomachache and a sensation that she has wet her bed. She knows what happens to a child who wets the bed at the commune. She sits up and feels between her legs. Wet. But the mattress is dry. She decides she caught herself in midstream. She puzzles over how such a thing could happen to her. She drank hardly anything before going to sleep. In fact, the practice among the children is never to drink before bedtime to avoid the humiliation that follows wetting the bed. It is too dark to see her hands, but she thinks to smell her fingers to confirm that telltale smell of urine. She sniffs once and must sniff a second time to allow the word for the smell that she registers to take up residence in her skull. Not urine but something more alarming, more pungent and distinct for being rare. Not urine that maintains a dull presence in all the children's dormitories scattered around the compound but something children know little about. She knows about urine. She knows how the children are made to drag a wet mattress into the sun and take the bedding to the laundry house and wash everything by hand and hang all the pieces on a line: the clothes the child slept in, the top and bottom sheet, and sometimes even a pillowcase if the accident is a big one. It takes over an hour for a prefect or adult to follow the child around and for everyone to know exactly what that child has done. The word for what Trina smells knocks on her skull to be admitted into the world, and she says it to herself, and again to confirm it, blood. She smells her own blood.

Trina jumps out of bed and hits her head on the top bunk. She brings her hand to her nose again and stares hard at it in the dark with the expectation that blood might shine above everything. She runs on her toes to Rose's bed. But Rose is not there. Her bed looks bulky with her pillow tucked in to replace her body. Trina decides to leave the dormitory and find her mother. She steps with care as if injured, afraid that if she walks, she might worsen her injury. She feels faint, thinking about her blood exiting her body.

—Trina. Trina.

She hears her name but fails to recognize the voice. She feels confused at the thought of her blood spilling from her body. She feels giddy.

—Trina.

The dark appears to thin, and minute by minute a gray veil becomes apparent. She thinks the smell of her blood spreads with this veil, her blood mixed in with this light. Everyone must smell it and, if awake, see it as well.

—Trina.

Her name again, in a voice she has never heard. She stumbles and falls, and two strong arms catch her and tip her back up onto her feet, and she sees Adam standing in front of her, steadying her, and his body that is big and broad and dark makes him look as massive as the night. Trina's eyes darken and she topples.

Ryan circles back on himself, not to dodge panther or jaguar but to find the compound. All the trunks of trees look the same. All the vines hide the face of the trees. The leaves decorate the giant body of the forest like scales. The scales shine green and iridescent in the changing light. Ryan laps up condensation pooled in a large leaf, and for a moment he sees the features of the man he will never become on the face of the boy he was never allowed to be. What are Rose and Trina up to now? And now? His parents must be worried. They stop being his parents out here among the trees, and he ceases being their son. He marks the trees to try and map his wanderings and comes back on old marks and makes new ones, sets out in a new direction. If he finds the compound, he will enter it a stranger to everyone and to himself.

He no longer runs from jungle noises. He stops hiding. More of him hungers to meet something inescapable and final, much more than any yearning to find the one place left that he can call home: the commune he ran from that now hides from him.

Trina opens her eyes or thinks the words, eyes open, and realizes her body is being transported. Her head lolls to the rhythm of walking, but her feet hang off the ground. She lies curled in the crook of a pair of arms. In the distance, a single jet trail scores against the sharpening blue. No sound makes it from the jet, and the tail of the plume disappears as soon as the front unfolds. She thinks the end of the jet trail must be tucked back into the beginning, and the lingering middle section of the trail represents the unending forward propulsion of a wheel. The white changes to red, and she jerks her head forward to check on her body.

Relax, young lady. We're almost there.

The sight of the nurse makes Trina relax. She is in the good hands of someone qualified to worry about her condition. Her mother runs to them, and the nurse eases Trina to her feet, and her mother hugs her. The nurse takes Trina's pulse and says it is fine and looks into Trina's mouth and peels back the lids of her eyes and pronounces her slightly anemic but otherwise shipshape. Joyce and Trina thank the nurse, who advises Trina to take a good shower.

—You have to be aware of time and your body from now on.

—I don't have a watch, Mum.

—Your inner clock, Trina. You'll have to listen to your body. You're a young lady now. We need to get you cleaned up.

—And my anemia?

—Nothing some spinach and greens won't cure.

—Chocolate contains iron, right?

—Less than prunes.

—Yuck.

In the washroom, Trina's mother tells her that she smells just like Adam on account of sleeping under his blanket.

—Did you sleepwalk to his cage?

—I was carried there, Mum.

—Who carried you there?

—I don't know. I'm not sure. It's a bit hazy.

Joyce shows her how to position a piece of cloth in her underwear to catch the blood. She advises Trina to pick long dresses, dark colors, at this time of the month and to take the pain in her womb as a sign to be prepared for her period. Trina should be proud, and much will be expected of her since she is no longer a girl but a young woman. Trina nods.

—What about my bed?

—Don't worry about that, someone will take care of that. This is not like wetting your bed. This is special.

—I feel tired.

—You never sleepwalk.

—I heard my name. Ryan calling me. He looked like a beast.

—That's some dream.

—It felt real, Mum. Why would I sleep on the ground covered by a stinky blanket next to Adam's cage?

—You tell me. Did you lose a bet?

—No, I—Never mind.

Joyce leads Trina past the dining hall and into the kitchen. Trina looks on as her mother boils a pot of water and reaches up to a shelf, extracts a clay jar fastened with a cork, pulls off the cork cover, and removes a handful of leaves. Trina cannot read the handwritten label. Joyce says it is an Indian remedy for women's troubles. Trina likes being seen as a woman even if she is in trouble. Her mother pours the leaves into the pot of boiling water, stirs the contents for a while, then hands Trina the job of stirring and says she hopes and prays that she will live long enough to see Trina do this same task for her own daughter someday.

Joyce ladles some of the greenish liquid into a cup and sweetens it with honey but does not add any milk. She says the milk would curdle. She hands Trina the cup and tells her to drink it all up to cure the pain.

Trina holds the cup in her hands and blows on the steaming concoction and sips it and savors the honey and the peculiar bitterness of raspberry leaf, black haw, chasteberry, kava kava, and ginger. She takes her time, to keep her mother with her for as long as she can. The pain below her stomach disappears, and hunger moves in. Her head feels light. She drinks more and cannot help smiling. She stares into the cup and wonders what her mother just gave her. Her bones feel hollow. She thinks if she pushes off the ground, she will float to the ceiling. Her mother smiles at her, and Trina tips the rest of the cup into her mouth.

The only time on the commune is the present, the here and now that the preacher pours his derision on, that deserves nothing of the people's inner selves. Trina dreams, but not in dreamtime or dream space, she acts not in or through space. Awake or asleep, all her thoughts and actions on the commune feel the same.

She dreams herself a spider. To turn into a spider, she runs on two legs and those two beanpoles double into four sprightly things, and those four whirl into six, and the wheel of six sprouts another two so that eight legs operate like spokes on a wheel, they spin so fast, and that child converts wholesale into a prickly spider.

Joyce sees the transformation in Trina over and over. In the commune's kitchen, as Joyce takes her turn to cook for one thousand hungry mouths, she speaks to Trina as she tends to her pots and pans.

—Don't hang your mouth around me.

Trina's mouth is always hungry for something. Joyce finds ways to feed that mouth without drawing rancor from the other cooks on duty. That is the last thing she needs. She does not want them to accuse her of showing favor to her child over all the other three hundred–plus children who belong to all the commune's men and women equally and without rank by blood.

—Open your mouth and take in a morsel, but don't chew, and try to look busy with it.

—Yes, Mother.

Joyce feeds Trina a piece of chicken. She holds it in two fingers and stuffs it into Trina's open craw.

—Now clamp your little beak tight and swallow.

—Yes, Mother.

Joyce fancies that she sees the meat travel in a lump down Trina's neck. Trina says something, anything, to show her mouthful of words, which are nothing, and so an empty mouth that contains nothing of meaning to anyone at the commune.

—That child can talk.

The women in the kitchen are talking within earshot of Joyce as a way to goad her to say something about their insult, calling Trina talkative. Hearing nothing from Joyce, they give up and turn after a slight pause to congratulate Trina on her first time.

—You're a young lady now.

Trina knows this about herself and does not care, or she cares but does not wish to show them that she does. She wonders if, in her light-headed spider condition, she can float above the trees and find Ryan. Why not just change into a creature with higher concerns than the talk of cooks in a kitchen? Trina finds little room left for her among the giant ovens and outsize pots and a nest of knives that chop and dissect. No room for a dreaming spider.

She waves her arms as she talks about her spider's view of a flock of parakeets chasing a giant hawk. She steps around Joyce. Her arms and feet move so fast, they become a blur and double in number, and she turns into Anansi, the trickster. Her mother playfully sprinkles some black pepper over Trina's head, and the granules settle on her and resemble stubble clothing her body. Joyce tells Trina she must do this very spider thing if trouble meets her and her mother is not there to help her fend it off. Joyce says she must busy her arms and feet and talk fast and she will stop whatever harm is about to befall her.

—Just like the spider in the captain's tales.

Trina smiles at the comparison her mother makes of her with a spider, and she smiles at her mother's mention of the captain.

Joyce notes how Trina's lips look just like hers but smaller. So her act of stuffing Trina's mouth amounts to Joyce feeding herself. The piece of chicken that Joyce scoops from the pot while she pretends to stir must cool for a few seconds before she grabs it and feeds it to Trina. Trina's tongue will burn and her eyes water if the food is too hot. She has to clamp shut and swallow no matter what Joyce stuffs into her mouth, so Joyce makes sure it is free of bones and spices and that it is cool enough for her child with a mouth like hers. As one hand busies itself by stirring a pot deliberately and lifting up and replacing a lid, Joyce's other hand grabs a morsel and feeds it to her daughter. As one hand reaches for another pot cover, the free hand steers to Trina's open mouth, agape as if about to speak or draw on air to launch words, not wait for food, not pause for longer than a second, which is all Joyce needs to feed Trina. Trina knows not to linger too long.

Trina must leave the kitchen soon. Joyce knows her daughter will return before too long unless she decides to help Rose finish a chore. The spider Trina becomes in front of Joyce's eyes turns Trina into exactly what Joyce thinks her daughter needs to be at a commune, a trickster just like Anansi. She reminds her daughter to be alert at mealtimes, to chew her food before she swallows, and to look carefully at what is on her spoon before she puts it into her mouth.

—What should I look for?

—Not all of what adults offer children is good for them.

—You mean poison?

—Not every cook means well or offers what's good to those who depend on her.

A guard intrudes on Joyce and Trina.

—Joyce, you put something in that child's mouth?

—No, sir, I just brushed a fly from her face.

—You just swallowed something. Didn't you, child?

—Yes, I swallowed the fly that my mother brushed from my face.

—All right, little miss spider. Out of this kitchen.

The guard marches off toward some other perceived infraction of commune rules. Joyce takes off her apron and tells the women nearby that she needs to do something, just one thing, for her daughter. Trina skips out of the kitchen ahead of Joyce. A child. A spider. Whatever of Joyce lives in Trina, Joyce wishes it to protect her daughter. Whatever remains of that trickster spider, Joyce hopes it helps Trina find her way alone, if need be.

—Trina, one day you'll have to find your own food. Remember the captain's stories? The spider always escapes from trouble.

Joyce thinks these things, and Trina hears them as if they are her own thoughts.

—Because I'm part of you.

It does not occur to Joyce that she will never feed Trina in this illicit way again. Joyce thinks that Trina will grow into a young woman capable of feeding herself who positively insists on finding her own food, and as her mother, she will eat from the same pot and at the same table.

Trina leaves the kitchen with her mother's lips on her face. Her body belongs to a spider. The captain's stories about Anansi the spider guide her just as the captain guided his boat from the capital to the settlement in the interior with Trina and her mother on board.

The preacher sends Joyce to the capital, to help organize the office and meet with ministers to discuss transactions between the government and local businesses and the commune. Trina accompanies her on most of these trips.

—Use that business-admin degree of yours to make this commune rich.

—Yes, Father.

As Joyce walks away from him, she feels his eyes on her back and a memory of his hands on her body from a time long gone and seemingly belonging to another life, not hers, not the one she lives in the commune away from everything she knows. Yet here she is, still answerable to the preacher she once worshipped and now simply wishes to keep at arm's length, a man whose wrath is the only incentive for her obedience. And if it were just a matter of her own safety, it would not matter, but she thinks of Trina's well-being in every move she makes and in all her dealings with the preacher. Trina first. Trina's life that is ahead of her. Trina above all thoughts of Joyce's own safety. Her child's life, to be lived not here in this remote jungle, under rules that rob children of their youth, but some other as yet unknown place for Trina to flourish beyond the strictures of the commune under the preacher. Joyce decides for Trina's sake to serve and bide her time and hope for some opportunity to arise, one she can seize with Trina that would transport both of them to a better place.

FOURTEEN

The commune business that takes her to the capital affords Joyce an alternate sense of time conjured by the river, a clock not of hours but of gestures, rainbow flocks, the seconds measured by the engine of the *Coffee* and its movement in the current. Joyce and the captain talk, and she rarely sleeps, just so they can. During a stop to stretch their legs along the riverbank, she joins the captain and other passengers for a swim in a tributary, and the captain says she has to see this great place a little way along. She walks with him on a trail with a towel wrapped around her swimsuit. They meet frogs the color of leaves, discernible only because of the peep-peep that makes her stop and stoop to give a closer look. He offers his hand and helps her over limbs fallen across the path. She hears the noise of water dropping from some height, and she strains to catch a glimpse of it and speeds up her pace in air that is now so full of moisture, it balms the skin. Into this gradual increase of water noise, she follows the captain and enters a clearing with him, and she looks and there it is, dropping from a promontory that resembles a giant skull with this water for waist-length hair. Mist rising in plumes, surrounding vegetation doused in it, no room in the air for anything but water. The next thing he asks her to do scares her, but he reads her face and slight hesitation and promises her it is safe. They will climb next to the falls about halfway up. For this he asks her to place her foot exactly where he places his, and she follows him up, and where she thinks the rocks must be slippery with moss, he finds a certain handgrip and foothold that provides a solid if somewhat clambering ascent. She watches him, his legs, his back, his arms and shoulders, to keep from craning at the height of the cataract. At the top of a ledge, he holds out his hand and helps her up beside him, and they step through the falling water and end up behind it and simultaneously move into a cave—just air and mist—with a feeling only of the cave's quiet hush and the tingle on their skin after being pummeled by water. And there she wants to stay and do nothing for the rest of her days but only if Trina can be by her side.

On another occasion on the *Coffee*, this time with Trina able to accompany her to the capital, the captain stops the boat at the halfway point to let passengers stretch their legs, and he takes Joyce for a walk while the first mate shows Trina how to make animals and birds by twisting and knotting bamboo leaves. The captain leads Joyce along a winding path, and at one point he stops and picks up from the path what looks like a squiggly stick, and he flings it away smartly and Joyce looks at how the stick becomes nimble and flexes and a head sprouts and a tongue tastes the air and it lands and wriggles out of sight into the undergrowth.

—Is it poisonous?

—No, but the bite's nasty.

They come to a clearing with a sky scraped clean and the two of them are under the bowl of this sky hollowed from trees. He tells her to imagine a gallery or museum in a city with the two of them let loose in it and given the run of it for an hour. First, she should close her eyes and listen to all the sounds around her. She says she hears the river and some parrots and a lone woodpecker chopping a tree.

—What else?

She cannot tell him that she hears her breathing and his, her heart so loud that it could be his.

—What else?

Now she stands as still as she can and holds her breath or slows it to a trickle of air and focuses on her ears.

—I can't hear anything. I feel you near me and I can only think of you next to me and I imagine it is you that I can hear, your breathing.

He says what she takes for her body, her breath, and her heart, and his body, breath, and heart is, in fact, the lungs and the pulse of the forest, the trees and every living thing in it. And for an instant her body loses its usual parameters and disperses among the trees and vines and flowers and insects, animals, and birds. She could not explain it if pressed, but she is no longer Joyce, the mother of Trina and member of the commune; she becomes every tree and leaf, each vine and the dirt under her feet and the river coursing over rocks and the rocks near the surface that resemble flesh underwater.

She returns to the commune altered by water, by the captain's touch, by the sight of trees and the textured light. She wants to put a name to how she feels, but she fears if she names the change in her, it will become public and she will lose it. She sees her future as a real possibility, someplace though without a name but with people she cares about, the captain and his first mate and Trina, able to live her childhood in this place that she must find and name, but not alone; perhaps with the help of the captain and his first mate.

People congratulate Trina. A group of four girls and a prefect, with an armed guard in case they meet some troublesome animal, walk with Trina and her mother to the river. They meet another guard stationed at the jetty and the two guards look on and chat. Luckily, the river is clear of the muck released into the water twice a day by the pig farm, which renders the water uninhabitable for the hour or so it takes the current to sweep the mess downstream. Joyce advises Trina to break the usual rule of swimming without disturbing the mud by sticking her foot into it and clouding the water. The group watches as Trina wriggles her foot and sinks a few inches into the mud and the water darkens around her ankle. Joyce asks:

—What does it feel like?

—Mud.

But it feels better than mud. The pull of the water is less than the sensation of her feet planted in the mud. The cloud raised by her feet sweeps downstream. She sees her body as a river whose current courses in her veins. Her blood comes into view as this mud kicked up by her. She wants to fall back into the river and sweep downstream with the current. As she leans back and floats off her feet, her mother grabs her and steers her toward the bank of the river. Trina closes her eyes and relaxes to the touch of her mother's hand guiding her, and with the current pressing at her side, the banks of the river tilt and Trina is a jet painting a trail on blue canvas and disappearing into the blue far from the compound and far above the tallest, biggest trees, walking upside down on the roof of the world.

—Mum, if I tell you something, will you listen no matter what it is?

—Of course, my darling. What is it?

—I think Adam carried me to his cage and covered me with one of his blankets.

—Trina. Listen to yourself.

—You said you would believe me.

—I did not expect you to say something so far-fetched.

—It was Adam. Or Ryan. I don't know.

—Look, I miss Ryan, too. Let's talk later, darling.

Word travels fast among the women, and each one congratulates Trina, and some add a gentle warning about her need to conduct herself like a young lady, no wildness. Trina thanks them all. She worries that boys next to her can smell what she imagines must be an obvious scent of her blood. She asks her mother:

—Can you smell my blood?

Joyce says Trina should not be silly about something as ordinary as a period. The older girls say the boys are not to see her private parts, as they call it, no matter what. And soon Trina will need a brassiere. But not yet. Buds toggle on her chest. She asks Rose if Rose can smell the blood on her. Rose shakes her head and sniffs the air and shakes her head again. Rose tells her to stop worrying about stuff that women have coped with since the Stone Age. The bleeding stops Trina from sprinting for the next couple of days. Instead she walks with small steps, one foot just ahead of the other, knees close together, hands ready to hold her dress down in case a breeze whips it up.

Trina heads to her music class. She clutches her flute and walks slowly past Adam's cage. She is sure the primate, with his extra-sharp senses, smells her blood. She stares at Adam and he stares right back. She holds out her hands to show that she has nothing for him, and he mimics her by spreading his fingers and showing her his palms. She mimics scratching his back, and he turns his back to her and moves to the bars of the cage. She stops and moves close to the bars. She thinks her blood might stir the creature into some kind of primitive rage. The thought makes her laugh and helps make up her mind to approach the cage and stick her hands in the bars and give Adam the scratching of his life. As she scratches and the weight of Adam leans on the bars, she closes her eyes and pictures her hand crawling up and down the gorilla's back. Her fingers are insects exploring the undergrowth. But the terrain is alive and makes her fingertips feel like they are playing her flute but without sound, just movement, her fingers moving and the back of Adam pressing against the bars of his cage.

—This may sound crazy, Adam, but I think you called my name. I fainted and you carried me from there to here and you covered me with one of your blankets. Am I crazy, Adam?

—Get away from that cage, girl.

Trina jumps a step from the cage and looks and becomes downcast at the sight of the young guard who likes to beat children for no good reason.

She looks around for another adult, but no one is near to save her. She decides that since it looks as if she is destined to get a beating from the camp sadist no matter what she says or does, then she better make it worthwhile.

—Girl, who you calling girl?

She says this with a sneer and waves her flute in the air, her fist tucked on her pelvis, her head cocked to one side.

—Can't you see with the two eyes God gave you that I am a young lady, not a girl, and don't you know with the head God put on your shoulders that I am allowed to scratch the gorilla?

The young guard, surprised by the girl's pluck, takes a moment to recover. He, too, steals a look around, and seeing no one nearby, he decides to enjoy the exchange.

—I don't care if you are the president, get away from the cage.

The guard lifts his stick, and Adam spins around and growls and bares his teeth at the guard. Trina takes another couple of steps from the cage, and the guard jumps back even though he stands a safe distance away.

—Come here, girl.

She glances at the long stick and then at the cage. She stands her ground and holds her flute up as if to use it to combat the guard.

—I said come here.

This time he is a little louder. Adam rattles the bars and growls. Trina takes two steps but not toward the guard. Instead she moves backward, closer to the cage and to Adam. The guard lifts his stick and stretches and swings at Trina. She steps back, and Adam sticks his arms through the bars and grabs her and pulls her against the bars. She relaxes in his grip. She keeps both hands on her flute. Adam growls at the guard. The guard shouts for help, and other guards and adults and some children run to meet them. Trina closes her eyes and thinks Adam must be able to smell her blood for sure. His arms feel as strong as the hands that carried her the night she fainted. Not like Ryan at all. But how? She has no idea. All she has to go by is the memory of a feeling. Adam's grip. The current of the river, her fingers on his back just like her feet planted in the mud of the river. His back stirs and muddies the clear air. She pictures both of them being swept far from the compound and no one able to follow them because the river becomes clear behind them, erasing all evidence of their trail.

—What's going on here?

The preacher's voice never fails to bring all activity to a standstill. The sound of his voice fills a person's head with the loud vision of the preacher's face. Bodies freeze and wait for his voice to instruct them what to do next or for the voice to become quiet. The spell woven by the sound of him holds everyone captive. No willful, independent action resumes until his voice ceases and makes it so. In moments of doubt, this voice helps to calm thinking. At times of self-doubt, all the members of the commune need do is conjure the instruction in the preacher's voice and the sequence of thoughts in that sound acts like a palliative on their own wayward thinking, calming them and banishing any notions of dissent. This extends to their dreams. Any place where their thoughts are not allowed to stray is guarded by his voice steering them back to the permitted pastures. Any sadness or longing is immediately burned from the mind by the steady flame of his teachings in his voice. Sadness, depression, longing are luxuries. How can any sane mind be sad at the prospect of the kingdom of heaven, unless the sadness is merely impatience?

All heads turn to face the preacher. He steps toward Trina in the grip of Adam. He takes the young guard's stick and orders the guard to follow him. He stops beside Trina, smiles at her, and asks if she experiences the slightest bit of pain. She shakes her head and he says:

—I didn't think so.

He taps the arms of the gorilla.

—Adam, release Trina now. She's safe with me here.

Adam drops his arms from around Trina, and she steps toward the preacher, who places his left arm around her shoulder.

—What happened here, Trina?

She explains. He looks at the guard.

—Is that right?

—Yes, Father.

Others arrive and the preacher tells his guards to open the cage and he orders the young guard who threatened Trina to go into the cage. The young man shakes his head but not in an impudent way. He begs the preacher to ask anything else of him but this. The preacher wants to know if the guard refuses to obey a simple request and to think very carefully before he answers. The other guards look at their friend, and it is clear from their faces that he has no option but to do as the preacher asks.

—Please, Father.

The preacher waves at him to be silent and indicates with an out-stretched arm that the young guard must step into the cage. Adam takes a few steps back from the bars and looks at the open door of his cage and at the guard inching his way forward. Adam backs away from the open door to leave room for the guard to step in and join him in his accommoda-tions. The guard's mother begs the preacher to have mercy on her only son. The preacher warns her to stop begging if she wishes to see her son alive.

—The more you beg, the more you show your mistrust and doubt of me.

She shakes her head and mutters no, and falls silent. She cries silently, a fine tremor throughout her body coupled to steady streams on her face. Adam looks from the preacher to the guard and back to see if there are any clues from either one about what will happen next. The preacher points his stick at the cage door. The guard, rooted to the spot, stares at the preacher, whose order stays the same and the meaning just as unequivocal. He locks eyes with the preacher a little longer, not in defiance but more in a plea for a change of heart from the man who brought him to this prom-ise of salvation. But the preacher raises his eyebrows, and the youth casts his eyes to the ground, slumps his shoulders, and drags himself into the cage, while the other guards quickly secure the lock behind him. He falls back against the locked door and begs the preacher to please forgive him and allow him to leave the cage and he will do anything to make amends for whatever wrong he committed.

—What do you think you did wrong?

The preacher is now shouting at the guard. Adam bares his teeth and takes a step toward the guard, and the guard lifts his arms in a gesture of surrender and presses back against the cage door. The guard cries for the preacher to please let him out. Trina breathes in deep and blurts out:

—Please spare him, Father.

The preacher touches Trina gently with the stick and shakes his head.

—Be quiet, Trina. Trust me.

She nods and searches the proliferating gathering for Joyce as more people drop their jobs and run toward the cage. They leave pots on very low flames and take pans off stoves in the middle of stirrings, percolations, stewing, brewing, and frying. Carpenters turn off drills and saws and drop their hammers and spit out the nails in their mouths and run out to the cage. A tractor idles, abandoned in a field right in the middle of turning over polished soil in which any and every seed that belongs to the forest springs up, impelled by an excess of nutrients in the untamed ground, while the commune struggles to make the most rudimentary of vegetables grow, and as heavy rains hose away rice seedlings, and as potatoes surrender to termites or harden into dense stones. They abandon wet clothes to languish in basins next to clotheslines. The nurses and the doctor leave their stations in the infirmary, accompanied by a few patients who can barely walk, and all head for the cage. The schoolroom hushes, and the teachers look out and order the prefects to take over, and they, too, abscond their classes. It takes one group of older children fifteen seconds of waiting on the edge of their seats for the teachers to disappear out of the building before these children push past the prefects, and another fifteen seconds for the entire schoolhouse to empty of children, followed by outwardly disconsolate but inwardly relieved prefects who do not wish to miss whatever lesson transpires outside.

Night watchmen and the bakery staff, asleep following a night preparing for the needs of the sleeping community, sense the uproar and stir from their slumber and vacate their warm beds and stumble to reach the scene at Adam's cage.

The preacher aims his stick at Adam, and Adam stops. The guard keeps his stance of pressing back against the cage door, his arms up in front of him, showing his empty hands and trembling fingers. He stops looking at the preacher and the other guards. His face muscles contract and compress his features. A preemptive look of distress takes over. A stranger emerges on the young guard's face, remolded by the anticipation of pain.

—Please, Father, mercy. Sorry. Please.

He keeps his eyes on the gorilla as he repeats his lament. The preacher maintains his aim at Adam, which proves sufficient to keep Adam still, and turns his head and addresses the impromptu gathering.

—Look at this, ladies and gentlemen, boys and girls. What have we here? A man full of remorse locked in a cage with an angry gorilla. Moments ago this man was about to beat this young woman with his stick for doing something he did not approve of. It did not matter what she was doing, it only mattered that he did not approve of it. He raised his stick to this young woman and would have beaten her but for Adam, our friendly gorilla here, who had to hold her to protect her from this young man's punishment. Now the situation has taken a twist. Now the guard is in the cage with Adam.

Adam hears his name and looks at the preacher and back at the stick and stays still. He waits for the preacher to move the stick in any direction. If the preacher aims the stick at the place where Adam sleeps, he will retreat there and ignore the intruder in his cage. But if the stick sends him toward the intruder, he will charge in that direction.

—What is mercy?

The preacher poses the question and pauses to survey his followers.

—Is it forgiveness?

He pauses for a deep breath. He waits deliberately to allow whatever emotions or thoughts to take hold and for his congregation to delight in and savor the effects of his reasoning.

—Is it restraint? Is it patience?

He glances back at Adam and adjusts his stick a little to keep it directed at the gorilla. The young guard with his hands held up in front of him appears soldered to the bars.

—Is it for one man to grant to another? Is mercy to forget? The Good Book tells us that the Lord is full of mercy and that His mercy lasts forever. Think of endless mercy at our disposal, brothers and sisters, endless mercy to match our insatiable appetites in this short span of a life. And yet all we have to do is bide our time to gain automatic entry into everlasting life. You see this stick in my hand. Is it merciful of me to point it from Adam to the overzealous young man locked in there and send the menace to him? Or should I point the stick from Adam and send him away from the poor youth begging me for mercy? How powerful is a man's mercy? I mean, how long can I keep this stick aimed at Adam and succeed in keeping his attention away from that poor fellow?

The preacher's voice, loud, strident, works its logic in the minds of the assembled. They watch him and wait to see what his voice will cause to happen next. His words take the place of the very air they breathe. His words are their reason for breathing. He promised them something that they dearly want to be true, that highest of ideals read about only in the Bible, and they can barely believe they are worthy to attain it based on the daily struggle of their humble lives. They have no choice but to see for themselves what will happen next in the cage, to find out the young guard's fate, but they want to hear what their leader wishes them to learn from it even more. Equally, the preacher's ability to hold the gorilla's attention becomes more important to the spectators than the fate of the young guard. The power of the preacher's command over the beast intrigues them more than the threat of imminent violence against one of their own, in part due to their desire for further proof of their leader's supreme ability to control events, from the smallest pleasures and luxuries of daily life to the ultimate promise of salvation.

The mercy that the preacher talks about, and the commune's sole focus, is his magic hold over the gorilla. His voice seems to control the beast in the same way that his voice controls them, making the women chaperone their children's behavior with inducements and punishments, and the men fire their weapons at birds and animals and daily chop and clear the trees. A pool of sunlight for each felled tree, a hole in the sky for cloud to fill.

The preacher turns his stick from Adam and directs it at the guard. The crowd inhales audibly, some of them scream, and Adam, in a leaping and bounding action that closes the gap between the two in an instant, charges at the guard. The young man ducks and covers his head and screams:

—Father!

Adam slams into him and bats him to the side, and he tumbles across the cage and stops in an untidy bundle. The guard tries to lift his head. He mumbles:

—Mother.

Adam rushes at the bundle and sweeps it up and throws it against the bars of the cage. The collision echoes around the compound. The young guard's mother screams and faints. A few guards raise their guns and aim at Adam. The preacher looks at the raised rifles.

—You'll have to shoot me before you shoot that beast.

They lower their guns and apologize. The gorilla lunges at the bundle again, and this time Trina shouts:

—Adam, stop! Stop!

Adam stops in front of the crumpled body of the young guard and looks at Trina and at the preacher and back at Trina. The preacher quickly repeats Trina's order:

—Adam, stop.

He points his stick to the back of the cage and Adam retreats to it and the guards unlock and rush into the cage and retrieve the unconscious young man. The doctor and nurses run back to the infirmary with the guards bearing the injured youth. The assistants lock the cage, and the rest of the commune, many of whom are crying, stand and stare at their leader and at Trina.

—Here is mercy, ladies and gentlemen, boy and girls.

The preacher feeds his hands into Trina's armpits and lifts her off her feet. Trina worries if the young man will be okay and if the preacher can smell her.

—Mercy walks among us in the form of this young lady.

He puts her down and begins to clap, and the congregation joins in the applause for Trina.

—Now return to your duties, and I shall see you all at tonight's service.

Slowly, the people disperse. They search around them as if they lost some personal item. They do not speak to each other, neither in the preacher's presence nor near his inner circle. The prefects and guards hurry them along.

The preacher calls to Joyce to come over and join him. He asks his assistants to write down everything he is about to say, since this is an edict from him to the community as a whole. He says the Holy Spirit moves in Trina. And Joyce is to devote her time to the care of her daughter.

Henceforth both are excused from the usual rotation of chores. They are permitted to work on the commune wherever they please, but they must not under any circumstances contact outsiders. The preacher looks knowingly at Joyce as he says the part about contact with outsiders. She lowers her gaze to the floor. He reaches out and lifts her chin.

—Do we understand each other?

—Yes, Reverend.

He nods and gives Joyce's chin a friendly push to one side before he drops his hand and adds that she should dress Trina in formal clothes for the evening service and they should sit at the front of the congregation and after the service they must join him at his house for a bite to eat. He pats Trina on the head and says he will make her a star. He smiles at Joyce. One of his assistants produces an orange and a banana, and the preacher takes the fruit and moves to the bars of the cage and entices Adam to come to him and take the fruit. Adam bounds forward, grabs the fruit, and leaps back to the farthest corner of the cage. The preacher says Adam needs music to calm him. Trina produces her flute and practices next to the cage. The reverend ruffles Trina's hair, winks at Joyce, and strides toward his house with his entourage of three assistants and two personal bodyguards. Trina thinks of Ryan somewhere in the forest and the image of him lost among the trees guides her fingers and her breath. Adam sits, his fruit in his hands, and listens without moving a muscle.

The talk throughout the commune never questions the preacher's motives. Most of the adults focus instead on the wayward nature of the young, their inability to follow simple instructions. What was so hard about following their savior in exchange for everlasting life? Why steal? And where is that boy now? Why couldn't he swallow his punishment and study his Bible? Why run away? And that young guard. He is lucky to be alive. Lucky he has to contend only with broken bones. Look what he put his mother through. Why disobey a direct command from Father and beat a child? The guard had no right to threaten the child, in particular that child. She was born twice. They conclude that the cage lesson is a hard one but necessary. Their leader remains the only supreme authority in the commune. He guides them along a lane they cannot see. He described it to them, saying that the lane will take them to paradise. All they have to do is believe him, follow him.

The children marvel at the flight of the guard around the cage. What a gorilla. And the smash of the young man's bones against the bars set their teeth on edge, worse than scraping long nails along a classroom blackboard. They say the preacher waved a magic wand that hypnotized the beast.

What a man. Man over beast. And the girl, Trina, newly turned young woman, what brazenness. She really must be as special as the preacher says.

The old makeup lady looks ashen, her body, rigid. Her friends double as morticians for the day and spoil her with a sponge bath. They stand on either side of her bed in a room dedicated to last offices administered to the dead. They dip washcloths in rosewater and wipe her face and neck and arms. They wash and comb her hair and rid it of knots and tangles and fix a bun in the back the way she liked it. Her friends hum as they work. Each holds the tune of the same hymn at a different pace. "Abide with Me." On occasion they coincide for a stretch of several seconds and sound like the same hymn before they break apart again. They clean and file her nails. No polish, she hated polish. They pluck a few stray hairs from her chin and add makeup, more than she would countenance, but they make her look ready for an important journey, in her best lace dress that she made for herself, stitched by hand without the need to take her measurements or without taking one look at herself in a mirror, seeing her dimensions in her mind and working by touch with lace, needle, and thread from the inside out, the dress she saved for special events such as important visitors or christenings, and for this day, her feet fit into the commune's best leather shoes, repaired by the commune's shoemaker, with a little bit of a heel that she would not be able to walk in at her age. But hers will be a journey of flight.

The carpenters make the coffin from local greenheart wood. No paint or varnish. A bright wood that, if someone did not know an old lady near ninety lay in it, would fool him into thinking that it conveyed someone young. But her youthful spirit justifies that brash wood. And for all her years devoted to the careful decoration of others, she appears now to be truly accommodated. They carry her to the congregation hall and place her coffin at the front on the makeshift stage and cover it with a green cloth and place three items on top of the coffin lid, a vase of wildflowers, a Bible, and a makeup compact from her trade. They leave the commune's most recent death ready for the evening sermon.

Two assistants collect Trina and Joyce and take them to a quiet room in the preacher's house. Trina has not been in the house in months. She stares at the indigenous Indian carvings of masks on the wall, and wood panels with paintings of hunting scenes and dancing around fires, and sculptures that resemble abstract human figures in the middle of various human actions, from dancing to chopping wood to hunting, all carved from wood. They sit around a table where the head teacher tutors Trina for the evening sermon. They enlist Joyce's help, and an accelerated lesson in public speaking ensues. Trina listens and repeats everything that they ask her to do and say, from the gestures with her arms, to the pauses between words, to the words themselves, all in the correct order and from memory. They reward her with soft drinks and chocolate biscuits. The public speaking lesson takes the rest of the afternoon and leaves Trina with just enough time to eat and dress for the evening service, where the head teacher says Trina will be reborn a star. Trina and Joyce walk to the dining hall.

—That would make it three times.

—What?

—That I'm born.

—What're you saying?

—Once from you. A second time by Father's miracle. And now this star thing tonight.

—Don't let it get to your head, young woman.

At the infirmary, the guard ends up in a complete body cast for twenty broken bones, and the nurses feed him through straws to bypass his wired broken jaws and several missing teeth. A broken nose and two black eyes shine on his swollen face. Both arms and legs are in casts, and the cast on his body starts at the top of his chest and ends at his pubic bone. The nurses rub the young man's neck, shoulders, hands, and feet to help with circulation. They tell him he should save his tears. He is young. He will heal fast. He must concentrate on finding myriad ways to show his love of his leader and regain his leader's trust. They tell him the medicine may be bitter, but the cure is Father's forgiveness.

The preacher visits the young man. He strides right up to the bed as if he intends to attack any place left on the young man's body not covered by a cast. The young man tenses his bruised face; his eyes narrow and his toes spread and his fingers curl into a fist. The preacher takes the hand of the youth and clasps it in his own and asks the young man for forgiveness. The two cry and pray together. The preacher thanks the young guard for his diligence on behalf of everyone in the commune, and before the guard can ask for his forgiveness, the preacher says he should focus on healing his body and spirit, that the whole community will be reassured to see him back on duty. The guard swears undying loyalty to the preacher and promises a speedy recovery. He asks for extra Bible study, and the preacher instructs the nurse to add Bible readings to the young man's nursing care chart.

The preacher orders his assistants, personal guards, the doctor, and other senior figures to gather around. He says with the recent public beating and with the death of the old makeup woman, there is altogether too much misery around. He asks them for suggestions to cheer the place. They need something to put in front of the commune and grab its attention, something that might act as a counterweight to the old woman's body and push aside the incident with the young guard. The head teacher posits a spelling competition with a prize for the best child and the best adult. The preacher says that would take too long to prepare. The head of security floats the idea of a shooting competition with the best shot winning a prize to be decided by the preacher. This makes the preacher smile, since he knows he is looking at the best shot in the community. Next. The nurse says a day of races with high jump, long jump, discus, and steeplechase, plus bag races and spoon-and-egg races and three-legged races and other fun things to promote community health and well-being. Not bad. The preacher rubs his chin and nods at the nurse as he gives her suggestion deep consideration. He thinks the games idea is too large-scale, requires too many people, and needs a lot of organization to make it work.

—Isn't there something small and miraculous that we can do?

The doctor says they could have a birth. There is a pregnant woman on bed-rest in the infirmary. The preacher likes this very much.

—How soon can a birth happen?

The doctor strokes his chin and scratches his head.

—In my professional opinion, I'd say we need another week or so to be sure the baby's lungs are fully developed before inducing birth.

The preacher looks dismayed.

—A week's too long.

The doctor and the preacher debate the merits of trying to contract a biological calendar to suit the commune's spiritual needs. The room empties as people edge away from them. They stand close together, and each time the preacher speaks, the doctor squirms and chooses his words very carefully. One is science, the other is art. One should balance the other. But in this case, only one can win.

FIFTEEN

As the preacher showers before the night's service, he sings "Tooty Fruity." He calls in one of his personal assistants, the one responsible for goods and services, to help with the zip of his jumpsuit. He says it is stuck. He says that he could use the expertise of his old makeup lady right now, God rest her soul. To powder the shine from his face, yes, and she was a talented seamstress. She took one look at the picture of the outfit in *Rolling Stone* magazine and made a copy of it for him, and it fits like a dream, but she was lousy with zips. He stands with both feet in the garment, which rests around his ankles. All he wears are his white briefs. He says his underwear is the only thing he would not let the old woman make for him. He grabs his crotch.

—I wouldn't let the old coot take these measurements. Now, if you were my tailor . . .

He trails off. His assistant locks eyes with him, smiles, and kneels at his feet, ostensibly to fix that tricky zip.

The preacher arrives at the tent feeling much too ebullient for the occasion. He curses the fact that his sermon has to be as solemn an occasion as a funeral service. His challenge, he thinks, will be to convert his glee to solemnity. Every impulse toward joy, he will steer to despair. He has held sway over people since his teens. He was born for this. You tell people something, anything, with enough conviction, and they believe you.

The preacher steps into the tent and the congregation hushes. He stands in front of the coffin, falls to his knees, and sobs. His assistants rush to him and help him to his feet while he wipes his eyes. He tries to speak and cannot get a clear word out. He turns to the front row.

—Help me. Help me find the strength to do this, brothers and sisters.

Trina and her mother and a few others at the front of the room rush to the stage and form a circle around him, hugging him and praying. The congregation wails. Someone shouts, God is love. Another voice launches into I Corinthians 13:

—Love is patient, love is kind . . .

The congregation takes up the verse at various points, some a few words behind, others a few words ahead, and together they create this vibrant humming in the room.

The assistants peel the arms off the shoulders of the preacher and free him from the collective embrace. The volunteers trickle back to their seats. Joyce tries to pull Trina with her before she feels the preacher's firm grip on her daughter's arm. Joyce releases, and after Trina gives her a reassuring look, she labors back to her seat. The preacher straightens, wipes his face, and keeps his grip on Trina's arm. He faces the congregation, and with each word, he shakes Trina so her wrist wobbles and her whole body shakes.

—Speak for me, my child, I am laid low with grief. My heart is heavy. My tongue is frozen with grief. Speak for me with your gift of tongues.

Trina looks at Father. He hands the microphone to her. She looks at her mother, Rose, the rest of the congregation ringed by guards, and last, the coffin next to her. She thinks of Ryan but cannot speak. The words will not come. If only she had her flute. She would play it for Ryan, the old woman, and for Adam.

—Speak for me, Trina, think of your happiest moment and speak from your heart for all of us.

Trina closes her eyes. She walks hand in hand with her mother along a tree-lined street in a small town on the west coast of another continent. What is her paradise. Sycamore seeds swirl down from the tall trees, and she tries to catch them with her one free hand. The seeds bounce off her and her mother, gentle prods by the very tips of very small fingers lowered by the trees. The seeds swirl down in whispers. Branches wave in the trees. The last slice of the day's sun climbs the trunks to nest for the night in the treetops.

—Father, yesterday I was a child. I did things without thinking what I was doing. Today I'm a young woman. I must think about everything that I do from now on. Tomorrow I'll be old and responsible for taking care of others. The day after that I'll be dead, just like Miss Taylor, lying here. And in all that time I'll do nothing to spoil my chance to get to heaven. I'll live like the example of Miss Taylor. I can do nothing to ruin my chance to enter paradise, not with you, Father, to guide me.

She hands the microphone back to the preacher, but he asks her to repeat what she has just said, every syllable of it, exactly the way she said it. She closes her eyes and closes her hand in the air around the microphone, and in her grasp she feels a sycamore seed newly plucked from the air. In her mind's eye she offers it to her mother. Her mother opens her hand and she, too, grasps a seed. They trade.

Trina repeats the words she said and remembers them all in the exact order. She opens her eyes and the congregation still has their eyes closed with their ears turned toward her as they wait for more. The preacher picks up Trina. Kisses her. Holds her high for the audience to see and appreciate her. Kisses her again. Takes the microphone from her, releases her, and steps away from her, pointing.

—Ladies and gentlemen! Boys and girls! Our very own Trina!

The applause deafens. Trina waves at her mother, who blows her kisses upon kisses with both hands. She draws an open hand toward Father, who bows. She points at the sky. The head teacher nods in approval. The band and choir begin.

—Yes, Jesus Loves Me.

The congregation changes the applause to handclapping and bursts into song. The preacher guides Trina to her seat and heads back onto the stage as Trina's mother hugs and kisses her. People reach over and pat Trina and congratulate Joyce. Trina asks the woman next to her to trade seats with Rose, who sits three rows back, and the woman obliges happily and Rose moves next to Trina. The preacher raises his arms and the singing quiets. He points with both hands down the center aisle to the back exit, and the doctor walks in with two nurses. The doctor holds a minute bundle in his arms. The audience stops singing altogether. The band ceases. A slight mewling sound emanates from the bundle, a distant alarm. The congregation cannot believe its ears. The doctor climbs onto the stage, and the preacher takes the bundle into the crook of his right arm, and with his left he brings the microphone very close to the baby's face and the alarm grows and fills the room and the audience holds its breath to listen and they hear, amplified over the loudspeakers, the small voice, hardly recognizably human, barely a breath, that can only truly be the cry of a newborn child. Pandemonium breaks out. People faint, fall into fits, howl, scream with joy, pull out their hair, and jump repeatedly on the spot, as if skipping to two ropes at once. The preacher holds the brittle bundle high in the air to cheers and applause, and a commune photographer snaps several shots with his flash. Adam runs to the bars of his cage and rattles them and hoots and cartwheels.

The preacher slowly relays the bundle to the doctor, who cuddles the premature baby and, flanked by two nurses, troops out of the tent. People stretch to touch the doctor, any part of his white gown. The nurses fend them off. They thank him for delivering a miracle to the commune. They keep shaking their heads to clear them but seem unable to manage even that small act of contrivance. Rose pats Trina and tells her she is great. Trina is not so sure. She buries her face in her mother's chest, and her mother hugs her.

—You're a beautiful and very smart young woman. You make your mother proud.

Joyce closes her eyes. The prayer hall bubbles with spirited chatter. The preacher stands and looks all around the hall and soaks in the success. Everything went as planned, but just in case Trina's part turned out wrong, the preacher had his Plan B and it involved the baby. The reverend takes a seat in his high chair and drinks a tall glass of ice water and motions for the coffin to be carried back to the infirmary for burial in the morning. The congregation hushes as four guards position themselves two on either side of the coffin, dip their shoulders under it, straighten up on the count of three, and walk in lockstep out of a side exit with people reaching in front or behind them to touch the coffin. Everyone applauds as the assistants leave with the preacher, followed by Joyce and Trina. They head for the preacher's house and one of his famous late-night parties.

—Don't worry, Trina, we won't stay long, you may be a young woman, but you are still my child, and you have to get your beauty sleep.

As they traipse toward the preacher's house, Trina tries to match her step with her mother's. The preacher invites the two to come closer to him and his assistants, Nora, Dee, and Pat. He rubs Trina's head and asks her to give him a moment with Joyce. The head teacher takes Trina's hand and slows her pace to allow the preacher, Joyce, and the three assistants to float ahead.

—You know I've decided to give you another chance, Joyce.

—Thank you, Father.

—Don't let me down this time.

—What do I have to do?

—Make a trip to the capital for me.

—Without Trina?

—Yes, without Trina. What kind of fool do you take me for?

—I don't want to leave her, Father.

—It's only for a few days.

—Couldn't I—

—I'm giving you another chance, woman. You want it or not?

—Yes, Father.

The doctor calls out in the dark, and the large group of assistants, guards, and heads of security, education, supplies, accounting, farming, community relations, trade, with Trina and Joyce and a few other special guests, all stop.

—Father, I need you at the infirmary.

The preacher waves the group on to his house with an order to have fun and adds in a mock-severe tone that they had better remember to save him a bite to eat and a drop to drink if they know what's good for them. He leaves with the doctor in the opposite direction. Whatever the doctor whispers to him makes him run his hands in rapid succession through his hair, and the two men increase their walking pace almost to a trot. Some of the group heading to the preacher's house notice the urgency, and they look at each other but think it better to say nothing in front of people who are present as guests and are not part of the inner workings of the commune.

This is typical of the two modes of talk in public. One kind is meant for the community as a whole and includes generalities about social and biblical conduct. The other talk is for all those privy to the intricacies of daily decision-making about the community. A speaker always takes stock of who is present before saying anything. If there were a third mode of talk, it might be the delicacy with which people in charge of the various operations critical for the smooth running of the commune never say anything to the preacher that they think may be judged by him as a bad career move on their part.

Music, food, and drinks break out at the house, soft drinks to begin with and church music. Trina and her mother eat fried chicken and cole-slaw, imported apple pie and cream, and drink as much reconstituted Kool-Aid as they can. Trina burps helplessly and covers her mouth with glee and hides a few treats in her pockets for her friends back at the dormitory. Joyce yawns, and Trina, triggered by her mother, yawns, too. An assistant notices and says they can leave and thanks them for their contribution to a successful funeral service. Several of the guests file out with Joyce and Trina. The music starts even before the front door closes. A few steps from the house, Joyce makes out the strains of Elvis intoning "Pork Salad Annie" and the clash of glasses.

A generator at the bakery outstrips the cicadas, the occasional bark of a dog, or hoot from the forest. Trina looks at Adam's cage and distinguishes his bulky outline standing at the bars, staring at them. Adam is fused to the night, the faintest seam of darkness thickening into flesh—the bold evening surrounding the bolder outline of the gorilla. She wonders how good his eyes are in this thick dark, if a creature like Adam might be able to look in a forest with Ryan lost somewhere and be able to find him. She waves at Adam just in case he can see her. Adam waves back and hoots to let her know, in case she cannot see him. His call makes her stop her mother and beg for three seconds and rush to the cage and say something to Adam that causes him to stare into the forest. She runs back to her mother.

—What's that about?

—Nothing, Mum.

Trina's mother kisses her good night at the door of the children's dormitory and leaves with the other adults for the women and men's accommodations. The moment Trina closes the door behind her, Rose and the others crowd around to hear about the party. She gives them the treats, and as they nibble, she answers as many questions as she can about the decor and the food and drink and the topics of conversation. She says the preacher got called away to the infirmary by the doctor, and knowing that the preacher was not at the house with Trina stops many of the questions that have to do with what it is like to be with him in his private space, since all they ever see of him is in public. Trina cannot tell them about her preparations for the sermon. The preacher made it clear to her, along with the head teacher and assistants, that all of her time in his house getting ready for the sermon had to be "our secret," as he, and they, put it.

—Ask me no questions and I'll tell you no lies.

This creates an awkward silence in the dormitory. Rose asks about her new dress. Trina says it was the last item made by Miss Taylor before she took ill and died. It is a dress for a grandchild the old woman dreamed about, one of her dream children, since she had none. The children ask Trina if she feels different with the Holy Spirit in her body. Is it a voice she hears that issues her instructions, or a force she feels that guides her, or is she in a trance, taken over and unaware of anything, the time she approached the gorilla, the other time she dared to answer back to the preacher in a way no other child has ever done, tonight as she addressed the congregation. Trina says she is tired and will talk to them about it another day, since she is not going anywhere and neither are they.

She climbs under her bedding, retrieves her pajamas from under her pillow, and changes out of her dress with a series of orchestrated maneuvers in the dark.

At the infirmary, the doctor and the preacher remain behind a curtain beside a couple of nurses with wet faces. The nurses disconnect tubes from the arm of a patient and cover her face by pulling the bedsheet. The doctor pulls back the sheet and reveals a young woman with eyes open just a tad and mouth slightly agape. He says the mother could not be saved, that she died during the service, not half an hour after the baby was cut from her. She was too weak for the sedation and operation. He tried everything to save her, but she hemorrhaged badly; only a total blood transfusion could have saved her. The infirmary does not stock that amount of blood. The doctor weeps. The preacher says it is a tragedy, but he needs the doctor to focus, now more than ever. He asks about the baby. The baby seems to be doing fine under the circumstances.

—Who else knows about this?

The doctor answers that only those present at the bedside know. The preacher says they should keep it that way, and he summons his assistants and two bodyguards. Everyone groups around the bed and listens as the preacher issues instructions. They stare at the young mother, who seems more asleep than dead. He covers her face and makes each person repeat specific parts of his plan. He says his instructions must be followed to the letter. He asks them all to bow their heads. He whispers a last prayer over the body of the dead mother of the miracle child:

—Absolve, we beseech Thee, O Lord, the soul of Thy servant from every bond of sin, that being raised in the glory of the resurrection, she may be refreshed among the Saints and Elect. Through Jesus Christ our Lord. Amen.

Everyone murmurs and makes the sign of the cross. They tiptoe away from the covered dead.

The young guard in his complete body cast and the other patients feign sleep. They keep very still and listen hard. They hear whispers and receive confirmation of their suspicion as a gurney is wheeled out in darkness and the bed stripped. They cry without making a sound by turning to a wall or burying faces in pillows. The nurses tiptoe and work through the night. Outside the infirmary, the bodyguards transfer the dead woman from the gurney and into a wheelbarrow. They aim torches into the night and, with shovels and rifles, head toward a clearing at the far end of the compound, cleared long ago during the commune's construction for the commune's inevitable dead, the first of whom happened to be the makeup lady and seamstress, Miss Taylor, who still lies in the coffin under the tent. The first dead but not the first buried: That honor goes to this mother. She is wrapped in the hospital sheet that lay over her at the time of her death. The guards drop her into the hole they've already dug and shovel dirt over her, not too much dirt, just enough to cover her so that if people were to look into the hole, they would see a shallow grave waiting for a coffin.

SIXTEEN

The young guard cocooned in his body cast enjoys hearing the nurse read aloud from the Bible his favorite passages about martial matters. She reads, and he daydreams not just about opposing armies but about the two of them, as generals facing each other. Before he became a prefect, he performed dull chores and daydreamed to pass the time. As a prefect, he watched over swaths of children working in a daze and guessed they daydreamed their way through those chores, while he dreamed where he stood. He became a guard and the dreams stayed with him. And here he lies, still relying on dreaming to make it through these long stretches of time. In this daydream he tumbles with the nurse, a synchronized pair, naked in moonlight. He stops abruptly in his fantasy with an erection pointed upward and stuck painfully under his body cast. He cannot move, and the predicament hurts and jolts him from his fantasy. He calls to the nurse for help, and she stops reading and takes a look at his troubles and calls another nurse, who takes a peek and calls a third.

—Vascular constriction is required, won't you say, Nurse.

—Yes, we could use a needle to extract some blood, perhaps.

—Too risky. How about a direct lowering of the temperature around the site?

The nurses introduce crushed ice to the young man's crotch and suggest he visualize his time in the cage with the gorilla to alter his circulation. He complains about the burn and they ask if he prefers them to draw some blood with a needle or cut off the offending object. That last suggestion works best as a visual aid. The nurse who reads to him uses her tongs to pull the willful object from under the cast and relieve the guard. The nurses leave him alone with the ice pack. He closes his eyes and soon his pain and embarrassment ease somewhat. Despite all his broken bones at least one thing on him is still working, and not an unimportant thing. He smiles. He is grateful to be alive.

He looks over at the young mother's bed that attracted so much attention during the night. He recognizes the nurse who has been reading to him. She lies propped up on the mattress, not wearing her usual nurse's uniform but dressed in the raiment of a patient, with a bassinet next to her. She folds her arms and looks around to see if anyone dares say anything. The young man says he read somewhere that a baby likes to listen to its mother's voice. He suggests that she read the Bible to the baby. He says if she feels up to it, maybe she could walk over to his bed and wheel the baby along with her and read to him and at the same time read to her child. The new mother likes this idea very much. She says movement is good for her after her operation and indicates her bandaged stomach. She moves in slow motion as she wheels the crib to the bedside of the young man. He asks if she knows her Corinthians and does she mind starting there. She says she knows her Corinthians back to front and is happy to oblige him.

The guards walk the coffin of the makeup lady to the hole prepared for her. Dressed in black, they march in step and pass people out early on chores to milk cows, feed and clean the massive pigsty, and cook breakfast for the multitudes. All pause and cross themselves as the funeral cortege passes. The guards lower the coffin sealed with the makeup lady's remains and her Bible and favorite makeup compact. The coffin sits lopsided in the depths. The men pick up shovels resting in a wheelbarrow beside the hole and shovel dirt onto the coffin until the hole fills to the brim and then pat the humped rectangle with the backs of their shovels.

The community carpenter hammers a wooden cross into the soft red earth at one end of the rectangle. The cross, made by him, bears the old lady's name and age. He wanted her year and place of birth and her favorite couple of lines from Scripture. But Nora, Dee, and Pat take turns reminding the carpenter of some crucial community tenets about the treatment of the dead.

—The past life of everyone at the commune is irrelevant, and all you need to know is her age.

—Everyone alive remains a child in the eyes of the Lord, and all their earthly lives will be over in the blink of an eye, and the only life that matters is everlasting life in the kingdom of heaven.

—Forget the convention of adoration of the dead with quotations and elaborate graves.

—That practice derives from a belief that this life, lived on a short fuse on this earth, is the only one worth living and therefore the only one in need of glorification.

—And that is devilishly wrong.

—And devilish.

The preacher keeps all legal documents belonging to the community, from birth certificates to passports, in a safe place close to him. Those paper markers from their former existences—full of sin and meaninglessness—do not apply to their new condition of rebirth as children of God, children of the Most High, in line for direct entry into the kingdom of heaven, children of paradise in waiting. And when they are delivered unto Him (not if, for this is the only certainty in a life of chance and accident, thanks to their trust of the preacher to steer them along the lane of righteousness), when they arrive, Miss Taylor will be there to greet them.

The preacher tells his followers that they are blessed like no other community on earth. He promises them that only the old die here and the young are happy and they live to a ripe old age. He says everything the people do is in preparation for their entry into the kingdom of heaven. Their physical and temporal lives on earth amount to a series of devout acts to prepare them for this stop of the physical clock and beginning of a spiritual eternity. The death of the young woman in childbirth upsets his philosophy and breaks his promise to his followers. He cannot inform them about it and her relatives overseas least of all. She joined his church and cut her ties with the world of disconsolate sinners. Her pregnancy was out of wedlock, by a man who had regular contact with the commune in his capacity as a delivery person but who abandoned her because she refused to leave the church and go with him. The life left behind is a blessing for everyone. The old woman dies, the baby is born. That is the equation. And if it means the death of the mother spoils the binary symmetry of one departure matched by one arrival, then the despoliation will be restricted and confined to a few minds. He will keep it from the heads of the community at large and maintain the purity of the equation. One death balanced by one birth.

He needs to get to his strong room, an underground cavern located beneath a back room in his house. Bodyguards move the eight chairs and long dining table and roll back the russet Persian carpet in the center of the room. They feed the end of a bayonet into a crease in the floorboards, a line that is difficult to discern as anything more than the join between two pieces of wood, and they lift a trapdoor. While one of them stands guard at the door into the room, the man and Nora, Dee, and Pat walk down the steep stairs with a rail to keep them from tumbling forward into a door. At that door, the man operates a combination safe and turns a handle and opens the door into a vault. He flicks a switch and the brightness blinds him. The shine in the room is almost audible. Bars of gold are stacked four feet high and ten feet along one side of the strong room. The preacher pulls his handkerchief from his back pocket and flicks it at the wall of gold to clear away imaginary dust. He blows a kiss at the burnished wall. He opens a metal trunk emblazoned with the large letters M–Z, and with the help of Dee, he locates the passport and birth certificate of Norma Riley. Dee shows him the passport photo and the birth certificate, and he nods. She closes the trunk. Pat and Nora heave one gold bar at a time up the steep steps and load ten into two attaché cases, five in each case. They mark a leather-bound ledger with the number ten and a minus sign and the year, 1978. The two of them sign and the preacher countersigns. The three assistants leave the room, and the preacher closes the vault behind him and climbs the steps, and the guards come back into the room and lower the trapdoor and spread the Persian carpet over it and replace the eight chairs and long table on the peacock-embroidered carpet.

The preacher grabs a pair of scissors and heads to the kitchen. He lights the stove and slams a frying pan on the fire and sprays the pan with a layer of lighter fuel. He cuts the passport into strips over the frying pan and tears the birth certificate into pieces and drops the bits into the oiled pan with the shredded passport. He grips the pan by the handle, jiggles and tilts it toward the flames, and the contents whoosh into a bonfire and he watches it burn to ashes. He kills the stove with a flick of the knob and waves the smoke toward the kitchen window. His assistants comb through the register of commune membership and the infirmary records and brush Wite-Out over Norma Riley's name and blow on it, just as they would on a fingernail if they brushed polish over it. They credit the baby to a young nurse, and for the father, they write unknown. They get the doctor to sign the necessary documents detailing the birth of a boy and the death of the old lady and address the large envelope to the country's registry of births and deaths. And they add the envelope to a pile of letters for the postman to collect when he arrives with his delivery for the community.

The captain sends messages to Joyce, but they appear to fall on deaf ears, since he hears nothing in return. He keeps writing and he waits for a reply but none comes from her. All he wants is a chance to clear the air with her. He cannot quite understand or accept that the commune can get in the way of what is just beginning between them. What is beginning between them? He wonders why an involuntary smile plays with the corners of his mouth when he thinks about her and how every thought of his duty as captain includes some reference to her for no reason, from her hair brushing his face to her rosewater smell, and something that bears no relation to her nevertheless brings her along with it so that she is there in his mind and she comes to him unbidden in kaleidoscopic ways and this continuous presence of her puts a spring in his steps and even the river takes on a sheen because of her image glistening in it and he wants nothing more than for her to be with him in person and for this feeling to be with him always.

The commune exerts a hold on her that baffles him. He is prepared to give up his boating life to be with her if she asks him to go away with her to another place. But to expect his total loyalty to a preacher in charge of a community is another matter. For her to ask him to follow, unquestioningly, a leader whose gospel makes him president and high priest, and who keeps a stranglehold on everyone around him, strikes the captain as too much to ask of anyone. He has to get a message to her. He must see her just once more to make certain he does not give up too easily on the woman who stirs in him the most unpredictable elation while he is in her company and the deepest gloom away from her. He cannot focus properly on his job. Every trip to the commune raises his expectation of seeing her, but she fails to appear and he leaves feeling disconsolate and listless for the entire voyage back to the capital, so much so that his first mate remarks on it and the captain makes a concerted effort to communicate with his passengers and conjure a cheerful disposition.

He inquires about Joyce and the information given to him—that she is busy with commune business or indisposed or not someone he should worry about or a woman way higher than his league—rattles him inside, and he fights to keep calm and look merely intrigued by Joyce rather than acknowledge his deep need of her. On many occasions he helps to unload commune cargo, but his offer to help carry it from the dock is always politely declined. The guards usually wait for help to arrive, and anyone on the boat who wants to visit the commune is told to make an appointment by writing to the spiritual leader. The captain jokes once about the high secrecy of the commune. Are they growing marijuana or something? The guards, Eric and Kevin included, become very serious and inform him it is no joking matter to belittle another person's faith unless he wants a fight on his hands.

—And don't expect a fistfight.

Eric touches a revolver strapped to his hip. The captain asks the guard to lighten up and apologizes for his bad joke. Eric says no problem, and they shake hands and return to talk about the scarcity of basic food items in the capital when so much of the country has arable land.

—We can't get any crops to stay in the ground; only weeds and vines flourish in it.

—I'm no farmer, but I bet the Waurá or one of the other indigenous peoples might be able to help your commune find the right crop for the region.

—I think the reverend is looking into that angle.

The captain says to the guard that they should not argue politics because the guard had a distinct advantage with his gun. Eric laughs about the ineptitude of political leaders. Other guards chime in that politics is a material undertaking doomed to failure unless wedded to the spiritual, to a belief in God. Their leader conceived of the commune as a social system with a spiritual core, and therefore as systems went, theirs was infallible. The captain senses that he should choose his words carefully, but something in him rankles at their certainty about themselves and dismissal of everything else.

—For me, belief is a private matter between a man and his God.

—Captain, you're naive. How can one person, mere flesh and blood, know a supreme being like God the Creator?

—I just steer my craft up and down the river and keep my eyes and ears and heart and mind open.

—You think organized religion is corrupt and has nothing to do with a loving God?

—I'm not sure people are able to act in God's name and get a result that is any different to someone acting out of self-interest. I think faith is too personal an experience to be organized into any system.

The guards, Eric and Kevin among them, ask him who would guide those lost souls wandering the streets and vulnerable to exploitation by the wicked, who, they might add, always seem to organize themselves into gangs and cartels and political parties. Here the captain says he agrees, but he has a ship to guide safely into harbor, so he must return to his work.

On another trip to the commune, he gives the wheel to his first mate and devotes his time to composing another letter, this time not to Joyce but to the preacher, and in his best handwriting.

Dear Reverend:

I write to request your kind permission to visit the commune to see the miracle of the settlement you and your followers have created. As you know I have served as boatman to your commune from its early days of construction to its habitation and to the present day. As you are aware I ferried the first expeditionary group to the interior and traveled back and forth with raw materials and saw the commune grow from a clearing to a community of buildings. The first planeload of community members sailed on my boat, and though every boat in the vicinity was commissioned to convey the group to the location, it was my sturdy craft that worked around the clock to help establish the community.

If there is any doubt about my reliability, then I should be dismissed forthwith from the privilege of doing any more business with your community, but if this letter contains a shred of truth about the beginnings of the commune and my relationship to it, then I know you will agree with me in saying that I deserve an audience with you, the spiritual leader of the community.

Sincerely,
Captain Aubrey Bryant

The captain licks the envelope, seals it, and writes across the front *Attention: The Reverend* and hands it to Eric as he disembarks at the commune's dock.

The captain's letter is delivered to the preacher, duly read, and consigned to the bundle of letters from the captain to Joyce in a larger pile of mail withheld from commune members placed on probation because of the unwelcome interest shown them by relatives in the U.S. or because the followers appeared less than enthusiastic about life at the commune. All incoming mail, no matter the addressee, undergoes careful scrutiny. If anything appears in a letter that obliquely criticizes the commune or seeks to entice a member away from the community or contains news deemed too upsetting to impart to the follower or offers information about the outside world that might capture the attention of the person and subtract from the total attention that must be paid to matters pertaining to the commune, that piece of mail never makes it to the name on the envelope but sits in the dead pile, waiting to grow to a size worthy of a trip to the incinerator, which covers just about every piece of mail addressed to every member of the commune.

The preacher refuses to see the captain. He relays a verbal message to the captain delivered by Eric.

—The preacher told me to tell you that you can keep up your work for the commune as a boatman, or you can quit and the commune will procure (that's the preacher's word, not mine) the services of another captain and boat.

The captain cannot believe what he hears. He struggles to remain calm. Instead of speaking right away and in a manner that might make things worse, he takes his hat off his head and runs a handkerchief across his forehead and on the back of his neck. He turns his hat around in his hands.

SEVENTEEN

Trina exercises her newfound freedom to work with whomever she pleases wherever she pleases by joining the garden crew for the day. She catches up with a dozen or so children, Rose among them, marching with their prefect to the fields.

Thank you for joining us today, Miss Trina.

The prefect hands Trina a hoe. She falls in behind him at the head of the line. A few steps later, she asks him if they ever sing as they march. The prefect suppresses a weary look and says that there is plenty of time to sing hymns at the sermons and in the classroom, and out here a walk in silence allows everyone to observe the bounty of God.

—Who said anything about singing hymns?

—Oh, what did you have in mind?

He looks over his shoulder at her.

—Well, we could start with something for the young ones and then graduate to other, more grown-up things.

He laughs.

—So you're a grown-up now, eh, Miss Trina?

—No. Since we walk all this way, we can make it more interesting for everyone.

—Take it away.

Trina gives him her hoe and falls out from the single file and walks backward and fires her instructions to the children.

—Okay, everybody, we are going to sing and whistle. I'll start us off, and as soon as you recognize the tune, join in. Got it?

—Yes.

Enthusiasm breaks out at the change in their routine trudge to the fields and back.

—First we have to march in step.

It takes a few adjustments by some of the children to get the march right. Trina watches the caterpillar feet of the line of children. She clicks her fingers, counts to three, and begins: Hi-ho, hi-ho . . . and with that, the dozen child laborers pick up their feet and sing and look at one another and compete to be the loudest in a jaunt toward the rows of unresponsive roots and vegetables, the beets, carrots, onion, potatoes, yam, cassava, okra, peas, and more, put in the ground and coaxed to no avail, all waiting for their attention. Or planted and weeded and sprayed with insecticide only to have a downpour kick the seedlings down the slope or float them away on instantly formed rivulets, or one time a plague of insecticide-proof locusts.

Well, this is fine, Trina thinks, but the song soon becomes a lot of whistling and not much else. The prefect asks if she knows any more tunes. She says: This old man, he played one, and the prefect replies while looking at Rose that Trina's song is too young even for the seven-year-olds among them. So Trina says: How about Chuck Berry's "My Ding-a-ling"? The prefect looks aghast for a second and intrigued for another second and, in no time, positively thrilled.

—Miss Trina, only you can make such a suggestion.

And with that Trina announces the new song and tells the girls to pretend for the sake of the song that they are boys, and the children slap each other on the arms and shoulders and laugh, and she launches into it with them at full throttle in a walk that is less of a march and more of a dance.

As they near the field, she signals to them to stop singing. They turn the corner and meet adults dotted about the rows of vegetable plants. All of the adults stop their work and stare in the children's direction. Trina's mother walks up to her.

—That was some show, young lady. It might not be a good thing to stray so far from the usual repertoire.

Trina apologizes and her mother tells her not to worry and they fall to work side by side with Rose. They weed, hoe, and pick at things. Joyce wields the hoe, and Trina and Rose clear and fetch and pluck. They pause to mop sweat with the end of their clothing and to stretch and lean back from the ache of constantly leaning forward. They take a break and queue for a drink from a drum of water on a cart pulled by a donkey. The cart rests in a shaded spot at one end of the field; the unharnessed donkey grazes close by. Each person lifts a ladle on a string, dips it into the drum, and drinks directly from the ladle, taking care not to slurp or spill a drop. They throw back heads and tilt the ladle into open mouths. They share according to the preacher's dictum that they must all eat from the same pot and drink from the same well. The younger children wet faces and necks and find the mess refreshing and amusing. Joyce steps in and holds the ladle for each child and directs the child to dip right into the barrel and open wide, wider, or to drink slow, slower, since the water is not going anywhere except into their little potbellies.

The donkey heehaws a loud neck-stretching bray that lasts so long, it causes everyone to stop and stare as the donkey winds down and falls silent. People hum, and some sing church songs to match the swing of a hoe or shovel or pull and throw of weeds. Most of the younger children assist the older children and adults. They fetch this or take away that and idle with a small bucket and stick and prod insects and block the path of worms and ants by placing stones and other obstacles in their path. The sky out in the field broadens and flattens for the child who lies back and looks up and waits for something to happen up there. And for Rose, something begins, small and brilliant to her eyes. A hawk drifts on a sideways moving loop, a flock of parrots swivels left and right with the precision of an aircraft made up of shuffling colorful pieces, a bunch of cloud shifts a city of towers, steeples, animals, and big heads with beards.

The final time Joyce and the captain made the trip to the capital together, neither one suspected it would be their last uninhibited meeting. Joyce is thrilled to see the captain, and he tells her that he spent every trip upriver looking for her and hoping she would be sent to the capital on commune business and not stay there but return a few days later on his boat, that what he ideally wants is to operate his boat and welcome her aboard as his permanent guest.

—That sounds like a marriage proposal. I thought you weren't the kind of man to commit to someone else.

—On my boat, I can do anything.

Joyce says that she is a package deal these days; Trina is a crucial part of her life. The captain says he means both of them and he is sorry to leave Trina's name out of his talk, he includes her in his thoughts. They pick up passengers along the way, but Joyce is the only person traveling from the commune to the capital. The captain maximizes his time with her by handing over pilot duty to his first mate. During a downpour on the boat, the captain and Joyce stand together in the rain, holding on to each other while sticking an arm out, palm up. An old woman shouts at the captain to bring his poor wife and himself under the shelter before the two of them catch their death of a cold. They obey the old woman's request, but neither bothers to correct her statement about their relationship. They just look at each other and smile. And the slow way they walk in from the rain makes it look as if they are reluctant to part from each other untouched by the inclement weather. It is not the first time a stranger views them as a couple and construes their easy intimacy to be contractual and far more practiced than is the case. They take this as a blessing that somehow an invisible charm is at work in their favor.

Joyce asks the captain to join the commune. They could be together more often than these periodic voyages. He says the faith that she has in God is one thing, but her faith in the preacher and the man's ideas for social living requires more from a convert than a simple leap of faith. Joyce breaks her half-embrace of the captain and takes a step away from him and turns to look at him squarely in the face.

—If you are prepared to believe in Christ just to be with me, how come you can't take the next, far easier step of taking an oath of loyalty to the leader of my commune? Why is that any more of a demand on you?

She wonders if his variety of love is nothing more than possession of one person by another, of a man wanting to own a woman, rather than the love that expresses a liberating emotion shared by two equal parties. The captain becomes serious. He knows he cannot couch his answer in his usual throwaway and affable manner, as is his custom for conversing on his boat, where his practiced neutrality encourages passengers into further conversation. This time he has to take a position and defend it.

—I see a god of some nature in all the complexity of living things around me, especially in the workings of the rain forest and river, never mind this planet in relation to the sun and everything else in the universe.

Joyce folds her arms and stares at the very river and forest venerated by the captain. Seeing her demeanor, he knows he has to say more.

—I believe—like all the songs on the charts—that love, more than any other force, powers this beautiful universe.

Joyce moves her eyes from the forest to the captain, and her arms drop to her sides.

—But I could never invest blind faith in another man who is flesh and blood like me. In a deity, for sure, but not in a fallible man.

This springs water into Joyce's eyes, not enough to run down her face but to fill her eyes, and she turns away and blinks rapidly to clear her sight. The captain's answer leaves her with the certainty that they can never be together, not in this life, because hers is sworn over to the preacher and the commune.

She says she understands his line of reasoning and leaves it at that. But the captain persists.

—What did I say?

—Nothing, you spoke from your heart, and that is all that I want you to do.

—Well, my heart tells me that religion should not get in the way of what we have.

This makes Joyce angry with him.

—As far as I am concerned, my faith is indistinguishable from my life.

He asks her to forgive him because his life up to now has been invested in hard work and honesty as the best way forward and not in a system where religion and one man control everything.

—I went to a church school, but I fail to see what God has to do with the gap between those who own everything and those who serve them. To my mind, subservience to God and to one man can only mean compliance to a bad kind of politics. I could never do that and live with myself.

—In that case, you will have to live without Trina and me.

Joyce storms off to the back of the boat and stays there, and the captain takes the helm from his first mate and stays there until the boat docks at the commune.

Rumor about Joyce and the captain circles the commune, rolls off tongues, and eventually settles within the ear of the preacher. He pulls her from the rotation of people allowed off the compound on commune business. He tells her that she will lose her daughter if she ever leaves the community to rejoin a life of sinning and meaningless pursuit of pleasures of the flesh. He reminds her that she came to him, and when she did, she was spiritually destitute and in dire need of guidance for herself and her child. Perhaps she forgets that despite her college education and ability to get by in the world as a single mother, she came to him seeking more than the material goal of satisfying the needs of the flesh, and she believed that she found what she was looking for in his teachings. He says she is a clever woman and worthy of a man's love and that she has his love and the love of every man in this community and her child will never be wanting of friendship and company and happiness.

This captain was one man. One destiny. Whereas, he, as her preacher, Father, savior, he was everything to her. No single human being he ever met could equal him, and no one man could offer more to her than the combined love of the community. And no love on this earth could match the love of Christ. Devotion to Him results in the coveted prize of everlasting life.

—Have you lost your faith in Christ?

—No, Reverend.

The preacher decides that the captain might prove useful to the commune. At least for now. His boat carries things that he never asks about, and no one seems to notice his business with the commune. He is reliable and cheap for a boat that size and a captain with that much experience. The guards say he never pries into their affairs, and he is pleasant and always voyages when they need him and waits for them when they are held up, at some cost to him of customers who leave for other boats. If the captain is a good man, then Joyce must be beguiling him. Her beauty must turn his head away from attention to his business. But the guards say that she is hard to like, much less love. Too ready to show she is smart. Too haughty with her intelligence. As if her body were a temple rather than the commune, which safeguards her existence. As if some hand cut her from a different cloth than everyone else.

The preacher asks Joyce about her relationship with the captain, and she admits to a warm friendship that goes no further than talk. He presses her about her feelings, and Joyce admits to liking him very much but says her feelings for the captain are cordial, nothing more. The reverend says she crossed a line by her association with an outsider.

—I'm disappointed with you.

—Sorry, Reverend.

The preacher asks Joyce to say good night to her daughter and to accompany him back to his house. He asks his assistants to stay with him along with three guards. They pass Adam's cage, and Adam stands holding the bars as he stares at them. The reverend does not even glance in Adam's direction. The group heads straight for his white house. He walks Joyce through the house to the bare and spacious meeting room and asks Dee to put on a record of Handel's *Messiah*. He stands opposite Joyce and waits for the music to begin. Once the choral voices start, he asks for it to be louder, and as it blares out, he says to Joyce that her time with the captain cannot go unpunished. He says he believes that he caught the relationship in its early development, and to prevent any irreversible acts on her part, some lesson has to be imparted to her to bring her back into the fold. Her temerity in cultivating such a liaison after her sworn allegiance to him and the community is an outrage.

Joyce tries to say something in her defense, but he holds his index finger over his lips, and when she persists in trying to speak, he grabs her by the hair and holds his hand over her mouth. He tells her she should know better than to ignore an order from him.

—Beat her.

His assistants and the guards surround Joyce and lash her with sticks. She tries to move away, but they follow her and swing at her body. She cries out and buries her head in her arms, tips over, but makes no attempt to thrust out her arms to break her fall. She lands hard on her right side and lies still. Her punishers pause and glance at the preacher and back at Joyce's unmoving body. The preacher takes a jug of ice water and throws it over her, and the cubes hit Joyce and scatter all around her. She moves in response to the cold shock, and the beating starts again. The preacher shouts at his guards—no more on the head and face. Joyce tries to get to her feet and grab the sticks. All she can muster is a repeat of the word "please," over and over, as she struggles to catch her breath. She makes it to one knee, and the guards push and kick her back down to the ground.

—Please.

Her eyes search the face of each guard. They pause and look at the reverend to verify if they should indeed stop. Blood runs from Joyce's nose and mouth, and the preacher throws a towel at her and waves the stick-wielding crew away. Dee, Nora, and Pat idle by the door, unable to watch. The preacher waves them away with an expletive uttered under his breath, and they scurry away and shut the door behind them. He kneels beside Joyce and hugs her. She feels wooden.

—I'm sorry, Father. Sorry.

—Hush. Hush.

He wipes blood from her face. He says that she is too smart to need this crude type of correction, but she forced his hand.

—I have such high hopes for you and Trina.

He wipes her arms and neck.

—I love you and Trina. Why would you want to risk leaving the community and losing Trina along the way?

Joyce cries and says she loves the community and understands the error of her ways, and she will do anything to earn his forgiveness and his trust. Again he tells her to hush. He kisses her cut lip, and she does her best to keep very still for him, but she trembles uncontrollably.

—You're on probation.

He says she needs to prove her loyalty to him and the community. He wants the devoted woman back. The one who dropped everything and rode a train and bus cross-country from Florida with her child and two suitcases and joined the commune in California. Who heard him preach and afterward walked into his office and handed over her and Trina's birth certificates and said their lives were his from now on. Who kissed his hand and thanked God for sending His ministry to his body and for guiding her to him in her hour of need. Even before they met, their personal correspondence in those early days convinced him that she was born to serve Jesus, but her recent waywardness throws everything into doubt, and in his opinion, doubt is the enemy of faith. He asks her to consider Trina. Would she want to see her daughter go through something like this? Joyce shakes her head. He touches his forehead to hers and stares into her eyes. Her full and overflowing eyes. His own well up, and he has to wipe them. He dries her face and his. He says if she passes the series of tests devised by him, he will restore her privileges to her as one of the shining lights in the community. She must past these tests to reenter his inner circle of people. Joyce agrees to forget the captain and to do whatever the preacher asks of her to win back his trust.

EIGHTEEN

—It's just for a couple of days.

—Why can't I go with you?

—Not this time, Trina. I must go alone this time.

Joyce looks at Trina, and her daughter knows not to argue about it. They collect Rose and walk back to the main compound. Rose hears an adult calling the name of another child. The voice sounds just like her absent mother's, forcing Rose to cover her ears and take evasive action by telling Trina that she will take care of her while Joyce is away. This jolts Trina out of her gloom and she hugs Rose. The two skip along in front of Joyce, who takes big strides to keep up with them. Joyce showers and packs an overnight bag. She receives her instructions from the preacher in the presence of his assistants, who advise her further after their Father has left.

—It's best if you don't talk to him at all.

Joyce agrees that this is the best course to take with the man in question on this particular occasion.

Two guards, assigned to Joyce's transport crew, take one case each and load them with great care into a wheelbarrow and throw a sheet over it. One guard pushes the wheelbarrow. The other guard carries their rifles, a strap over each shoulder. Joyce walks in front, followed by the guard pushing the wheelbarrow, with the armed guard at the back. They walk in silence along a zigzag path that leads from the compound down to the dock. The dock belongs to the commune, with posted Private Property and Keep Out signs as well as a daytime security guard. On seeing each other for the first time in a long time, Joyce and the captain can only stare into each other's eyes. The armed guard explains the situation to the captain and his first mate.

—She's not allowed to talk to you, so please don't talk to her.

They leave the empty wheelbarrow in the custody of the guard stationed at the landing pier and board the craft for the flight to the capital. The journey takes a day, and the river twists and turns and seems to double back on itself. Most of the time Joyce finds herself intently looking at the passing scenery as her way to avoid catching eyes with the captain. His skin, wrinkled at the corners of his eyes, makes him appear as if he smiled his way through difficult days. Unlike the captain, the first mate tries to get close to Joyce and flash her a smile. Joyce smiles but keeps her eyes fixed on the water or the thick trees on the riverbank. The water changes color from brown to clear to dark metal. The boat chugs past various indigenous tribes fishing at the banks and women washing clothes and children swimming. Men throw fishing nets in perfect circles that plop down on the water and sink out of sight, and the men haul the nets with care and shake out the pieces of dancing silver on the banks. The children chase the bounty, grab at it two-handed, squeal if the fish slip from their grasp, and hurl into buckets what they succeed in keeping. They wave and Joyce waves back, thinking how happy Trina and Rose would be to play out here and whether Ryan might be somewhere among other children. The children run along the path for a short distance to keep up with the boat. The people on the banks recede and the wild succeeds them. Egrets stand one-legged on the banks and in the shallows, apparently admiring their reflections until they dart forward and spear a fish. Caimans sun on the banks and drape half in and half out of the water, their traps slightly ajar to show teeth, as if posing for a camera. Overhanging trees seem to steer the current left and right. Darkness and sunlight appear to be born somewhere in the middle of the river. The only sound at night is the engine of the boat, but in the day it competes with other motorized traffic and with birds and monkeys on the shore.

They pass other vessels and wave, and the captain and his first mate, in their matching khaki outfits, exchange information about the water and a quick fact about someone or something at the port. A punt overloaded with sugarcane passes close to them, and the cane cutters, baked by the sun and covered in cane sap and dirt, greet them and hand over sticks of cane to the guards and other passengers, and the soporific air on the boat switches to animated splendor. People peel the hard outer husk from the cane with their bare teeth; others produce pocketknives. There is much chewing of pulp and spitting of sucked dry husk into the water. Fish flick up from the depths and snap at the husks. A caiman pushes away from its moorings on the bank.

As they approach the capital, the river narrows and traffic grows, and the waves from other boats, some speeding past on both sides and in both directions, cause the *Coffee* to bump and sway and force the captain to slow down and shout to the passengers to hold on. The first mate throws an anchor rope to a man posted on the dock, and he pulls the *Coffee* port side to the boardwalk. The first mate steps off and offers his hand to each passenger. Joyce accepts the help and squeezes the first mate's hand as she clambers from water to land. The two guards thank the captain and hand him a few extra notes. He thanks them in turn and says he will see them in a couple of days. He looks at Joyce, who averts her eyes.

Three men and one woman (fieldworkers, as those who work away from the commune refer to themselves) greet Joyce and the guards. The four operate out of the commune office in the capital. They shake hands and wish each other blessings. The guards surrender their heavy briefcases and position their rifles across their chests with both hands. The group walks quickly in loose marching formation, slicing through the crowded port to two jeeps. Heads turn, and talk stops in the crowd. The speculation about the group ranges from military in plainclothes, to government secret service, to a new opposition party, to commune people. Some among the group carry handguns, but the sticks carried by most of the men, a trademark of the commune, settle the question. A commune driver hands a few notes to some youths hired on the spot to watch over the vehicles, and the youths step away from the jeeps and admire their easy money.

The guards and Joyce drive direct to the commune's office building in the city center. Getting out of the port requires a near-continuous laying of hands on the jeeps' horns and countless near misses of pedestrians who dash across the road at the last second. The jeeps slow to a crawl for herds of sheep grazing by the roadside and spilling into the path, for goats dragging shredded ropes and making unexpected leaps into the middle of traffic—hunting food scraps that appear inedible to untrained eyes, for children who fetch water from standpipes with basins and buckets on their heads or in both hands, and along stretches of road with rickety stalls selling fruits and jars of honey whose proprietors wave at the jeeps to stop and buy, and slow for short stretches of the roadside covered with pieces of coconut laid out to dry in the sun. Near the city, the traffic increases and houses cramp near the road. The rearview mirrors of the jeeps pass inches from people nonchalantly walking along. Occasionally, the jeeps are forced to steer around perilous potholes so deep and wide that they must enter the lane of oncoming traffic to avoid blowing out a tire.

The jeeps pull up and park at two reserved spaces in front of a large four-story building. The armed guards jump out first and stand by the jeeps as Joyce and the others bearing the briefcases file out of the jeeps and into the building. They greet each other, and the office manager welcomes Joyce back into the fold. One receptionist asks how Trina is getting on, and Joyce says very well, and the receptionist says she keeps hearing great things about her daughter.

A person curious about the building can walk in off the street and pick up a leaflet about the commune and meet two friendly receptionists in the front office, decorated with framed photos of land being tilled and a band playing and a congregation singing and several portraits of the spiritual leader in action shots, preaching with a smile, holding up a baby, surrounded by older pictures of him shaking hands with world-famous dignitaries. The two receptionists know to smile and offer warmth and courtesy always, no matter who walks through those doors, since it can be anybody: a potential recruit or a spy. A camera at the door captures footage of the comings and goings downstairs, and a guard in an upstairs room watches the live feed on a monitor. Another armed guard sits all day at the door that leads from reception to the rest of the building. Joyce climbs to the top floor and selects a bunk bed on which to rest her bag. She hops into the shower and exhales at the luxury of warm water and the absence of a time limit. She stands still, inviting the water to do any damage it can. Her skin wakes up, and the tingle forces her to banish an image of the captain for one of Trina, then hurry out of the shower. She gyrates into a light-blue knee-length pencil skirt and a cream sleeveless nylon blouse, runs a brush through her hair and pins it back by touch alone, since she cannot face a mirror, and heads down one floor to join the group strategizing about the imminent meeting with the interior minister.

They run down their checklist of who says what and where the minister must sit. Remember not to interrupt and pause to allow the minister to have his say and listen and do not rustle papers or make unnecessary background noises. And remain seated. Do not leave the table. Let the minister do most of the moving and talking. The office manager reminds Joyce to observe and keep quiet and deflect any direct questions from the interior minister to someone else. Joyce says she is not stupid. The office manager says she knows Joyce has a university degree, so if it was not stupidity that got Joyce into a big mess with the captain the last time, what was it? Did she act out of self-interest against the interests of the commune? Surely that could not be it. Joyce says the office manager must sleep really soundly at night, knowing what a perfect person she is. Someone else begs Joyce not to argue.

The interior minister's Mercedes pulls up in front of the building and settles in the no-parking zone behind the two jeeps. The guard at the monitor alerts everyone in the house to take up their allotted positions. The driver stays with the car. A secretary accompanies the minister. A receptionist holds the door, and the minister steps inside, followed by his secretary. Right away he asks the receptionists how Joyce is keeping, and one of them replies that she has just come back from the interior. The minister looks pleased. The second receptionist whips up a tray of iced Cokes and slices of cake for the minister and his secretary. The guard takes the tray and leads the VIP guest and his secretary upstairs to the second floor. That same offer of an iced carbonated drink and cake is extended to the very appreciative driver, and the receptionist explains something to him as he nods and feeds his face. The receptionist returns inside and locks the front door and turns the open sign to the closed position. The group gathers around a large mahogany table in a second-floor room and launches into their affairs from chairs padded with soft velvet. The minister and secretary examine the contents of two briefcases on the table. Both pat the bars of light and smile. The minister's secretary transfers the gold to ten plain burlap sacks previously used to store paddy. The minister speaks.

—Gold suits these strong bags much better than rice. The piper must be paid, and there are plenty of them.

The guards repeat the preacher's concerns about prying eyes and the need for this payment to guarantee strict noninterference.

—Of course, of course. You people speak my language. I hear you loud and clear. It's a pleasure to do business with you.

And with handshakes all around, the minister tells Joyce how good it is to see her again and how attractive she looks. Joyce remains placid and says nothing. He tells her she must come out and see the town sometime. Joyce looks around the room to indicate to him that she has too much work to consider his invitation and perhaps to remind the minister of their location in the capital headquarters of the commune. She wants to say something much more rude. But she cannot speak. He looks at her and asks if he should read her silence as agreement. The office manager steps forward and shows the minister's secretary the door. The minister and his secretary grab the sacks with help from the guards and ferry them downstairs and out the front door. The driver pops open the trunk of the Mercedes and hops out of his seat to help them. But the minister insists that they stack the two bags around him in the backseat.

—It isn't every day that I get to play Monopoly with real bullion.

The moment the minister's car pulls away, a guard extracts the videotape from the machine, copies it and places the copy in an envelope, seals it with a kiss, dates and labels it *Interior Minister*, and hands the envelope to Joyce for her return journey. The office manager radios the compound and tells the preacher that everything is taken care of just as he stipulated. The preacher asks for Joyce and checks to see how things went. Joyce confirms everything the office manager said, and she asks after Trina. The preacher says Trina is doing perfectly fine. Joyce asks if she can have a quick word with her. The preacher says absolutely not, that this is not a social, and Trina feels more at home on the compound than Joyce gives her credit for. His tone is irritable. The office manager edges Joyce from the microphone. Another of the office staff casts her a stern look.

For the return journey to the compound, Joyce helps a receptionist fill the empty attaché cases with U.S. currency (low-denomination dollar bills to trade for gold) collected from pensions for the two hundred or so elderly at the commune and for goods produced by the commune, principally pork, and for unspecified security services provided to the government. The commune pays the government under the table. The government pays the commune over the same table.

NINETEEN

The captain stays on the docks for two days and two nights. He dwells on the woman whose company he missed for months only to see her and have her on his boat and not be able to say a word to her, a failure not his but a forced compliance that amounts to rejection, and he watches her leave his boat with a certainty that she will return and give him the same silent treatment and perhaps disappear from his life for several more months. Unless he can come up with a plan. Over a lunch of a shared half-chicken, he tells his first mate that he should take the time off but get back early or miss the boat, since commune folk do not like to linger.

—They keep their own sense of time, and the setting is always on fast forward.

The captain daydreams about Joyce, wonders about Trina, breaks a wishbone with his first mate and wins the bigger portion, and secretly wishes to be reunited with Joyce and Trina. The first mate asks about his wish, and he says it is bad luck to share it but adds that he asked the gods for a boat that never leaks. His first mate waves and struts off the jetty. For two days the captain performs rudimentary repairs and touches up the paintwork of the vessel, repaints the letters on the hull: *Coffee*. His body performs the actions of boat repairs, but his mind is elsewhere. At each part of the boat where Joyce stood, he stands and broods over the fact of their proximity and talks to her as if she were there.

He remembers the many ways he devised to make discreet inquiries about Joyce and Trina in front of the commune guards. At the time many of the guards pretended not to understand his questions or recognize the pair. But two guards who make the trips to the capital on a regular basis are on friendly terms with the captain. He asks them and at first they pretend they have no idea what he means. They play with him. They say there are literally hundreds of young women and children at the commune and that he will have to be more specific.

His past with her must be summoned in her absence, every detail of it, as his way to get around the silence between them. His mind reaches out to Joyce with his memories of them together. The guards must hear the desperation in his tone.

—Relax, man. We're kidding with you. We know who you mean. Joyce and her daughter, Trina. The child talks a lot.

—Yes, but smart talk, not just a chatterbox.

Both guards nod at his distinction and take turns to volunteer more about Joyce and Trina.

—They're doing fine. The child's a godsend.

—She's special.

The captain asks some more about Joyce. He says he cannot figure out why she stopped going to the capital on commune business:

—I haven't seen her for a while.

Both guards warn him that Joyce is married to the commune, and unless he is thinking of joining, he will be better off if he forgets about that particular woman. There is a lull in the talk. He stands with the guards, and they watch the river flex and ripple its muscles as it turns this way and that. The warning in the tone of the guards curtails any further inquiry about Joyce and Trina. The men listen to the water slapping the side of the craft for some time before small talk ensues. And what if he listens to their warning and leaves things right there? He will be a poorer man. He takes a different line in his questions.

—How does a man join an organization like yours?

The guards say that first, the captain would have to believe in God, and second, he would have to believe in their leader or the other way around, certainly both.

—What's third?

—No third, just those two things.

—But they're enough, my friend, let me tell you, more than enough.

The guards remark that the captain does not strike them as a man who follows orders without question.

—Perhaps that's why I run my boat and work my own hours.

He cannot help himself, and despite their warning, he returns to the subject of Joyce.

—Joyce is the kind of woman a man would give up quite a lot for, though, don't you think, boys?

—Yeah, we heard all about your many letters to her, but you know we cannot deliver any messages from an outsider to someone in our community.

The guards tell the captain that they like him but he has to drop his interest in Joyce or it will cost him his business with the commune. The captain says he would not want to jeopardize his lucrative work for the commune, ferrying goods and people back and forth, and he will not mention Joyce again, but he has a last question if they will be kind enough and indulge him one more time. The guards feel obliged to hear him out. The captain gives the wheel to his first mate and walks with the guards to a quiet corner of the boat.

—All this time I wonder why I don't hear back from Joyce or someone at the commune. Why string me along all this time? Why not just tell me to get lost?

—The reverend thought you would lose interest in Joyce if she ignored you.

—You people are playing with a man's feelings. That's sad.

The guards say he cannot repeat what they are about to tell him, since it can get them into trouble. The captain leans closer to hear what they have to say. He has no idea what to expect. One second they are warning him to avoid some danger for his own good; the next they seem more than willing to threaten him.

—Our community's not built to last, not solid like your boat.

The guard raps his knuckles on the port side of the *Coffee* for emphasis.

—You're different from us. You're busy planning for the rest of your life. But it's only a matter of seventy, maybe eighty, years if you're lucky. Our reverend's plans are for an eternity. One day you'll arrive at the port and find us missing.

The guard says this with such finality that the captain holds back the ten new questions that immediately came to mind. He regrets confiding in them. Their loyalty to the commune sounds just like Joyce's, almost as if their community is a species apart from everything else. He has to be careful not to lose his business by falling out of favor. He feels inferior. For saying too much to men who look like him but who think about the world in an alien fashion, as if this life, given in part and shaped by human endeavor, amounts to no more than a staging post for an as yet unrealized other realm of existence, and so does not merit the attention to alter or improve it, much less do something to help those who might care about the here and now.

He sees how she cannot help thinking and feeling that their spiritual leader miraculously made the rain forest welcome more than one thousand souls. He tried during their first meetings to listen to Joyce's religious reasoning. What else could he do? She stood close to him as she spoke, needing both hands to keep from her face the masses of her long black hair, its thickness and sheen. Even without makeup she looked clean, her proportions just so, beautiful, yes, a beauty that needed no adornment or embellishment of any kind, just light for his basking eyes. A face so open and keen and ready to smile.

Trina seemed a miniature of Joyce, with just the same quick mind and keen look at things. He loved them both right away. He wanted their trips to last for a lifetime. He watched them sleep and could not wait for them to wake and start again with their questions about the river and the life around it and even the light, they notice the light, and they make him notice it, too, how it changes around every bend and, with clouds on the move, takes on the same quality of a gossamer fabric spread over the landscape. Joyce asked him what is the single most important thing about the place, and he wanted to say the people or the flora or fauna, but after all her talk about the way the light changed minute by minute as the boat cut upstream and around each corner, the surprise of a pool of light among trees or light churning up the river or light falling through her hair, all her talk made him answer that it is the light, yes, the light, and she smiled as if she knew he meant her, that she is the best thing he could think of as he stood with her and her daughter on his boat.

The captain turns everything over in his head while he works on his boat. The story of Joyce in his life takes the shape of his beloved *Coffee* that he cleans, spruces up, and patches. There, somewhere, in his work and reflection, a solution to his problem stares at him and waits for him to meet it face-to-face.

His first mate returns and they refuel and stock up on supplies for the journey and passengers trickle on board and barely catch their attention. The five commune staff arrive with a flurry, four guards with two attaché cases and Joyce flanked by them. They are serious and in a hurry. The air of languid preparation for departure turns tense. Joyce looks everywhere but at the captain while the guards seem to look at him and nothing else as a way of ensuring that he has no contact with Joyce. His first mate whistles Peter, Paul and Mary's "Leaving on a Jet Plane," as he runs around in friendly mediation between the captain and the commune people, principally Joyce. The boat passes the places that mean something to just the two of them because of the way they were together in those places: where they swam, where they climbed a waterfall, and where he asked her to listen to the trees. At each landmark the captain looks out at the forest and it seems to brighten just in those places and he wonders if Joyce sees what he sees. If she does, it means they are talking in a language available to no one but the two of them. The captain realizes that for him to share with Joyce in this way makes it more than memory. Their pooled memories, though independent of each other, amount to new experience.

The boat speeds to the commune dock. The clouds race by overhead, and the current rolls at high speed along the wake of the boat. Everything takes on the hurried time of the commune. Every time the captain glances at his watch, the time left for Joyce to be on his boat has dwindled. The first mate sees the captain at the bow and Joyce at the stern, and the guards close to her with their eyes on both the captain and Joyce, and the first mate whistles more and busies himself more between bow and stern.

The captain looks up from his watch and the commune port appears to be marching toward the boat to reduce the time it takes him to dock. The guards and Joyce stand ready to disembark, attaché cases clamped under arms. Joyce looks dead ahead and unsmiling. The first mate whistles Otis Redding's "(Sittin' on) The Dock of the Bay" as he readies the rope in loops he will swing and fling to the guard already standing by the water's edge on the tip of the dock.

The captain looks at the wheel. He cannot bear to lift his eyes to the forest only to see Joyce marching into it between the guards. The forest brought her to him and now the forest takes her away without so much as a goodbye.

That evening the preacher calls a meeting of his emissaries who work in the capital. He tells them to use the opportunity of their trips to advise the captain in ways that make it unequivocally clear that he must forget Joyce and respect her wishes to serve Christ and renounce the world of flesh and sin. He waves the company out of his sight. The preacher summons Joyce and reminds her of her contract with the Lord, the commune, and Trina, who is inextricably bound to the commune. He says before she gives a thought to doing anything stupid, she should consider those things. He tells her to get out of his sight and to watch herself. One good trip proves nothing. She is still on probation.

The preacher's disapproval of the captain results in a marked change of attitude by the guards. They are decidedly cool on his boat and say only the most perfunctory things to him and his first mate. They rarely look at him, and the few times that he catches their eyes, they do not smile and they look away quickly. He senses the change but is reluctant to pursue the cause of it, partly due to his suspicion that it has to do with Joyce and the preacher and also just in case his inquisitiveness might make matters worse. Part of him hopes that the whole thing will blow over, given time. He assumes another reason for their hostility has to do with his letter to their spiritual leader, in which he is sure he wrote nothing malicious or slanderous. He sticks to piloting his craft. His first mate whistles the Beatles' "Let It Be" as he fraternizes with the noncommune passengers in the captain's stead.

One of the commune guards deliberately bumps into the first mate. The first mate says nothing, only retreats with a look of surprise. The commune guard asks if he finds people from the commune contaminated or something. The first mate says he does not know what the guard means. The guard says that his community is viewed by some people as a prison camp and the good work that the commune does goes unheralded while scandalous lies abound about it, and he wants to know if the first mate might be one of those people wagging his tongue. The first mate draws back from the guard and peers at him, not quite sure he heard him right. A cousin of the captain, he came straight from high school to be apprenticed on the boat at about the same time as the commune began. Like the captain, he knows the commune people well and assumes a certain degree of informality in his dealings with them.

—Come again?

—I said you look to me like one of those loose-tongued fellas who go around maligning the good name of the commune.

The first mate says that if he did not know the guard was from the commune, and therefore a declared teetotaler, he would mistake him for a drunk. Before the first mate can say another thing, the guard fishes a knife out of his pocket and slashes the face of the first mate, who does not have time to lift his arms to avoid the swift blade. He screams and covers his face. The knife has sliced from his left earlobe down his jaw to the corner of his mouth. He grabs his face and screams for the captain to help him. The captain dashes from the bridge area, leaving the steering wheel unmanned, an act of madness, he knows, but he cannot help himself, and he runs to his cousin's aid. He uses a short stick to hit the knife from the guard's hand. Other guards lunge at the captain and his cousin, and the two men fight off four commune guards, who kick and punch at them. The first mate begs them to stop, but they seem motivated to hurt not just the first mate but the captain as well. Passengers who have nothing to do with the commune rush to the aid of the first mate and one of them fires a pistol into the air, which makes the commune guards stop and draw their guns. The captain shouts at everyone:

—Cool down. Please. Just stop.

He says the boat will hit a bank at any moment and jeopardize all the passengers if he does not attend to it right away, and he says he will allow the boat to crash into the rocks and let them all go to hell if that is what they want. He will resume his captaincy only on condition that all weapons are set aside and if the commune guards promise to stop their assault on him and his first mate. They agree and the captain leaves his first mate with a couple of passengers who attend to the young man's cut face. The captain dashes back to the wheel. The first mate keeps saying:

—The man cut my face; the man cut my face.

He seems unable to believe the sting of the cut and the blood pouring down the left side of his face. The guard who brought the original message from the preacher advises the captain to make himself scarce; it would be unsafe for him to be seen in the capital and on these waters, that locking horns with the commune would bring trouble, that the preacher views altercations with his enemies as a life-and-death situation.

—You're threatening me?

—We're past making threats, Captain. You need to watch your back.

At the port, the captain tells the guards that this is the end of his working relationship with the commune. He puts his first mate in a taxi headed straight for the hospital, and he knocks on the door of the office of the port authority. He complains to the port authority police about the conduct of the commune guards on his boat. He says he wants the men charged with assault of his first mate and explains that the men made an explicit threat to their lives as well. The port officer calls the capital's central police station, and the central police station calls the chief of police, who advises the central station to direct the port authority police to scrap the charges. The captain waits for two hours to hear that nothing can be done about his complaint. The captain asks the police officer if, in addition to donning the uniform of his profession, he swore an oath to serve the people and to uphold the law. The officer says yes, he did. The captain says if that is the case, how can this officer stand there in a uniform in an official capacity and tell a citizen he has no rights. The officer orders a few of his men to bring the captain from the area of the front desk to a more discreet location inside the building. They try to grab the captain, but he assures them that he will cooperate and they do not need to manhandle him. Once in a back room, the officer says to the captain that if he wishes to practice his trade on this river and keep his prized boat, he had better forget about this incident. They leave him for a couple of hours to think it over.

When the officer returns, the captain tries to say something about checking the arrogant power of the commune, whose members behave as if they are above the laws of the land. The officer raises his voice. He says the captain should persist with the complaint only if he really wants more trouble than he bargained for. Two more officers show up at the office door. The officer wants to know if his uniform is official enough for the captain to comprehend his meaning, because if it is not, they can talk a different language, one less decorous, one more rudimentary. He stares at the captain, who returns his gaze. The two police, poised at the office door, step into the room. The captain looks at the three men and shakes his head and raises his arms in a sign of surrender, shrugs. Before he leaves the building, they copy the details of his boating license.

The commune office in the capital calls the port authority and lodges an official complaint of incompetence and endangerment of the public against the captain. They say they have four men willing to sign an affidavit. They ask for his license to operate a boat on the river to be revoked. The port authority police promise to look into the matter and examine the license of the captain. The guards want to know if they need to take the matter higher up, to, say, the chief of police, or whether the port authority can handle the matter. The port authority police assure the commune guards that it will not be necessary to go higher up, since the matter is in the right hands and they should not worry about it. The guards invite the officer to drop by the commune office at his earliest convenience for a thank-you gift. The officer thanks the guards for their generosity and wishes them a good night.

On his walk home, the captain decides to take a shortcut through the city's oldest graveyard. The graves are so ancient that some of the tombstones list to one side and the mounted concrete graves look vacant, as though their occupants have risen up and left for the evening. Footpaths twist through the graveyard and resemble corridors in places with graves stacked as high as an adult's chest and arms' width apart. In these spots a person can turn a corner and come face-to-face with some stranger whose intentions may not always be good. Robberies and stabbings occur frequently. A person must be in some big rush or entertain some kind of a death wish to take the graveyard shortcut at night. But the captain is not in a hurry and he does not want trouble. He needs time to think, and this place, for all its claustrophobia and dilapidation, seems to offer him solace. Ever since he was a young man, he found the graveyard the best location to be in a crowded city, to capture that isolated feeling in the most splendid and luxurious of ways, because it cost nothing, just a little courage in the dark.

As a young man, he tried to bring women he courted to the graveyard, but all of them except one thought him a little eccentric if not downright creepy. He walks east to west and cuts a leisurely path through the intersecting passages, wanting to emerge into the city street, refreshed in his mind, having succeeded in undoing some Gordian knot of a worry that accompanied him into the graveyard, a worry that he left behind in the unkempt graves.

Tonight he wants to decide on a course of action for Joyce and Trina— and how, if there is a how, he should deal with the violence of the commune guards against his first mate and their threats to him and his livelihood. He feels unafraid for himself, but his young cousin carries a scar for life. And although he feels fine, he knows that Joyce and Trina might really need his help if they are held captive at the commune. Even if his young cousin prevails over the incident and is keen to move on, as well and good as that sounds, there will remain the matter of Joyce's and Trina's safety at the commune. He would go back to navigating the river and its tributaries and resuscitate the old pleasures of life on his boat with no one to bother him and only the tides to govern his movement from one day to the next. But the river would be spoiled for him. He would see Joyce and Trina around every twist and turn.

He crossed paths with some powerful and dangerous people, and yet he knows he cannot walk away and pretend to forget about everything. If he persists, he realizes he is guaranteed to meet calamity of some kind from people whose tentacles stretch deep into the politics of the city. At least that is how it is put to him, and he has to believe that is how it would turn out if he ignored the warnings and pursued the matter. Would the preacher try to harm him? Where in the land could he hide to evade the clutches of the commune?

The moon falls on the graves and casts deep shadows that seem more defined than the graves themselves. Shadows crisscross and create the impression of three or four torchlight moons shining on each grave. The captain sees how each step he takes elongates his shadow ahead and to the side of him, and as he turns a lighted corner, his shadow compacts to a dwarf and gathers under his feet as if darting back from tentative exploration to a safe haven. On evenings like this, the capital courts a light and cool breeze that refreshes everything it touches. The dead all around him could not be blamed for going on walkabout; it is too good a night for even the dead to pass up. Do they walk around with him right now? They occupy another dimension and ignore the likes of him. In the distance, the captain makes out what he counts as three or four adult shadows, which retreat from view as he approaches a narrow walk between looming graves. The captain stops and considers turning back and heading for another intersection.

—What's going on there, boys?

He waits for a reply but none comes. The captain pulls his trusty baton from his belt and picks up a large stone. He walks forward and tries to keep his breathing steady. He quells an impulse to turn on his heels and run. His years of walking at night in the graveyard will not allow him to flee. He thinks this place will be as good as any for trouble to find him.

—I know you're there, you may as well show yourselves.

He commits himself to the narrow path, just one way back and one way forward, with two walls of old tombs on either side. About halfway along it, four men step in front of him, and he glances back to see two others walking fast to meet him. The captain turns and runs at full speed toward the two men approaching him. The four others who stand blocking his path give chase. A few steps from the two men, he notices that they hold large wooden clubs and he thinks he catches the glint of a knife in one of their hands. The captain calculates that if he can bring down one of his assailants, he might create an opening for his escape. He directs his attention to the man flashing the glimmering blade. He kicks the man in the crotch and whacks the man's hand with a stick and frees the metal from the man's grip. The captain and the man tumble to the ground, and with the man under him, the captain swings his stone down into the man's face. But he feels lashes on his back and kicks to his ribs. He rolls to one side and curls up in an instant to protect his face and ribs. He absorbs a flurry of boots and fists and sticks.

—Captain, you need to listen.

A voice shouts through its exertions delivering an assault on the captain.

—This is your one and only warning.

The voice punctuates its warning with hits to the captain's body as an arm grips the captain's neck and chokes him.

—Keep away from the commune.

The captain tries to pry the arm from around his neck, but the other men have him pinned. Though he kicks, he cannot budge the stranglehold. The moon swoops down toward him and brings its bright bulb close to his face, not one moon or two or three, but four or five of those moons run up close and swerve from him at the last possible moment and leave him in darkness.

A call from the office at the capital to the commune reports that the captain has been put in his place for good.

—He won't be seen on the river again.

The office manager asks that the rest of the conversation with the preacher be conducted in private. The preacher says they are all one family and the office manager should go ahead and say what is on her mind. She recommends strongly that the preacher hears in private what she has to say before he divulges it to the rest of the group, since what she has to tell him will determine how he strategizes with the rest of the commune. The preacher, intrigued by the request for privacy, puts on a pair of earphones and sits in front of a microphone. The office manager says her call concerns the organization formed by relatives of people in the commune. The preacher dismisses the organization as a lot of hot air, a bunch of losers, and a campaign in search of a cause. The office manager informs the preacher that recent activities of the organization have taken on new meaning for the commune. The preacher interrupts and says he will be the judge of whether those miscreants huffing and puffing at his brick house are really to be considered a cause for concern. That he doubts it very much. And so should she, if she has any faith in him. She apologizes and swears that her faith is intact but he should listen to the rest of what she has found out.

She says that letters smuggled out of the commune make various allegations about cruelty and imprisonment of those who express a desire to leave. The preacher wants to know what letters. He demands proof. She says an official affidavit, hand-delivered to the office in the capital, names a dozen children at the commune, Rose among them, whose relatives want them back on the grounds that they are minors. The office manager adds that the California-based pressure group has convinced the state government to launch an inquiry into the affairs of the commune. Despite the commune's many gifts to various ministries in the capital, a U.S. delegation not only expressed a strong desire to visit to make the determination whether people lived there voluntarily and not against their will, as claimed by the relatives' pressure group, but the delegation was granted permission to visit the country in an official capacity, with a view to gaining entry to the commune.

The preacher swears. He thinks there must be some mistake. He asks her who in the government ratified the U.S. delegation's visit. What the office manager says next surprises the preacher.

—Permission came from the very top, Reverend.

—The very top?

—Yes, Reverend, the very top.

The preacher tears off his headphones and slams them to the floor and tips over the microphone. He storms out of the radio room and shouts at his assistants to gather everyone for a meeting. The radio operator collects the headphones and tidies the microphone on the desk. The preacher decides his next sermon will be about this onslaught from hostile outside forces determined to destroy the commune's way of life.

Dressed in a khaki suit, the preacher asks the congregation to imagine that he is on a safari hunt to capture souls. He asks if they would like to be the prey hunted by the power of the Lord. Everyone cries out to be hunted by Him. He says his other reason for dressing in khaki, as if ready for a hunt, concerns their location. The jungle offers a natural refuge for his community, but there are mercenaries hidden out there in the trees who might attack the commune, and while his soldiers, their brethren, can hold off mercenaries for a while, there is not much hope of success against a hired professional army bent on their destruction.

—But I am a soldier of Christ, and every single one of you here tonight is here because you are willing to be commissioned into my army to serve Christ. Every one of you is willing to serve as prey for Christ and allow yourself to be captured because you want to serve the Lord. True or false?

—True, Reverend.

He asks Joyce, seated with Trina in the front row, what she would do under such circumstances:

—Remember, you're about to be overrun by mercenaries whose mission is to destroy your refuge and take you back to the bad old ways of your former life and shame you in front of everyone for your willingness to follow in the path of righteousness. They would lock you in prison with common criminals and throw away the key for following Christ. They would take your precious children and institutionalize them in decrepit government detention centers for lost children.

He pushes the microphone under Joyce's nose, and she says through her sore and cut lips that she would use any weapon she could lay her hands on to defend herself.

—But you cannot defend yourself, Joyce. Not against overwhelming odds. So what would you do?

Joyce thinks about her reply for a moment. If the preacher says there is nothing to do, meaning no earthly course of action, that means there remains only one thing to do. She knows what she must say by the way he stares at her and half-smiles, that same look and expression multiplied on the faces of his assistants and personal bodyguards.

—I would kill myself, Reverend.

—Say that again and louder this time.

—Kill myself, Reverend.

—You hear that, people? To evade certain capture and to stay pure and true to her word, Miss Joyce would deny her enemies the ultimate victory and satisfaction derived from her capture and defeat by killing herself. Joyce, you are a genius.

He kisses her on the forehead and asks her what about the little princess seated beside her.

—What about Trina, Reverend?

—What becomes of her after your inspired escape from the oppressors?

His question startles Joyce. She wonders why ask something if everyone in the room already knows the answer. She realizes she must play her small role in the preacher's method of roping his audience inexorably into accepting the conclusions of his reasoning. Some important lesson in his head requires her cooperation for it to be instilled among the congregation, of which she is just one expendable piece in a larger puzzle of nearly one thousand pieces.

—Remember, you've killed yourself to deny your enemies.

—Yes, Reverend.

—And what becomes of your precious daughter without her mother to protect her? You would leave her to her fate, to a life in the hands of our worst enemies? The very people who are out to imprison us and separate us from our children?

The congregation shouts a unanimous no. Joyce nods in agreement. She feels trapped in a form of reasoning she has heard many times and never succeeded in finding a way around and so could never offer any effective resistance. She knows her participation needs to be unequivocal to convince the preacher of her reinvigorated commitment to him and the commune.

—You see the dilemma, don't you, Miss Joyce? You do the right thing by evading capture and robbing our enemies of victory when you take your own life, but you leave your most precious girl to her fate at the hands of the wicked.

—No, I wouldn't leave her. I'd take her with me.

The preacher thrusts the microphone under her nose:

—Say that again, Miss Joyce.

—I would take her with me, Reverend.

—And how would you do that, Miss Joyce?

—I would kill her first and then myself.

—Say that again, you brave woman and devoted mother.

—I would kill her first, then myself.

The congregation erupts into applause and affirmative shouts of yes, yes, yes.

—Look around you, people. Let us be realistic. We've a lot of children here. How many? What, three hundred and twenty, fifty, or more? Should I as your leader expect each of you to take it upon yourself to kill your own children? In the heat of being under attack, it takes enough just to think about yourself, never mind your children. What kind of a leader would I be to you if I abandoned you to your enemies? What would you think of me if I left you to your own devices at the very moment when you needed me most? You can say it. I won't hold it against you. You would be within your rights to curse the hell out of me, damn my name. Wouldn't you?

The agreement is a little tentative. It does not sit easily with the congregation to condemn their leader to his face even if he invites them to do it. They know he has the memory of an elephant and he summons details about everyone and everything going back years, to the inception of the commune. Sometimes these details make their reappearance verbatim, but with a slight shift of emphasis, that turns a compliment into an insult or an invitation to criticize him into uninvited betrayal.

—As your leader, I've made contingency plans. Just as the enemy plans our destruction, so I am planning our escape from their clutches. We view death altogether differently than the outsiders, don't we? We are fortunate in our faith in the Lord our Savior to know that death is not a final precipice. Aren't we lucky to have this faith, people? Are we not blessed in the certainty of our faith? We know that death is a transition and not finality. What is it? Repeat.

—Death is a transition, not a finality.

—Death is a transition. Don't think of it as final. We know that we leave this life to walk through the gates of heaven into everlasting happiness. We know when the enemy rushes out of the forest, we will be ready to make that journey together, won't we, people?

The congregation stamps feet and claps hands and shouts in unison:

—Yes, yes, yes, yes.

He waits for the chant to die down. The congregation settles for him.

—Imagine we have sounded the alarm all over the community. You have all been summoned to meet here. You know that the guards are doing their best to keep the enemy from overrunning this refuge. All you have to do to escape your enemies and reunite with your children in paradise is follow my instructions. Imagine this is the moment, people. Right here and now. What do you have to do? How can you escape imprisonment, separation from your children, and their imprisonment?

—Tell us, Father. Tell us.

The preacher sticks out his arm in the direction of a corner of the stage and asks the congregation for volunteers to be the first to come up and drink a fast-acting potion that will take them quickly and painlessly to the other side.

—Who will lead this community to the kingdom of heaven?

The people in the front row switch into emergency mode and rush to be the first on the stage, and the rows behind the front trample and push forward. This results in a crush at the front. The children cry and the guards push people back from the stage. The preacher shouts for order:

—Stop, stop, stop.

Not in anger does he tell them to stop; he seems satisfied with the serious response by the congregation. Rather, it is a cursory show of concern for the children.

—Form a line, children first. Come up and take your portion and be saved from tyranny. There is plenty for everyone.

Encouraged by their leader, the congregation slows, their collective demeanor changing from a show of emergency to a calm display of poise under duress. They cry and laugh at the same time, look at each other, unsure what to expect next in the hands of their savior. They form two queues and drink from two ladles dipped into the vat by two assistants and try hard not to spill a drop and they drain the portion fed to them and say thank you through tears and with a broad smile. The preacher takes a turn to dip a ladle and fill a cup, and he blesses each one who drinks from it.

—Honor thy father and thy mother that thy days may be long.

After they drink dutifully, they turn and scurry to a seat as directed by the guards and pray and sing and wait for the effects of a transition from the body to begin and for the soul to surface in paradise. The members of the congregation look at one another for a sign of alteration, and seeing none, they exchange hugs and kisses. For this time they walked through the valley of death of their own making. They filed up to a vat at the invitation of their leader and drank what they took on trust to be the means that would carry them through a portal from this world to the next. They grew terrified and elated at once with the feeling that this time might be real rather than a rehearsal. They disperse from the meeting and drink deep from the night air that tastes like their first air of this life.

They forget about Adam. He senses that something important is happening. A kind of incessant crying replaces the usual commotion of singing and chants and some tears. The children cry loudest and sound afraid. Adam growls and rattles his cage. A couple of guards on night duty rap on the bars with their rifles and sticks for Adam to be quiet. He retreats to his corner, plants his hands over his ears, and rocks back and forth. He conjures his running dream, first on the forest floor, next with his feet off the ground and higher up on a lane cut through vines, until he reaches a sprint and collides into the open arms of his mother and the two tumble together before coming to a standstill and neither one releases their grip of the other.

TWENTY

The captain wakes battered and bruised in St. Joseph's Mercy Hospital. His first mate is by his bedside. The nurse tells the captain that some men in a jeep dropped him off at the main entrance without a word to the nursing staff.

—You were unconscious. Do you remember anything?

The captain barely manages a shake of his head. A detective steps into the room and asks if he could identify his attackers. The captain says he did not see or hear anything. That his attackers surprised him. He cannot remember anything. The detective places his card on the stand next to the hospital bed and says the captain should find safer avenues for his thrill seeking. The detective's card has the same address as the port authority police.

—Use that number if you remember anything.

The detective wishes him a speedy recovery and leaves. The captain is too tired to say anything.

Alone with his first mate, he asks how their shared sweetheart, the *Coffee*, is doing. The first mate says she is moored and safe and waiting for her captain to come back to her. The captain says he misses her and he cannot wait to take up his station behind the wheel. His first mate sits with him for a while and works up the courage at last to break the news that an injunction has been placed on the *Coffee*, an injunction that revokes the license of the boat to operate in national waters until further notice. The captain grits his teeth as he tries to turn in the bed and face his first mate, who leans a little closer. The captain whispers that they need to move the *Coffee* right away to a less public place, and the first mate should do it under the cover of darkness but exercise the utmost caution and stay out of sight of the port authority police and anyone from the commune.

He tells his first mate that his encounter in the graveyard was with the commune guards and they need to move fast. He asks his cousin how his face is doing. The cousin says he is fine and rubs the protective bandage that covers fourteen stiches on his left cheek. He says his cheek aches and itches a lot and serves as a constant reminder of his scrape with the commune. He says if any other man on earth cut him like that, the matter would not be over but just the first round of a ballistic affair. The captain says he feels the same way, but fourteen stitches and a serious beating later, maybe the two of them should reconsider their position. The captain eases a bruised arm around his first mate's shoulder and pulls himself into a seated position.

—Captain, we in some deep water here with these commune people.

—I'm more worried about Joyce and Trina.

—Maybe we should take that trip upriver that you been putting off.

—How's your Portuguese?

—About the same as my Wai-Wai.

Ryan finds fruit in his path. He falls asleep in the crook of a branch and wakes with fruit planted in the branch next to him. He cannot believe his eyes: The trees have sprouted oranges and bananas and even vegetable peels conveniently near him, all of which he eats. He tries to stay awake all night to see how trees bear fruit just for him. He wonders if he should talk to the trees and tell them he could really use some warm bread, not butter, that would not be necessary, just the bread. He tells the trees:

—Trees, bring me some bread.

He sleeps and dreams of the bread he shared with Trina and Rose, and as if by magic, he wakes to a strong smell of bread and sees an actual loaf next to him and a column of ants marching toward the loaf, which he snatches up just in time and runs from the tree with his bounty to escape the ants. He thinks he might be going mad. That the bread in his hands is so real, surely his mind is playing tricks on his senses. Nevertheless he eats fast and looks around and hardly chews before he swallows and wonders if he really might be mad and in his madness somehow able to conjure the things he most needs. But how?

Only one place bakes bread like this, and this bread can come only from that one place. The commune must be nearby. He must have help from someone in the commune able to come and go at will and move in the forest like the wind with only a whisper of leaves. He shouts at the trees that he wants his bed and his friends.

The commune office in the capital works through the night. Office staff acting on the preacher's authority place calls to ministers regardless of the hour to ask about the progress of their efforts to curtail the hostile activities of the relatives of commune members. The preacher insists that his staff request verification from each minister that no foreign government official will be invited to visit the commune. He wants reassurance that they still agree with the mission of the commune: to worship and live a righteous life free from bureaucratic interference. Each minister agrees that the preacher and his followers are in complete compliance with the government's policy for development of the area. Foreign interference will be resisted with all the might of the government on behalf of the commune. The office staff members thank the ministers on behalf of the preacher, and they promise the usual reward for their continued efforts on the commune's behalf.

Commercial and private traffic strafes the city, from rugged jeeps to prancing Mercedeses, from battered buses to hand-decorated vans chockfull of paying passengers, from bicycles conveying two people and motorcycles with up to three people, to horse- or donkey-drawn carts stacked with tons of bags and men pushing or pulling smaller carts or standing next to them shouting for customers to slake thirsts or fill holes in stomachs and throngs of schoolchildren marching along the sides of roads with their eyes glued to and feasting on these carts. And no reason for the constant blaring of horns except to warn pedestrians of the impending approach of a vehicle or for one vehicle to tell another that it is right there behind or beside it and at jammed junctions to try and clear a path or tell others that another inch or two to left or right risks a collision, horns at the start of traffic from lights that change from red to green to say get out of my way, here I come, ready or not.

The convoy of three commune jeeps makes urgent deliveries of gifts to secure the cooperation of important persons. The vehicles succeed in cutting paths through all of this pulsating, epileptic activity with a combination of horns, flashing lights, shouting, and rude or imploring gestures. People stop and stare at the jeeps, and some wave, but most utter curses under their breaths. Far from hurrying people along, the horns, dense traffic, the sun, and the exhaust fumes seem to slow pedestrians to a leisurely, loping walk. They move sideways, as if to navigate a narrow passageway or to avoid colliding with oncoming shoulders. This way of moving in the open creates the effect of dodging or sidestepping the heat and saves them from sweating. The locals swear they can identify newcomers to the city by the way they rush under the overhead sun and always seem drenched in sweat and never stop mopping brows and necks.

Commune people rush everywhere, covered in sweat. People look at them and say hurry, hurry, make bad curry. In addition, commune people are notorious for moving about the city in packs. Not one jeep but two or three, no police or army escort but each one of them packing a pistol or rifle as permitted by their special VIP security status, besides their trademark long sticks. When commune people travel on foot or in vehicles, they have the same effect on a crowd as the president's convoy. People stop and stare and curse silently.

On an errand for his captain, the first mate moves among the corridors of the city's covered market, where it is said that anything that can be sold is on offer and someone with purchasing power can buy anything from guns to roses, from cocaine to kidneys. Stalls with imported clothes and woodcarvings from the interior showcase their wares on wire hangers and wood pegs sticking out of tall, flat boards. Someone browsing can touch and hold things up to the rays funneled into skylight windows. The more sophisticated stalls resemble arcades with ornate windows and glass shelves with finger-length soldiers from every army whose clothing a very patient and steady hand has painted while looking into magnifying glasses and whose details must be examined that way to confirm the originality of the artistry, soldiers from Thermopylae to Gallipoli.

Having a fresh scar on his face emboldens the first mate, who shows it as proof of his toughness to anyone he deems even remotely challenging by inclining his head to the right so that the bold worm under his skin catches the light and shady men in pairs, stationed at every twist and turn in the warren of corridors, take a step back from his path. At one of these military mini-shopfronts, the first mate notices a crossbow and a samurai sword and certificate of authenticity and a license granting permission to barter and trade. He opens the door and a bell rings. He waits at a counter no wider than the span of his arms. A metal stairway that may have been salvaged from a scrapped submarine twirls up into the ceiling, which is very low and undulating, as if it once were truly underwater.

A door behind the counter cracks open, and a shaved head peers around it. The woman's giant earrings, two empty circles of bright gold, seem large enough to entertain a parrot on a perch. If she retained hair on her head, it would be gray, but she carries herself like a memory from her glory days. The first mate clamps his jaw to prevent it from hanging open and nods at her and searches for the right words to begin his inquiry. She raises her eyebrows and looks at him and waits for him to speak.

—I hear that a man can buy anything here, no questions asked.

—Heed a bit of advice from an old woman. Ears are open, and anything can pour into them.

—If I wanted something special, could you help me?

—I'm an old woman, you're a young man. I'll do my best.

—I need a commercial boating license. And enough of that old-woman crap. You're fit and you know it.

The woman smiles and lifts a hatch in the counter and squeezes past the young man and bolts the shop door. She invites him to follow her up the submarine steps, and they crouch down inside a room full of locked metal drawers. She asks him for details about the boat. He begins to say that some people bothered him and his captain, but she raises her open hand in front of his face and says she does not want to hear why he needs the license, just what type of vessel he intends it for and the necessary details about the captain. He says the license is needed right away. She says she is a craftswoman, not a magician. He says lives are at stake. She says all her business is a matter of life and death. He says his life and his captain's depend on how fast she can make the license. She says it is none of her business, but whatever grand scheme he and his captain are in it is not worth a red cent if it means throwing his young life away.

—Who spoiled your pretty face?

He is about to answer, but she raises an arm to silence him:

—Don't tell me.

She lowers her arm and he decides not to say anything. They are silent for a moment or two.

—Unless you really want to.

He tells her his story. She says she can help him, but he has to come back in two hours, and she demands half the payment up front and half when he picks up the goods. He asks if she cares to recommend a place nearby where he might spend two hours. She says it depends what he wants to do with his time.

—Sleep. I'm tired.

She steps close to him and he holds his ground. She squints at him.

—Whoever stitched your face must have used a knitting needle.

Her breath smells of cardamom. She runs her index finger along the ripe scar on his left cheek and he closes his eyes.

The captain, meanwhile, finds the dock that is no more than a clearing next to the water and does not appear on any map. There he climbs into a canoe, which conveys him in darkness as two paddles scrape the boat and lick and caress the river. He moves toward a lamp far out in the water. The light stretches over the pliant surface from bright strips to faint tentacles that grasp at the canoe. These tentacles seem to grow as they nose toward the lamp, and they pull the boat slowly, as if hauling in a delicate catch by even more delicate means. The captain sees a familiar figure holding up the lamp as the canoe nuzzles up to *Coffee*. The first mate helps the captain up with a hug and a slap on the back, which draws a sharp intake of air and a wince and sincere apologies from the first mate.

Across town at the commune's city office, the guards, field officers, and receptionists make calls to the commune at various times to report calls received at the office from abroad, and they pass on messages from their leader to various government dignitaries. The guards, receptionists, and field officers hold hands around a dinner table and pray and give thanks for their leader and for the dinner of fried chicken with chips and squash, all from abroad, chased down with cans of Jamaican ginger beer. The carbonated drink causes one of the younger guards to belch loudly, and this inadvertently triggers a belching competition among the men. The women call them juvenile. One of the young men tries to belch and vomits ginger beer through his nostrils. An older guard orders them to stop.

Six of the guards pile into a pair of jeeps and drive to the port and ask the whereabouts of the boat named *Coffee* registered to a Captain Aubrey. The port police on duty say the boat is moored nearby and not accessible in the dark. The commune guards say they will wait right there until they hear from the officer that the *Coffee* is secure. After several phone calls, the officer shakes his head and says that the *Coffee* is not moored in the city, otherwise he would know about it, that the first mate and captain must have taken the craft upriver, and since the two have done so without jurisdiction and without declaring a destination, that would be two arrest-worthy offenses. The commune guards say arrest and imprisonment would be too good for those scoundrels and they want to be notified the minute anyone spots the boat.

The senior commune guard gives the senior officer an envelope to be shared with his colleagues, and the uniformed men offer effusive thanks. The guards say they look forward to hearing some good news sooner rather than later. They wish the captain, his first mate, and that boat to be out of sight and nowhere near the delegation visiting from overseas.

TWENTY-ONE

—Mum, will we die here?

—No. Stop worrying.

Joyce's swollen and cut lips barely move, but she sounds clear and defiant. She squints through bruised, bloodshot eyes, and these purple islands from her assault disrupt the even tan on her arms and legs. She pulls Trina close and whispers to her about the things she must remember in case of an emergency. As her mother speaks, Trina moves her lips, knowing all the words and hearing the sounds in her mother's voice. River. Boat. Captain. Adam. She speaks as her mother says them, but in her mother's voice. Trina's eyes light up as she hears her mother declare her belief that Trina was right about Adam the morning she woke in front of his cage. Adam. Captain. River. Boat. Heard as if said in front of a mirror.

The preacher doubles security around the settlement. He orders his guards to turn away anyone who appears at the gates without an appointment, and if the person claims to have an appointment, the guards should radio the main house and confirm it with him personally. He broadcasts on the community-wide loudspeakers about the outside forces determined to destroy them all for no other reason than these forces swore allegiance to the devil against the commune's shining example of divinity. He pauses to take or make phone calls, to eat, drink, and freshen up. Otherwise he sits and talks to his followers on the loudspeakers about the short pit stop of this life compared to the eternity that awaits them in the next. About the need for them to trust in him and believe that those who operate in this life on the assumption that seventy-odd years is all this great design of a universe is set up to bequeath humanity, these folks labor with a false belief, and theirs will be a hell of fire and eternal damnation for promoting this paltry flesh against the Holy Spirit. About how only the commune people's belief can open the gates of paradise and grant them entry to eternal salvation.

The preacher cries as he speaks into the loudspeakers. If only their songs of praise really meant that their voices lifted in veneration of the Most High. He wakes the entire commune in the small hours to remind them that they chose him, needed him, and wanted the things he talked about. Slaps the desk in front of him and says now he makes the choices and now he chooses them, handpicks each and every one of them for paradise. He asks if they do not recognize him as a messenger of God, if they intend to fail the small, short test of their flesh and blood. His tears cause a flood of wailing in the commune. Even Adam howls. The preacher's followers berate themselves for making their leader cry, for making him doubt their loyalty, for proving themselves unworthy of his beneficence, for seeming unfit for paradise, for their weak flesh that houses their weak spirits, for their persistent dreams of doughnuts and burgers despite the promise in heaven of myrrh and frankincense, for the magnet of desire in the fragile body that makes them lose sight of the eternal polarities of the spirit in heaven, for hunger, always the hunger of their bellies that snuffs the mind's flame of a vision of heaven and a hell competing for their eternal spirits, for their failure to see the beauty of a parakeet in its glory of flight and bounty of colors as evidence of God's plenty, for the preacher's twenty/twenty vision in all things pertaining to this world and the next and their own continued myopia.

The nurse selected to nurture the motherless newborn says she feels uneasy about her role as a surrogate, and in God's eyes surely her false claim will not go unpunished. She speaks her mind to the young guard nursed back to health with the help of her readings of military verses from the Good Book. He agrees with her in private, he says, but he will not say that he does in public, so she should keep it to herself. He proposes that the two of them make a child of their own. She brushes him aside and says there will be plenty of time for that if his devotion is more than to just the flesh. He says he loves her and perhaps he could help her care for the baby she feels bad about, a destitute soul they could learn to love as they love each other. She thanks him for his offer of help and says it is not the loving of the child that bothers her but the false premise that she birthed it. He tells her it is one of those things that must be done, however uncomfortable, because Father wants it done that way.

Nevertheless, she confides to the other nurses about her concern for her soul. One nurse, elected to watch over the others, reports back to the preacher about her colleague's objections. The preacher flings his glass across the room. His assistants and the other guards around the house rush in. He asks the reporting nurse to repeat to the assistants and guards what she just told him. She says that the mother of the baby dislikes her foster-mother role on the grounds that it might look false in God's eyes. The man says that this is the last straw. Is it such a great sacrifice for the stupid nurse to look after one child? Did he really ask too much of her? The reporting nurse and the assembled eyewitnesses all say no, of course not, Father, and that the woman is selfish.

—What if I complain about all the things that I must hold my nose and perform on behalf of this community? What if I pick and choose what I will and will not do for all of you here? Where would you all be? I'll tell you. Back in a ghetto in that materialist nightmare of a country, wringing your hands for deliverance from your living hell, that's where.

He stamps his foot and walks over to a guard, punching him in the stomach as if he is the cause of the whole problem. Nora, Pat, and

Dee usher the guard away and encircle the preacher in an effort to calm him.

The preacher pushes them away and announces over the community public address system that everyone should gather right away at the congregation hall. He makes the announcement several times, and people respond by putting out fires and turning off engines and removing overalls and marching to the tent. Trina stops her flute practice and Joyce collects her and they head for the meeting hall. The preacher tells Pat, Nora, and Dee that he wants the offending nurse to appear before the congregation. He does not bother to select a costume for his appearance before the impromptu gathering. He simply washes his face and grabs his Bible and marches out of his house with his guards at a respectable distance and his assistants in a rush to collect a towel and a jug of water for him. He walks into the hall and stops the singing and asks the choir and band to put aside their instruments, for there is no joy in his heart today about what he has to tell them. He says that as a young man, he was called by God to devote his life to spreading the good word, and as a young man with many competing ambitions and passions, he embraced God's calling and turned his back on all temptations.

—It was not easy. If it was easy to renounce this world, there would be no need for proselytizing to humanity, God's word would be obvious to one and all, and it would be a question of simply waiting for the flesh to give up on this world in order to gain automatic entry into the next.

The congregation nods and shouts assent.

—You all agree with me to my face, but behind my back, I know you grumble. What am I asking of each of you? Am I asking too much?

The members of the congregation look around, puzzled and in search of the right response to the preacher's question; not sure of one, many resort to shaking their heads and holding up their hands.

—What do I want from you that you find it so hard to give?

Again the nods all around but fewer hands in the air, since they are afraid to answer incorrectly and earn his opprobrium. The preacher searches his pocket for a handkerchief and finds none, but Nora steps forward with a towel. He wipes his face and neck with it and throws it back at her.

—Would you believe it, people, that what I ask of you is not something you cannot give to me, and I am not the one doing the asking. I am a messenger, and what is asked of you comes from God, and what you have to give is so little compared to what you will receive. What is asked of you is a little sacrifice in this life, and what you get in return is eternal life. Here is an example from your sinful past. Imagine buying a lottery ticket, just one, and the number, the one you pick, a birthday, a zip code, an anniversary, whatever it may be, that number comes up. Well, all you did was take a short walk to the store and put up a dollar, and what do you get in return? Millions. Well, that is what is asked of you in this life to gain entry into the next. For one dollar of sacrifice, each of you gains eternal life. Now, our nurse here, well qualified, a gifted healer, a soothing voice to many, has her dollar but refuses to place the bet of a lifetime, even though it is a gamble she cannot lose.

The preacher calls the nurse to step forward and tell the congregation why she cannot in all good conscience place the dollar-bet sacrifice asked of her in order to win eternal millions. He gives her the microphone. The nurse stands on the stage and looks at the preacher and his assistants, unsure whether she should tell the congregation of the exact nature of the sacrifice she needs to make. The nurse covers the microphone and asks the preacher if she is allowed to go into all the details of the case. He tells her she has the floor and she should use it as she sees fit. The nurse says she is not cut out to be a mother. She feels too young for the responsibility. She says she chose geriatric nursing as her specialty because she could not bear to work in maternity and witness daily the many things that go wrong with such fragile human beings. The preacher nods, and seeing his approval, the majority of the congregation nods as well. Some faces in the audience look bewildered, unsure where the nurse's talk might take them. Many of the people watch the preacher more than the nurse, just to be sure that they react exactly how they should as events unfold in the hall.

—I'm not the mother of that child. I slept with no man.

Pat grabs the microphone from the nurse, and the guards surround the nurse, and she fights with them as they wrestle her to the ground. The preacher informs the people that the Holy Spirit moves in the nurse. He says if her last statement is true, then hers has to be only the second virgin birth in human history. The audience is clearly confused. They want to see why the guards pin the nurse to the ground and why she cannot speak. The preacher says the community is blessed but not that blessed. This stops the audience, and they wait to hear how the preacher will follow that last remark.

—The truth is she is overworked, delusional, suffering from postnatal depression. Or else the devil speaks through her.

He orders the guards to put her in the cage with the gorilla. A few people scream. The nurse redoubles her efforts to break free from her captors, but each guard holds on to a limb, and a fifth grips her around the torso and clasps a hand over her mouth. They carry her out of the tent.

—Don't worry about her, worry about your salvation. If the child she just renounced dies right now, its soul will go straight to heaven for having done no wrong but to be born into a world of greed, ambition, selfishness, and pride. Name the cardinal sins, people.

The congregation lists them for him, in alphabetical order, but in their usual manner of rushing ahead or falling behind to create a hum of assent, a mantra familiar only to those uttering it, a spell with a hold over the already enchanted. The preacher claps and they applaud with him. The members of the congregation turn to the left and to the right and shake hands and hug. They leave the tent, beginning with rows nearest the exits, and hurry to the area in front of Adam's cage.

Joyce and Trina match the responses of the crowd step for step. Joyce explains to Trina that they should disappear in the crowd, become an indistinguishable part of it, and hope that the gaze of the preacher falls on others. The preacher's favor, granted freely and easily to both of them, can be withdrawn just as freely and easily. There is no way to please him and keep him pleased. Mother and daughter linger at the back of the crowd gathered at Adam's cage. The nurse appears much calmer, or at least she no longer fights the guards who surround her near the entrance to the cage. Adam moves away from the chained gate. He touches one corner and runs to the next and touches it and repeats the back-and-forth move between two points. The preacher walks to the cage with his assistants and guards around him. He tells the nurse she has two choices. She can do this the easy way, or she may decide to opt for the more difficult course of resistance and end up taking her life into her own hands and out of his safekeeping. Did she understand?

—Yes, Father. Please forgive me. I'll take care of the baby.

The preacher shakes his head and says it is too late, the damage is done, he will find some more willing and grateful mother for the baby, she needs to be quiet and take her punishment, because her words make it clear to him that she does not understand the gravity of the situation facing the commune. The nurse begs him to explain and she will make sure she understands and follows him. He tells her again to be quiet, since her speech amounts to resistance. He turns to the crowd and says that if people do not understand why the nurse is about to be punished, this is the moment to raise their hands and let him know and he will furnish them with a full explanation. He surveys the crowd, along with his assistants and guards, many of whom, armed with sticks and guns, form a perimeter around the crowd. Joyce and Trina glance at each other, and Joyce hopes that no one is foolish enough to take the bait. Even if rampant puzzlement troubles the assembly, there is no way anyone among them should declare it to a man with a tendency to interpret confusion as insolence, lack of clarity as a liability.

—Good.

He faces the guards around the nurse and flicks his hand from her to the cage. The nurse screams and begs for mercy. A guard unlocks the padlock and pulls the chain from the bars. The guards near the nurse push her to walk into the cage and as she turns to run, they grab her and lift her off the ground and the nurse holds on to the bars and the guards pull her hands away and steer her through the open cage door. Adam stops his run from side to side to watch the open door with the nurse framed in it and the preacher. Adam knows this means only one thing, and he wonders how he can avoid a direct command from the preacher. Adam covers his eyes and looks through his fingers, swaying from left to right. The nurse trembles and leans back into the grip of the guards. The preacher raises his arm and levels it at Adam and then moves it from Adam toward the nurse.

Three rapid shots ring out and freeze the scene: the guards' fight with the nurse, Adam's sway rooted to the spot, the crowd's mix of grief and wild expectation, all cease. Several guards drop to the ground, rifles and pistols ready. Everyone looks at one of three places: the first, at the end of the crowd nearest the infirmary, where the injured guard, with pale and emaciated limbs from his six weeks in a plaster cast, aims a rifle at the two guards nearest him; the second, at Ryan's father, who stands midway between the preacher's house and the crowd and aims similarly at the preacher; and third, at Ryan's mother, also armed, her rifle pointed at the two guards closest to her. The guards nearest to Ryan's parents and their former colleague all throw away their weapons and stick their arms into the air. The young guard shouts at the men surrounding the nurse:

—Move away from her. Do it now or we shoot.

The guards look at the preacher but do not wait for his direction. They release their grip on the nurse, who wriggles free and runs to the side of the young guard. The preacher tells them to wait a moment. He begins to walk toward the young man aiming the rifle. His assistants and bodyguards take a step with him and he lifts his arm at them and they stop. He talks to the young guard as he walks up to him, and people back away from the young man and part to make way for their leader.

—Aim that rifle at me, young man. You two as well, aim at me. I'm a more valuable target than your comrades, don't you think? Go ahead. Aim. Look at this, people. This young man and his two helpers are armed and dangerous and intend to test us as a community today.

All three aim at the preacher, and all the guards aim at them. The preacher stops a few inches in front of the rifle and eases his chest forward until he comes into contact with the barrel. The young guard steps back and the preacher steps forward to maintain his contact with the young man's rifle. His mother steps forward and begs her son to put down his weapon. Others appeal to Ryan's parents to do the same. The preacher holds an arm in the air and puts an index finger over his lips and the crowd falls silent.

—What's your problem, son?

—I won't let you hurt her. I love her, Father. You can't put her in there. Please.

—Don't beg, son. You have all the cards in your hands. Okay, what should I do with a liar and a cheat in our midst? You be the judge and jury. You tell me what I should do with her.

The young man appears to search for words. He looks at the nurse and at Ryan's parents. Ryan's father speaks:

—Forgive her just like you should have forgiven my son. Forgive her and give her a chance to make amends.

—And if I don't? If I decide, in my limited wisdom, that she needs this lesson, that we all need it to stop another case of insubordination like yours right now, what do you say to that?

—We'll shoot, Reverend. I swear to God we'll shoot you and anyone who tries to stop us. We don't care about our lives anymore.

—You swear to God you'll shoot me? I plucked you three miserable excuses for humanity from certain oblivion and guide you to the gates of paradise, the very brink of entering eternity, and now you declare that you'll shoot me? Go right ahead. You three decide the destiny of this community.

The three stand and aim and look at one another and at the preacher and his guards. The congregation begins to edge closer to the three rebels. The nurse walks from the young man slowly at first, and he calls her back, but she ignores him and picks up her pace and strides into the cage and slams the gate behind her. The young guard drops his rifle and tries to run to her, but the preacher holds him, though not in a restraint; it takes a simple laying of hands on the young man for him to stop. Ryan's parents lower their rifles, and the nearest guards grab and wrestle the two to the ground. The preacher orders Adam to attack the nurse. Adam pauses and looks at the preacher, who repeats the order with a wave of his arm toward the nurse. Adam knows his fate is tied to the preacher, in whose good graces he must remain or perish. Adam runs at the nurse and bats her to one side. She screams and the crowd turns its attention back to the cage. The guards closest to the preacher charge at the young man, and a rifle discharges as they pile on him and throw him to the ground. People scream. Adam pounds the nurse with his fist and she remains motionless on the ground. The preacher instructs the guards to take the young man and Ryan's parents to his house, and he walks back to the cage and calls Adam's name several times before the gorilla stops hitting the bundle at his feet and turns to the voice whose commands he obeys always. The preacher steps into the cage and pushes Nora, Dee, and Pat away from him as they try to stop him. He digs into his pocket, retrieves a bar of chocolate, and hands it to Adam, who grabs the bar and retreats to the back of his cage. The preacher gestures to his guards and assistants, and between them they rush into the cage and gather up the nurse and jog with her to the infirmary. The preacher secures Adam's cage and dismisses the crowd with a sweep of his arm and tells his assistants and the guards around him:

—Make sure everyone gets back to work. Trina, where are you, my child? Trina.

—Here, Father.

—Play your flute for Adam until he calms down.

—Yes, Father.

The preacher strides in the direction of his house as his followers shrink from him and open a tunnel.

Joyce waits with Trina as she plays her flute for Adam. He seems to slow in his movements and rocks to the music of the flute. As she plays, Trina pictures the trees with Adam roaming free beside Ryan. She imagines thick undergrowth, long vines, a waterfall, and Adam and Ryan able to make a bed of leaves at night anywhere under the canopy, rising with the sun to find fruit and leaves with salt and no one to interrupt them. By the time she finishes, Trina sees herself with Rose and Joyce in the company of Adam and Ryan, all together in that forest. Adam dozes off.

Joyce stores Trina's flute at the library building, and mother and daughter walk to the pig farm. The worst job after cleaning the commune toilets happens to be the most convenient one for Joyce's plan. She has picked the pig farm for two reasons. It is farthest from the central part of the commune, and, located as it is on the edge of the land, of all the cultivated sites on the property, the pig farm is nearest to the river. People stay away to avoid the stink on their clothing and their skin, which retains a pigskin smell even after washing with carbolic soap. And when the smell disappears, the nostrils invoke a memory of it, leaving pig workers in permanent doubt about the status of their hygiene.

From the pig farm, it is possible to see a boat arrive at the jetty. The crew is not as easy to identify from a distance of four hundred meters, but the boat can be discerned, and with good eyesight, the lettering on the side, while not legible, suggests either a single name or a double-barrel name. By this process of elimination, Joyce hopes to tell whether a boat about to dock is the *Coffee* and, at four hundred meters, whether the boat's specious captain dons a distinctive captain's hat; at least that (specious) was how the preacher described the captain and his many messages to Joyce. The beating Joyce took for messages she did not see and whose contents she can only guess at makes the captain seem like an unlucky talisman for her, but the severity of her punishment and her wholesale condemnation make her believe in the meaningful nature of the captain's messages, meaningful for her and Trina's chances away from the commune.

She finds it intriguing that the captain continues his campaign of epistolary worship of her (assuming he did not go through all that trouble just to pour his scorn on her) despite not a syllable of return from her. Could this be love? Can this be what the captain talked about on their river trips, the thing that looks and feels so different from her faith, though just as loyal and blind and persistent? Her gamble: If his love is real and true, this means the captain should interpret her silence not as a rebuttal but as something forced upon her. And if his love is of the fighting kind, as the man himself appears to be—and here her gamble seems biggest—then he will do something to make sure she is not in any danger.

On the walk to the pig farm, Joyce plays a game with Trina where one or the other makes the trip with closed eyes and tries to guess along the way where they are on the trail and how much farther they have to go. This gives each of them an accurate mental picture of the walk. All that remains untested is the trip from the pig farm down to the river. They allow an inquisitive pig to escape under the wooden fence, then take their time retrieving it in order to reconnoiter the area between the farm and the river. Most of the paths are circuitous trails with all manner of hoof and paw prints. Some trails lead to dead ends and make no sense except to a pursuer in a chase.

Kevin, whose guard-duty rotation brings him to the pig farm, tells another guard he will follow the mother and daughter. The other guard watches him as Kevin watches them, so the chain of eyes makes it impossible to do anything but look officious while on duty. He walks along and observes from a little distance as Joyce and Trina slow-chase a squealing piglet, corner it, and drag it, by holding on to one ear each as it screeches blue murder, back in the direction of the pigpen. The guards follow commune workers if they stray for any reason from their designated posts. The official reason given for this close scrutiny—safety—appears legitimate. On two occasions commune workers needed to be rescued by guards from the clutches of a viper and a panther, and once a commune worker became sunblind and walked into the forest and was lucky to bump into a hunting party of Waurá who returned him to the compound late that night.

The guards stop and question anyone who seems to be unattached to a work party. The policy of the commune is to keep people in groups of four or more and to switch the groups on strict rotation and move people from one task to the next, ensuring that there is no group cohesion that might foster negative schemes of any kind. Even the armed guards work on rotation from night to day, from front-gate duty to the pig farm or another part of the compound perimeter, and the group makeup is never the same on consecutive rotations. Kevin misses what he considers the best job for a guard on the compound, duty at the front gate, because only one other guard works with him and it is easy to persuade one other person to go along with a scheme than two or three others, as he persuades Eric to bend and twist the rules of the commune whenever they happen to be posted together. He asks Joyce over the squeals of the piglet why she and her daughter have picked the worst place to work when they have special dispensation from the preacher to work where they please. Joyce says she prefers to be outside, and pigs may be smelly and sound like poor-imitation banshees, but they are very smart, much smarter than cows or chickens. He says he heard that somewhere, but for him the stink cancels all that wisdom.

Joyce and Trina march the warbling pig back to the sty and leave Kevin standing some distance from them. Trina asks her mother why she was so hostile with this guard, who seems so much more polite than the others. Joyce looks at Trina quizzically and says she did no such thing. Trina said she heard anger and there is no denying it. Joyce shakes her head emphatically. Trina wants to know if a view of the river empty of a boat that shall remain unnamed might be Joyce's reason for being mad. Joyce casts her daughter a sad expression and says she misses the captain every day, but

Trina must never mention his name to anyone or within earshot of anyone. Trina says she misses him, too, and his whistling first mate. She suggests that they come up with a code word for the captain in case they are overheard talking about him. But what? They launch into a list of captains from fiction and history. Trina kicks off:

—Hook. Ahab. Kirk. Scarlett. Drake. Blackbeard. Raleigh. Morgan. Cook. Silver. Bligh. Columbus. Cabral. Vasco da Gama.

—How do you know so many?

—We studied them in school.

Joyce tells Trina she is too smart for her boots. Trina says she does not have any boots. She holds up a foot to show her lace-up canvas shoes, a size too big, then hops on one foot to keep her balance and puts that foot down to keep herself from toppling to the ground and raises the other foot. She keeps switching feet in this dance until her mother laughs and doubles over, holding her midriff and wiping her eyes, and begs Trina to stop before she makes her poor mother split her sides open. Kevin watches them from behind a tree.

The pigs seem to know what happens if men in overalls separate one pig from the rest and pull it into a hut. That pig launches high-pitched screams, hollering, and near-articulate cries for help, that someone who hears must set aside as coincidence based on a belief that a pig does not really understand its fate. How could it? Pigs root in the ground for grubs, roll in mud and eat anything poured into a trough, including their young. Joyce and Trina follow the practice of sticking tissue in the ears to reduce the volume of pigs screaming at the slaughterhouse, nothing like the compliant moos of cows, nothing like the bleat of sheep; pigs cry and beg for mercy. The man who wields the knife must be efficient with a sharp knife and a brisk stroke of the throat for that scream to stop. The pig's scream ceases in midflow. The legs paddle the air and freeze midstride. The open throat bleeds. The long knives sever the head from the body, slit the stomach, and strip the vitals from the corpse, and the carcass, hung with a hook through it, surrenders its meat to an inquisitive blade. Blood runs down gutters to the river along with the waste of hosed pigpens. Blockage of the drains causes the water to gush back into the sinks and holes in the ground, and the whole operation comes to a standstill as someone traces each drain to find the choke.

Joyce and Trina follow the drain from a sty and find the plug in the drain and move it along until they come to the river and look at each other and know how many steps it will take them from the pig farm to reach the water in the dark. A guard stationed at the dock challenges them, aiming his rifle. He wants to know who gave them permission to come to the river. Joyce begins to explain about unblocking the drain by tracing the blockage from one drain to the next, and she looks for Kevin just as he steps from the trees and calls to the guard, Eric, at the river.

Kevin tells Joyce and Trina to continue their task of unblocking the drain and give him a minute with his friend. Eric apologizes for his stern manner and says he hopes they understand that he has a job to do, and if he appears soft, it will land him in big trouble. Joyce nods. The two men debate whether they should take a dip in the river before the sluices from the pig farm open and mess up the water, as happens twice daily. They look around and appear to assess the risk of such a venture in front of Joyce and Trina. Kevin says he needs a swim to clear his nostrils and hair of the smell of pigs. Eric adds he will swim to keep his friend company. The two men decide to invite Joyce and Trina to join them. Joyce says she does not have a costume, and Trina says the same, but seeing how the guards strip down to their underpants and dive in, they decide to tuck their dresses into the legs of their underwear and wade in up to their thighs and scoop the cool water onto their arms and necks and faces. The guards ask Joyce if with all her influence high up, she might be able to pull a few strings to get them on the same work rotation. Joyce promises to try. They dress and wish each other a good day and swear mother and daughter to secrecy. Joyce and Trina follow the drain up the slope to the pig farm with Kevin a few paces behind. Trina asks: Cook? And her mother says Cook it is.

TWENTY-TWO

At the preacher's white house, in the spacious meeting room with little furniture, Ryan's parents and the young guard sit strapped to chairs, blood on their clothes. Dee injects the three captives with a sedative. They look asleep, heads bowed. The guards tell them they have signed their death warrants by their actions. They slap the captives and nudge them hard with rifles. The prisoners cease making the usual sounds of bodies under duress. The guards talk with the assistants about the outrage of someone in their ranks pointing a gun at their leader. As if there were not enough guns aimed at the commune from the many enemies in the surrounding bush, in the capital, in the country they left to get some peace.

The preacher appears and the assistants throw glasses of water over Ryan's parents and the young guard to wake them. The preacher walks over to the young guard and unties his hands and feet.

—You're free to go.

The guards and assistants look at one another and at their leader, and a couple of them say no involuntarily. The preacher repeats his announcement. The young guard raises his head, surprised. Ryan's parents muster a look of vague interest. All three try their best to feign alertness. The young guard tries to stand but cannot. His arms grab at the air and his legs splay from under him. He falls back into the chair and almost topples it backward. He slurs his speech:

—Father, I'm sorry. I love her, wanted to save her. Love you, Father.

The preacher asks the young man if he needs help to walk. He nods. The preacher helps him to his feet and he clutches the preacher and sobs.

—Father, please forgive me. I love her. Didn't want her to get hurt.

The preacher says he understands. He, too, loved someone a long time ago, before he found Christ and his love became the service of saving souls for the kingdom of heaven. He chastises the youth for putting the life of the nurse in danger by distracting him from his careful orchestration of her punishment.

—She understood the situation better than you. She walked into that cage all by herself. Didn't she?

The young guard nods and cannot stop his tears.

The preacher asks him what should happen next to maintain order in the community. He wants the youth to put himself in the shoes of a leader and imagine that leader's responsibility for the lives of so many and make a determination what should be the best course of action to maintain order. The young guard asks for water. The preacher flicks his fingers and an assistant produces a full glass, which the young man empties in one uninterrupted tilt of his head. His mind seems to clear for a moment. He asks the preacher's permission to prescribe his own punishment to show everyone in the community the error of his ways. The leader says that will not be necessary, he is free to go. The young guard says the preacher saved his life and his mother's by taking them in from the streets, and therefore his life is nothing without the preacher's blessing. He says he lost his mind. The nurse helped him while he lay in a cast. She washed him, took away his bedpans, read the Gospel to him. He loves her and he acted out of fear for her safety and his actions came from that wrong impulse, wrong because it went against his greater love for the preacher and the commune and the chance of everlasting life.

The preacher nods his approval. He kisses the young man on the top of the head. The young guard sobs and collapses, and the preacher holds him and eases him back into the chair.

—Father, tell me what to do to make things better.

The reverend looks at Ryan's parents and tells the youth that the situation is grave. To have any guard aim a rifle at him in front of everyone, with the help of two adults who should know better despite having a wayward child, puts the preacher in a predicament. If he does nothing about it, even if he forgives the three of them as he did in his heart the moment the incident occurred, despite his forgiveness, if the three of them try to walk out of the commune and the people do not feel the same generous disposition, the people will pounce upon them and tear them from limb to limb. Even he, as their leader, enjoys limited control over the members of the commune.

—Witness your own behavior toward me. I could not win your total trust and loyalty after all your years of seeing for yourself the proof of my devotion as your leader. Well, just so the wider community, who feel differently about me than you do, may find it too difficult to accept three of their own pointing a gun at their leader and may not find it in their hearts to forgive your transgressions.

The young guard says he knows what he has to do to fix the mess. Ryan's parents look at him with eyes full of appeal. But the young man avoids looking at them. Ryan's father speaks up:

—Boy, don't throw away your life.

The preacher instructs his guards to gag Ryan's parents. The young man watches as the guards tie cloth around the mouths of Ryan's parents, both of whom move their heads about and make it difficult for the guards to knot the cloth at the back. The young man does not react; he just looks at them with his wet face and red eyes, turns away slowly, and heaves himself out the front door.

A guard helps him to navigate the three steps off the front porch into the yard. People stop and rush over to meet him as he staggers in a wavering line toward the dried well. The people, guards among them, carry sticks and stones and guns. They set their faces against him in angry expressions, from gritted teeth to scowls. Not a single face shows pity for him. Not yet. He reaches the well and realizes it is not fitting for the damage he did to the commune. The well will not satisfy them. He looks back at the house just in time to see the front door close and the preacher no longer on the front porch to oversee things. Those nearest to him hold their sticks and stones and guns above their shoulders, ready to bring down those weapons on his head. He hears some of them say that he tried to shoot their leader. Part of him wants to argue with that assertion and say no, not shoot, just protect his sweetheart from the cage that she walked into of her own accord to stop him from intervening on her behalf. He blames himself. He wanted to serve, and his idea of service took a wrong turn, a dead end. He walks past the well, and more people hem him in. He feels tired. There is nowhere else to go, no room left for him to take another step, and no other place where he wants to be. He stops and sits on the ground and falls back on the grass and clasps his hands in prayer and shuts his eyes against the harsh light and waits for their sticks, their rifles and stones. His mother stands at a distance, turns her back, and buries her head in her arms.

The sound of an ax splitting logs, the sound of a paddle beating clothes on the stone bank of a river, many axes, many paddles, of firewood ablaze, of two stones crashed together, of doors slammed repeatedly, of a hammer driving a nail home, of a carpet brought outdoors and beaten, of plates dropped on the kitchen floor, of glasses toppled off a tray, of a wheelbarrow full of stones tipped over, of a tin can stamped underfoot, many cans, many feet, of newspaper tearing, of a slap and another slap, of a firecracker, one and one hundred, of an exhaust's backfire, and no pig squeal, no bleat, no moan, no cry, except for Adam in his cage, except for a mother with her head in her arms, unable to shed another tear.

They disperse, breathless and still angry with the young man for what he made them do to him, and with themselves for killing him, and they pray for forgiveness and beg for his lost soul to gain entry into paradise. The guards drag the young man's lifeless body on an old sheet to the mill and from the mill in pieces to the incinerator, where he is reduced and picked up by the wind and lifted into cloud and sails mountain ranges before his precipitous fall miles from the commune and far from his limited body, and free.

The preacher tells his guards that he wants Ryan's parents out of his house. The guards look a little unsure about the inexact nature of the preacher's wish. But he has a headache and he must lie down immediately. Nora, Dee, and Pat take over the job of issuing orders. They confer, and Nora leaves to assist the preacher. Pat and Dee talk to the guards. Pat and Dee apply blindfolds to Ryan's parents. Four guards take them by the arms and lead them out the back door and to the mill.

At the infirmary, the nurse wakes from her sedation and asks for the young guard. She expects him to be in a bed not far from hers, recovering from some punishment or other meted out for his public defense of her. She worries that she cannot see him. A nurse on duty reminds her how badly the young man has acted and advises her to forget about him and save herself a lot of trouble. She asks for something for her pain, which the nurse gives to her and hurries away. She lies in a cast, her body aches, but she knows the young guard will turn up and read to her whatever she asks him to read, just as she did for him. A baby cries and someone soothes the child with a song. Both sound far away. Perhaps the young man sings to the baby. And in that restored world, she counts the child as their own, soothed to sleep by the young guard's song and placed in a bassinet by her bed and soon the young guard's voice reading to her and reading her asleep. The verses in his voice set loose in her head and in the baby's head. She closes her eyes for him to come to her bedside and read what she wants to hear, just the way she wants to hear it. She has only to wish for this to be the case and it will be so. She swallows her hoard of tablets and waits for sleep to claim her and to wake with the young guard by her side, restored, healed, unblemished, with the book open at random and his eyes picking up the words and his voice seeping into her ears.

All evening the breeze holds his skin tight, the crisp air carves out Ryan's lungs. At dawn he studies steam as it rolls from his mouth and spreads a thin translucent veil to make the sky look etched by the gray left over from the trees. He lies in some enclosure and has no idea how he came to be in there. Bread and a banana rest on a broad plate-sized leaf next to him. He tries to speak, but his swollen tongue fills his mouth.

—I want my bed, please.

He closes his eyes and inhales his surroundings, pulls the whole scene inside his rib cage, and hopes the next time he opens his eyes, none of it will be there, no trees, no vines, no thick vegetation underfoot, and no distant sky and its circus parades. He trembles and curls up around his meal, unable to eat a morsel. He thinks himself into the bed he dearly wants, back in a place he ran from and now wishes he could find.

The overseas mail of pension checks and letters from concerned relatives includes a subpoena, lodged by the relatives of three children, for a court hearing in the capital concerning the well-being of the children reputed to be held against their will by the commune. The subpoena names the preacher, and the mailman delivers it personally. It holds the preacher responsible. The reverend calls the capital and tells his lawyers he absolutely will not appear in any court, and his lawyers counsel him that he may deputize his role to another commune member. Though the subpoena names him and he should be there in person, his lawyers say he can supply an emergency medical reason with matching proof signed by a qualified doctor declaring his inability to travel to the capital.

The preacher gets his doctor to produce the diagnosis of incessant diarrhea. The lawyers say this is not a joking matter. Isn't there some malady less liable to be viewed as a parody of the legal process? The preacher's doctor says the preacher has lots of things wrong with him and diarrhea is the least of them. He needs more sleep or less fitful sleep that could be sleep apnea. He retains water in his feet. He suffers from recurring bouts of malaria. Palpitations and chest pain rack his body. He recently expelled a kidney stone. His nose bleeds as if it has a mind of its own. Headaches surround and assail him awake and asleep. Nightmares wait for him to surrender to sleep in order to pounce on him.

The lawyers succeed only in getting the court to postpone the date for one month, which annoys the preacher, who does not feel he should have to answer to anyone outside the community and no one in it other than God. His legal counsel warns him that too many postponements might lead to a court order for a compulsory visit of relatives to check for themselves that the children are doing okay and a warrant for his arrest for contempt. The preacher produces letters written by the children testifying to their well-being. He says the subpoena is undue harassment from forces hostile to their objectives. He mentions the countless relatives aggrieved by the fact that they lost people to the commune, but these people voluntarily sided with the commune over their earthly blood.

Is that my fault? Are the persuasive powers of the Gospel to be held against us?

Since he has no intention of answering the subpoena, the preacher calls the foreign minister to ask if he can provide warning to the commune well in advance should any delegation arrive in the capital. The foreign minister suggests to the preacher that any such visit should be an easy win for the commune, whose operations provide a model of how to live a harmonious and Christian life. He asks the preacher to consider staging a welcome to dispel the rumors among relatives. The preacher counters that he knows these people. They are out to destroy the commune, not reform it or rescue one or two people from it. That is why he lives in a remote location, for the peace of being far away from interference. Can the government stop a foreign delegation from landing on its soil with the specific intention of destroying a community that the government holds in high esteem? The minister says it can, but the negative publicity will outweigh the benefits of such a move. The best course by far is to show the international delegation that there is nothing to worry about and be rid of them once and for all. That would be the diplomatic course of action and the one that the foreign minister strongly recommends. The preacher says he will consider it. His chosen vocation is not politicking but the Bible, and politics and the Bible, like oil and water, do not mix. The minister wonders if all of it is not in fact thrown into the same pot, meaning both politics and the Bible, and everyone eats from that pot.

The tribal council pulls up in two jeeps at the main gate of the compound. They say they have something to return to the leader of the commune. The guards on duty, Kevin and Eric, tell them that they cannot arrive unannounced and expect to be seen right away. They radio the main house and then inform the council that the preacher cannot see them today or tomorrow, no room in his diary for another appointment. The speaker for the council says they will wait right there at the gate until the preacher sees them. Kevin and Eric radio the main house and the preacher slams the receiver on the desk. Sid accompanies the tribal council, which helps to keep things cordial. Even so, after another spell on the radio, both Kevin and Eric stiffen toward Sid and refuse his offer of cigarettes. They apologetically inform Sid and the rest of the group that the order from above says if the tribal council insists on waiting, they are free to do so but not on commune property, which includes the last mile of the approach road to the main gate. Sid shakes his head and wishes Kevin and

Eric a good day. They nod but do not reply. Sid sees that both guards have his mosquito remedy plastered on their faces, necks, and arms.

—Good to see the mosquitoes don't bother you anymore.

Eric and Kevin nod and want to say more to the mosquito apothecary and his miracle remedy, but the instructions from the main house ban all fraternizing with outsiders. The guards confer and quickly switch back to being cordial and tell Sid they are sorry but they have their orders and they hope he understands. Sid says he knows all about orders and they should not worry about it. He adds that he can see the mosquito remedy bushes around them are running out fast. The guards ask him where they might find more of the plant. Sid says the plant likes plenty of water and there must be an underground spring for it to grow near the hut and more of it can be found by the banks of the river. Kevin and Eric thank him and say they will keep checking with the preacher about his availability if Sid comes back every couple of hours. Sid offers his cigarettes once more, and this time Kevin sheepishly takes two while Eric bullishly declines and Sid climbs back into the jeep. Eric asks Sid if his friends have enough water to endure a long wait, since they could spare a few bottles for the group. Sid thanks him and says there is water all around for his friends to find for themselves, and he appreciates the invitation to return for an update. The tribesmen turn their vehicles around and retreat about one mile from the commune's grounds, their two jeeps raising a red dust cloud trail behind them.

The guards radio to the preacher that the tribal council really intends to wait all day for an audience. He curses and says he hopes they bake in the sun. But he calls a meeting of his managers to talk about the ramifications of having a group of indigenous Indians camped on the perimeter of the grounds. The meeting concludes that they should let the tribesmen wait for a while and then the preacher should agree to see them briefly and in the open at the gate of the compound.

The preacher decides to bring everyone back to the commune for a large meeting, and this means leaving a skeleton staff at the commune's office in the capital. He sends a truck to the airstrip at a nearby town to pick up office staff returning from the city, and he curses the expense of flying back and forth since his ban on the *Coffee* and the inconclusive search for a replacement boat and crew. The truck drives past the two jeeps of the tribal council without stopping or waving. Sid waves anyway. Two specially hired small planes circle and land as children stand on the side of the airstrip along with a couple of grazing cows. A senior guard briefs the commune staff about the tribesmen squatting on the perimeter of the commune since the morning and orders the staff to ignore them. On the drive back from the airstrip, the loaded truck passes the two jeeps and Sid waves again. A receptionist from the office forgets the instructions about the delegation and lifts an arm automatically and a senior guard slaps it back down.

—What about that damn tribal council out there?

The reverend waves in the direction of the compound's main gate. The head of security raises his hand, not meaning to ask permission to speak but, rather, emphatic dismissal of the idea that the tribesmen should be a cause of worry.

—To hell with them, Reverend. Let them roast.

The head of finance slaps his thighs in disgust:

—They took our money.

—Thirty pieces of silver.

The head of security smiles satisfactorily at his witty response, but the preacher remains exasperated and runs the fingers of his left hand through his Elvis-styled hair.

—Gold.

His commune suffers from too many gross humiliations of late, from dissension within the ranks to subpoenas by outside hostile forces. Now the commune faces a direct assault and effrontery with this tribal council camped on the edge of its property. The preacher speaks in an almost distracted way, not loud or reprimanding, more like a thought uttered:

—How much failure should a leader tolerate from his first line of defenders before losing hope for his community? Is God's calling too much for us to answer?

The head of security shakes his head and wonders if his guards cannot shoot the entire group of tribesmen and feed them to those pigs they are complaining about. Everyone laughs. But the head of security says he is serious, and they all laugh again, and he says no, really, and they laugh a little less vigorously, and he admits he is joking, and they laugh loudly again, and he says actually, he is serious, and no one laughs. The preacher hugs the head of security. The head of security smiles and wipes away tears. He breaks the preacher's embrace and struts out of the meeting room. A pause ensues among the managers, assistants, and guards. The assistants and managers look with stern disapproval at the guards, clearly placing the blame on them for the present crisis and making them feel responsible for finding a solution. The guards do not know where to place their gaze. Their heads swivel from side to side and their eyes settle on each other and a collective responsibility gathers in the looks they exchange, looks pooled in this way until they become emboldened to act.

—What do we do with their jeeps?

—Strip them for parts for our vehicles, then burn or bury the rest.

The guards form a circle, raise arms and touch hands, and shout together:

—For the commune!

They break formation and grab their rifles and file out of the house to see their head of security standing by the truck.

—What took you all so long?

Commune members at various tasks around the compound stop and look to see what the commotion is all about. Joyce and Trina hear nothing of the guards shouting and see nothing of the pairs of guards piling their rifles onto the truck bed and climbing up into it before offering helping hands to those who wait to board. Stationed at the pig farm, Joyce and Trina pretend to work as they count the exact number of steps from the sty down to the river. They count with their eyes closed, as if in the dark. Adam shakes his cage and jumps on the spot and hoots at the guards. The truck peels away from the center of the compound and races to the main gate and digs up a red dust cloud, which drifts and paints the grass and trees. Stationed at the main gate, Kevin and Eric see the truck approach at high speed, and they work fast to pull the log from the road just as the truck speeds past and speckles red on the two guards, who turn their heads and shield their eyes.

TWENTY-THREE

The captain, helped by his first mate, renames the boat and registers it with the port authority, using a proxy at huge expense, to carry freight, not passengers, and they declare a bauxite-mining town far upriver as their base. They feel out of reach of the port authority, two days downstream in the capital, and far from the commune, one day away. The *Coffee*, re-named *Many Waters*, immediately gets nicknamed *Muddy Waters*, not after the American bluesman but due to the nation's seawater. It sports new paint in natural bright colors, as if a piece of the vegetation, detached from the surrounding flora, is being carried by the river. Parrots passing over the boat might be forgiven for mistaking it for a floating flock. In fact, many houses in the countryside bear the same bright palette, and many commercial passenger minivans in the city try to distinguish themselves by sporting outlandish and brash primary colors.

The city is carved out of the landscape. The rainbows that begin as bright buses and houses and boats become features of the moist air and make the city new all over again. Through this land, stained with mineral wealth rising to the surface—minerals that stir and provoke a response from the land that the land refuses to surrender—a truck full of armed commune guards races to add another gradation of red to the green world beneath sunsets and dawns. But the red of the truck not seen in the dust is a color born of violence and necessary conviction. The red intent of the guards signals a compulsory sacrifice to restore their pride and prove their loyalty to their reverend leader. They cross their fingers that what they are about to do will be hidden by the miles of dense forest, the lack of a city for many more miles, and the concealing penchant of the jungle. If they fail to win back the approval of the preacher, their own paltry lives will be worth even less than the little it takes to make them feel they are worth anything at all. Their future, and that of the commune, which the preacher fights to secure, will not be theirs if the guards disappoint the reverend by failing to solve this problem of a tribal council demonstrating on the steps of the commune, and by failing to prove themselves worthy of the inheritance he fights for on their behalf. Succeed in ridding the preacher of this tribal problem, the guards believe, and they will win back his confidence. This small thing that they must do will serve them better than anything they ever did for their spiritual leader. They promise not to ask any questions when they reach the place. They take oaths to fire and keep firing until the job is done and after that to clean up the evidence. Each swears to empty his rifle into a target, and they all say not one of them will leave without firing a weapon into an enemy of the commune. The tribal group displeased the preacher and, in so doing, fashioned itself into an enemy of the commune.

The truck arrives at the T-junction where the group is supposed to be waiting for permission to visit the compound, but the guards find nothing and no one there. Tracks lead in both directions: To the right is the route to the small mining town and airstrip, to the left more forest and eventually the river and the Indian villages settled not far from the banks. The guards debate whether they should wait for the group, which surely must return at some point, or pick a direction and drive in the hope of meeting the two jeeps. If they take one direction, the tribal council might return from the other. If they sit and wait, there is no telling how long it will be before the jeeps return.

They decide that since they are there, they might as well wait for a while rather than risk going in the wrong direction. As they wait, they debate about the commune and where it is going and how things will end. Everyone sings and prays as much as they ever have, but there is no shortage of misery in the air, with each new drill surrounding the imminent doom brought about by each new crisis. At first these men guarded the commune against wild animals and intruders, and now their duties involve just as much policing of the residents as guarding against the jungle and the threat of an invasion from mercenaries. The tribal council is just such an invading force, and this is a test of conviction. Their action will restore the equilibrium of the commune. Things are out of balance for them as a community. They find themselves on their back foot, but they should be pivoting on the balls of their feet and toes and leading the charge.

Sid and the rest of the council watch the truck from their hiding place among the trees. Their jeeps, reversed off the road and camouflaged by bush and vine, cannot be seen by someone driving past. The tribesmen sit on sheets on the ground and discuss this response by the commune to their friendly visit. Sid scratches his head slightly, at a loss for words in his effort to square his personable interactions with people at the commune with the grievous intent of sending armed guards in a truck to pursue the council.

—Not very hospitable.

Sid suggests they have some fun with the commune guards, since both armed guards and council are out in the forest with time to kill:

Didn't the commune try to kill time way back by shooting up that poor time seller's cart?

The laughter all around, tempered by worry and irritability at the commune's decision to ratchet up hostility, fades when the elder of the council considers Sid's proposal and agrees. Sid, always the clown, especially in the face of tension, rubs his hands together in mock glee.

—Let's go native.

The tribal council shrugs and strips to just underpants, applying dye squeezed from leaves and scraped from bark to their bodies. They tie small branches to their arms and legs and heads, examine one another from head to toe, and add finishing touches, asking someone to close both eyes and swiping the eyelids with a thumb dipped in black dye, adding the right stripes and circles on each other's back and behind the knees. Sid starts a low, rhythmic, guttural chant, to get in the mood, he says, rubbing his hands together, and the chant spreads to the rest of the group—even the usually serious elder joins in—and together they sound like an odd gaggle of geese, wild turkeys, and bullfrogs.

The temperature in the back of the truck is enough to melt the glue binding a book. The commune guards sweat and their tempers flay. A guard peers into the bush.

—You hear that?

—Hear what?

—That hyena.

—No hyenas here.

Only one other guard says maybe, but he hears less of a bark and more of a wild boar grunt. The guards look out at the thick vegetation. It reflects so many gradations of green and so much variety of texture that staring at the bush with wet eyes plays tricks on them. If the light hits the eyes one way, the bush assembles a giant face resting its chin on the ground with its forehead in the trees, or at another angle a herd of galloping horses, or a savannah shifting with so much wildlife grazing on it.

—See that?

A guard shouts and aims at the bush, and the other guards look in all directions and agree that there is movement out there. There is not just something out there but many things all around them.

—Look.

—Where?

—Over there.

—Yes, I see something.

—Over here, too.

—Yes, I see it.

—Must be a lot of them.

—Of what?

The guards aim their rifles in many directions. A senior guard reminds them to hold their fire until something definite shows itself. The bush all around them shakes without a breeze. The guards hear grunts and barks in the bush. Not grunts of wild boar or hyena barks but something bigger and unknown. And the sounds match the movement all around the truck. One guard suggests:

—We should get out of here.

The senior guard says they are to stand their ground, since whatever is out there cannot be bulletproof. The bush rattles, and the grunts and barks grow louder. The senior guard orders his men to fire at will and the guards aim their rifles, some at the movement in the bush, others in the direction of the sounds. They shoot from the truck in all directions and break tree limbs, shredding leaves and twigs and pockmarking tree trunks. They pepper a bird that accidentally flicks into range and send feathers flying and bring down the bird in a heap. They keep firing until their rifles empty and shell casings litter the ground. The trigger clicks cease and the forest seems stirred by something that passes through in a hurry and upsets things, but the forest is far from disturbed. The trees stop shaking, and the men imagine faces in the bark and in the clusters of leaves. Then the shaking of the vegetation starts again, along with the grunts and barks, and the senior guard shouts that enough is enough and he orders the driver to get them out of there. The driver reverses at high speed for a mile and does not stop in time for the two guards at the main gate to lift the barrier out of the way, and they crash through it, stop, call the two guards onto the truck, and turn and speed back to the compound.

The council members regroup at their camouflaged jeeps, laughing at the reactions of the commune guards. Sid sounds a triumphant note:

—The ancestors will be laughing at this one for a long time.

They shake hands, drive down to the river, wash off their paints as they sneer at the smelly water poisoned by the commune's pig farm, dress, and head back home with their report about the negative response of the commune to the council's second visit. The indigenous tribes who depend on the river cannot ignore the commune's pollution. Fish are dying; the water irritates the eyes and causes rashes on the skin of the children who bathe in it at the wrong time; it stains clothes yellow and orange; and at different times of the day, the water stinks like a pigsty. The fishermen throw their nets in the river and joke that they pull out mutant fish.

—Fish the color of pigs.

—Fish that smells like bacon when you fry it.

—Stink fish that no amount of juice from lemons or limes can neutralize.

The entire commune hears the gunshots and people run from their chores in the kitchen, the fields, the farms, the mill, incinerator, and infirmary, to gather in the central area in front of the preacher's house and Adam's cage. The truck pulls up and the guards bail out, their faces drained of blood, their eyes showing too much white and their mouths stuck open. They run in all directions and talk about the jungle coming alive in front of their eyes, and the shaking trees and the big faces formed by tree bark and broad leaves. The preacher listens to the senior guard recount the events. He asks him to go outside and calm his guards before they panic the community. The preacher asks his managers, the doctor, the head of security, the head teacher, the accountant, what they make of this latest debacle. Do they think the commune is under attack? Not one of them thinks that it could be, though everyone agrees that something odd happened out there to spook the guards.

The preacher says they should use the opportunity to have another drill in case an attack may be under way. He orders his assistants to mix the vat of concentrated powder diluted with water. He sounds the compound sirens: The community is under attack. Joyce and Trina join the other stragglers rounded up at gunpoint and ordered to stay in the open area. The people obey instructions to form a long line and to drink fast and to pray. Children drink first and Trina cries and Joyce looks puzzled and she keeps staring at the managers to see if this ninth drill is real. Every one of the managers and assistants move fast, to Joyce's eyes, but their actions of filling up the ladles is too careful and lacks the edge of a believable emergency. Joyce tells Trina not to worry, just go along with it. This surprise gathering is not one they should worry about. Trina says the drink is just warm water with coloring. Joyce warns Trina to make sure when she tells Rose that the whole thing is a drill and not the actual thing that Rose acts normal and keeps it to herself.

Joyce, Trina, and Rose find it hard to watch the other children cry and ask for their parents in the belief that this is their final drink, and parents drink to join their children and promise them that they will meet again on the other side. They sing hymns. The guards, always the last to drink, set down their sticks and rifles. Rose looks at Adam and wonders, if this time were the real thing, what would become of him. Would the preacher make Adam drink as well? Adam howls and grabs the bars of his cage and jumps up and down.

Captain Aubrey and First Mate Anthony rehearse their manufactured IDs and tug and itch their recently grown beards as they steer the freshly painted and newly registered *Many Rivers* toward the jetty that belongs to the commune and wave at Eric, the guard stationed there. He waves back. The captain asks Eric how things are going, and he says fine as long as they do not plan on bringing him and his Kalashnikov any trouble. The captain says he would not dream of disturbing the beautiful day's peace. He offers the guard some ginger beer, cold, he says. The guard invites him to pull in but to be ready to leave at a moment's notice if anyone from the commune approaches the dock. The captain promises to keep the engine running should such an eventuality arise. They answer the guard's preliminary questions about the boat and their location upriver; soon he seems satisfied. They chat and drink not one but two cans of ginger beer. The captain breaks out some of his special black cake, and Eric thinks it is the best cake he has tasted in his life.

—What's it made of?

—Well, it's a Christmas recipe started a full six weeks before, with raisins soaked in rum.

—But it still tastes fresh.

—An old family-secret.

—One day I'd like that recipe to try for myself.

The captain says he will bring some more the next time he sails by:

—How is life at the commune?

Eric says if he speaks honestly, it has to stay between the three of them. The first mate nods and pretends to attend to matters on the deck.

—Not good, Captain. Not good. Tense. Hardly any laughter, and the prayers are desperate, whereas before when we prayed, it was ecstatic.

The captain says he understands what Eric means, but he wonders what could cause such a big change in the atmosphere.

—Paranoia. Pure and simple.

Eric's eyes moisten, and he says he cannot talk because he is stuck with it, and if things do not improve, his nerves are done for. The captain strokes his beard and looks Eric in the eye and tells him if it ever comes to his nerves not able to withstand living in the commune, he should come to them and they will help him, he should turn to them first before he thinks of anything else. Eric thanks them but says he is in with the preacher for the long haul. He loves Christ and loves the reverend and gave up too much to walk away from it all.

The captain scratches his beard again and says he understands about the sacrifice, but faith should not be stubborn, and maybe sometimes faith is the midwife of doubt. Eric nods in deep thought about this.

From his elevated vantage point at the pig farm, Kevin spies his friend Eric in conversation with someone whose multicolored boat is docked at the landing. Kevin's engrossed stare attracts the attention of Joyce, who tries to look without looking by keeping her gaze trained on a spot far ahead of her, making a series of small movements of her head toward the river. She picks up the vibrant boat, about the same size as the *Coffee*, with two people in charge of it, but they are too far away to see features. She asks Trina in a quiet, matter-of-fact tone to pivot her body and direct the same practiced stare and steal a look at the wharf to see if younger eyes might pick up a trace of Cook on the water. The word causes Trina to become very attentive to her mother. Trina looks in the same covert way and catches sight of the colorful boat and the two figures, and one of them, she thinks, even with her way of having to look without seeming to, one of them, this one man for sure, moves like Cook. She knows this little nugget of information will excite her mother, so she takes extra care with reporting it, to keep her mother's reaction safe; she says the bigger Cook of the two, with the full beard, reminds her of a clean-shaven Cook, who ran a somewhat plainer kitchen compared to this spicy one, and she misses this Cook quite a lot but she knows her mother misses this Cook even more. Joyce asks Trina if she is sure and if she will kindly drop the whole Cook thing, since no other ears linger near enough to eavesdrop. Trina glances at the guard. He seems mesmerized by the scene of his friend contravening orders by fraternizing with people from outside, though from this far, how can he be sure the talk is not all about commune business?

Joyce inhales heavily and says they must send a signal to the captain that they can see him, even if they cannot get to him or he to them. Trina thinks they should stage an escape. Not just one pig but a whole brood of piglets, to make rounding them up quite an enterprise. She opens the pen a fraction and ushers the piglets out, and once they start to scatter, she shrieks and runs at them to make sure some of them head toward the river, and her mother follows her, grabbing at the piglets and failing to grip even one, as if the little pink slip of a thing is greased and this is a game of catch the greasy pig. Kevin can hardly believe his luck, a chance to get a closer look at Eric in some animated conversation with strangers down at the landing pier. So he joins in the chase of the piglets with not much effort to catch the pigs so much as scatter them nearer the river to get a better look. And with that, the three commune people and the screaming pigs spread out and draw near to the dock.

Eric, the captain, and the first mate look up and see them, and Eric suggests it is time for the captain and his first mate to leave, and the captain thinks so, too, when he spots the woman and her daughter and recognizes both of them right away but hides this from his first mate, who hides it from his captain in case the sight of the mother and child makes the captain lose his head. The captain shakes Eric's hand and departs. Joyce and Trina run after pigs and do their looking without seeming to, which is quite dangerous while on the move. Surely he can see me now, thinks Joyce. How much more of an exhibition do I have to make of myself? Two more guards come on the scene to help out, and Kevin has to stop pretending to catch the pigs and really try to catch them, and so do Joyce and Trina, and with the extra help, the job is done in no time.

Eric shouts at the captain and first mate that the next time they stop, he would like to know about the significance of the boat's painted colors. The captain promises to explain everything next time if Eric promises to greet them with a wave instead of an aimed rifle. Eric smiles and nods.

—Child, it was him. We have to find a way to get to him. The next time he turns up, we have to make our move. Help me to think, Trina.

—I'm thinking, Mother.

The rest of the afternoon flies by as they work with half a mind on their task, which can be dangerous around pigs notorious for never missing an opportunity to bite a careless hand or foot. Piglets jump at the chance to chew on the end of a dress. Fortunately for Joyce and Trina, the piglets beat the sow and boar to the tape of mischief, and Joyce feels a tug on her dress and tugs back, thinking it must be Trina playing with her, and the tug gets stronger, which makes her look behind her, and she sees the three little pigs, each with a bit of her dress in their mouths, pulling and chewing at the same time, and she tugs back harder and shakes her dress and the piglets hang on and squeal and Joyce screams and Kevin runs to help drag them off her dress and Trina tries to help as well. Another piglet rushes at the open gate and another guard uses his stick to block the piglet's path. Kevin helps Joyce to free her dress, but she loses three chunks from it, and the piglets chew and swallow their little cotton treat. Kevin, Joyce, and Trina do all they can to stop themselves from laughing; they wipe their faces in their hands to snuff the flame of a smile and avoid each other's eyes, since one look can spark the next into a smile, and once the eyes surrender, the mouth follows and the face and torso contracts and converts the throat into a trumpet. They pretend to cough a volley of coughs and study the patch of ground in front of them but stay to share the collective restraint and the shared joke in a place where such things are frowned upon.

On the walk back to the buildings, Joyce and Trina hold hands and want to skip along but keep their walk to a trudge to match the other farmworkers'. Joyce offers to give Trina a piggyback, since they are leaving the piggy farm. Trina holds her canvas shoes and points at her sore foot and even hops a couple of steps to indicate pain or blister, in case a guard or prefect is looking. Then she climbs aboard. The piggyback is as close as she comes to hugging her mother to celebrate the fact that the captain showed up. Joyce walks slowly with her daughter on her back. She tells herself she will get them both away from this place and the captain will be there to help them. And if she fails, then this act of carrying her daughter will be the last thing they do. If she has to join a commune line to drink along with her daughter, she promises herself to find a way to carry her just like this, and if the preacher is right about paradise, then this walk will never end.

—That was her, wasn't it?

The first mate puts this to the captain as they steer the boat back into deeper water.

—To whom do you refer, señor?

—The Princess and the Pea.

The captain straightens his hat and stares ahead with a smile and replies in his best faux Australian:

—No idea what you're talking about, mate.

The first mate slaps his captain on the arm and takes his hand and keeps hold of it.

—Captain, that was Joyce and Trina up on that hill, chasing those pigs for the world to see, well, a world with just you in it. That was the two of them!

—Yes, oh yes, that was my Joyce and Trina.

And right there the two men grab each other and perform a little jig, sticking out their legs and circling by linking arms, before they check themselves and run back to their stations in case the boat drifts into a sandbank. They talk about how many guards were on the scene and how far away Joyce and Trina were from the wharf and how long it would take to reach them or for them to make it down to the boat. The captain asks his first mate to forget that they are relatives for a moment and forget that he is the captain and tell him honestly, man to man, if the idea of devising a plan to rescue Joyce and Trina from the commune strikes him as a madcap notion.

—Man to man?

—Yes. Plain, no varnish.

The first mate says if the captain forgets about Joyce and Trina and does nothing but pretend the river is his life and life is the river and everything else a distraction, he will be one first mate short and one cousin fewer and will have one less friend in the world to watch his back. Aubrey cannot leave his captain's post, as he dearly wants to right then, so he waves a raised fist in the direction of Anthony, his first mate, his cousin, his friend. Both men scratch their itchy new beards.

The first mate asks the captain, if he could be one thing in this life, what would that be. Aubrey takes no time to reply:

—Water, of course. How about you?

The first mate says wood.

—Wood?

—Yep. I start as a tree, and I turn into practical things like this.

He slaps the boat.

—What made you ask that?

The first mate says partly because he loves the boat and river and working with the captain, he would not want to be too far away from that trio. The captain bows and waves his fist in a gesture of solidarity with the first mate. They steer *Many Waters* down the middle of a bend enclosed by trees that funnel the boat through a green-lit bottleneck. The river opens into a straight; on both banks a panorama of rolling savannah tilts into the distance all the way up to greet the horizon, and the two banks blend with the surroundings and with the sky to become a river somehow lifted into space.

Today the water appears smooth, its usual wrinkles ironed out by the sun. Almost as if thinking aloud, the captain says that the way the river flows with a quiet power tells him a thing or two, that for power to do real good, it need only be deployed quietly.

Captain says there are places, ports, jetties, whatever, all along the river for people to board and disembark as they choose.

—And sometimes those arrivals and departures are chosen for us.

Aubrey pauses and Anthony rolls his hand in small circles for Aubrey to elaborate.

—The river grinds a stone to dust and washes bones clean. It runs but it can fly to great heights and fall to great depths. If that isn't a library for a lifetime's study I don't know what is.

The first mate nods, but says nothing, can say nothing, looks at the expanse of water in front of him and wipes his eyes.

Ryan thinks as he is conveyed from cave to bush to clearing.

Wind to the left and to the right blows away things stuck in the eye of the sun. Sun eye open but moon eye shut and the two share the same face. And birds fall, one for each teardrop from the bright eye of the sun and the darker eye of the moon, from the bearded face of sky, from cotton wool squeezed dry and swiped to the left and to the right until those two eyes become clear. Clean sun eye shine and dull moon eye, too. Sky face shines bright and blue.

Ryan keeps looking up as he is carried, and his head that is too heavy for his neck hangs and lolls and lollops to another's bounds and strides.

Joyce volunteers to work at the bakery to get some extra baked goods squirreled away at short notice in case she and Trina need them. She wants to see how things work during the night. Since most of the sermons occur at night and run very late on many occasions, it is entirely probable that the final communal drink could fall during an evening, in which case Joyce wants to know that she can secure some rations in a hurry for a fast exit. As she mixes flour and water and begins kneading dough and greasing pans, she wonders if Trina can sleep with so much to store in her young head. She asks herself what kind of a mother gets herself and her daughter into a situation like this.

Her tears fall into the dough that she mixes even as she dabs her eyes on her sleeves and tells herself that she is stupid to cry over a situation that needs her resolve, not her tears. She leans in to the bread mixture with all her strength and rolls and twists it. The table creaks and shakes under her weight and she turns over the dough with the same, slamming it down again with a loud thump that causes loose flour to flare upward like smoke from a blast, and she keeps doing this over and over. Then she tears the dough to pieces and forces those portions into baking pans. And from flour, water, baking powder, and a pinch of salt mixed and forced around in this way, she makes bread. Just like the preacher made a disciple of her and everyone around her.

Trina looks around her dormitory and wonders what will become of all the children. Not like Ryan. She realizes that her family extends to everyone in the room and on the compound, and for them to die would mean the end of her family. What will become of Adam? Is Ryan alive or dead? She faces the wall and keeps very still and tries to sleep. She counts the times she talked with Ryan and thought their time together would never end. His legs to help her run in the game he played so well. His bread in her mouth. She hears Ryan call her name. She wants to turn around and whisper to him for a while about whatever he chooses to talk about, but she knows he is not really there. He calls her name again. Without changing her position, she whispers that he should shut his mouth and his eyes.

Another voice, Rose's this time:

—Yes, go to sleep.

And another and another and Trina adds her yes to the chain and they begin to giggle and become noisy and Ryan begs them to stop and sleep or they will get him into trouble and he will get another beating. And all the children jump up with Trina and Rose and leap on Ryan. He falls to the floor and they cover him with hugs, and under the pile, Trina's face ends up near his.

—Why didn't you answer me the first time?

TWENTY-FOUR

The captain and his first mate spend the night at an indigenous Indian village carved out of the forest a short walk from the river. Hammocks slung between trees hold dozing adults or children in pairs or a parent rocking a sleeping infant. Huts fenced in by logs form a semicircle, and a central clearing supports a large fire with a roast turning on a spit attended by a couple of men and a woman. The first mate pulls off his cap and puts it on the head of a child, and the other children chase the child to take a turn. The next child to get the hat runs off with it on his head, pursued by the group of children.

The captain talks with the elders, Sid among them, about ways to persuade the commune to stop polluting the river. The commune, it emerges, is the principal culprit but not the sole one. The international logging companies' alarming rates of deforestation add their share of bad practices. Sid shares the joke with the captain about his unarmed indigenous council taking on a truckload of armed commune guards and how the guards retreated from the scene, shouting the names of clothes, blouses, skirts, trousers, and panties. Sid asks the captain if he knows the significance of the items. The captain shakes his head and says that the commune works in mysterious ways. Sid and the elders laugh. The talk returns to logging. They knock around ideas about how to control the numbers of loggers, since their machinery clears so many trees so fast that they create massive dead zones in the forest. Those responsible happen to be foreign companies, blessed by the government. They talk about saving the country from itself before the entire rain forest ends up parceled off and sold to the highest bidder from overseas.

The cooks add pieces of the roast to a large pot of vegetable stew and ladle the stew into wood bowls and pass around cassava bread that everyone tears and dips into the stew. Wooden cups of warm rice wine never seem to get more than half empty before being refilled. Neither the captain nor the first mate smoke, but as the pipe comes around the circle and it reaches the captain, he takes a symbolic puff and coughs, which draws laughter, and his first mate puffs and does not cough even once, which earns him cheers. They join in a dance around the fire to drums and chants, and their dances make the shapes of birds and animals of the forest. Perhaps it is the wine and the smoke, but the moment of circling the fire slows, overtaken by a faster spin of the dark and the shadows of flames licking the leaves and rubbing against the trunks of trees. The captain and the first mate feel indistinguishable from their surroundings. The captain thinks he moves because the person in front of him and his first mate behind him move, that he can stop only if they stop and the forest and the darkness in a faster spin stop at the same time. The chanting and the drums match the flames. The people and the forest shape the dark. All of them move in concert. None of them wants to be the first to stop the dance.

They sleep in a guest hut on beds made of grass and leaves, and the room smells of baked clay. They remove their shoes and their hats, and the moment their heads touch the bedding, they drift off. The forest can be a noisy place at night if a person listens to it, but the ears get tired just like the body, and though ears remain open, they stop being consciously receptive. The captain and his first mate hear monkeys and frogs, but in their end-of-a-long-day state, they cease putting names to sounds and therefore stop hearing the names. Their bodies join the shadows of a dying fire. They hear but do not listen to the drum of their hearts and they feel a stranger's heart as it synchronizes with their own. They dance but with wings for arms, which makes their gyrations weightless, freeing them from the limits of their bodies and casting them into the air above the trees. And instead of falling they simply drift with no up and no down and with stars all around them that they can reach out and touch if they have the energy or inclination.

In the morning it is almost sorrow to resume their former selves, but it is sweet to feel renewed, in a new body, and therefore in a new set of circumstances even if they face the same things. They eat cornmeal porridge and drink green tea and thank their hosts and offer a few dollars. The first mate asks the captain's permission to give away his cap and the captain says yes and the first mate drops it on the head of a child who immediately attracts many small hands that try to pull it off and the child runs away pursued. The two men promise Sid that they will return soon. They dip in the river and brush their teeth with the chewed end of a twig from a special bush with oil in it that polishes the teeth and leaves the mouth feeling fresh. The captain asks his first mate if he is ready. The first mate says never more so.

—Let's do this.

The first mate nods slowly and spins the wheel. In the morning light, as the boat leans into the current, it looks like a perfectly formed flock of parakeets swooping low over the water. The *Many Rivers* cuts across the river current, set on a course for the commune.

Trina brings Ryan a bowl of cornmeal porridge. He crawls out of his hiding place under the bunk bed but refuses to eat. She tells him the trouble she went through to walk from the kitchen with a bowl of porridge that every hungry child wants to take from her and every prefect and guard she meets questions her about. Still Ryan shakes his head and looks at the bowl as if it might be poison. She tells him she might get into big trouble for telling everyone that the preacher asked for the bowl of porridge so that he can sample the quality of the breakfast being fed to his flock, but Ryan remains unmoved. Trina dips the spoon in the porridge and eats a little and tries to feed the rest to him. He pulls his head away and keeps his lips sealed. She brings the spoon to his mouth and presses it to his bottom lip and he takes the spoon's contents and swallows. She feeds him again and again until the bowl empties.

—Next time you feed yourself, you big baby.

TWENTY-FIVE

The president of the land of many waters dictates a letter that he wants flown and delivered forthwith to the commune leader with the date—two weeks hence, is how he puts it—of the U.S. delegation's arrival and its composition. Next to the list of names, he writes "press" or "VIP" or "concerned relative" and the kind of access each wants at the commune. His letter advises the reverend to take this one on the chin and he will be rid of foreign interference, since half the things said about the commune concern outside access and this visit would settle that question and quiet the negative publicity. The president argues that this could be a positive public relations exercise if the commune handles the visit with professionalism. Much can be accomplished in the few days before the delegation arrives. He recommends that the commune spruce up the place, mow grass, a lick of paint here and there, put out flags, bunting, that sort of thing. Plenty of schoolchildren in neatly pressed uniforms always do the trick with the media.

Finally, he offers the assistance of the highest office of the land to the commune leader to facilitate the urban aspects of the visit.

We have a zoo with the largest collection of anteaters on the continent. Our botanical gardens abound with Rafflesia, the largest single flower on earth, some opening only once every twenty years, with a twenty years' smell to match; to witness one of these rare specimens opening is to remember that time and day for the rest of your days. The largest wooden building in the southern hemisphere that is a miracle of engineering is here, and cloth, we are a land of weavers, and the best indigenous Indian wood carvings at bargain prices, the best curried goat, the most prized blood pudding, the most precious gold and diamonds at a steal given the exchange rates, the most mouthwatering cow foot, pig foot, and offal stew, and the world's longest single-drop waterfall in the free world, not to forget calypso, everyone needs to dance every once in a while, and we have cricket.

The preacher's assistants divide themselves between checking the radio to see if the connection to the president's office is still open and making sure the reverend is okay. The preacher looks around for something else to throw, and seeing nothing within reach, he stamps his feet, jumps up and down on the spot, and rushes at the radio again, but his assistants and the guards restrain him. They release him and he warns them all never to lay a finger on him when he has a mind to do something. He turns to the nearest guard and punches him hard in the stomach. The guard doubles over and vomits into his hands and darts out of the room, still leaning forward and leaving a trail of bile and a sour smell in his wake.

The people roam around the commune, guided by chores. All appear to wait for something, an order to switch tasks, another summons to meet, or a message on the broadcast system. They do what they think the preacher wants them to do, but he asks something different of them. They move as if the preacher were standing in their midst, directing them this way and that. They move against each other at the slightest provocation or report of dissent or any accusation of impudence or a lack of effort. Adam watches them as if he stands in their place and they in his and he acts for them.

Adam spots the woman in an apron covered in flour, coming toward his cage, and he sways from side to side and grips the bars. He holds his open hand through the bars and Joyce places an aromatic chunk of

warmth in his palm. Bread, she says, and she spells it for him, b-r-e-a-d.
He looks at her, retracts his arm with the spoils, and scoots to the back
of his cage. He sits on his bed and nibbles the bread to make it last. Soon
enough, though, the bread disappears. He sniffs his hand for the bread
smell. Soon that goes, too. He considers asking her for some more, with
a sound for bread and an open palm pushed through the bars of his cage
and perhaps a gesture of that hand to his mouth. If not Joyce, someone
else will come along soon with a banana. The preacher or Trina. Or both.

The guards believe their gunfire repelled a mercenary attack on the commune. They say the assailants manipulated the jungle according to their
training, but the superior firepower of the guards saved the day. These
hostile forces will regroup and launch another, more direct attack on the
commune, so preparations need to be made to repulse them. And if this
line of defense fails, there is always the ultimate escape route from capture
and imprisonment and separation of parents from children and dissolu-
tion of the commune. The preacher asks the guards if they accept his
assessment of the situation and his remedy for it. They all agree that they
want to evade their persecutors and be by their leader's side in paradise.
They will mount an armed defense of the commune as a first response to
any hostility, and this should create a diversion and help to facilitate the
orderly departure of everyone in the commune from this world to the next.
The leader says theirs is a win-win situation. Faith is the only requisite
ingredient in a recipe to win the kingdom of heaven.

Over the community loudspeaker, the preacher announces the imminent arrival of a delegation from the U.S.:

—Soon Satan will set foot in our holy refuge.

It galls him to say the name of the land that banished them all. He asks
the faithful if they want prying eyes and hostile minds to walk all over the
commune that their labor built from nothing, the order that they carved
out of the chaos of the jungle, for these intruders to judge them as if they

were common criminals. No one wants that, and they all pause in the middle of their chores to shout and gesticulate at the nearest loudspeaker.

At the evening sermon he talks late into the night and orders the commune to rise at dawn to purge their sins and pray. People faint in the congregation. Many need medication to sleep, to stay awake, to eat, to stop eating, to stop biting their nails and pulling their hair, to stop their hair from falling out, to cure inexplicable rashes, for shingles, for mono, for nervous exhaustion, for not knowing which way to turn and not being able to tell their up from their down, their left from their right. They need to sleep but the preacher will not let them. He broadcasts night and day and at irregular intervals. His people's nerves are frayed, their minds rendered incapable of making the simplest decisions. They ask someone in charge what to wear, what to do, and when to do it. They stand in one place for ages, unsure what to do next or what to think. They walk around and bump into furniture, each other, drop plates of food and glasses with milk and clean clothes that need to be rinsed all over again, and which they'll wear back to front and inside out.

He marches them around the commune and points out where vipers and tarantulas and scorpions might nest and bite a child, and idle pools where mosquitoes might hatch and spread malaria, and worms that eat between the toes and flesh-eating mites that crawl into the crotch. He reminds them their children belong to God and their lives will be better in God's hands and not his and not this commune, and no place on this godforsaken earth is good enough for his flock, only the kingdom of heaven, only everlasting life. For their vigilance in this life against the temptations of the flesh, they will garner freedom of the spirit in the next. This life in this commune tests their bodies every day, but the real test is their faith in a spiritual life that lasts forever.

He tries to get them to comprehend forever. Old men and women in the commune stand during the sermons and face the young people nearest, and they swear to those youth that time is an illusion, one day you are young, the next, old, and that their earthly lives will run away from them like quicksilver, will pass through their fingers like the river's water. That yesterday they are young, less than yesterday, a moment ago, that they blink and open their eyes and, lo, they are old. That they find the days shorter and shorter. That this time they are in, this present, is just a trick, chump change, funny money that is robbed from them in an instant of daylight. The old testify to the young that the afterlife has no truck with conventional hours, days, weeks, months, and years. They believe it is true because there must be a reason for this trial by time of the flesh at the expense of the spirit.

The old take their seats, and the preacher thanks them and takes over:

—Forever exists outside of time.

He asks them to examine the second hand of a clock, and he gets two guards to hold up a large clock borrowed from the schoolhouse. He says that time in God's mind is so slow that in terms of creation and all of human history, only one second elapses on this clock. Imagine that, he says, one second to get from the beginning of time to where we are at this moment. That is time in God's hands. There is no way to measure seventy or eighty or ninety years on this scale, those human years are too infinitesimal to count for anything in God's time.

—Now you have an idea about eternity. That is what waits for each of you because you chose to be here with me today. Eternity is your reward.

Joyce, Trina, and Rose add their praise the Lord to the chorus and a part of them finds the preacher's reasoning irresistible. Rose applies it to Ryan's disappearance and return and concealment, all in one blink, and to her own mother, whom she trained herself not to think about to avoid feeling dejected from the day her mother had to leave the commune and was forced to leave her behind as insurance. They leave these meetings in a daze and find that they, too, weep in the moment for no reason and feel numb and walk in a sleep of some kind. Joyce tells Trina again and again to think of the boat and the captain and the river and not to listen too closely to the preacher, since his voice stays in the head and steers independent thinking in unpredictable directions.

The only thing the two listen for is the amen responses required from them, and they mimic these without thinking. Trina thanks her lucky stars that most nights the preacher seems too busy with others to call on her for support during his sermons or demonstrations. But tonight he pulls a scorpion from a box and asks the nearest child, who happens to be Rose, to open her hand and to be very still while he places the insect on her hand. Rose pees her pants as the preacher lowers the insect toward her hand and the preacher castigates Rose for her fear that is deeper than her faith and dismisses her. The preacher calls on another child, who stands, wide-eyed, and faints or pretends to faint even before taking a step toward the stage.

The preacher asks for Trina:

—She'll show you kids what faith is.

But a young prefect jumps to his feet and says he will do it, he has faith, he believes in Father. And the preacher smiles, hails the young man forward to the stage, and lowers the scorpion onto his hand, which shakes abysmally until the scorpion begins to slide off his arm and he screams and flicks it away and the scorpion lands somewhere between the fourth and fifth rows, which causes a stampede from the area, and the guards restore order with their sticks.

The scorpion cannot be found and the two rows remain clear, no one wants to go near the area until the guards agree to sit in the chairs themselves to reassure the congregation. The rows fill up again and people keep looking around their feet and twitching their legs just in case. Pat produces another box and the preacher pulls a tarantula from it and turns his hand over as the spider crawls along his hand. He invites two other assistants, Nora and Dee, to do the same, but they recoil and he takes their hands and keeps hold as he repeats the same motion of turning the hand over to keep the spider on it. He calls Trina again. Another young prefect jumps to her feet and begs to prove her faith. The preacher agrees and she bounds onto the stage and perhaps it is her proximity to the tarantula that causes the change in her from sprightly volunteer to someone rigid who wishes she could change her mind. She holds out her hand and shakes so much that the preacher has to steady it. He tells her to keep still so he can place the spider on her, and recommends that she think of a calm place, since a tarantula easily senses fear and lack of faith and will bite her.

He decides to place the spider on her shoulder and reminds this young prefect to keep her head still and trust him. She nods and offers her hand again by holding the hand with the other to keep it from shaking, but the preacher says his choice of her shoulder is better than a shaky hand and all she needs to do is obey him. He holds the tarantula in a pincer grip between his thumb and index finger and lowers it onto her left shoulder. For a few seconds she closes her eyes and holds her breath and sways a little and the spider moves from her left shoulder toward her face with these slow legs picking up and touching down lightly like fingertips on piano keys and perhaps the prefect feels something from the movement through her dress that makes her forget that the material sits between her skin and the tarantula, maybe the hairy feet feel just as if the tarantula crawls on her skin. She strains her neck upward and toward her right shoulder and into tense cords to keep the creature in view of her wide disbelieving eyes and to increase the distance between its prying, hairy legs and her face. As she leans, she tries her best to remain still and model obedience to the reverend. She sees the tarantula grow in her sight as the only thing present in the congregation, and from its becoming giant in size with its many legs on her skin, she thinks that somehow it succeeds in dividing itself into two and then four spiders and at any moment they will crawl all over her body.

She springs from her position of frozen consent and cooperation and beats her neck and shoulders with her hands and brushes hard and rapidly to clear away as many spiders as the feel of those legs on her skin. She bolts off the stage and the guards try to hold her but she pokes them in their faces with her wild arms and slips from their grasp and they follow her out of the tent and into the dark as she screams and hops and waves her arms around to fend off many nightmare tarantulas. The real arachnid sheepishly crawls along the stage where she knocked it off her, and the preacher retrieves it and places it back in the box.

The guards chase the girl but not the way an adult pursues someone in an emergency; theirs is a casual pursuit, more a case of follow that girl's scream and her noisy progress from the tent toward the gorilla's cage. A few lights dot the commune and make it possible to see the prefect's shadow sprint into the circumference of a lit area and then out of it and back into the dark. They wonder where she thinks she is going at this late hour. Rather than heading for the children's dormitories, she sprints toward the field to the right of the gorilla's cage. A pothole might break her ankle or a viper bite her foot. Prefect, young lady, hello, where are you, the guards call into the darkness. They run faster now because the field is no place for a child at night and she needs to be rescued from herself.

Adam runs at the bars of his cage and throws his body against them. He jumps on the spot and shakes the cage and howls. The guards beat the bars of the cage with their sticks to silence Adam. He retreats out of sight. The guards discuss the girl's disappearance:

—She knows what's in that field.

—Headed straight for it.

And the words barely leave their mouths before they say blouse and skirts and pick up the pace, followed by the rest of the group. They hear the girl's scream cut short with an echo, not in the air, as before, but from under their feet, up from the ground, and they collide with the well and shine their torches into it, but the well is so deep it swallows the rays.

The guards fetch more lights to shine into the well. One or two still call: Prefect, young lady, hello, and point their torches at the forest, hoping she might emerge from it. A guard returns to the tent and whispers something to Nora. She orders the guard to pull himself together, but she has to do the same. Nora, Dee, and Pat confer and decide to allow the reverend to finish his preaching before they inform him. But he turns from the middle of his tirade against the enemies of the commune to ask where the girl is and why a bunch of grown men cannot catch a teenager and must he do everything himself. He sees the glum expressions of his assistants and pauses and asks his congregation to excuse him for a moment. He walks to

Nora, Dee, and Pat and asks them to tell him what all the chaos is about if they care one iota about him. They tell him that the prefect who ran from the tent did a stupid thing.

—What stupid thing would that be?

The nurse says the young woman ran and jumped into the well. The preacher spins away from his assistant and slaps his forehead with his open hand. He barks into the microphone:

—No, no, no, no, no. Do not go before me, wait for me. I want you all to repeat. Do not go before me, wait for me. Repeat.

—Do not go before me, wait for me.

He falls quiet. He covers his face, and his shoulders shake as he sobs. He wipes his face with a handkerchief fished from his back pocket, tucks the kerchief back in place, straightens and breathes and exhales into the microphone.

—Forgive me. Even I'm overcome sometimes. People, do not fear this world or anything in it. Believe me, you have the kingdom of heaven, and this world's nothing to you. Don't fear a scorpion or spider or snake. These things can't harm your everlasting spirit. Believe me. The young woman did not understand. Parents, make your children understand, please. The child ran from here in her fear and confusion. She ran from me and the safety that we all provide to each other in our unity. She ran from us and into the night. They tell me she jumped into the well.

Shouts ring out, no, no, and screams from the young woman's parents, her immediate circle of friends, and pockets of the audience. The prefect's parents clutch each other and crumple in their seats and beg the preacher to say it is not so, that their little girl is all right. But he shakes his head and says he wishes it were otherwise.

—Is this flesh so precious to you that it overrides your faith in the kingdom of heaven? Is this body so much in need of your protection that you would forgo everlasting life? Answer me, people.

—No, Father.

—Our enemies want us in disarray. They want us to commit individual acts of fear and panic and fall apart as a community, but we're stronger than that. We've come a long way, haven't we? Think of where each of you was before you were saved and how far each of you has come and where you are now, think of that journey of your spirit from ruin and loss and wandering to sure salvation. Do not lose heart at this late stage. Do not mistake the actions of a confused child for defeat. Our spirits, people, cannot be conquered in this world, only our bodies die. Parents, look at me. There is nothing I will not do for you. Look at me.

The parents obey and the preacher takes a knife from his pocket, flicks open the blade, and before Dee, Pat, and Nora or anyone near him can react, he slides the blade across his wrist and holds his arm out for all to see the red slice weep. The prefect's parents look at the preacher's face and at his open wrist without releasing their grip of each other. Their faces are wet, their mouths open, and their eyes wide. The preacher pulls out his handkerchief and steps off the stage and Nora grabs the handkerchief and his arm and straps it tightly. He walks to the parents and they fall at his feet and he kisses them.

—You've every right to grieve for her and miss her, but don't feel sorry for her or for yourselves. She's ahead of you in paradise, and that's where we're all heading. Not here in this temporary flesh but with her in eternity. Do you believe?

—Yes, Father.

—Don't grieve. Let's lift our voices and sing. We'll meet your daughter on the other side.

—Yes, Father.

The choir and band strike up the hymn "In the Sweet By-and-By." The parents hug each other and cry.

As the band, choir, and congregation rage with hallelujahs and praise the Lords and sing at the top of their lungs and throw their arms in the air and some people topple onto the floor and gyrate in paroxysms of bodily transportation, the preacher moves to one corner with his assistants and asks them to confirm that the girl—the stupid little devil of a girl, is how he puts it—really jumped down the well, because he cannot trust those fools who call themselves his bodyguards after their unlikely shaking-bush story. The doctor examines the preacher's wrist and tells him that although there is no damage to the tendon, he needs stitches, but the preacher says that will have to wait, so the doctor tightens a bandage around the cut. He walks back to the center of the stage with his microphone.

—Trina, Trina, Trina, Trina, Trina. Where are you, my child? Come up here.

Joyce holds on to Trina, who looks at her mother and touches her mother's arms for Joyce to release her grip. Joyce prays inwardly. God, spare my child.

Trina raises her hand and shouts from the middle of the congregation:
—I'm here, Father.

People steady her and pat her all over as she steps across many legs and picks her way out of her row to continuous applause from the congregation. Trina reaches the stage, transported by these hands touching her and pushing her forward. The preacher leans over and offers his bandaged hand and Trina kisses it and smells his blood and thinks of how blood smells as though the body manufactures vegetation of its own, green leaves, brown bark, tree sap, and she steps up onto the stage. The preacher kisses her on her head.

—Now, children, look at a real demonstration of faith and trust. Trina knows what I mean by the body as a temporary house for the eternal spirit. Don't you, Trina?

—Yes, Father.

—You know that if I ask you to do something, I make the request as your loving Father who means you no harm and who intends to give his life for your safety, don't you?

—Yes, Father.

—You hear that, people. Can each of you say that? Without reservation. That you know I mean you no harm; that everything I do is for your
well-being?

An array of replies flits around the congregation:

—Yes, Father. We do. We love you. We trust you.

The preacher waits for his followers to quiet and they take their time
for each one wants to voice love and loyalty beyond measure, since everyone believes someone watches. Even the stragglers who shout praise feel
compelled to stop and allow the preacher to resume his lesson with Trina
and discover if the child can produce another miracle.

—Trina, hold out your arms, palms facing upward. Look at me. Don't
take your eyes off me.

—Yes, Father.

Joyce looks around to think what she should do to save Trina. She wants
to jump to her feet and scream at the reverend to leave her daughter alone.
She wishes she sat closer to an armed guard so she could grab his gun and
fire. She feels the arms of the women seated around her, and she looks at
their faces and realizes they know what runs through her mind and crawls
all over her body, and their touch lets her know that nothing she can think of
as a mother will change things for her daughter except a mother's hope and
prayer and surely things will turn out right. The women around Joyce begin
the Lord's Prayer and she joins them. The best she can do for Trina, she
decides, requires the most of her, to be strong and keep calm, to remember
their plans laid over a long time, sound plans, if they get through this test.

Trina knows what she must do to help herself. She sees herself beside
Joyce, hanging clothes in a theater of bodiless shapes. Joyce closes her
eyes, unable to look at Trina on the stage with her arms in front of her,
palm up, waiting for the preacher to do whatever he plans for her. Trina
supplements the hanging of clothes with a walk she takes with her mother
through an avenue of big trees with seeds raining down on them and each
trying to catch one. Late-afternoon light basks in the tops of the trees.
The seeds fall from this high orange-colored harvest.

The preacher asks for two small cardboard boxes, and Nora and Dee step forward, each holding a box. He gives his microphone to Pat, rubs his hands on his trousers, and lifts the lids of the boxes and pulls out a tarantula in one hand and a scorpion in the other. The audience in the rows near the stage leans back. The guards take a step closer to the front rows. The preacher moves swiftly and eases the two writhing creatures onto Trina's hands, the tarantula in her right and the scorpion in her left. Trina floats away from her body, like one of those seeds departing a tree, and she leaves just a dress, no one inside it and no breeze to enliven it. She locks eyes with the preacher. She follows her mother's instruction to pick her favorite scenes and keep them in her mind, stay with them, and Trina adds to the theater of clothes on a line and the big trees releasing their produce another picture, of the *Coffee* with the captain at the wheel and her mother next to him and the two of them talking as Trina sketches.

She hardly feels the arachnid and anthropoid's crawl from her palms to her wrists and over her wrists that she turns to keep the preacher's pets from falling. They feel their way, one on the left arm and the other on the right, along her warm skin, goose-pimpled but still for them. Trina sees the preacher's black eyes as pools with nothing in them, just black water, so it is easy for her to see the *Coffee*, the captain, her mother, and her, and she adds the first mate walking to and fro with a rope or a tray and a whistle and winking at her, as is his habit. The creatures reach Trina's inner elbows about the same time. Her arms are slightly bent and provide a crook for the tarantula and the scorpion to pause and turn around and get the measure of their location. Perhaps her strong pulse there attracts them. And her veins sit up proudly and make the skin there seem thinner than elsewhere. Several people faint, some double over and vomit. Others cover their eyes. Joyce keeps her eyes closed and prays aloud. The preacher holds up his hands for silence and a hush falls on the congregation. In silence the guards attend to those keeled over in their seats or slumped to the floor. The ones who vomited are pulled out of the crowd and offered towels and water. Those who can bear to look crane their necks to get a view of Trina's outstretched arms. And those at the back who cannot see ask others to tell them what is happening, and the whispered reports, from those who take in the scene on the stage, sound like a secret being divulged in public.

With her eyes locked on her leader's, and her alternating visuals of the captain and her mother adrift on the *Coffee*, the theater of clotheslines, and the walk with her mother among falling helicopter seeds, Trina tries to keep each breath calm, not too labored a draw on the air, but a gentle outpouring as from a ladle into a jug with her long neck and body. In that way Trina's mind remains alert and she stays upright. Both creatures make a U-turn in the crook at Trina's elbows and pause as if to get their bearings and amble methodically back along her forearms, tapping with their front feet to test the soundness of the soft terrain until they reach her palms.

The preacher gestures for assistance and Nora and Dee bring the boxes and hold them under Trina's palms and the preacher tilts her hands in a swift move and the tarantula and the scorpion drop into the boxes and Nora and Dee are only too happy to snap the lids shut. Trina remains on the spot with her arms outstretched and the preacher grabs her and holds her close to him and kisses her and everyone applauds. Joyce clambers out of her row, and encouraged by everyone, even the guards, she rushes to the front of the assembly and climbs onto the stage, and Nora, Dee, and Pat move to block her path but the preacher waves them away and she runs to Trina and the preacher includes Joyce in his embrace.

—People, faith comes in all shapes and sizes, and tonight you have seen a giant demonstration of faith from Trina.

The continuous applause and repetitions of amen and praise the Lord reverberate for an age and several people faint and are fanned and fed water to revive them.

—Suffer the little children . . . the reverend begins and trails off and the congregation picks up the rest of the verse in a loud and enthusiastic recitation, not quite synchronized, filling the assembly with an air of hypnosis.

Three rows from the stage, a squeamish teenager believes the hairs on his legs stirred by a gust really must be a scorpion and the young man leaps straight up from his seat and shouts the words "scorpion" and "blouse" without even a glance to be sure and the people around him take him at his word and leap from their seats as well and rush, scrambling over one another, each person convinced of the scorpion by the last person's response to the person before in a chain of panic that results in pandemonium that the guards themselves succumb to by lashing with sticks at any dark patch on the ground. Only the preacher's voice over the microphone slows the scramble sufficiently for the guards to begin to hit people rather than dark patches, and only after hearing the preacher plead with them for order does the crowd stop and look at him.

Nora approaches the preacher and whispers in his ear. He pulls back from his assistant and looks at her and leans forward again and offers his other ear so that she can tell him her message a second time. He walks over to the guards and tells them to meet him at his house right away. But first he walks down the center aisle and hugs and kisses as many people as he can reach. He pauses twice to launch a verse from the Bible and leave the group to finish it among themselves as he propels himself toward the back exit with more embraces and kisses and more snippets of verse to inspire his followers. His assistants leave the stage by a side exit and run around the outside of the tent and meet him at the back, along with two armed guards. They hurry to the main house, ablaze with more lights than any other building apart from the bakery.

Once inside the front door, he curses and summons the guards who chased the girl. As the doctor and a nurse stitch his wrist at an improvised sterile station set up on a table, he has the guards recount the exact details of their report that the girl jumped into the well. Did they see her jump? Have they found a body? What makes them conclude that this is the most likely action taken by the girl? He fires his questions and does not wait for answers. The guards shrug and glance at each other.

—So, my trusty guardians, you know these people here.

He sweeps his arms to take in his assistants and two guards, and the search party follows his sweeping gesture.

—How come they searched the same well with lights and found nothing?

The guards who chased the girl swear there must be some mistake, since the child ran toward the well and she screamed as if pitched to the bottom of it. They say she disappeared after her screams cut short and echoed. One guard says they could see her ahead of them until they reached the well. Another guard suggests that she sank to the bottom of the little amount of water that remains in the well.

Nora shakes her head:

—No, we lowered a prefect on a rope with lights and a stick, and he found nothing but rancid water and cobwebs.

The preacher lifts his arms above his head for quiet. He pauses for a moment and speaks in the most even tone he can muster:

—There's a child out there and we need to find her before our erstwhile delegation arrives and don't tell me she might be killed by a panther, jaguar, or boa constrictor, or she can't get far in the dark. No more ifs and buts, just find her and bring her here to me tonight. Now get out.

He asks Pat to stay with him, and after almost everyone clears the front room and leaves the house or moves to the kitchen or the back rooms, he slumps into his favorite armchair with the leg rest and asks her to give him something to calm his nerves, which he says are about to break. Pat rolls up his sleeves and flicks a syringe and injects his arm. Next she maneuvers to the back of the armchair and massages the man's temples, and he hums for a short while, and his head lolls to one side as he slides into a stupor.

A child in a blind sprint in pitch dark, swatting at her shoulder, neck, and torso, soon runs out of breath and risks running at full pelt into something. Suppose this something looks as dark as night, weighs four hundred–plus pounds, and squeezes through a tunnel dug under its cage and catches that child in its arms just as she scrambles over the retaining wall of the well. In her rush to stop the sensation of something crawling all over her skin, almost under her skin, she tries to dive into that well and end everything.

Her screams from the tent and her mad exit alert Adam, who is stationed at his usual spot, listening to the sermon over the loudspeakers and swaying to the songs of the congregation. Adam sees the girl in distress and the guards in search of her and he dashes to the back of his cage, determined to help her, no matter the consequence. He squeezes into the tunnel he has dug over several days, careful all that time to spread the dirt around his cage and fling some of it between the bars into the grass, and he emerges out of his cage. His eyes know the dark. His mind pictures the well and the terrain around it, and he runs to that place to intercept the girl. He reaches her as she clambers over the side of the well, and he grabs her, covers her mouth, and runs with her to the perimeter of the compound. She passes out. He follows the fence to one of several gates dotted along it. He holds the girl under his left arm and slightly behind him to keep her safe from the impact, and he breaks through the fence post by dipping his right shoulder and throwing his weight against it.

In his dreams he flies through this forest unimpeded. In this dark he takes the nearest path down to the river. The prefect wakes and Adam covers her mouth and moves his hand away slowly and she tries to scream and he covers her mouth again and once more moves it away and this third time she remains quiet. She shrinks from him, but he grips her around the waist.

The guards, charged with finding the girl, comb the area and widen their search until they include Adam's cage and think he must be asleep in it, but as a formality of their search they shine torches at his bed and find nothing and inspect the entire cage and, to be doubly sure, unlock it and, with sticks and guns ready for any surprise, reach Adam's bed and come upon the large hole against the back wall of the cage. They sound the alarm with the permission of Nora, Dee, and Pat. They decide not to wake the preacher from his sedation. Pat says it would be unwise to give him such bad news in his drowsy condition. He cannot hear the alarm in his deep sleep, and it is important to get the entire commune to help with the search, since Adam must be somewhere on the property, hiding in a corner.

TWENTY-SIX

Thirst wakes the preacher. Mouth dry as caked cotton wool and head groggy, he calls for drink as if a drink might come rushing, but no one responds. Always two guards at their station at the front door and Nora, Dee, and Pat milling about the house. He opens the front door to the entire commune rushing about left and right and shouts to the nearest person to tell him what is going on, has everyone gone mad in the night? Only one guard is in the yard at the front of the house with his rifle poised and swinging it in all directions as if he expects to be attacked from all quarters. The reverend lifts his arms questioningly.

—Reverend, Adam's gone.

—What do you mean, gone? Where can a fucking half-ton gorilla go? Pat! Dee! Nora!

He feels wobbly on his feet and leans on the porch railing for balance. He staggers down the steps and crosses the area between his house and Adam's cage. A second guard rushes forward to join the first, and they accompany the preacher. The cage is unlocked, gate open. The preacher walks into it and shouts for Adam. Pat runs to him and he leans on her and asks her what happened. She shows him the hole next to Adam's bed. This new piece of evidence makes the preacher alert. He pushes his assistant from him and curses.

A few more guards arrive on the scene. The preacher says if the gorilla can dig a hole and disappear around the same time as the girl, then there must be a connection. He says if they find Adam, they will solve the mystery of the disappeared girl. No one around the preacher believes him. Pat thinks he must be speaking under the influence of the narcotic. The guards cannot square the beast they are accustomed to seeing in the cage with any demonstrable intelligence that extends to an intervention of the kind described by the preacher. The notion that Adam escaped from his cage and took the child with him and that he performed his escape undetected by digging a hole under the noses of the guards and everyone else seems too much, too fast, for them to process.

The reverend invites them to think about it, then not to think about it but leave the thinking to him and just do as he asks—find the gorilla and they will find the girl. He suggests a plan for the search, but a guard interrupts him with a report that there is a breach in a side gate and it looks like it was made by a powerful animal of some kind. The preacher says with a degree of triumph in his voice: That spot is as good a place as any to begin your search, gentlemen. He says Adam is no ordinary gorilla and he should not be harmed in any way. They should use tranquilizers to subdue him. The preacher falls to one knee and the guards are about to copy his action, thinking he wants to pray, but Pat asks two guards to help her carry the reverend back to the house.

Joyce and Trina take the opportunity of the confusion at the commune to find each other and head for the pig farm. The path is dark and they hope nothing else roams on the trail. They hold hands with a tight grip and stay close to each other. After two hundred paces, Joyce stoops and feels in the bush and picks up the two sticks she placed there in the weeks of planning. She gives the smaller of the two sticks to Trina. At another four hundred paces, Joyce turns left, and after another four hundred, they find the drain that leads down the slope to the landing pier.

On their way down the slope, they hear the grunts and think it might be a wild boar. They raise their sticks, and the plan is to strike them together and make as much noise as they can. But Trina recognizes the grunts as something other than a boar and tells her mother things will be fine now. Joyce asks Trina what she means by her declaration. Trina says that grunting can belong to only one creature, the one who carried her when she fainted and covered her with his blanket so that she might sleep and be safe near his cage.

Joyce cannot believe her ears, but she knows not to argue with her daughter anymore. Mother and daughter creep out of the bush, and there is Adam shielding the young prefect with his body and baring his teeth and grunting at them. Adam spots Trina and releases the girl and bounds toward her. Joyce raises her stick, but Trina pulls her mother's arm down and drops her stick and opens her arms and Adam sweeps her up into his embrace. The prefect runs to Joyce and the two of them watch Trina and Adam hugging each other. Adam turns his back and Trina scratches it. Trina bows her head toward Adam and he ruffles her hair. They do this a few times.

A guard shouts that they should put their hands up and step away from Adam. A second guard repeats the order and warns them they will be shot if they do not obey immediately. Adam tenses to charge at the two men but Trina stands in front of Adam and says no, very firmly and with pleading in her voice. Adam keeps still for her. Joyce holds the prefect and calls to Trina to come to her. The two guards walk closer and both aim at Adam. They order Trina to step away from Adam. Joyce recognizes them.

—Kevin, Eric. Don't do this.

—We have our orders.

—Don't obey mad orders from a madman. Leave us. Search somewhere else.

Kevin asks Joyce please not to say another word and get herself and her daughter into trouble and to obey his instructions. Eric says they have no choice but to return to the compound. No good can come from seeking the life they abandoned. Kevin tells Eric to take a shot if he can. Joyce begs them to wait. Eric orders Trina to move away from Adam, but she refuses to move.

—Trina, my gun has tranquilizing darts. Adam won't be harmed.

Kevin says only his gun carries live ammunition and he will use it if Eric's darts fail. Best to give him a clear shot. They should listen and come back to the commune. Adam looks at Trina and Joyce for direction. He can reach the men in a few paces and put an end to the argument. But Trina or Joyce needs to instruct him. Kevin promises that neither he nor Eric will say anything about the dissent if Joyce gets Trina to cooperate. But they must do so without delay, since other guards will soon arrive. Joyce turns and looks at the river. There is nothing on the water but a layer of darkness. She half-expects to see a rainbow boat materialize on the water in the wake of that harvest and gather Trina, the prefect, Adam, and her into it and disappear from this place. But the surface of the river keeps still for the first light to pick the dark from it.

A shot and another in quick succession send Adam reeling backward and clutching at his arm and leg. He turns to charge at a group of men who run out of the trees not far from Kevin and Eric. Joyce screams at the men to stop, and Trina grabs Adam, who holds on to her and keeps her to one side as his legs buckle under him. Joyce asks Kevin to remember his promise. She tells the prefect to say nothing about any of this to anyone, not even her parents, since it will get them all in big trouble. The prefect looks at Joyce but does not respond. The guards get on their radio and say mission accomplished. About eight men lift Adam onto a cart and bind his hands and feet, and the men, helped by a donkey, pull the cart back to the compound. The doctor shines a light into each of the prefect's eyes. She fails to respond to any of his questions or to her parents, who stop asking her if she is all right and just hold her while the doctor pronounces that she is in deep shock. He prescribes a sweet drink and a sedative to help her rest. The preacher tells the community that this reappearance of the child is nothing short of a miracle and they should pray. He says he cannot explain it to them, that God's infinite work is a mystery, more often than not, to the limited minds of humanity.

—The child was lost and now she is found. God's power is supreme.

He asks them to pray hard, for this is surely a sign from God of things drawing to a close, some big event on the horizon for the commune. The preacher questions Kevin and Eric at length, and whatever they say to him induces him to thank Trina and Joyce for their good work.

The guards reinforce Adam's cage with staves hammered deep into the ground. They pour cement into the tunnel dug by Adam and attach a shackle to his left leg. A long chain on the shackle allows Adam some restricted movement in his cage. They padlock another chain around the bars of the cage. Adam snoozes in his drugged condition while the preacher whispers and Trina plays her flute. The preacher says that Adam is special, but how would he manage in the wild when all his life was spent in captivity? He wants to know, if Adam truly understands his sermons, how could the gorilla attempt to escape?

Kevin and Eric march to the pig farm. They debate the merits of their decision to stay with the preacher. Kevin says it is a matter of faith.

—If Joyce lost hers, that's her loss.

Eric wonders if their love of God and their love for the reverend and for each other are all three reconcilable. Kevin says he cannot imagine a heaven with a God whose love is anything but unconditional. He says Joyce can do what she wants with her daughter, but she must not implicate them in her plans. At the farm Eric touches Kevin's arm, a quick furtive gesture, and walks on toward the landing for his guard duty. Kevin walks over to Joyce and Trina, who rake pig muck and turn their backs on him. Kevin wants Joyce to know that she can do what she wants, but it must not involve him or Eric. He apologizes for spoiling her plans but says that when he and Eric found them, they were stuck on the wharf with nowhere to go and the other guards arrived just a few minutes later. He tells her she needs a better plan. And just so she knows, he says, his good friend Eric has just two more days of duty at the dock before the rotation puts some strange guard in his place. Kevin walks away and Joyce stops raking and utters a quick thank you. She nudges Trina and points with her chin in the direction of the jetty, where Eric marches.

The captain and his first mate meet Eric at the pier. The captain asks Eric if he is all right. Eric twirls a used tranquilizer dart between his fingers.

—What happened?

Eric says it would be unwise to pursue the issue, but no one got hurt in the incident, it was all a misunderstanding. The men drink ginger beer and the captain breaks out a few precious slices of his black cake. Eric asks what they would say to him if he told them of a miraculous attempt to flee the commune by a gorilla as smart as a man who grabbed a child and took off with it. The captain replies that if he were not the source of the ginger beer and cake, he would think the bearer of such a tale was drunk or having visions, but knowing the source of the story, drink and cake or no drink and cake, he has no choice but to believe it.

The captain asks Eric if he cares whether Joyce and Trina leave the commune. Eric says he does not care but he cannot risk being blamed for their departure. The captain asks, if Joyce and Trina were to slip past Eric and he did not see them and so could swear they did not pass by him while he was on his watch, would that absolve him of blame in their departure. Eric says that in all good conscience he would have to be unaware of their presence if he is to be in a position to swear before his leader and before God that he knows nothing about such an event. The captain thanks him and wishes him a good day.

The preacher announces to the commune that they must prepare the place for the delegation even if it is true that their worst enemies are about to descend on them. He says they must meet these evil people and show them once and for all that commune life is sacred. He instructs his carpenters and painters to spruce up the place, from the hut at the main gate to the pig farm. He asks that all schoolchildren wear commune insignia, yellow and green, as a uniform. The choir puts together a repertoire and the band polishes its brass. He reminds them that cleanliness is next to godliness. The hammering and painting start right away, along with the cutting of cloth for yellow shirts and green trousers and yellow blouses and green skirts for the children. He walks through the campus with his managers, and they list the things that need immediate attention. He doubles the gardening contingent. He asks for guards to work at their stations on one other task in addition to their guard duty.

The guards at the front gate paint their hut while on duty. The bakers double up as spring cleaners of the bakery. The preacher sets groups to work on the infirmary, his house, the schoolhouse, and the library as the main buildings earmarked for a brief tour by the delegation, and these buildings are whitewashed and the paths leading to them weeded and cleaned. He doubles the rations for the children and asks the doctor to get as many patients as possible out of the infirmary to create an impression of a healthy environment, even if that means putting those bedridden patients in secluded buildings.

The schoolchildren practice greeting important personages and learn special songs and recitations of key Bible and Shakespeare passages to impress the delegation. The doctor and nurses order patients to look as if they are more recovered than ill and not to disclose their true diagnoses but to offer milder, less debilitating diseases. Most are told to use the flu as their preferred ailment, and most are to say they expect to be up and about the next day. The managers stock the pharmacy to capacity, and an odd aroma of almonds emanates from it. They overflow the kitchen shelves with all manner of imported goods, and meat appears on the menu every day leading up to the delegation's arrival.

The preacher explains the importance of creating a good impression to get the devils off his back and ensure the commune a future free of out-side interference. He draws a circle on the ground and says the commune is that circle and outside of the circle are the forces determined to break the sovereignty of the commune. Those in the circle are fortunate because they are saved, those outside of it are damned and determined to drag the saved to hell. He says he spent his life fighting evil and this delegation is just another manifestation of it. And he will continue the good fight and protect the circle and everyone in it from those evildoers.

He asks people if they are happy, and if they say yes, as they invariably do, he makes them elaborate on the exact source of their happiness. A guard says he is happy because he lives in the commune. The preacher cor-rects him and says the guard should say the commune lives inside of him because of his faith, that his faith is the first source of his happiness and the second is his location in this veritable paradise. He makes the guard repeat that exact thing. He asks Rose if she misses any aspect of her former life but warns her she cannot say ice cream trucks and chocolate bars and cotton candy and hamburgers. Rose thinks very hard because she knows her answer must have some bearing on her new life as a saved person. She says she misses or rather does not miss the gunshots in her ghetto and she still dreams about hiding under her bed while a battle rages between drug dealers and the police, and this commune makes her pinch herself every day to make sure she has not died and gone straight to heaven. The preacher kisses her and presses a chocolate bar in her hand.

He tries similar bribes to induce the prefect to speak. Since her rescue by Adam, she has not uttered a word, and though she washes and dresses and eats and attends school, she begins a task only if some supervisor tells her to start one and stops only when directed to stop. If someone tells her to sweep a room and leaves her with a broom, she will sweep until the person returns, no matter how long the interval or whether the job is complete. If she is forgotten at the task, then that is where she will be found hours later. Her need for constant supervision makes her the baby again to her parents, and the preacher takes it as a personal challenge that he should get the prefect to say her first words. He offers a chocolate bar, and when she takes it, he keeps hold of it and says thank you, hoping she will understand that his release of the bar is contingent on her saying thank you. She keeps quiet and he tugs at the bar as she tugs at it and the bar breaks, with the prefect getting the lion's share, and the preacher flings away his piece and walks off.

Another time he asks Trina to offer the prefect chocolate, but Trina should keep hold of it until the girl says thank you or something that approximates civil speech. Trina tries to catch the prefect's eye by stooping to look up at her bowed head. But the prefect keeps her head lowered and the chocolate in Trina's hand seems to provide no incentive. Trina tells the prefect that the chocolate is really a gift from Adam and not from the preacher and Adam worries about her and all she has to do is take the chocolate and look at Adam's cage and smile and that will put Adam's mind at ease. The prefect looks at Trina and then at the cage, and sure enough Adam in chains stands in his usual posture, gripping the bars and looking intently through them with his head inclined to the left and to the right in small adjustments, depending on what he looks at and where the action is located.

The prefect takes the bar and holds it up toward Adam, who pushes his hand through the cage. The two girls walk to the cage and the prefect breaks a piece of the chocolate and hands it to Adam, who pops it into his mouth. She breaks another piece and another. Adam takes the last piece and stops just short of putting it in his mouth and offers it back to her. The prefect takes the morsel and smiles and pushes it into her mouth and nods at Adam.

Rose looks on. She asks Trina how she managed to tolerate a scorpion and a tarantula. Trina says what Ryan did, taking bread from the bakery for all of them, was brave. They must keep him hidden and remember to bring him food and water. She tells Rose that she is bravest of all for helping to keep Ryan safe. An insect or two is nothing, Trina says, compared to finding fresh bread and sharing it and taking a beating for the whole group, as Ryan did.

Rose agrees but still wants to know how Trina tolerated the scorpion and tarantula crawling up and down her arms. Trina says she thought about something altogether different from those insects on her arms, and her arms belonged to the preacher for the duration of his experiment. Rose says that Ryan must have put something good in his head when he walked in the dark to the bakery. He imagined everyone in the dormitory with him, linking arms and making a chain of steps in the dark, and that carried him there and back with the loaf of fresh bread.

—He carried us with him in the dark forest.

Rose likes this idea. Trina adds to it. She says that while the body may be trapped in this place, the mind is always free to roam wherever it feels safe.

Later that night, Trina asks her mother if the two of them are the only ones who might try to leave the commune. Joyce looks at her daughter and says nothing. Trina wonders if there is room for two more. Joyce says it would jeopardize a lot of carefully laid plans and Trina must be a hundred percent certain of what her suggestion means, since it could ruin everything. Trina says two more adds up to little more, since the two she has in mind are trustworthy. Joyce says if that is the case, then Trina is correct, but the fewer people who know about the plan, the smaller the risk, so Trina should wait for the time being and not divulge any of it to anyone else. Trina says there might be a way of including others without telling them what is going on. Joyce feels that presents a moral dilemma, since the persons would be fooled into a course of action for their own good rather than out of personal choice. Trina says her faith took away her choice and her loss of faith returned it. If the act of deception saves the person's life, surely it is a good thing. Joyce says it will not be seen as such if the person believes in an afterlife as a better place, that some people think any effort to extend this life on earth merely defers their appointment with paradise.

—Mother, I want to live, but I feel bad that my future will be without my friends.

—Child, the two of us can barely save ourselves, never mind others.

—If there's a way to save everyone who wants to be saved, would you agree to it?

—Of course, Trina. Everyone deserves the chance to live, but we have to be careful; we are in a dangerous place.

—The more I want to leave, the more people I want to take with me.

—Let's put our minds together and see what we can come up with.

The preacher tells his assistants to watch the prefect for signs that her mute condition is but insolence. How else would she smile for Trina and not say thank you to him? Lucky for her he has bigger fish to fry, with the impending arrival of the delegation. This visit promises to be the biggest test of the commune since its arrival to the interior of the country five years ago. But he says he has a bad feeling about it. Politicians typically use one move as a way to get to another position rather than admit defeat to the opposition. Politicians act because their survival matters more than loyalty to a group or idea. And sending this delegation to the commune is a political act, nothing more. He says while the commune fights for its spiritual survival and entry into heaven, the politician merely seeks to protect his material well-being in the here and now. In addition, the preacher worries that no matter how good a show the commune mounts for the delegation, it might leave the place and redouble its opposition.

He asks Nora to give him a shave and cut his hair. He reclines in his armchair and says all the men in the community should cut their hair and shave:

—No long hair, no Afros, no beards, no ponytails, no plaits, this is not a hippie commune.

Nora asks him to please keep still. He keeps muttering about the need to look like a tidy church no matter how big the challenges posed by the environment. Nora nips him with the razor, a small cut that produces a droplet of red over the white soap. She apologizes as he jumps out of the armchair, half of his face clean and half covered in soap and bristles. She drops the razor and he snatches it off the floor and chases her around the armchair and she runs to the front door screaming for help. He stops at the front door and she bounds down the stairs and he pelts the razor at her. He asks the guards at the door to retrieve his razor blade stuck down in the yard and to tell his assistant to come back to the house and to stop making a spectacle of herself.

Trina, Rose, and others bring Ryan food saved a little at a time from their meals. He thanks them but they remind him that he stole bread for them, the sweetest bread they ever tasted, and their scraps are nothing in comparison. He leaves the dormitory in a work detail with other children and never singles himself out from the group and the other children surround him so that he blends in as one of over three hundred children going about their daily chores.

TWENTY-SEVEN

The delegation of concerned parents and relatives, politicians and community leaders, and members of the press arrives at the capital to a full parade organized by the president's office. They stay in the best hotel, with a view of the sea, as guests of the government. The hotel is the only tower of its kind for miles and boasts a bird's-eye view of the muddy Atlantic shoreline. Children bathe in the surf and emerge with mud heads. The delegation watches the children cavorting, and once in a while a breeze lifts their voices to the twelfth-floor balconies. A seawall curves out of sight and couples walk arm in arm along a path on top of it. A fisherman riding a bike on the wall looks like a circus act. The entire lower half of his body and his bicycle draped with a fish net make him and his bicycle resemble a fresh catch getting away on two wheels.

The delegation arrives early to talk to locals who know the commune, to hear what they can about how the commune residents appear to outsiders. The woman who cleans the commune offices in the city says the building is always a hive of activity, even at five-thirty A.M., when she turns up to start cleaning the building from top to bottom—people of all shapes and sizes coming and going, meetings lasting all manner of hours, and lots of prayer, loud and persistent and liable to break out at any moment but nothing sinister. The electrician says the place uses a lot of electricity and has more electrical outlets and surveillance equipment than usual for that size property and for an ecclesiastical undertaking. The parking meter attendant says they always have cars coming and going, but they always beg him for grace when he tries to write a visitor a ticket. They carry guns, but they never make him feel that he cannot write them a ticket if he wants to write one.

No children are ever seen at the offices. No one in the city ever converts to the discipline because the terms of surrendering everything to the commune exceed by far the usual tithe or midweek Bible study or any of the extra demands of a church on its community to serve, to worship, to testify, to sing, and to bring in others. The delegation asks to tour the building, and the commune says the place has been recently mothballed and all activities moved back to the commune. The official date for their visit must be respected.

The president's office outlines the social and economic benefits of the commune to the country. The delegation sees flowcharts and graphs of facts and figures about the jobs the commune creates for the country and the money it spends. Chief among the benefits to the young and the old, the ungodly and the materialist, has to be the commune's Christian faith; it presents an enduring and convincing model of a productive citizen. The president's office wants to know how a delegation can find fault with people who read the Bible and worship daily.

The American politician leading the delegation says he has testimony that those who join the church can never leave it and must cut all ties with relatives outside of it. If people really associate with the church of their own free will, then why the secrecy and remote location? Why the hostility to scrutiny from outsiders? What about the parents who have left the church and say their children are still being held captive? These are some of the questions that a visit will settle. Has the commune committed some crime, crossed some legal line, or contravened some rule? The delegation lists contempt of court and some shady financial dealings back in the U.S. The delegation must see the place to ascertain whether the inhabitants, who are still U.S. citizens though far away, remain there voluntarily. And there is the unresolved issue of the subpoena for the three children and the preacher's dismissal of a court order. The delegation and the president's office debate this for a while:

—Your police force, bound by the courts, needs to enforce these court orders.

—But our police force has its hands full chasing dangerous criminals. The commune leader is no danger to society.

—Not to your society maybe, but what about his thousand followers?

—They're American citizens.

—In that case, a conscientious American is well within his rights to make a citizen's arrest of this man.

—Have you traveled all this way to make a citizen's arrest?

—No, the delegation's mission is a fact-finding one.

The delegation tours the botanical gardens. They admire the gigantism of Rafflesia, and right on cue, a flower as big as a hand basin and sealed for twenty years opens its vault and emits the strongest and most nose-pinching rotten-meat smell south of the equator, to the delight of the delegation, who reach for cameras and handkerchiefs to cover their noses and mouths. The gardeners tell them that this is a lucky omen for their visit and that they should make a wish. Many people pause and think of something that they dearly want to happen. If only this sealed flower were the commune waiting to open its gates and reveal all to the delegation. At the zoo, they stop and wait for the sloth to stop imitating a carbuncle on a tree trunk, but to no avail, and an anteater snorkeling a viand of ants earns applause and shudders from the delegation. Many nibble at blood pudding but draw the line at souse—pig feet in a clear lime stew. And mutton in a bun proves too stringy for some. The biggest hit is the country's red rum, for its sweetness and the traces of molasses. The iced tea, brewed from a root, tastes too medicinal; the shavings of sugared coconut, fried with a touch of spice, too distinctive. Most of the delegation tries to limbo but give up about waist-level and marvel at the locals scraping the floor with their backs to make it under the stick.

The delegation walks along Market Street outside the covered area with its cavernous alleys and lopsided shops of dubious commercial brokerage. They interview vendors and shoppers alike, and each time they ask about the commune, they are painted the same picture of efficiency and beneficence. But then the handpicked guides of the delegation confuse a right turn with a left, and by the time they get their bearings, it is too late. The delegation is halfway along a row of diminutive shops and overstocked stalls belonging to the government opposition, and the same question to shoppers and vendors results in talk about commune men moving around the city in packs, wielding Kalashnikovs and big sticks and buying favors from high-ranking ministers, and in one instance armed commune guards look on as a woman from the commune whips a grown man in public for going about his humble business in ways of which the commune does not approve.

—The government hires them to break up our demonstrations.

—They run people out of business and out of town if you cross them.

An old woman lifts the blouse to show the delegation the scars on her back from a beating she claims she received at the hands of commune guards at the central office, who accused her of stealing. Like judge, jury, and executioner, they just decided she must be guilty, and they beat her black and blue and threw her into the street half-naked. No police would take her case, she says, when they heard from her mouth that the commune had beaten her up like that.

Others say that pork-knockers embark on diamond prospecting trips into the jungle and emerge months later from the bush with precious stones and with stories of a commune where people disappear.

—They walk into the place and are never seen again, and the ovens smell of burning flesh.

—The children have no parents, and the adults behave as if they were born full grown and self-sufficient and never needed suckling.

A man with long dreadlocks and a crooked staff (to correct a limp he says he got from a snakebitten ankle) describes how he worked as a guide in the jungle interior for a U.S. government agent who told him that the commune is a mind-control experiment.

—How else can so many Americans commandeer so much of our land and do whatever they please without any inquiry from our government?

—They're there to mount an attack on the neighboring country because they occupy disputed territory.

—They have enough guns and chemicals to defeat our army and take over our country.

The delegation makes copious notes. Their time in the country has been managed so well that, to this point, they have encountered only citizens held under the government's mesmeric influence. But the picture of the commune painted by these eyewitness accounts, even if partially hearsay, adds to the troublesome one the delegation left their own land with and crossed the sea to find corroborative evidence about. Nearly a thousand lives are at stake, many hundreds of them children.

—I don't want to give my name. My child is held captive at the commune. I made the mistake of walking into their office and asking about their commune after they gave me food and money to get me through a bad patch I was going through. I took the boat ride with my child, and we got there, and after a day or so, no more, I realized my big mistake. The food was scarce and the children trained to punish each other for the slightest mistakes, and the adults worked from sunup to sundown and the kids were put to work before and after school, and the one sermon I heard made me believe I was in hell and waiting to get to heaven. I wanted to take the next boat out of there. But they would not let me leave. They surrounded me and asked what made me such a weak woman and a bad mother for a child who needed guidance. They said I had to stay. That faith in the commune was a process. They carried long sticks, and I could see I was next in line for a beating. But I kept saying I wanted to leave. Then they told me: Okay, you can go, but your child must stay. They insisted I was free to leave and they made my child tell me to my face that I could go but she wanted to stay there. I was chased out of the place with big sticks, and my poor girl had to stay behind. No one in charge in this city wants to hear my story. Thank you for coming all this way to do something about it. My girl's name is Rose. She's seven now, this was taken a little after her sixth birthday.

She hands them a passport-sized color photo of a little girl with a broad toothless smile. Other mothers and fathers press similar pictures of their missing children into the hands of the delegation. The government officials, with help from the police, chase off the surprise petitioners and herd the delegation back onto the official path to the isolated privacy of the luxury hotel. The next thing the delegation knows, the time arrives for their long-anticipated visit to the People's Commune.

A twin-propeller Cessna chartered from an ex–military officer turned entrepreneur waits for them at the capital's private airport. The same flight operator organizes tours of the country's interior for dignitaries from abroad who invariably want to fly over the rain forest and land near a waterfall for lunch, meet a local indigenous tribe, buy a few arts and crafts, and fly back in time for a sumptuous dinner at the best hotel in the city.

As a result of the eyewitness accounts at the market and the pictorial evidence of several children in captivity, the leader of the delegation requests a last-minute meeting with the country's president. Granted a mere fifteen minutes, the delegation leader presents a number of questions. First, does the delegation require security for their visit to the commune? The president replies that he thinks it would be overkill to send a peaceful delegation under armed guard to a Christian camp. The leader of the delegation agrees that their intention is peaceful, a fact-finding mission, and perhaps they have nothing to worry about. Second, can the president guarantee the delegation's safety? And third, what about the rescue of those captive children? The president replies in his most legal voice, tinged with thinly disguised irritation, that because the delegation's visit is not from government to government, and because both delegation and commune are guests of his country and welcome guests so long as both obey the laws of the land, the answer has to be no, his government cannot guarantee the safety of the delegation even if, in his government's humble estimation, no such security is necessary. The president explains away the use of guns by the commune guards this way: One, commune guards have security clearance to bear arms; two, they carry guns as a result of their remote location frequented by wildlife, bandits, and pork-knockers; and three, with no proper police presence in the area to summon in an emergency, it makes sense for them to police themselves. The president even tries to make light of the situation with an anecdote. He says the only rumor he ever hears is about some drunkard watch repairman whose sole complaint against the commune is that the guards fired on him and destroyed his precious timepieces. The president can hardly contain himself as he chuckles and concludes by saying that by firing on the watch repairman's merchandise of various and sundry timepieces, it is clear that the commune guards were not trying to kill the watch repairman but trying to kill time.

—These aren't dangerous people. They're holy crusaders—idiosyncratic mavericks, I grant you, but not sinister in any way.

The president reduces his chortle to a smile and looks at his watch as the more persistent members of the delegation wave their petitions from concerned parents. He gives up on getting rid of the delegation and orders tea and tells his secretary to cancel his next meeting. The president asks if the parents of the children will be satisfied with evidence that their young offspring are happy at the commune. If the minors elect to remain at the commune, will the relatives accept their decision? The relatives, between accepting finger food off trays pushed at them by young men dressed from head to toe in white, feel it fair for an adult to choose to do as he pleases but not a good thing to leave such a choice up to an impressionable child, given the very high probability of coercion. The president, who prefers white sugar to brown, provides both kinds for his guests. He directs a waiter to add spoon after spoon to his cup of tea, and he speculates aloud if it would not be wiser for the concerned relatives to act at that future time when such a change of heart occurs rather than cause a fracas now.

The relatives respectfully inform the president that he has way too much regard for the preacher, who masks his bad actions with the holy cloth. The president sets aside his very sweet tea and sits back in his high chair. Surely the president must have heard about the preacher's claims to cure the crippled and the diseased, feats of chicanery performed with the collusion of trusted followers to lure new and gullible followers into the organization. The highest office in the land says that the man he knows as the commune's leader never claimed such powers on this soil and never performed any miracle healings to win gullible converts. The president encourages the relatives to eat and drink as much as they wish, but he has another appointment, and will they kindly excuse him. The relatives of the delegation protest that the preacher preys on the poor and the weak and collects the pensions of the old and vulnerable. The president pauses at the door and says that sounds a lot like taxation, but the relatives do not find his quip the slightest bit funny.

The moment the president returns to his office, he makes a private call to the leader of the commune and asks how he is keeping. The preacher hears the smirk in the way the president says his name, but nevertheless replies that his feet are bothering him, fluid retention, and he cannot sleep well, worrying about the delegation coming to disturb the peace of his community. The president wants to know if he should worry about the safety of this high-level delegation or whether he can trust his old friend to handle the matter. The preacher says he would be insulted by the insinuation that he and his members were prone to violence had it not come from the trusted leader of the country where he and his members were honored to be guests, no, the president should not worry, and no again to any notion of violence on the part of his members against the delegation. He hopes the delegation is not coming all this way to stir things up and disrupt his peaceful community. Has the president heard of any violence within the community? No. Has any indigenous Indian in the area complained about any disturbance at the community or received any violent threat from members of the community? No.

—Well, actually, now that you mention it, there is the matter of the pig farm polluting the river, and there are rumors of commune guards forming some sort of firing squad and shooting down the forest.

The preacher ignores this altogether and asks the president to imagine what it would take to drive the commune to violence against anyone, what type of threat and what manner of provocation.

—I don't know. What would it take?

—A lot, Mr. President, a whole lot.

The president wishes the reverend good luck with the visit and promises him all the help of the highest office in the land to see that the delegation departs the capital expeditiously upon its return from the commune. The preacher thanks him, but the call ends without the usual cordial goodbye. The president pelts his chewed cigar across the room. The preacher pounces on a guard and pounds him with his fist.

Trina wishes to secure permission from the preacher to rehabilitate the prefect struck dumb by the tarantula. The prefect's parents express gratitude for the help with their daughter from someone gifted with insects and animals and people. Trina asks the preacher for the scorpion boy, so called by the other children, to be included in her therapeutic plan to cure him of wetting his bed and to stop his hair loss, both maladies inflicted upon him by the insect sermon, as the commune has come to call it. The preacher asks her what she has in mind. She says she will not stray off commune property, but she has a plan to reintroduce the girl and the boy to the rewarding side of life in the forest, lessons she has learned herself from the commune's schools.

She wants her mother to be her assistant. The preacher says Trina understands him more than most; she cues into his ideals better than most. And if she plays her cards right, one day she can lead lost souls, just as he does. With that, Trina and her mother walk to the river with Ryan, his head shaved, included in the therapeutic group of Rose and the two prefects. Kevin guards them. As they pass Adam's cage, Trina, Rose, and Ryan run their hands along the bars and touch Adam's hands poking through. Adam's chain is removed from his ankle to allow the torn skin to heal. The group marches toward the pig farm, and Trina looks back at Adam several times, and each time he waves at her with a flick of the back of his hand, and Trina thinks he might be ushering her away from this place. She waves at him, copying his gesture of shooing flies from a surface.

The party turns right at the pig farm and eases along the trail that slopes down to the pier. Joyce and Trina try to remain calm and act casual and avoid each other's eyes just in case seeing one or the other's glee triggers some uncontrollable reaction that might make Kevin suspicious. Joyce stops in the path and tells the children to look closely at a broad leaf, and they bunch up close and peer at it, and the blemish on the leaf sprouts a head and legs and hops away and croaks at them. They hear more frogs than they can see. Guided by an expert Ryan, they shout at each other about their sightings: a caterpillar with bands of flesh and feet like waves coming into shore, a butterfly as big as a dinner plate mistaken for a large piece of bark on the ground until it flaps and lifts away from them, a colony of bees formed in a black cloud around a newly hatched queen moving overhead in a promenade of kazoos.

The group meets Eric at the wharf. Soon Kevin and Eric wander a little away from the dock, engrossed in conversation. The children search for flat stones on the riverbank and skip them on the water to see who makes the most skips. Ryan enjoys this right away and counts for everyone. He asks where Kevin and Eric got to, and Joyce says they are sure to be nearby, spying on them. Ryan watches everyone's attempt with a stone and counts the result aloud each time. Trina tells him that she can do her own counting, thank you, and she looks at the mute prefect for solidarity, but the prefect looks away. The five youngsters search for the best stones to skip, choosing and discarding one for another, and straightening from their search to watch each other taking turns skipping the flattest stones on the water.

Joyce divides her time between scanning the slope for signs of Kevin and Eric, watching the children, and looking up- and downriver for any traffic as she sits on the landing pier and swings her legs and her toes just skim the water. The mute prefect finds a particularly flat stone that fits into her hand as if molded by her palm. She aims at the river and swings her arm and sends the stone skidding on the surface, one, two, three, four, five, six, seven, eight times. And that is how the prefect counts aloud and for herself and smiles. Everyone looks at her and she covers her mouth and they nod approvingly and she takes her hands off her mouth and smiles. They hear a hum and turn toward the water, wrinkled by a faint breeze, and they see this rainbow vessel tacking toward them with the captain and first mate waving. The children hold on to each other and on to Joyce and do everything in their power to keep calm and still rather than jump up and down and wave.

Kevin asks Eric if his love for the commune is greater than his love for him.

—I love God, and He sent me to the preacher and this commune, where I met you.

Kevin counters that their love cannot thrive here, that there is no place here for their kind of love.

Eric declares that this situation may be a test:

—If we're patient, we'll be rewarded.

—Are you certain about the afterlife?

—As certain as my love for you.

The first mate throws a mooring line to Joyce, who catches it, kisses it, and ties a layman's knot around the anchor post. The first mate aims a stick with a hook at the landing pier and pulls from the back of the boat, which swings in a perpendicular arc from the river to the dock. The captain leans and looks aft and stern as he maneuvers with a series of reverse and forward engine thrusts; the river boils around the propellers. The first mate jumps off the boat, followed by the captain. Everyone hugs and exchanges hurried introductions. The first mate jumps back onto the boat, and the captain lifts the children over the side to the first mate. The prefects say they cannot board the boat and they prefer to return to their parents at the commune. There is an awkward pause in which the captain looks at Joyce and she says fine and tells them to stay on the wharf until the boat is out of sight. She hugs them, and Rose and Ryan lower their heads, but Trina looks agitated. The captain and first mate glance around to see if anyone might be coming to the pier. Each takes Joyce by the hand and helps her, one handing over to the other as Joyce takes a big step from the dock into the boat. The captain jumps aboard and takes the wheel as the first mate unties the mooring strop with a raised eyebrow at the terrible knot, flings it aboard, and climbs on.

Eric says they should get back to the landing pier just to show their faces and keep Joyce in check, in case she has something up her sleeve.

—What can she do out here? One more question: What if the preacher asks us to die for him?

Eric replies that it won't be for him but for Christ.

—I wish you could feel my certainty.

—I do when you talk about it like that. I hope you are right.

Joyce hugs Trina, Ryan, and Rose, and the captain opens full throttle upstream from the pier. They wave at the prefects on the dock. Trina shouts at her mother, and her mother hears her but asks her to repeat it to be sure she heard right.

—Mother, we have to go back for Adam and the other children.

—Darling, we are free of this place. We should count our blessings.

—We must go back for Adam and the other children. Please, Mother. We must.

—It's too late, darling.

The captain looks at the first mate for help with the talk, since he cannot hear, and the first mate is positioned much nearer to Joyce and the children. He tells the captain that Trina wants to go back for some Adam and all the other children. The captain shakes his head at Joyce to indicate that this one is her area of expertise and responsibility. Joyce holds Trina and asks her to think very carefully about what they just achieved and how close they came to courting disaster and what luck they had in securing the safety of Ryan and Rose.

—I dreamed this very moment, Mother, us on this boat with Adam and the other children, otherwise we don't make it.

—But Trina, we cannot go back, not now, darling, please be reasonable.

Trina breaks from her mother's embrace, runs to starboard, and leaps into the water and disappears. Joyce screams and the captain shouts to everyone to hold on and he throws the engine into reverse, which jolts the boat and throws everyone forward. The captain swings the wheel several revolutions to the right to cut as steep a curve as possible without taking on water. The first mate grabs a buoy attached to a rope and dives into the river and swims as hard as he can to the spot where Trina disappeared. His head ducks under the river and his back curls up and under as he propels himself down.

Joyce lunges to the side of the boat, but Ryan and Rose hold on to her and cry for her to stay with them and barely succeed in keeping her on board. The captain shouts at Joyce to wait for his first mate to do his job. She stops fighting to free herself and they all come to a standstill and stare at the water, and apart from the buoy rope attached to the boat, there is no movement. The captain calls Joyce to take the wheel and he pulls his shirt over his head and kicks off his boots. He runs aft and starboard, and just as he is about to dive overboard, up pops the first mate with Trina in one arm and the buoy in the other. The captain extends his arm and pulls Trina out of the river and passes her to Ryan and Rose. He helps his first mate up and pats him and they retrieve the buoy and the captain takes the wheel from Joyce, who runs to Trina and hugs her. The captain sets the engine in neutral and turns to Joyce to see what he should do.

—Take us back to the pier. Trina's right. We can't leave all those children behind.

The captain opens his eyes wide and inhales deeply to hold his tongue. His first mate looks at him and shrugs. The captain aims the boat back to the wharf, where they are met with puzzled looks from the prefects. The captain passes the children to the first mate before helping Joyce out of the boat.

—Aubrey, you owe my daughter an Anansi story, remember?

—When shall I come back?

Joyce stares at the captain, unsure what to say, having heard exactly what she needs to hear from him.

—Stay close to here if you can.

Kevin and Eric walk out of the trees and meet Joyce, Trina, Ryan, and Rose and the two prefects at the dock. Kevin asks Joyce what in hell's name she is doing back on commune property. Joyce says she must go back and save the children. Kevin says there is no time left to save everyone and she should save herself, that this is Eric's last shift before another guard takes over the area. Joyce thanks Kevin and tells him he is a good man to distract Eric for her. He says she should stuff her thanks, because all his efforts are in vain now that she and Trina are right back in the lion's den.

Trina cries all the way back to the compound. She apologizes over and over to her mother for dragging her into more trouble. Joyce tells her to stop apologizing for doing what is right. As they walk into the clearing by Adam's cage, Adam jumps up and down and shakes the bars. He seems simultaneously mad and glad to see them. A few people ask why Trina is soaked through. Joyce says a minor mishap at the pig farm. Joyce asks Ryan and Rose to stick close to Trina and to her, since the next few hours will be vital for all of them. Ryan and Rose ask what they should say when asked about the trip to the river.

—Tell them you skipped stones on the river. Come with me, young lady, you need to change out of those wet clothes.

Joyce heads for the laundry house and tailor shop with a drenched Trina trailing after her.

—She fell in a pig trough. I had to hose her down.

Joyce slows and pulls up beside Trina and drapes an arm over her daughter's shoulder and pulls her close. Trina puts her arm around her mother's waist. As they walk, Joyce leans toward her daughter's ear and divulges a few things of such importance that they widen Trina's eyes and trigger the seventeen muscles that it takes to smile and return the sprightliness to her steps.

They wave simultaneously at Adam. He makes synchronized pendulums of his arms. Joyce waits on Trina as she washes away the smell of the river, fusses with a towel, and wriggles into dry clothes. Joyce zeroes in on Trina's head with a mother's mix of comb strokes, gentle tugs, and prods with her articulate fingers, her eyes steeped in thought as she divides her daughter's hair.

—My darling daughter, you must outlive me.

—No, Mum, let's grow old together.

Joyce sticks the comb in a tuft on Trina's skull, and with free hands, her fingers interlace and scissor as she plaits a neat row along Trina's scalp from the front, where her child's hairline meets her forehead, to the back, at the nape of her neck.

—Where're we from again, Mom?

—Redwood.

—Where's that?

—In San Mateo County.

—California.

—West Coast.

—U.S.A.

—North America.

—Western hemisphere.

—Earth.

—The galaxy.

—The universe.

Joyce stands and steps aside from the chair and away from her daughter, who looks up at her. She sets the comb on the chair and stoops down and grabs her daughter tightly. Trina pauses for a moment, then throws her arms around her mother and soaks up the kisses planted on her neck and the whisper of love and love and you, you, you, which she says back to her mother in an echo of love and you and I and you too.

TWENTY-EIGHT

The preacher calls the president:

—Can't you do something, anything, to stop them from coming?

—What should I do with the eyes of the world watching?

—Fuck the eyes of the world. Throw all of them off the twelfth floor. Just don't fob them off on me.

—You know these people cannot be harmed. The best course is to show them what they want and be rid of them. You have a self-sufficient community—show them that; show them your schools, your choir—

The preacher cuts off the president:

—Don't tell me how to do my job when you can't do yours.

The president's earpiece hums, killed at the other end.

The president asks for all calls from the preacher to be blocked.

—Who does he think he's talking to? Two-bit con man lording it over a bunch of losers.

The president knocks his portrait of the preacher off his desk, and the framed glass smashes on the floor.

At the same time, the preacher looks for something to throw against a wall or someone to grab and hit, but Dee, Nora, and Pat slide out of reach and the guards make themselves scarce.

The preacher takes off his dark glasses and flings them.

—You pay for what you never get in this country.

He storms outside. The guards at the door jump to attention. He leaps off the front porch and squints skyward and throws up his arms and shouts at the glare of the sun:

—Let them come! Let them come and see what I can do!

He feels around him, hardly able to see in the open. He scoots back into the house.

—Pat! Dee! Nora! Bring me my dark glasses. Dammit.

The pilot of the twin-engine Cessna informs the passengers that the journey to the compound involves a small detour, by popular request, past the country's famous falls. The passengers applaud. The plane taxies and climbs off the runway in sixty thunderous seconds. The pilot reports excellent weather but warns that his forecast is subject to dramatic change in this mountainous, forested terrain. In no time the buildings thin out, with the capillaries of dirt roads running in crisscross fashion among voluminous trees. Trees fill the windows, and a river twists out to an expanse of sea.

The plane crosses the river at a wide juncture in its course, and at some point the water seems as wide as a sea, with its own islands and small powerboats dragging their tails up- and downstream. A passenger who tried too much of the country's signal red rum the night before reaches into the back of the seat in front of him just in time to catch the contents of his bilious stomach in the waxy bag that he quickly unfolded. People around him squirm and cover their noses to quell the contagion of stomach juices. They pretend not to notice anything, and he holds up a piteous hand as he continues to retch into the bag.

For the next hundred miles, a host of greenery looms. As far as sight, the ground looks stuffed with broccoli. The bulbous, crumpled, inflated, vibrant, slumbering, towering, seemingly endless jungle makes the plane feel like a toy that, if dropped into the wild arrangement of greenery below, would be swallowed and never found. A clearing opens up: brown and red naked earth like a scar, with bulldozers pressing into the giant trees, felling them one by one and wounding the forest. Columns of smoke dawdle above large brick ovens dedicated to burning trees to make charcoal. Other clearings reveal huts and half-naked figures staring up with a hand in salute to shade the eyes. And just as the passengers begin to talk about their business at the commune, some of them wonder what they will find. They pass through cloud and the windows streak with rain and the plane banks and emerges from cloud and beside them the wall of water drops and turns to mist far below. A rainbow arches over the plane and the passengers crane their necks to catch the colors as they fly through the rainbow and for a moment the banked aircraft, the endless waterfall, the plunging rainbow above and below scramble their bearings and invert polarities so they have no idea if the falls they see go down or up and the rainbow loops like a skipping rope for the plane to jump over.

The compound strings a banner that welcomes the delegation to the commune. The residents hang yellow and green commune flags, alternated with flags of their adopted country and flags of their home country. These strings of three flags drape over entrances and between buildings and signal the commune's alliance to three places. Each flag represents a distinct geography, but taken together, as an amalgamation, they amount to no place found on earth. The residents break into opposing groups. Most people say they should obey the preacher and not listen to the delegation, whose visit spells trouble for everyone, but some think this may be their only opportunity to break with the commune, whose leader seems to be in meltdown. They debate in fierce whispers: He cried when they hit the children, he made children beat their parents, he cut his wrists to prove a point, he thinks he is impervious to bullets, he lies down with a gorilla in its cage. Perhaps the jungle experiment is a failure. Maybe their faith needs some other communal outlet. What loving God asks parents to poison their children as a means to salvation? Can a delegation made up of the press, politicians, and blood relatives really be such a dangerous entity and pose a threat to the commune? How? These questions rage among commune members as they work side by side, so the talk in the compound is at a higher pitch, and the preacher and his managers put it down to excitement about the delegation's imminent arrival.

Various scouts and prefects report the growing dissent to the preacher, who says he has a special surprise in store for those in the commune who want to be deserters. He reminds everyone over the loudspeakers what happens to deserters in the military during a time of war—and this is a time of war for the commune, as they are about to face the most serious assault ever mounted against them.

—This is our last stand, right here. Anyone comes here, our rules apply. People ask me all the time why we don't turn the other cheek to our attackers, like good Christians. Why? So they can slap that side as well? And if they run out of sides to slap and want to keep hitting us, what else is there for us to offer up to them? I say we are not just passive Christians. We do not just turn the other cheek. The Good Book says, "If mine enemy smite me I shall smite him back with interest." We are crusaders. We are soldiers of Christ the Savior. We do not turn the other cheek. This is where we make our last stand. Repeat after me. We are soldiers of Christ.

—We are soldiers of Christ.

—We do not turn the other cheek.

—We do not turn the other cheek.

—If mine enemy smite me I shall smite him back with interest.

—If mine enemy smite me I shall smite him back with interest.

He calls together his senior guards and announces that any of his followers in the commune who elect to leave with the visiting delegation must not be allowed to do so under any circumstances. He says the result of any defections would be an endless stream of official visits and renewed scrutiny and the beginning of the end for the commune. He reminds them how far they have all come since their days scratching out a living in a country that throws away its people by the boatload: in wars, in prisons, in high homicide rates, in abject poverty, in ghettos, in godless materialist pursuit. The commune was born out of this necessity, to save the souls of the few left in the country who believed in the kingdom of heaven. They ran from terrible destructive forces to find peace in this jungle as they prepared for salvation, and now the day looms large as the devil's emissaries near the compound.

He turns on the commune's loudspeakers and announces that the Day of Judgment is near. People stop last-minute preparations for the delegation and begin to pray. He says the delegation's arrival will drive a wedge between parent and child, brother and sister, husband and wife, and as their protector, he must launch a final counterattack to save them from suffering and assure their passage to eternity.

—You know what we have to do, brothers and sisters, you know how we can escape the devil coming in disguise to tempt you and rob you of your place in heaven. You know what we must do. You must answer the call when you hear it. You trust me in this, and we shall meet again in heaven. Don't be afraid. Something scares you, and you come running to me with your tails between your legs. You know what I have to put up with, alone, every night? You want to know what I have to face on account of all of you? Death. Death walks up to me and says it is my turn to go on a little trip with him, to a place he set aside just for me. I look at his animal shape and hoof feet, horns on his head, and I nod without a word of protest or any hesitation. I want to say to him, I've been expecting you, what took you so long? But he knows my thinking even before I know it, and knowing me the way he does, he just walks up to me and claims me as his prize. We do not waste air with words after he identifies me. I nod. You want Father? The devil nods. And I say, Father dead, family done. And we stroll off together.

—Our walk to end all walks builds into a trot until next thing we are flying. Instead of a journey skyward, we tunnel to the center of the earth. I feel none of this, numb from head to toe. The tips of my fingers feel numb. I want to take the devil's hand. Not that he offers it. But I do not. That, too, would be a waste of energy. I want to attack him in the name of Christ, but I think better of it, unsure what he would do to me in my flesh-and-blood state. I do not feel pain. My numb body registers nothing, but I remember pain, and the memory is enough to serve as a warning to be careful. I know from stories about the devil that death has a lot of bad things in store for me and that I deserve them all.

—To tell you the truth, I expect God to come and claim me, not the devil. I expect life, eternal life, not hell and damnation. I disguise my mild surprise at seeing the devil as intrigue, too tired to muster the suitable level of outrage. God, I did all this for You, and this is how You repay me? I think this. My evil escort glances at me as if to encourage me to think something complimentary about him fast, or I will face the consequences. This time flying headlong downward, with the earth parting for us, takes time and no time at all. I think the way we move appears to be outside of time, looking at a fish tank populated with varieties of time. I tap the glass to see a piece of time dart from me, a colorful piece with long fins and large eyes and rainbows for scales. I tap the glass again and a sign looms up that says: Do Not Tap Glass. No please, no explanation, but I cannot disobey. Once I read it, I must comply with it.

—I could have written it myself. I say it enough times. I say enough to fill a library. I do not write a word. I want my books to boil in the blood of my people, to fill the seashells of their ears with their constant roar. All my life I need one book and one book only, the Good Book. And from it, I spin my talking books. Not one man or woman tells me to my face that I am bad for them or their children. Not one. My enemies attack me from a safe distance. Across the sea. In courtrooms. What kind of fight do you call that? Spineless. Bloodless.

—God comes to me in my sleep. He takes the form of a branch scratching against the windowpane. The branch writes on the glass, and I read the writing, and though written from the outside, the words flow nevertheless from left to right and join up. The branch says, "Do not eat of the fruits of man. Eat from the orchard of the Lord. Do not drink from the well, drink from the spring that feeds the well." I wake and read it, not once but a few times, before it fades. I take the teaching to mean that I should listen to my voice and not the clamoring voices of others. It gives me permission to open the Good Book and speak directly from it as I see fit.

—Why a branch? I was a young man, a teenager poised at seventeen between the boy I was and the man I would become. The writing on the window thrust me into manhood. I did not look back. My mother tried to beat me for repeating the dream. She said it should never be made public, since the whole thing blasphemed against all the known teachings of the Lord. I left home. I slept in shelters. It took me a long time to make people listen. They thought me mad and a swindler. I made it plain that I was out to capture their soul for God, and if that was a swindle, I was surely a swindler with a capital S and proud of it. Not dangerous pride. God would stem the flow of all falseness of spirit, like pride. I would rather hold my hand in a naked flame than harbor one ounce of pride.

—As I say in my nightmare, I fly with the devil, and I think deep underground should be hot, but it is cold. I picture steam, hot springs, volcanoes in subterranean tunnels lit by spontaneous flames shot from lava, but it is pitch black. It is so dark, we seem to cut through the blackness to make our way. Perhaps the devil takes me to the North Pole rather than the center of the earth. Or the devil has lost his bearings. I have a compass around my neck, tucked under my shirt. I should offer it to him if he keeps pretending he knows where he is going. I reach for it and the pointer spins and spins. I shake it and still it rotates. The devil is not taking me forward, sideways, slantwise, or even backward; the devil revolves on the spot and the revolutions spin so fast they throw off the world, chunks of it at a time, for something that is not a world at all. And the moment I work this out for myself, the devil begins to slow down, but my compass keeps spinning.

—Is the devil tired? I think not. The devil must be near home. I have to make my move. Devil, I shout as we come to a standstill, before you roast me or freeze me or tear me to pieces, I have a statement to make in my defense. The devil without a face always looks taller, thinner, than his victims. The devil favors black attire, a simple black gown and hood, hooves, and a staff nearly his height with special powers. That is my comic-book version of the devil. In truth, the devil operates out of me, and that's why he succeeds in directing my every move. I follow his lead and yet I seem alone with my thoughts. The compass continues to spin. I may be standing on a magnetic field. I almost throw it away and remember I am not in the usual place with a left and right and up and down. I am in a world of my own making, with my own rules and regulations. Everyone in my world must do what I say or face my punishment. And now here I am, at the mercy of the devil in this same world. Here I may be upended because all around feels solid, no air and no light.

—Devil, do not show me mercy. I do not want your mercy. There cannot be room for mercy if this world of mine is to work for everyone in it. World without end. El Dorado. Shield for all my followers. Show me justice. That I can swallow however big the pill you have for me. In everything I do, let justice be my guide. Real justice has no truck with mercy. Mercy is too much like pity.

—The devil with no face throws off his hood and I see every face from the commune, young and old, man, woman, and child. The time for all those faces to show on the devil's head takes a lifetime and is over in the blink of an eye. I see them all, nearly one thousand people lined up before me as for police. The faces say things I cannot hear. The thousand mouths make shapes for words, single words. I make out a why, and once I recognize it, other words become clear: please, don't, help, God, Father. Mouths that say nothing in life, baby mouths, take shape on a death mask and form words: no, Jesus, devil, mercy.

The preacher wipes his wet face repeatedly and keeps it hidden for several seconds in his handkerchief. Nora, Dee, and Pat surround him, and he pushes them away. His shirt sticks to his skin. The room of faces, all in tears, stare at him and some of them make the sign of the cross. The commune, frozen during the preacher's speech, mobilizes slowly and the people dry their eyes and add a small prayer of their own for a painless transition from this world, across the terrain patrolled by the devil, and into the safety of paradise. Most of them think they will be fine, the preacher has seen it all, has foretold all, has done it all, and he is their leader and he will guide them to the other side.

Trina hurries to the main house to see the preacher. The guard tells her to be a good child and go away, since the preacher is very busy with last-minute preparations for the U.S. delegation. Trina says her wish to see Father concerns these very plans. The guard begs her to leave and says if he disturbs the preacher and makes him angry, he will have to pay a price and it is more than his job is worth. Trina says what if she guarantees to him that the preacher will be pleased and he will be rewarded for interrupting the meeting, would that change his mind?

—He'll be pleased and I'll get a reward?

—Yes, sir.

—But how, Trina?

—I can't tell you. You have to trust me.

He shakes his head and opens the front door and walks in and the preacher shouts at him to get out and he is about to turn and leave when Trina barges past the guard and bows to the preacher and asks him for two minutes of his time, please, please, please. The reverend's face changes from fury to a smile.

—Okay, Trina—just two minutes.

The packed room steams with the sweat of senior guards, managers, and assistants. All of them think Trina has something about her that they cannot pin down and therefore grudgingly respect, but none of them understands what possesses her to walk in at this busy moment, except some inflated sense of her own importance to the commune, fed by the preacher's overindulgence.

—Father, I want us to hold a parade for the delegation. No one in this room has to lift a finger. I know you're all very busy. My mother and the children will help me.

—Go on.

—I want us to hold a parade of the children, the bright future of the commune, all the children of paradise, acrobats, musicians, dancers, all led by Adam dressed up as our mascot.

—I don't know, Trina. I like the idea very much, but Adam and lots of children loose around the place . . .

The once mute prefect pokes her head into the room:

—Father, I will help Trina.

The preacher jumps up out of his chair and rushes over and places his hands on the prefect's shoulder and stoops down and looks up at her and then at Trina.

—How did you do it, Trina? How?

—We played together with the friendly things of the forest, Father.

The prefect nods and speaks.

—I'm sorry I didn't stand still for you, Father, but the tarantula has itchy feet.

The preacher bursts out laughing. He topples backward and rolls on the floor, and the entire room convulses with laughter. The preacher holds his stomach. He points at the prefect.

—Itchy feet. You all hear that, not doubt, not the devil, but itchy feet.

He rolls around and laughs and his assistants help him up. He grabs the prefect and kisses her face several times and sinks into his chair and wipes his face and chuckles all the time and shakes his head. Blood springs from his nostrils and he grabs his face in his handkerchief. He waves her away.

—Go on, Trina. Have your parade. Do whatever you want. You are something else, Trina.

Trina turns to leave, but the preacher remembers something. He beckons to Trina to wait for a second. He examines his bloody handkerchief, and Pat stuffs cotton wool up his nostrils. He waves Trina to come closer and she steps into his embrace and he plants two kisses on her forehead and gives her the key to Adam's cage. Trina hands the preacher her handwritten announcement for him to read over the commune-wide loudspeaker system. She says goodbye and bows to everyone, turns on her heels, and departs with the prefect. The preacher announces to the room of his senior guards and managers and assistants that he cannot wait to see the radiant light that will shine from this child in heaven.

The preacher passes Trina's announcement around the room and solicits the opinion of everyone present. A heated discussion ensues. The majority of the managers, senior guards, and assistants say Trina really has gone too far this time. The preacher says a parade of children might be the very trick needed to thwart the malice of the delegation toward the commune. He reminds them that Christianity should honor children, who are the only ones predisposed to enjoy the fruits of Christ's teachings here on earth because of their innocence. He thinks Trina's plan might be a fine counterpoint to the serious business at hand of matching the delegation strategy for strategy. Fewer guards will need to watch the children. All the children will be in one place and readily accessible. The preacher moves that they pass Trina's motion to hold a parade and that he reads her notice over the PA system as is, no edits. Pat seconds the motion and changes the cotton wool in his nose. The ayes win the motion. There is not a single nay. Several people appear to withhold their vocal support despite no formal abstentions. The preacher claps his hands.

—Motion carried, unanimously.

He reads Trina's announcement over the commune's loudspeakers by first of all calling everyone to attention and adding that this concerns Adam as well.

The commune freezes, taps are turned off, hammers pause over nails, someone stops halfway up or down a ladder, someone pushing a red wheelbarrow rests it on the spot, someone stirring a pot lifts the spoon and lets sauce drip from it. Adam ceases rocking from side to side when he hears his name.

—All children with the following skills are excused from their chores and must report immediately to Trina and her mother, Joyce, in front of Adam's cage for a special meeting: all children in the band, all players of a musical instrument even if it is the kazoo, all gymnasts, dancers, acrobats, jugglers, baton twirlers, clowns, mimes, comedians, orators, singers, magicians, Hula Hoop experts, whistlers, and willing marchers, please report immediately to Trina and her mother, Joyce, in front of Adam's cage.

The commune springs back to life, and the children cheer and run from mops, brooms, laundry, fetching this or that for some adult or other. Of all the noises at the commune, the hymns, the applause, the choir, the band, school rote learning, breakfast, lunch, and supper bells, Trina's flute lessons by Adam's cage, the daily industry of the place, hammering, sawing, jabbering, two-stroke and four-stroke engines, the wildlife of the forest, Adam treasures above all the children's voices unleashed in joy. He jumps up and down and rattles his cage and hoots his own version of happiness. The group of children, over three hundred strong, cheer all the way to the front of Adam's cage.

The parade crowns Adam its king. He wears a crown made of calabash cut to resemble a castle with an elastic strap under his chin; a velvet cloth partly covers the crown and partly hangs around the sides of it, with beads and false precious stones sewn into it. A king's cape trimmed with sequins hangs on Adam's shoulders, and Trina ties it in place with a bow around his neck. Adam holds a scepter, which happens to be a guard's stick covered in fabric fitted at one end with velvet to simulate royalty and authority. Trina plays her flute and marches next to Adam, accompanied by the rest of the band. Gymnasts and acrobats, jugglers and dancers, and characters from cartoons, Halloween, Day of the Dead, and Carnival troop behind Adam and Trina or occasionally break rank to tumble or display an elaborate dance move. A child in a wheelchair and two others on crutches, armed only with whistles, seem happy merely to be part of the procession.

Kevin and Eric guard them to ease many adult minds balking at the idea of children marching around without adult supervision. Trina passes along the instruction to march once around the compound before they process along a special route.

—Once around the compound, then we follow Trina.

Ryan, disguised as Humpty Dumpty, appoints himself cheerleader, complete with megaphone, and although another child twirls a baton and spins around and flings it high and kicks and falls into a split and straightens in time to catch the baton, it is Ryan who shouts the titles of hymns while Trina with her flute plays the Pied Piper and leads the band at the front of the procession. "Onward Christian Soldiers," Ryan says, or "I've Got That Joy, Joy, Joy, Joy, Down in My Heart." The audience sings that line, prompted by Ryan's drawn-out shout—Deep—into the megaphone.

They somersault, dance, juggle, and sing around the campus with adults looking up from their toil and shaking their heads in disbelief. Joyce walks up and down the procession, keeping everyone busy and roughly in place. Adam carries the scepter and heads the parade. Older boys and girls who are not performing carry younger children on their shoulders and dance with them or push the wheelchair or assist someone on crutches. A blind girl walks chaperoned by two children, a boy on one side and a girl on the other, both holding her hands and telling her about everything.

They complete the circuit of the compound before Trina veers onto the path in the direction of the pig farm. Here Joyce asks the children to pick up the pace and the band goes allegro. According to Joyce's gamble, it will take the adults about three minutes to miss the parade and realize the children have not disbanded but disappeared. In this three-minute period, she hopes to create a gap between the children and guards large enough to convey everyone to the pier. She calculates that other guards will head down the three other paths that splay out into the forest from that side of the compound.

Joyce acts as timekeeper and counts the seconds. After two minutes she nods at Kevin, who turns his attention to Eric. Kevin asks Eric if they can have a chat in private. Eric says he has a job to do, so it needs to be quick. Kevin promises it will not take long. They walk off into the woods.

—I've been thinking, Eric, that we should choose how we get to heaven. I don't like the idea of poison: too slow and painful.

The second Kevin and Eric disappear, Trina stops playing and begins to run. Adam follows and all the children trot along. The music stops. Joyce runs back along the line to make sure the children in the wheelchair and on crutches and the blind girl all have assistance and can keep up. Joyce reminds them not to rush and risk a fall, just to keep moving at a comfortable pace, since no one will be left behind. At the pigpen, Joyce opens as many pens as she can, and with the help of some children, she steers the pigs onto the path that leads back to the compound. Trina runs ahead of the group and blows short bursts into her flute.

The slope down to the wharf is easiest of all, and here the children break formation and race to see who will be first to reach the dock. Some drop deliberately to the ground and roll, others tumble, and this creates a competition among the children to see who can make the descent fastest in unorthodox fashion, either a mix of run and roll, or tumble and run, or cartwheel and run, or hop, skip, and jump. The boy in the wheelchair balances on two wheels by leaning back on the move downhill, which affords him a giddy view of the sky. The blind girl takes her cue from the change in the gradient and shakes her hands free of her guides and falls into a vibrant roll and cartwheel. The only rule Joyce insists upon is silence. Adam has the greatest difficulty with this rule, even with inducements of fresh fruit. He drums his chest, throws his teeth to the sky, and cackles. He loses his crown as he puts together the most impressive sequence of cartwheels and somersaults.

At the landing pier, Joyce, Trina, Ryan, and Rose look in both directions of the river, and Adam glances around, too. Joyce seems most anxious of all:

—Come on, Captain, where are you?

Trina scratches Adam's back, and Ryan and Rose inch nearer and add their hands to Adam's back, arched in bliss. Trina says the captain and his first mate will turn up as sure as salvation. They hear engines and search the river but look up just in time to see the sky empty of birds except for one airplane, which crawls past on its way to the nearby airport. A few minutes of palpable quiet pass before the first bird chirps and others pick up and the usual volume of birds resumes, augmented by frogs, cicadas, and monkeys.

A single shot makes them all jump, and Adam becomes agitated. They look in the direction of the trees, and Kevin emerges from a thicket with his hand over his face and his rifle slung crosswise on his midriff. Instead of walking to meet them, Kevin heads up the slope.

—Kevin! Kevin!

But he ignores Joyce and walks faster away from them. The children look at Joyce, and she tells Adam and the children that everything is fine, help will arrive soon and take them all to safety. Trina repeats this to Adam and to the children around her as she continues to scratch his back and he stays calm. Joyce shouts for Kevin and he stops, turns, and waves before disappearing on the trail that leads toward the compound.

—What is he doing?

She does not expect an answer. She wants to go and look in among the trees to see what has become of Eric, but Trina begs her not to leave them and says there is nothing anyone could do now. They turn their attention back to the river. Trina, Ryan, and Rose think of their flung stones skipping on the water and how good it would be to have the properties of a flat stone right at this moment to simply up and cross the river with quick little steps, like so many stones, all the way to the other shore.

They expect the guards at any moment. But looking at the water, how its muscles ripple and make things seem soft and slow, affects the passage of time itself, slowing it to an undulation that might without notice head into reverse and take away from the time they lose standing on the wharf. This trick with chronology means the captain and the first mate could appear at any time, and that would be the right time for them to climb aboard and head out into the river where time stands still.

Three or four shots echo from the area around the trail between the pig farm and the compound. Birds spill from the trees. A volley of gunfire replies to the single shots. Pigs squeal. Joyce thinks it sounds like an exchange from one person to a group and back, Kevin meeting other guards on the trail. The children turn from the water and look up the slope and wait for the guards to appear near the farm and begin the descent to the pier. They look at Joyce for some clue about what they should do other than simply wait to be returned to the compound at gunpoint.

Joyce glances up- and downriver, and seeing nothing but coins in the water and a neat picket fence of green on either side, she turns to her last option for buying time. She walks to Adam, takes his face in her hands, and begs him to do something, anything, to delay the guards and save the children from lining up to drink from the vat. Adam nods. She picks up his scepter and hands it to him. Adam bows his head as he takes the decorated stick and bounds away from the landing, not directly up the slope but adjacent to it, into the trees, to reach the trail between the farm and the compound by the most direct route.

Trina covers her face and sobs, but Joyce asks her to be strong for Adam, and Trina stops and looks at her mother, whose eyes take in the gathering of children, and Trina knows she has to keep calm, not only for Adam. She places her flute to her lips and begins to play one of her spontaneous tunes, and the rest of the band listens and cannot help but improvise with her. Ryan appoints himself conductor, and the musicians look at him periodically as they play. The children hold each other and sway to the music.

Adam drops from a tree in front of the guards. The front few members of the group of fifteen or so backpedal and bump into those following. A couple of guards run from the front toward the back to get away from Adam. A handful of the senior guards aim their rifles at Adam and encourage the other guards to do the same. Adam raises his scepter with both arms over his head. The guards take their eyes off their aim toward Adam and stare at the raised scepter. They appear puzzled by the clarity of the signal for them to pay close attention to him. They glance around and at each other to make sure they are all witnessing the same scene: Adam the commune gorilla in his parade regalia, holding his scepter over his head as if to alter the guards' course of action.

—Stop.

The men hear and do not hear. They register the word, and because it defies logic, many refuse to believe their ears. The bass of the voice, close to a roar, and a growl stretch the word and snap its clarity beyond comprehension. Several of them drop to their knees and begin to pray. They stare at each other and back at Adam. They look into the trees, half expecting the vegetation to spring into action against them. A senior guard tells the others to hold their fire and addresses Adam:

—What did you say?

The senior guard hushes the men, who pray and cry to be spared, from what, they cannot be sure. Guards pull the ones on their knees to their feet. They huddle and begin to organize into a group of armed men. The senior guard speaks to Adam a second time:

—What did you say?

The group waits to hear from Adam. If he remains silent, the first sound will be consigned to chance, a fluke, some trick of the senses. But he dug a hole and escaped from his cage and rescued a girl from jumping into the well and ran from the compound with her. They wait because a part of them is already convinced that Adam really said what they thought they heard him say, and given time, he will oblige them with a repeat. Adam brings the scepter straight down in front of him and pounds the ground.

—Stop.

The repetition, though half expected, brings many more guards to their knees than the first time. They pray and beg for mercy. The senior guards shout at their distressed juniors to stop and stand like men. But many say God is speaking to them through Adam. This is a sign sent by

Him to them, and it is plain as day. The senior guard ignores the protest and the prayers and shouts at his men to take aim as he lifts his rifle and points it at Adam. Adam pounds his stick on the ground once more.

—God.

This definitive speech from Adam being coterminous with the thinking of many of the guards seals the disarray among them. Some pray. Others aim their guns at the few among them, who side with the senior guard and take aim at Adam. Adam advances and pounds his stick with each step and the guards begin to retreat from him, some guards still on their knees scramble to keep their distance.

—God.

The first senior guard to throw away his gun and drop to his knees creates a domino effect of surrender among the rest of the guards. They drop their guns and fall to their knees and clasp their hands and pray, asking for forgiveness and guidance. They cry. Adam stands and watches them, and they alternate between keeping an eye on Adam and imploring the heavens. Adam walks up to the guards in a slow rolling gait, his staff hitting the ground with each step, and though they shrink from him, he reaches out and touches them and passes between them as he walks toward the compound. The guards understand they must abandon their pursuit of the children and follow Adam.

A second contingent of guards comes upon the scene. They puzzle over what they see—their colleagues in the middle of prayer, apparently to a gorilla carrying a colorful stick and wearing a regal cape. But Adam stands in the path of the second group of guards and advances toward them, and they do not wait for an explanation of the puzzle. The senior guard aims at Adam and fires. Adam falls and pushes himself upright, compensating for his wounded left shoulder. The guards in the middle of supplication shout at their colleagues to stop shooting, but the senior guard fires again and someone in the prayer group grabs a rifle and shoots the senior guard and a firefight breaks out between the two groups with the shouting of God and murder.

Adam crawls into the trees. At some point, reason prevails among the guards and the two groups cease their fire and talk with a degree of urgency about Adam and the children and the delegation and God. They count their dead and injured. They split into two smaller groups, one to raise the alarm at the commune, the second to continue to the dock and collect the missing children. The group returning to the commune gathers the injured and leaves the dead for later. The guards heading for the dock redouble their efforts to get there. They blame the whole incident on Joyce and Trina. Only Adam has paid; so, too, will that woman and her witch of a daughter pay for sowing chaos.

At the pier, a shadow appears on the water. Instead of silver in a treasure chest on the water, a dark line takes over. The line breaks into smaller shadows, and the pieces crawl toward the jetty and grow in stature with each moment of looking at them. Trina points and the children begin to ask what the mass might be, not a boat, but yes, there is a boat in front, and all the smaller things are river creatures, or what, or yes, canoes, dozens of canoes surround the disguised *Coffee*, and the captain lifts his cap and waves it twice, then puts it back on, and the children wave and jump up and down and hug each other. The canoes vary in size from long, with two paddlers, to small, with a single paddler. The indigenous Indians who steer them work very fast to keep up with the *Coffee*. The strong swimmers among the children move along to the end of the pier and wade out to meet the canoes. The younger children and those who need assistance wait on the *Coffee* to dock. They discuss if they should leave without their parents or return to the compound, and they wonder what will become of them.

Adam cuts through the forest and reappears at the top of the slope, cutting off the guards and watching the children board the boats from where he sits on the path that leads to the compound. The guards stop at the sight

of Adam, who is between them and the escaping children, and a guard
asks him to let them pass and do their work for the commune and save
the children led astray by the devil. Adam shakes his head. This confirms
his language capability for the guards who heard him earlier, but for those
who did not hear him, it is a revelation. They react with disbelief and
seek reassurance from one another and look at Adam as if he might be an
apparition whose original incarnation as a man could be restored at any
moment.

Blood trickles from Adam's left shoulder and from his stomach. He
sits in the middle of the path and faces the guards. His stick keeps him
upright. He decides not to let them pass. They will have to shoot him
again. The guards plead with Adam to move aside, to join them, to bring
the children back, to speak again, to tell them what they should do, to
come back to the commune and show the reverend the miracle of a beast's
tongue moved by divine will.

—Stop.

Adam shakes his head slowly. His lips move again, but no sound
emerges. The guards debate whether there is another way to get to the
dock or if they should just wait for more help to arrive or simply shoot
Adam and put him out of his stubbornness and wounded misery. They
decide to shoot him and cook up a story that the shots were fired by the
dead guards and they happened upon Adam's body. They lift their rifles
and steady them at Adam and pray for forgiveness for what they are about
to do. Adam closes his eyes. His body leans on his stick, but his mind
propels him from a sprint along a forest floor to a miracle of legs running
on air up among the trees, a headlong sprint, a blur of speed, a figure in
the distance waiting to greet him whose open arms will be his finish line.

TWENTY-NINE

Green. Masses of open umbrellas vying for elbow room. Numberless heads of broccoli that cover the ground in every direction as far as the curved horizon. All green. Except for the occasional hairline fracture, drawn higgledy-piggledy, of a resplendent brown river. The twin-propeller cruises over the rain forest of the Amazon Basin and cuts a ribbon of dense moisture between blue sky and green earth. The shadow of the plane ripples across the forest in a close race. The monocot trees stand tall, with wide-rimmed sombreros for canopies. Clumped together in this thick jungle setting, the majesty of each tree is eclipsed by a jam-packed show of open umbrellas.

The fear is if the plane crashes here, it will disappear forever. Imagine a farmer in the Middle West of America who climbs a silo's ninety-foot ladder and accidentally drops the cross from a broken necklace into a large space full of grain, and you get the picture of our plane over the Amazon. That farmer simply gives up on ever being able to recover his cross. If they crash now, the trees may open a small incision for them to enter and close back around them.

On the surface of it, the inquiry sounds straightforward. The government-sanctioned committee must ascertain that all the thousand-odd U.S. citizens who are members of the religious commune belong to it of their own free will. The journalists among the travelers, unlike the others, perform double duty as reporters and as members of the committee. Three women are among the group. All worry that the children at this remote retreat may be suffering at the hands of grown-up religious zealots. All think a child who suffers alone and abandoned remains a bad omen for any society intent on calling itself adult and civilized.

The pilot banks the plane to the extreme right over a large clearing that reveals itself with a flourish among the giant trees. From the plane, it is possible to see a long road leading to the rough-hewn gated entrance to the commune and rows of dormitory-like buildings and a single white painted house around a square and many outlying buildings, one with a large chimney and a farm and fence leading this way and that, and not far from the commune, the wavering brown scar of the river, now clear of trees, now hidden among greenery, now defined as a gap that the trees might lean across and bridge. Lower in its flight path, the Cessna straightens for a few quick miles of hurtling greenery before the pilot makes his approach to land. His maneuver tilts the delegation buckled in their seats, and the runway looms up ahead. Bodies tense as the undercarriage grinds open and brace against seats and stop looking out the window at the green ground rushing up to meet the plane.

The last things seen from the air are four children with satchels slung crosswise on their bodies, loping along the side of the runway on their way home from school, and some cows grazing in the long grass, and six or seven men, some in shades, milling about in plain clothes with rifles slung over their shoulders.

Breathe, people, breathe past the knot in the chest and try not to think of the axle of the plane shearing off with all the jolting and noise and rumble of the chassis as the engines shut down fast to a relatively quiet cruise in the direction of the armed men.

Do not be alarmed by the sight of guns or by your proximity to arms and the people who bear them. The simple geometric shapes of weapons advertise deadly intent but only as a remote prospect. They seem to mean serious business only when poised and warming against a man's flesh. Do not become nervous, seeing how the rifles become an added appendage to these men, who look as if it would take surgery to separate the two, or some deadly conflagration.

Tell yourselves it is just two nights and three days out of your lives and away from what you know as civilization. Picture yourselves as moral stalwarts on a fact-finding mission to save the children, assuming, from the many negative reports about the commune, that they need saving.

The welcoming party from the commune, armed men, are vibrant in their own way of being easy with their bodies' musculature, though they lack, somehow, the vibrancy of the surrounding vegetation. One of them, dressed in dusty and patched imitation army fatigues and, improbably, old flip-flops, smiles as he cleans his dark glasses with a rag and, before reinserting the rag in his back pocket, lovingly wipes the barrel of his rifle. He smiles and nods. Mirror his smile. Keep inhaling past the hitches in your breath as you try to hold back tears.

A flock of the brightest and noisiest parrots, all primary colors, shrieks, and squawks, swoops across the clearing between trees by the airport, and the members of the delegation shade their eyes to follow them. The flock disappears as it plants itself in the trees.

THIRTY

The ladle lifts and empties into cups. My head feels just as though my mother lifts me up above her head until her arms are straight, and keeps her grip on me as she lowers me and repeats her lift. Not quite giddy but a blur, trees seem to haul up roots and lift skirts of vines and swing through the air with me. There is a sound to go with this swinging, but I do not hear it. What tune goes with this feeling? My flute knows it. I feel the impression of the holes of my flute on my fingertips. I breathe in and out and both in and out breaths make a tune on my flute. I do not know how this can be. One kind of music is for outside, another for inside, not both the same. I have no words for it. We reach the open. I find myself next to Ryan and Rose. Our shoulders touch. We line up in front of a large vat. Women bring their young, nurses feed the babies with syringes, men guard the older children to keep them in line, and not a dry eye among the guards, who sleeve their faces to keep them clear, and mothers and fathers feed their youngest first, as ordered, and the work of parents is done, and not much noise at first besides our church sounds and this deep output of air all around me. Mother. I think this without saying it. I am sure my lips move, but no sound for Mother happens. Not even a whisper. Or I say her name and it cannot be heard above the moan, the hymns running up and down the long queue, the cries of the very young picking up volume, orders shouted by guards, and gunshots, their two-four dying echo.

—Children!
   —Yes, Captain.
   —Do I have your ears?
   —You have our ears.
   —Your good ears.
   —Our good ears.
   —You looking at me?
   —We looking at you, Captain. But how did we end up on this ship, and where are our parents and friends?
   —All of your questions will be answered with this story. You ready for my Anansi story?
   —We ready!
   —You know about Anansi. Who don't know about Anansi? A human and a spider wrap up in one, a house and a web in the house for a bed. Anansi walk upright on two legs and he use two more legs for arms and he hide the last four on his travels among people. A man tangled up with a spider. But at night and in the spirit world, where he often play tricks and win and lose fortunes, he need all his limbs and all his wit to survive.
   —Imagine, children, how much we would get done around this ship if we all had Anansi limbs. Anansi got big eyes. He can see all around him, three-hundred-and-fifty-nine-degree point of view except for a one-degree blind spot no thicker than a silver thread that run from the back of the point on his head, a single strand of web for a blind spot. In the world of people, that don't sound like a weakness at all. But in the spider world, it count for something.

—Children!

—Yes, Captain.

—You sure you want to hear this?

—Yes, Captain, we sure.

—You can see and hear me, right?

—Yes, Captain. But we can't see where you're taking us.

—Don't worry about your journey. Let me be your captain.

—Yes, Captain.

The ladle catches the light, the cups turn and drain. Throats exposed. I am four places back from the front of the queue. Two for Ryan. Three for Rose. She grips my hand. Hers shake. Hers sweat, and if I did not return her grip, our sweat would free our hands. Ryan glances back at me for the last time. He stands at the head of this queue about to consume itself. His eyes stay on mine, and for a moment the flicker of a smile upsets the compressed corners of his lips. The smile of the three of us, about to embark on another game of run, run and never stop, and hope never to be caught. The line packs tight, shoulders touching, almost impatient for a turn to drink from the ladle, but not us, Ryan, Rose, and me, we are caught up in the web of it, the line as a sticky web, made up of pieces of us. I do not have to move a muscle. The queue moves me along. Its push and pull forward. Songs run up and down it, crying chases the song and the two catch each other in one throat and then another as both hymn and crying, and neither one the same.

—Children!

—Yes, Captain.

—I need your ears and nothing else.

—You have our ears.

—Your eyes on me?

—Yes, Captain. We're looking at you. But where're you taking us? And why don't we remember how we found our way on your ship?

—Don't worry. Keep your eyes locked on me and your ears tuned to my words, and all your questions will be answered.

—Yes, Captain.

Cups drain. The front of the queue collapses. More people add to the queue. Ladles refill cups. Heads throw back to swallow and the back of an arm wipes a mouth and a boy makes the sign of the cross and moves to the side and it is Ryan, and I am next, and Rose who steps in front of me at the last moment, and I cannot even lift an arm to stop her, my arms and feet leaden, her look begging me to let her be first this time, one last time, my body moving as one piece on a web made up of many bodies, and after Rose tilts her head back and steps to the side, I stand at the head of the line barely able to stay upright, and I am next to drink.

—Children!

—Yes, Captain.

—You can look and listen at the same time?

—Yes, Captain.

—Where are your eyes pointing?

—On you, Captain. Are we there yet?

—We will soon be there.

—Will our parents be there to greet us?

—Yes, trust me, children.

—Yes, Captain.

Trina! Two armed guards press close to me. A face, ladle in hand, fills a cup, holds out the cup with not much in it, and says my name and nods at me to go ahead. Take. Drink. I hear my mother. Trina! Calling me back to my name. Her tone above all the wailing. She tells me to do as I am told. She says, I love you, Trina. I see her combing my hair as clear as if I looked into a mirror. A comb in her hand over my head of hair. She says, Child, hold your head still and let the comb do its work. I hold my head quite still for you, my mother. The comb, guided by your gentle push and tug of my head, does its work. I love you, Mother.

—Children!
    —Yes, Captain.
    —I got your ears.
    —You have our ears.
    —Where are your eyes?
    —On you, Captain. We look and we listen.
    —You doing well?
    —We're doing well. But this journey's taking long.
    —We have all the time in the world.
    —Will we be there soon?
    —Soon. You ready for more Anansi!
    —Yes, Captain.
    —Children!
    —Yes, Captain.
    —You all ready for more Anansi?
    —Is Anansi real, Captain?
    —Yes, children.
    —Is he more real than us?
    —No. Let me finish the story and all will become clear.

Sometimes I think I am Anansi, the spider. I shift into any shape to suit my dilemma and escape. Not just me but Adam, Rose and Ryan, and all the children. All of us shape-shift and escape. I hold a mirror to the sun and redirect one beam into several hundred, from one place where no good comes of the light to another place that welcomes the shine. Light, splinter for me now, if not for me, for my mother, and if not for her, for love.

Acknowledgments

I am grateful to everyone at HarperCollins who played a part in publishing this story, book cover artists, copy editors, publicists, one and all. I single out Jonathan because he ran with the manuscript. From the early 1990s he has shown an expert eye for a good story and by now he knows all about the art and craft of the novel. And Barry. He rolled up his sleeves and aimed at the body of the text with a ninja's accuracy. He is a gifted editor. My friends Geoff, Peter, Grace, and Douglas read with cold eyes and warm hearts. My brothers Andrew, Patrick, and Greg said I could do it and I was foolish enough to believe them. My thanks. I sat with Wilson Harris and talked about my project and explained how much his books inspired my attempt at this tragic story. He urged me to do it. He is the presiding spirit behind my writing of this novel. Bless him. My children served as daily reminders of the hundreds of children who perished at Jonestown. Bless them. The result is a novel inspired by Jonestown rather than in strict adherence to it, and for that I am solely responsible.